Fairperoo

Book One of the Dark Inventions

Fairperoo

Book One of the Dark Inventions

by

Mark Lamb

with

Illustrations by Matthew Armstrong

Cover Graphics by Claudio Grilli

Farperoo

Book One of the Dark Inventions

Volume One

Published in Great Britain by Mark Lamb
The Madriax Press

This illustrated, limited edition first published
March 2005

ISBN 0-9548356-1-1

Printed and bound in Great Britain
by Biddles Limited, King's Lynn, Norfolk

Set in 13pt Garamond

10 9 8 7 6 5 4 3 2 1

For Marion

Who knows the end of all stories…

Arcanum the First

Arcanum the Second

Arcanum the Third

An Accident With the Weather

by Lucy Blake - Class 2ae
(Short Essay Homework)

First angel: Sorry I'm late Gabriel. There was a traffic hold-up at the pearly gates – now, where are you up to?

Second angel: I'm doing the 'Gs' – I've just finished Grimston-on-Sea.

First angel: Grimston-on-Sea in *Inguland* you mean?

Second angel: That's the one – the only town in the book that's underlined in red.

First angel: And you gave them the usual I suppose?

Second angel: Ah! Well not *exactly*. Actually, I wanted to have a word with you about that. You see there was this particularly interesting iced bun on the tea trolley…'

First angel: And?

Second angel: And, erm, *well*, I rather got distracted.

First angel: *And?*

Second angel: Well, I *sort of* pressed the wrong button – this yellow one *here*, to be exact.

First angel: (*sounding rather annoyed*) – I *sincerely* hope this is another one of your practical jokes. That's the *sun* button, you idiot!

Second angel: Joke? Erm, no, not exactly – but it was an easy mistake to make. And it won't hurt them to have nice weather just for once, will it? It'll make a nice change.

First angel: No, it *won't* make a nice change – take it from me, they'll absolutely *hate* it. What they like best in Grimston is four black buttons. Then we follow that up with a grey button, just to give them hope. Are you with me so far? Then, just as they get their expectations up, we give them a dozen black buttons, one after the other. After that, they get a grey and four blacks and we're back to where we started. It's what they're *accustomed* to. Trust me on this – I'm an angel.

Second angel: Well *so* am I, and I happen to think that everyone deserves a little bit of joy now and again – even if it *is* an accident.

First angel: I tend to agree – *unless* they happen to live in Grimston-on-Sea – and unless the entry is underlined in red.

Second angel: Well it's done now, so they'd better enjoy it whilst it lasts.

First angel: (*he takes a metal cover from his pocket and screws it down over the yellow button*) - Yes, they better *had* enjoy it, because it's going to be an awfully long while before they get any more…

The Department

Nothing is ever lost which can be imagined…

On the day the five-fold quest for heaven began, the small town of Grimston-on-Sea was squatting beneath a heavy, doom-laden sky. Down on the promenade, a fisherman was leaning hard into the wind, steadying himself against the iron fence posts as mountains of sea-spray crashed over onto the paving. His bright yellow waterproofs shone like a beacon in the storm-light – in fact, they positively *glowed* in comparison with *some* people's garments.

Professor Ordinax was the only other person mad enough to be out in such a storm and to prove it the wild-haired numerologist had dressed in his customary black-silk gown and mortarboard hat. He gave the fisherman a friendly wave and opened his mouth to speak, but the words of greeting were whisked through his teeth – stolen by the tempest. They weren't wasted though; instead, they became an essential part of history in the way that *all* words do – woven into the fabric of eternal happenings, alongside the soggy newspaper that whizzed past and stuck to a nearby lamppost.

'What chew doin' down 'ere then?' shouted the fisherman. He was struggling to make himself heard against the roar of the waves and the rusty creak of the fence chains. 'Erm, you're not feeling *strange*, are you? Only I'd *hate* to see you get carted off to Saint Mallydick's again.'

'My head is perfectly *well*, thank you Ned,' yelled Ordinax. 'And I've seen enough of Saint Mallydick's to last me a lifetime, thank you *very* much.' He gave a toothy grin and turned his back on the raging sea, staring up and down the deserted esplanade in the hope of spotting a customer. At his side, a makeshift table supported a large crystal ball. The seeing-glass was encircled by thirty-six yellow prediction slips, each one spiked by a rusty nail.

'Erm, yeah, *right*,' shouted Ned, still uncertain of the professor's sanity. 'So if you *haven't* gone mental again, then why ain't you wearin' a proper coat?'

'You think I should worry about *clothes*, with all *this* is going on?' yelled Ordinax.

He gestured towards the storm-filled sky, as if there might be something *else* worth seeing. 'Just *look* at it all Ned.'

'Erm, all *what* exactly?' shouted Ned.

The crystal ball moved slightly, rocked by the unseen hand of the wind.

'The vault of heaven,' shouted the professor. 'It's all *happening*.'

'Yeah, *very* nice, I'm sure,' yelled Ned. 'But why do you need to be out here to look at it? Can't you see it from home?'

'I'm here because someone *needs* me,' yelled Ordinax. A sudden severe gust tried to claim his hat, and then turned its attention to the prediction strips. They flickered and chattered amongst themselves, whirring impatiently like three-dozen racing locusts.

'*Yeah?*' shouted Ned. 'Well I reckon they should be ashamed of themselves, bringing you out here in this weather.'

The wind gusted again, slicing through the taut cables of the Ferris wheel with a moan that would melt even the bravest of hearts. The two men studied each other, looking for signs of fear in the other's face.

'*Ah!*' said Ordinax. 'Erm, *ye-es*, but they don't necessarily *know* they need me.'

'Oh, so you're just hangin' around hoping for customers then?' yelled Ned. He flinched as a massive wave crashed over the end of the pier. For a moment it seemed that the famous 'exhibition of curiosities' would be destroyed, but eventually it reappeared, surfacing like a rusted-iron monster, seawater pouring and hissing off its domed back.

'*You* might think of it as hanging around,' shouted the Professor. 'But there's a lot more to it than that – I'm providing what we in the prediction trade call an essential service.'

'Oh *yeah?*' shouted Ned.

'*Absolutely,*' bellowed Ordinax with a wild look in his eyes. 'If there's the slightest chance that a member of the public will need a forecast then I must be here to bestow it.' He leaned across to steady the sign on the front of his table – as soon as he let go though, it carried on flapping in the wind.

The Department

'I Predict the Future,' it proclaimed. 'The One and only Ordinax – Counted Amongst the Few; This man is a renowned Master of Numerology – admired by the stars and consulted by the rich and famous.'

'Sounds like you're just desperate for a few customers,' grinned Ned. 'Have you run out of money again?'

'Yes, well cat food is *so* expensive these days,' yelled Ordinax. 'And the Great Mysterio would never forgive me if I didn't buy his favourite brand. It's the new Mete-o-Chunx, with Snacker-Mouse gravy.' He gave a thin smile, but even Ned could tell that something *else* was going on – and it was something *much* more important than cat food.

'Why don't you go home and get out of them soakin' robes?' the fisherman yelled. 'This storm's settling in for the duration – although I suppose you already *knew* that, *didn't* you?'

'*What?*' shouted the Professor, his silks flapping like bat's wings. He'd been distracted by the rain-soaked newspaper that was stuck to the lamppost. The banner headline was only partially visible:

"riory,

ective,

case."

'I *said* you must've *known* about the storm,' yelled Ned, grinning and pointing at the professor's sign. 'You must have seen it coming in your predictions.'

'Erm, ye-es,' shouted Ordinax. 'I suppose I did.'

'Yeah,' said Ned. 'I reckon you must, because it's the *biggest, hoogest* storm Grimston has ever seen – and *he* reckons it's going to get worse.'

As if to prove that it was indeed going to worsen, a sudden bolt of blue-white lightning gave shape to the Grimston skyline. The single blazing strike split into four burning ribbons as it approached the ground, each of them striking one of the four rusting domes that capped the Winter Gardens. For just a fraction of a second, the entire town was aglow – connected by brilliant streamers of light to the great vault of Heaven. All around them, the salt-laden air was suddenly filled with the magical, burning smell of Lectric.

'He?' shouted the Professor, shielding his eyes. 'Who is *he?*'

The newspaper was suddenly whipped away for good – now he was *never* going to find out what it had said.

'Old Hubert,' shouted Ned, 'the fisherman's weather predictor. He's never been wrong – not even once.'

'There's always a first time,' yelled Ordinax. He glanced nervously into the sky and decided it was time to leave. He slipped the crystal into his pocket, and was just about to gather up the prediction slips when they were torn from their nails by a vicious gust of wind. Then, as he attempted to fold the embroidered table covering, a massive wall of spray crashed down. It ran straight off Ned's waterproofs, but soaked the Professor to the skin.

'Looks like the weather's beaten you at last,' shouted the fisherman.

'It most certainly has *not*,' yelled Ordinax, watching the slips disappear over nearby rooftops. 'It's something *else* entirely – and I don't rightly know if I even want to hear it.' His eyes narrowed as if he was listening intently – but not with his ears. Some *other* part of him was tuning into the skies.

'Hear *what*?' bellowed Ned. 'Is there a good show on the wireless?'

The Professor tilted his head, like a puzzled dog. Suddenly a look of horror spread across his rain-washed face, as if he'd found the missing piece of some terrifying jigsaw. Then he slowly shook his head, unable to believe what his senses were telling him.

'The show is out *here*,' he yelled, 'beneath the canopy of heaven.'

'You *what*?' said Ned looking puzzled. 'Erm, have I *missed* something, or have you gone potty again?'

A large piece of seaweed flew in on the wind and wrapped around the Professor's neck and arms, one end sticking itself in his mouth.

'I've been out here all day Ned,' he spluttered. 'So I've had lots of time to think – and to *listen*.'

'Listen?' shouted Ned. 'Listen to *what*?'

'*Voices*,' whispered the Professor. His words were swallowed by the wind, but the fisherman read his lips without difficulty.

'*Ah*,' grinned Ned, 'now you wouldn't be trying to *scare* me by any chance, would you?'

'I'm afraid not,' yelled Ordinax, his face the colour of cold ash. 'Actually I'm doing quite a good job of scaring myself.' He glanced into the sky, and then looked back at the fisherman with an expression of panic. 'They're getting *closer*,' he cried. 'I thought I was imagining it, but I heard them again, just now – as clear as anything.'

'Yeah, *right*,' grinned Ned. 'This is one of them *special* predictions, *innit*? The ones you charge double for.'

'*No*, it's *not*,' howled the professor, 'I think we *both* know I make those up as I go along. No, this is something *real* Ned, and it's going on up *there*, high above the storms.'

'*Above* the storms?' shouted fisherman. 'In space you mean?'

'No, of course not,' yelled Ordinax. 'It's happening in a place that no mortal mind has ever imagined.'

'Whoo-hooo-hooo,' grinned Ned, 'it's just like a ghost story.'

'I'm *serious*,' insisted the Professor. 'There are voices up there – in the weather.'

'Yeah?' said the fisherman. 'So what're they talkin' about then?'

Ordinax hesitated as a toothy grin spread across Ned's face.

'*The future of all creation*,' he whispered solemnly.

'Creation eh?' said Ned, slowly shaking his head in disbelief. It was turning out to be the story of the Dragon Teapot all over again. Only *this* time they were going to keep the old fool in Saint Mallydick's for good.

'You don't *believe* me, do you Ned?'

'Erm ye-es, I *do*,' said Ned unconvincingly. 'I believe whatever you say Professor – it all sounds very, erm, *interesting*.'

Suddenly, the wind speed dropped and the silence that followed sent a shiver down both their spines.

'Well it's interesting for *someone*,' said Ordinax seriously, 'because they're back – and this time they're coming through as clear as a bell.'

'*Nah*,' said Ned, swallowing hard and suddenly looking quite nervous. 'You're imagining it *aren't* you? You're *mad* – everyone knows that.'

'Do they?' said Ordinax, looking somewhat disappointed.

Ned took a single pace backwards and removed a large silvery fish from inside his waterproofs. He stared into its dull, lifeless eyes for a moment, and then held the creature up to his ear, as if receiving some fishy words of wisdom.

'Yeah, that's *right*,' he said, nodding eagerly. 'You're *imagining* it – *and* you're mad – and what's more, Hubert agrees with me.'

In the distant future, when events surrounding the great storm had finally unwound themselves and the full story was known, this fateful day would be celebrated as '*Drix Luciftias*' – 'The Bringing Down of Brightness'. And *in* that same future, if anyone cared to look, there would be a record of the professor's lost words, and an account of the headline on that soggy piece of newspaper. For now though, there was no such entry. The events to be filed under 'D' had not yet happened. Nothing had yet been written. Eternity itself was waiting for the hand of the Architect.

There was a voice in the air. It was composed of one hundred and seven layers of wind and a dozen fragments of whispers, all of them woven together by a single malevolent thought.

'*This* is the place,' it hissed. 'I can *sense* the effects of a great work of invention.'

'It's *possible* your instincts are wrong,' said another, his speech given form by the pattern of spaces between raindrops. 'But there *is* a feeling of great darkness here – and the world *has* been woven with a great deal of skill.'

'Such is the work of Magdala,' whispered the wind. 'Light wrapped within darkness and then shrouded in light – layer within layer, and layer upon layer, until none but the Architect can tell which is truth and which is invention.'

'And if it *is* the work of Magdala?' said the rain. 'Then what of the prize – is *that* here too?'

Before the wind could answer, a bolt of lightning created a bright, blinding arc between two huge clouds. The air was filled with the sound of distant trumpets and the crackling discharge of Lectric and for a fraction of a second, a vast, high-ceilinged interior was illuminated. It was a wood-panelled office with hundreds of dissimilar doors on one side and thousands of tiny glass panes on the other, many of them broken or boarded up. It was dark outside, but even so, there was a suggestion of a vast, uncharted space beyond these windows, capable perhaps of swallowing entire universes.

The area nearest to the voices was packed with ten thousand-year-old filing cabinets, whilst stretching away into the distance were hundreds of desks, each creaking under the weight of dusty paperwork. In the far distance, and keeping well clear of the source of the conversation, a group of shadowy figures was tending a complex mechanism.

'I believe it *is*,' said the wind eventually. 'Can you *imagine* a better sanctuary than a place which is forever wrapped by shadows?'

'But if the world *does* enclose the cherished item,' said the rain, 'then those shadows will be filled with intricate mysteries and hidden dangers, and *you*, above all, cannot afford to become ensnared – the consequences of failure are unthinkable.'

'My plan is rigorous and without flaw,' hissed the wind. 'As we speak, six of my most loyal followers are already established in the haven.'

The storm seemed to disapprove of this and delivered a lightning bolt that made a reasonable attempt at ripping the skies apart. The windows glowed incandescent with the effects of the strike, and the machine-tenders stopped to gaze as the discharge spread a brilliant web of filaments amongst a number of small clouds. The flash also illuminated the two speakers, who were floating at the other end of the office. They were flowing and eddying like clouds of gas, their forms outlined by boiling clouds of electrons – but nobody dared to look.

'No plan is without flaw,' said the rain, 'and there are powers at work here that even the Architect cannot control. You must proceed with great caution.' He descended towards a circular screen that formed the upper surface of a huge drum-shaped machine, his formless body mingling with the image displayed there. As parts of him flowed and joined with the device, he drew various elements of the picture into his body, supplementing his own dark plasma with storm-light and starlight and moonlight. Even the feeble yellow light from Grimston's Lectric street lamps contributed.

'No,' hissed the wind. 'We began slowly in the *other* worlds, and where did *that* get us? Years of painstaking work have yielded nothing.'

'And if you are mistaken?' said the rain. 'What then?' As he withdrew from the device, the images of Grimston and the storm separated from his body and returned to the machine with a loud sucking sound, like someone emptying a bath.

'The Architect Elect is here,' hissed the wind. 'I am certain of it – and the *light* is here too.' He formed a gaseous appendage that looked like a deformed hand, scooping a portion of the image out of the machine. Then he tipped the claw up and let the picture flow back into the pool, spreading great ripples across its surface. 'We must act with all speed,' he said. 'The benefice of heaven depends on it.'

'Then descend into their realm,' said the rain, 'and may the Grand Architect watch over you, and guide your actions.'

The Coat of Raziel

It was a Thursday, and it was raining, *again*. And the luckless inhabitants of Grimston were so busy controlling umbrellas and navigating around the world's deepest puddles that none of them noticed the shape of the wind as it descended. So when the creature flared his wings and made a perfect landing behind a rain-lashed winkle stall, nobody noticed *that* either. They were too busy drying their coats and looking for clean towels to be worrying about a spirit who had suddenly become flesh.

And *that* was their first mistake; because once an angel was on the ground and had concealed his wings, he was virtually undetectable. For all *they* knew, he might just as well be one of them.

The line where Grimston ended and the Cherman Sea began was usually obvious, but today, with the town in the grip of a northerly gale, the sea looked as though it had finally conquered the land. The waves were attacking the promenade as if the onslaught were part of some personal vendetta, constantly crashing over the iron railings and flooding the road beyond in a knee-deep tide. Their swirling waters had already carried off a sign that said '*Welcome to Grimston-on-Sea, Home of the Bleevil*', and now they were amusing themselves by filling the Bowling Green with seaweed and converting the crazy golf course into a submarine dock. Not to be outdone, the gales were playing their own part in the drama. They had other jobs to do, of course, but today there was an extra special task. They had to form the droplets of rain into diamond hard pellets and fire volleys of them at the windows of the sea-front boarding houses.

For the children who were imprisoned behind those panes it really was a most distressing time, but not because of the storm. They were upset because they had been banned from inventing humorous and abusive names for the other guests, being forced instead to play endless games of *Snork-my-Ludo* and *Filch* and *Broddle-your-Neighbour*. The alternative was to get out their coats, gumboots, and umbrellas and venture into town with their parents who would pass the time competing for jars of gherkins at prize bingo. And after that, if they hadn't thrown themselves into the sea with despair, it was time for tealeaf reading by genuine gypsies or perhaps a visit to the daily mermaid-smelling pageant in the underground aquarium. And finally, when all other forms of entertainment had been exhausted, there was the greatest suffering known to man – having to endure a four-and-a-half hour banjo concert in the aptly named Winter Gardens.

In an instant though, there was a dramatic change in the weather. Pavements that had soaked up the rain for weeks were suddenly dry. The flags on the promenade were hanging limp instead of being ripped from their poles by howling gales. And the moody, sulking clouds had vanished, revealing a pure blue sky and the bright yellow disc of the seldom-glimpsed sun.

Nobody knew why this might have happened, but they were *far* too busy to stop and ask if it was all due to some heavenly accident. Down on the foreshore people were competing to see who could wear the silliest sunhat, eat the most ice cream, or lose the greatest amount of money on the penny amusements. On the beach it was much the same story, where sunbathing in stripy deck chairs and building sand castles and wearing hats made from knotted handkerchiefs was the order of the day. One group of adventure seekers was even attempting to eat a special type of cucumber sandwich – the very distinctive kind that tastes as though it has been made with real sand. And they were pretending to *like* it. All over Grimston it seemed, people were enjoying the unexpectedly fine weather.

Which was why nobody noticed the birds.

High above their unsuspecting heads, the embodiments of spirit had begun massing in their thousands. There were gulls and oystercatchers and redshanks, kittiwakes and fulmars and curlews, all gradually converging on a single point below. And it wasn't just the seabirds that were drawn to this strange attractor. There were crows too, and rooks and magpies and every other kind of loud-beak. And they in turn were joined by hordes of smaller birds, the wagtails and swallows and flycatchers and goldfinches, all of them spinning and turning with a single mysterious purpose.

And *still*, nobody noticed their gathering.

If people *had* looked up though, they might have noticed how the birds were circling – slow and high to begin with, turning in a wide, sweeping arc, then gradually speeding up and spiralling inwards towards a precise focus. And if they had paid *particular* attention to that vortex of beaks and wings and claws, they might even have noticed what was happening directly below it.

The main pier was busy, but the wooden gangway that separated Nurk's amusement arcade from the *Bleevit* was unusually quiet, as if people were staying away but didn't know why. Perhaps they *saw* what was happening there but their minds told them it was something else? Or maybe they looked straight through the scene, their gaze drawn to much happier sights in the fairground beyond? Whatever the reason, the two lone figures were left to themselves, untouched by even the slightest form of joy.

The girl was pretty, perhaps twelve or thirteen, and had waist length blonde hair that had a habit of looking windblown even in a gentle breeze. Watching her, *staring* at her in fact, was a pale, much older man with a waxen face. He stood in silence, absorbing every detail of the girl, as if he needed to commit her features to memory before she was lost forever. He noticed, for instance, that she was wearing a thin, white summer dress, and although it was quite warm, she appeared to be shivering.

In contrast, the pale stranger was overdressed, especially considering the unusually bright weather. He wore a heavy black coat across his narrow shoulders, and a tall hat that cast a shadow over slow moving eyes. It was an *old* hat too, the girl was thinking, just like the ones in the faded brown photographs in her grandmother's album.

Suddenly, about twenty feet away, the "talker" appeared on the steps of the *Bleevit* – a large, newly erected wooden shed with a corrugated tin roof. The girl recognised Mungo from the fairground – it was his job to coax people into the attractions, supplying them with an enigmatic description of what they might find inside, once they'd parted with their money.

The Coat of Raziel

'*Rool up, Rool up,*' he bellowed, to nobody in particular. '*Yewl be amazed at what you'll find. Come on now ladees and gennermen, boys and girls, step inside and witness the marvels and mysteries of Grimston's newest attraction. It's so real you'll think you were there. Who needs reality when the Bleevit has so much to offer? Rool up, Rool up, for the experience of a lifetime.*'

Mungo stared into the middle distance for a moment, as if someone had crept up and stolen the crowd when he wasn't looking. Then he scratched his head and went back inside, wondering if he hadn't imagined it all. The girl's heart sank as he disappeared, and she suddenly had the strangest impression that her body was floating. She wanted to look down, to make sure the wooden boards were still there – but she was unable to move, suddenly transfixed by those dark, smouldering eyes.

'My name is Rasmussen,' whispered the stranger. The words leaked between his teeth with a subtle hiss, as if his mouth was filled with snakes.

He extended a cold hand, and the girl politely grasped it, realising too late that he didn't intend to let go. She looked straight into his eyes as she'd been taught, but instantly turned aside in disgust. Rasmussen reminded her of a partially melted figure she'd seen the day the wax museum caught fire.

'And *your* name?' he said, smiling as if he already knew the answer.

The girl shook her head and pulled back, finally releasing her hand from his clammy iron grip.

'You *have* no name?' he said with a thin smile. 'Ah well, it's no matter, *is* it? Sometimes, if we name a thing, it can lose its mystery. And sometimes the names we give to things can never begin to describe their beauty.'

He touched the girl's cheek with a surprisingly gentle motion, then reached up and felt his own paste white complexion.

'So *very* pretty,' he whispered. 'A girl with the face of an angel, yet surrounded by so many dark winged daemons.'

The girl smiled nervously and followed Rasmussen's gaze. The dark funnel of birds was still spiralling above them, circling, watching, and apparently laughing at her stupidity. You should *never* have responded to him, they seemed to screech. You should have carried on walking, or called out to the others.

'Are you s-s-selling something?' stuttered the girl. There had been a vague idea that the sound of her own voice might break the spell, but it was a forlorn hope.

'*Selling?*' said Rasmussen, spitting the words. 'What do you take me for, a purveyor of *baubles?*' He seemed deeply offended, wounded almost, and for a moment, the girl thought she had misjudged him. 'I'm *giving,*' he hissed.

Just a short distance away the girl's friends were enjoying themselves, eating candyfloss and sucking on gobstoppers the size of hens' eggs and suspecting nothing of the dark play that was unfolding nearby. She knew they were there *somewhere* and tried to call out, but all that emerged was a whimper that sounded like an injured puppy.

'Shall I tell you a little of what I have in store?' said Rasmussen. He spread his arms to discourage her from running. The coat billowed in a slight gust of wind, blocking even more of the girl's already limited light. She was beginning to disappear in his shadow.

'Are you t-talking about the *Bleevit?*' she said, nervously. 'D-do you just want me to go inside?'

'Inside, outside, it's all relative, isn't it?' said Rasmussen. 'I simply want to show you something – an item of great interest.'

The girl shook her head, catching sight of the newly painted sign on the wall behind him.

"*You Won't Bleevit.*"

"*So real you'll think you were there!*"

'I don't want to see it,' said the girl. 'And I don't want to *buy* anything either – there's nothing I need.' She was pressing her back up against the wall now, breathing heavily, with beads of sweat forming on her brow. Although she was pushing her hands tight down by her sides they continued to twitch as if they belonged to someone else.

'I find that *very* hard to believe,' hissed Rasmussen, the words scarcely escaping from between tight-pursed lips. 'Unless you're the only girl in the world who has everything she needs? I picked *you* out in particular, because I believe I have something you want.'

'You *p-picked* me?' said the girl nervously.

'Of course,' he said. 'You look like a young lady with imagination – someone who might appreciate a mystery.'

The girl shifted her weight from one foot to the other, which was always a dead giveaway. People who knew her could tell when she was nervous, even from a distance. They wouldn't know why of course, not unless they knew something about her that only two other people in the world knew.

'*Come on now ladees and gennermen, don't be bashful, step right up, and sample the delights. You won't Bleevit, it says on our sign, and we guarantee that you won't. Come and see the Madgy-Cull things we have for you inside. Rool up. Rool up.*'

'Don't worry, about him,' said Rasmussen, nodding towards Mungo. 'He doesn't see us – not in the way people normally see.'

'*You'll be agog,*' shouted Mungo, '*you'll stand in wonder, gob-smacked and completely open-mouthed. Rool…*' He stopped suddenly and looked in their direction without the slightest flicker of recognition, pausing just long enough to scratch his head and pick his nose. The two strangers in the alleyway might have been made of glass or composed entirely of air for all he cared.

Even though Mungo couldn't see her, the girl gathered confidence from his return, as if he'd broken a spell that the pale man had cast around her. She could hear the world again, and her resolve was suddenly reinforced by familiar sounds that flooded her senses. Not far away, the fruit machines were whirring and clunking, swallowing ten pennies for every one they paid out. And there was laughter too, and the sound of the Lectrical Romance machine singing its mechanical tune.

You are so Bee-Yoo-Ti-Full…
I think you're so Cute-Ti-Full…
Please don't be Snoo-ti-full…
And give your heart to meeee…

The girl paused for a moment, glancing at Rasmussen's gut. His soul was clothed in a deep blackish violet, and she hated *that* colour most of all. Especially when it was surrounded by lilies, and smelt of sulphur.

'I'm *going* now,' she said confidently.

'So soon?' said the stranger. 'Before you know what I have to offer?'

'I don't care what you have,' she insisted. 'I told you, I don't want anything.'

'No?' he said quietly. 'Not even to be back with your friends?'

The girl cast her mind back to the moment when she'd heard that strange mechanical melody, only just audible beneath the cries of the gulls. It had floated on the air like notes plucked at random from an old music box, and as she had turned to locate the source of the refrain, Rasmussen had caught her eye, beckoning her into the narrow alley. Like a fool, she had followed.

'Alright,' she said. 'Yes, I want to be back with them.'

'You *see*?' said Rasmussen in a soft voice. 'That wasn't such a long way to travel, *was* it? We began our journey in a place where you wanted for nothing, and yet just a short distance away we find that you want to be with your friends. If we were to travel just a little further along that road, there's no telling *what* we might discover – in *here* for instance.'

One by one, Rasmussen undid the buttons that held the two parts of his coat together. There was an intense look of concentration on his face, as if the fastenings needed a spell to undo them and the magic required for each was ten times stronger than the last. Beads of sweat appeared on *his* forehead now, giving the impression that the effort was almost too much to bear.

'He's weakened,' the girl thought, 'so I might just be able…'

'*No*,' he hissed, 'you will *not*…' Rasmussen moved quickly, ending the girl's escape even before her muscles had a chance to respond to the thought. 'That's *better*,' he said, placing a bony hand on each wing of the coat. 'Now, pay *attention*.'

His left hand remained stationary for a moment, holding the dark fabric against his breast as he moved the right, just as an illusionist might. He was not as relaxed as a magician though, in fact his long fingers gripped the cloth so tightly that the knuckles had turned purest white.

'Watch the hand that remains still,' the girl whispered to herself.

'Watch *nothing* but the coat,' hissed Rasmussen.

'No,' she whispered. She *knew* that when watching an illusion you should never pay attention to the moving hand – she was unable to take her eyes from it though, the waxy skin and the blue veins and swollen knuckles suddenly swelling to fill her entire universe.

'Watch,' hissed Rasmussen. 'Watch and *learn*.'

The girl did exactly as she was told – her willpower folded like a worn-out concertina. There was no choice now, but to witness whatever trick he had in store.

Somewhere in the lining of the coat, a soft light was calling to her and she was unable to resist its message. Her eyes widened as Rasmussen continued to reveal the interior of the garment – and by the time it was open wide she was totally relaxed. Suddenly, there was nothing to fear – she had been *right* to trust him, *hadn't* she? Because there, floating in the brilliant lining of the stranger's coat, was everything she had ever dreamed of.

'It's just as you promised,' she whispered, 'but it frightens me.'

'*Frightens* you?' said Rasmussen softly. 'How can that be? This is what you *want* – the coat is never wrong.'

'Yes,' she said, 'but people aren't *supposed* to have everything they want, are they? And *that's* why I'm afraid.'

'Nothing of value can be had without fear,' said Rasmussen. 'And we could never learn to be brave, could we, if there were only joy in the world?'

The girl tried to look away, searching right and left for somewhere to run, trying to catch a glimpse of her friends. Each time though she was drawn back to the glow. She had nothing to fear from *him*, did she? He'd brought her the coat and set her free. And he'd shown her the thing she most desired – there were *beings* in there, moving about in the brilliant folds of cloth, coiling and un-coiling their bright, star-filled bodies. They were creatures of light, and they had stolen her tongue with their incandescent beauty.

Rasmussen gave a self-assured grin, the wrinkles spreading across the surface of his face like fractured ice. Nobody in this shallow, materialistic world could resist the sight of the thing they most desired – or *could* they?

He'd been certain she was his, but for some reason the girl's gaze had shifted. Her eyes had moved away from the lining and she was watching *him* now, focusing on the fire that burned inside every creature who laid claim to a soul.

'My, you *are* a strong one, *aren't* you?' he hissed. 'But you'll watch the raiment all the same, *won't* you? Now child, look at the *coat.*'

This time she was eager to obey, because his violet soul and its gallery of dark reflections was causing her *such* great pain. With the smell of sulphur burning in her nostrils, she looked back towards the coat. And with an indescribable feeling of joy, she returned to the creatures that swirled, swooped, and dived there, frolicking in the depths of its peacock-coloured lining.

ΩᚸⵝⵊⵁⴽⵝⲤ

'If you can *see* it, then you can *have* it – all you need to do is keep looking.'

The girl was still under the influence of the spell he'd had woven, but even so it was clear to her that something wasn't right. Her thoughts were flying with the winged creatures now, soaring in skies that could only ever exist in dreams – but even so she managed to find her voice.

'My name isn't Lucy,' she said in the faintest of whispers. 'It's Fenny.'

'Fenny?' hissed the tempter. '*Fenny?* What kind of name is *that?*'

'The one I was given,' she whispered meekly.

'But you were walking with the boy,' hissed Rasmussen, his eyes smouldering with rage. 'How can you *not* be the one?'

'I'm *me*,' whispered Fenny, 'isn't that enough?' She began to cry, torn away from the company of creatures by her own sadness.

'*No*,' screamed Rasmussen, 'it is *not* enough.'

Fenny's eyes widened in horror as his fingers encircled her neck, his bony, powerful thumbs pressing harder and harder against her windpipe. He pushed the girl's head back as he throttled the life from her, forcing her to look up – first into his wild face and then at the dark funnel of birds. They were spiralling closer and closer now, their shadowy wings almost blotting out the sky.

'Please, *no*,' she cried. 'I don't want to die – not yet.'

In the desperate struggle for breath, her eyes flooded with tears and her vision faded and blurred – and *that* was when she imagined the enormous vein-scarred wings. They floated like black-stained veils at the outer edge of her vision – moving with a grace that suggested intelligence and poise and a deep, sinister beauty.

'Please, *no*,' she gurgled, struggling to break free. 'If you let me go I promise I won't tell.'

'No child,' grinned Rasmussen, 'you *won't* – I can guarantee that.'

She screamed as the pressure on her neck grew beyond all endurance, but all that emerged was a gurgle that spoke of approaching death. Rasmussen hissed as he watched her eyes flicker and close. When she finally blacked out and turned limp in his grasp, he looked deeply disappointed - but then, as her lifeless body fell at his feet in an untidy heap, an idea began to germinate within him, its growth marked by a sneer that gradually crept across his face.

'I appear to have missed the fish I was angling for,' he whispered, 'but there may *still* be a small chance. Can it be that the fortune of heaven still smiles upon our undertaking?'

He knelt down on the hard wooden boards, listening to the sea for a moment as it shifted the pebbles beneath the pier. Then he cradled Fenny's motionless head in the palm of one bony hand and exhaled – first into her ears, and then into her nose and mouth, his breath hissing like a leak in the walls of hell.

'*Apila*,' he whispered. '*A-pi-laaaaaa…*'

Fenny coughed and choked as she regained consciousness, gagging on the cloud of foul breath that surrounded her. She struggled for a moment and tried to stand, but fell back against the wall, her eyes crossed as though they belonged to a drunken puppet.

'Who are you?' she whispered, trying to make out the blurred shape that crouched over her. 'Where am I? Am I *dead*?'

'*No* child,' whispered Rasmussen. 'You are *bait*.'

The Prisoner of Panoptica

As the dusk began to lay a mantle of shadow over Grimston, Lucy Blake was prowling the limits of her tiny bedroom, searching for the source of an annoying squeak. It was one of those noises that was difficult to pin down. Her current feeling was that it was outside somewhere, despite the fact that the turret room was on the third storey – and *that* of course, was what made the Panopticon the perfect spying place – as well as the perfect prison. The only way into her sleeping quarters was a trapdoor in the middle of the floor, and it was here that the 'food' tray occasionally appeared – unless she dragged the bedside cabinet across to stop them lifting the flap. Sometimes the rations were actually edible, but mostly she preferred to stay hungry – it primed the thoughts and concentrated the mind. At least that was what her Uncle Byron said, and he *knew* a thing or two about thinking. He'd told her for instance, that 'Panopticon' meant 'all seeing', which was why her bedroom had acquired the name all those years ago. The room was a perfect cube, with a differently styled window in each of the four walls – and according to the compass that came free with 'Phoenix', her favourite comic; the windows were perfectly aligned on the cardinal points - north and east, west and south. What she *didn't* know at this precise moment was just how important those compass points *were*, and what a large part they might play in her future. *If* she managed to survive...

Eek, eek, eek, eek…
There it was *again*, somewhere out *there* – or in *here*. She really wasn't sure. It wasn't just the 'eek' that worried her though. There had been an 'oof' too, which sounded like a field mouse trying to lift a house brick. And judging by the strained nature of the noise, it was either a very small mouse or a very large brick.

Eek, eek, eek…

Lucy lifted the sash of the east-facing window and stuck her head out to survey the garden. It was clear of intruders, as she'd expected. There was a fair bit of storm debris lying around though, including a number of small, yellow tickets that had become snagged in the holly bushes.

'*Hello?*' she whispered. There was no answer, just the distant sound of the Cherman Sea breaking its waves on the south-bay shore. As far as the eastern window was concerned, the storms had finished and it was just another boring night in Grimston.

Oof, oof, oof. Aah…

Hmm. It had come back again, *hadn't* it? And this time it was coming from the south, however unlikely *that* might seem. The main body of the house lay in that direction, so whoever or whatever was the source of the grunting would have to be on the roof. Lucy looked anyway. It was clear, except for a pair of friendly seagulls who were keeping surprisingly quiet.

'*Hello?*' she whispered, just in case.

There was no answer, unless she counted the satisfied bird gurglings.

'*Hello?*' she said again, slightly louder. She didn't dare call out. The lampstand had ears like foghorns, and if she heard the slightest disturbance from the tower then the prison sentence would be extended for sure. And that was the last thing she needed, now she'd decided to share her discovery.

'*Hello?*'

There was still no answer, and nothing to be seen either, except for the distant lights of the golf club and the sand dunes beyond. Sometimes, as night drew in, they would appear closer to the house, looking as if they went on forever.

Eek, eek, eek…

A-ha! So the '*oofs*' had gone again, had they, only to be replaced by the '*eeks*'? There was a clue there somewhere, but with only two windows left to check, the mystery wasn't going to take *too* much working out.

She turned towards the north-facing window, where the brass telescope was mounted. There was no time for spying on the Malmaison tonight though, not with a mystery in progress. She raised the window and stuck her head out, pausing for a moment to watch the slow-moving traffic on the road coming in from the North, where a sign read:-

"Welcome to Grimston-on-Sea, the home of 'You won't Bleevit'."

After a brief glimpse at the North Bay and the headland, she peered down into the physic garden and found nothing but the wind. Three quarters of the 'all seeing' windows were open now, and as the night crept up, she began to feel the cold. She didn't bother to close them though, because a mystery was always more exciting when you were cold and shivering and felt a chill running down your back.

Eek, eek, eek...

There was just one possibility remaining.

She turned to the west, convinced that she was ready for anything. On the way to the window though she caught sight of herself in her mother's mirror, the one that Maggie had called her 'Psyche'. As usual, it proved a bit of a shock, because in her own mind, Lucy was at *least* five foot six, a flaxen haired beauty who could be mistaken for an opera singer if the wind was in the right direction and it was slightly foggy. The reality was slightly different. She was just five feet tall, quite slender and with short, mousy hair that could be used to hide her pixy-like nose in an emergency. One thing the mirror *couldn't* show though was her strength. There was practically nothing to see when she flexed her biceps, but she was *still* the best arm wrestler in her class. And if anyone ever dared to accuse her of cheating again she was going to rotten-well pin them to the floor and sit on their heads until they changed their minds.

Oof, oof, oof...

Right, that was *it*, she thought. The noise *had* to be coming from the west, possibly from the railway lines. Perhaps they had installed some new piece of machinery at the inland factories? She wanted it to be closer than that though, but not actually *inside* the room, because that would be just *too* scary.

She took a deep breath and warily approached the window, as if someone might suddenly appear on the other side and scare the living *bejasus* out of her. That was one of Percy's favourite words, and was perfect for times like this – when the hairs were standing up on the back of your neck and your palms were beginning to tingle.

Eek, eek, eek...

Oof, oof, oof...

Eek, eek, eek...

When she opened the curtains, the mystery was finally solved.

Her friend Toby was teetering around in the garden, trying to balance an extremely long pole he'd made by lashing three clothes props together. There was a wheel attached to a vee shaped notch at the top of the contraption, and looped around it was a piece of string, disappearing down into the darkness.

'*Shh,*' hissed Lucy, 'they'll *hear* you.'

Eek, eek, eek, eek, eek, eek, eek, eek, eek, eek…

The string started to move, and eventually a note appeared at the top. Lucy leaned out to read it. It said simply:-

'I *know* that stupid, that's why I'm using a pole and not waking the neighbours by shouting.'

'Oh,' whispered Lucy, 'erm, *yes*, what a good idea.'

'*Shh,*' came a hissing sound from below.

Eek, eek, eek, eek, eek, eek, eek, eek, eek, eek…

The note disappeared, and after a lot more 'eeking', it returned, this time with a new message.

'How long have you been in prison *this* time?' it said.

Lucy leaned out and pencilled a reply at the bottom of the note.

'Just three days, but it *seems* like three weeks.'

Eek, eek, eek, eek, eek, eek, eek, eek, eek, eek…

'Why?' said the reply.

Eek, eek, eek, eek, eek, eek, eek, eek, eek, eek…

Lucy leaned out, but before she could add her next contribution there was a disturbance down below. Moments later the pole disappeared, and seconds after *that* there was a crash that sounded like a greenhouse being bombed. The back door flew open, illuminating the garden path with a creamy-yellow rectangle of light. It revealed two adult sized shadows, although one of them looked a *bit* on the thin side.

'What do you think *that* was?' said a man's voice, filtering up from below.

'Which bit?' said a woman's voice. 'The squeaking or the smashing?'

'The squeaking – it sounded a bit like a mouse on top of a flagpole.'

'I really wouldn't know,' she said, 'but it seems to have stopped. I'm more worried about the other noise. What do you think *that* was?'

'The really loud *crashing* one?' said the man. 'Oh, that's *easy* – it was the greenhouse being destroyed.'

There was an agonising pause, during which Lucy imagined her stepmother surveying the widespread damage. And *then* came the horrible screeching. It began gently enough, as a raucous, ear-splitting wail, and got steadily worse after that.

'And I wonder who *that* could have been?' she screamed. 'Have we any ideas do you think? Do we have the slightest notion of just *who* might be responsible for such a destructive act?'

'Erm, yes, well let's see,' said the man nervously.

'Let's see *nothing*,' screamed the woman. 'It's *her* again, isn't it?'

'I don't *think* so dearest – she's securely locked up.'

'*Don't* argue with me,' snapped the angry female. 'Locked up or not, *she'll* be the one to blame. You *know* that, *don't* you? It's *always* her. Well she can stay in that bloody-well tower until I get an apology – and the repairs to the greenhouse are coming out of *her* money.'

The woman ran out into the garden and looked up towards the Panopticon, but Lucy leaned back just in time, desperately trying to think of a brilliant plan. As soon as the adults went inside she slid the bedside cabinet over the trapdoor so she could pretend to be asleep. Then she ripped a page from a school exercise book and scribbled a quick note, tying it around the first heavy thing that came to hand. It was a glass paperweight with a model of Grimston pier inside – she had never liked the horrible thing, and it suddenly seemed like the ideal item to be throwing out into the bushes.

A loud '*oof*' from Toby confirmed that the souvenir had reached its target, which meant that all Lucy had to do now was apologise to Lily – not because she was particularly sorry, but because she was going to explode if she didn't tell someone her secret – and it had to be *soon*.

Playing the Empire

Lucy sat on the end of her bed, smiling as Toby rummaged through her treasured collection of theatrical memories. He remained silent, but there was obviously something on his mind, and eventually he could bear it no longer. He picked up an unusually ornate hairbrush and turned to her with an enigmatic grin, waving the item at her like a wand.

'Alright Luce,' he said. 'I admit it – I'm mystified. Why do you want to spend your first day of freedom in the same room you were locked up in?'

'I *like* it up here,' she smiled, 'haven't I always told you that?'

'True,' said Toby, 'but I never really believed you until now. So three days in high security chokey wasn't really much of a punishment, was it?'

'Not really,' said Lucy, 'in fact I enjoyed it even more than usual, because I discovered something rather interesting.'

'A new piece of theatrical junk?' said Toby.

'I only discover new pieces on a Sunday,' grinned Lucy, 'and since you've got your green T-shirt on this must be a Monday.'

'It's not *my* fault she makes me wear colour-coded clothes,' said Toby.

'And licks your hair to stop it sticking up,' grinned Lucy.

Toby ruffled his sandy hair as much as possible and gave her a broad grin. 'There, that's the way I like it,' he said.

'Me too,' said Lucy. She grabbed the hairbrush and made out she was going to comb it straight again.

'That's your mum's old brush, isn't it?' said Toby, grabbing it back.

'Yes,' said Lucy, 'now give it *here*.'

'Wow – she must have been collecting this stuff for ages,' said Toby. 'There's absolutely tons of it – I bet it's worth a fortune.'

'No it's not,' said Lucy, 'because it's not for sale.'

'*Oh*,' said Toby. 'I stand corrected.' He picked up an old handbill that advertised a summer show at the Grimston Empire. It was from years ago, and featured strange acts he'd never heard of, like Maisie Barnacle and her amazing performing fleas. Below that, in smaller letters, were the Testudo Brothers and their Totally Terrific Talking Turtles, and then, in even smaller writing were the Grand Imperator and his troupe of Lectric Angels.

'That poster was one of hers,' said Lucy, pointing to the microscopic script at the bottom. 'Look – Maggie Blake as Mistress Angelique.'

'Oh yeah,' said Toby, squinting at the almost invisible writing. 'But that was *ages* ago, wasn't it? Didn't they demolish the Empire to build a warehouse for storing underpants or something?'

Lucy smiled but said nothing, and as Toby's attention turned to a poster advertising an end-of-pier curiosity show, she stroked her mother's written name, as if it might somehow connect them once more.

'Yeah,' said Toby, picking up a palmistry hand and examining the strange symbols that covered every part of it. 'I keep forgetting your mum was an artist. Is that why she collected all this junk then?'

'She was an *actress*,' said Lucy, 'and it's *not* junk, it's memorabilia.'

'Memoro-*what*?' said Toby.

'Things that bring back memories,' said Lucy quietly. 'People collect them because they wake up the past.'

'Yeah,' said Toby, 'but they'd be great for playing tricks.' He picked up a wig and tried it on, briefly bringing a smile to Lucy's face.

'You look totally ridiculous,' she said.

'Yeah,' he said, 'but we could use this to fool…'

'*No*,' insisted Lucy. 'I think we need to wait a while before we try any more trickery. It'll be at *least* a month before they forget about the last episode. And there's the small matter of the bomb-damaged greenhouse too, which you *might* want to avoid mentioning in front of Lily.'

'Oh, erm, *yeah*,' said Toby. 'Sorry about that. So, why did she put you in prison *this* time?'

'I invented a story about a jar of make-up cream that was haunted by a creature with a thin face and red hair,' said Lucy.

'Is that *all*?' grinned Toby. 'But you're making up stories all the time aren't you? Like that one you did at school, before the holidays.'

'Yes, but *she* doesn't like them,' said Lucy, 'and anyway it wasn't just the invention that got me locked up.'

'No?' said Toby.

'Erm, *no*,' admitted Lucy. 'I put one of Byron's Lectric speakers in the precious child's bedroom. Then I frightened him to death, by making ghostly noises in the night, and doing all sorts of whispery voices.'

'Oh, *brilliant*,' grinned Toby.

Lucy half expected to be asked what the lovely Tarquin had done to deserve the punishment, but Toby had been distracted by the huge brass instrument that was mounted in the north-facing window.

'Hey, Luce, this is a *great* telescope,' he said, with a broad grin. 'I can see all sorts out there. Look at all those molehills in your garden – and there's that awful sign of yours, down by the road.'

'The sign isn't anything to do with me,' said Lucy. 'And Percy says we have to live and let live as far as the moles are concerned. We *tried* getting rid of them, but... *hey, Lindstrom*, are you listening to me?'

'Four Havens,' said Toby, 'that's what it says on your sign.'

'Toby! Will you please give up with that rotten thing?'

'B and B,' said Toby. 'I know that one, it means Bed and Breakfast.'

'*Toby?*'

'H and C running W,' he said. 'That's hot and cold running water.'

'Toby! Will you stop that? Telescopes are for looking far off. If you really *must*, you can read the sign without it.'

'Ah, yes,' said Toby. 'But you can't see all the detail, can you? Look at the way the paint's flaking off. You can't see *that* with the naked eye, can you? And anyway, what's SV?'

'Sea views,' said Lucy.

'Oh, right,' said Toby, 'it's obvious I suppose, once you know.'

'Isn't everything?' smiled Lucy.

'Yeah,' said Toby, 'so what does 'Cruet extra' mean then?'

'I haven't a clue,' said Lucy. 'You'll have to ask the vicar. He's supposed to be an expert on ancient Grimston. And it was probably the Vikings who put the original sign up, so he's bound to know.'

'Did Vikings have cruet then?' said Toby.

'Maybe,' said Lucy. 'Or perhaps *they* didn't know what it was either.'

'*Aaagh* – they're coming,' said Toby, spying into the telescope. 'Look, it's Erik Bent-Axe and his rampaging cruet invaders – they're hurdling up the high street with theatrical memory-billy-o strapped to their helmets.'

'Yes, *very* funny,' sighed Lucy. 'Now, are you going to leave that valuable instrument alone?'

'I've just thought,' said Toby, 'if you *really* want to know what cruet is you could ask my mum. She's always wanted to run a boarding house. In fact I think she fancies this one, even if it *is* falling down.'

'Hey,' said Lucy, 'you're not supposed to say things like that.'

'Why not?' said Toby, 'you do.'

'But I live here,' said Lucy, 'so I'm *allowed*. Anyway, your mum's welcome to it. Your whole family could move in and we probably wouldn't even notice. Some of the rooms downstairs haven't been opened for years.'

'Wow,' said Toby, 'a house with unexplored rooms – cool.'

'They certainly *are*,' said Lucy. 'It's like the frozen wastes down there – all cold and barren and complicated. It's such a maze that even the rats get lost. I *know*, because the other day I saw one of them looking at a map.'

'What, *really*?' said Toby.

'Of course,' grinned Lucy, 'but they're not as clever as you think. It was the wrong way up.'

'The rat?'

'No, the map,' grinned Lucy.

'Really?' said Toby.

'No,' she said, 'not *really* at all.'

'You're *always* doing that, aren't you?' grinned Toby. 'I reckon you couldn't *stop* doing it even if you wanted to.'

'Doing what?'

'Telling lies,' he said.

Lucy stared, screwing her face up into the wrinkliest frown she could muster.

'They are *not* lies, they're *inventions*, and there's a great deal of difference. I get quite enough of that *liar* stuff from my stepmother, thank you very much.'

'Erm, sorry,' said Toby.

'Hmm,' said Lucy, raising an eyebrow.

'No, *really*, I am,' he added, thinking of the time he'd found her in the school stationery cupboard, her chalk stained face running with tears. 'Anyway,' he said, 'speaking of stories, how's your stepmother getting on with her book?'

'It's a total disaster,' said Lucy. 'She turned up for a signing at Rockfire's bookshop and there were mobs of angry parents trying to break the windows. One of them even shoved a burning book through the letterbox.'

'Wow,' said Toby, 'and what could be worse than *that?*'

'Erm, well there *was* something worse as it happens. They found out the book had been published by accident.'

'You're kidding,' said Toby. 'How did that happen?'

'There was a slight mix-up at the printing company,' said Lucy. 'They were supposed to print one with a similar name, but the manuscripts got swapped over and twenty thousand copies of hers got printed.'

'And what was hers called?' said Toby.

'Mambo Rumbletrouser and the Mystery of the Lizard Skin Folio,' said Lucy, grinning like a cat in a tree.

'It sounds *awful*,' said Toby.

'It's worse than that,' said Lucy. 'Do you want to read some of it?'

'Have you got a copy then?' said Toby.

'We've got loads. The coal shed is stuffed full of the horrible things. The publisher said we could look after them until they were needed.'

'And have they been back to check on them?' said Toby.

'Not unless they came at night,' said Lucy. 'Percy – that's my step-step-dad – called to ask how long we should keep them and the telephone operator said the company had gone out of business.'

'Because of her book?' said Toby.

'See for yourself,' said Lucy. She bent down and extracted a battered copy from under the bed leg. Toby took it and glanced at the cover.

'I don't think I'll bother,' he said.

'I don't blame you,' grinned Lucy. 'We sent twenty signed copies to the charity shop along with a pile of Fred Nebbley long-players. They sent a note back saying they'd made the records into plant pots but they'd put the books in the coal shed, thank you very much, and they never wanted to see them again, yours sincerely etc.,'

'It sounds like a fantastic read,' said Toby.

'The characters are based on people who stay with us,' said Lucy. 'But Lily didn't even change their names, so I hope *they* don't buy it. She used to sit at the breakfast table eavesdropping on their conversations and scribbling notes on anything that came to hand – sauce bottles, paper napkins, table cloths – I once caught her spelling out someone's name with baked beans.'

Toby was about to accuse Lucy of lying, but thought better of it. Then he remembered some of her other stories.

'You get *lots* of weird holidaymakers here, *don't* you?' he said.

'Oodles,' said Lucy. 'Percy says it's because Grimston is trapped in a time warp, but I reckon it's because the lamp-stand advertises in strange places.'

'*Lamp-stand?*' said Toby. 'Is that your new name for her then? I *like* it. She *is* a bit on the thin side, isn't she?'

'I'd say she was like a rake,' said Lucy. 'Only I don't want to give rakes a bad name. Did I ever mention that she's got a nose like a razor blade?'

'Once or twice,' smiled Toby. 'But what was that about advertising?'

'Oh, *that* – well, we were driving through a town in the middle of nowhere once, and she just wound the window down and threw a pile of postcards at the people standing in a bus shelter. Percy said it was the worst case of saturation advertising he'd ever seen.'

'Well he should know,' said Toby.

'You'd think so,' said Lucy, 'but we got quite a few bookings that year, and so he had to keep quiet about it.'

'Was that the time you had the family with an ugly baby that had ginger whiskers? And the couple that sat up all night with the light on, howling?'

'Might have been,' smiled Lucy.

'And there was that man from Lundern who had two heads,' said Toby. 'You told me the smaller one kept popping out of his shirt pocket and starting arguments with the main head.'

'Erm, ye-es,' said Lucy with a sly grin, 'but that was quite a while ago, wasn't it? I'm surprised you remember.'

'Oh *no*, I haven't forgotten *any* of them. They were the best ever.'

'Erm, you *do* know I made some of those up, *don't* you?' said Lucy.

'*No way,*' said Toby, 'erm, which ones?'

'All of them mainly,' said Lucy, 'apart from two.'

'And which two were those then?'

'I'm not saying,' said Lucy, 'I don't want to spoil your fun.'

'But what about that bloke who licked people's cutlery when they weren't looking?' said Toby. 'The one who used to blow his nose on the corner of the tablecloth – that one's true, *isn't* it?' He sounded slightly desperate, as if this particular story was his favourite.

'It *might* be,' said Lucy, not wanting to let him down too much.

'Oh good,' said Toby, 'because I told Miss Simmons about that one.'

'I bet she was impressed,' grinned Lucy, 'did you get detention?'

'No,' said Toby, 'but *you* might when we go back after the holidays. She asked where I dredged up such a load of old filth, and I told her – *sorry*.'

'Oh, *brilliant*,' said Lucy. She folded her arms tight and pushed her lips out in a sulk, like the lamp-stand often did. It was something her stepmother was *much* better at though, because she was a lot older and had had a lot more practice.

They sat in silence for five minutes or so, staring each other out. Toby rolled his eyes so that only the whites were showing, but Lucy held firm, pretending to push a finger up her nose as far as the second knuckle. And she finally managed to crack Toby's guard by waggling her left ear whilst keeping the right one completely still.

'Come on then,' he grinned, 'I *know* there's something going on.'

Lucy pushed her lips out even further and crossed her arms even tighter.

'Go on,' he said, 'you're dying to tell me, I *know* you are.'

'I'm not,' said Lucy, wondering whether to give in. If Toby went home now she'd have to wait even longer to tell the story – and she couldn't *bear* to go another week without sharing her secret with someone.

'You *are*,' laughed Toby, 'your lips have gone all slack.'

'Alright,' admitted Lucy, 'but if I tell you, then you've got to swear to keep it a secret. You have to swear with all the worst words you know, including all those new ones we learned last term.'

'Alright,' said Toby, holding his hand up. 'I swear.'

'Nope,' said Lucy, 'on second thoughts that's not good enough – hold your right hand up.'

Toby did as he was told and Lucy gave a little grunt. Moments later, she burst into a high-pitched chant.

'*Surzas, surzas, surzas. Stretch forth and conquer. I, Toby Lindstrom, under pain of mortal death, do hereby swear that I will always, hail, seal and never reveal any mystery, obscurity or secret entrusted to me. So help me God, and keep me steadfast, in this, my most solemn undertaking.*'

'Erm, yeah, *right*,' said Toby, repeating the words. 'And where did you get all *that* from?'

'I made it up,' grinned Lucy. 'Now, are you ready to hear the secret?'

'At *last*,' said Toby. 'Well *go on* then.'

'Right,' said Lucy, 'but before that we need to have another look through that telescope.'

Toby swung the great brass instrument so that it faced roughly east, out over the Cherman Sea where the drowned village was supposed to be. The image in the eyepiece moved so quickly that he felt sick, so he used the tiny winding handles instead, moving the optic much more slowly. First, he located the harbour, and then the chain-link bridge to the hermit island, and finally, as he swung through due north, he came across the amusement arcades and whelk stalls on the promenade.

'I can see the pier,' he said, 'and the ferry boat.'

'Red or blue funnel?' asked Lucy.

'Red,' said Toby, suddenly hesitating. 'Erm, isn't that the one your dad…'

'*Yes*,' snapped Lucy, 'it *is* – or rather it *was*. Now, why don't you just move away from the ferry?'

Toby wound the telescope over to the west, crossing the railway line and the close-packed roofs of the huddly houses and finally reaching the pong factories further inland. This was the oldest part of town where columns of smoke constantly belched from the brick-pile chimneys at Snogg's Brown Sauce and Pickle-a-Torium. It was also where Lucy's Uncle Byron had his laboratory, which was buried in the maze of streets near the gasworks – a place where the weather was always ten times worse than anywhere else. Her uncle had a theory that it was all the fault of the local corporation, and if people paid more taxes, they'd get more sunshine. But then they'd be happier, and *that* didn't seem right either, because he'd always maintained that Grimston had been created for a particular purpose, and it definitely wasn't enjoyment.

'You've gone too far,' said Lucy, realising that she'd used her stepmother's favourite phrase. 'You've gone too far this time, Lucy,' she'd say. 'There's a limit to how much the truth can stretch, and you've just passed it.'

'Look,' she said, 'all you need to do is line up the marks.'

Toby located the two red arrows on the mount and lined them up so that the telescope was pointing in the right direction. Then all he had to do was move the thing up, until the green arrows were aligned.

'There's a house Luce, with a room at the top – and it has four windows, just like this one.

'And what can you see in the window?' said Lucy.

'Erm, another telescope?' said Toby. 'Only it's a lot bigger than this one. And there's a label on it that says *The Mundus Magni-Ficat*. Wow, if I can see that well with *this* one, just think how good the Magnificat is. I bet you can see insects pulling faces ten miles away.'

'Not quite,' said Lucy, 'but if they stand on their tiny little suitcases and get up on tiptoes you can just about see them waving.'

'How do you know?' said Toby, 'have you been over there and used it?'

'Nope,' said Lucy smiling, 'not to the room *you're* looking at anyway.'

'And what exactly do you mean by that, oh mysterious one?'

'Just be patient,' said Lucy, 'and tell me what else you can see.'

'The room's empty,' said Toby.

'No it isn't.'

'Well *I* can't see anything – maybe if we had a bigger telescope?'

'Good idea,' smiled Lucy. 'So why don't we go over and use that one? Or perhaps one just like it? First though we'll be needing some peanuts.'

'But I don't like them,' protested Toby.

'Keep them in your pocket then,' she said, 'in case we need to tempt an elephant out of a tree.'

Lucy unlocked her bedside cabinet and pulled a toy theatre out from under a blanket. It had solid panelling at the back and slots in the sides, where the actors-on-sticks could be pushed in. There was a winding handle too, which cranked a paper roll and allowed the scenery to change.

'This is the Empire,' said Lucy proudly. She pulled back the flowery curtains on either side of the stage to reveal the interior.

'Is that *it?*' said Toby. 'The big secret you've dragged me here to see?'

She handed the model over to Toby who turned it this way and that, looking for some sign of a trick or practical joke. It was exactly as it seemed though, just a simple model theatre, the stage of which had obviously been decorated by hand. It was painted with an ornate symbol that had four main sections, picked out in red, blue, yellow and green. The segments of the symbol were lower than the surrounding wood, suggesting that they were designed to hold an item of the corresponding shape. And if you looked long enough it was even possible to imagine that they formed some kind of rotating puzzle, where the various pieces revolved about the centre. The middle of the symbol was similar, in that it too had a slightly mysterious and interlocking feel to it, but the dish-like indentation was semi-spherical in shape, as if to support a giant marble.

'Alright,' grinned Toby, 'what's special about it? I *know* you Luce – you wouldn't drag me all this way just to look at some old lumps of plywood.'

'And what if I have?'

'Luce, it's just a stupid toy theatre and it's not even very well made.'

'It *is* well made,' frowned Lucy, 'but even if it wasn't, it doesn't matter – just *watch* will you?'

'Right,' said Toby, 'but I'm willing to bet I've seen the play before.'

'Not *this* one, you haven't,' smiled Lucy. She tilted her head back and pursed her lips, as if she was going to blow a soap bubble through a hoop.

'*Phenuu,*' she hissed, almost silently.

There was a brief, almost invisible glow in the middle of the stage.

'What was *that* all about?' said Toby, 'and, erm, what's *that?*'

A peanut had appeared in the central indent of the stage, as if a spell of invisibility had suddenly been removed.

'It's a peanut,' said Lucy with a smile.

'I can *see* that,' said Toby, 'but I still don't like them – and especially not *that* kind, with the shells left on.'

'Never mind whether you *like* them or not,' said Lucy, 'just *think* for a moment – where do you imagine it came from?'

Toby picked up the Empire and turned it upside down, rapping his knuckles on the base, in case there was a cleverly concealed compartment.

'There must be a hollow space inside,' he said.

'There *isn't*,' sighed Lucy.

'It wouldn't need to be very big,' said Toby, 'just room for one nut.'

'Let's see then, shall we?' said Lucy. She pursed her lips again and closed her eyes this time before uttering the words.

'*Mag Phenuu*,' she whispered. There was a slightly brighter glow this time, accompanied by a sound like tissue paper being rustled.

'Oh,' said Toby, counting the nuts that had appeared next to the original one. '*Twenty* peanuts. Well you could still fit twenty in there, no problem.'

'I think you're what Uncle Byron calls a doubting Thomas,' sighed Lucy. She closed her eyes with a mad squint, as if concentrating on an impossibly long division. Then she took a deep breath and pushed it all out at once.

'*Beeee Mag Phenuu*,' she gasped.

There was an embarrassing silence where nothing seemed to happen, and then, just as Toby began to wonder if the theatre might be broken, the surface of the stage glowed even brighter, lighting up like the inside of an old wireless radio. The sound of rustling paper returned too, but louder this time – and it was followed by a brilliant flash of light that temporarily blinded them both.

When the pair recovered their vision the theatre was still there, but it was now covered in a pile of nuts about a foot deep.

'*Gordon Bennett*,' shouted Toby. 'Alright, *please*, no more nuts – I *believe* you. So where the hell did they all come from?'

'I thought you'd never ask,' said Lucy. She retrieved the theatre from beneath the pile and placed it on the bed, laying the palm of her hand on the painted symbol.

'*Now* what are you doing?' said Toby.

'Give me your hand and you'll find out,' said Lucy.

'Not until I know what's going on,' said Toby with a suspicious look.

'It's something I discovered when I was locked up,' said Lucy. 'Come on, I promise it won't hurt – *much*.'

'Oh well that's it,' said Toby, 'I'm *definitely* not playing.'

'But I think it might be the message,' said Lucy, offering her hand again.

'*Message?*' said Toby. 'What message is that?'

'Don't you remember? You said my real mother should have left a message before she disappeared. Well I agree – she *should* have, and I think this might be it. So *now* are you ready?'

Toby took her outstretched hand and watched as Lucy closed her eyes. She whispered so quietly this time that he was unable to make out the word, even though he was listening intently.

'*Empaaah,*' she mouthed, forming her lips as if to blow a gentle kiss.

There was a short delay, followed by the sound that dried-up leaves make when they rustle along a concrete path.

'What was *that*?' said Toby. 'And what's that *smell*? It's like toy trains.'

'It always happens,' said Lucy. 'Byron says that magic *always* smells like Lectric. Or Lectric smells like magic. One or the other.'

'*Magic*?'

'Well maybe it's not magic,' said Lucy, 'but *I* don't understand it, so it might as well be.' As she spoke, the bedroom walls became darker and less distinct, like distant skies in dusk-light. Finally, they disappeared altogether, leaving the pair standing amidst a black void.

'Luce?' said Toby, 'I don't like this – what's happening?'

'Don't worry,' said a reassuring whisper, 'just stand still.'

The floor began to vibrate, as if a thousand elephants were stampeding past them just a few feet away. There was nothing to see though – just a gentlest of draughts on their cheeks, and a strange impression that it was *them* and not the elephants who were moving.

'I've managed the standing still bit Luce, but I still have a problem with the worrying. What was that noise, and why has it gone dark?'

'Don't panic,' she whispered, 'it'll be over soon, and *then* you'll see.'

After a few seconds, the sound of marauding elephants died away, replaced by a gentle, almost heavenly chant that seemed to be trying to coax the light back into existence, banishing the shadows to far away corners. Then, a drift of something like dandelion seeds floated past, shedding a soft glow on their faces. The spheres of light did not actually touch, but were drawn to each other's gravity – constellations that wandered across an inky sky, pulling their wonderment behind it.

'This is *brilliant*,' said Toby, reaching for the lights with his free hand. The glowing balls circled his fingers, avoiding his grasp and humming gently.

Then they went to Lucy, tenderly grazing her cheek before accelerating off through the wall, as if they had urgent business elsewhere.

'We're not in Grimston any more, *are* we?' said Toby. 'It feels *different* – like that story where the children go through the coats and find a new world in the back of a wardrobe.'

In the distance, they heard the sound of thunder and roaring, and a fanfare of trumpets.

'Something like that,' smiled Lucy, suddenly realising that she was still holding Toby's hand. It had seemed necessary in order to bring him, even though she didn't know where the thought had come from. 'It's much better than that,' she grinned. 'Just wait, *you'll* see…'

Now that the level of light had increased, Toby could see what she meant. They were standing in a smooth-walled, cubical room that measured about ten feet on each side. Three of the walls were blank, but the fourth featured a large, panelled door with a big brass lock. Toby didn't pay much attention to the exit though because the central part of the room was *much* more interesting – it was crammed with twisted pipes and bendy tubes, all of which were connected to a complex-looking machine. The metallic casing of the device had a dull sheen to it, and seemed to vibrate in sympathy with the hum that filled the room.

'It's full of nuts,' said Lucy.

'Yes,' grinned Toby, 'and so are you.'

'Well thanks a *lot*,' snapped Lucy. 'I thought you might be a little more impressed than that. And it would be *such* a pity if you went back to Grimston never having learned anything, wouldn't it?'

'Erm, yeah,' said Toby, glancing at the locked door. 'Sorry – it's all just a bit of a shock.'

'You're forgiven,' said Lucy.

She placed her hand on a part of the machine that was surrounded by an engraved rectangle. A flat metal plate jumped inwards slightly, and with a hiss of compressed air, it disappeared to reveal a small control panel. There was a switch that could be set to 'shells' or 'no shells' and a button marked 'test'. The only other items were two lights, one red and one green.

'Are you going to press it then?' said Toby.

'Nope,' smiled Lucy, 'you are.'

'Erm, no thanks,' said Toby, 'it doesn't look that friendly.'

'*Friendly?*' said Lucy. 'It's a peanut machine, not a Lectric chair.'

'Hmm,' said Toby, considering the possibilities, 'alright then.'

He reached over and pressed the button, but before he could release it, a small blue spark leaped out and danced around on his fingernail.

'Ouch, it *bit* me,' he squealed. 'I thought you said it was friendly?'

'Don't be such a pussy,' grinned Lucy. 'It *always* does that – now just listen, and wait.'

There was the usual short pause, followed by a sound like a mouse blowing up a paper bag. Then the red light came on, and somewhere above them, a Lectric motor started up.

'Have I broken it?' said Toby.

'Be patient,' whispered Lucy, 'these things take time.'

Just then, the room started to vibrate, gently at first but becoming much more violent, as if the elephants had decided to play a return concert. Then the noise died away again, and the heavenly voices returned.

'Hey,' grinned Toby, as the chanting reached a climax, 'I reckon this is going to be *really* good.'

As the sound of trumpets came and then finally went, the red light went off and the green light came on, accompanied by a loud bang.

'Erm, wait a minute,' said Toby, 'is that *it?*'

'Why don't you have a look around?' suggested Lucy.

Toby gazed about, desperately searching for something wonderful.

'Alright,' he said eventually, 'I give up.'

'You'd better be quick,' smiled Lucy. 'It'll be going soon – look, it's there, just above your head.'

Toby looked up, and there, floating about two feet above him, was a single peanut. It was encased in some kind of transparent shield – and as he reached out to it, his hand was engulfed by a sheet of blue flame.

Tzzzzzzzzzt.

'*Owwwww,*' he squealed, 'you could have warned me.'

'Shush,' said Lucy. 'Just watch.'

Seconds later the transparent shell turned opaque and then disappeared with a loud crack. The peanut hovered for a moment and then it too disappeared.

'It's an awful lot of trouble to go to just for one nut,' said Toby. 'Have you ever thought of just buying them in packets?'

'Why bother,' said Lucy, 'when I can have as many as I want?'

'So they disappear from here and reappear on the stage of your toy theatre?' said Toby.

'I *think* so,' said Lucy, 'but I've never been in both places at once, so I can't be certain.'

'So what's the story then?' said Toby. 'Is it your job to fill the machine up or something?'

'You don't *get* it, do you?' said Lucy. 'The machine never runs out you idiot, it just goes on and on, for ever and ever. I've been eating them for days now and the needle never goes lower than this mark.'

She pressed another panel, which slid aside to reveal a brass dial with a picture of a nut engraved on it. The silvery needle was quivering in a region of the scale marked 'plenty'.

'Well they must come from *somewhere*,' said Toby.

'If you say so,' smiled Lucy.

'But they *must*,' said Toby, 'otherwise they'd run out. I reckon they probably come from up there, where the big pipe comes through the ceiling.'

'Yes,' grinned Lucy, 'that's what I thought, at least to begin with.'

'*Well then?*' said Toby. 'Have you *tried* looking outside on the roof?'

'There *is* no roof,' said Lucy, 'and there's no outside either – at least not in the way you mean. Now, would you care for another nut?'

Nether

Grimston

Lucy took the key from her dress pocket and turned it in the well-oiled lock. The mechanism gave a gentle click and the door sprang open slightly, as if it had been anticipating her actions.

'And where did you get *that*?' said Toby, pointing at the key. 'Or do they hand one out with every toy theatre?'

'I was patient,' smiled Lucy. 'On first couple of visits the door was locked and there was no key – and I used to lay awake at night wishing there was. Then one day I came here and it was just lying on the floor.'

'So you *kept* it?' said Toby.

'I don't think anyone will object,' said Lucy. 'You'll soon see why.'

She pushed the door open and they stepped from the peanut room and into the space beyond. They were greeted by the smell of salt spray in the air and the raucous sound of seagulls.

'There,' she said, 'what do you think?'

'Erm, we're back in Grimston,' said Toby after a short pause. 'At least I *think* we are.'

'Something like that,' said Lucy, 'but it's not Grimston.'

'But this is exactly the same as your bedroom.'

'It's a mirror image of it,' said Lucy. 'We're in the Malmaison – this is the room you were looking at through the telescope.'

'It's a trick, isn't it?' grinned Toby. 'I don't know how you did it Luce, but it's like that new attraction on Grimston pier – the one you invented.'

'I've told you before, I *didn't* invent it,' sighed Lucy.

'You *did* Luce, in a way. You wrote that story about the '*You Won't Bleevit*' and it was read out in class. Then Biffo Perkins told the story to his dad, and old man Perkins used the idea to build the attraction on the pier.'

'Yes,' said Lucy, 'but that's not the same as inventing it.'

'Well *I* think it is,' said Toby. 'You had an idea, then you wrote it down and suddenly it was all real – that's good enough inventing for me.'

'Thanks,' said Lucy. 'I appreciate your confidence.'

'Yeah, and another thing – old man Perkins' place is nowhere near as good as the one in your story,' said Toby. 'They just get you inside and use mirrors and smoke and stuff to make you think you're somewhere else. And they blow fishy smells through holes in the wall to make you think you're at the seaside.'

'But you *are* at the seaside,' smiled Lucy.

'You know what I mean,' said Toby. 'It's a big con trick, like this place.'

'It's *not* a trick,' said Lucy. 'You thought we'd moved, and we *have*. Come and look through this telescope if you don't believe me.'

'And why will *that* change my mind?' said Toby.

'Because if this is the Malmaison house then you'll be able to see my room,' said Lucy.

'I *can*,' said Toby, lining up the instrument just as he'd done earlier. 'It's all there; just as you'd expect – the house, the sign, and your bedroom window – what's so unusual about that?'

'Aren't you forgetting one tiny detail Toby? This is *all* unusual – unless you think travelling half way across town using a toy theatre is normal?'

'Erm, I s'pose not,' admitted Toby. 'Now you come to mention it.'

'*Right*,' smiled Lucy. 'So, just from memory now, tell me what colour my bedroom curtains are.'

'That's easy,' said Toby confidently. 'They're bright yellow.'

'Correct,' said Lucy. 'Now have a look through the telescope.'

'*Oh*,' said Toby. 'They're a sort of grotty brown, like dried gravy. But how can that be?'

'It can't,' said Lucy, 'if that's really my room.'

'So *is* it?'

'I don't know,' said Lucy. 'The only way to find out is to go over there.'

'Right,' said Toby, turning to go. 'I'll go back the way we came and when I get there you can look for me in *that* thing. I'll wave at you.'

'There's just one small problem,' said Lucy, wearing a broad grin. 'The door leads back to the machine room.'

'So?' said Toby. 'We just go in there and… *Oh*. I see what you mean. There's only one door, and it connects *this* room to the one that contains the peanut machine. So we *can't* go back, can we?'

'Correct,' said Lucy. 'So why don't you stop worrying about gravy coloured curtains and come with me? I've been here before, remember?'

'Erm, alright,' said Toby. 'But what if we meet someone?' He scanned the telescope along the foreshore but the promenade was completely deserted.

'Did you see anyone?' said Lucy.

Toby shook his head.

'So do you feel any better about coming along?'

'Not really,' he replied. 'I didn't think it was possible for anywhere to be grimmer than Grimston, but this place is certainly having a good try. It gives me the creeps.'

'Me too,' said Lucy. 'I came here every day when I was locked up and I never saw a soul. It's like being inside one of those glass dome things full of water and snowflakes – only without the snow – and the water.'

She pushed Toby away from the eyepiece and squealed the telescope around on its mountings, eager to move on.

'Hey, don't do that,' said Toby. 'I'd just found something interesting.'

'Really?' frowned Lucy. '*Where?*'

'To the left of your house,' said Toby, 'right at the end of the promenade, near the golf course – it looks like a sort of bandstand.'

'Impossible,' said Lucy, 'there's nothing out there except sand dunes.'

'Well there is now,' smiled Toby.

'Let *me* have a look,' said Lucy. She lined the telescope up on the clubhouse and then swept slowly from side to side, scanning the grass-topped dunes and the wild marshes beyond. And sure enough, she saw something that hadn't been there before. The question was, why had it suddenly appeared? Or had she simply not noticed it before?

'I *told* you,' grinned Toby. 'It looks like a bandstand, doesn't it?'

'I suppose so,' admitted Lucy.

'It's a good job you brought me along then, isn't it?' grinned Toby.

'Not really,' said Lucy. 'Whatever that thing is, it's miles away.'

'*So?*' said Toby.

'So it's no use to us,' snapped Lucy.

'Hey,' said Toby, 'there's no need to bite my head off.'

'Sorry,' said Lucy, 'but this feels like *my* place, and if anyone was going to find something new then it should have been me.'

'Yeah, right,' said Toby, 'but hey, I've just thought of something. If there *was* someone else here then they could go back to the real Grimston, and they'd end up in your bedroom, wouldn't they?'

'Oh,' said Lucy nervously. 'I hadn't thought of that – erm, wait, no, it's alright. They couldn't, could they? Not without the Empire.' She breathed a great sigh of relief that they couldn't reach her, whoever *they* were.

'Yeah, but how do you know they *haven't*?' said Toby.

'I never thought of that either,' said Lucy, suddenly glad of his company. She'd spent so much time exploring the town that she'd completely ignored the room itself – and it had taken Toby's curiosity to wake her up.

'Alright then,' she said, 'let's see shall we?'

She started pulling things down from the shelves and examining each item in detail. Eventually she concluded that the room was the same as her own – but with one significant difference. When she opened the bedside cabinet and pulled back the blanket there was no sign of the Empire.

'That's a relief,' she said, slumping into the armchair.

'Right,' said Toby, 'but it's a bit of a worry too, because if there's no theatre then how do we get back?'

Lucy smiled. Now *she* was the one with the answers.

'That's easy,' she said, 'but first we're going for a look round.'

'I'm not sure I want to,' said Toby, 'this is all a bit too scary.'

'I know what you mean,' said Lucy. 'I felt sick the first few times, but I got used to it. And you *are* looking a bit green around the ears.'

'Yeah?' said Toby. 'Well I'll be alright in a minute.'

'Good,' smiled Lucy, 'so we can go then, can we?'

'Once you tell me about the houses,' said Toby. 'Why are there two big houses in Grimston, both exactly the same?'

'*Nearly* the same,' said Lucy. 'My great-grandmother built hers as a mirror image, like a reflection.'

'Your great-gran? But I thought…'

'Look,' said Lucy, 'you know the black house – the one they call the Malmaison? Well that was built by my family about a hundred and eleven three years ago. But there was this huge argument and my great grandmother moved out. She took all her money with her and built another house, right where it could be seen from the first one. And then she bought this huge telescope, so she could spy on the rest of the family.'

'So *they* bought one to spy on *her*?'

'Exactly,' said Lucy.

'Families eh?' said Toby.

'Quite,' said Lucy, 'but not happy ones – anyway they all eventually died from eating too many winkles or got murdered or threw themselves under buses or trams. My great grandmother outlived them all, and that's how we ended up living where we do today – it got passed down the generations.'

'So the Malmaison house was sold?' said Toby.

'Quite often,' said Lucy. 'The last time was a few years ago – it was bought by those two old ladies – the ones nobody has ever actually seen.'

'Right,' said Toby, 'but it doesn't explain any of this, does it?

'No,' said Lucy, 'not really.'

'Unless it's meant to show that things which look similar can actually be opposites,' said Toby. 'Like if you imagine Grimston to be heaven then this place is a sort of hell.'

'It's not *that* bad,' said Lucy. 'Actually I quite like it here – it's peaceful.'

'Yeah,' said Toby. 'But do you see what I'm getting at? Maybe it's a sort of lesson, to tell you how different things can be.' He bent down to examine something he'd spotted under a chair. But after picking it up, he was none the wiser. 'What's this for?' he said, handing the item to Lucy.

'It's a toy boxing machine,' said Lucy. 'Just like the one in my real room.'

'But there are four boxers,' said Toby. 'Isn't that a bit strange?'

'I don't know,' said Lucy. 'Perhaps it is, now you come to mention it. I never play with it. It's silly.'

Toby took the toy back and examined it in detail – and the closer he looked the more interested he became. There were four winged fighters, one in each corner of the ring, and dressed in shorts that were red or blue or green or yellow. The four sides of the ring were painted with text in matching colours. Two of the sides said '*Not all angels are good*', and the other two sides said '*Not all daemons are bad.*'

'This is *very* unusual,' said Toby. He clicked at each of the trigger paddles in turn, causing the angels to throw punches at each other.

'Of course it is,' said Lucy. 'But it doesn't *mean* anything.'

'I wouldn't be too sure about that,' said Toby.

'You can have it if you like — there are loads more where that came from. My mother collected all sorts when she was on tour.'

'But I didn't even know angels *liked* to box,' said Toby. He turned the toy repeatedly, as if viewing it from every conceivable angle might force the secret to reveal itself. Suddenly though, he seemed to lose interest, as if he was frustrated at not being able to work it out. He handed the toy back and wandered over to the wall, tapping it gently and listening to the echoes.

'*Toby*? What on earth are you doing *now*?'

'I'm feeling the ornately carved panelling,' he said with a grin.

'*Why*?'

'There's *always* a secret passage behind the panelling — haven't you read any mystery books?'

'Not many,' said Lucy. 'I prefer to make up my own stories. *So*, have you found the secret way out?'

Toby patted the wall again, as if a door might appear at any moment.

'Well?' said Lucy.

'Not so's you'd notice,' admitted Toby.

'I thought as much,' said Lucy. 'Then shall we try it my way?' She opened the south facing window and stepped out onto the tiny wooden balcony, and then, to Toby's surprise, she vaulted over the low wooden handrail and disappeared from view.

The Malmaison was perfectly situated at the top of the Olivier's Mount and had one of the best views in Grimston — from the grassy area in front of the house they could see things now with the naked eye that Toby had needed a telescope to spot from Lucy's house. There was just one thing missing.

'Where *is* everyone?' said Toby. 'If I was going to have my own private world I'd at least make sure there was someone to talk to. And I'd make sure there were doors too, so people didn't have to climb down the outside of their houses.'

'I *like* climbing,' said Lucy. 'It's more interesting than doors and stairs.'

'And exhausting too,' added Toby. 'Which reminds me, I'm starving. Is there anything to eat in this place?'

'There isn't time,' said Lucy.

'I don't want much,' said Toby, 'practically nothing in fact.'

'Good, because that's exactly what you're going to get,' said Lucy. 'You should have eaten those nuts I offered you.'

'But I'm *dying* for a bag of chips,' said Toby, 'with vinegar.'

'I don't believe it,' said Lucy. 'Ten minutes ago you were absolutely amazed by all of this, and now you're complaining because you can't stuff yourself full of fried potatoes.'

'Don't forget the vinegar,' said Toby, 'and lots of salt.'

'This is just like Byron's talking dog story,' said Lucy. 'The first day it happened people were amazed it could speak at all, but by the end of the second day everyone was complaining about how monotonous its conversation was – all about bones and the like.'

'Well it's not the kind of place you'd come for a holiday, *is* it?' said Toby.

'Neither is the real Grimston,' smiled Lucy, 'unless there's another accident with the weather.'

'Good point,' admitted Toby. 'Although while we're here there *is* one thing we *could* do – one very *exciting* thing.

'And what's that?' said Lucy. 'Does it involve chips?'

'No, it's better than that,' said Toby. 'We can go to your house – the one *here* that is, not the real one.'

'No we can't.'

'Why not?'

'Because there isn't enough time,' she replied.

'No time?' said Toby. 'So *now* who's the moaner? Just *think* about it. If the telescope room had all that stuff in it then maybe your room has too. And if there's a toy theatre in *that* room then maybe there's another world like this one inside that. Are you getting confused yet?'

'No,' said Lucy, 'because I've already thought of all that.'

'So what are we waiting for then?'

'Are you any good at running?' asked Lucy.

'Why?' said Toby. 'Is there someone coming?'

'No – there's never anyone here, I *told* you.'

'Why then?'

'So you can reach my house before the horizon rolls up.'

'Eh?' said Toby. 'What the *hell* are you talking about?'

'There's a limit to how long we can stay,' said Lucy. 'About twenty minutes.'

'And then what?'

'There's a thundering noise,' said Lucy, 'and then the sky gets rolled up.'

'Like a carpet you mean?'

'If you like,' she replied. 'And there's nothing you can do to stop it. I've hidden in telephone boxes, hung onto lampposts, and tried tying myself to fences. I even waded into the sea once and put my head under the water, but once the thunder comes and the sky begins to move that's it. And *that's* why we can't go to my house or visit that bandstand you found.'

'What about a bike?' suggested Toby. 'If we can't run fast enough then perhaps we can cycle?'

'I thought of that too,' said Lucy. 'There *is* a bike, leaning against the railings near the pier. I know, because I ran down there once. It took about twelve minutes.'

'Aha!' said Toby. 'So that's *it* then.'

'Sorry,' said Lucy, 'you reckon we can move the bike and come back to it next time, right?'

'Yeah,' said Toby.

'I've tried it,' said Lucy. 'When you come back next time the bike will be back at the pier.'

'What a *swizz*,' said Toby. 'Fancy giving you all *this* and then fixing it so you can't do anything interesting.'

'Yes, *fancy*,' said Lucy. 'But perhaps I don't *want* it to get any more interesting? My Uncle Byron reckons that the more fascinating things are the more dangerous they get, and he should know.'

'*Hmm*,' said Toby. 'Alright, so what happens when the carpet rolls up?'

'Well,' said Lucy. 'If we make it down to the sea front in time you'll find out, won't you?'

The streets that led from the Malmaison down towards the promenade were the steep, cobbled remnants of the old fishing town, overlooked by dozens of tall, narrow houses and oak-beamed inns. But there was no time to explore any of them – not if they wanted to get to the sea-front in time.

Their rapid descent started gently enough, near the graveyard where Angora Bunty, the famous writer was buried. It was *fairly* level as it ran past 'Paradisio', the old sea captain's house, but then it turned sharp right, racing down a long steep hill where the stones were as smooth as glass, polished by hundreds of year's worth of sailors' boots. They paused for breath at the bottom, and then started to run again, turning right at the Old Cross Inn and then left at the seamen's chapel, finally emerging onto the promenade.

'Do you think we'll make it to the pier?' said Toby. He was breathless and ready to drop.

'Stop talking and keep running,' gasped Lucy. 'You'll see, soon enough.'

She could never get used to seeing the promenade like this. Even in winter there was always someone mending a net or selling crabs or even just walking their dog. Here though, in the place she called 'Nether Grimston', there was nothing of the sort. Every detail of the real town was present, except for its inhabitants and their livestock. There was just one exception to that rule, and as they both looked up, they could see exactly what that was. There were *always* plenty of birds.

'This is *exactly* like Grimston pier,' said Toby grinning widely. 'But we've got it all to ourselves.'

'You'd better enjoy it while you can,' smiled Lucy. 'We've got about three minutes.'

'Alright then,' said Toby, 'let's go and have a look at the new attraction.'

Lucy had seen it all before and was still out of breath, so she sat on the marble horse trough while Toby ran across the road to the pier. He was looking for a sign that read '*So real you'll think you were there*', but he came back less than a minute later wearing a disappointed look.

'What's wrong?' said Lucy.

Toby shook his head, apparently not wanting to speak.

'Come on,' she smiled. 'What is it?'

'It's gone,' said Toby. '*The Bleevit* – it's as if it was never built.'

'That's because we're not in the real Grimston any more,' said Lucy.

'I *know* that now,' said Toby. He was wearing a worried look.

'You mean you weren't sure?'

'I was hoping it was just a dream Luce – but it's not, is it?'

'No,' she said seriously, 'but don't worry.'

'I *am* worried Luce – but not about *this* place.'

'Then why the long face?' said Lucy.

'I was thinking about yesterday, when we all went down to the *real* pier.'

'There's no need to rub it in,' said Lucy. 'The first day in ages we've had sunshine in Grimston, and I was locked in my own private prison.'

'Yeah,' said Toby, 'sorry about that, but *listen,* Luce – I think something *happened* when we were there. I kept hearing strange noises, like music, and there were birds everywhere – and then Fenny disappeared.'

'We've got about ten seconds left,' said Lucy with a nod.

'But I think she might be in trouble Luce.'

'Five seconds,' said Lucy, no longer listening. Her eyes were fixed on the distant horizon where for all *they* knew the Cherman Sea flowed out over the edge of the world.

'Four…'

Toby stepped towards the edge of the promenade, still thinking about their friend Fenny. Just for a moment though, she disappeared from his thoughts and he found himself staring at the thick bronze paint on the posts that marked the edge of the pavement. It *looked* to be newly applied, but there was no way of telling, and he suddenly had the strangest feeling that in Nether Grimston even brand-new paint might be thousands of years old.

'Three seconds,' said Lucy.

'Two…'

'One…'

There was a disturbance out at sea, like a shimmering in the air. If they had looked away and then back again, they might even have believed they had imagined it. A few seconds later though all doubt evaporated as the shimmer became real. At first, it looked like a flock of birds, but with every passing second, the sky became darker and darker, and the creatures got closer and closer. Finally, it became clear that they weren't birds at all.

'What *are* they?' said Toby, suddenly wishing he hadn't asked such an obvious question.

'I don't know,' said Lucy. 'That's as close as they come.'

As she spoke, the flock stopped about a mile offshore and began to hover. Even so, it was difficult to make them out because of the haze.

'But they've got *wings*,' said Toby nervously.

'I know,' said Lucy. 'I think they might even have more than one pair. When I came yesterday it was colder and I could see them more clearly.'

'But they look, erm, sort of human,' said Toby. 'What do they want with wings? And what are they doing?'

'I've never managed to work it out,' said Lucy. 'They get so bright it's difficult to keep looking.'

It was almost as if Lucy had been talking to Toby on the telephone and the tall, heavenly looking creatures had been listening in on another line. As soon as her words were uttered, the winged host spread themselves out in a line and dipped towards the sea, getting brighter and brighter as they went. And when they reached sea level they simply picked the water up by its edges, as easily if they were rolling up a rug.

'We're going to *drown*,' screamed Toby, as the sea arched above them. '*Luce*, it's coming over the top of us – and there are *things* in it.'

Sure enough, there *were* things. The sea was curled into a crystal curtain like a paper-thin wave, and there was a light coming from behind it, perhaps from the sun, or more worryingly, from the creatures. And silhouetted in that glowing light were thousands of lobsters and crabs and fish, all swimming around as if nothing was happening.

'Luce, I don't want to drown – for God's sake, *run*.'

'Stay where you are,' said Lucy calmly. 'But don't just look at the water.'

'*What?*' said Toby. 'What are you talking about?' As he turned to face Lucy, it became obvious what she'd meant. Towards the west, the houses, the railway, and the factories were rolling up too, preparing to dump the contents of a thousand smoke-filled chimneys on their heads. To the south, the broad, wet marshes were approaching their zenith – they could see the golf course too, like a map, laid out above them. Lucy managed to spot the bandstand as well, still torturing herself with the idea of getting to it when she couldn't even get as far as her own house.

'Oh, God, *no*,' shouted Toby as he turned northwards. 'Luce, just *look* at all those birds.'

The scene to the north was composed of rippling air and glowing clouds and hundreds of thousands of birds – not just Grimston's creatures but everyone else's as well – all packed into a maelstrom of beaks and feathers, flying wingtip to wingtip but never colliding.

'Earth and Air, Fire and Water,' whispered Lucy.

'*What?*' shouted Toby.

'Nothing,' said Lucy, 'just take a final look – we're about to leave.'

The four horizons had rolled up completely now, meeting at a point directly above Toby and Lucy. There was no sign of the winged creatures that had carried them though – they had disappeared behind the surfaces of earth and sea, cloud and marsh that now enclosed them completely.

'I've changed my mind,' said Toby. 'I want to stay – isn't there anything we can do to stop it?'

'No,' said Lucy, taking hold of his hand.

As she did so, the sound of invisible elephants returned, thundering past them and brushing their cheeks with the breeze. As the strength of their stampede-wind increased, the pair knelt together, clasping each other around the waist and looking straight up into the heart of the vortex. The point where the four edges met was rotating now, the walls of their private world spinning in sympathy, like a whirlpool with nowhere to go.

'Not long now,' whispered Lucy.

She gave Toby's hand a reassuring squeeze, and with the sound of trumpets and a sudden ear-splitting crack of thunder, the entire world turned black.

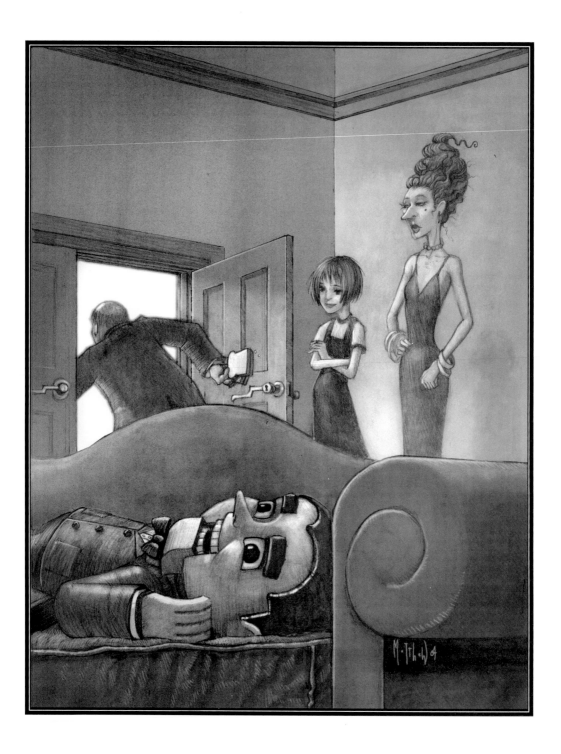

The Man With the Wooden Teeth

The darkness, the birds, and the rotating world were suddenly and distressingly *gone* – wrapped up by the sound of thunder and transported to a place that for now existed only in their memories. They were back in Lucy's bedroom, surrounded by thin blue layers of smoke and the deep, metallic smell of Lectric.

'Oh, *wow*,' grinned Toby, 'what *happened*?'

'We came back,' said Lucy plainly.

'I guessed that much,' he laughed, 'but *how*?'

'We got rolled up with the carpet,' said Lucy, making sure the toy theatre was still in one piece.

'Incredible,' giggled Toby, 'and that smell, it's just *amazing* – like when you blew up all the Lectric equipment in the physics lab.'

'Excuse *me*?' said Lucy. 'I think you'll find that it was *you* who blew the place up, when you…'

'Loooo…cy?'

The argument would have to wait. There was an infuriatingly familiar sound coming from downstairs – a bit like a shrieking thing that had recently given up screeching and decided to go into something much more terrifying.

'Loooo..cy?' it wailed. 'Are you *up* there, girl? Stop making all that noise *now* and get down here.'

'What noise is she talking about?' said Toby.

'I don't know,' said Lucy. 'Maybe it happens when you come back. I've never been here to hear it, remember?'

'Loooo…cy?'

'We'd better go,' said Lucy, 'if she comes up to check she'll want to know where the smell and the smoke came from.'

They climbed through the hatch and slid down the ladder onto the dusty upper landing, which was populated by hunting trophies and hundred-year-old plants in tall glazed pots. And as they crossed the threadbare Persian carpet and ran downstairs, it suddenly occurred to Lucy that her friend might give their secret away.

'Erm, *Toby?*' she said. 'Just remember that what happened in the Panopticon is a secret – so keep your BFM shut.'

'You know me Luce,' he said with a grin.

'Yes, I *do* know you, and that's why I'm saying…'

'Yeah, but *God* it was *brilliant*, wasn't it?'

They swung round the ornately carved newel post at the bottom of the stairs and found themselves in the huge baronial hallway, where stuffed animals gazed down from every possible nook and cranny.

'This place gives me the creeps,' said Toby.

'Me too,' agreed Lucy, 'but they're heirlooms, so we have to keep them.'

'Yeah, well I wish they wouldn't keep staring at me,' said Toby, skidding on a rug and breaking into a sprint again.

'Wait for me,' shouted Lucy, 'I…'

As Toby ran into the huge draughty kitchen, he collided with a thin, hawk-like woman who was mopping the tiled floor. She was wearing a sickly yellow housecoat and a disgusting floral pinny.

'Are you alright, Toby?' she said.

Toby was temporarily struck dumb, trying not to stare at the sharp nose and mass of flame red hair that belonged to Lily Winnet-Blake, Lucy's stepmother.

'*Well?*' snapped Lily, tapping an impatient toe on the tiles.

'Erm, *yes* Mrs. Winnet-Blake, I'm just feeling a bit pale – I think we came down the stairs a bit too quickly.'

'I see,' said Lily. 'Then perhaps you should try walking?' She gave Lucy a frown, as if Toby was her responsibility – then she went back to the tiles, paying particular attention to the red one.

'She only mops up when we're expecting guests,' whispered Lucy. 'So I reckon there's *something* going on – look at Percy, he's even more anxious than usual.'

Lucy's step-step-father was sitting at the big oak table, puffing on an empty pipe and obviously deep in thought. Lucy and Toby sat down opposite him so they could whisper to each other if they needed to.

'Percy? This is Toby – he's in my class.'

'What? Oh yes, pleased to meet you old boy,' said Percy. He had the kind of face that would look better on a very sad dog.

'And what have you two been up to?' he said. 'I heard noises – it sounded a bit like a brass band, although I might have imagined that bit.'

'We've been exploding things mainly,' said Toby.

'Hmm,' said Percy, absent-mindedly. 'Well *that* certainly sounds interesting – just mind you don't blow up something you'll need later.'

Toby looked surprised, as he'd been hoping for the kind of reaction Lucy got with *her* stories.

'He's thinking about work,' whispered Lucy. 'You can say practically anything to him when he's trying to come up with new ideas. The lamp-stand reckons it's the first sign of madness, and she should know.'

'So what do you think about my blowing things up idea?' said Toby, whispering to Lucy behind his hand.

'Not bad for a first effort,' whispered Lucy. 'Three out of ten.'

'Is that all?'

'You're lucky you got that many,' she said. 'A really *good* lie has to have an element of truth in it and I don't recall us using any explosives. If you *really* want to invent a story then you have to weave believable ideas in with the implausible stuff – but at least you're trying.'

'Yeah, well you're definitely the expert when it comes to porky pies.'

'Eh?' said Lucy. 'What's a porky pie?'

'It's Cockernees rhyming slang,' said Toby. 'My dad says they talk like that all the time down in Lundern – *porky pies* rhymes with *lies*.'

'Why?' said Lucy.

'Because they end in the same sounding letters,' grinned Toby.

'No, stupid, *why* do they talk like that?'

'Dunno,' he said with a shrug. 'It must be like a secret, so nobody knows what they're saying.'

'Well it can't be much of a secret if Toby Lindstrom knows it.'

'What are you two whispering about?' said Lily, exchanging her mop for a mysterious new cleaning device.

'Erm, nothing Mrs. Winnet-Blake, we were just keeping secrets,' said Toby. 'About Lundern. And spies. And secret languages.'

'See?' he said to Lucy. 'It's easy.'

'*Right then,*' said Lucy. 'We'll just have to see about that, *won't* we?'

'Oh,' said Toby. 'So it's a *competition* then, is it?'

'Not if *that's* your best effort,' said Lucy. 'That was another three out of ten.'

'*Feet* Percy,' commanded Lily, wanting to Swipp underneath him.

Percy lifted his feet and carried on sucking his pipe. His brain was now fully committed to the exploration of thirty-seven different flavours of sauce, and his wife's mood went completely unnoticed.

'She's *amazing,*' whispered Toby.

'Yes, *isn't* she?' hissed Lucy.

Her stepmother didn't *like* modern technology and the new Swipp-o-Matic that Percy had brought home was far too modern. It had a *switch*, for one thing, and she didn't like switches. It had a squeezy plunger too, and she definitely didn't like those. She didn't like knobs either, or germs, or things that were painted black or green or certain shades of red, or anything to do with Lectric. *Especially* things that were to do with Lectric. And there were certain kinds of small car she hated too, and typewriters, clocks, brass letter openers, budgie seed trays…

'And where were *you* earlier this morning?' said the lamp-stand. She knocked Lucy's feet out of the way with the Swipp, then glared at Toby whilst waiting for an answer. 'I suppose you were at that Byron's again?'

Lucy nodded.

'Well *I* don't know what you find to do around there,' she said. 'Do *you* know what she finds to do around there Percy? *Percy?* Pay *attention.*'

'Eh?' said Percy.

'What does she *do* all day?' screeched Lily.

'Does it matter?' said Percy. 'She's happy, aren't you, Luce? And it keeps her busy.'

'I've told you a *thousand* times,' said Lily. 'She is *not* called *Luce* – and just because she's happy, it doesn't mean it's good for her. That Byron is a bad influence.'

Lucy smiled – dear Lily always called him *that* Byron.

'Well *I* spoke to that Byron once,' said Percy, 'and I quite liked him.'

'Don't talk such nonsense,' said Lily. 'How could you possibly like him? The man is a complete idiot. What is he?'

'He's an idiot dear,' said Percy. He was dreaming of what a quiet life might actually be like, and whether anyone he knew actually *had* one.

'That's *better*,' smiled the lamp-stand, 'now, what was I doing?'

'Testing a broom,' said Lucy.

'*What* did you say, young lady?'

'Sweeping the room,' said Lucy.

'*Did* you?' said Lily, her eyes narrowing into tiny disbelieving slits. 'Well in that case I've a mind to make *you* finish the job – but I want it done properly, so I'll do it myself. We want to be presentable for our guest, don't we?'

Nobody said anything.

'I *said* we want to be presentable Percy – *don't* we?'

'Yes dear,' sighed Percy. As his wife turned away, he knocked his pipe on the edge of the table and a column of ash fell to the floor. Then he winked at Lucy and nodded at the teapot in the centre of the table. It was a secret sign of some kind, as though she had just been admitted to his private club. She was glad to be a member too, just as long as they didn't have to talk about sauce.

'*Luce*,' whispered Toby. 'I've just noticed something funny about your kitchen floor.'

'You've finally noticed the red tile then?' said Lucy.

'Erm, ye-es,' said Toby, 'and I was just wondering – why would you want a black and white chequered floor with just one red tile?'

'Why wouldn't we?' grinned Lucy. 'Perhaps they ran out of tiles and that one was left over?'

'Eh?' said Toby.

Lucy smiled, but didn't bother to explain. It would do him good to be kept in the dark – that way she'd have something to bargain with if he ever had a secret that *she* wanted. The red tile was a trap, and she knew *that* for a fact. She had once watched her stepmother stand on it, and imagined a coconut rolling from a high shelf onto her head. The next day it had actually happened and Lily was steamrollered by a runaway pineapple. Unfortunately, Lucy had been unable to stop laughing, which had meant *another* day in the prison tower.

'Tell me,' whispered Toby, *'please?'*

Lucy shook her head and nodded towards the horrendous yellow-brown teapot. It was the colour of dog vomit and shaped like a dragon's head, with a huge spout formed by the flames of the animal's breath.

'You only get that teapot out when the vicar comes,' said Lucy.

'Well in *that* case the vicar must be coming, *mustn't* he?' said Lily.

Lucy elbowed Toby in the ribs. 'Now's your chance,' she whispered. 'You can ask him what a cruet is.'

'*You* ask him,' said Toby. 'I won't be here, will I?'

'Erm, is it alright if Toby stays for tea?' asked Lucy.

'No, it is not,' said Lily.

'Go on, let the boy stay,' said Percy. 'He'll be no trouble, will you Toby?'

'Alright,' said the lamp-stand, 'but only if he promises not to be sick.'

'So that's a yes then?' said Lucy.

'Sick?' whispered Toby. 'What does she mean…'

'*Shh,*' grinned Lucy. '*Look.*'

Lily had checked to make sure that Percy wasn't watching and was now primping her hair, using the big mirror over the hearth to admire herself. She was muttering too, just under her breath, but it was clear to everyone what she was saying, even poor Percy.

'*He said I was like a perfect rose you know, a beautiful thin stem, and a luxuriant red bloom for a head.*'

Lucy kicked Toby under the table, grinning as her stepmother became more beautiful by the minute.

'The vicar's *always* complementing her,' she whispered. 'He's always asking what she likes to do and where she likes to go. That's why he comes to the house so often – I think he fancies her.'

'Do you think he wants to marry her?' whispered Toby.

'Don't be *stupid*,' said Lucy, 'she's married to Percy – although he might agree to loan her out for a while, just to get a bit of peace. The vicar would need a big bathroom though.'

'Why's that then?' said Toby.

'For all her beauty preparations,' said Lucy. 'Last time I checked there were at least half-a-dozen bottles of Skruntley and Farmer's wrinkle cream – and about a ton-and-a-half of Boggley's *Re-Joov-e-Nate*.'

'Yeuk,' said Toby, 'my mum never uses stuff like that – but she never seems to look any older.'

'She'll look different in photographs though, won't she?'

'Dunno,' said Toby. 'We haven't got any – my dad has a collection of old cameras, but I don't ever remember seeing any photographs.'

'We've got *loads*,' said Lucy. 'But most of them are of *her*. I've got just one of my real dad, and none at all of my real mother.'

'That's a bit of bad luck,' said Toby.

'Byron says there's no such thing as luck,' said Lucy. 'He told me once that if you find a tortoise on a fence-post it didn't get there by accident.'

'Yeah, *right*,' said Toby, 'and what exactly does that mean?'

'That things happen in this world for a reason,' said Lucy.

Toby was watching Percy now, because he'd taken out a silver scraping thing and was cleaning the bowl of his pipe. It made a kind of scratching noise like a mouse walled up inside a pilchard tin.

'Are you looking forward to seeing the vicar, Percy?' said Lucy.

'Enormously,' he said, suddenly more alert.

'And have you had any more ideas for the sauce thing?' she said.

'A few,' replied Percy.

'Sauce?' whispered Toby.

'I'll tell you later,' said Lucy, glancing at the mirror again.

'*A lovely thin stem,*' said Lily. '*Yes. And a luxuriant bloom. Oooh. With a captivating and gorgeous scent. Ahhhh.*'

Toby giggled and mimicked Lily's actions, smoothing his face and patting his hair. Then he noticed Lucy – she was shaking her head furiously and silently mouthing something. It looked like the word 'no'.

'The thing with *mirrors* Toby is that they reflect,' said Lily. 'Which is probably what *you* should be doing, especially if you want to stay for tea.'

'Ah,' said Toby, 'erm, *sorry*, it was just a joke.'

'Yes,' said Lily. 'Well you'll be joking out in the street if I have any more of your cheek. It takes an enormous effort to keep up one's appearance you know. Beauty doesn't come cheaply.'

'Right,' said Toby. 'I'll remember that.'

'I *said*, Percy, beauty doesn't come cheaply.'

'No dear, you're absolutely right there,' he said. 'It certainly doesn't.'

Lily had been crowned Miss Creme-e-Lushus fifteen years ago and had never looked back since, although Byron once said that if she *had* looked back, she might have seen a lot of people giggling. He'd told Lucy that the only reason she won was that her father owned the Happy Friars chip shop and the judges had been bribed with free haddock for a month. They *still* hadn't been sure, but apparently an offer of a month's supply of mushy peas had been thrown in at the last minute and that had finally swung the deal. Lucy imagined them throwing tubs of bright green peas around and smiled to herself.

'Are you two plotting something?' said Lily. 'You *are*, aren't you? And I'll bet it involves Lectric, doesn't it? I've *heard* the stories about you trying to blow the school up. And *then* of course there's that bit of trouble we had with the greenhouse getting demolished.'

'Erm, the school thing was an accident,' said Toby. He was desperate to divert the conversation away from washing-line poles or anything remotely connected with the sound of breaking glass.

'Yes, and anyway, nobody was killed,' grinned Lucy, 'apart from two teachers, so there was no real damage.'

'Have you *heard* this Percy?' screeched Lily. 'She's at it again.'

'It's just an innocent bit of fun,' said Percy. 'And I'm sure it was an accident, like Toby says – at least I think the first *three* times were an accident.'

'There's nothing innocent *there*,' said Lily, 'it's inherited, and it's going to be stopped – she's just as bad as that Byron.'

'I'm *not*,' said Lucy. 'Anyway, you don't even know Byron. You only know what you make up, or what you've been told – he won't even speak to you.'

'Have you *heard* this Percy?' said Lily. 'It's that Byron's influence, I know it is. That Byron has just drifted through life, wasting his so-called talent, and if you're not careful Lucy you'll go the same way.'

'He's not like that at all,' said Lucy. 'He *has* got talent. And he invents all sorts of useful things.' As she was sticking up for her uncle, she realised that she only half believed it herself – Byron *was* a bit on the unpredictable side.

'I *see*,' said the lamp-stand. 'So what about the machine for talking to the dead? Did *that* work?'

'Erm, that was a joke dear, wasn't it?' said Percy.

'He's going to try it out again, very soon,' said Lucy with a wink. 'And he's going to let me help.'

'He most certainly is *not*,' said Lily. 'You're not to go anywhere near that thing, do you hear?'

Lucy gave a sheepish look and turned to Percy for support.

'You *haven't*,' said Lily. '*Have* you?'

'No,' said Lucy, shaking her head and crossing her fingers at the same time. It didn't count as a lie in any case. Lily was only worried about all the questions that would be asked if she got her brains fried in Byron's machine – that and all the paperwork they'd need to fill in.

'She *has* been messing with it,' said Lily, wagging a bony finger. 'I can tell you know, just by looking at her. And don't think I didn't see you crossing your fingers either my girl – this time you've gone too far.'

Lucy stared at the teapot and found herself hoping the vicar would turn up soon. And if not him then anybody really, just as long as they provided a distraction.

'There's nothing wrong with telling tales,' said Percy, 'as long as they're good ones. Her mother was always telling stories, so that's probably why Lucy is so good at it – and, er, erm…'

There was a sudden look of panic in Percy's eyes, like the reflections of approaching storm clouds. He'd seen dark weather approaching and was now regretting opening his mouth.

'*Uh-oh*,' whispered Lucy. 'Here it comes.'

Lily took a long deep breath and then held it for a moment before emitting a horrendous, ear-splitting screech. It began innocently enough, like a parrot asking for chocolate – but it ended up sounding like a banshee with all its scariest bits being mangled in a vice.

'I've *told* you about that before, *haven't* I?' she screamed. '*I'm* her mother now, and I'll not have you mentioning that other woman under my roof.'

'Yes, but it's *my* roof,' shouted Lucy. 'Dad left the house to me.'

'That's right, he *did*,' snapped the lamp-stand. 'And we're never allowed to forget it, *are* we? But you'll have to wait until you're twenty-one before it's properly yours, and an awful lot of things can happen in eight years.'

It sounded a bit like a threat, and Lucy was just about to say something she'd regret when her prayers for a distraction were answered. There was a loud knock at the front door, and she leapt from the table to go and answer it. Lily was even quicker though, and pushed her back into her seat.

'You stay there,' said her stepmother. 'I'll deal with this.'

Lily must still have been muttering under her breath when she got to the door because the vicar seemed to have heard something.

'*What* was it that should have been left to you Mrs. *Winnet*-Blake?'

'Erm, the arrangements,' said Lily, blushing. 'For the summer fete.'

Toby winked at Lucy and grinned. 'She's a quick thinker,' he seemed to be saying. 'You'll have to watch yourself.'

'Oh yes, of course Mrs. *Winnet*-Blake – the fete, how could I ever forget? The cakes you organised last year were an absolute triumph.'

The vicar gave a weak smile and placed his leather suitcase on the sideboard, patting it, as if it were a small dog.

'Ah, tea,' he said, spotting the pot and rubbing his hands. 'We *are* blessed, *aren't* we? But you haven't gone to the trouble of making your, erm, special fancies have you? Only I've been having a bit of stomach trouble recently.'

'It's no trouble at all for *you* vicar,' smiled Lily. 'I've prepared just a few of my choicest items.'

'Oh dear,' mumbled their guest. 'Erm, *really*, you shouldn't have, Mrs. *Winnet*-Blake.' Whenever he pronounced Lily's name he emphasised the Winnet instead of the Blake, which annoyed Lucy intensely. Her stepmother was definitely a Winnet, that was for certain, but Lucy didn't want *that* name anywhere near hers. The Blakes were noble, courageous, and caring, and the Winnets were, erm, well, they were just *Winnets, weren't* they?

'Well they're done now,' said Lily, 'all we have to do is enjoy them.'

'Erm, *quite*,' said the vicar, 'and speaking of enjoyment, do I notice a certain lovely difference? Unless I'm very much mistaken Mrs. WB, you seem to have done something with your hair.'

Lucy snorted and felt a bogey loosening. The lamp-stand's hair looked like it always did – an empty magpie's nest, filled to the brim with old twigs, and just waiting for the bird to return.

'It's a new cut, vicar,' said Lily. 'I saw it in a magazine.'

Lucy looked sideways at Toby.

'*Hamster and Furry Rodent Monthly*,' she whispered.

'Incorporating *The Weasel Gazette*,' added Toby with a broad grin.

Lily shot a venomous look at them.

'*Right*,' she said, 'Lucy, I want you to stop whatever it is you're plotting and help me put the plates out. You too, Toby – you might as well do *something* useful whilst you're here.'

'Yak,' said Toby, turning his nose up as they carried the plates to the table. 'What *is* all this disgusting stuff?'

'Those are pilchard and whipped-cream vol-au-vents,' said Lucy, 'and these are turnip surprise pasties.'

'What's the surprise?'

'There's nothing in them,' said Lucy, 'except for the turnip.'

'Great,' said Toby.

'And watch out for the chilli-pepper truffles,' said Lucy. 'They look like chocolate but they taste like something for sending your ears in opposite directions.'

'OK,' said Toby, poking at something that had once been alive. It was quite a while ago though, judging by the slimy green skin. 'Erm, what's…'

'Don't ask,' said Lucy. 'Or you really *will* be sick. You know how easily you throw up.'

'Right,' said Toby. 'I won't – and I won't be having any either.'

'Nobody will,' said Lucy. 'It'll go back in the cold room and stay there until Percy pretends to have it for supper. Then he'll chuck it in the sea, next time he's passing.'

'But why does she keep bringing the same things out?' said Toby.

'To save money of course,' said Lucy. 'So she can spend it on making herself more beautiful.'

'She'll need to save an awful lot of money for that,' said Toby. 'And I don't think she'll do it by telephoning Gorbin and Swabb, you know, that big posh shop near the police station? I heard her calling them once when I came to see you – she was ordering a stuffed pheasant and quails eggs.'

'Yes, but we never actually get any of it,' said Lucy. 'She orders those fancy things if someone's listening – then she calls back later and changes the order to cooking fat and baked beans.'

'Oh,' said Toby.

'She takes the labels off the tins too, so if someone looks in the cupboard they won't be able to see what we eat.'

'Doesn't that make it slightly confusing at mealtimes?' said Toby. 'How do you know what's in them?'

'We don't,' grinned Lucy. 'That's why we get such interesting meals.'

When the table was finally stocked, groaning with hideous food known only to certain remote hill tribes, they all sat down and watched Percy fiddling around with his pipe.

'That's quite a pungent tobacco you've got there,' said the vicar wrinkling his nose.

'It's called devil's guts,' said Lucy. 'I have to go down to the post office to collect it, don't I Percy? I *like* going down there, because I can visit the python – the one the post-mistress has trained to lick the stamps.'

'That's right,' said Percy. 'Strange woman that, she keeps the shop key on a piece of string above the cat flap.'

'Really?' said the vicar. 'Isn't that rather unusual?'

'Is that right?' whispered Toby. 'About the snake and the devil's guts?'

'Of course it is,' grinned Lucy. 'What do you take me for, a fibber? Would you care for a spinach cornet?'

'No thanks,' said Toby, 'I'm trying to give them up.'

The vicar took a loud slurp of tea, trying to get rid of the taste of a garlic, peppermint and anchovy fancy. He pushed the offending article around his plate, desperately trying to think of something that didn't involve the food.

'Have you found a new publisher yet Mrs. WB?'

'Not yet vicar,' said Lily. 'I want to make sure I get someone who's a good match for my unique talents.'

'*Ah,*' he said, his brow knitting up with puzzlement. 'I *see*. And what is it you're working on at the moment?' He flicked the anchovy fancy onto the floor when nobody was looking, but everyone heard it drop.

'It's volume two of the Mambo Rumbletrouser series,' said Lily proudly.

Lucy tried to stifle a giggle, but it slid out of the corner of her mouth and started dancing around on her face.

'*Lucy?*' said the lamp-stand, 'Why don't you make yourself useful and pass the vicar a jelly fancy?'

'Not just now thank you Mrs. WB. I do *like* the raspberry jelly but I think it clashes with the cabbage – only slightly of course.'

Lily frowned, but then remembered it would show her wrinkles – she smiled again, as the vicar tried to change the topic of conversation.

'So,' he said, 'how is the bed and breakfast business doing?'

Lucy winced, because she knew what was coming.

'You do well to ask,' sighed Lily. 'And now that you *have* I don't mind telling you that the holiday trade is simply horrendous at the moment. Even when we *do* manage to get people in you wouldn't believe the things they get up to – drying their filthy underpants on the radiators for instance.'

'Not that they actually work,' said Lucy.

'Drying their disgusting underclothes on the radiators, working or *not,*' said Lily, correcting herself. 'Green fig and spaghetti rondello, vicar?'

'Erm, not just yet, thank you,' he said. 'Have you thought of trying to attract a better class of clientele? I'm sure Mr. *Winnet*-Blake could help with the advertising – what with being in the trade.'

'I'm too busy old boy,' said Percy. 'We've just finished the Meet-o-Chunx cat-food account, and now I'm up to my ears in the new Snogg's proposal.'

'Snogg's the sauce works?' said the vicar.

'The very same,' said Percy. 'It'll be a very lucrative contract if we can put the deal through. I was thinking of something of the lines of…'

Sauce, sauce, everyone needs sauce,
and you can get it - from Snogg's pickle-a-torium,
of course.

'*Hmm,*' said the vicar, using his most diplomatic tone, 'I *like* the tune, but the lyrics might need some work before you present it to a wider audience.'

'That's *exactly* what we need,' said Percy, 'a wider audience – we could move inland perhaps. The problem with being in advertising at the seaside is half your potential customers are fish, and they just don't have the disposable income.'

'Yes,' said the vicar. He was uncertain whether Percy had actually cracked a joke and was far too polite to ask.

'What *you* need Percy is a machine to convert your customers into believers,' said Lucy, 'then they'll buy anything you tell them to.'

'That's a cracking idea,' grinned Percy. 'I must ask your Uncle Byron if he's got time to make me one.'

'You'll do no such thing,' said Lily. 'The girl's head is filled with enough rubbish already. I don't want you going round there and encouraging him.'

'It's alright,' grinned Lucy. 'There are bound to be other inventors – you could talk to one of those.'

'He's not going anywhere,' said Lily. '*Are* you, Percy?'

'No dear,' said Percy, 'apparently not.'

'And another thing,' said Lily. 'We are *not* moving – *this* is our home.'

'Then we need to bring in more money,' said Percy. 'The advertising game is practically dried up – unless we get the Snogg's deal of course.'

'You could try improving the sign outside,' suggested Lucy.

'We can't afford a painter,' said Percy, 'you know that.'

'Well just take it down then,' said Lucy.

'I haven't got the time,' said Percy. 'I'm too busy with sauce.'

'But it gives the wrong impression,' said Lucy, 'it looks a mess.'

'Ah yes, the sign,' said the vicar. 'I saw that when I came in. It *does* look as though it could do with a lick of paint. And what's cruet by the way?'

'That's funny,' said Toby, nudging Lucy in the ribs. 'We thought you'd know that, didn't we Luce?'

'It's something to do with sauce,' said Percy. 'And salt and pepper. I think it's to discourage the visitors from using up lots of ketchup.'

'How strange,' said the vicar. 'Charging extra for sauce – still if the Snogg's deal comes off you'll have more sauce than you can handle.' He started to laugh through his nose, but stopped when he saw that nobody else thought it was funny. Then he got up and took a newspaper from his coat pocket.

'Is that the Daily Phibber you've got there, vicar?' asked Percy.

'Yes,' said the vicar. 'In fact it's the main reason for my visit – that, and coming to pay my respects to the most attractive woman in Grimston, of course. You're a very lucky man Mr. *Winnet*-Blake.'

Lily patted the back of her head and smiled at the vicar. And when she looked away, he hid another one of her special fancies under a plate.

'Yes, I am, *aren't* I?' said Percy with a wrinkly grin. 'So, what is it that interests you in the newspaper?'

'Well,' said the vicar, looking first at Lucy and then at Toby. 'You know that young Fenny Savage has gone missing, don't you?'

'But the stories in the Daily Phibber are usually wrong,' said Percy.

'Usually,' agreed the vicar, 'but every so often a real story comes up, and that means that they don't have to invent any of the details.'

'Sounds like you, Luce,' whispered Toby.

'So it's true?' said Lily. 'The girl really *has* disappeared?'

'From the pier,' said the vicar seriously.

Lucy and Toby tried to look surprised, but they knew instinctively it was true, and that it had something to do with the birds.

'Did *you* see anything Toby?' said Percy. 'I thought I saw you down there yesterday.'

'He *might* have been,' said Lucy defensively. 'It depends if you're going to accuse him of kidnap.'

'Don't be like that,' said Percy seriously. 'Young Fenny's parents will be worried sick – I just thought he might have seen something.'

'Sorry,' said Lucy. 'Only we don't know that she's actually missing, do we? The Phibber probably just made it up.'

'I can assure you they haven't made this one up,' said the vicar. 'Although I can certainly remember a few that they did. Do you recall the one about the chocolate-covered kipper factory?'

'Yes,' said Percy, grinning widely. 'And the body of that murdered circus performer they found buried in the seam of coal. The paper said all along that the police should have gone straight for the Juggler Vein.'

'Ah *yes*,' grinned the vicar. 'Those were the golden days of newspapers, weren't they? When an editor could write anything he liked.'

'What about Kolley Kibber?' said Percy. 'Do you remember him? He'd walk around the town waiting to be recognised, and if someone identified him, they won five pounds.'

'And if they were carrying a copy of the newspaper they got *ten* pounds,' said the vicar enthusiastically. 'Yes, *those* were the days alright.'

'It's all rubbish if you ask me,' said Lily. 'Now, let me have a look at that article.' She snatched the newspaper from the vicar and began to read about the mysterious disappearance.

Lucy leaned over her shoulder and sneaked a look at the front page. There was an out-of-date picture of Fenny and a few words about how the police were searching high and low. Underneath was an advertisement for hair-restorer that had all the hallmarks of Percy's work. There was a picture of a bald man and a cheesy ditty with musical notes dancing around the words.

'Bentley Priory does it again,' said Lucy, reading the next article aloud. 'Grimston's premier detective solves another long standing case. He…'

The paper was suddenly whisked away and rolled up.

'That's enough of *that*,' said Lily. 'We don't want you getting any more ideas for stories, *do* we?'

'Ah yes,' said the vicar, 'the famous story-writing competition. Are you going to tell us about that, Lucy?'

'Yes,' said her stepmother. 'Why don't you tell us all? *Again*.'

'I don't want to,' said Lucy. She was getting bored telling people the same thing over and over. She had written an essay about a mad inventor called Uncle Byron and sent it off to a magazine because everyone had said how wonderful it was. They had even congratulated her on having something called a bizarre imagination, although most of it wasn't made up. In fact, some of it was frighteningly real.

'Oh *go* on,' sneered the lamp-stand. '*Do* tell us Lucy.'

'No,' said Percy, sensing another argument brewing. 'Why don't you just go upstairs Lucy, and play with the Empire?'

'*Empire*?' said the vicar, sensing an opportunity to dispose of another Dribble Fancy. 'My, *that* sounds awfully interesting. I'll bet it's tiger hunting and gin and tonics and tea with the Major. No, on second thoughts perhaps you're a little young for gin and tonic. Tea then? That would be nice.' As if to prove how nice the tea might be, he took an especially loud slurp, draining the cup.

'It's a complete waste of time, vicar,' said Lily, refilling his cup from the dragon pot. 'She spends *far* too much time with that Empire thing, and not nearly enough time with her school work.' She turned to Lucy, who knew exactly what was coming. 'You're not going to get a good job because you can do silly voices you know – and jiggling puppets around isn't a proper qualification either.'

With that, they all looked at the vicar's suitcase.

'*Sorry*, I didn't mean you vicar, I erm…' said Lily, turning a brilliant shade of red.

'The Empire is a toy theatre,' explained Percy. 'Lucy's father made it – and I made some of the actors.'

'Ah yes, the late father,' said the vicar. 'Now I must confess I get rather confused just thinking about that – it all seems terribly complicated.'

'It's not complicated at all,' said Lucy. 'My *real* mother disappeared and after seven years they declared her legally dead. Then my dad married Lily, that's Mrs. Winnet-Blake to you – then *he* died and Lily married Percy. So she's my stepmother, and he's my step-step-dad.'

'I *see*,' said the vicar, 'and what was it you were saying about the actors? It all sounds very interesting.'

'It can be as interesting as you want, can't it, Luce?' said Percy.

Lucy nodded.

'Sometimes I make it deliberately boring though,' she said. 'I once did a play where the characters didn't talk to each other for a whole hour.'

'Oh,' said the vicar, somewhat curious. 'And why was that?'

'They'd had an argument,' said Lucy. 'It was just before the play started, so they just sat about staring at each other, waiting for the other one to talk.'

Lily frowned and then smiled again quickly. It was obvious what Lucy was up to. The arguments, the staring, and the silences were something she'd seen quite a lot before her father had finally left them.

'Is this in real life Lucy?' said the vicar, 'or was it the characters who had the argument?'

Lucy grinned and Percy gave a phlegm-loosening snort.

'In the *play* silly,' said Lucy. 'The actors are made out of lolly sticks and old pieces of paper – *they* couldn't have an argument, could they?'

'I suppose not,' said the vicar, looking embarrassed. 'I don't know what possessed me to even ask.'

'I think you need to apologise Lucy,' said Lily. 'For calling the vicar silly.'

'No Mrs. WB,' he said. 'That won't be necessary – it was my fault for asking a stupid question – and it's good to know that Lucy has an interest.'

'If that's *all* it is,' said the lamp-stand. 'I think she carries it just a bit too far though. I think it might be one of those obsessions we hear about, where children become addicted to games and can't tell fantasy from reality – or truth from lies.'

'Really?' said the vicar, 'and what do you think, Lucy?'

Lucy wanted to tell the vicar how life was much less complicated in the worlds she invented but Lily was glaring at her with a piercing stare. It was the kind of look she'd seen once in a film. She shook her head instead, fearful of what she might say, and what might happen after the vicar had left.

'Well I think it's wonderful,' said the vicar. 'Fancy, having a special place where only you can go – just think of the adventures you could have.'

Lucy thought for a moment and decided to tell the truth, just to see if Lily preferred it. She paused for a moment though, to watch Percy. He had managed to get his pipe going again and sent four interlocking smoke-rings floating towards the ceiling.

'Actually we were there just now,' said Lucy, 'weren't we, Toby?'

'Erm, ye-es,' said Toby, 'but I thought we weren't going to tell anyone?'

The words came out past a half-chewed ball of bread and marmite. It was like looking into a concrete mixer. Toby spat the stuff onto a side plate and cleared his nose. 'But *yeah*, we just got back. The way it happened, as I see it, was that we sort of went into this parallel world.'

'*Oh?*' said the vicar.

'Yeah,' said Toby enthusiastically. 'We had to climb down the side of the house, and we couldn't get back because the bike was back where it started.'

'I see,' said the vicar, rubbing his nose and looking somewhat bemused.

'Yeah,' said Toby, 'because it goes back to the same place every time you visit the world.'

'Erm, ye-es,' said the vicar. 'I can see how that might be necessary – and you visited this world as well, did you, Lucy?'

'Of course,' she smiled.

'So how do you get out when you're finished?' said the vicar.

'You don't actually *finish*,' said Lucy. 'You just wait for the horizon to roll up and then you sort of *pop* out.'

'Interesting,' he said. 'I might be able to make a sermon out of that...'

'Yes, well that's *quite* enough rubbish for now,' said Lily.

'But it's not rubbish,' said Lucy. 'For once it's the truth.'

'Of *course* it is dear,' said Lily, glowering. 'Now vicar, will you have another carrot, peach, and Marmite sandwich?'

'Erm, no thank you, Mrs. WB. I've had all the excitement I can take for one day, and I really do need to get back to the manse. I'm expecting a telephone call from the police, regarding this Fenny affair. There are certain outstanding questions.'

'Yes, well you've seen what happens when you ask questions in *this* house vicar. All we get is lies, lies, and nothing but lies.'

'That's not true,' protested Lucy. 'Even when I do tell the truth it's not enough for you. You just want me out of the way – and you don't care how.'

Percy saw the storm clouds gathering on Lily's brow and blurted out the first question that came into his head.

'Why don't you tell us something about the missionary position in Africa vicar? Or perhaps you can tell us what's happening in far Peru?'

There was a grunting noise from Toby that sounded like a dragonfly being breathed up.

'Shut *up*, Percy,' said Lily. 'And will you *please* stop going on about far Peru all the time? It's about time we had this matter out in the open.'

'Yes,' said Lucy. 'It is.'

Lucy and her stepmother stood glaring at each other, ready to tear flesh and gouge eyes, but before they had a chance to begin there was a distant, muffled sound. It sounded a bit like a voice, but coming from a long way off, like someone trapped under a pile of blankets, or inside a thick canvas bag.

Everyone stopped breathing, just for a moment, as if the sound of their breath might mask the sound. Then they realised what was happening and turned to stare at the battered suitcase on the sideboard. The vicar walked across and opened it, keeping the contents hidden behind his body. Suddenly though, he turned to reveal a ventriloquist's dummy sitting on his arm. It was desperately trying to smile.

'I sometimes find that my little friend here can be a great help in calming violent situations,' he said.

'Uurrgh,' said Lucy, staring at the grinning wooden face. 'It's *horrible*.' One of the puppet's eyes appeared to be following her, and his bottom lip was quivering, as if it was upset with her.

'*Brilliant*,' said Toby. 'But scary.'

Lucy shook her head, unable to take her eyes off the dummy. It had big staring eyes and thick black eyebrows that looked like giant caterpillars. The worst thing though was the mouth. It opened and closed like a sliding door that was possessed by an evil spirit – and it was crammed full of painted wooden teeth.

'For once I agree with the girl,' said Lily. 'It *is* horrible – and it's not natural either, keeping something like that locked inside a case. I could swear I heard it talking just now.'

'Well we *all* know that's not possible, don't we?' said the vicar.

'Do we?' said Toby. 'I'm not so sure. Those things give me the creeps.'

'He's perfectly harmless,' said the vicar, 'just as long as you give him the right sort of chocolate biscuits – he can be *very* choosy you know.'

The vicar was grinning, as if it were a joke. Probably.

'Well I *like* it,' said Percy, 'there was one on the radio once.'

'What?' said Lucy. 'A chocolate biscuit?'

'No,' replied Percy. 'A dummy - it had its own show.'

'And what would be the point of *that*?' said Toby.

'It's true,' said the vicar. '*Educating Archie* the program was called.'

'Pull the other one,' said Lucy, grinning all over her face. 'There wouldn't be much point having a ventriloquist on the radio, would there? He could move his lips as much as he wanted and nobody would know.'

'If you like to take things literally,' said Percy, 'but you can make up your own world when you listen to the radio.'

'That's right,' said the vicar. 'The pictures inside your head are *always* better than anything you see at the cinema.'

'Are they?' sneered Lily. She folded her arms, which was a sure sign of trouble ahead. 'And I suppose this Archie could juggle as well, could he? Because you'd never know if he dropped a ball, would you?'

'I *can* djuggle acksherly,' said the dummy. 'Gut I nedder geen on der gradio.'

'Will you please *stop* that vicar?' said Lily. 'You're frightening Lucy.'

'No he isn't,' said Lucy. 'Erm, hello ugly puppet – what's your name?'

'Genjanin,' said the dummy.

'Genjanin?' said Lucy. 'That's an unusual name.'

'No,' sighed the dummy. 'Ny nane's not Genjanin, it's *Genjanin*. You skell it wid a G.'

'But I *did* spell it with a G,' smiled Lucy.

'No, a *G*, not a *G*,' said the puppet.

'Pardon?' said Lucy.

'Look,' said the dummy, apparently getting annoyed, 'ny nane is skelt wid a G – der second letter od de alserget.'

'The second letter of the alphabet?' suggested Toby.

'Yes,' said the dummy triumphantly.

'But G is the seventh letter,' said Lucy.

'No,' said the dummy. '*G* is the seventh and *G* is the second.'

'I can't skand this,' said Percy. 'Erm, I mean I can't *stand* this any more. He's called Benjamin, but he can't say the letter B.'

'Oh, I knew *that* all along,' smiled Lucy. 'I just wanted to see if *he* knew it.'

The vicar heaved a great sigh of relief as Benjamin's mouth dropped open – his wooden head swivelling around towards Mrs. Winnet-Blake.

'Can I hag a choc-lit giscuit kleese?'

'This should be good,' Percy whispered to Lucy. 'I've never seen a block of wood eat a chocolate digestive before.'

'Ere,' said Benjamin, 'less of the glock of good if you don't nind. And while you're at it why don't you nake yourself useful and anser der door?'

Moments later a desperate knocking came from the hallway. It sounded like someone was being chased by a herd of wildebeest and urgently needed to be let in.

'*I'll* go,' said Lily, glowering at absolutely everyone.

She returned a few moments later, arranging her hair and smiling at the vicar. 'Erm, it's something that requires your immediate attention vicar.'

'Where?' said the vicar. 'Is it the police?'

'I'd rather not say,' said Lily.

'Oh,' said the vicar, 'well surely you can tell us *where* the emergency is Mrs. WB?'

'You're wanted at the chapel of rest,' she replied.

'*Oh?*' he said. 'Now that *is* a surprise – it's usually quiet down there.'

'Usually,' grinned Lily. She leaned over and whispered in the vicar's ear. His face remained solemn and straight as he received the news, but Benjamin waggled an eyebrow, opening and closing his lips slowly, as if repeating what the vicar was hearing. Then his face suddenly stopped moving altogether and he was flung onto the sofa, face up and motionless.

'*Ah,*' said the vicar, looking somewhat distressed. 'Erm, do you think I might use your telephone, Mrs. *Winnet*-Blake?'

'Of course,' she said, ushering him into the hallway.

Everyone lifted their bottoms from their chairs, as if moving a few inches closer might allow them to overhear the conversation. As it happened, they needn't have bothered.

'*Still alive?*' shouted the vicar. 'But that's impossible – the poor chap was *embalmed*, wasn't he?'

'Percy?' whispered Lucy, 'what does embalmed mean?'

'Don't ask,' said Percy, 'you really don't want to know.'

'Go on,' she said, 'tell me – please?'

'Ah, *well,*' said Percy, 'I'm afraid it's when they take all your insides out.'

'*Oh,*' said Lucy, trying to picture the scene.

The vicar stumbled back into the kitchen looking rather pale, as if he'd just seen the man-with-no-guts walking in the front garden. He paused for a moment, obviously intending to speak, but the most his flapping mouth could manage was a disturbing parody of Benjamin's efforts. Eventually though, he drew inspiration from somewhere, and as he turned to flee, he grabbed one of Lily's carrot, peach, and Marmite sandwiches.

'Erm, *bye* then,' said Lucy, as he gathered speed.

A solemn silence descended as everyone tried to take in what had just happened – and when the front door slammed, they all turned their eyes towards the sofa. Benjamin was still lying there, just as he'd been left – and he was staring up at the ceiling and grinning.

Flaming Panties

It had seemed like a good idea at the time, but now that Toby had met Lucy at the pre-arranged spot, he wasn't so sure. She was wearing her old school rucksack, and it looked to be quite full – and if he knew anything about Lucy that was bound to spell trouble.

'Erm, *where* did you say we were going again?' he said. 'Only my dad reckons that all sorts of characters hang around near the railway. And I don't like going near those dark arches either.'

'We're going to Byron's office,' said Lucy. 'I want to show him my new doll. And if you're so worried about going through the arches then I'll hold your ickle handy-wandy. Or you can cuddle my dolly if you like.'

'Shut your face,' said Toby. 'I don't need my hand holding, and I certainly don't want your poxy stinking doll.'

'*Don't* you?' said Lucy. 'Not even when we get to the middle, where the snot monster lives?'

Toby went suddenly quiet – there was a gulping sound, like somebody swallowing a large boiled sweet.

'Erm, yeah, that's the worst bit, right enough,' he admitted. 'When you get so far inside that you can't see daylight at either end. And those Lectric lamps are about as much use as fireflies in a jam jar – I didn't know they even made three watt bulbs.'

'They don't,' said Lucy, hitching up her rucksack. 'The lamp shades are covered in spider poo and bat droppings – that's why they're so dim. Now, are you coming or not?'

As they reached the partially bricked-up entrance, Toby looked back nervously towards the road, as if he'd seen something.

'What was that?' said Lucy.

'I thought I saw the hedge move,' he said.

'It'll just be the wind,' said Lucy nervously.

'Yeah, that's right,' said Toby, 'it'll be the wind.'

The arches in question ran under the main lines, linking the holiday part of Grimston to the factories on the other side of the railway. And although they were the best shortcut, they had a certain reputation for dark deeds. They had only gone about twenty feet when Toby stopped.

'Erm, this *doll* you mentioned Luce – it's not the vicar's dummy is it? This place is scary enough in the daytime, so I don't really fancy being alone in the dark with that thing.'

'*Aah*, well don't worry,' grinned Lucy, pushing on ahead. 'I'll be there to hold your hand.'

'Get lost,' said Toby. 'Anyway, I thought you were supposed to take it back to the vicarage? Doesn't he need it for his sermons or something?'

'I expect so,' said Lucy. 'I'll take it back just as soon as Byron has seen it.'

'Erm, yeah, and why would he want to do that?' said Toby.

'I want him to take a look inside,' replied Lucy.

'Oh *great*,' said Toby. 'The vicar *will* be pleased when he hears you've been poking around his friend's insides with a soldering iron.'

'Byron won't damage it,' said Lucy. 'He's a genius with things like that.'

'Yeah? Well I've heard he went a bit loony,' said Toby. 'And I bet that dummy's going to end up broken, like all his other inventions.'

'Such as?' said Lucy.

'What about the thing he designed for magnetising chutney?' grinned Toby. 'Do you remember that day we borrowed it and took it over to our house? We got all those pickles stuck to the ceiling and my dad had to switch the Lectric off at the mains to get them down.'

'Alright,' said Lucy, 'maybe I should just go on my own? And you can go back the way we came.'

'Doesn't bother me,' said Toby. 'I'm not interested in seeing inside it anyway. It's probably full of bits of string and old saucepan lids.'

'You *will* be interested,' said Lucy. 'If I'm right.'

'No I won't,' said Toby. He turned to leave but suddenly froze. 'Shhh – *Luce* – can you hear something?'

'It's the trains,' said Lucy. 'They steam right overhead.'

'No,' said Toby, 'it wasn't a rumble; it was more like a sort of laugh. And there were *voices* – I definitely heard voices.'

Lucy examined Toby's dimly lit face for signs of lying. 'Is this another three out of ten?' she said.

'No,' he said, 'honest.'

Above them, thick, slow water was dripping from the brick ceiling, and a squadron of flies was circling a solitary light bulb, their tiny shadows dancing about on Toby's face. He looked so serious that Lucy decided he might just be telling the truth – and then, just as she decided he wasn't wearing the liar's mask, she heard the voices for herself. She had been to a church in Lundern once, where whispers on one side of the dome could be heard hundreds of feet away on the other side. And now, here in this rat-infested tunnel, the same thing was happening. She could make out certain words as they clung to the roof and skittered along the walls like marauding insects.

'*Stop them before…*'

'Uh-oh,' said Lucy, 'we *are* being followed and I have a good idea why.'

'Then let's go,' said Toby. 'I don't like the sound of this, and I don't want to stand around in the dark with that puppet thing nearby.'

There was a rumble as a train passed overhead, temporarily blocking out the voices – but once it had passed, they heard them again.

'*Won't be telling any more…*'

'Luce? Come on – *run.*'

For once Lucy agreed with one of Toby's plans. It hadn't been worked on for weeks at a time, or drawn out on huge blueprints or approved by three different committees, but it made good sense all the same.

'What are we waiting for?' she shouted, 'Let's go.'

Lucy made it to the other end of the tunnel in record time, bursting out into the sunlight and blinking in the short-lived brightness. As soon as Toby emerged though, the clouds moved in front of the sun and the whole world seemed to darken, as if it were his fault.

'Now what?' he said.

'Keep running,' panted Lucy, 'come *on.*'

They ran through the sardine dumps without pausing to look back – and when they finally reached the great rusty Gas-O-Meter, Lucy fell back against a chain-link fence, gasping for breath.

'We can't stay here,' panted Toby. 'They'll see us easily.'

Lucy scoured the landscape, looking for a place to hide. It was like a scene from some old film where a mysterious force had reduced the town to rubble and killed all the inhabitants. And now that everyone was gone, every possible hiding place was either knocked down or surrounded by barbed wire, in case people wanted to pinch the bricks.

'Alright then,' she said, 'we'll just have to keep running.'

'Erm, no,' said Toby, 'wait a minute.'

'What now?' said Lucy.

'Who are we running *from*?' he said. 'The arches are a quarter of a mile back and nobody has even come out yet.'

Lucy scanned the fishy graveyard. It was deserted – just a stinking mass of bones and skin and a lot of contented-looking cats.

'Alright, we'll walk,' she said, sounding relieved. 'But we still need to keep watching our backs, don't we?'

'If you say so,' said Toby.

As they entered Chapstick's yard, the sauce works began to flush the automatic puree injectors, making the whole place stink like an incontinent elephant's bedroom. Lucy sighed. They'd be switching on the giant vinegar accelerators next, and *everyone* knew what those smelt like.

'What a *dump*,' said Toby, holding his nose. 'Do you come here a lot?'

'Only for my holidays,' said Lucy grinning. 'But not for much longer though – there's a rumour that the whole lot's going to get pulled down to make way for a new picture house.'

'Great,' said Toby. 'When?'

'It's *not* great at all,' said Lucy. 'Byron says the buildings in this yard are hundreds of years old – they're full of history.'

'And full of disgusting stink too,' said Toby.

'Well I like them the way they are,' said Lucy, 'apart from the smell. Anyway, why would anyone want to watch four films at once?'

'What are you talking about now?'

'The new picture house,' said Lucy. 'It's going to have four screens.'

'Yes, but you don't have to watch all of them,' said Toby, shaking his head in disbelief. 'Sometimes Luce, for a bright girl you can be a bit thick.'

'I suppose,' said Lucy vaguely. She was thinking about being able to see four places at once, and suddenly the idea appealed to her – but just the one place would do for now, *if* she could manage to see through all the grime.

She cupped both hands around her eyes and peered into the window of what used to be her uncle's toy shop. The interior was completely dark and there were just a few scattered remnants of stock, as if they'd been left behind to remind people of what the place had once been. There was a doll's pram with three wheels, a toy theatre like the Empire but not so well made, and hundreds of different-sized marbles scattered across the muck-strewn floor. There was an angel boxing machine too, which she hadn't recalled seeing until today.

'Why's it closed?' said Toby. 'It looks like it's been shut for years.'

'It has,' said Lucy. 'Percy said it happened when they built the stench works for Snogg's sauce factory – people just stopped coming.'

'I can understand that,' said Toby, waving a hand in front of his nose. 'I don't know what they put in that sauce but *I* wouldn't buy it.'

'Don't tell Percy,' said Lucy. 'He's trying to work out how to sell it to people. Or maybe you *should* tell him? Then he'll know what he's up against.'

'But it smells of farts,' grinned Toby. '*That's* what he's up against.'

'Hmm,' said Lucy, 'it's just as well he appreciates a challenge, isn't it?'

'The *ultimate* sauce challenge,' laughed Toby. He peered through a gap between the boards that had been nailed across the window of the shop next door.

'That was Eastman's Butcher's,' said Lucy. 'If you stare through the hole long enough your eyes will get used to it and then you can see inside.'

'Oh, yeah,' said Toby. 'There's a bacon slicer, and a big silver dish and a load of those two ended hooks – it's gruesome.'

'That's what Percy reckons,' said Lucy. 'He said the shop closed because people didn't want to eat meat any more, but the lamp-stand reckons it was because Eastman short-changed his customers. Erm, and *then* of course there was the rumour – the one about someone finding a nose in their mince.'

'A nose?' said Toby, squirming. 'Oh my *God.*'

'That's not the worst part,' grinned Lucy. 'It was a *human* nose, and it was full of those snotty tufts of hair.'

Toby stared at Lucy, trying to decide if she was joking. She wasn't giving any clues though, and with an enigmatic smile, she turned away and squinted through the narrow green door that led up to her uncle's workshop. There was a draught coming through the letterbox, as if there was a window open somewhere inside. But it was the lack of a certain smell that told her the place was deserted – when Byron was home, there was always a smell of Lapsang Souchong tea.

'Is this it then?' said Toby. 'The famous office?'

'It's not really an office,' said Lucy. 'It's more like a laboratory.'

'Like a place for taking people's brains out?' said Toby enthusiastically.

'Don't be stupid,' said Lucy. 'Byron does proper science, with valves and Lectric.'

'But brains *are* proper science,' insisted Toby.

'Well *your* brain isn't, Lindstrom. If brains were dynamite you wouldn't have enough to blow your ears off.'

'Yeah, that's *right*,' said a voice. 'You *wouldn't*.'

They spun around in surprise, to find some very unwelcome visitors. It was Lucy's snivelling stepbrother Tarquin, and his two friends, who, unlike their skinny companion, were built like brick outhouses.

'Erm, Biffo, Warren, Tarquin,' said Lucy, 'what are *you* doing here?'

'We're following you two idiots,' said Biffo. 'Not that it was *that* difficult. We could've jumped you any time. It was soooo easy.'

'So it was *you* in the dark arches?' said Lucy.

'You're the one with all the answers Blake,' grunted Biffo. 'Why don't *you* work it out?'

'So you didn't want to catch us, you just wanted to know where we were going?' said Toby.

'Clever, aren't you?' said Biffo. 'It's a pity you weren't bright enough to catch on earlier – then you wouldn't have led us here, would you?'

'Yeah,' said Tarquin. 'So now we all know where the famous laboratory is. I *told* you we'd find it eventually, didn't I lads?'

'Yeah, that's right Tarkers,' said Biffo. 'Now shut up will you? *I'm* the one doing the talking.'

'It won't do you any good,' said Lucy. 'My uncle won't talk to anybody with a skull as thick as yours – and anyway he's not in.'

'Yeah? Well that's the way we like it,' said Biffo. '*Isn't* it lads?'

Warren and Tarquin both nodded. Lucy didn't like the sound of this and realised that she needed a plan. Byron often disappeared for days at a time, and if these three knew when he was away…

'Yes, erm, well I'm coming here to live,' she said suddenly, much to Toby's surprise. 'So there'll be someone here the whole time, making sure the windows are kept closed and the doors are properly locked.'

'You're coming to live here on your own then?' said Biffo, his eyes narrowing in disbelief.

'Of course not,' said Lucy, 'I'm going to live with my uncle.'

'No you bloody-well aren't,' said Tarquin. 'I'd know if you were – mum would *never* be able to keep something like that quiet.'

'Then you'll be getting a nice surprise *won't* you lovely non-brother? And I'll finally be getting some peace.'

'Yeah, right,' said Biffo. 'Well I don't see how, even if you *have* managed to fool Tarquin – your uncle has done a runner, just like your mum.'

'He hasn't,' said Lucy, 'and neither did my mum – she wouldn't just go off and leave me for no good reason.'

'You reckon?' said Biffo. 'So what happened then? You don't believe all that stuff about her disappearing from a locked room do you? My dad says they made all that up, so the Daily Phibber could sell more newspapers.'

'She *did* disappear,' said Lucy, 'it was all true.'

'Yeah, well my dad says it wasn't,' said Biffo. 'It's impossible for one thing – not that the Phibber ever let the truth get in the way of a good story.'

'Eh?' said Warren. 'What does that mean?'

'It means they're always telling lies,' said Biffo. 'Unless they get it right by accident now and again, a bit like Lucy here, and her stupid stories. Oh, and by the way, my dad told me to thank you again for the *Bleevit* idea. He's making a fortune thanks to you.'

'Yeah,' said Warren. 'The paper said the *Bleevit* is an overnight success story and it's all due to the genius of our brightest local entrepreneur. And that's Biffo's dad.'

'And I suppose it was your dad who told them that?' said Lucy.

'That's right,' said Warren. 'His dad's *always* talking to the newspapers. He got an absolute *stack* of money for that story about your mum.'

'Shut *up* will you?' said Biffo. 'She didn't *know* about that.'

'No,' said Lucy, 'but I do now, *don't* I? Thanks Warren.'

Warren suddenly found something very interesting stuck to sole of his shoe. In fact, it was *so* interesting he didn't want to look up.

'Yeah,' said Biffo, 'thanks a *lot,* Warren. No wonder they call him Warren Idiot – even his own family have started to do it.'

'So your dad got money from the *Daily Cheet*, did he?' said Lucy.

'Yeah,' grinned Biffo, 'and the *National Lyre* too.'

'Well thanks a lot,' said Lucy. 'That was exactly what I needed, just after my mum went missing – all those horrible reporters sticking their noses through the letterbox, and their stupid smudgers photographing the insides of our dustbins.'

'Potty wife spirited away from locked room,' laughed Biffo. 'That was one of the headlines – my dad saved them all in a big scrapbook.'

'Yeah,' said Tarquin, 'mad mother disappears for good – I've got *that* one stuck on my bedroom wall.'

'Stop it, stop it,' shouted Lucy, 'and get *lost* – I *hate* you – all of you.'

'Now, now, let's not lose our rag, shall we?' grinned Biffo, 'otherwise we'll get Warren to demonstrate some of his old-fashioned wrist torture.'

'Best not,' said Tarquin. 'We need to keep the torture in reserve.'

'Yeah, that's right,' said Biffo, 'I almost forgot – Tarquin here tells us you won a prize in a story competition.'

'So?' said Lucy.

'So let's bleedin-well *see* it then,' demanded Biffo.

'I haven't got it yet,' said Lucy. 'I'm still waiting for the post.'

'Yeah,' said Tarquin, '*if* you ever won it in the first place.'

'I can prove it,' said Lucy. 'I had a letter from the magazine.'

'Yeah? Well *I* didn't see any letter,' said Tarquin, 'and I'm *always* nosing through your stuff.'

Lucy growled inside at the thought of him sneaking around the house and messing with her things.

'I hid it,' she said, 'just like all the other things you don't know about.'

Toby gave Lucy a sideways glance, and she knew exactly what he was thinking. He was wondering if Tarquin knew about the *other* Grimston.

'No you didn't,' said Tarquin. 'Nowhere in that house is safe from me – and anyway, it'd be too big to hide.'

'And how do you know *that*?' said Lucy. 'You don't even know what the prize is.'

'I *do*,' said Tarquin. 'You told me it was a sort of machine.'

'*Did* I?' said Lucy. There was a sudden vague notion that she *might* have told him that, just to make him jealous. And what was it her Uncle Byron had said? To be a good liar requires an outstanding memory, otherwise your previous lies come back and haunt you.

'Yeah,' said Tarquin. 'You told me it was a Lectric reality machine – you said it was about the same size as a packet of Lemerny-Puffs.'

'Lectric reality eh?' said Biffo. 'Wow, just think what we could do with a machine like that. It'll have a direct brain interface and a three-dimensional thingummy generator. And there'll be a sympathetic pattern inducer, and it'll be crammed full of switches and coloured wires.'

'There'll be an alarm clock too,' said Lucy, 'to wake up idiots like you. Don't you *see*? My lovely stepbrother has gone soft in the brain, and that's why he can't tell when I'm making things up for a bit of fun.'

'Well you'd better pray you *weren't* making it up,' growled Biffo, 'because Tarquin promised to pinch it from your bedroom and lend it to us.'

'No I didn't,' protested Tarquin.

'Yes you *did*,' grunted Biffo. 'So she'd better have it, or else. Now, let's just have a look inside that bag.'

'It's empty,' said Lucy. It was the weakest lie she'd managed for weeks.

'Well you won't mind if we have a look then,' said Biffo, ripping the rucksack from her back and pulling it open. 'Oh, *look* everyone – it's a *dolly*! You're a bit old for dollies, aren't you, Lucy?'

'It's *not* a doll,' protested Lucy.

'Well it looks like one to me,' said Biffo, 'even if it *has* got an ugly mug. Just *look* at the thing – it has a grin like a burned-out piano.'

'It hasn't,' said Lucy, suddenly realising that she'd actually grown to *like* the dummy. 'He's special, and he's mine – and he's called Genjamin.'

'Yeah,' said Tarquin, 'but you were supposed to take him back.'

'I did,' lied Lucy, 'but the vicar said I could have him.'

'Well in that case you won't mind giving us a go,' said Biffo. 'We could do with a giggle, couldn't we lads?' He went to hold the dummy above his head, but Lucy lunged just in time, grabbing the puppet by the torso. There was no other choice – she *had* to pull hard or give him up completely.

'Stop it,' she screamed. 'You're hurting him.'

'Yeah, well I'm not the one doing the pulling,' said Biffo. 'So any pain he's going through is your fault.'

'You *are* pulling,' said Lucy. 'Stop it. *Stop* it.'

The stitching around Genjamin's neck began to creak, but just before it gave way, there was a loud splintering sound. Biffo was left holding a pair of trousers and a painted wooden leg with the shoe still attached.

'Aaah, *look*,' he laughed, 'the little leggy-weggy has come off – and the tiny wickle shoe as well. What a shame.'

'*Give* me those right now,' demanded Lucy.

'Nope,' said Biffo, displaying the broken parts to his friends. 'I don't think so, do you? It's not as if it needs to walk anywhere, *is* it?'

There was a sudden squeal of bicycle brakes, and they all turned to look, temporarily forgetting the dummy.

'Is there something I can help with?' said the vicar, screeching to a halt. 'Only you seem to be having some kind of disagreement.'

'Erm, er, yes, *hello* vicar,' said Lucy. 'I erm, I was just showing Genjamin to my friends.'

'So I *see*,' said the vicar with a disapproving stare. 'It's just as well I came along then, isn't it?'

'I expect it was,' said Lucy, glaring at Biffo.

'Yeah, well thanks for showing us the dolly,' growled Biffo. 'We'll be going now.'

'Yes,' frowned the vicar. 'I think you should. And as for you Lucy, I think you should *keep* Genjamin, especially in view of his recent modifications.'

'Erm, yes, sorry about the leg,' she said. 'And thanks, I *would* like to keep him if that's alright – perhaps I could replace him?'

'*Replace* him?' said the vicar. 'I doubt if *that* would be possible. There can't be many puppets who can move their very own 'licks' and 'gody', can there?

No, Benjamin is a unique creature, and you can repay me simply by taking good care of him.'

He mounted his bike again and with the briefest of smiles, cycled off into the stench, in search of the few parishioners who had not yet moved house.

'Erm, yes, thanks,' said Lucy, waving goodbye and quickly turning to Toby. 'Come on, let's get inside,' she hissed. 'I don't trust Biffo to stay away.'

'Have they come back yet?' whispered Lucy.

'I don't think so,' said Toby. He was peering through the letterbox, looking for signs of Biffo and his friends. 'Anyway, they wouldn't dare to do anything now – not until it gets dark.'

Suddenly there was the sound of a singsong voice coming from outside.

'*Liar, liar, knickers on fire.*'

'Oh, they wouldn't do anything *now*, would they not?' said Lucy.

'Anyone can make a mistake,' said Toby with a shrug.

'*Liar, liar, knickers on fire.*'

'Shut your face Biffo,' shouted Lucy. She pushed Toby out of the way so she could get her lips behind the letterbox.

'Yeah, shut it Biffo,' echoed Toby.

'Are you talking to me storm boy?' shouted Biffo. '*Are* you? Well why don't you come out and try to shut it *for* me?'

'What's he saying?' said Lucy. 'And what did he call you?'

'Nothing,' said Toby. He closed the letterbox but it was no use. There was a short pause and then the taunting song began again…

'*Lucy, loosy, loose e loose elastic…*'

She pushed Toby out of the way and shouted through the letterbox at the top of her voice – like four opera singers, all bellowing at once.

'Get *lost* Biffo,' she screamed, wishing she'd thought of something cleverer. Then she decided she didn't *want* to be clever, she just wanted to cause him pain – to make him feel the same agony he had inflicted on Genjamin.

'Yes, get lost,' she shouted again, 'or I'll set Byron's dog on you.'

'Erm, he doesn't have a dog, does he?' whispered Toby.

'Yes, but *they* don't know that,' said Lucy.

'*Liar, liar, smokin' panties – your mum disappeared and you've got no aunties.*'

'Or uncles,' added Tarquin.

'Yeah, that's right,' said Biffo. 'Or *uncles*. Good one Tarky.'

'So they've *gone*, have they?' said Lucy, turning to face Toby.

'Well *I* couldn't see them. Anyway never mind them — what *I* want to know is how you made the vicar come along at just the right time.'

'It was just a coincidence,' said Lucy.

'Yeah?' said Toby. 'And how often does he come round here? Never, I bet.'

'He might,' said Lucy.

'Yeah, he *might*, if one of his parishioners was hit by an asteroid and he needed to come and comfort them.'

'Or bury them,' said Lucy helpfully.

'Yeah, well even if he did,' said Toby, 'there's no way he was going to give you that puppet.'

'No?' said Lucy. 'Then maybe you ought to believe in serendipity?'

'I might do,' said Toby, 'if I knew what it was.'

'It's a lucky accident,' said Lucy, not quite believing it herself. 'Oh, and by the way, did you *hear* something earlier, when the puppet's leg got pulled off?'

'Nope,' said Toby. 'Did you?'

'Erm, *no*,' said Lucy uncertainly. 'I didn't.'

They decided to lock the door and leave Tarquin and his friends to shout at the empty hallway, hoping they'd eventually get bored and go home. In any case, the laboratory was at the back of the building, so they wouldn't have to listen. As they walked up the stairs that led to Byron's workshop a strong draught came down to meet them, and when they reached the top landing, it was easy to see why. The window that overlooked the railway-shunting yard was wide open and the dirty lace curtains were soaked with rain. On the slate roof outside there were damp footprints leading to a ladder that was propped up against the guttering.

'Someone's been here,' whispered Lucy, 'in Byron's private laboratory.'

'I know,' said Toby nervously. 'Are you sure you want to go inside? They might still be here.'

Lucy shivered at the thought. There was an uneasy feeling about the place, as if someone had died and the house had gone to the grave with them. Finally, though, she raised the courage to open the door and they stepped through into a scene of desolation and utter destruction. There was a brief sound of laughter from outside, but when she looked out into the yard, it was deserted.

'Oh, *no*, just *look* at all this mess,' she whispered.

She picked her way through the piles of glass and twisted metal and broken instruments, looking for just one thing that might have survived – but the tears that flooded her eyes made it difficult to pick out shapes. Even so, she recognised the outline of some of the machines. The Penny All-Wins were still mounted on the wall but smashed beyond repair. On the floor, there were dozens of others – machines where you had to turn wheels to race cars or horses, lung testers fitted with giant bellows, four-penny Diddle-Oh machines, and even a mystical future-wife predictor. And in the middle of it all, broken into hundreds of pieces, was Byron's favourite – the Green Ray Device – a machine that claimed to read minds using the power of television.

'It's broken,' she sobbed, 'the whole lot – all completely smashed.'

'Yeah,' said Toby. 'But it was all old stuff though, wasn't it? There's nothing here that's of any use.'

'That's the whole point, you idiot,' sobbed Lucy. 'It's a collection of antique amusements, so it's *bound* to be full of old stuff – and *now* look at it.'

'Well it's certainly a bit of a mess,' admitted Toby.

Lucy wiped a tear and nodded, picking up a piece of a model crane that had once been part of a 'Grabb-o-Prize' machine. It was snapped in half, and would never be able to grab another prize – not that it ever had when it was in one piece.

'I reckon this must be part of your happy accident idea,' said Toby.

'And how do you work that out?' sniffed Lucy.

'Well this is the other side of the coin, isn't it? We got lucky when the vicar arrived, but there has to be a balance. Someone has to get unlucky, and I think it was your uncle. Do you reckon it was Biffo and that lot?'

Lucy wiped her eyes again and gave a weak smile. She was thinking of what Byron had said about Percy, and how he should have used the future-wife predictor before marrying Lily.

'I don't think so,' she said. 'Old man Perkins loves this kind of thing just as much as Uncle Byron. And so does Biffo – he's always going on about them, isn't he? I could imagine him stealing them, but not this.'

'You're right,' said Toby. 'You remember that day Biffo was really friendly with me because he thought my uncle owned a fruit machine company? He took me to see their collection – they have *loads* of those old penny scenes, where you put the money in and the burglar creeps in and opens the safe, or the graves open up and ghosts fly everywhere. He was really proud of those – and so was his dad.'

'I know,' said Lucy, with a broad grin. '*I* told him that fib about your uncle – remember?'

'Oh yeah,' said Toby, 'I forgot about that.'

Lucy picked a twisted metal plate off the floor and read the inscription:-

"Princess Mumtaz – the Lectric Mind-Reader"

'What does this one do then?' asked Toby. He took the plate from Lucy and held it up against the front of a gaudy wood-and-glass cabinet that was just about managing to stand upright.

'It reads Lectric minds,' smiled Lucy. 'What do *you* think?'

'Yeah?' said Toby. 'Well how does it work then?'

He tapped on the glass that imprisoned poor Princess Mumtaz. She was quite attractive for a dummy, but her eyes seemed to be *watching*, encouraging him to look at the cards that were spread out in front of her.

'It's broken,' he said, tapping on the glass again.

Suddenly though, the figure burst into life and the princess began to wave her arms, signalling her desire to escape. It looked as though she was breathing too, but that was impossible, *wasn't* it? Toby moved closer, to be certain he wasn't seeing things. As he came face to face with the princess she rapped her mechanical hands against the cabinet window – luckily he managed to jump back just before the glass shattered.

'It wasn't me,' he shouted.

'Don't worry,' said Lucy. 'It doesn't really makes much difference, does it? Everything else is broken or bent, so why shouldn't this be?'

Mumtaz was still moving and leaned forwards now, coming to a sudden halt as her robes snagged against the broken glass. Her head continued to move in a graceful arc though, falling forward to reveal a series of rotating wheels and push wires buried in the hollow of her neck.

'The wires work her eyes,' said Lucy. 'She watches you when you pick a fortune card out of the slot.'

'What,' said Toby. '*This* slot?' He jammed his fingers into the narrow brass aperture, trying to extract the card that was lodged inside. It was like a bus ticket, only much stiffer, and printed with a short message:-

"Amidst confusion can be found the light…"

'I've seen these before,' said Toby. 'They don't mean anything though, *do* they? There's never anything that matters to you personally, is there?'

'*Amidst confusion can be found the light*,' said a shaky voice.

'What was that?' asked Lucy.

'Well it certainly wasn't *me*,' said Toby.

'Then *who*?' said Lucy.

Before they had chance to work out *who* had said *what* the cabinet pitched violently and they were forced to jump smartly out of the way. The princess fell too, and as the whole lot toppled over, she came flying out of her private world. Or at least her head did – the rest of her was trapped under the wreckage as it fell with an almighty crash, shaking the ancient foundations. Lucy looked about nervously, firstly at Toby and then at the head which had rolled across the floor. It had come to rest under Byron's favourite sofa, and now it was lying on its side, looking out at them – and *blinking*.

'*Am-idst con-fusion…*' it croaked. Then the mouth stopped moving and the eyes closed and it seemed to give up trying.

'I didn't know it could do that,' said Lucy.

'Well I hope it doesn't try to do it again,' said Toby. 'It was *far* too freaky – I had this sudden horrible thought about being stuck inside one of those things myself.'

'You'd better behave then,' said Lucy. 'Otherwise I might just get my Uncle Byron to arrange it. He'll probably…'

'Erm, *Luce*,' said Toby, 'what are you looking so worried about?'

Lucy had turned quite pale and was staring at Toby as if she'd just seen Princess Mumtaz get up and walk out of the door.

'The head,' she screamed, 'it said something about confusion, didn't it? Oh, hell's bells – with all this business I completely forgot about the Lectric confuser. I hope *that* hasn't been damaged too.'

'The *what?*' said Toby, looking extremely confused.

'Just wait there,' said Lucy.

'Don't worry,' said Toby. 'I wasn't planning on going anywhere.' He was still keeping a nervous eye on the severed head – if it was going to start talking again he wanted as much notice as possible.

Lucy dragged a chair across the room and climbed up on it, feeling around in the dust on top of a cupboard. When she got down again she was holding a key attached to a string. There was a yellowed label attached too, that read:-

"Confuser room."

"Property of the McGuffin Company Limited."

And pinned to the door of the confuser room was another note. It was handwritten in bright green ink, and seemed to carry on where the note on the key left off-

"If it ever gets finished that is…"

The room beyond the door greeted them with a strange odour, a combination of cricket bats, old dust and the burning Lectric smell that had once hung in the air in Lucy's bedroom. Toby's nose twitched like a field mouse's, and Lucy knew instantly that he was thinking about their adventure in Nether Grimston. It was almost as if he'd been deliberately ignoring it, but now the smell was evoking the memory whether he liked it or not.

'Wow,' he said, wondering what kind of strange science they'd stumbled upon. The room was crammed from floor to ceiling with metal racks – their shelves packed with valves and transformers and control knobs.

'Your uncle invented all *this?*' he said.

'On an envelope,' said Lucy proudly.

'Excuse me?' said Toby.

'Byron reckons that all the best inventions are written on the back of an envelope,' said Lucy. 'Or sometimes you can use a beer mat.'

'Or a very small postage stamp?' suggested Toby.

'You're impressed *really*, aren't you?' said Lucy.

'Nope,' said Toby. 'I was just thinking that I've never seen so much junk in one place.'

'It's *not* junk,' said Lucy, somewhat deflated. 'This is a proper scientific thingummy.'

'That's the technical term is it? A *thingummy*?'

'It hasn't got a name yet,' said Lucy. 'Byron wanted me to think one up but I haven't been able to.'

'Now *that* I don't believe,' said Toby, '*you*, the great fibbing Lucy Blake? The world famous porky pie machine having trouble inventing a story?'

'But that's just it,' she said. 'It's not really a story, just a name, and every time I think about it I just hear a whole barrage of words and I get confused. That's why Byron wrote confuser on the door – it's a kind of joke.'

'Hilarious,' said Toby, kicking at a line of brass stair rods that were nailed to the floor. He looked at the ceiling directly above them – there was a line of rods there too, linked to thick, heavily insulated cables that wound their way down the walls and into the Lectric racks.

'So what does this confuser thing *do* then?' he said.

'I don't know,' said Lucy. 'It might be for putting the jam inside those round biscuits for all I know – although Byron *did* once mention that he was working on a machine that allowed you talk to dead people.'

'*What, really*?' grinned Toby.

'Yes, really,' said Lucy, 'but I'm almost certain it was a joke.'

Song of the Thermionic Triodes

For a moment, Toby actually considered how a machine like the confuser might be used for inserting jam. Eventually though he decided that Lucy was joking and turned his attention to the other idea – the rather bizarre thought that you could talk to people on what his mother called *'the other side'*. But surely, that had been a joke too, hadn't it? He looked at Lucy for inspiration and she seemed to know exactly what he was thinking.

'Your guess is as good as mine,' she said.

'Well it's *Lectric*,' said Toby. 'I can tell *that* much.'

'Maybe it's a secret weapon?' said Lucy. 'Or perhaps you just plug yourself into it and then think of something, and it does what you tell it?'

'I like the jammy biscuit idea best,' said Toby. 'It sounds a lot less dangerous.' He walked over to the main rack and examined the rows of tiny glass bottles, which were sitting quietly in their sockets, minding their own business. To Toby though, 'examining' meant poking and prodding and getting sticky finger-marks over everything.

'Hey *Lindstrom*,' said Lucy, 'don't do that, this is a delicate machine.'

'Oh?' he said. 'I thought you didn't know what it was?'

'I don't,' snapped Lucy, 'but I'm pretty certain those great fat fingers of yours can damage it.'

'Hey, these bottle things look like miniature light bulbs,' said Toby. 'But their insides are a lot more complicated.'

'They're valves,' said Lucy. 'But the Mericans call them toobs – and they have this sort of dull amber glow when the machine is working.'

'You've seen it switched on then?' said Toby.

'Just the once,' grinned Lucy, 'for my birthday.'

'Some birthday present,' said Toby. 'Still, it's better than yellow and green striped socks. So why do they glow? Is there something wrong with it?'

'That's how the machine works,' said Lucy. 'It's full of something called thermions – or perhaps it was onions?'

'Never heard of 'em,' said Toby.

'Well when it's running,' said Lucy, 'there are millions of these little thermion things racing around inside those bottles.'

'Valves,' corrected Toby.

'Yes, *thank*-you, *valves*,' said Lucy. 'And when the machine is almost ready to work they start to sing.'

There was a tiny delay – just long enough for Lucy to speak.

'*Don't*,' she said.

'Don't what?' said Toby.

'You know very well – you were going to ask me what tune they sang.'

'I *wasn't*,' protested Toby.

'Well that's just as well then,' said Lucy, 'because there *is* no tune as far as I can make out, and anyway it wouldn't have been very funny.'

'It *would*,' said Toby, 'if I'd had the right audience.'

'Yes, well *some* jokes don't have a right audience,' said Lucy.

'That's where you're wrong,' said Toby, continuing his exploration of the confuser. 'Everything's funny to someone – you just have to find them. Erm, and what do you think this bit's for?'

The wooden frame in question was about five feet high and wobbled when pushed – and it was the only thing in the room that wasn't jammed full of Lectrical gadgets.

'I don't know,' said Lucy with a slight frown. 'It wasn't here last time I came. It looks like someone is supposed to fit inside, but the door's stuck – I can't move it more than a foot or so.'

'It looks like a shower cubicle,' said Toby, 'for a midget.'

Lucy took her rucksack off so she could squeeze through the gap. There was a small seat inside and when she sat on it, her head came almost level with a curved glass screen that looked like a goldfish bowl. She sat up slightly, spinning the seat so it got taller. Then she read the inscription on the engraved plate that was stuck to the front panel with tape:-

The Gecko Junior Ampliphonic Televisual Apparatus. 405 lines VHF.

'It sounds like someone made that up,' she said.

'They probably did,' replied Toby. 'Now *tell* me patient fifty-seven, has your head started to feel numb yet? And have you still got just the one pair of arms?'

'Shut up, Toby. It's not even switched on *is* it? Anyway, my uncle wouldn't invent something like that. I *know* him; he'd make it funny or educational.'

'Great,' said Toby. 'So why don't we just power it up and see what happens?'

'Oh,' said Lucy, 'you're an expert all of a sudden, are you? *Let's just power it up and see,*' she mimicked. 'And see *what* exactly?'

'Actually I was joking,' said Toby. 'If you put power into this thing it'll blow us all up – I know, because I've done loads of physics.'

'I know,' said Lucy. 'I've *seen* you doing it, remember? I even had to stay behind to help you clear up the mess.'

'So I know what I'm talking about, don't I?' said Toby. 'Because that's exactly what's going to happen if we switch it on. It's held together with old bits of sticking plaster, and… oh *yuk*. This bit has blood on it, Luce – your uncle's Lectric confuser is held together by old bandages and plasters.'

'He doesn't like to waste things,' said Lucy, feeling as though she ought to defend Byron in his absence. 'And he was always cutting himself.'

'And blowing himself up, by the looks of it,' added Toby. 'Still, at least he'll never run out of parts. He can always go to the dump and get more equipment when he explodes this lot.'

'It doesn't bother *me* if you don't like it,' said Lucy. 'Because I'm going to switch it on anyway.'

'You'll be *so-rry*,' chanted Toby.

'Maybe,' said Lucy, 'but it feels like something I've got to do – don't you think so?'

'No, I don't,' said Toby, 'but if you're determined to go ahead then I'm going to stand over here behind this big piece of wood.'

'No you're not,' said Lucy. 'You're going to help – have you got any money?'

'No,' said Toby.

'Erm, right,' said Lucy, 'well have you got a hammer then?'

'No,' he grinned, handing over a large piece of iron piping. 'Will this do?'

'That will do *very* nicely,' grinned Lucy.

They returned to the amusement room and rolled one of the fruit machines onto its back so that Lucy could jam the pipe into the door. She eventually succeeded in breaking the hinges, and after a couple of gentle taps, closely followed by three *not* so gentle ones, the floor was covered with hundreds of silver sixpences.

'Do you know,' smiled Lucy, 'that's the first time I've ever seen the Brodwick Plum-n-Cherry-Matic pay out?'

'I take it we need the money for the Lectric meter?' grinned Toby.

'Hmm,' said Lucy. 'They were wrong about you Toby – you *are* clever.'

'Yes, very funny,' said Toby. 'So where is it?'

'That should last us for a while,' said Toby, returning from the cupboard under the stairs. 'And I reckon *this* is going to be the lever we need.' He was pointing at a huge Nife switch – the kind that usually supplies the Lectric to a monster in a horror film. Lucy nodded, and he threw the bar to the 'ON' position, expecting to see a shower of sparks as the current began to flow.

Nothing happened.

'Erm, *that* was impressive,' said Lucy.

'I'm tempted to agree,' said Toby. '*Most* disappointing.'

'Try the light switch,' said Lucy.

'But it's still daylight,' protested Toby.

'Just *try* it,' insisted Lucy.

Toby flicked the switch, but instead of the room lights coming on, a single yellow light appeared on the panel in front of Lucy. The last time she'd seen *this* piece of gear it had been part of a 'romance' machine on Grimston Pier. The idea was to put your hand on the metal plate and then a needle would indicate whether you were a warm kisser or a red-hot lover, or something in between.

Lucy dithered for a moment, but finally settled her fingers on a three-way switch marked '*CWPWHPO (OKAD)*', '*Dangerous*' and '*Experimental*'. It was already in the '*CWPWHPO (OKAD)*' position, so she decided to leave it there, mainly because the other possibilities sounded a bit dangerous – especially the one that was helpfully labelled '*Dangerous*'.

'Touch the hand-thing,' suggested Toby. 'I want to see how romantic you are.'

For once Lucy did as she was told and put her hand on the metal plate. And as soon as her flesh made contact, the machine began to hum.

'*Wow*, it's working,' giggled Toby. 'I think it's a bit confused though – according to the dial over here you're about to meet a tall dark stranger.'

'Good,' said Lucy. 'I hope he knows something about Lectric.'

'Do you reckon it's going to do anything else?' said Toby.

'Give it a chance,' replied Lucy, 'it needs to warm up first.'

Sure enough, over in the main racks that covered one entire side of the room the valves were beginning to glow and tiny mysterious noises were building up. Suddenly there was a *frubbling* sound, like a six-inch ruler whizzing through the air, and without any further warning the wooden frame that surrounded Lucy collapsed and disappeared into a hole in the floor.

'Erm, I don't want to worry you or anything Luce, but your hair's standing on end.'

'And it smells horrible,' said Lucy. 'The confuser that is, not my hair. I bet you recognise it, *don't* you?'

'It's just like your toy theatre,' smiled Toby.

'Yes,' giggled Lucy, '*great*, isn't it?'

'Not really,' he said nervously. 'It reminds me of a magic show my dad took me to. Whenever the illusionist did something mysterious the people behind the scenes burned this stuff called Lycopodium and Ether on a hot shovel.'

'Was it exciting?' said Lucy.

'Erm, yeah, actually it was a bit *too* exciting,' said Toby. 'Even though I knew it wasn't real, I still felt really scared – and it made me want to pee.'

'Oh, *lovely*,' said Lucy.

Suddenly, all hell broke loose and the room was filled with the sound of tiny glowing angels, each one singing at the top of its voice.

'It's the thermionics,' shouted Lucy. 'Can you hear them?'

'Are you *kidding*?' screamed Toby. 'I think my eardrums have burst.'

'Don't worry,' yelled Lucy, 'they'll settle down in a minute.'

Somewhere nearby a large oil-filled transformer began to whine. Then a heavy-current relay clicked over. It was almost certainly a sign that the device was ready, because the room was suddenly filled with a curtain of lights, like a miniature Aurora Borealis. The yellowy-orange sheets of flame danced in the air between the rods in the ceiling and their counterparts on the floor – and whenever they moved it sounded like distant thunder. Every so often, they would flex and touch at their edges, and whenever they did so tiny blue sparks would leap between them, as if information was flowing back and forth in a Lectrical language that nobody else could understand.

'Wow,' yelled Toby, 'now I really *am* impressed – I reckon this machine does a *lot* more than just put jam inside biscuits.'

'You're probably right,' grinned Lucy. 'Something with *this* much power could probably manage to squirt the cream in as well.'

After a minute or so, the room finally stopped shaking and the singing from the valves gradually reduced to a gentle hiss. The curtain of lights remained for a while, but it was thinner and dimmer than before, like a wall of tissue that was in the process of disappearing. And *that* was when they noticed the gentle flickering of the lights on Lucy's panel. As they tried to think what the patterns of illumination might mean the Gecko Junior burst into life. Moments later though, it seemed to lose enthusiasm and the picture on the screen dwindled to a patchwork of flickering lines and dithering dots. Then, just as it seemed they were about to disappear for good, the pattern gathered strength again and began to form the rough outline of a face.

Lucy stared at the screen in surprise – just able to make out the features of her missing uncle. He was much thinner than she remembered him, as if he'd been struck by some terrible tragedy. The poor man was grey-faced and deeply worried, just like their physics teacher at the start of a lesson.

Lucy felt a strange sensation in her stomach, and just for a moment, she pressed her palm flat against the screen. It was exactly the same feeling she'd experienced when her mother disappeared. Her scalp tingled and her hair stood on end, the tips of each filament crackling with impatient energy.

'Is that your Uncle Byron then?' said Toby.

'Shush,' said Lucy, nodding and removing her hand. 'I think he wants to say something.'

They watched as the face on the screen mouthed silently, occasionally looking off to the side as if he was expecting to see someone. There was no voice though, just a fizzing sound from a Lectric speaker buried deep in the gubbins.

'It sounds like a broken kettle,' said Toby, 'in fact it wouldn't surprise me if it was *made* out of one.'

'Shhh,' said Lucy, turning a knob marked 'volume'. The sound got louder but was no more intelligible – just a *lot* more annoying.

'Why do I need to shush?' said Toby. 'There's nothing to hear – and anyway, when he realises we haven't heard he'll say it again.'

'I don't think so,' said Lucy. 'I think this is a bit like a record – I'm guessing that this picture was taken some time ago.'

'Eh? How's that then? I don't think you can record pictures, *can* you?'

'Maybe that's what the machine does?' suggested Lucy.

'It's an awful lot of trouble to go to,' said Toby, 'just so he could leave you a message – it would have been simpler to put a note in a milk bottle.'

'Shush,' said Lucy. 'I'm trying to concentr…'

Suddenly the machine made a noise that sounded like a *Ker…floppp*.

'It's gone,' observed Toby, 'and all the lights have gone out.'

'I can *see* that,' said Lucy. 'The Lectric must have run out – you need to go and feed the meter again.'

'Do I *have* to?' complained Toby. 'It's dark under those stairs – and anyway, what did your last slave die of?'

'Disobedience,' said Lucy. 'Now do as you're told and *this* time no talking. I want to listen to the whole thing.'

When Toby returned, they repeated the entire procedure. This time though, the song of the valves seemed even more fervent, and when the curtain of light appeared, they touched it – gently at first, just with their fingertips, but eventually pushing their hands and wrists into its cool fire. And finally, feeling braver than ever, they joined hands and leaped through the glowing veil, stumbling out the other side laughing and giggling, with their hair standing on end.

'Come on Luce, it's ready – get back in the swivelly chair.'

Lucy went back to where the non-waterproof shower cabinet had once stood and sat down in front of the screen.

Sssss. Zzzzz. Snackle. Freeeeeeeee……poppp.

'See?' said Toby. 'I *told* you – it's all just hiss.'

'Shut *up* Toby.'

Vzzzzzzz.

Snuzz.

HISSSsssss….

Nnnnoonngg.

Vzzz.

Gronk.

Phartsss. Pharties.

Bnnnzzsssalbumzzssskkk…

Zzzz.

Sssszzitt.

Sput.

'What was that?' said Lucy.

'I think it was *Sput,*' said Toby.

'No, before that.'

'Sssszzitt and Zzzz,' he replied.

'No, *earlier* than that, it was just after…'

Bnnnzzsssalbumzzssskkk…

'There it is again,' hissed Lucy. 'I told you there was something, didn't I? I definitely heard him say the word *album.*'

Ffrrrappp!

'Have we run out of money again?' said Toby.

'Erm, actually no,' said Lucy, watching the smoke rising from the valve racks. 'We ran out of luck – I think we may have just broken it.'

'*Broken* it?' said Toby. 'But it was *knackered* already.'

'Well now it's broken *and* knackered,' said Lucy. 'Byron will never forgive me.'

'Don't worry,' said Toby. 'I still reckon a hand-written note is more obvious.'

'Well I don't see any of them around here, do *you?*' said Lucy. 'So I suggest we go and look for that album.'

'Erm, *right,*' said Toby, 'and where are we going to find one of those?'

Lucy thought for a moment before replying, her eyes darting around as if she was rifling through a mental filing cabinet.

'Erm, next door,' she said. 'I *think*…'

They returned to the amusement room and began the heart-breaking task of searching the wreckage of Byron's collection. Fortunately, it wasn't long before they found something.

'I think this might be it,' said Toby. He lifted one end of a *Fizzo* Lectric shock machine and nodded towards the book that lay beneath it. It was a big leather photograph album, covered in dust and with a heavily dented cover. Lucy dragged it out just as Toby dropped the machine with a crash.

'*Oops,*' he said, 'sorry, it was heavy.' He rubbed the dirt and grime from his hands and stood up beside Lucy who was staring at their find.

'I reckon that'll be the one,' smiled Toby. 'Look at the design on the front cover – it's the same as your toy theatre.'

'It's *called* The Empire,' said Lucy.

'Yeah,' said Toby. 'Well whatever – it's exactly the same.'

'I suppose it *could* be,' said Lucy.

'Don't be dense,' said Toby, 'there's no *could be* – it's the same.'

'Apart from the title,' said Lucy, 'and that's been rubbed away.'

'You can still read it though,' said Toby. 'If you tilt it up towards the light you can still make out the letters. Look, it says '*Behold these flaming stars which stand before you*'.'

'Oh,' gasped Lucy, 'well *that* sounds impressive, doesn't it? Perhaps we should have a look inside?'

'Go on then,' grinned Toby.

Lucy found a place on the floor that wasn't covered in debris and placed the album at the centre. Then she settled down in front of it, and holding her breath, she turned the first page.

'It's rotten-well empty,' she said, unable to hide her disappointment. She held up the semi-transparent protector leaf, looking at it first from one side and then the other, as if she expected to see something through it.

'And what did you expect?' said Toby.

'I don't know,' said Lucy, 'photographs I suppose. That wouldn't be *too* much to hope for, would it? In a photograph album?'

'Have a look on the next page,' suggested Toby.

Lucy expected another blank page, so she wasn't too disappointed when that was exactly what she found. There was a slight difference here though, because there were four adhesive paper corners that had once kept a photograph in place. And there was a faint difference in colour too; a dark rectangular patch that suggested a picture had been removed. Below it, written in faded red ink was what she assumed to be the title.

It read ⅂ᒐⱽᒐᗡ.

'Uh-oh,' said Toby. 'I'm getting a funny feeling about this.'

'You mean the symbols?' said Lucy.

'Yeah, it's like I've seen them before – only I know I haven't.'

'Same here,' said Lucy.

It was a similar story on the next page. But the interlay sheet had been torn away, so the word ᒐⱯⱯᒋ jumped out at Lucy as soon as she turned over – even though the blue ink was almost invisible. There was just the faintest of outlines, like the marks left behind when the tide goes out.

'These are *great* photographs,' said Toby trying to sound unimpressed. 'I wonder what sort of camera they used – a Yawn-O-Mat f64? Or the Snoozo Roll Film model with built in alarm clock?'

'Probably,' said Lucy, 'and I'll bet your dad's got both of them in his collection, hasn't he?'

'Actually, no,' said Toby. 'I made them up – they're not real cameras.'

'I *know*,' said Lucy. 'But you can have two points for trying. And I *know* you're only making jokes because you're nervous – don't worry, so am I.'

She ran a slow-moving finger across the faded blue ink and then gently turned the page. The contents of the ᒐⱭᙠⱯᒋ page had also been removed – and all that remained was the pale yellow ink of the title.

'Come on,' said Toby nervously, 'let's get to the end and then we can go home. It's bangers and mash for tea, and…'

'Oh…,' he said, as Lucy turned the page again. 'What's *that*?'

'I don't know,' said Lucy, lifting the protective sheet.

'Wow, now that *is* something,' said Toby, 'but *what*?'

They had been expecting to find photographs, so the scruffy bit of paper mounted on the next page came as a bit of a shock. It was a piece of rough-edged parchment that looked like it had been torn out of an old Bible – and it was covered in a strange, loopy-handed text.

'What is it?' said Toby. 'Poetry?'

'How should I know?' said Lucy. 'I don't even know if it's a language. It looks more like doodles to me. The letters are nothing like the symbols used for the titles, but they're not Ingulesh either.'

'Maybe it's poetry in a different language?' said Toby.

'Or perhaps it's a shopping list?' suggested Lucy.

Suddenly a vague look spread over her face, as if she was trying to do the square root of minus one in her head.

'*Luce*? You alright?'

'Erm, ye-es,' she said. 'I've just realised – it's *Babage*.'

'What is?' said Toby.

'*That*,' she said, pointing at the word V⩑V⩗⊓. 'It means South, and it's pronounced *Babage*.'

'*Does* it?' said Toby, sounding surprised. 'Are you sure?'

'Positive,' she said.

'Ah, *wait* a minute. This is just another invention, *isn't* it?'

'No,' said Lucy. 'Honestly – it means south.'

"Air in the north and earth in the south,
Call out to me by word of mouth,
Wet in the east and hot in the west,
Call out to me; I will do my best.
Lucal, Sobol, Babage, Raas,
These four points will come to pass."

'And what was all *that* about?' laughed Toby. 'I thought you said it wasn't poetry?'

'It's a rhyme my mother taught me,' said Lucy. 'Lucal is north, Sobol is west, Babage is south and Raas is east – which means that the first four album pages represent directions of the compass.'

'And suppose they do?' said Toby. 'We're still none the wiser, are we?'

'No, we aren't,' admitted Lucy with a smile. She was *so* pleased that the memory had chosen to come back to her at just the right time.

'Perhaps there'll be more clues further on?' said Toby.

'Maybe,' she replied, turning the page.

It was another empty slot, accompanied by a damaged and unreadable title, and following that were a further ten pages, all of them empty and all without titles. The last page was black though, rather than brown, and the word 'Daath' was scribbled there in thick pencil, hardly visible against the dark background.

'Now *that's* spooky,' said Toby.

'What is?' said Lucy.

'*Daath*,' said Toby with a shiver. 'It probably means death.'

'Actually it probably *doesn't*,' said Lucy. 'If they'd meant death then they'd have written death wouldn't they? Unless they're as bad at spelling as you.'

'Who?' said Toby.

'Who? *Who*?' she said, sounding like an owl. 'Whoever wrote it, that's who – my uncle probably, or my mothe…'

Toby had been thinking up a good response to her dig about spelling, but changed his mind as tiny patches of damp appeared on Lucy's cheeks.

'I hadn't thought of that,' she sniffed. 'This really *could* be my mother's album, because Byron took a lot of her stuff after she disappeared. He said the lamp-stand couldn't be trusted to look after it properly.'

'So he brought it here and used it to prop up his furniture?' said Toby. 'Well that's *really* taking good care of your inheritance, isn't it? And I suppose he keeps the priceless figurines in the toilet?'

'No Toby, just shut up and listen – I'm *sure* this belonged to my mother. Do you know that feeling you get when you've seen something before? Well I can recall my mother showing it to me now. That's how I recognised the symbols and knew how to pronounce them.'

Suddenly her thoughts took flight – and the book before her was as clear as day and completely free from dust. She was sitting on a wooden floor in her nursery, turning the pages over and over. Each newly turned leaf contained something of interest, and the titles were all written in bright, unfaded colours. There was a shadow too, cast on the floor beside her. Its owner stroked the five-year-old Lucy's hair, and as each page was turned anew, a comforting, musical voice pronounced the title below the script. *Lucal*, it said, almost too gently to be heard. *Sobol* it whispered. *Babage. Raas. These four points will come to pass.*

There was a rustle of crinkly paper, and for a moment, Lucy imagined the breath and the smell of her long-lost mother. She was standing behind one of those protective album sheets, her features reduced to a smiling blur –

and it looked as though she was trying to say something. Suddenly though, there was nothing – her imagination had turned off again, just as surely as if someone had pulled a plug out.

'It *is* my mother's,' she said eventually, 'and it was left here for a reason.'

'Something to do with your silly rhyme?' said Toby.

'It's *not* silly – especially not if my mother taught it to me.'

'Alright, so what does it all mean then?'

'I don't know,' said Lucy, closing the album. 'But I have a feeling we're going to find out.'

The Illustrious
Doctor Veracifer

As Lucy stepped off the bottom stair and into the hallway, she paused and gave a wistful glance at the iron hook where Byron hung his coat and walking stick. They were still there, along with his overshoes and a copy of *Practical Caber Tossing*, which he always reckoned would be handy if he was summoned to Scottlund in an emergency. With a deep sigh, she decided it was time to go. She peeped through the letterbox to make sure it was safe, then slipped quietly into the street, closing the thin green door behind her. As she turned though, the vast bulk of a policeman blocked her escape.

'*Going* somewhere, are we?' he said.

'Erm, ye-es,' said Lucy, her eyes only coming up to the level of his whistle chain. 'I was thinking of going home actually.'

'And where would that be?' said the constable. 'Somewhere warm I hope? Only you don't appear to be dressed for the weather, and that bag isn't going to keep the chill off.'

'Ah, *yes*,' said Lucy, feeling a sudden urge to lie. 'But I only live around the corner.'

'*Do* you now?' he said. 'And which corner would that be?'

'That one there,' said Lucy, pointing across the street. 'Number six.'

'Mrs. Boggins' house?' said the constable. He raised one eyebrow.

'*Ye-es*,' said Lucy. The will for invention was suddenly strong, because of all the time she'd spent on her own. 'I'm her niece,' she said. 'I'm visiting – from erm, down south.'

'*Niece*?' said the constable. 'You do know she's ninety-three, *don't* you?'

'We have a very complicated family,' said Lucy, suddenly regretting the fib. She was beginning to shiver now, the wind cutting through her clothes as if they were made from old bits of string. And the poor quality of her latest invention had made her even colder.

'Yes, it *does* sound rather complex,' said the constable. 'Anyway Miss, you get yourself off home and get warmed up. You don't want to be hanging around outside, now the bloomin' weather's back to normal – in fact they say it's going to get worse.'

'Yes,' said Lucy, glancing skywards. 'It's lucky we all have a sense of humour, isn't it?'

'It certainly *is*,' smiled the policeman, 'but just one thing, before you go though.'

'Erm, ye-es?' said Lucy.

'There's no need to feel guilty and start telling fibs as soon as you see someone in uniform,' he said. 'Especially if you haven't done anything wrong.'

'Erm, no, I suppose not,' said Lucy, looking rather embarrassed.

As the constable returned to his beat, she stepped back into the toy shop doorway, wondering how he'd known. And then she remembered that the houses in that street had been demolished the previous week. It was her very first zero-point story, and for her penance, she decided that she'd confess everything to Toby – *if* she could ever spare the time to meet him again. Because at the moment she was *extremely* busy.

She'd arrived at the laboratory today just as she had on the previous six mornings, each time hoping for the faint aroma of Lapsang Souchong wafting down the stairs. There had been no such smell though, just a cold feeling of desolation waiting behind the door – *and* of course the page with the mysterious writing on – the one she and Toby had found in the photograph album. She'd realised, even on that first day that the scribble-filled page was a *far* more potent device than the Empire – she could *feel* it in her sinews. The only difference was that she knew how to use the theatre, whereas the album page had resisted all of her attempts to unlock its secret. Or at least it *did*, for the first couple of days. Then, on the third visit, she had stumbled across the words it was waiting to hear – and she had discovered exactly what it was capable of.

Names have power, she was once told, and once again she'd found that it was true. Just as the theatre responded to the word *Empah*, the album page was expecting to hear a name – and when that name was pronounced, it revealed a gateway to another new world. The new place was darker and far more threatening than Nether Grimston though, judging by what little she had seen. Or rather *hadn't* seen – and that was one reason why she hadn't told Toby – because there was nothing to look at.

She'd been to the new world four times now, and found nothing but the smell of dust and shadows. She had felt her way round in the dark, only to trip over objects that she couldn't begin to guess the identity of. She had searched high and low for some means of lighting the room but had given up in despair. She had even laid on the floor near the door, inhaling the draught that blew underneath. There were no smells from the other side though, and no light either – just the sound of the wind as it navigated the great corridor beyond. Or maybe it wasn't a corridor? It was *so* frustrating – like sitting in a waiting room for an appointment she knew nothing about. Only there were no magazines to read and someone had blacked out the windows and stolen all the light bulbs.

She shivered and stepped back into the shelter of the doorway – but then realised that if Byron turned up he wouldn't see her. She stepped forwards again and noticed that the sky had darkened even further. If it carried on like this then soon it would be as black as the room on the other side of the album page.

During today's visit, she had tried sitting still for what seemed like hours, waiting in the dark in the hope that someone might come and open the door. She had even failed at *that* though, eventually overtaken by the fear that whoever she was waiting for might not be friendly. Apparently, the room had no intention of giving up its secrets, and if there *was* a world on the other side of the door then *that* was going to remain a mystery too.

'Are you *still* there?' shouted the constable. He was standing on the other side of the street, examining a tiny car that had seen much better days.

'Erm, yes,' shouted Lucy, 'but I'm going home, right now – I promise.'

It was true. She *had* decided to leave; finally satisfied that Byron was going to remain missing for a tenth day. It wasn't just that she was tired of waiting for him though – she was starting to feel the cold, her whole body wracked by the kind of deep-rooted shiver that was impossible to stop. If she didn't get warmed up soon then the weather was going to wrap her in its sinister arms and take her away from the world forever.

'What *you* probably need is a nice warm coat,' said a voice behind her.

Before she could object, a shabby black skin had been wrapped around her shoulders. It was still warm from the man's body, and heavy too, the hem of it almost reaching the ground.

Lucy turned and smiled at her benefactor. The rest of his clothes were even tattier than the leather coat, and it was clear that he hadn't bothered to shave today – or perhaps even this week. His bottom lip drooped as though it usually supported a cigarette, making him look like a detective from an old black-and-white film.

'Thank you,' said Lucy. She was far too cold to consider refusing his kindness – and something about the man told her it was just that – kindness. As he returned her smile, the skin at the corners of his eyes wrinkled up, just like Lily's.

'It's getting quite dark,' he said with an upwards glance. 'Have you noticed that? Awfully, *awfully* dark. I think there might be something strange going on. Remind me to make a note, will you?'

'Erm, yes, I did notice,' said Lucy. 'And as for your note, erm…'

She looked at the sky again, not that she needed to. It *was* getting awfully, awfully dark, as the stranger had kindly pointed out. But it wasn't just the sky that was more sinister. She felt a greater darkness in her heart too, and wondered if that was what he'd really meant.

'What was that about a note?' said Lucy.

'Don't worry,' he said, taking out a pencil and a cigarette packet. 'I'll write it on here.'

'Oh,' said Lucy, trying to see what he was scribbling.

'Right, well that's it,' he said suddenly. 'I think I can go now.'

'Go? *Already?*' said Lucy. 'But…'

'I just wanted to wait until that copper finished nosing around my car,' he said. 'Just in case.'

'Just in case of *what?*' said Lucy.

'Nothing,' he said, pocketing the note. 'Right, I'll see you later.'

'*Will* you?' said Lucy. She hoped she would, but it didn't seem very likely. 'Hey,' she shouted, 'wait a minute – what about your coat?'

The owner of the garment was already inside his car, and after a few seconds of mechanical coughing and spluttering, he managed to coax the wreck into life. As he drove away, he wound the window down and called out to her.

'You can have it on loan,' he shouted.

'*Loan?*' said Lucy, watching the red tail-lights disappear round the corner. 'That's lovely, but I don't even know who you are.'

As she turned to leave for home, Lucy noticed a queue at the butchers next door. Just a few hours ago, the place had been boarded up, but now, despite the weather, people were queuing up to buy half a pound of mince. Where had they all come from? The street had been deserted not five minutes ago and now it was full of people with raincoats and umbrellas. As she approached the doorway, Lucy spotted a middle-aged woman inside the shop. She was talking nineteen-to-the-dozen to the butcher, rummaging in the depths of a handbag that looked big enough to swallow a goat.

'I'll have a snot brain,' said the woman, 'and a couple of slabs of frappy skenk. Oh, and I'd better take a few ounces of chicken insides too.'

The butcher nodded and smiled, his greedy little eyes fixed on the woman's huge purse.

'And is that a pig's head you have there Mister Eastman? I think I might take one of those too, for my Eric's tea.'

'Erm, no Mrs. Fortescue,' said the butcher with a grin. 'I'm afraid it *isn't* a pig's head – it's a mirror.'

There was a horrible silence, and then everyone inside the shop burst out in a frightening kind of laughter. The woman calmly clipped her handbag shut and turned towards the door with a look of despair, breaking into a run as her tears began to flow. Lucy dived out of the way as she rumbled past, shaking the pavement, and filling the gutters with teardrops. Actually, it *had* been quite funny, thought Lucy, but it was also terribly cruel, and she suddenly felt guilty for even thinking about laughing. It was no wonder Mr. Eastman had gone out of business – only he *hadn't*, had he? Because the big man with the ruddy face was still here and still dishing out the compliments.

'*Well?*' he said, coming to the door and shouting after her. 'You *did* ask, didn't you? And I was only saying, *wasn't* I?'

He looked at Lucy as if everything that had happened was her fault —
then he turned back to his other customers who had begun to applaud.

'That's *right*,' he said, taking a bow. 'I was only *saying*.'

With the memory of the butcher's grinning face stuck firmly in her mind,
Lucy ran all the way home, her lungs finally giving up just as she reached the
guest house steps. As she paused to regain her breath, she noticed the new
handiwork on the sign. Someone had painted out the words 'Cruet Extra'
and left a nasty blue splodge; just to prove they had done the job. There was
another nasty splodge too, waiting for her on the top step — it was Tarquin,
and he was looking extremely pleased with himself.

'Just *wait* till you get inside, Lucy Lastic. There's a *brilliant* surprise.'

'Is it Uncle Byron?' she gasped. 'Have they found him?'

'Don't be thick,' grinned Tarquin, 'it's *much* better than that. *You'll* see.'

'I'm not going in then,' said Lucy. 'Or if I do then I'm going to tell them
about you and Biffo and Warren Idiot — I'll tell them you wrecked my
uncle's laboratory.'

'That's a great idea,' said Tarquin, 'and then you'll *really* be in it.'

'And why should I get in trouble for *that* you little weed? *You're* the ones
who did the damage.'

'No we didn't,' said Tarquin. 'But even if we had they wouldn't believe
you. Nobody's going to believe anything you say, ever again. Go inside and
find out if you don't believe me.'

Tarquin sniggered as he watched Lucy creep through the hallway and
sidle up to the living-room door. She could hear voices inside, but unlike the
strange, soundless words uttered by her uncle in the confuser, she could hear
these as clearly as if she were in the room. She breathed as gently as possible,
not moving an inch in case she stood on a creaky board.

'What about the money then, Doctor?' It was Percy's voice.

'Ah, well that was merely a misunderstanding Mr. Winnet-Blake. As I
said to your wife earlier, we intended the money to go into the charity fund
all along, but my secretary made a ghastly blunder. I don't profess to
understand how it came to happen but the cash ended up in my personal
account by accident. It's a complete mystery. The stupid girl swears blind
that she wasn't to blame, but I simply *had* to give her the sack. I can't have a

complete liar working in a position of trust, particularly in *my* position. You *do* see, don't you?'

Lucy heard Percy mumble some reply or other. It didn't sound like he agreed, but he probably couldn't think of a reasonable response. The lamp-stand had no such problem though.

'And that's precisely *our* problem,' said Lily. 'With Lucy it's *all* lies and stories, *isn't* it? But mainly just lies.'

There was a pause, during which Lucy imagined her stepmother's face screwing up into a hateful grimace.

'*All* those *horrible* lies,' she screeched again, as if she was having difficulty believing it the first time. 'In fact,' she said, 'I can't remember the last time I heard the girl speak the truth.'

Lucy pushed the door open just a fraction, frightened that she might miss something important. There was a tiny squeak from the floorboards, but nobody seemed to notice.

'No, look, I'm sorry,' said Percy, 'but I can't have you saying things like that about Lucy. She's just inventive – look at the writing prize for instance.'

'Ah, yes,' sneered the lamp-stand, 'the famous writing prize – now *tell* me, do we even know if there *was* a competition?'

As Lucy leaned forwards the door creaked slightly, but again nobody appeared to notice.

'Well, we *don't* know, *do* we?' hissed Lily.

'No,' said Percy. 'I suppose not.'

'There you are then,' said Lily triumphantly. 'I'm telling you, there's something deeply *wrong* with that girl. There's something dark and deep and slimy living inside her, and if you ask me it needs to be dragged out into the light and beaten to death with sharp sticks.'

Lucy couldn't stand it any longer and gave a great sob as she burst through the door, almost falling into the room. She was close to tears, and breathing hard again – but most of all she was confused.

'Percy? *Dad?* What's she talking about? And who's *this?*'

She closed the door and leaned back against it, allowing the great brass knob to dig into her spine as she surveyed the scene.

'Don't be so rude,' snapped Lily. She was standing behind the sofa, watching Lucy with the kind of smile that could only mean bad news. 'And don't point at people either.'

Lucy lowered the accusing finger and even found time to close the mouth that had dropped open in surprise. She had expected to see one of the family doctors, but was greeted instead by a short, fat man in a dark suit. Someone, in fact, who looked as though he'd been involved in an accident with a bicycle pump, because his cheeks were blown up like balloons. The rest of his head had fared no better, with just three tufts of hair trying to cover his baldness, and eyebrows that looked like badly stitched wounds. It was his eyes that distressed her most though. They were like a couple of miniature walnuts buried in raw cake mix.

She stood away from the door, swallowing hard and realising that her tongue had dried up completely.

'Don't worry Luce,' said Percy. 'You just need to answer a few questions and everything will be all right.'

Lily nodded and smiled – Percy had *finally* done something to please her.

Lucy wanted to trust him, especially as he seemed to be on her side, but despite his assurance things seemed very far from alright. She could *feel* it, somewhere deep inside her, in an organ that dealt only in fear – and she'd called him 'dad' too, which never *ever* happened.

'This is Doctor Veraciter,' said Lily, staring at Lucy's newly acquired coat. 'He's from the surgery.'

Lucy thought she saw a wink pass between her stepmother and the doctor but couldn't be sure. But even if she hadn't imagined it, there was still something funny going on. She could remember every detail of the brass plaque outside the surgery, and there was definitely no mention of a Doctor Veraciter. There was Dr. Pomfret Edgar, FRCS MA; the bone doctor from Boxford, and below him, there was Dr. Sanjay Dilip, the Ear, Nose and Throat specialist from Bombay who also knew quite a lot about making mango chutney. Then there was… Well it didn't actually *matter* who else was there, did it? There was *definitely* no Veraciter.

'Excellent,' said Lily, suddenly looking much calmer. 'Now, why don't you two get to know each other whilst I go and get some tea?'

Lucy squirmed uncomfortably as her stepmother left the room. She had been looking at the coat the whole time and hadn't mentioned it, but the thought was *there* now, stored up inside Lily's twisted mind until the time was right.

Percy looked worried. To prove it he filled his pipe with some disgusting new tobacco mixture, and then paced about the room puffing out great stinking clouds of smoke. Veraciter just sat there, clicking his tongue against the roof of his mouth, looking like an overweight preying mantis. He was staring at Lucy as though she was a prize in a bingo competition – a prize he simply *had* to have.

When the lamp-stand finally returned with the tea things Percy sat on the sofa next to the doctor, and Lily took up position behind. Lucy was placed in front of them on a rickety kitchen chair, and since she alone faced the window, she was the only one to notice the disturbance outside. Tarquin's head was just showing at the bottom of the window, and a pair of hands, his own presumably, were reaching up from below, and pretending to throttle him. He disappeared though, just a fraction of a second before the doctor turned to look.

'What was that?' he said.

'Nothing,' said Lucy.

'Very well,' said the doctor, scribbling a note. '*No-thing*. Now, let me tell you why I'm here.'

'Yes,' grinned Lily. 'Tell us all.'

'*Well*,' said Veraciter, 'sometimes Lucy, when people aren't completely right in the head, they begin to have strange thoughts.'

'Oh?' said Lucy. 'What kind of thoughts?'

'We doctors call these things *errant imaginings*,' he said. 'Awful, dreadful thoughts that aren't particularly true, and certainly aren't *right*.'

'That's right,' said Lily, 'and it takes an expert to sort things out.'

'Quite,' said the doctor.

'I see,' said Lucy, 'and who is it that's in charge of deciding which thoughts are right?'

'Experts,' said the lamp-stand, '*that's* who – *good* people like the doctor, who, under the circumstances, has kindly agreed to visit you at home.'

'And what circumstances are those?' said Lucy.

'You'll know soon enough,' said Lily with a sneer. She looked at Percy for encouragement but he was nervously sucking on his pipe. It had gone out again. Any minute now, thought Lucy, he'd be knocking it on the heel of his shoe.

'*Yes, thank you* Mrs. Winnet-Blake,' said the doctor. 'But will you allow *me* to do the talking?'

'Erm, *humph*, yes of course,' said Lily with a shrug. The idea that she should let someone else do the talking seemed to cause her almost physical pain. When *she* wanted a say there was nothing that would keep the words behind her lips. Except perhaps the thought that her plan was finally about to work. Now *that* just might be worth keeping quiet for.

'Now, Lucy,' said the doctor, 'can you imagine what the world would be like if all the people who had these thoughts were to act on them? Just *think* how much discomfort and distress that might cause the rest of us.'

'I don't care,' said Lucy, 'there's nothing *wrong* with the way I think.'

'Yes, well that's what I'm here to find out Lucida,' said the doctor.

'It's *Lucy.*'

'Is it?' he said. 'Ah, well no matter – now, with your permission I'd like to go through a few things. Shall we begin?'

Lucy thought of refusing to co-operate but realised they would win in the end, so she decided to sit patiently through the questions and then perhaps write a story about it afterwards – one where the three interrogators met with a grisly death. Or perhaps just two of them. Percy would only fall down a deep well and break both legs. And he'd have to stay down there for six weeks before he was finally discovered, surviving only by eating raw frogs and drinking slimy black water.

As Veraciter began to sort out his clipboard, Tarquin bounced back into view at the window. He was managing to get quite high too, so Lucy guessed he was using the little trampoline. Each time he re-appeared he crammed a gobstopper into his mouth until finally, after six ascents, his cheeks were stretched to bursting point. Lucy managed a thin smile – it might *even* have been funny if things weren't so serious on this side of the glass.

'What was that?' said Veraciter, looking round.

Tarquin had disappeared once again.

'It was nothing,' said Lucy.

'Hmm,' he said, fishing around in his briefcase. He pulled a familiar looking buff folder from the cavernous interior. 'In that case let's have a look at these, shall we? These are reports from your school, Saint Frideg's.'

'What are you doing with those?' said Lucy, staring wide-eyed. 'That's confidential information.'

'And it *is* of course being treated confidentially,' he said. 'Only the most trusted members of my staff will ever see it. Now, let's see what it says.'

Lucy squirmed at the thought of Veraciter examining her personal details. It was like finding a peephole drilled in your bedroom wall – you could never be quite sure what people might have seen.

'Mister Snoad, your form teacher seems to think that you have an above-average mathematical ability,' said Veraciter. 'And you have an exceptional gift for physics and the other sciences. Then again, you appear to be rather less than magnificent in geography, and well below standard in history and religious studies. It seems that your particular *bete noir* is physical education though. That's a black beast Lucy – what we in the medical profession might call a particular weakness.'

'I don't like games,' said Lucy plainly.

'*Don't* you?' he said. 'Hmm, from what *I've* heard, games are a *particular* favourite of yours – and drama too – I've heard you can be *very* dramatic when you want to be.'

'That's right,' snapped Lily, 'she's a real drama queen, aren't you? As well as being a liar. And what about that coat she's wearing – what *is* she up to with that? Coming in here all dressed up like a spiv – where on earth did she *get* something like that in any case?'

'It was loaned to me by a friend,' said Lucy.

'And what kind of friend has a coat like *that*?' spat Lily. 'A coffin stealer? Or a graveyard haunter perhaps?'

'Erm, he's a *magician*,' lied Lucy. 'And, erm, *that's* why the coat has such deep pockets. He went away for a few days, and needed someone to look after it – erm, in case the police wanted to look inside it.'

'Steady on old girl,' said Percy. 'There's nothing wrong with telling a few tales now and again, but this isn't really the time, is it?'

'It most certainly *isn't*,' screamed Lily. 'I've had just about all I can take of this nonsense – which is fortunate really, because when the doctor has finished listening to what you have to say, he's going to lock...'

'Mrs. *Winnet Blake*,' interrupted Veraciter, '*please*, try to let *me* handle this.'

'Yes dear,' sighed Percy, 'let the doctor deal with it.'

Lily gave a subterranean growl and glared at Lucy, her eyes glowing like tiny pits of molten fire.

'So, *Lucy*,' said the doctor, with an artificial smile, 'the school documents tell me that you have an excellent understanding of scientific principles and a very firm grasp of morals. That's the difference between right and wrong – but you knew that already, didn't you?'

'Of course,' said Lucy.

'*Yes*,' said Veraciter, 'I rather *thought* you might – but you can't always believe everything you read in a school report now can you?'

'A firm grasp of morals?' said her stepmother, spitting the words. 'Does that include lying and chea...'

'*Please*,' said the doctor, 'will you allow *me* to conduct the interview?'

The lamp-stand nodded and fell silent. It was a *very* worrying sign.

'Now Ludmilla,' said the doctor, 'let's think about your school subjects again, and language in particular. It *seems* that you have a quite extraordinary aptitude for words – why do you think that might be?'

'I don't know,' said Lucy. 'I was born with it I suppose.'

'Interesting,' said the doctor, pausing to scribble some notes. 'Alright, now let's take a look at some other aspects of your behaviour.'

Lucy frowned. She didn't like the sound of that. Tests on paper were fine, but behaviour was a matter of opinion, and if it was Lily's opinion that counted then she was in deep trouble.

'Tell me about the ventriloquist's dummy,' said the doctor. 'Why have you taken to carrying it everywhere?'

'It's *only* a puppet,' replied Lucy. 'Or did you want me to say that it was my best friend and that I talk to it all the time?'

'So you *don't* talk to it?' said Veraciter.

'Of course not,' smiled Lucy. 'It's just a block of wood – look.'

She unhitched the rucksack and brought Genjamin out into the light, covering his eyes so that he wouldn't have to squint. It was supposed to be a joke, but the doctor made another hurried note, glancing at the doll with vague distaste. It had a face like a giant leprechaun and a rogue eye with a mind of its own — almost as if it was capable of looking around the room independently.

'And what *do* you do in your spare time, Lucy? If you don't talk to this *thing*? This doll?'

'I write stories,' she said.

'*Stories*?' gasped the lamp-stand. 'I don't *think* so. The only talent *she* has is for telling tales, doctor. She's the only person I know who can lie out of both sides of her mouth at once.'

'*Really* Mrs. Winnet Blake — I'll do the jokes from now on, *if* you don't mind. This is a very serious matter — serious but deeply, deeply interesting.' He paused to fill an entire sheet of paper with notes, underlining one particular phrase in red ink. Lucy was good at reading upside down though and managed to decipher the scrawly handwriting. It said simply '*The Word*'.

'Erm, what are you writing?' said Mrs. Winnet-Blake, craning her neck for a look at the notes.

'Just a few observations,' said Veraciter, covering his writing. 'What we doctors might call the salient points.'

'Well as long as your salient points include lies, lies and more bloody lies,' said the lamp-stand, 'I think that should just about cover it.'

'They *aren't* lies,' protested Lucy, 'they're inventions.'

'Oh, well *that* makes all the difference, doesn't it?' said Lily. 'Now I feel *so* much better about the time you came home from school and told us that everyone in the class apart from you had died of Beriberi.'

'Well *most* of it was true,' grinned Lucy, 'and I survived, didn't I?'

'*Everyone* survived,' said Lily, sounding almost disappointed, 'the outbreak of disease turned out to be a rat stuck up a pipe in the girl's toilets.'

'Well, you can't have everything, can you?' smiled Lucy.

'No, indeed you *can't* have everything,' said the doctor. It sounded like a thinly veiled threat — as if he was promising she wouldn't have *anything*.

A kind of uneasy truce was declared whilst the vicar's dog-sick teapot was pressed into service and the doctor treated himself to an entire packet of assorted biscuits. Lucy wasn't offered anything to eat though and sat waiting, her hands thrust deep into the pockets of the borrowed coat. And *that* was when she noticed they weren't empty.

'Wonderful biscuits,' said Veraciter. 'These ones with the raspberry jam in the middle are my favourites.'

'Oh *good*,' said Lily. 'Well why don't you have another – and perhaps next time you come I can tempt you with some of my special fancies?'

There was an almost inaudible groan from Percy who was still attending to his pipe. He winked at Lucy, but she didn't feel much like responding and gave him a frown in return. Then she spotted Tarquin at the window – he was wearing a cycling cap with two torches strapped to it. They were positioned to shine through his ears, which he was waggling about with pieces of string. Just as Lucy began to smile, he pretended to vomit and fell off the trampoline.

'What was that?' said the doctor, spinning round, and dropping a biscuit in his tea. Tarquin had disappeared though, and Veraciter was left poking around in the teacup, trying to rescue the sopping dunker.

'Nothing,' said Lucy, deciding to get Tarquin later. She would wire his bed up to the Lectric, and see how he liked *that*.

'Nothing eh?' said the doctor. 'Then why don't you tell us about your hobbies?'

'I've told you,' said Lucy, 'I like writing.'

'Anything else?' he said. 'What about the cinema? Everyone your age likes to go the pictures, don't they?'

'Sometimes,' said Lucy, 'but real life is better.'

'*Is* it?' said the doctor, scribbling furiously. 'And how do you know that this *real life* as you call it is actually real?'

Percy and the lamp-stand looked at each other, suddenly puzzled by the doctor's line of questioning. Surely, this kind of deep philosophy was lost on a thirteen year old?'

'Life is as real as you make it,' said Lucy firmly. 'And if *I* say it's real, Doctor Veruca, then it *is* real.'

'Interesting,' said Veraciter. 'Erm, just talk amongst yourselves for a moment will you? My fountain pen appears to have run out of ink.'

They watched in silence as the pen sucked noisily at the green fluid. And none of them, not even Lucy, was prepared for the announcement that followed – it was almost as if they'd been hypnotised by the movements of his nib as it hoovered around the recesses of the ink bottle.

'I *think*, Lucy,' said the doctor, 'that you are probably what we in the medical profession call a pathological liar.'

'Erm, *no*, you can't say that,' gasped Percy, 'she's nothing of the kind.'

'No?' said the lamp-stand. 'Well *actually* I agree with the doctor.'

'And *I* think you might all be over-reacting,' said Lucy, trembling. 'I just like to tell stories, that's all – erm, I mean inventions.'

'Evidently,' said the doctor. 'But consider *this* – a liar *knows* when they are lying, but pathological liars are usually unaware of their actions. And they frequently believe in their own inventions, as if they were real.'

Percy seemed upset with the idea but the lamp-stand looked pleased, because it proved that she had been right all along. Her dear-darling Lucy was terribly, terribly sick, and might *even* be a criminal.

'It's easy to explain though,' said the doctor, 'because lying, especially if we don't realise we're doing it, can often be to our advantage. A good lie is worth twenty shallow truths any day. And of course, the very *best* lies are those that the liars themselves believe. Poor unfortunates like young Luca for instance, who *obviously* believes everything she tells us. She probably even believes all the things she *hasn't* told us – *don't* you, Luca?'

The doctor glared at Lucy, daring her to tell a much *bigger* story – because if she did take the bait, then *he* would have an answer for it. It was all there, written in the piggy little walnuts he used for eyes.

'I see,' said Percy. 'But how does all this come about?'

'I was hoping you'd ask me that,' said the doctor. 'The condition often arises as a result of challenging situations in the home.'

'Challenging situations?' said Percy. 'Erm, do you mean mistreatment?'

'Wait a minute,' shrieked the lamp-stand. 'Are you suggesting that *we're* the ones to blame?'

'Surely not,' said Percy, 'we take the very best care of her.'

'*Excuse* me,' said Lucy, 'can you not *talk* like that please?'

'I'm sorry,' said the doctor, 'are some of the big words confusing you?'

'No they are *not*,' said Lucy. 'I can understand the big words perfectly well, thank you very much. I just don't want you chatting about me as if I'm not here. It's not polite – I'm not being studied in a laboratory you know.'

'Not *yet* you're not,' whispered Veraciter.

'Pardon?' said Lucy. Everyone looked at her as if they'd misheard. Then she realised that the doctor's words hadn't actually been spoken. It was as though his lips had moved by accident and his ideas had just leaked out and insinuated themselves into her ear.

'Well,' sighed the doctor, 'it's obvious that we need to find out more.'

'No we don't,' said Lucy. 'There's nothing *to* find out. I like telling stories, and that's all there is to know. They're *not* lies – they just aren't.'

'Then tell us about last Friday,' said Veraciter, 'the day you were confined to your room for wiring the front doorknob to a Lectrical accumulator.'

'You've obviously been told about that,' said Lucy. 'What more is there to tell? It was meant for Tarquin. I didn't mean to hurt Lily.'

'No,' said Lily, rubbing at her injured fingers. 'You didn't mean to hurt *me*, but it was alright to electrocute my child, *wasn't* it? It was perfectly alright to fry your poor brother with Lectric.'

'I told you,' said Lucy, 'it was an accident.'

'Alright,' said the doctor, 'let's just say we believe you; now why don't you help us with another little question?'

'Erm, what?' said Lucy suspiciously.

'Well,' said Veraciter hesitantly, looking first at Percy and then at Lily. 'Perhaps you'd like to start by telling us how you got out of the room?'

'I didn't,' said Lucy. She had a horrible feeling she knew where all this was going.

'Erm, we checked, old girl,' said Percy. 'The room was empty.'

'*Oh*,' she said. It was time for some of the doctor's pathological lying and it needed to be good – but not *too* good. She didn't want them actually believing there was another Grimston somewhere.

'I was writing a story,' she said, 'and I must have fallen asleep.'

'But the room was empty,' hissed Lily. 'We checked – *didn't* we Percy?'

'Erm, ye-es,' said Percy, 'and you weren't there.' He sounded reluctant, as if he didn't want her to get into trouble. But there was no other answer he could give – if he *did*, then his life would be made hell for weeks.

'I was probably under the bed,' said Lucy desperately.

'Under the *bed*?' said the doctor. He scribbled another note.

'Yes. I go under there to sleep sometimes.' She smiled sweetly. It was such a little lie, and it didn't seem to matter. In fact, it was almost as if someone else was telling the story and she was just listening.

'Under the *bed*?' fumed Lily. 'I've never *heard* such a ridiculous story.'

Yes, but you've *written* them, thought Lucy as she spotted a movement in the bushes. Tarquin's bouncing face had appeared again – this time there was a birds' nest tied to his head.

'This is *just* how her mother used to be,' said the lamp-stand. 'And that uncle of yours is exactly the same. Or at least he *was*, until he disappeared. If you ask me the whole family are completely potty.'

'I think I'll be the judge of that,' said Veraciter. 'I studied psychiatry for seven years, so I think I'm probably going to be better at identifying the potty ones.'

'We're *not* potty, *or* mad,' screamed Lucy, directing her anger at Lily. 'None of us is mad – and anyway, how do *you* know what my mother was like? You didn't even know her.'

'No, I didn't, but I was married to your father,' said Lily calmly. 'Or have you forgotten that already? And *he* was always telling me what a complete fruitcake your mother was.'

'He bloody-well *didn't*,' squealed Lucy. 'He just wouldn't *say* things like that.' It was suddenly more than she could stand, and she burst into tears, thinking about the loss of her parents. And now Byron had left her too, and she was being forced to relive those awful experiences all over again.

'It all keeps coming back to the mother, doesn't it?' said Veraciter. 'A deep-seated emotional problem, brought about by the constant disappearance of members of her family – first her mother, then her father.'

'That was different though,' said the lamp-stand with a smirk. 'We all know where *he* went, *don't* we? Down a steaming great funnel.'

'Quite,' said the doctor.

Lucy felt the muscles twitching at the corner of her left eye. At school, she'd overheard Mr. Snoad saying that her poor father had probably thrown himself off the pier and into the funnel of the ferry because it was quieter in there – and it was probably true.

'He was just trying to get away from *her*,' snapped Lucy.

'*Ooh*,' hissed Lily, 'you ungrateful little guttersnipe…'

'Can we *please* get back to the point?' said the doctor.

'And what's that?' said Lucy.

'Your disappearance,' said Veraciter.

'But I've already *told* you what happened,' insisted Lucy.

'I see,' said the doctor, 'and is that what I should write? *Under the bed?*'

'Put whatever you like,' snapped Lucy. 'It's the truth.'

'Well it's certainly a version of it,' smiled Veraciter. 'And if you don't mind me saying so, it's a version that bears an uncanny similarity to the story of your own mother's disappearance. *She* disappeared from a locked room, didn't she? Even though there was no possible means of escape.'

'Then I must have inherited her talent,' smiled Lucy.

The doctor gave a great sigh and turned towards Lily.

'*Well*, Mrs. Winnet-Blake, I'm afraid we appear to have reached what we doctors call an *impasse*. In spite of everything we've tried to do for her, our young patient still insists that her stories are real.'

'They *are* real,' insisted Lucy, 'and I can *prove* it – and I'm *not* your rotten patient.' She was thinking about showing them Nether Grimston – then they would *have* to believe her, and it would all be over.

'You little liar, you can't prove anything,' hissed Lily. 'Now just shut up and listen to the doctor – because this is your very last chance.'

'Erm, ye-es,' said Percy, 'I'm afraid she means it old girl.'

'Means *what*?' said Lucy. '*Why* is it my last chance?' She looked at Percy for an answer, but he wouldn't meet her gaze – he just played nervously with his pipe.

'You should listen to your mother's advice,' said the doctor.

'She's *not* my mother,' spat Lucy. 'She's my *stepmother*, and I don't ever want to forget it.' She was shaking now – the blood draining away from her face.

'I think we ought to consider the use of drugs,' said Veraciter. '*Strong* ones – most cases of pathological lying respond well to extreme medication – but only when it's administered in *very* large doses.'

Lucy looked firstly at Percy and then at Lily, expecting some kind of reaction. But they were staring at her as if Veraciter hadn't said a word. She took a deep breath and tried not to imagine the scene, but the picture came bursting into her head without permission. She was going to be strapped down to a bed and stuck full of sharp needles. And she knew exactly what kind of needles they were going to be – the kind that were big enough to fit a drinking straw inside. And the worst part of it was that nobody seemed to mind. They all seemed perfectly happy for her skin to be pierced and damaging chemicals to be pumped into her veins.

She began to scream, but before the sound of terror could emerge, Tarquin appeared at the window again. He'd coiled a jute washing line around his neck and was pretending to hang himself. The stupid boy had even gone to the trouble of staining his lips a horrible purple colour and making his eyes bulge out of their sockets.

Lucy leapt from her chair, pointing furiously at the window. The doctor and Percy moved in their seats, and Lily spun on her heel, but before anyone had turned far enough the rope snapped and Tarquin disappeared from view. They all turned back and stared, as if they had been locked in a room with a raving lunatic. Percy looked disappointed, but Lily was wearing a triumphant grin, as though she was ready to open a bottle of champagne – only in her case, it would be fizzy apple juice with the label steamed off.

'Well,' said the doctor, making a few final notes. 'I think I've seen *quite* enough for now – and I've certainly *heard* enough.'

'Good,' grinned Lily. 'So it's all settled then?'

'Yes,' said Veraciter with a malevolent grin. 'I rather think it *is*.'

Kolley Kibber and the Mechanical Turk

Lucy hated hospitals. They smelled of ether, and that, along with the scent of sparks reminded her of magic. And although that was a good thing, it reminded her of what was going on in her life, and how little she currently understood. There was one thing she *did* know though – she didn't want to be here, surrounded by people dressed in white and carrying clipboards around draughty, antiseptic corridors. And she didn't want Lily, Percy, and the rotten doctor for company either. It was all *very* depressing, especially as she'd been woken at dawn for an early visiting session. If it had been anyone but Tarquin she wouldn't have minded so much, but the accident had been his own stupid fault – or so she kept telling herself.

The thickest of the plastic tubes was carrying some sort of pink fluid up dear-brother Tarquin's left nostril – and *that* was the quiet one. It was the one stuck in his mouth that provided most of the entertainment, sounding a lot like one of those huge trucks that suck sludge up from the sewers. Her stepbrother didn't seem to mind the *schluurrrp-snork-snorky-snorky-schluurrrp* noises though, because it was two days now since he'd tried to hang himself and he *still* hadn't regained consciousness. It was probably just as well too, because if he could actually *see* the great purple wound around his neck he'd probably faint all over again.

'Well,' said Veraciter, sitting down on the bed. 'We had a narrow escape there, *didn't* we Lucia?'

'Where?' said Lucy, ignoring the repeated slur on her name.

'Young Tarquin of course – accidentally hanging himself like that. He might have died if we hadn't got him to the hospital in time.'

'It was his own fault,' said Lucy.

'*Was* it?' said the doctor. 'I'm not so sure about that.'

'Well *I'm* certainly not to blame,' insisted Lucy.

'No,' said the doctor, 'of *course* you aren't – absolutely not.'

Lucy winced. She was unable to look Veraciter in the eye, because there was a tiny part of her that didn't feel quite so innocent. The other day, when Veraciter had come to the house and threatened her with drugs, she'd imagined Tarquin in some sort of awful peril, and suddenly he was. It had been just a brief angry thought, but what if she really *was* to blame, as Veraciter seemed to be suggesting? No, she finally decided, how could it possibly be her fault?

The lamp-stand plumped Tarquin's pillow for the fifteenth time and then mopped his brow with a monogrammed handkerchief. And when she was happy that the precious child was comfortable, she turned her attentions to Lucy, glaring at the girl who had somehow engineered the whole situation. Even though she couldn't work out how it had been done, she was certain that Lucy was to blame, and was equally sure that she was going to get to the bottom of it.

'Come on,' said Percy, noticing his wife's stare. 'Let's go home, shall we? They're taking good care of him, aren't they?'

'Yes,' said Lily, suddenly full of enthusiasm. 'Let's go home.'

'An *excellent* idea,' grinned Veraciter.

'Erm, *is* it?' said Lucy.

'Of course it is,' said Lily with a sinister smile. 'And as a special treat we're going to ride in the doctor's car.'

It had been raining heavily when they arrived at the hospital but it had stopped now, and as they gathered next to Veraciter's chauffer-driven limousine the sun came out, bathing them in a beautiful golden light. Normally this would have made Lucy happy, but ever since they left the ward, she had been sensing some kind of hidden threat – and a bit of sunshine wasn't going to put *that* right.

The car was a masterpiece of engineering, and naturally, it had Percy's eyes out on stalks. Thousands of raindrops were laid across the polished chrome and the peacock-coloured bodywork, each of them reflecting a perfect blue sky and puffy white clouds.

'It's an Alvis Crested Eagle, *isn't* it?' enthused Percy as he climbed into the back with everyone else.

'The Mayfair model,' said the doctor proudly.

'Naturally,' said Percy, 'and such lovely coachwork too – and you even have a luggage carrier, and just look at that dashboard, and…'

'Aren't you supposed to be up front *dear*?' said Lily. 'With the *driver*?'

'What?' said Percy. 'Oh, erm, yes, I suppose I am.'

'Percy is getting out at the greengrocer's, *aren't* you dear?' said Lily. 'We urgently need spinach – and turnips.'

'Yes,' said Percy, 'and cauliflower stalks.'

Lucy's stomach began to roll. She hated turnips and spinach almost as much as she hated the back of the Veraciter's car. It smelt of stale cigars and sweaty armpits, and the deep blue upholstery was leathery and squeaky, just like its owner, but without the squinty eyes.

They dropped Percy at the shops and as they pulled away, he gave a weak little wave. Lucy thought he looked upset, but it was hard to tell these days. He was always miserable, because he *still* didn't have the contract from Snogg's sauce. His other campaign was going badly too – it was for something called Billy Bungham's Bilious Beans, which as far as Lucy could work out was a product with absolutely nothing going in its favour.

She tried to wave, but Doctor Veraciter was squished up against her, and the best she could manage was a half turn with a quick look out of the side window. Lily's smug face was reflected there in the glass, and as the car made its way slowly along the high street, Lucy realised that the events she was worried about were beginning to take shape. It was like she was sitting in a theatre on her own, and somewhere behind the scenes, people were doing things that concerned *her*. But they weren't telling her about it, they were just leaving her to sit and worry. She would know soon enough though, once the play started – and *that* was what worried her the most.

'I've just remembered,' said Lily. 'I need to see Mrs. Pobjoy about the summer fete. Could you ask your driver to drop me at the chemist?'

'Of *course*,' smiled the doctor. 'As long as I'm invited to the fete.'

'Naturally,' said the lamp-stand. The car pulled up outside Pobjoy's Health and Chemist Emporium and sure enough, Mrs. Pobjoy was there, waiting for Lily and polishing the big coloured glass bottles in the window.

'Oh, and I *do* hope that everything turns out alright,' said Lily, slamming the door and glaring at Lucy. Then she changed to a smile and waved at the doctor as they pulled away again.

'What did she mean by that?' said Lucy, her eyes narrowing. 'What *is* it that she hopes will turn out alright?'

'We'll *see* about that shortly, won't we?' said the doctor.

The car had reached the end of Beach Road now, but instead of taking the road to the boarding house, they turned left, towards the sea front.

'We're going the wrong way,' said Lucy, suddenly aware that the mystery play had begun.

'*Are* we?' said the doctor. He leaned forward and tapped his walking cane on the window that separated them from the driver. The panel slid open.

'Are we going the wrong way, Bruno?'

'No, sir,' he said, 'this is the road we need.'

Lucy didn't like the look of the driver. His head joined straight onto his shoulders, just about where his neck should have been.

'*There*, you see?' said Veraciter. 'This is the road we need.'

'I thought you were taking me home,' said Lucy desperately. Suddenly, the strange look that Percy had given her made sense. He'd known about the plan all along, and obviously hadn't been happy with it.

'*Yes,*' grinned Veraciter. 'Well you know what *thought* did, don't you?'

'Then where *are* we going?' pleaded Lucy.

'We're heading for Saint Mallydick's of course,' grinned Veraciter. 'Where else do you imagine we'd find a suitably equipped laboratory?'

Suddenly the car had become a prison and Lucy needed to escape. She panicked and grabbed the door handle, but then recalled the driver locking it before they set off.

'No, *please,*' she squealed. 'I don't want to go to Saint Mallydick's. That's where they took Adam Knox after he set fire to the school.'

'Quite right too,' said Veraciter. 'We can't have people going around lighting fires just because they feel like it, now *can* we?'

'No,' said Lucy, wringing her hands, 'I suppose not.'

'There, you see? You *are* capable of being sensible sometimes – despite what your mother tells me.'

'She's *not* my mother,' yelled Lucy.

'Aah,' said the doctor, 'just for a minute there I thought we were making some progress, but now we appear to have slipped into denial again.'

'I don't *care*,' said Lucy. 'We could be slipping into a pile of pigeon poo for all I care. I'm *not* going to Saint Mallydick's just for telling a few stories – it's not as if I've hurt anyone.'

'That will be for the authorities to decide,' said Veraciter. 'Who knows what kind of damage your lies might have caused? There might be children lying in a gutter somewhere, mightn't there? And they might be bleeding to death, all because of your mania for fabrication.'

'Don't be so *silly*,' said Lucy. 'There can't be – erm, *can* there?'

'Ah, I sense a little bit of *doubt* creeping in,' said Veraciter. '*Excellent.*'

'This is all my stepmother's idea, isn't it?' said Lucy. 'She wants to have me declared insane.'

'Oh *please*,' laughed the doctor. 'That's the most preposterous idea I've heard this year, and believe me, I've heard quite a few – what possible motive could she have?'

'If I'm mad she'll get my house,' sobbed Lucy, 'and she'll get my mother's house, and my grandmother's house, and my great-grandmother's house.'

'Well that certainly *is* a lot of houses,' said Veraciter with a smirk. 'What do you think, Bruno? It's a lot of houses, isn't it?'

'Erm, yeah,' said Bruno, furrowing his brow. 'That's a lot of houses, right enough.'

'No it's not,' said Lucy. 'They're all the same one – and that's what she wants. She's after my house and the money that's tied up in trust until I'm twenty-one. It was all left to me by my real mother.'

'Ah,' said Veraciter, 'the *real* mother again – the one who disappeared in mysterious circumstances from a locked room.'

'That's right,' said Lucy, 'she did.'

'It sounds a bit unlikely,' said Veraciter. 'What do you think, Bruno?'

'It doesn't *matter* what he thinks,' snapped Lucy. 'And anyway it wasn't even my story – it was in the newspaper.'

'Indeed it was, but you can't believe *anything* you read in the Phibber, and only about a tenth of what you see.'

'Then we agree on one thing at least,' said Lucy.

'It's a start,' said the doctor, 'but there's still a major problem.'

'Is there?' said Lucy innocently.

'Of course,' said Veraciter. 'You didn't print that story yourself, I accept that, but you *still* insist on the truth of it, even though it's just a figment of someone's vivid imagination.'

'But it's *true*,' said Lucy.

'There you are, you see?' said Veraciter. 'We're back to square one – insisting on the impossible.'

The car had become stuck in traffic as they got onto the promenade but they were moving again now, albeit very slowly. As they approached the pier, Lucy had an idea.

'Right,' she said with newfound determination. 'Do you remember I said that I could prove it?'

'Prove what young lady?'

'That my stories were true,' said Lucy.

'Ah, *that* old chestnut,' said Veraciter. 'And how can we prove them? Unless we go through them one by one and look at the evidence?'

'We *could* do,' suggested Lucy.

'I fully intend to,' said Veraciter. 'You needn't worry about *that* – but we'll be doing it under my terms Lucida, not yours.'

'It's *Lucy*,' she hissed.

'Yes I know it is,' said Veraciter. 'At least that's what *you* say.'

'You mean you don't even believe me when I tell you my own name?'

'Well, it's difficult to know exactly where the lies end and truth begins, wouldn't you agree? Just think of all those possibilities out there – all we have to do is decide which of them is true and which isn't. You could build a world from it, couldn't you?'

'But it's my name,' said Lucy. 'That's a fact – it just *is*.'

'Your other inventions are 'just' something as well,' he smiled. 'But we can no more prove *them* than you can prove to me that your name is Lucy. Names have power you know.'

'*Right* then,' said Lucy, her eyes narrowing. 'Stop the car right now and I'll show you.'

'Here?' said Veraciter. 'In the midst of all these holidaymakers?'

'Yes,' said Lucy. 'I'm going to tell you a story – one with a *name* in it.'

'I see,' said Veraciter. 'And what name would that be?'

'Kolley Kibber,' said Lucy. 'That's him over there, by the railings.'

'Kibber?' said the doctor with a frown. 'But that was years ago.'

'Are you going to stop or not?' said Lucy.

'And what if I do?' said Veraciter.

'Then I'll come quietly and do all your tests,' said Lucy. 'Otherwise I'm going to kick and scream all the way.' She took a deep breath, as if preparing to demonstrate her lethal screaming weapon.

The doctor gave her a suspicious look but decided to take a chance. It was the ideal opportunity to prove that Kolley Kibber didn't exist – and if *he* didn't exist then by extension none of the girl's other inventions existed either, and the whole house of cards she'd created inside her head would come tumbling down.

'Alright,' he said, 'but no tricks – I'll be watching you.' He tapped his cane on the window, signalling Bruno to stop.

'No tricks,' said Lucy. 'I promise.'

'Lies are alright,' she whispered as she climbed out of the car. 'As long as they're in a good cause.'

'What was that?' said the doctor.

'Erm, *nothing*,' said Lucy with a sweet smile.

She ran up to a middle-aged man who was dressed in a shabby brown suit. He was wearing a trilby hat and carrying a newspaper. Whilst he was still wondering what was going on she grabbed the paper and whispered to him, using it to cover her mouth.

'A horrible man has kidnapped me,' she hissed. 'And he wants to put me into an asylum.'

'I see,' said the trilby wearer, 'And why exactly did you pick me?'

'Because you've got a kind face,' replied Lucy.

The man smiled with his eyes and Lucy knew that everything was going to be alright.

'You are Kolley Kibber,' she shouted, 'and I claim the ten pound reward.'

'That's exactly right young lady,' he said, 'I *am* Kolley Kibber – you have just won today's ten pound prize. Congratulations.'

Lucy looked back towards the car where the doctor was scribbling furiously in his notebook.

'*See?*' she shouted. 'I *told* you it was him, didn't I?'

A crowd began to gather as Mr. Kibber dragged a small orange box across the pavement. Lucy was ready to swear that it hadn't been there a moment earlier and stood in amazement as Kibber got up on the box and began to attract attention to himself. That was the idea of course – the more people who saw him giving away today's prize, the more likely they were to buy a newspaper tomorrow.

The doctor leapt out of the car, suddenly eager to talk to Lucy again – and the man in the shabby suit *too* – he was going to have some very strong words with *him*, if he could manage it. More than anything, he wanted to know how Lucy had won him over so quickly.

'*Bruno?*' he shouted. 'Keep an eye out – I might need your help.'

Lucy saw what was happening and decided on her plan.

'I want you to give the money to *him*,' she said, pointing at the doctor.

'*Really?*' said Kibber.

'Yes,' said Lucy, 'he likes money, and it might slow him down long enough for me to escape. *Please*, will you help me?'

'The young lady says I should give the money to you,' said Kibber, blocking the doctor's path. 'Is that right?'

'Money?' said the doctor, looking suddenly pleased with himself. 'Erm, *yes* alright – how much are we talking about?'

'Well now, let me see,' said Kibber. 'That's one and erm, two, and one and three, and erm, two, and one – it comes to nine pounds.'

'*Ten*,' said Veraciter with a frown. 'It *comes* to ten.'

'*Oh*, so it *does*,' admitted Kibber. 'Ten crisp whole pounds – now, if I could just ask you to fill in the form? It's for my office you see, to prove I didn't pocket the money myself. You *know* what it's like, don't you? All that red tape. People just can't be trusted nowadays.'

He reached into his pocket for a pen and a piece of paper, winking at Lucy as he did so. It was almost as if he knew she needed help, and exactly what he had to do to provide it. He winked again and nodded, encouraging her to run.

'Form?' said the doctor. 'Oh, well I don't know about that.'

'No form, no money,' said Kolley with a wink. 'It's paperwork that keeps the world running smoothly, *isn't* it?'

The doctor nodded, desperately trying to decide on what was more important – ten pounds for a few second's work or getting his hands around the Blake girl's neck. In the end, he decided it was possible to have both – he turned to grab her, but Lucy had already begun to push her way through the crowd.

'*Pharty*,' shouted the doctor.

'Pardon?' said Kolley, watching Veraciter closely. He seemed to be trying to take off, waving his arms about madly, and gesticulating towards the car.

'*Pharty*,' he screamed, 'get out of that car now and get that bloody *girl.*'

'Don't go worrying about her,' said Kibber, 'I just need a signature and the money's all yours.'

'I'm not interested in your rotten money any more,' screamed the doctor. 'I want the girl.'

'Oh *do* you now?' said Kibber, stepping into his path. 'Well, if you ask me she's well out of it – she said you were trying to drag her off to an asylum.'

'*What?*' shouted Veraciter.

'That's right,' said Kibber, 'she told me she didn't want to go and would I mind helping out.'

'You mean you're *not* Kolley Kibber?' blustered Veraciter.

'Oh yes, I'm *him* alright. That was a bit of luck, wasn't it? She probably didn't even realise – uncanny, don't you think?'

'But, but…' said Veraciter, looking very red in the face.

'But what?' said Kolley.

'But you don't *exist*,' said Veraciter. '*Do* you?'

Mr. Kibber raised his eyebrows.

'I've got a wife at home who might disagree with you there.'

'But she, erm, she made you up,' said the doctor.

'She's a gifted girl then, wouldn't you say? What you might call a rare talent. I'd take good care of her if I were you.'

'Yes, Mr. Kibber, I intend to take *extremely* good care of her. Just as soon as I can get my flaming rotten hands on her.'

The smell of free money was in the air and the crowd were all pushing and shoving to get some for themselves – but they were interfering with Lucy's escape plans. Every step she took was blocked by people waving buckets and spades or pushing prams, or lugging those inexplicably battered suitcases that everyone seems to take to the seaside.

'Gangway,' she shouted. 'Can you let me through please? It's urgent.'

'It's more urgent in this direction,' said a man wearing a Kiss-me-Quick hat. '*Look*, it's Kolley Kibber – and you're going the wrong way.'

'I'm not interested,' protested Lucy, 'now will you *please* let me past?'

The man ignored Lucy's request and picked her up, hoisting her up to shoulder height to give her a better view.

'Can you see him now?' said the man. 'He's over there.' He pushed Lucy even higher, giving her a simply *splendid* view of the promenade.

'Put me *down* you idiot,' squealed Lucy. 'They'll see me.'

'There she is,' shouted the doctor. 'Some kind passer-by has caught her for us – hold onto her sir, and I'll pay you ten pounds.'

'What was that?' said the stranger. 'Something about ten pounds?'

'I don't know,' said Lucy. 'Now will you *please* put me down?' She gave him a gentle back kick in the chest, just to prove she was serious.

'Ouch,' he said, 'watch what you're doing with your feet, will you? And try to *understand* what I'm telling you about Kolley Kibber.'

'I *do* understand,' said Lucy, issuing another smart kick. 'And I'm not interested in Kolley Kibber *or* his money.'

'Not interested in money?' said the man, finally putting her down. 'Well *there's* a thing. Did you hear that Monica? There's a girl over here who's not interested in money.'

'Barmy,' said Monica, 'completely barmy – and just *look* at the way she's running.'

With her feet firmly planted back on the earth Lucy was on the run again, turning off the promenade and ducking under the penny barriers to get onto the pier. It was one of the longest in the country and her favourite haunt, even if some of it *did* belong to the rotten Perkins family.

You are so Bee-Yoo-Ti-Full…

I think you're so Cute-Ti-Full…

As Lucy drew level with the Lectrical Romance machine she realised her mistake – but she got down on her knees and spied between the planks, just to make sure.

'Damn and blast,' she hissed.

Please don't be Snoo-ti-full…

The tide was in, so the only way to get off the pier was back the way she came – but if she turned back now, they would catch her for sure.

And give your heart to meeee…

She sprinted past the amusements and the '*You Won't Bleevi?*' exhibition, almost colliding with the fortune-telling gypsy as she emerged from her lace-curtained lair. In front of her now was the usual sea of deck chairs and beyond *them* was the long, thin section of the pier where there was absolutely no chance of hiding.

'Scuse-me, scuse-me, scuse-me, scuse-me,' she chanted as she forced her way through the crowds. 'Scuse me,' she said.

'*You're* in a bit of a hurry aren't you?' said an old gent in a deck chair. He was sucking very carefully on an ice cream.

'Yes, erm, I'm just *dying* to get to the end of the pier,' said Lucy, not wanting to be rude. She looked back towards the amusements where Bruno was shoving his way through the crowds and gradually catching up.

'You ought to be in less of a hurry,' said the ice-cream licker. 'Where are you going in such a rush?'

'Erm, the theatre,' she said, pointing to the end of the pier. It was a huge structure, hunched over the cast-iron piles like a malevolent dwarf squatting on a park bench – and nestling in its shadow was the exhibition of curiosities.

'Ah, it'll be the *exhibition* you're after,' he said. 'I suppose you'll be eager to see the Flaming Hindoo and the Water Tank of Death?'

'Actually it's *something* like that I'm trying to avoid,' said Lucy.

Bruno was almost on top of them. She could hear him shouting, even though she couldn't make out the words.

'Sorry,' she said, breaking into a run. 'It was lovely talking to you, but I really must go.'

She sprinted off again, but after fifty yards or so, turned to check on Bruno. He'd tripped over the gent in the deck chair and there was some kind of disagreement. But Bruno didn't have time to argue – he snatched the man's ice cream and threw it over the railings into the sea.

'Whoops,' said Lucy, turning to run.

At the ticket booth, she turned again, and found to her horror that Pharty had closed the gap. He was badly out of breath though, sounding like a piano accordion that had been punctured with a shotgun.

'*Out of my way*,' he bellowed. 'I'm on important medical business and if you don't shift your fat arse I'm going to break your rotten nose.'

'Erm, do you see that man doing all the shouting?' Lucy said to the man in the ticket booth. 'Well he's my uncle, and he'll pay for us both.'

'Well,' said the ticket man, 'I don't rightly know if I should let him in – he's of a type, that one.'

'He certainly *is* a type,' said Lucy, 'but he's got plenty of money to spend – he just won ten pounds from Kolley Kibber.'

'Did he?' said the ticket-seller. 'Now *that's* interesting, because I recall Kolley Kibber from years back – well before *your* time of course young lady…'

'Yes, *very* interesting,' said Lucy as she ducked under the turnstile. 'But I need to go in now, thank you very much…'

'*Oi*, Miss! You can't go in there until you have a ticket. It's not allowed – and I wanted to tell you an interesting story about Kolley Kibber.'

'It'll have to wait,' shouted Lucy. She was already deep inside the exhibition, running past the rows of shrunken heads that were supposed to be famous composers. She ducked under the ribcage of a three-headed elephant that had been found living in someone's attic, and that was when she ran into the gang of holidaymakers. The women were all wearing transparent plastic raincoats and the men were dressed in string vests and had knotted handkerchiefs on their heads, all pushing and shoving to get a look at the giant bonsai tree. Unfortunately, they formed an impenetrable wall – a heaving mass of bodies that was packed together like sardines.

'If you want to see something interesting,' said Lucy, 'why don't you come and have a look over here?'

There was no response. The wall of bodies remained tightly packed — uttering the occasional '*ooh*' or '*ah*' as they studied the exhibit. Finally, though, one curious soul turned towards Lucy.

'That's right, look over *here*,' she shouted. 'This is *much* more interesting.'

Suddenly everyone turned in her direction, and as their gaze fell upon her, she realised that some quick thinking was required. She'd been in such a hurry to clear a passage through the crowd that she hadn't bothered to look at the exhibit behind her. She turned and stared at the cabinet, and a feeling of dread descended over her.

'It's empty,' said a child with greasy hair and a half sucked lolly.

'Yeah,' said the child's father. 'What do you take us for? Idiots?'

Lucy took another desperate look. It *was* empty, except for a slimy pool of brown liquid in the bottom that looked like melted wax.

'Ah,' she said. 'It's empty *now*, but, erm, *well*, just you wait until it's *time*.'

'Yeah?' said the awful child. 'And then what?'

'Erm, well,' said Lucy, 'do you see all this brown slime?'

'Yeah - go on,' said the child's father.

'Well if you're patient, you'll see them rise up out of the swamp.'

'Who?' said the child. 'Who's in there?'

'Erm, it's *Lulo*, the mother of vinegar,' lied Lucy. 'And if you're really lucky then after her you'll see erm, *Mondragoni*, yes, that's it – the man with four faces.'

'Is that all?' said the child.

'*All?*' said Lucy, glancing towards the turnstiles. 'What do you expect for a threepenny admission, the FeeJee mermaid?'

'Ah, now *that* would be more like it,' said the father. 'A mermaid – that's proper exhibiting that is. I can remember once, when…'

'Look, I'd *love* to stay and chat,' said Lucy. 'But I've just remembered an emergency appointment.'

Without giving anyone chance to ask what the appointment was for, she dived between the two bodies that were furthest apart and actually managed to squeeze through. Mercifully, the crowd didn't bother to follow her – they were all too busy studying the cabinet, eager for the slightest sign of a mermaid.

Lucy scanned right and left, desperately looking for a hiding place and finally deciding on a cabinet with two skulls inside. The deep shadows behind the exhibit hid her completely, so she paused for a moment to get her breath back. And that was when she read the tatty piece of cardboard placed next to the larger skull. It said, '*William Snake-speer, The Bard of Avon*'. The other note, next to the smaller skull, read '*Snake-speer when he was a boy*'.

She smiled and peered back towards the ticket booth through a double thickness of glass. She could just make out the ticket man, who kept looking nervously towards the interior of the exhibition. He seemed to be thinking about coming to look for her, but a queue was building up, and for each moment he dithered a new face arrived at the ticket window – and now, one of those faces belonged to a man with no neck – it was Bruno.

Lucy squatted down, peering out between the two skulls, her heart thumping in her chest. *So*, she thought, that made a mad doctor, an angry driver and a ticket-booth man after her now. And it was only ten sixteen-and-a-half in the morning. She *knew* that, because the man standing over her said so.

'Ten sixteen-and-a-half is a little early to be studying anthropology isn't it?' he said. 'Shouldn't you be out on the beach enjoying yourself?'

'Anthropo-what?' said Lucy.

'The science of the nature of man, my dear – skulls and such.'

'They aren't real you know,' said Lucy, 'none of the exhibits are.'

'Aren't they?' said the man. He sounded a little disappointed.

'Of course not,' replied Lucy, 'they make the heads out of papier mache. Then they paint them with varnish and leave them out in the sun until they turn this horrible old bony colour.' She stared in horror at the man's head as he took his hat off. He had a large bony skull with no hair, and his skin was exactly the same colour as the exhibits.

'Erm, look,' she said, 'I don't want to be rude or anything but I'm being chased by three people and I haven't got time to stand around talking. That man with no neck wants to strangle me.'

Her new friend peered towards the entrance and must have been impressed with Bruno's appearance because he decided immediately that Lucy was in need of help.

'In that case might I be of some assistance?' he said. 'Why don't you precipitate the removal of your good self from the immediate environs, whilst I remain in my present location and engage your pursuers in various idle speculations concerning the spurious and unpredictable nature of meteorological phenomena?'

'Pardon me?' said Lucy.

'You make a run for it,' he grinned, 'and I'll bore them to death talking about the weather – and if that doesn't work I'll pretend to have a heart attack or something.'

'*Brilliant*,' said Lucy, rushing towards the emergency exit. '*Thanks.*'

Once outside, Lucy realised that her problems weren't over. She was standing on a narrow platform that jutted out over the side of the pier. Below her, the waves were rolling in towards the promenade, slicing around the iron supports like butter round a heated knife. She closed the escape door behind her and leaned over the handrail, only to confirm her worst fear – there was no way down.

With a sigh that sounded like wind in the trees, she made her way to the metal gate at the other end of the platform. It was unlocked, but she didn't rush to open it straight away. Instead, she stood looking through the tight, rusty mesh, imagining what might happen if Veraciter managed to get her to the hospital. She had dreamed about the horrible place once, when Adam Knox had first been committed. In her nightmare, the boy was lying in a laboratory having his teeth pulled out with oily pliers, and when the last of those little bloodstained stumps had dropped onto the surgery floor, she had woken in a sweat. And in her dream, just as now, there were two men dressed in brown janitors' coats, waiting to sweep up the dark, bloody mess.

'We can't just leave it *here* Vern,' said the owner of the first overall.

'No?' said the second. 'And why's that then Crumpy boy? It's *their* fault, innit? Look, it definitely says so on the docket.'

'*Mechanical Turk, Pavilion of Curiosities, Grimston Pier.*'

He showed Crump the docket, then pointed to the rotting gable end where the name of the attraction was picked out in gaudy metal letters.

'Pavilion of Curiosities,' he said. 'Now I *know* that's where we are because that's exactly what it says up there, and rusted up to buggery or not, you can't argue with writing that's twelve foot high, now *can* you?'

A small crowd began to gather around the workmen, interested to know what it was they were shifting – and from the safety of her peephole, Lucy was equally curious. The ornately carved cabinet was about the size of a small desk, with sliding doors at the front and an inlaid chessboard on top. The most unusual feature though was the figure of the man, a Turk, who looked like he was standing behind the cabinet but who was actually built into the back of it. He was dressed in a brilliantly jewelled robe and wore a turban with a giant ruby fastened to the front. It was the expression on his face that interested Lucy the most though – he was completely impassive, as if nothing in the world mattered, except for the study of his next move.

'Yeah, it's right enough,' said Vern. 'But look, I've just noticed. See on the bottom here, underneath that last item, where it says head pickling fluid.'

'*Head* pickling fluid?' said Crump.

'No, *underneath* that,' said Vern, 'don't you ever listen?'

Whilst the two men argued over the docket, Lucy opened the gate and slipped quietly through the crowd – and when nobody was looking, she opened one of the sliding doors and climbed inside. She was just in time too, because as it slid closed, Bruno burst through the rusty gate, nearly battering the thing off its hinges.

'It *says*,' said Vern, 'quite clearly I might add, that the pavilion is the invoice address. The delivery address is '*You Won't Bleevit*', Grimston Pier. And we just came *past* that, didn't we? I thought you said you could bleeding-well read?'

'Yeah? Well I can,' said Crump. 'I thought it was someone back at the office having a laugh. So what *is* a *You Won't Bleevit* anyway?'

'If I told you that,' said Vern, 'I don't think you'd believe me.'

'Oh *ha* bloody *ha*,' said Crump.

'Yeah,' said Vern. 'Well you can have a laugh at *this* as well, because you're carrying the heavy end this time – now shut your great cakehole and get lifting.'

'Not so fast,' said a voice in the crowd. 'I want a word with you two.'

'Yeah,' said Bruno, 'in fact, we want a *few* words.'

'Eh?' said Vern. 'And who the hell are you?'

'Erm, Inspector Snodgrass,' said Veraciter. 'I'm from the Metropolitan Lying Squad – and this is Sergeant Bacon, my hippo.'

'Oppo,' corrected Bruno.

'Yes, sorry,' said Veraciter, squirming slightly. 'He's my oppo.'

'*Lying* squad?' said Crump, putting the heavy end down.

'Flying squad,' said Veraciter. 'Are you deaf?'

From her hiding place inside the machine, Lucy peered through the gauze-covered opening in the Turk's clothing.

'You *do* know that obstructing the police in the course of their duties is a serious offence?' said Veraciter.

'I was only *saying*,' said Crump. 'It just *sounded* like lying squad.'

'Well it wasn't,' said the doctor. 'Now, we've got a few questions for you. Erm, no, actually we've got just the one. Have you seen this girl?'

Lucy gasped aloud as the doctor produced a photograph of her – and she was even more shocked when she realised where it had come from. It was out of the pearl frame in her bedroom – the one she folded up at night, so that she and her dad, her *real* dad, were as close as they could possibly be.

'*Girl*, you say?' Crump examined the picture as if he'd never seen a girl before – or even a photograph come to that. 'Erm, *this* girl?'

'Yes *that* girl,' snapped the doctor. 'Good *God* man, how many girls do you see in the picture? She's a danger to the general public and needs to be captured at once.'

Lucy squirmed, which was difficult, given the cramped conditions inside the box. 'Rotten liar,' she thought. '*I'm* supposed to be the one that makes up the stories – he's a dirty rotten, filthy, stinking *liar*.'

'Yeah, that's right,' grunted Bruno. 'She's a danger, and she's a crinnimul too, and if you're hiding her then there's going to be trouble.' He cracked his knuckles, as if to demonstrate the exact form the trouble might take.

'Yeah, *well*,' said Crump, 'just because you're the police, there's no reason to get all threatening.'

'Never mind that,' said Veraciter. 'Have you *seen* her?'

'I *have* seen her as it happens,' said Crump.

'*Ah,*' said the doctor, grinning at Bruno. '*Have* you now?'

Lucy shifted uncomfortably, trying not to make a noise. They were just a couple of feet away, and the slightest creak would attract their attention. If the cramp in her legs would hold off for just a few minutes, she'd be safe.

'Oh yeah, definitely,' said Crump. 'It was her we saw alright. She was running along the pier, wasn't she Vern?'

'Yeah,' said Vernon. 'And your sergeant was chasing after her. Come to think of it I just remembered something else.'

'Oh?' said the doctor.

'Yeah – that Sergeant Bacon there, he chucked some old bloke's ice cream in the sea – I seen him do it.'

'*Saw* him do it,' corrected the doctor.

'You saw him do it too, did you?' said Vern.

The doctor frowned and looked accusingly at Bruno. It wouldn't do to be leaving evidence around – not at *this* early stage.

'Erm, I tripped,' said Bruno.

'Yeah, well it looked like a Cornish wafer to me,' said Vern.

'It was a trick of the light,' said Bruno, flexing his knuckles again. 'Now, why don't you just answer the inspector's question? *Have* you *seen* the *girl?*'

'I told you once,' said Vern. 'You were chasing her and you…'

'*After* that,' screamed Veraciter, '*after* the alleged incident with the rotten-well, stinking, blasted Mivvi lolly.'

'Nope, I'm sorry,' said Vern, 'but it was *definitely* a Cornish wafer – and no, I didn't see her after that. Did *you* see her Crumpy?'

'Nope,' said Crump, leaning on the machine. His hand was just inches from Lucy's face.

'Right,' said the doctor with an accusing stare. 'Then we'd better have a look inside *this* thing, hadn't we?'

'Ah, well I don't know about *that* inspector,' said Vern. 'You see we're on private property – and this machine is private property too.'

'And *we* are on urgent police business,' said the doctor, poking at the jewel in the Turk's turban. 'What *is* this thing anyway?'

'It's the world's first chess playing machine,' said Crump.

'*Is* it?' said Vern, looking surprised. 'How did you work that out then Crumpy boy?'

'It says so here,' said Crump. He produced a sheet of paper that had been taped to the side of the cabinet. 'Made by Wolfgang von Kempelen,' he read. 'The chess playing automaton is fashioned from wood, powered by clockwork, and dressed in the style of a Turk.'

'All very interesting,' said Veraciter, 'but I think we've had enough of the boring details, don't you? Let's just have a little look inside, shall we?'

He whipped open one of the doors, his broad grin turning to a look of deep disappointment as he surveyed the insides of the machine. The space behind the door was filled with a mass of gears and belts and cogs. It looked like the inside of a hundred-year old cash register.

'See?' said Crump, closing up the panel. '*Told* you so.'

'And the other door?' said Veraciter, certain that it would reveal his prey.

'*This* one you mean?' said Crump. He opened the other door, exposing even more of the machine's internal gubbins. He *knew* it was gubbins, because Vern once told him that whatever kind of machine it was, the technical insides were always called gubbins — and Vern knew about these things.

'*See?*' he said.

The doctor bent down with some difficulty and peered into the space — and was surprised to find that he could see all the way through to the back.

'But there's nobody in there,' he said. 'It's completely bloody-well empty. I was *certain* that…'

'Certain of what?' said Crump.

'The erm, the girl…' said Veraciter. 'She was erm…'

'So that's settled then,' said Vern with a smile. 'Everything is just as it should be — so perhaps me and Vern here can get on with our delivery?'

'Erm, yes, I, erm, *suppose* so,' said the doctor.

Crump and Vern picked up the cabinet and began a slow, lumbering walk towards the landward end of the pier. From her hiding place inside the Turk, Lucy smiled as she watched Veraciter scratching his head. He looked as though he'd just witnessed a magical illusion, and was furiously trying to work out how it had been done.

The Grobbley Manuscript

Lucy sprinted like her feet were on fire, diving in front of traffic, leaping over small, yapping dogs and barging her way through the crowds in a desperate search for somewhere to hide. Finally, she found her way to the relative safety of the maze of narrow streets that nestled behind the promenade – and that was where she bumped into a miserable looking Lavinia Lindstrom.

Toby's mother seemed slightly detached, sad almost. She was staring into the travel agent's window, her nose pressed against the glass like a hungry dog staring at a butcher's display. Lucy guessed she was thinking about all the ruined holidays they'd had – because whenever the Lindstroms arrived at their destination, the clouds immediately turned black and the rain came hammering down in buckets – some of them still with mops in. And it *stayed* like that until the day they left, when the sun would venture out to celebrate their departure. Lucy knew *exactly* what was going through the poor woman's head. She needed a holiday alright, but definitely not in Grimston.

'It was good of you to let me tag along, Mrs. Lindstrom,' she said nervously. For the moment at least, Lucy had shaken off her pursuers – and she had latched onto Lavinia, so that if Bruno caught up she would have someone dependable to stick up for her.

'What was that?' said Mrs. Lindstrom absentmindedly. 'Oh, *yes*, tag along, yes; well it's no trouble at all. I do enjoy meeting Toby's friends, even if it *is* just to be sure that they do actually exist.'

'Erm, *right*,' said Lucy, 'and where *is* Toby? Will he be coming along to erm…' The question trailed off as Lucy realised she didn't have a clue where they were heading. Not that she cared – as long as it wasn't Saint Mallydick's.

'*What?*' said Mrs. Lindstrom. 'Oh, erm, yes, I *expect* he'll be along later. He went with his father to look at the model yachts on the boating lake. And what have *you* been doing this morning Lucy – anything interesting?'

Lucy rolled her eyes and gave one of her enormous sighs. Even if she answered, she wasn't certain Toby's mother would hear – the poor woman seemed to be off in a world of her own.

'Not really,' Lucy replied eventually. She was thinking back to when Vern and Crump had stopped near the *You won't Bleevit* exhibition. 'No, I haven't been doing anything even remotely interesting.'

It wasn't *much* of a lie. Or if it was, then at least it wasn't a bad one. She just didn't want Toby's mum to look any sadder.

'Really?' said Mrs. Lindstrom. 'Now that's curious. I could have sworn I saw you down by the pier earlier. You were talking to a strange looking man who was standing on an orange box.'

'Erm, n-o,' she replied. 'I think I would have remembered that. It must have been that girl who looks a bit like me.'

'Ye-es,' said Mrs. Lindstrom, not sounding too convinced. 'I *see*.'

Lucy didn't know exactly *why* she wanted to lie about her morning's activity, but the thought of being anywhere near the pier suddenly made her feel very unhappy. It had all started when Crump and Vern stopped for a rest. They had put the Mechanical Turk cabinet down at the side entrance of the new 'Bleevit' display, and Lucy, still squashed up inside, had been overtaken by a feeling of great sadness. It was like something terrible had happened there and the evidence of it was still hanging in the air. And she knew exactly why that was – it was the last place that anyone recalled seeing Fenny Savage.

Just before they reached Grimston's one and only set of traffic lights, Mrs. Lindstrom steered them down a narrow alley that Lucy hadn't noticed before. The shops here had all seen better days – most of them had yellowed blinds pulled down inside dusty windows and a tatty 'closed' sign showing in the door – it was difficult to believe that they were ever going to open again.

'It's down here,' said Mrs. Lindstrom. 'At the end of the ginnel.'

'Are you sure we're not lost?' said Lucy. 'I don't think I recognise any of these alleyways.'

'Lost?' said Lavinia vaguely. 'No, I don't *think* so. This is very definitely where you need to be – where *we* need to be I mean.'

'*Oh,*' said Lucy, recalling that she was still on the run, 'erm, alright then.'

They emerged into a brick-paved courtyard, surrounded on all sides by buildings that were much taller and older than those she was accustomed to seeing. Most were closed for the duration, but there was a long stream of customers queuing outside one of them, most of whom were filling their time by reading from sheets of paper. From a distance, it looked like a list, but it was impossible to see any details unless she was extremely rude and peeped over someone's shoulder. When they joined the queue though her curiosity got the better of her and she sneaked a look. Unfortunately, she made the mistake of reading it aloud.

'*Bumblebee's salerooms,*' she said, '*a sale of unusual artefacts, certain to appeal to the more discerning collector.*'

'Hey, do you *mind?*' said the man in front. 'I had to *pay* for this catalogue.'

'Erm, yes, well *we* bought one too,' lied Lucy. 'But we forgot to bring it. The police had to cordon off our street this morning because of a gas leak. We had to evacuate the house in a hurry and didn't have time to pick it up from the hall stand. That's where we put it for safe keeping, between the painting of the Watery World and the model of the Mechanical Turk.'

'*Gas?*' he said. 'Evacuation? Oh, you poor things – how you must have suffered. Here, take mine, I've finished with it.'

'Thanks,' said Lucy, taking the sheaf of printed sheets. 'I expect we'll need something to read later – I think we're sleeping at the railway station with all the other refugees.'

'*Lucy?*' hissed Toby's mother. 'I think that's *quite* enough of that, don't you? I've heard about your stories.'

'Have you? Hmm, well in that case I must remember to have a word with Toby about secrecy.'

Mrs. Lindstrom placed her hands on Lucy's shoulders, and in a show of disapproval propelled her through into the lofty warehouse. It was filled to the ceiling with treasure, or at least it *would* have been, if it had been one of *Lucy's* inventions. Instead, it was packed with rolled-up carpets, Lectrical appliances, and the kind of stuffed animal heads that Lily would have killed for. Whatever piece of household junk someone might want, *this* was the place to come and find it. Lucy imagined the saleroom men being sent out with instructions to bring back ninety-seven old wardrobes, half a gross of lamp-stands and thirty-five assorted carpets, beds and occasional tables. And now here it all was, lined up in neat rows, each item tagged with a number that corresponded to an entry in her catalogue.

'Are they going to sell all this furniture today Mrs. Lindstrom?'

'No Lucy, I don't think so. There's a house clearance sale next week. It's art and curiosities today, so they'll be busy with the items at the other end of the room – the ones behind the auctioneer's podium.'

'I see,' said Lucy, not bothering to look. She was distracted by a small boy who was bouncing up and down on a leathery green sofa. Every time he landed, a cloud of dust puffed out of the cushion, like a bellows – and it sounded exactly like the wheeze that Pharty made when he ran. Suddenly she was worried again – what if he was just keeping out of sight until it was safe to grab her? She couldn't stay with Mrs. Lindstrom forever.

'Are you expecting someone?' said an unfamiliar voice.

'Pardon?' said Lucy, turning to face the stranger.

'You seemed agitated when you looked over at the door just then. As if you were expecting something unpleasant – or some*one*.'

The voice belonged to a tall, slightly built man. He was dressed in a huge black cape and wore a top hat that cast a shadow over his eyes, emphasising his waxy pallor. He was either very pale skinned or his face was covered in some sort of make-up, like a clown's. Lucy shuddered and glanced over at Toby's mum. She was busy reading the catalogue and hadn't noticed what was happening. But if she *had* noticed then she wouldn't have left Lucy alone with the man, *would* she? One glance of *him*, and Lavinia would be whisking her out of the nearest exit.

'Expecting someone?' said Lucy nervously. 'Me? Erm, yes, I mean no.' She desperately tried to think of a lie, but her mind froze under his gaze. He had a thin, cruel mouth and large bony ears and his nose was fat in the fleshy parts but came down to a sharp-chiselled point. Then she spotted the hands, and her eyes refused to budge from them. They were like birds' wings – light and delicate but stripped of feathers – and they had far too many bones too, the outlines of which could be glimpsed through his semi-translucent skin.

'I've just escaped from a mad psychiatrist,' she said finally. Byron had once told her that if you couldn't think of a good lie then the truth would often serve as a temporary solution.

'Escaped?' said the stranger.

'I know it sounds unlikely,' gabbled Lucy, 'but he wanted to take me to a hospital for liars and perform all sorts of experiments on me. I managed to escape though, by making him think he'd won money from Kolley Kibber. Then he had to fill in a form to claim the ten pounds and whilst he was doing that, I ran away and hid behind a cabinet full of heads. There was a man in a ticket booth too, but it's the other two I'm worried about – the driver with no neck and the doctor with walnuts for eyes – and that's why I keep checking the door.'

'Well that seems to have clarified the situation,' he said without a shadow of a smile. 'And the driver you're running from – I suppose he had an iron fist and gold teeth?'

'Actually no,' said Lucy, 'he was quite ordinary.' She glanced over at Lavinia for a moment, and as she did so, she imagined a feather growing out of the stranger's hat. When she turned back though it was gone – or might never have been there.

'Ordinary?' he said, studying her gaze. 'Then why were you running?'

'Because I don't want to be poked and prodded and jabbed in that rotten hospital,' said Lucy. 'That's why I hid inside the automatic chess machine.'

'I see,' said the stranger. 'What a wonderful imagination – but aren't you a bit young to be attending a sale like this? Are you *alone?*'

The way he asked that last question made Lucy's hair tingle. The pale man's manner had changed. Suddenly his voice had an edge that belonged to a far more fearsome creature – as if he kept a part of himself hidden, but occasionally it slipped out.

Lucy suddenly realised that her palms were sweating. She waved desperately at Lavinia, who was examining an item of tea-ware that was even more horrendous than Lily's vicar-pot. To her great relief Toby's mother noticed and waved back.

'I'm not on my own actually – I'm with my mother,' said Lucy, sighing with relief. 'That's her over there.'

'And is your *mother* interested in artefacts like these?' said the man. He was craning his thin neck, trying to see what Lavinia was showing an interest in. 'Has she come to bid for curiosities?'

It was time for another lie. Lucy didn't know *why* exactly, but it just was. He'd been pleasant enough to begin with, but a change had come over him and now he deserved it. Because if she *did* tell him the truth he was liable to take it away and do something awful with it – he was more than capable of twisting truth into lies, she was certain of that much.

'She's a curator,' said Lucy without a trace of guilt.

'I see,' said the stranger. 'A curator of what? And where?'

'The National Museum of Antiquity,' said Lucy, saying the first thing that came into her head. 'It's in Lundern – she's in charge of loads of old things – and not just skulls made from old bits of paper either.'

'Is that so?' said the man. He looked unimpressed and Lucy found herself wishing she'd put just a little bit more effort into the lie.

'I'm staying away from her though,' said Lucy.

'Oh?' he said.

'Yes, she thinks I don't know about her plan, but I discovered the truth by listening at keyholes.'

'Really?' said the man. His interest in Lucy seemed to be wandering but he was still watching everything else that happened in the room, as if he was expecting some unusual event.

'She's in on the plot,' said Lucy, mixing a bit of truth into the lie, 'her and that mad psychiatrist. They've got some strange ideas about what happens when I tell stories and they want to put me in Saint Mallydick's.'

'*What* did you just say?' hissed the man. '*Stories?*' Suddenly, all of his attention had come back to her – he was staring hard now, holding his eyes in a dark, steady squint that furrowed his brow.

'Erm, ye-es,' said Lucy timidly. She looked for Lavinia again, and for a fraction of a second, she imagined a great pair of *wings*, just visible out of the corner of her eye. They were like the thinnest kind of filmy gauze – so delicate they were almost invisible, fluttering in the air above and behind him, supported only by the heat of his breath. When she looked directly at him though the mirage vanished, like the constellation that Byron had shown her once. If you looked at the 'Sisters' straight on you could see just seven bright stars, but if you looked with the corner of your eye there were dozens of them, perhaps even hundreds.

'*Stories*,' hissed the man.

'Erm, ye-es,' said Lucy nervously. She waved flamboyantly at Mrs. Lindstrom again, hoping the pale man would turn and give her a chance to escape. He did, and when he eventually turned back, she was gone.

'*Pssst – hey, Toby*.'

'Eh? What?' said Toby.

'Don't say a word – it's *me* Lucy – I'm in the wardrobe.'

'Luce?' he smiled. 'What are you doing in there?'

'Shhh,' she hissed, 'just shut *up*, and don't turn around – pretend to be interested in the sale or something.'

Toby leaned back and rested his head on the door so he could hear. If anyone was watching though, they'd be certain to spot that something strange was going on. He was staring into space and grinning like an idiot. And when he heard what Lucy had to say, he grinned even more, like a split on an old suitcase.

'I'm running from a mad psychiatrist and a strangler with no neck,' she whispered, 'and there's someone *else* I'd rather not meet too. I think he might be an angel, only he doesn't have wings or anything – at least not all the time – and he's not glowing either.'

'Yeah, *right*,' laughed Toby. 'You'd better stay in there a bit longer in that case. I think the King of the Spiders is around here somewhere too. I tell you what; we'll wait until he eats the other two, and then when he starts to feel sick we'll make a run for it.'

'Toby, *don't*,' hissed Lucy. 'I'm *serious*.'

'Alright,' he said, 'I'll go for a look around, but first of all just let me confirm the details. We're looking for a mad doctor and someone with no neck and a man without wings who isn't glowing, and who may or may not be an angel. That shouldn't be *too* difficult – and what do you want me to do when I've found them all? Get their telephone numbers?'

'*Lindstrom*,' she hissed, 'when I get out of here, I'm going to do things to you that'll make your eyes water – unless…'

'Alright, alright,' he said, 'just tell me what they look like; but if you ask me, you've been dreaming about that bloke on your mum's poster. The one with the troupe of Lectric angels.'

Lucy described the three pursuers in detail, then settled down to wait, holding the door on the inside and listening to the muffled announcements of Mister Bumblebee, the auctioneer. When Toby still hadn't returned after ten minutes or so, she sat down on a box full of knitting magazines, trying to work out what else was in the wardrobe with her. It wasn't easy, but she guessed that one item was a machine for making tea. Then there was a tennis racquet, which was almost *too* easy, and something that felt like a giant corkscrew with extra twiddly bits. Before she could decide though, there was a knock on the door and a welcome crack of light illuminated her prison. She could see the item plainly now, but it was still a mystery, and after a moment's thought it was discarded. It ended up being thrown into a cardboard box along with the plans for ten of the world's most fiendish woolly cardigans.

'Luce? It's alright,' laughed Toby, 'you can come out now. We managed to get hold of some angel repellent and they've all flown off.'

'That's right,' grinned Toby's father, 'the saleroom is completely angel free, so why don't you come out and join us?'

Lucy blushed and peered out into the light. Toby and his parents were standing there with broad smiles – there were other nosey parkers too, all craning their necks for a look at the strange girl in the cupboard. Fortunately though, Bumblebee was announcing the next lot and they soon turned their attention back to that. It looked like the thing in the wardrobe, but slightly bigger and with less twiddly bits. There was a description of the item too, but Lucy couldn't make it out because Toby's dad was too busy making jokes at her expense.

'Were you looking for anything special in there?' said Mr. Lindstrom.

'No,' said Lucy, confused by the sudden brightness. 'I'm er, I'm here with my Uncle Byron – he's over there.' She waved in the general direction of the door, where there was absolutely no sign of her uncle – or anyone else for that matter. Mrs. Lindstrom frowned and shook her head slowly.

'I *see*,' said Mr. Lindstrom. He was watching his wife, who was still shaking her head. 'And is your uncle going to be bidding?'

'What do you mean?' asked Lucy.

'Is he trying to buy any particular item?' said Mr. Lindstrom.

Lucy looked at Toby for some inspiration. He was trying to stifle a huge laugh, but not doing very well. The noise sounded like a pig that had got itself stuck inside a Sukk-o-Maxx vacuum cleaner.

'Erm, ye-es,' said Lucy, suddenly feeling inspired. 'He *is* as it happens – he's going to be bidding for *that*.'

She pointed up at the raised platform where Bumblebee was sitting behind a high, old-fashioned desk. His assistant, a bespectacled old biddy, was seated at a smaller desk to his left, whilst to his right was an armoured glass case with brass fixtures and fittings. And standing next to *that* was a security guard with a key around his neck. '*Suspect everyone*' he'd been told – at least that was what Lucy imagined. He was eyeing the bidders as if they were all master criminals who were intent on just one thing – stealing the book.

'Ah,' said Mr. Lindstrom, 'the Grobbley Manuscript – yes, I *thought* it might be that. There's a great deal of interest in it you know. Although I'm surprised they aren't trying to sell it at one of the big auction houses in Lundern. Do you remember, Lavinia? We saw it during our first holiday to the capital – I remember it distinctly, because it rained the whole time.'

Mrs. Lindstrom nodded and then frowned at Toby as if it was his fault.

'That's it,' said Lucy. 'That's *exactly* what Byron is going to bid for.'

'Well, there are some very big dealers here,' said Toby's father, 'so your uncle will need an absolute shed load of cash to be in with a chance. He'll have to get his skates on too, because it's the next lot.'

'And *now* ladies and gentlemen,' said Bumblebee, 'and *children*,' he added, looking in Toby and Lucy's direction. 'We come to the highlight of today's sale – an unusual, if not unique work, considered by some to be of mediaeval origin. At various times, the Grobbley Manuscript has been owned by the Great Emperor Rudolph, Count Etienne the Unworthy of the province of Urr, and of course Detritus Phlegm-Bucket, the Great Wizard of the North. And there are *some* who claim it was once the property of Doctor John Dee, the renowned alchemist, scientist and angel speaker.'

'Never heard of them,' said Toby.

'Me neither,' said Lucy. 'But I like the sound of the alchemist.'

'I like the bucket of phlegm best,' grinned Toby.

'*Shush*,' said Toby's father. '*Look*, they're bringing out the Grobbley.'

The guard removed the key from around his neck and unlocked the cabinet with far too much ceremony, as if a film director was in the audience and he was auditioning for a part. He gently opened the book so that two of the pages were visible then presented them to the audience. Lucy squinted, but it was too far away to see any detail. It was *just* possible that there were some drawings of plants though.

'Gordon will now pass amongst you,' said Bumblebee, 'and as he does so, I shall tell you more about this fascinating article. The manuscript is approximately nine inches by seven, with calligraphy and drawings in both ink and pigment, presented on approximately two hundred and forty vellum pages. It is illustrated with many unidentified plant forms and pictures of nymphs in bathing tubs. Even *more* interesting though are the numerous charts and mysterious diagrams, which nobody has yet managed to decipher. The text is presented in an unknown alphabet, and all attempts to decode *that* have also failed. It might be a cipher or a code of some description – it *might* even be a lost language – perhaps we will never know.'

'That's *it*,' whispered Lucy, 'that's why the angel's here.'

'Yeah, *right*,' grinned Toby, 'I suppose they've read all the books in heaven so he's been sent down to pick up something new.'

'Don't be stupid,' hissed Lucy. 'You heard the auctioneer – he said that Doctor John Dee was an angel speaker, and *that's* why the man with wings has come to claim the manuscript.'

When the guard reached Toby's dad he stopped for a moment and held out the manuscript for his inspection. It was just a few feet from Lucy now and she could see it in perfect detail. And when she *did*, her mouth dropped open in complete surprise. She shot a look across at Toby, just to check she wasn't imagining things. He nodded, silently confirming her suspicions – some of the writing was like they'd seen in the photograph album, and in the middle of the left hand page was a diagram exactly like the one on the stage of the Empire.

'I've *got* it,' said Mr. Lindstrom, turning to his wife. 'I've just realised why the Grobbley is being auctioned here in Grimston.'

'*Have* you, dear? How nice.'

'No,' he said, 'listen to me – what if this is the *real* one?'

'But *of course* it's real dear – you just heard the auctioneer…'

'No,' said Mr. Lindstrom. 'The *real* Grobbley manuscript is a fabulous work of art. It's a unique treasure, and as far as I know it spends most of its life buried in a vault at the Lundern Museum of Antiquities.'

'You mean there really *is* a museum called that?' said Lucy. She stared longingly at Gordon as he went off to show the manuscript to someone else. It actually hurt to see the thing go, as if the book had somehow become attached to her heart by invisible threads.

'Museum of Antiquities?' said Mr. Lindstrom. 'But of *course* there is.'

'But I made it up,' said Lucy, still watching the manuscript.

'I'm sorry, Lucy,' said Toby's dad, looking at his wife for help. 'I don't quite understand – how can you make up a museum?'

'Don't worry about it,' said Lucy, her eyes following the book around the room, 'honestly, it's nothing, *really*. Why don't you tell us your idea about the Grobbley?'

'Ah, yes, the manuscript,' said Toby's dad. 'Well how about *this* for an idea? What if the one in the museum is a forgery and *this* is the real one? They wouldn't try to sell it at Christo and Botherbies or any of those big Lundern auction houses would they?'

'Wouldn't they?' said Toby.

'No,' said his father, 'it'd be too obvious – but if it *had* been stolen then the thieves might choose a quiet town like Grimston and let it be known that the item just *might* come up for auction. They'd only tell people they could trust though – *dishonest* people I mean.'

'And anyone else who heard would assume it was a forgery?' said Toby.

Mrs. Lindstrom gave a little laugh as she looked around at the bidders.

'Well if these are the ones we can trust Robin, I wouldn't like to meet the criminals. Look at those people over there for instance.'

Nobody looked though, because Lucy had made a loud squeaking noise.

'Oh *no*, it's *him*,' she said, diving back into the wardrobe.

'Him?' said Toby's dad.

'Who is it you've seen, dear?' said Mrs. Lindstrom, opening the door.

Lucy tried to pull it closed again but Toby's dad held it firm. He wasn't going to have any more nonsense and Lucy realised it was useless to resist.

'It's the angel,' she said, 'erm, *no*, I mean the man I saw earlier.'

'What man?' said Mrs. Lindstrom. 'And what's all this about an angel? Is this another one of your silly stories?'

'No,' said Lucy, 'I just *thought* he was an angel when I first saw him, that's all – a bad one.'

'Is there such a thing as a bad angel?' said Mrs. Lindstrom.

'I don't know,' said Lucy. 'It was just a silly idea.'

'That's right,' laughed Toby, '*very* silly.'

'So what about the symbols and the secret alphabet?' whispered Lucy. 'Or have you forgotten that already?'

'*Acksherly* you *can* have bad angels,' said the boy who'd been jumping on the sofa. 'They're called daemons.'

'Oh yes, that's right,' said Toby's mum. 'You *can* have bad angels – that's what all that business in heaven was about. The bad angels were all thrown out, weren't they?'

'Well I'm glad *that's* sorted out,' said Robin, staring intensely at his wife. 'It wouldn't do to have gangs of angels running about the place, now would it? Good *or* bad.'

'Yeah, that wouldn't do at all, *would* it?' sniggered Toby. 'We can't just let them go roaming around, especially if they don't glow and they haven't got wings.'

Lucy folded her arms and decided to say nothing. Her Uncle Byron reckoned that people sometimes appeared cleverer when they kept quiet, and this seemed like the perfect occasion to try out the idea. The dark angel was staring at her, and looked far less friendly now than he had earlier. For one awful moment, it seemed as though he was going to come over to Lucy and speak to her. Just as he began to move though, a bell sounded and he turned to the face the auctioneer – the sale was about to start.

'I'm looking for an opening bid on this *most* unusual item,' said Bumblebee. 'Will someone start me off at five hundred?'

'Hush Lucy,' said Mrs. Lindstrom. 'They've started.'

'But I didn't say anything,' said Lucy.

'Makes a change,' whispered Toby.

'*Shush*, Toby,' said his mother. 'Listen.'

'Five hundred,' said Lucy's angel, raising a numbered card.

'Thank you, sir,' said Bumblebee, somewhat nervously. 'I have an opening bid from the gentleman in erm, er, black – five hundred pounds.'

Lucy smiled at the auctioneer but he didn't notice. He was too busy looking for further bids – but he had already begun to sweat, and Lucy guessed that he felt the same as she did about the angel.

'One thousand pounds,' said a man in a pin-stripe suit.

'He'll be a dealer,' whispered Mr. Lindstrom.

'Two thousand,' said the angel.

'Three thousand,' said the suit.

'Three thousand I'm bid,' said Bumblebee. 'Do I hear four anywhere?'

'Four,' said the angel.

'Five,' said the suit.

'Six thousand pounds,' said Lucy's angel.

'*Thank* you, sir,' said Bumblebee, grinning all over his face. 'The bid stands at six thousand, from the gentleman in black.'

There was a long pause, filled only by the sound of anxious breathing – and it suddenly dawned on Lucy that the men in the suits had lost their nerve.

'He's going to win it,' she whispered.

'Yeah, the evil angel is going to buy the book,' sniggered Toby. 'He'll be needing something to read on the train back to heaven.'

'But we mustn't *let* him,' hissed Lucy.

'Shush,' said Mrs. Lindstrom, 'it's about to be sold.'

'Going once, to the man in black.'

'We can't let him have it,' whispered Lucy.

'Going twice.'

As Bumblebee raised his gavel something somewhere deep inside Lucy cracked – it felt like a jar of hot oil, breaking and spilling into the pit of her stomach. The angel was going to win the bidding and she just *knew* that he was the wrong person to have the manuscript, whoever *he* was, and whatever *it* was. And to make things even worse he was staring at her with an evil smile.

Lucy stood up on the creaky green sofa, and as she trampled her feet back and forth to keep balance, the dust shot out from the punctured corner of the cushion, as if breathing in time with her movements. Then the springs began to creak, warning of the insanity that was welling up inside her.

'Ten thousand!' she shouted, holding a hand in the air.

'*Lucy! Shush,*' said Mrs. Lindstrom. 'You can't possibly make a bid; you haven't even got a number – *or* money.'

'A number?' said Lucy, still fighting to keep her balance.

'You need a number to *bid,*' said Mr. Lindstrom. 'It means you've registered your credentials with the auction house. Otherwise anyone could just walk in from the street and start offering ridiculous amounts.'

'Is that child attempting to *bid?*' said Bumblebee. He didn't look happy, and neither did the angel. And now everyone in the room was turning to look in their direction.

'No, erm, I'm terribly sorry,' said Mr. Lindstrom. 'It's just that she was, erm, she was, erm, er...

'I was being pestered by a nasty looking wasp,' shouted Lucy.

'*Really?*' said Bumblebee, 'now *that's* one I haven't heard before.'

'No, honestly, it's true,' said Lucy. 'It was a great big one, and it was all yellow, and erm, black – that's it, yellow and black – and it was going *zuzz.* Look, there it is, up there in the roof.'

Every pair of eyes in the room turned skywards, as if they were at an aerobatics show – and sure enough, there was the wasp that Lucy had promised. It was bouncing in and out of the old glass lampshades, dislodging puffs of dust that fell like tiny sandstorms onto their upturned faces.

'So,' sneered Bumblebee, 'you were fighting off this vicious looking wasp, were you?'

'Erm, ye-es,' said Lucy. She was feeling a little more confident, even though everyone was still staring at her.

'I *see,*' he said, 'then perhaps you wouldn't mind telling us why you also shouted out *ten thousand?* Purely as a matter of interest you understand.'

'*Ah,*' she said, thinking hard. 'Erm, well, I was sneezing, and it just sort of *came out* like ten thousand.'

The idea raised a patch of muffled laughter in the audience, but the entertainment came to a sudden halt when the angel raised his voice. The words came with such authority that it was hard to resist.

'*If* we could return to the proceedings?' he said. 'We have *not* come here to listen to the ramblings of a stupid child, no matter *how* amusing she thinks she is.'

'Quite right,' said Bumblebee, 'shall we resume the bidding? Always assuming that we can keep Miss Fibalot quiet?' He stared at Mr. Lindstrom who turned bright red and nodded his agreement. And *then* he turned to scowl at Lucy, who was already being frowned at by *Mrs.* Lindstrom. Finally, to add insult to injury, Toby raised a single finger to show Lucy the score he had awarded for her story.

'I was under pressure,' she whispered.

'Will you two please *shush*?' said Mrs. Lindstrom.

'The bid stands at six thousand,' said Bumblebee. 'The *real* bid that is. Now, do I hear seven anywhere?'

'*Ten,*' said the suit, obviously wanting to end matters.

'*Twenty,*' said the angel confidently.

There was a sharp intake of breath. Nothing had *ever* sold for that much, at least not in Grimston. The Lundern suits looked at each other nervously, and finally, after a lot of whispering they appeared to reach an agreement.

'Thirty,' said their representative, waving his bidding card at the angel, as if to signal his victory.

'Thirty thousand from the Lundern Consortium. Do I hear forty?'

'Merchant Banker,' whispered Mr. Lindstrom. His wife looked at him sideways, with one of those disapproving glances she did so well.

'What was that?' said Lucy.

'He's a Merchant Banker,' said Mr. Lindstrom. 'The man who just bid thirty thousand pounds.'

'Oh,' said Lucy, 'yes, I've heard of them, they...'

'And how do you work *that* out, Robin?' said Mrs. Lindstrom.

'He reminds me of Watkins-Basset that's why. *You* remember him – he was the manager at Bling, Bling, Thompson, Crudlow and Knackerbee – we shared an office once. We were very close.'

'But I thought you said you didn't like him?' said Mrs. Lindstrom.

'I didn't Lavinia – it was a *very* small office.'

'Fifty,' said the angel with a grin. '*Fifty thousand pounds.*'

Lucy noticed the sweat on his brow – suddenly the room seemed a lot more crowded. The banker raised his card again – it bore the number seven.

'Sixty thousand,' he said, sounding a little nervous.

'*Sixty* I'm bid,' said Bumblebee. 'The bid is with the Lundern Consortium at *sixty thousand pounds.*'

The room fell silent as the man with the gavel looked first at the angel and then at the banker. Lucy's angel raised a hand, signalling that he wanted a moment to consider. He reached inside his coat to remove a scrap of paper – and as the coat fell open slightly, Lucy caught sight of a flash of colour, like a kingfisher darting from a low branch and disappearing into a sunlit stream. Then there was a splash, like the tinkle of laughter, and her imaginary bird was gone. Even though the saleroom was packed with warm bodies, Lucy shivered, as if someone was standing on her grave. For the fraction of a second the colour had been visible, she'd experienced a feeling of deepest joy – but now it was gone she felt as though a cold, rusty knife had been slipped into her stomach. And with a sudden horrifying clarity she realised she would give anything to see the bird and the stream again. *Anything.*

'*One hundred thousand pounds,*' said the angel. He shot a venomous look at the bankers' spokesman, as if daring them to continue. Lucy was hurting and still slightly confused by the disappearance of the bird, but she hadn't imagined the hatred in his look. The angel was threatening them – they were going to lose far more than just money if they continued to defy him – much, *much* more.

The man entrusted with the Consortium's card looked terrified. The rest of the group were whispering and prodding him in the back though – *they* were all prepared to go higher, but *he* was too scared to say the words.

'The bid is against you sir,' said Bumblebee, 'at one hundred thou...'

'Yes, I *know* it is,' said the angel's adversary. He scratched his head, then ran a trembling finger between his collar and a neck that was drenched with sweat. Finally, a savage poke in the back prompted him to speak.

'One hundred and fifty thousand,' he said, stepping forward.

'And *that*, I think you will find, is the final bid,' said one of the other bankers.

Bumblebee raised an eyebrow but said nothing. He'd seen some unusual things in his time but *this* was shaping up to be one of the strangest.

'You *think* so?' hissed the angel.

'It's not worth any more than that,' shouted the banker.

There was a general nodding of heads and a murmur from the crowd that suggested he might be right. But what did they know?

'Then why have you bid so much?' said the angel.

The banker remained silent. His friends were all smiling now, thinking of the champagne celebration that was certain to follow. The angel simply stared at each of them in turn, and then slowly turned his gaze on Lucy.

'It depends how you measure worth,' he said. 'I expect that in *your* world the value of an artefact is governed by the profit you can make by selling it again.' He turned towards Lucy. 'Is that not so?'

Lucy shrugged her shoulders. She could see the angel's point, but why was he asking her?

'You think we want to sell it again?' said the banker.

'Well *don't* you?' said the angel. 'Or do you value the manuscript purely for itself? Is it an investment or a treasure? Because if you are buying it to sell again then you might find that you have wasted your precious money. It is worth only what a buyer is prepared to pay, and tomorrow there might *be* no buyers.'

'We'll find one,' said the banker, 'you needn't worry about that.'

'*Will* you indeed?' hissed the angel. 'But just now you claimed that you weren't interested in reselling.'

There was another round of nodding which seemed to suggest that the crowd were swaying over to the angel's side.

'And of course there's the *other* issue,' grinned the angel. 'The one tiny remaining flaw in your plan.'

'Yeah?' said the banker. 'And what's that then?'

'You have not yet won the auction,' said the angel, raising his card. He must have made some kind of pre-arranged signal to the auctioneer, because the gavel-master appeared to understand exactly.

'Ladies and Gentlemen,' he announced, 'the bid now stands at *five hundred thousand pounds.*'

The banker gasped, unable to contain his surprise, and the crowd burst into a spontaneous round of applause – a sound which was rapidly replaced by the noise of eager chattering.

'*Five hundred?*' said the banker, 'but…'

Somewhere at the back of the room, a flashbulb went off. The angel shielded his face from instinct, apparently eager to prevent his photograph being taken.

'Ladies, gentlemen, *please*,' shouted Bumblebee, 'the auction is still in progress. Can we have *order* until the sale is finalised? The bid, I think, was…'

He stopped in mid sentence, trying not to think *too* hard about the commission he'd get from a half-million pound sale. There was some kind of disturbance at the back of the hall, and if he couldn't finish the sale, he wouldn't get the money.

'Please, *can* we have some order back there?' He stood up to get a better view and *that* was when his jaw dropped. He looked like a giant aquarium fish, but a *lot* more surprised.

'Hmm,' said Mr. Lindstrom as another flashbulb went off. 'Now that's the first time I've ever seen Mr. Bumblebee lost for words. I wonder if we can get a copy of that photograph.'

The auctioneer turned to his assistant, Miss Borrowgrove, who had been writing down the details of bidders and prices – and suddenly he found his voice again.

'*Mimsy*, what the gut-rumbling hell is going *on* here? Call security at once.'

'Erm, they, I mean *he* is looking after the book,' said Mimsy.

'Well give it *here* then,' he grunted. He snatched the Grobbley Manuscript from Gordon who then proceeded to wade through the crowd towards the disturbance.

'Suspect everyone,' he mumbled as he pushed his way through the crowd. 'And that includes *you* matey boy.'

The troublemaker in question had climbed on top of a wobbly-looking wardrobe. He was holding one end of a silk banner, whose delicate white fabric was embroidered with gold letters that spelled out the word 'elis'. The rest of the writing, if there was any, was probably still furled up inside the banner, because the agitator at the other end was still climbing into position. He'd stacked a coffee table on top of a large dining table and was trying to climb *that* to make his way onto another huge wardrobe. The whole lot wobbled precariously, but eventually he managed to scramble up.

'The *light* is not for sale,' he shouted as he reached the top. 'The *light* is not for…'

'Look out,' screamed Lucy, 'the wardrobe – it's collapsing.'

'*Ah*,' said the banner carrier, looking down at his temporary perch. There was a loud creak as the doomed furniture splintered and began to fall apart, pitching him headlong towards the crowd.

'Well he's not going to fall on *me*,' shouted a woman who'd bought an aspidistra.

'Me neither,' said a dozen or so people all at once. The two halves of the crowd moved smartly apart like a zip fastener, and the unfortunate banner carrier fell between them, issuing a loud 'uurgh' as he hit the floor. As soon as he was down the photographer pushed his way out of the crowd and took a picture of the back of his head. His companion, a lady reporter, whipped out her notebook and pencil, presumably in case the poor creature regained consciousness and managed to say something. Lucy recognised them both immediately – they worked for the Daily Phibber.

'*What* was it he said?' asked the reporter. She spoke to the crowd as if she was accustomed to this sort of thing.

'Apparently the *light* isn't for sale,' said a voice from the crowd.

'Yeah? And what light's that then?' said someone else.

'Dunno,' said another. 'I think he must have a screw loose.' He turned to the lifeless form that was stretched out across the floor. 'Which loony bin did you escape from mate? Was it Saint Mallydick's?'

'Leave him alone,' said a clear voice, ringing out from the top of a wardrobe.

'And who are you?' said the lady reporter.

'My identity is not important – but my message is.'

'I *see*,' said the reporter, 'and what exactly *is* your message?'

'The *light* is not for sale,' said the man. He heaved desperately at the banner, but the other end was stuck under the motionless body of his companion.

'Boring,' said someone at the back. 'Borrrringgg… That's exactly what *he* said.' The one who was bored pointed at the crumpled figure on the floor. He was still lying face down, and there was a trickle of blood leaking from the corner of his mouth.

'Is the value of a message diluted simply because of repetition?' said the wardrobe man. 'Or do the words not mean exactly the same the next time they are uttered, and once again, the time after that? Is not the word eternal and unchanging?'

Lucy winced. It was exactly the phrase that Veraciter had written down and then underlined in red – '*The Word*'.

'You shut your face mate,' said the cocky voice. 'Tell us something we *don't* already know.'

'The message is *just* as valid,' said the wardrobe man. 'No matter how many times it is repeated and no matter who hears it.'

'Yeah, well not here it isn't mate,' said the security man. 'Come on now, down you come.'

Before Gordon could get there, the loud mouthed one and a couple of others tried to pull the man down from the wardrobe. At least they had *thought* it was a man – now he was a bit closer though, they weren't altogether sure. There was a pale greyness to him and an unsettling look in his eyes – and there was even a suggestion that they might be able to see through his ashen skin.

'Erm, I think we'll leave the job to you Gordon,' said the loudmouth. 'I don't like the look of that one.'

'Yeah,' said one of his friends. '*Something's* not right.'

Lucy nudged Toby, and when she had his attention, she nodded towards her dark angel. He was glaring up at the remaining protestor.

'Keep an eye on him,' she said.

'*Hello up there?*' shouted the reporter. 'Yes, I'm talking to *you*, Mister Wardrobe – I'm Zenda Freggley of the Daily Phibber. Can I quote what you said about the *light?*'

There was no answer, so she scribbled a few notes down and then shouted across at her smudger, who was still taking pictures of the back of the other one's head.

'Tenby,' she screamed. 'Don't waste any more film on him; get over here and get some shots of *that* one up there.'

'*No!*' bellowed the wardrobe percher, covering his face. 'No images – and no more quotations.'

'It's a public place, isn't it?' shouted Tenby. 'So I can take photographs of whoever I want.'

'Actually it's *not* a public place,' said Mr. Bumblebee. 'So if you wouldn't mind leaving?'

'No mate,' said Tenby, 'I *wouldn't* like to leave as it happens – haven't you ever heard of the freedom of the press?'

'That's right,' said Zenda, 'we have a duty to serve our readers, and from where *I'm* standing this story is very much in the public interest – so you can't throw us out.'

'Well *I* can't,' said Bumblebee, 'but my security men can.'

'Yeah, if you can find him,' shouted the photographer.

'I, erm, oh, I *give up*,' said Bumblebee, thinking about his commission. 'Just take your rotten photographs and *leave* will you? We're *trying* to conduct some business here.'

He glanced down at the manuscript and stroked it, smiling at the thought of its sudden increase in value. Yesterday it had been a cheap junk-shop knock off, put up for sale by a local madman, and today it had become a valuable relic. Suddenly though he wasn't so sure – it was either a priceless gem or a complete piece of junk, so he was going to hold onto it until he had the truth.

'At *last*, we have some *sense*,' said Lucy's dark angel. 'We are attempting to conduct a sale here. So, if we could just get rid of *those* two?' He pointed at the two interlopers, the unconscious one who had been rolled onto his back and photographed from every angle, and the one who was still rather attached to his perch on the wardrobe. 'Yes, and perhaps we ought to get rid of *those* two as well?' he said, pointing out the Daily Phibber team.

'No mate,' said Tenby, 'we're staying put.' He raised his camera and threatened to photograph the angel if he didn't back off – and rather surprisingly, it had the desired effect.

As Tenby turned away, the wardrobe percher saw his chance and peeped out between his fingers, bellowing down at Lucy's angel.

'You think you have *won* Raziel? Well remember this, and remember it well. The *light* cannot be taken by force – it must be lost, or given freely.'

Lucy's angel frowned, his face blackening as he listened to the idiot balanced on the furniture.

'I *know* that only too well,' he spat. 'Do you not think I *know*?'

'Then *remember* it,' shouted the percher as he launched himself into the air. It looked as though he was intending to reach the auctioneer, and if *that* didn't work, he was going to try to reach someone else – anyone really, just as long as they were going to provide a soft landing. For the first few feet of his flight the percher's expression was supreme. The next couple of feet saw a slight change in confidence though, coupled with a considerable loss of height. And during the last twelve inches of the flight, his expression turned to one of utter disbelief – he was going to eat dirt, or more precisely, he was going to eat one moth-eaten corner of a very shabby carpet.

Bumblebee stepped back a couple of paces, just in case the intruder fell on him. At the same instant, he put the Grobbley in his jacket pocket – it must have been an old jacket though, because the book dropped straight through the lining and onto the floor. It came to rest at Lucy's feet, almost as if it *wanted* to be stolen.

'Here,' said Lucy, as the creature splatted into the floor. 'You dropped this.'

Without looking or even saying 'thank you' Bumblebee took the book and put it in his other pocket.

Lucy smiled and closed up her rucksack. Then she began to look for her angel, suddenly worried that he might have been watching. He was nowhere to be seen though, and *that*, she decided was a good reason to be leaving. She waited until Toby and his parents were distracted, and then melted into the crowd, turning for one last look at the grounded wardrobe creatures. Zenda Freggley was prodding one of them with her pencil, and the other wasn't faring much better – Tenby Yates was hovering over the body like a vulture, taking pictures from every conceivable angle.

Lucy gave another little smile, and slipped quietly away.

The Angel Loft

Lucy had never visited the shantytown before, because that particular area of Grimston nearest the railway sidings had a reputation that was even worse than the dark arches. The patch of scrubland behind the railway cottages wasn't *really* a town though, and nobody actually *lived* in the sheds, so they didn't really count as shanties. Nevertheless, it was a good way to describe the various shacks and lean-tos that had grown up from old planks and doors and bits of rusting metal. Some of them, particularly those made from discarded window frames, looked almost palatial, but it was difficult to see how any of them stood up – they appeared to be held together by string and nails, and the odd prayer. Lucy counted at least a hundred of them inside the barbed wire perimeter, but fortunately, there was only one with an 'Old Father Time' weathervane – and if her sources were correct then *that* was the one she needed.

As Lucy reached the path leading down to the loft, she hesitated for a moment, suddenly unsure if she was brave enough to go ahead with her mad scheme. And *that* gave her time to wonder how many people were out searching Grimston for her, now that she was an asylum runaway *and* a criminal. It was hours since the incident in the saleroom, so her little deception was certain to have been discovered by now, which meant Mr. Bumblebee and Gordon the security man and probably even the police had joined the manhunt – or girl-hunt. She had left the auction rooms with a huge grin on her face, trying to imagine the look on Bumblebee's face as he pulled a copy of *The Geography of the Sahara* from his pocket. A fraction of a second later though she was wearing an expression of horror. She had been in such a rush to keep the manuscript out of the angel's hands that she'd made an *incredibly* stupid mistake. Inside the geography text book, written neatly in pencil, was her name and address.

The Angel Loft

At one time, the dilapidated shed had been painted sky blue, but the decorations were flaking off now and turning green with mould. The only part of the place that retained its original colour was the white criss-cross lattice on the roof, preserved that way by the constant passage of wings. She paused for a moment to listen to the sounds of the place – then quietly made her way to the porch, stooping half-bent in the frame of a tiny doorway. Inside the shed, dozens of birds were flapping to and fro, manipulating shafts of sunlight with their wings as they put on a show of light and shadow for her. The darkened interior was filthy, and no matter how hard she tried, Lucy found it impossible to believe that a manuscript worth half-a-million pounds really belonged in such a place.

For a moment, she stood in silence, wondering if anyone was about – and suddenly she felt compelled to take the manuscript out and examine it again, as if it might be the last chance she'd have. She slipped her rucksack off and eagerly pulled the Grobbley from its hiding place, her expression turning to a broad grin as she touched the timeworn cover. The thing seemed to glow in her hands – not with light, but with a presence that spoke to her in a silent voice – and in a language she didn't understand. It felt right for her to have it though, just as it would have been wrong for it to fall into the hands of the angel. But stealing it had been wrong too, even when it had been done for the right reasons – and *that* meant it had to be returned. She only hoped the owner would understand, because it would have fetched a good price if she hadn't interfered. And *that* was going to make things all the more difficult.

'Are you looking for me?' said a soft voice. It belonged to a dumpy figure who was standing in the dark interior of the loft. He shielded his eyes from the light and stepped forward to shake Lucy's hand, his podgy fingers like a row of beef and tomato sausages.

'Erm, I might be,' said Lucy, stuffing the Grobbley away and quickly slinging the bag onto her back.

'*Might* be?' he said. 'Well *that'll* be a good start, won't it?'

'Actually no,' said Lucy. 'I was erm, just out for a walk, and I saw some pigeons landing on your loft thing. I'm interested in birds you see.'

'*Are* you now?' he said. 'Well *that* I can believe – there's a lot to be said for winged creatures. But strolling through the shanties for fun? I don't *think* so, do you? I reckon you came to see someone specific like.'

'Alright,' admitted Lucy. 'It wasn't a very convincing lie, was it?'

'No,' he said with a smile. 'How did you find me?'

'Erm, I made an invention.' She still wasn't sure of her plan, but the bit about the invention was a good start.

'An *invention*? You mean like a special machine?'

He was probably the oldest person Lucy had ever met, with a lovely fat nose that looked like a handle for something – his face probably, which was like a knobbly potato, sprouting tufts of untidy white hair. It was a kindly face though, and Lucy suddenly felt a lot better about handing the manuscript back – *if* the old man was the rightful owner.

'No, it's not a machine,' she said, 'an invention is a story – or at least that's what I like to call them.'

'Ah,' he said. 'Well that's very important, isn't it, getting the right name for things? They works better if you calls 'em right. So, what was this story you'm on about then?'

'Erm, I telephoned the newspaper with my adult voice,' said Lucy. 'It's a sort of party trick I can do – that and whistling with three cream crackers in my mouth. My mother could do it as well, but I think she used digestives.'

'Your mother sounds like a noteworthy person,' he said with a smile. 'But that still don't explain how you come by my address – and what about this trick you can do?'

Lucy started to breathe in and out so rapidly that the old boy thought she was having an attack of the vapours. She lifted a hand though, to show she was alright, then coughed and coughed until she made herself hoarse. Then she picked up an old piece of wood and held it against her ear like a telephone handset.

'*Hello?*' she said in a much deeper voice. '*Is that Grimston Seventy Seven? And is that the news desk?*'

'*Yes, and yes again,*' said another voice. She was pinching her nose to make it sound like someone on the other end of a telephone.

'*I'm calling on behalf of your reporter, Zenda Freggley,*' said the deep voice.

'*Good, it's about time,*' said the squeaky nose voice, '*where the hell is she? I need that story now.*'

'*She said to tell you to be patient.*'

'*Oh did she?*' said the telephone voice.

'*She told me to say that she's onto something big, and needs some urgent information. There's been a disturbance at the auction rooms and she needs an address.*'

'*And how do I know this isn't a trick?*' squeaked the nose editor.

'*You'll just have to trust me,*' said Lucy's deep voice. '*Zenda said something about winning a prize though – a poo-litzer or something.*'

'I think I can guess the rest,' said the old man. 'That bloomin' editor was so excited about getting a scoop that 'e gave out my private name and whereabouts to a total stranger. What *I'd* like to know is how he got 'em in the first place though. I'm Harry by the way.'

'The newspapers know all sorts,' said Lucy. 'More than they have a right to my step-step dad says – that's why I thought of asking them.'

Lucy wrinkled her nose as she caught a whiff of the most horrendous stink. It had been there all along, but she'd been too excited to notice.

'It proves they exist,' said Harry.

'Pardon me?'

'The rotten stink – it proves the birds exist – because if there wasn't any smell then we'd like as not think they was perfect, wouldn't we? As if they was flying spirits or something. Birds *know* spirit, see? They know about air under their wings and the freedom of the skies. They have the light of *angels* in 'em, see? And you *learn* a thing or two about angels when you work with birds – it's only natural.'

'Is it?' said Lucy. She felt suddenly light headed at the mention of angels, so she took a deep breath, trying not to let it show.

'Course it is,' said Harry. 'Flying's the most natural thing in the world. So if there's ever anything you want to know about winged creatures, just you come back and see me, alright? I'm not promising I'll *tell* you mind – not unless you bring a bag of corn.'

'Thanks,' said Lucy, not quite sure what to say.

'That's good then,' said Harry. 'We got *something* sorted. *Now,* before we goes on any further, do you want to see a secret thing?'

'Erm, maybe,' said Lucy uncertainly. 'What is it?'

'You ain't getting no clues,' said Harry. 'You got to *trust* me – do you want to *see* something or not?'

'Alright then,' she smiled.

'Right,' said Harry, 'then come and take a gander at this.'

He reached into a rickety wooden framework that had been built from a load of old nailed-together cupboards. Suddenly though, he stopped, frozen in mid-movement, with his arm still buried inside.

'What was that?' he hissed. 'Did you hear something just then?'

'Erm, *no*,' said Lucy, tilting her head to listen for a noise.

'Well *I* did,' said Harry. 'I'll bet it's them rotten kids again. Sneakin' round all the time and callin' out names. They sometimes bangs on the sides of the loft, and it frightens the birds somethin' terrible – do you *know* them?'

Lucy said she didn't, but had a good idea who it might be. And now that she was concentrating, she *could* hear voices.

The sun had gone in too – and it felt like an omen.

Harry looked slightly comical, standing with his ears perked up and his hand stuck inside the cabinet, but he wasn't laughing. In fact, he was furious, and just for a moment Lucy felt scared of him. She put her ear against the door, not daring to go too near the window in case she was seen. She *thought* she heard the word 'spirit', but wasn't certain. Perhaps they were going to get methylated spirits and burn the loft.

'I reckon they've gone,' said Harry.

'I'm not certain they have,' said Lucy, listening for a disturbance.

'They've gone,' insisted Harry. 'I know when there's danger and when there's not – now, come and take a look at this.' He withdrew what looked like a large, rectangular biscuit tin from the cabinet. There was a dim-looking light bulb attached to the lid, but no sign of a hole for it to shine through.

'The bulb's for warmth,' said Harry. He opened the lid with a great deal of care, and there, nestling amongst a confusion of shredded tissue paper, was a tiny, pink chick.

'Oh, it's beautiful,' said Lucy.

'No it *ain't*,' snapped Harry. 'It's certainly a few things, but beautiful ain't one of 'em. In fact, it's *ugly*, that's what it is – even 'is own ma wouldn't call him beautiful. They're *all* ugly when they're that young and no mistake. Until they gets their feathers mind — and *then* they becomes beautiful. And some of 'em, well *they* becomes exquisite.'

'Can I touch it?' said Lucy.

'Best not,' said Harry, 'he's a bit fragile — or *she* is. I can't sex it for a while yet, so he could be anything. Just *think* of it, a few days ago, he was nowhere to be found, not *in* the sky or *under* the sky — and now look at him. He's got no idea where he is, but his wings are still impatient. He wants to be out flying, even though he doesn't know about the air yet. Can you *imagine* that? Being so eager to explore a place you know nothing about?'

Lucy shook her head, but then remembered the door in the dark room she'd been visiting. She *certainly* wanted to explore beyond that, but Harry didn't know anything about *that*, did he? Nobody knew about it — only her.

'If I was him,' said Lucy, 'then yes, I *would* go.' She felt a bit of a fraud saying that, because every time she went to the darkened room she failed, and came back even more afraid.

'Even if it was dangerous?' said Harry.

'It's bound to be dangerous,' said Lucy, feeling even more of a hoaxer.

'Oh, it *will* be,' said Harry, 'definitely — there'll be certain mortal peril.'

'Well I might get taken by a sparrow-hawk on the day I learned to fly,' said Lucy, 'but at least I'd have felt the sky beneath my wings.'

'Right, well that's excellent to hear,' said Harry, 'because…' He jumped suddenly and replaced the lid, pushing the light-tin back into the frail looking cabinet. As he stored it away, Lucy saw the Lectric cable that fed the lamp. She hadn't noticed it before, but it was so obvious now — it was like the chick's umbilical cord.

'*Shhh*,' whispered Harry, 'they're *out* there again — can you hear 'em?'

'No,' whispered Lucy.

'Maybe not,' said Harry. 'I hear 'em so often I starts to imagine it — but when they *do* come the birds get upset, and they don't fly right.'

'Fly right?' said Lucy.

'They don't come back,' said Harry, 'because them's afraid. Or them'll come back all confused, like Oscar here. He was away for three weeks once, but I knew he'd come back, 'cause I had faith see? That's what you need in times like these — *faith*.'

'Erm, what do you mean?' said Lucy. 'Times like what?'

'Disturbing times,' said Harry, 'the kind of times when birds don't sleep – they just flap and worry all night long. They always know when things aren't right with the world – and that's when they get sick, see? They *know*, them birds do, because them's connected to creation like no other being – you'd do well to remember that.'

Oscar certainly *did* look unhappy. Lucy couldn't say what the difference between a happy bird and this one was exactly, but he blinked at her ever so slowly, then stared at her before beginning the next blink. It was like he'd *seen* something, and was trying to tell her about it in the only way he knew.

'And that's the worst part of it right enough,' said Harry, 'because when they gets sick then they's got to go.'

'*Go?*' said Lucy. 'What do you mean?'

'Go,' said Harry. '*You* know.'

'No,' said Lucy. 'I don't – *where* do they go?'

'Wherever creatures go when they die,' said Harry.

'You mean you *kill* them?' said Lucy.

'We don't like to use the 'K' word round here,' said Harry, 'or the 'D' word neither, come to think of it – anyways, it's only natural.'

'No it isn't,' said Lucy, 'dying of natural causes, *that's* natural.'

'They don't *feel* it you know,' said Harry. 'It's *me* that feels it. It's all over in the blink of a beady black eye for them, but for me it lasts a *lot* longer. I'm the one that's got to watch 'em kick and twitch.'

A tear appeared in the corner of Harry's eye, and although Lucy didn't agree with the idea of killing the weak and the sick, she could see that *he* believed it, and even thought it proper.

'But *why?*' said Lucy. 'You say it's got to be done, but *why* has it?'

'Reasons of performance,' said Harry, 'and reasons of perfection.'

'I don't understand,' said Lucy.

'Whether you understand it or not, that's the way things are. It's like Mother Nature – *she* chooses the best and the fittest to survive, and sends the weak to their deaths.'

'And did the birds agree to this great plan?' said Lucy.

'No more than any of *us* agrees,' said Harry. 'Anyways, just *look* at the way this loft sings – every bird is a perfect one, and some of 'em are exquisites, and it wouldn't be like that if they was all croaking and vomiting and hobbling around on gammy legs, *would* it? Or if they was all riled up with disease, or trying to see out of a half-blind eye?'

'Erm, no,' said Lucy. 'I didn't think of that.'

'Well then,' said Harry. 'You should allus think beforehand, see? No use thinkin' after, is it? This loft is right because of the cull, and there's only the birds who get taken out who would disagree with that. Have a look at this one and see what I mean.'

He reached into a roosting box and drew out a brilliant white bird – then he turned the creature over onto its back and gently spread one wing until the tips of the feathers seemed to reach out for distant air.

'This one's a dark,' he said.

'But it's beautiful,' said Lucy, 'and so bright – why do you call it a dark?'

'You're just lookin' at the colour of him,' said Harry. 'It's what you find in his soul that counts, and it's a place he'll seldom let you look, because he's as black as coals. He's called Lucifer, this one, from the Lattinn – his name means *Light Bringer*.' As Harry turned the bird back the right way Lucy caught sight of a single steady eye that seemed to be watching her soul.

'So why do you keep bad birds then?' she asked.

'I don't do nothin' of the sort.'

'You *do* – you said he was bad, just now.'

'I never said anything of the kind,' protested Harry.

'Yes you did,' said Lucy, 'you said he was a dark.'

'That's right enough,' said Harry, 'but I never said nothing about him being bad, did I? *You're* the one who thinks that light is good and dark is bad.'

'Oh,' said Lucy, 'and *isn't* it?'

'Well that depends – there's a bit of dark in the brightest white – and some brightness in the deepest black. They *need* each other see? Dark needs light and bad needs good – otherwise how would they measure themselves, if there was nothing to compare against? That's why you need dark birds amongst the brights. Nature needs balance – always has and always will.'

Lucy shuffled uncomfortably, increasingly aware that she was being drawn deep inside a story that she knew nothing about. And now there was all this talk of dark and light, good and bad – it was beginning to worry her.

'Will you put him back in the box please?' said Lucy. 'I think I want to go now.'

'Alright then,' said Harry. 'But you mustn't go without seeing Lilith – she's Lucifer's mate – what we call a singular.'

'A singular?' said Lucy nervously.

'Yup,' said Harry. 'And when a bird's *that* special then we give 'em plenty of names. Now Lilith, well *that's* a bird that's got seventeen. Do you want to see her? It'll only take a minute.'

'*No*,' said Lucy, rather forcefully, 'I don't care *how* many names she's got and I don't want to see her either – I just want to go.'

'Alright,' said Harry, 'keep yer hair on – Lilith can wait. We'll just get on and conduct our business and then you can go.'

'Erm, what business is that?' said Lucy.

'Getting forgetful are we?' said Harry. 'You know perfect what I mean, otherwise why did you come to see me?'

Lucy blushed and wanted to turn away, but something in Harry's stare held her gaze. In all the rush of explaining about telephones and looking at birds, she'd forgotten the reason for her visit. She had come to return the Grobbley, but now she wasn't so sure – there was something about Harry that reminded her of the angel.

'I've changed my mind,' she said.

'No you haven't,' said Harry.

'I *have*,' said Lucy, 'and I'm going.'

'Tell me what you've got in the bag,' insisted Harry.

'Bag?' said Lucy innocently.

'The one on your back,' said Harry. 'Every time I move, you turn away slightly so I can't see it.'

Lucy thought of making an excuse, but knew it would sound feeble.

'Sorry,' she said.

'So what's in it?' asked Harry, ignoring the apology.

'School things,' said Lucy.

'In the holidays?' laughed Harry. 'You *must* be keen.'

'And a puppet,' said Lucy, realising he wasn't going to be fobbed off.

'A *puppet*, you say?' said Harry. 'And would that be the kind with strings, or one that fits on your hand?'

'Neither,' said Lucy. 'Well, no actually, I suppose it *is* the kind that fits on your hand, but he takes up some of your arm as well.'

'Ah! A *vent* dummy is it? Like the one the vicar uses.'

'It *is* the vicar's,' said Lucy. 'I was supposed to return it, but things kept happening.'

'Happening?' said Harry.

'All sorts of things,' said Lucy. 'I don't suppose you'd understand.'

'Try me,' said Harry. 'You might get a surprise.'

'You wouldn't be interested,' said Lucy, 'they're just silly stories – at least that's what people keep telling me. One moment they say I'm stupid and childish and making things up, and the next thing they want to cart me off to the madhouse and do all sorts of experiments on me that I don't even want to imagine.'

'Ah, well *that's* what it's all about,' said Harry. 'If you ain't got the power to imagine, then you ain't got the gift to live.'

Lucy frowned. Just for a moment, the old man hadn't seemed quite so old or quite so grey, as though a light had switched on inside him. But now it was gone again, like someone had rushed to the window and swiftly pulled his curtains together – as if there was a room inside him that nobody was supposed to see.

'These *stories* you're accused of,' said Harry. 'What are they about then?'

Lucy told him the whole story, beginning with the car turning the wrong way and ending at the moment she entered the saleroom. Nothing was missed out, even when they paused occasionally to listen to noises from outside the loft. When the tale was finished, Harry just looked at her and smiled, wiping away the tears as soon as they began to appear. The girl had to see strength, *didn't* she? Because *that* was what she needed for herself.

'It's a story within a story,' said Harry. 'And another one inside that.'

Lucy nodded.

'And how deep do you think those stories go? How far down can you burrow, looking for one tale inside another?'

'I don't know,' said Lucy, 'but the time is coming when I might find out – and I think the manuscript is a part of that.'

'Ah, so you *do* have it,' said Harry. 'And how much do you know?'

'Nothing,' said Lucy. 'I was hoping *you* could tell me about it.'

'No, girl – I'm afraid I can't be doing that.'

Lucy had known what his answer would be before he ever floated the words on the air. Whatever the nature of the approaching voyage she was going to have to navigate her own way.

'So I'll never know why it's important?' she said.

'That's up to you,' said Harry, 'the manuscript is yours to *keep* – but mind you don't go losing it though.'

'You don't really mean that, do you?' said Lucy, her eyes widening.

'Of course I do,' said Harry, 'take it and keep it safe – and study it.'

'But it's so valuable,' said Lucy.

'Oh?' said Harry, 'and how do you know that?'

'There were people at the auction who were willing to pay thousands of pounds for it,' said Lucy. 'Just think what you could do with all that money.'

'*Money?*' hissed Harry. 'Does money make my birds any more beautiful? Or make me love my wife any more than I do already?'

Lucy looked surprised.

'Love don't stop when you gets older,' laughed Harry. 'It increases if anything – and that's why I don't need money.'

'Then why were you selling the manuscript?' said Lucy.

'Ah,' said Harry, 'so you think it was up for sale, do you?'

'But it was in the auction,' said Lucy, 'and people were bidding for it – and if there hadn't been an interruption then it would have been sold. I'm no expert, but I *think* that's how it works.'

'But the auction *was* interrupted, wasn't it?' said Harry.

'I suppose,' admitted Lucy, not even stopping to wonder how he knew.

'No supposin' about it,' laughed Harry. 'There was never any danger of the *light* going astray.'

'So you were using the auction as a sort of advertisement?' said Lucy.

'*Might* have been,' said Harry.

'*Hmm*,' said Lucy. 'My step-step dad might be interested in that technique – he was the one behind the chocolate kipper advertising campaign.'

'Oh?' said Harry, raising an eyebrow. 'It don't sound much like a combination that many would enjoy.'

'They didn't,' said Lucy, 'the campaign went down like a cast iron bedstead, but people enjoyed the adverts. My favourite was the one they put on that big hoarding near the railway station. They had a big Lectric speaker behind it, and whenever anyone walked past it played a jingle.'

'I heard about that,' smiled Harry. 'The people living opposite set fire to it one night.'

'It was never proved,' said Lucy, 'anyway, everyone else liked it. And Percy said the most important thing was that it got people's attention – a bit like your sale.'

'Like you say,' said Harry, 'it got people's attention – yours for instance.'

'So you knew I'd be there?' said Lucy.

'It was written,' said Harry.

'Written?' said Lucy. 'Where? And by whom?'

It was the old man's turn to frown now – he began shaking his head as if he'd already said too much.

'It was written,' he said, 'that's all.'

And that *was* all – Lucy knew that the final word had been spoken.

'But what if something had gone wrong?' she said.

'There's always a chance,' said Harry, 'but sometimes you have to take risks. Life isn't life without risks – you just have to be careful, like that pigeon chick poking its head out for the very first time.'

'That's why I stole the manuscript,' said Lucy. 'It was a risk, but it was better than letting the man with wings get his hands on it.'

'You *spoke* to him?' said Harry quietly.

'Erm, *ye-es*,' replied Lucy. 'He seemed quite nice at first. He said that some things were beyond value too, so you two might even get along if you met.'

Harry winced. It was like that far off school day when they'd wired batteries up to frogs' legs to make them twitch. Because now, someone, somewhere, was applying those same copper wires to his face.

'Listen to me,' said Harry. 'This man might *seem* friendly, but you should be very careful if you ever find yourself near him again. Better than that, you should be *afraid*, because fear is a good defence. Now tell me, did he *show* you anything?'

'No,' said Lucy, 'erm, well, not *deliberately* – I saw inside his coat, just by accident, when he was reaching into his pocket.'

'His *coat?*' hissed Harry. 'Yes, *that* would be it – and what did you see?'

'A sort of bird,' said Lucy, 'flying in a bright sky – a kingfisher maybe, or possibly a peacock – but they don't fly, do they?'

'You've heard them *crying* though, haven't you?' said Harry. 'You know that loud wail they do? Creatures cry like that because they forgot *how*, that's why. They all knew how to fly at one time – they was *made* for it, only some of 'em got lost along the way. They got too tied up with themselves and thoughts of what they could do, and that's when they forgot. Some of 'em forgot complete, and some of 'em forgot partial – but they could all fly once, and some day you'll know the truth of it. Now, tell me straight – when you looked inside the raiment, was that *all* you saw? Just the bird?'

'Yes,' she said.

'And you felt nothing peculiar?'

'Like what?' said Lucy. 'And what's the raiment?'

'Just tell me what you felt,' said Harry. 'Was there ever a great feeling of sadness that came over you?'

'Afterwards,' said Lucy. 'But when I was looking I felt happier than I'd ever been.'

'Tcchh.' Harry spat into the corner of the loft, adding moisture to a pile of swept-up droppings. 'That's one kind of happiness you can do without – now tell me girl, how do feel right this minute?'

'I'm alright,' said Lucy. 'A bit weepy, but it might be the smell of poo that's doing that.'

'Might be,' said Harry, 'and if it is, then you're lucky – we both are.'

'How?' said Lucy.

'Never mind how,' said Harry. 'Just trust me – you ain't known me long, but you can trust me. You know *that* much don't you?'

Harry was right. She *did* trust him. In fact, she felt as though she could put her life in his care and he'd never let her down. He'd called the manuscript the *light* too, so he knew at least *some* things that she didn't.

'I trust you,' she said simply.

'Good,' he said. 'Now listen – this man's name is Raziel. It's not his real name, because he stole it, like he steals everything else. But it's the monicker he goes by so it's what I'll call him. Only *you* don't need to call him anything.'

'Don't I?' said Lucy. 'Why not?'

'Because you ain't goin' anywhere near him, that's why. And if you do happen to get close then don't you *ever* speak to him – or even listen. And don't for pity's sake *ever* look inside that coat of his – *promise* me.'

'Alright – I promise.'

'Good girl,' said Harry, cocking an ear towards the world outside.

'They're back, *aren't* they?' said Lucy.

'Yes,' said Harry, 'I think they might be.'

The whispering voices that had suggested themselves all along had grown to a murmur now, as if a great crowd had begun to assemble outside the loft. The birds hadn't been certain earlier, but now they had decided – the foe was at hand. Before Harry had a chance to close them up, they burst from their roosting boxes, their wings carving the air in a panic, raising a veil of dust and feathers that swallowed the light and seemed intent on choking them both to death.

'Here,' said Harry. He handed Lucy a handkerchief flecked with crusty green flakes. At any other time, she might have refused it, but the wing-panic was increasing and she needed to breathe. She forced the cotton square against her mouth to keep the dust out, squinting so that only the smallest part of her eyes was exposed to the airborne debris. In the confusion, she could hardly tell what was air and what was wing. But she was certain of one thing – there was a noise outside like a thousand deep voices, all of them humming a single note.

'No time to explain,' said Harry. 'But don't let it touch you.'

'Don't let what…'

The sound increased ten-fold, and a brilliant yellow-green light suddenly burst upon them, forcing its way through the ill-fitting slats of the loft walls. It was accompanied by a strange rustling sound, like a thousand ivy-clad fingers scratching at a window pane.

'You know what to do, *don't* you?' said Harry.

'We have to fight, don't we?'

Even through the dust, she saw the look of horror on Harry's face.

'*Fight?*' he shouted. 'You want to fight *that?*'

'We could *try,*' said Lucy.

'And what would you try *with?*' shouted Harry. 'Have you any great power within you? Do you have some talent that goes beyond whistling with a mouth full of custard creams?'

'It was cream crackers,' said Lucy, realising she'd wasted a vital fraction of a second correcting him – but *he* was wasting time too, wasn't he?

'Listen closely chick – there's an unknown force outside the door and a known weakness inside – so I ask you again – do you know what to do?'

'Erm, run?' suggested Lucy.

'*Good,*' said Harry. 'Now take your bag and your puppet and your manuscript and *go,* and may the Grand Architect protect you. And remember – peacocks *can* fly, as long as their wings aren't clipped – *that's* what they're crying about.'

He pulled a trapdoor up and Lucy jumped through it without hesitation. She dropped about four feet into a mound of soft black earth that swallowed her shoes and crept up over her socks. It didn't take long to realise that she was shin-deep in pigeon waste.

'I'm afraid it's worse than you think,' smiled Harry. 'You need to crawl on your hands and knees to get out.'

She smiled weakly, and was about to bid him goodbye when she realised that she hadn't even introduced herself.

'My name's Lucy Blake,' she said, offering to shake the old man's hand.

'I *know* who you are,' he hissed, 'now get off and hide yourself, before Raziel realises what's going on – and *stay* hidden mind, until you *understand.*'

The Fifth Gate

Lucy stood behind the door of Byron's laboratory, trying not to breathe too loudly. She was balanced on a chair and holding a large, bent piece of metal – preparing to clobber whoever was coming up the stairs.

'Erm, Luce, I can *smell* you,' said a voice on the other side of the door.

'*Eh?*' she said, 'Toby, is that you?'

'Yeah, were you expecting someone else?'

'Yes, erm, actually *no,*' she lied. 'How did you know I was here?'

'I went round to your house,' he replied, 'and when you weren't there, I guessed this would be the most likely place. I didn't expect to track you down with my nose though – you *stink* like a rotting whale.'

'And how do you know it's me that smells?' protested Lucy.

'Well,' he said, rattling the doorknob, 'of all the people I know with a key to this place I reckon you're the one most likely to reek of poo.'

'Yes, *very* clever,' said Lucy as she unlocked the door and let the odour-detective in.

'My *God*, Luce, it really does *stink* in here.'

'So you keep saying.'

'Yeah,' said Toby. 'Erm, so what *is* it?'

'Pigeon droppings,' she admitted.

'And you're covered in the disgusting stuff,' said Toby. He pulled a large spotted handkerchief out and covered his nose. 'What have you been *up* to?'

'It's a long story,' said Lucy, 'I'll tell you later.'

'I'm sure it'll be very interesting,' said Toby. 'Oh, and speaking of stories, Lily grabbed me when I called at your house – she told me to give you a message.'

'But I'm supposed to be hiding,' said Lucy.

'I think she *knows* that,' said Toby. 'She said to tell you that there'll always be a next time.'

'*Did* she?' snarled Lucy.

'Yeah,' said Toby, 'what do you think it means?'

'That I can't go home for a while,' said Lucy.

'Why not?'

'Because they're going to try to put me in Saint Mallydick's again, *that's* why. And this time they'll probably succeed.'

'*Ah*,' said Toby. 'Speaking of mad people, what about those two loonies on top of the wardrobes? I managed to get a look at that banner as they were being piled into the police van – it said *Lux Angelis*. What do you reckon that means?'

'Erm, dunno,' said Lucy.

'I think *I* might be able to help with the translation,' said a deep voice. 'It means *Light of the Angels*.'

They turned back towards the doorway, staring open-mouthed at the uninvited guest – it was Lucy's auction-room angel.

'*You?*' she hissed.

'Perhaps you were expecting someone else?' said the angel. He gave a flap of his coat tails that sounded like a crack of thunder, then closed the door and stood with his back towards it.

'But how did you find us?' said Toby, 'and how did you get in?'

'You needn't bother yourself with such irrelevances child. The point is that I *have* found you and I *am* here.'

'Yeah, but why?' said Toby, trembling slightly.

'I would have thought *that* was perfectly obvious,' snarled the angel. 'I believe you *have* something of mine.'

'Erm, I don't think so,' said Toby.

'Not *you,* boy. How would an idiot like you come into possession of such a relic, unless it happened to drop from one of the heavens and fall into your lap? *This* is the person I'm referring to,' he said, pointing at Lucy. '*The Fake Bidder. The Wardrobe Lurker. The Light Stealer.*'

'Hey, less of the idiot, *if* you don't mind,' protested Toby.

'Yes,' said Lucy, '*I'm* the only one that's allowed to call him that – and anyway, neither of us has anything that belongs to you.'

'Oh, but you *have*,' said the angel, fixing them with a sinister stare.

'No,' she insisted. 'We have *not*.'

'No?' said the angel, forcing a smile.

'*No*,' said Lucy defiantly, 'didn't you hear me the first time?'

'Ah,' he said, realising her game, 'so we're playing with words, are we? Or are you messing with fire? Either way you run the risk of getting burned.'

'Don't you go threatening us,' said Toby, trying to sound brave.

'I will threaten whomsoever I like,' said the angel. 'Now, regardless of whether or not I purchased it from the auction, the manuscript belongs to me – and *you*, young lady, are going to return it.'

'No I'm not,' said Lucy, moving back a step.

'I can *hear* you breathing,' whispered the angel, as he put his waxy face next to hers.

'Yes,' said Lucy nervously, 'I do quite a lot of that.'

'But it's probably not usually quite so laboured, is it?' said the angel. 'You've *heard* it, haven't you?'

'No,' she said, swallowing visibly. It was a lie, and not a very good one. She could hear a soft rustle, like a beast creeping through undergrowth.

'I can't hear it either,' lied Toby, 'but whatever it is you're doing you'd better stop it, right now.'

Lucy shook her head in disbelief. What a giveaway *that* was.

'I'd better stop it, had I?' grinned the angel. 'Or else what?'

'Or it's two onto one,' said Toby uncertainly. The rustling sound was getting louder, and there was a growing smell too, like rotting vegetation.

'Two quarters against one and a half?' said the angel. 'Let me *see* now. I was never very quick with numbers – there's no particular need for it in my line of work, but I *think* that means I outnumber you by three to one. Do you think those are good odds?'

'We're *not* quarters,' objected Toby.

'Yes, and you're not one and a half,' added Lucy.

'Am I not?' said the angel. 'But you know so little about me – how can you possibly judge, when you have so little evidence?'

'I've got evidence,' she said confidently. 'I know things.'

'*Do* you now?' smiled the angel. 'And exactly how much of this pathetic microcosm are you familiar with?'

'A micro what?' said Toby. 'What's he on about?'

'Shut up, Toby,' said Lucy, 'I'll do the talking.'

'As long as you are able,' threatened the angel. '*Now*, this evidence you claim to possess. Why don't you enlighten us all with it?'

'Alright then,' said Lucy. 'I know what you want.'

'So you know *that*,' hissed the angel. 'And what else?'

'I also know *what* it is,' said Lucy. She tried to swallow, but her mouth had dried up.

'I doubt that very much,' said the angel. 'Scholars have spent their entire lives studying it, and even *they* would not claim to understand its mysteries.'

'I said I knew *what* it was,' said Lucy, 'I didn't claim to understand it.'

'That much is true,' admitted the angel.

'In fact,' said Lucy, 'I haven't even had a chance to look inside it yet. I've been too busy running away from you.'

'Then why don't you *have* a peep?' suggested the angel.

'*No*,' said Lucy, 'it's staying where it is.'

'Well *I* fancy a quick look,' said Toby.

'No you *don't*,' snapped Lucy, 'you don't even know what we're talking about so just *shut it* will you? This is serious.'

'I bet I *do*,' said Toby. 'You're talking about the thing in the auction. You've only gone and nicked that Grubby Manuscript, *haven't* you?'

'Grobbley,' nodded Lucy, 'but I only pinched it to begin with – it's mine properly now.'

'Oh, brilliant,' said Toby. 'And how does that work? Does it get to become yours if you can run faster than the rightful owner? And how did you get your hands on it anyway? It was guarded and everything.'

'I'll tell you later,' said Lucy. 'For now just *look* at me and listen. This man is dangerous.'

'Yeah? Well he doesn't look all that threatening to me.'

'That's because he wants the book,' said Lucy. 'He's trying to appear friendlier than he really is.'

'But he's bigger than us,' said Toby. 'He could just take it.'

'The boy is correct,' smiled the angel. 'All I want is to have a look, that's all – and then you can have it back.'

'Go on, Luce, let's all have a look. Then we can get off home for tea.'

'That's right,' said the angel, 'give us both a look, Luce.'

'Don't you *dare* call me that,' she said. 'My name is Lucy – and don't treat me like a child either. You can fool poor Toby here, but you're not going to sweet-talk me – because I remember *exactly* what they said at the auction rooms.'

'What *who* said at the auction rooms?' asked Toby.

'Those, erm, *people,*' said Lucy. '*You* know.' She was beginning to suspect they hadn't been real people at all, but Toby didn't seem ready for the truth – at least not yet. In fact, it felt like *she* wasn't quite ready for it either.

'You mean those two that jumped up on the wardrobes?' said Toby.

'Yes,' said Lucy, '*them* – just try to think what they said.'

'Oh, yeah,' said Toby, 'something about the *light* not being for sale.'

'That's right,' said Lucy, glaring at the angel. *The light is not for sale.* But they said something else as well.'

'Yeah,' said Toby. 'It was, erm, err, nope, sorry, I can't remember.'

The angel looked suddenly relieved, until Lucy spoke again.

'You needn't smile like that,' she said. 'I didn't ask Toby because I couldn't remember. I just wanted to remind him what we saw, so he'd realise what we're dealing with.'

'How touching,' said the angel. 'So you want your little friend to become part of your crusade do you?'

'If you like,' said Lucy.

'Aaaah – well then why don't you tell *me* as well? Just what *did* they say that was so important?'

'The *light* cannot be taken by force,' said Lucy. 'It must be lost or given freely. *See*? I'm good at remembering things like that. It's one of the three things I excel at.'

The angel's face dropped for a moment, as if he was making hundreds of mental calculations, each of which required the utmost concentration. The girl was obviously cleverer than he'd thought.

'Yeah,' said Toby, 'cracker whistling, remembering things, and doing deep voices. Oh, and telling lies.'

'Stories,' corrected Lucy, '*not* lies.'

'Yeah, right,' said Toby. 'Only I thought you said they were inventions.'

'*Inventions then,*' hissed Lucy, beginning to sound agitated, 'stories, tales, legends, or whatever – anything you like, as long as it's not lies…'

The angel suddenly lost patience and flung his dark hat into the corner, his face emerging from its shadow for the first time. His skin was paper thin and ghostly white, and through that almost transparent surface they were able to glimpse the actual fabric of him, a dull white sub-flesh that looked as though it was fashioned from melted candles.

'ENOUGH OF THIS DRIVEL,' he screamed. 'Now *give me the light.*'

'I don't think so,' said Toby. 'Like the girl told you, it's not for sale, and neither are we.'

'Then prepare yourselves,' said the angel.

'For what?' grinned Toby.

'For a glimpse of that which you claim to already understand.'

'Eh?' said Toby. 'It's funny, but I thought you were going to threaten to kill us just then.'

'He was,' said Lucy, listening for the noise they had heard earlier. The rustling sound had all but died away though, as if one threat was subsiding, only to be replaced by another.

The angel crossed his hands on his breast, gripping at the lapels of his dark coat with bony fingers – he was preparing to open up the garment.

'Don't look,' said Toby. 'I'm not sure what he's doing, but I've got a bad feeling about it.'

'I have no intention of looking,' said Lucy, turning her head to the right and shielding her eyes with the back of her palm. 'I know all about the angel and his raiment.'

The angel hissed violently, and Lucy felt traces of his spittle running down her face. She was too terrified to wipe it away though, because he had stopped talking and begun to act, and that was *always* a bad sign. His hands fell to his sides, but he immediately began to lift them again, his outstretched fingertips describing a sweeping arc in the air. The motion filled the room with the sound of thunder and the smell of Lectric, like a more powerful version of Lucy's theatre.

'Such insolence,' he hissed, 'and such *arrogance* – and do I take it from your mention of the raiment that you have spoken to the bird-keeper?'

Lucy nodded. There was no point in denying the obvious. She was better off saving her inventions for things that mattered.

'I thought as much,' said the angel. 'I sensed your presence when I visited his stinking spirit house. But he was cleverer than I gave him credit for, masking you with the *smakkabosh* of those disgusting creatures.'

'*Told* you,' whispered Toby with a nervous half-grin. Suddenly though, he realised that the time for jokes was gone.

'Laugh while you can,' hissed Raziel. 'Your friend is no longer masked, and no longer protected.'

The angel's arms were high above his head now and when his palms finally joined, the sound of weather and the sparking of Lectric doubled and then redoubled, forcing the smell of burning atoms into the air. It was like all the sea air Lucy had ever smelt, but squashed together into the last few seconds of her life.

'Raziel is *come*,' said the angel with a thin smile.

Behind him, almost invisible and shimmering like the northern lights, was an expanse of golden wings that reminded them of Nether Grimston.

'I don't like the look of this, Luce,' cried Toby. He was pointing at a host of glowing dandelion seeds. 'Those things floating around him look a lot like the things in the peanut…'

'Shut up,' said Lucy, stamping on her friend's foot and winking. 'Because if you don't shut up then I'm going to wire *you* up, *like I wired up Lily.*'

She stared at Toby as if she hated him. Then she transferred her gaze to the angel, trying to look suitably awed by his appearance.

'You really *are* an angel, aren't you?' she said, watching Toby from the corner of her eye. He *seemed* to have got the message, and was slowly edging around the room, forcing Raziel to alternate his gaze between them.

'I am,' said Raziel. 'The first and last heavenly creature you will ever see.'

'Erm, wait a minute,' said Toby. He'd moved around to the door now, and was standing within easy reach of the monster switch.

'What is it *now*?' hissed Raziel. He turned towards Toby, just enough to allow Lucy to creep towards the shower cabinet without being noticed. And as Toby continued to distract the angel, she sat down at the console, still unsure if their plan would work.

'Whistling, right?' said Toby. 'That's one, innit?'

'WHAT?' said the angel.

'One of the things she's good at,' said Toby, 'and telling stories – that's two.'

'BE QUIET,' screamed the angel.

'And doing those deep voices,' said Toby, 'that's erm…'

'THREE,' screamed Raziel.

'Oh, and erm, magic tricks,' said Toby, 'that's another one.'

'SO?' said Raziel. 'For your last utterances in this mortal realm you choose *stupidity*?'

'Not exactly,' said Toby, 'because I make that four things she's good at – and if you hang on for just a moment, you'll catch a glimpse of number five. She's a dab hand at science, and *especially* good with Lectric.'

The angel looked puzzled for a moment, as if dumbfounded by the boy's nonsense. It was always possible to speak out against a rational argument, but there was little to be said in the face of complete idiocy. He had even seen it written on a wall once:

"Bullshit baffles brains"

There was a tiny click from the control panel, hardly audible to earthly ears. Raziel heard it though, and leaned forward to identify its source.

'Don't be nosey,' said Lucy, placing her hand over the switch.

'What was that?' said the angel.

'It's the way out,' said Lucy.

'*Is* it now?' said Raziel, looking a little worried. 'You don't think this pile of rubbish actually *does* anything, do you?'

'It's like a lot of things,' said Lucy. 'Perhaps it has more than one purpose? It *might* be a machine for talking to the dead – or maybe it's just like you said and it does nothing at all?'

'Or maybe it *is* the way out,' said Toby. 'For us that is, not you.' He threw the Nife switch to the 'on' position and prayed there was enough money left in the meter. For a moment, nothing happened – and since Raziel knew little of thermions and their habits, he began to grin, like a cat in a tree.

'I think that might be the end of the story,' he said, 'don't you?'

On the previous occasion when they'd switched the confuser on, the light on the control panel had glowed yellow – but this *time* Lucy had moved the switch to '*dangerous*' and it was now showing a deep, ruby red. Toby studied her expression closely, hoping they were thinking the same thing – they *had* to get the angel to stand near the rods.

'Amuse yourselves while you can,' said Raziel. 'But when you have finished playing with this ridiculous toy, you will *still* have nowhere to go – and *then* you will give me what is rightfully mine.'

The valves had begun to glow now, and the dial near the wall switch was reading 'luscious kissing lips'. Toby prayed that it was a good sign.

'Alright then,' said Lucy, her hair standing on end. 'I'll give you the *light* if you let us go.'

'And you think I will *agree* to that?' said Raziel in a mocking tone. 'There is usually trickery whenever an earth-bound is involved. All I need to do is work out what it is.'

'Then keep your eye on the hand that's not moving,' said Lucy, as she climbed out of the cabinet. 'Who knows, you might even see the secret?'

'You really *are* a confident one, aren't you?' said Raziel. 'I have no doubt now that you are the one I seek. It will be *such* a great pleasure to take you both back with me – you *and* the *light*.'

'Whatever you say,' said Lucy, 'but the only way you're going to take both of us is by getting the *light* first. And you can only take it when I offer it – so why don't you take it now?' She took the manuscript out of her bag, but kept it down by her side.

Raziel thought for a moment, and then waved her away. He'd become aware of a heavenly singing building up around them, and for a moment it seemed to Lucy that he recognised the sound.

'*More* distractions?' he said. 'Do you think this sort of childish nonsense impresses me?'

'No,' said Lucy. 'I've already agreed to give you the *light* – what could we hope to gain?'

As she moved towards the angel, her hair began to wilt. Now, instead of standing bolt upright, it merely stuck out at either side of her head.

'You look stupid like that,' said Toby. 'But it's no reason to be *acting* stupid as well – don't give it to him Luce. He can't touch us, can he? And he can't take the book by force.'

'Ignore the boy,' sneered the angel. 'I may not be able to take the *light*, but I can certainly harm you if I wish.'

'He's right,' said Lucy. She took a pace forwards, so that the floor rods were between her and the angel. 'I'm going to hand it over.'

'No, Luce, *don't.*'

'Be *quiet,* imbecile,' hissed Raziel. 'She has made the right decision.'

Lucy paused, her face suddenly blank, like an actor who has forgotten the next line. She was just delaying though, waiting for the whispered voice that would prompt her actions. After a few seconds it came – somewhere inside the machine, a transformer began to whine.

'Here,' she said, holding the manuscript out to Raziel.

The angel smiled, but it wasn't an *ordinary* smile – the kind you might expect someone to use when patting a baby, or watching an enemy getting a poke in the eye – this was a much deeper expression, like the satisfaction that accompanies the very last of a million actions, each of them part of some great plan.

Raziel reached out to grasp the manuscript, stepping towards Lucy so she could not snatch it away at the last moment – he was *far* too clever to fall for *that* kind of stupidity.

Somewhere deep inside the confuser though, a relay clicked – and now it was Lucy's turn to smile.

'What was that?' said the angel, suddenly suspicious.

'Just a thing for inserting jam,' she said with a grin.

'And squirting cream,' added Toby.

The two friends had expected the machine to perform as it had done on the previous occasion, so they both jumped in shock when it gave a low grumble and a deep crack resonated around the room. Raziel smiled at their discomfort, but then began to sniff the air as the brass rods began to fizz and crackle. And then he made the mistake of looking down, searching for the source of the noise when he should have been looking up. A thin blue curtain of flame sliced down from the rods in the ceiling and caught him at the back of the neck. And a fraction of a second later a burst of deep red flames erupted from the floor, catching him in the chest and holding him like a pair of Lectrified shears. Where the two curtains met, a ball of violet flame exploded around him, expanding from a point centred on his stomach and wrapping him completely in a fizzing, purple torment. Toby was already standing at a safe distance, but as Lucy leaned back to avoid the outer edges of the sphere, she stumbled and fell.

'We should have tested it first,' shouted Toby above the continuing noise of the valve-song.

'Shut up,' hissed Lucy, 'and get down.'

She didn't really know *why* they should be on the floor, but suddenly it seemed like the safest place to be – it was certainly better for seeing what was happening inside the sphere. Raziel was resting on one knee, pressed down by the force of flame issuing from the ceiling rods. He was shouting something at her, but there was such a noise it was impossible to hear his words. But even if it *had* been quiet, Lucy was guessing that the sphere sealed him off from them, at least for the moment. One thing was clear though, the angel was in the grip of an uncontrollable rage. His face was even whiter now, wrenched this way and that by sheets of flame that distorted his features into grotesque masks. His intent was clear enough though, and Lucy was glad of the glassy wall of fire that separated them.

Raziel bent his other knee now; sitting back on his heels and reaching towards Lucy, demanding that she hand over the manuscript. She shook her head violently, leaving him in no doubt of the answer. Then she reached out a leg and looped a toe into her rucksack, finally managing to pull it over from where it had fallen. She displayed the manuscript to Raziel for one last time and then pointedly placed it back in the bag. Her defiance only seemed to enrage him more though, encouraging him to fight back against the flames.

'I don't like the look of this,' shouted Toby.

Lucy could do nothing now, except nod and watch in horror as the angel resisted the power of the firestorm. Toby could leave if he wanted, but there was no way out for her. The sphere surrounding the angel had completely filled the space between floor and ceiling now, and extended all the way to the equipment racks too. Lucy was trapped *behind* the wall just as effectively as Raziel was trapped *inside* it.

The angel rose from his heels into a kneeling position, forcing the blue sheets of flame above him to compress and glow brighter, as if they were sentient and annoyed at his resistance. He rose on one knee, glaring at Lucy as he did so, then he smiled slightly, as if anticipating his joy at the exact moment of her death. And it was that very same thought that convinced Lucy that what they were doing was wrong.

'*Toby?*' she shouted, 'We have to stop, – we mustn't kill him.'

'It's a bit late for that,' he shouted, 'and anyway, *he* wants to kill *you* – just take a look at that face if you don't believe me.'

Raziel had managed to stand now, his features distorted into a sea of snarling rage. His knees were buckling under the pressure, the curve of his back making him look like an old man – but *still* he appeared to be winning. Whatever force the confuser possessed, it no longer seemed a match for the angel's resistance.

'We've no right to kill him,' said Lucy. 'I don't care what he's done.'

'What about self defence, Luce? I think we can do *that,* can't we?'

'We don't know that it *is* self defence,' said Lucy. 'He threatened us, for sure, but it's not the same as actually killing us.'

'It's pretty close,' shouted Toby. 'And it's going to be a bit late to change our minds once he's done away with us, *isn't* it? Anyway, oh *bloody hell…*'

Toby was suddenly struck dumb by events inside the sphere. Raziel had fallen forwards again, pressed down by the force of flame – but there was something *else* going on. If there had been any doubt in their minds before, then it had completely evaporated now.

Raziel *was* an angel.

They were difficult to make out, because of the sudden brightness of the light, but it was clear now that he had three sets of wings. One set was attached to his back, obviously intended for flying, but there were other sets of feathered stubs – one pair covering his feet and another wrapping his eyes. Not that he needed eyes to see them any more. Lucy could tell that he was aware of their every movement, whether he looked at them or not.

The man-figure was still there at the centre of the maelstrom, but another being had appeared – a glowing spirit, superimposed onto the earthly body. And the spirit was raging against the entrapment, its huge wings sweeping against the low ceiling like some wild, feathery cleaning machine.

'When he gets out he's definitely going to *kill* us,' said Toby. 'You *have* to use the switch Luce.'

'No,' she hissed. 'That's how we got *into* this mess. Don't you remember all those things Lily and the doctor said, about judging people? They were judging me, just like you want me to judge the angel.'

'Yeah, but that was different,' shouted Toby. 'They were only going to put you in a hospital – this thing wants us dead.'

Lucy watched the creature increase in brightness until she was no longer able to look. Then she shielded her eyes with her hands, forming a tiny hole between her fingers that she could barely see through. The angelic outline was still there amidst the glow, but it was smaller now, the wingtips no longer pressing against the ceiling. The dark shape at the centre was there too, but less confident, fearful almost, as if the effort had been too much. Raziel had fallen flat on his face, twitching and trembling and obviously in great distress. But once again, he managed to draw himself up into a kneeling position.

'We've got to switch the thing off,' said Lucy.

'But he'll kill us,' shouted Toby.

'We have to take a chance,' said Lucy. 'I'm not going to take the life of another creature, even if it *is* dangerous – not if there's another way.'

'And what way is *that* then?' shouted Toby.

Lucy wasn't listening. She crawled over to the cabinet and climbed inside, to reach the control panel. Moments later the room went silent as she placed her hand on the switch. With a soft cracking sound the sphere of flames 'popped' out of existence.

'Uh-oh, Luce, I don't like this. I hope you know what you're doing.'

Lucy climbed out of the cabinet and tiptoed over to where Raziel was kneeling. The angel was stripped naked, his clothing burned to smoking tatters by the aurora. His hands were resting near his knees and his forehead was flat against the charred wooden floor, as if he was praying to some invisible God.

'What do you think *those* are?' said Toby, pointing at Raziel's back.

'What do *you* think?' said Lucy. 'We didn't imagine those wings you know.'

'No,' said Toby. 'I don't suppose we did.'

He prodded at Raziel's back, then stepped away as if he'd suddenly realised that the angel might not actually be dead. On either side of the ridge formed by his backbone a row of short stubby quills protruded from the skin, making him look like a plucked and grossly overcooked turkey. The ends of the protrusions were burned and charred and smelled like an old horsehair mattress in flames.

'You decided not to turn it off then?' said Toby, prodding the body.

'I was *going* to,' said Lucy, 'but then the Lectric meter ran out of money.'

'You're *kidding* me,' said Toby. 'You intended to save this thing's skin? But he was going to *have* us, Luce, and I don't mean have us around to tea.'

'We'll never know, *will* we?' said Lucy.

'Never know what?' said a muffled voice.

'Oh God, *no*,' cried Toby, 'he's still *alive*.'

The pair exchanged urgent looks. Whatever they were going to do, it had to be quick, before Raziel recovered. It was obviously a lot harder to kill an angel than they thought.

'Luce, we've got to run.'

'No, he needs help,' said Lucy, 'look, he's twitching.'

Sure enough, Raziel's burned body was wracked with convulsions, as if hundreds of tiny creatures were burrowing away beneath his skin.

'Fine,' said Toby, 'then we'll call for an ambulance – but let's do it from somewhere safe, shall we?'

Lucy stared at Raziel, and then shook her head slowly – suddenly unable to believe what they had done.

'Come on,' hissed Toby. 'Let's help ourselves for once.' He ran into the amusement room, leaving Lucy to stare down at the burned angel.

'I'm sorry,' she whispered, 'but it was your own fault.'

'No,' hissed Raziel, keeping his face to the floor, '*your* fault Lucy Blake, and now you will give me...'

'*Give?*' sighed Lucy. 'You just don't know when to give up, *do* you?'

'No,' groaned Raziel, '*never* give up...'

'Well I think you should try,' said Lucy, 'because I'm going to take the manuscript to a place you'll never find. And it's going to *stay* there – for *ever*.'

'No such place,' he croaked. 'Raziel knows *all* places.'

Lucy bent down, trying to get a closer look at the angel's face. He cupped his charred, bird-like hands at either side of his head though, hiding his flame-crisped features.

'Then we'll have to find a place you *don't* know about,' said Lucy.

'I *told* you,' hissed Raziel, collapsing towards unconsciousness, 'there *is* no such place…'

Snogg's Number Two Stack

'*Luce*, we've been sitting in the dark for *hours*,' whispered Toby. 'When do you reckon something's going to happen?'

'Perhaps it already *is*?' said Lucy. 'Maybe there are things going on right in front of your face, and you don't even know.'

There was a gulping sound, somewhere in the dark.

'Erm, *yeah*,' said Toby bravely, 'but I wouldn't be scared, even if there *was*. Erm, *Luce*? Are you there?'

Lucy made a choking noise as if she was being strangled by some great hairy thing that had crept out of the shadows.

'Oh yes, *very* funny,' said Toby.

Silence.

'Luce?' whispered Toby. 'You are there, aren't you?'

'*Aaagh*,' shouted Lucy, after a long pause.

'Oh *very* funny – but I *knew* it was you.'

'Yes, of *course* you did,' laughed Lucy.

'Yeah, right, so when are we going home?' said Toby. 'This is boring.'

'Boring, but safe,' said Lucy. 'The angel hasn't followed us, has he?'

'True,' said Toby. 'I think I'd rather be bored than go through *that* again.'

There was a pause whilst they considered the idea. Neither of them said anything, but they knew it wasn't going to end as simply as that. The angel would find them eventually, and then all hell was going to break loose.

'It must be well past teatime,' said Toby eventually, 'which means I'm going to get skinned alive when I get home.'

'That's nothing compared with what *I'm* going to get,' said Lucy, 'if I ever *go* home that is.'

'Oh, *yeah*,' said Toby, 'that was great, wasn't it? The way we ran through your front door and straight up the stairs with Lily screaming her head off at you. What will she do when she finds out you've disappeared again?'

'Celebrate,' said Lucy, only half joking. 'Then she'll call Doctor Veraciter, to see if she can get a concrete cell for when I come back.'

'Do you think she'll work out where you went then?' said Toby.

'Where *we* went you mean?'

'Oh yeah, where *we* went,' admitted Toby.

'I don't think so,' said Lucy. 'She didn't believe us about the Empire, did she? And she doesn't even know about the album, and even if she *does* find it, it's just an old book, isn't it? She's not going to pull it out from under the bed and guess that the mad step-daughter and her stupid friend have climbed into page four and disappeared.'

'She *might*,' said Toby, 'but I don't think she'd describe me as stupid.'

'No?' smiled Lucy. 'You had a chance to back out, didn't you?'

'What, and miss this great opportunity? I've *always* wanted to sit for hours in a dark room. We seldom talk about anything else in our house.'

'I'm not surprised,' said Lucy. 'Compared to your usual fun-filled misery breaks this must seem like a luxury holiday.'

'Yeah,' sighed Toby, 'well I've got a theory about that – I might even tell you about it some day.'

'Tell me now,' said Lucy, 'it's not as if we've got anything else to do.'

'You'll laugh,' said Toby, 'I *know* you will, because you're just sitting there in the dark – and it'll seem a whole lot funnier with the lights out.'

'If there *are* any lights,' said Lucy. 'I never managed to find any when I came before. Anyway, I promise not to giggle – *look*, cross my heart and hope to die.'

'Very funny,' said Toby, squinting into the bible blackness.

'Go on then, *tell* me,' said Lucy. 'Get it over with.'

'Erm, right,' said Toby, 'well, don't laugh or anything, but I first got the idea from this weird dream.'

'Ye-es?' said Lucy.

'Erm, well,' said Toby. 'I, erm, dreamed that I could control the weather.'

There was a sound of gurgling, which was obviously the noise that Lucy made when she was trying not to break a promise.

'*Nurse?*' she giggled. 'Nurse? You remember that strange patient you warned me about? Well I'm afraid he's out of bed again.'

'No, Luce, I'm *serious*,' he said. 'It was just a dream at first, but then I realised it was true. Only when I say *control*, I don't mean control *exactly* – I mean more sort of *influence*.'

'And that's why it always rains when you go on holiday?' giggled Lucy.

'I *think* so,' said Toby. 'It only ever happens when they take me.'

'Remind me never to come away with you then,' said Lucy. 'And by the way, I'll give your story four out of ten.'

'Thanks a lot,' said Toby. 'It's an improvement on my last score, but I expected a five at least – maybe even a six if it turned out to be true.'

'*If* it turns out to be true,' said Lucy, 'then you can have a five – but then I *definitely* won't be coming on holiday with you.'

'There's not much chance of that Luce, not after the show you put on at the auction rooms. If Lily ever needed help to get you put away in Saint Mallydick's, I reckon my parents would be at the front of the queue. They were a bit taken aback by all that stuff about wasps and making up museums. They're not used to your stories like Lily and Percy are.'

'Yes, well that's rather *unfortunate*,' said Lucy, impersonating Percy sucking his pipe. 'I *had* to make an invention to get out of the situation.'

'I know that *now*,' said Toby, 'but *they* won't see it that way – to them you're just some barmy school kid with a mania for hiding in wardrobes and a sideline in silly stories.'

'That about sums me up,' admitted Lucy. 'Apart from the fact that we've electrocuted a real, honest-to-goodness angel and we're sitting in a darkened room in what might turn out to be another world.'

'*Hey*, wait a minute Luce – did you just touch your hair then?'

'Yes,' she said, 'how did you know?'

'I think it's getting lighter,' said Toby. 'Give me a wave, will you?'

Lucy waved, suddenly worried about the sights that might greet them when the light finally came.

'It's definitely getting lighter,' said Toby. 'And I think *that* was more of a rude gesture than a wave.'

'In that case you're right,' laughed Lucy. 'It's definitely getting lighter.'

'Then let's celebrate,' said Toby. 'Why don't you break out all the food in your rucksack?'

There was a long pause, followed by a familiar voice that sounded nothing like Lucy's.

'Der isn't any foog in ger gag,' it said.

'Oh yes, *very* funny,' said Toby. 'I didn't even see your lips move – now hand it over.'

'There isn't any,' said Lucy. 'You *heard* what Genjamin said, didn't you? What with him and the manuscript and all the rest of the junk I carry around, there really isn't much room.'

'Haven't you even got one of Lily's creations?' said Toby.

'*Sort* of,' said Lucy, 'but it's for emergencies – because it's not real food.'

'That depends,' said Toby. 'What is it?'

'A pickled gherkin and cream cheese sandwich.'

'I'll take it,' said Toby. 'It sounds almost edible.'

'But I haven't finished the list of ingredients yet.'

'Uh-oh,' said Toby. 'You mean there's more?'

'Erm, there's mint sauce,' said Lucy. 'With cauliflower stalks and a load of that horrible green jelly you find inside giant sea monsters.'

There was a pause whilst Toby went through the possibilities. Using it as a weapon perhaps, or holding his nose and eating it anyway, in the knowledge that he was going to be violently and colourfully sick. Eventually he decided on the bravest course of action.

'Keep it for emergencies,' he said. 'I think I'd rather get some sleep.'

'But we have to stay alert,' said Lucy. 'We don't know *what* might happen if we fall asleep.'

'Same as when we're awake,' said Toby unenthusiastically. 'Nothing.'

'Tell me about your dream again,' said Lucy, trying to think of a way to stop him dozing off.

'I've told you once,' he replied. 'Why don't you tell me one of yours?'

'Oh,' said Lucy.

'You don't want to then?'

'Erm, no,' said Lucy. 'I just wasn't expecting to be asked.'

'So tell me then,' yawned Toby.

'It was the last time I was locked up in the Panopticon,' said Lucy. 'The day before you demolished the greenhouse.'

'Hmm,' grunted Toby.

'Toby?' she said, 'Are you still awake?'

'Yeah,' he grunted again. 'Green-n-n-houses…'

'Well it was the night before that,' said Lucy. 'I dreamt I was standing at a great height, looking out over Grimston.'

'*Nnn?*' said Toby.

'The town was spread about below me, like a map. And I was perched on top of Snogg's number two chimney – the one with the name written down the side. I was wearing a long coat that floated in the air, and there was a wind blowing in my face – I was thinking about jumping, and there was this voice telling me to *do* it…'

'*Nnnggghhh,*' mumbled Toby. '*Grunfff…*'

'Toby?' she hissed. 'Are you awake? I'm *trying* to tell you my best-ever dream here.'

There was nothing but silence – but suddenly the peace was shattered by the sound of snoring – a *lot* of snoring.

'Oh well,' she sighed, curling deep into the chair, 'I *suppose* it can wait until the sun comes up.'

Garderobius
Janiforum

When she woke, Lucy was curled up in the armchair and Toby was lying on his back on the floor, staring at the cracked plasterwork on the ceiling.

'*Great*,' he said, 'it's half way through the school holidays, and we discover a fantastic new world, only to end up back in school again.'

'Really?' said Lucy. 'How can you tell?'

'I can smell the custard,' said Toby with a smile.

'Well I can't smell anything.'

'No?' said Toby. 'Oh well, I must have made it up.'

'Two points,' smiled Lucy, 'and that's only because I'm feeling generous.'

She got up and stretched, and as the fresh morning air entered her lungs, she felt suddenly elated. This was *it* – the place she had been wondering about for so long. This was – erm, well *actually* it was a complete *dump*, like the very worst museum they'd ever visited, only with an extra three inches of dust.

They were in a square room. It measured about twenty feet on each side and had a small window high up on one wall and a solid-looking door on the opposite side. Toby wandered over and tried it, hoping that by some miracle it might have opened itself, using the morning light as a key.

'Solid,' he said. 'There's still a draught coming from underneath though.'

'That doesn't matter so much now,' said Lucy.

'Why?' he said. 'You want to get out, don't you?'

'Eventually,' said Lucy, 'but I want to find out where we are first.'

'Good idea,' said Toby. 'Why don't we ask *these* ugly mugs?' He indicated the paintings that were arranged at regular intervals around the walls. All twelve were portraits, and each of the stern-looking big-nosed faces bore a strong family resemblance. 'Professor Glassbone Haddock the first,' he said, reading the nameplate aloud. '*Braneskule Beak – 1ˢᵗ year AC.*'

'And this is Professor Glassbone Haddock the third,' said Lucy, reading another. '*Braneskule Beak – 3rd year AC.*'

'They've all got the same name,' said Toby looking at the rest. 'All twelve of them are called Professor Glassbone Haddock and they've all been a Braneskule Beak, whatever *that* is.'

'And they're all *incredibly* handsome,' laughed Lucy. 'Perhaps that's why they're stuck in a store room? I expect they'll keep the good-looking ones upstairs.'

'If there *is* an upstairs,' said Toby, 'and assuming they don't *all* look like this – all the people that live in this world I mean.'

'Is that likely then?' smiled Lucy.

'They *might*,' said Toby.

'Well if they do,' said Lucy, 'then *we're* going to stick out a mile.'

She studied the portrait of Professor Glassbone Haddock the twelfth, trying to work out if his eyes really *could* have been that close together, and wondering how they were going to remain inconspicuous when they finally got out. Then she noticed something a *lot* more interesting than the professor's face. Behind the figure in the portrait was a flag which bore a remarkable resemblance to the one stood up in the corner. It had caught her eye earlier, but she'd been happy to see just a part of it and imagine the rest. Now that she had noticed it in the picture though she wanted to see more, as if it formed a link with the unseen world on the other side of the door.

'Flag,' she said, pointing at the centre of the room where she wanted the pole to be.

'Yes, I know,' said Toby, 'your last slave died of disobedience.'

He dragged two desks aside and shifted a huge pile of leather-bound books to gain access to the corner. As each of the volumes fell at her feet, Lucy tried to read the titles but gave up when the dust started to rise.

'Nearly there,' grunted Toby. He unhooked the pennant from the pole and threw it across to Lucy who spread it out on the floor.

'It's embroidered, isn't it?' he said, settling down next to her.

'Yes,' she said, feeling the silky smooth texture of the golden tassels. 'And it must have taken quite a while to finish too – just look at all the detail.'

'Mmm, yeah,' said Toby.

'And before you say anything else,' said Lucy, 'I know exactly what you're thinking.'

'Do you?' he asked.

'You were going to tell me that the symbol in the middle looks a bit like the one that's painted on the Empire.'

'Nothing gets past you, does it Luce?'

'I hope not,' whispered Lucy, still in awe of the needle mistress who had created the flag. She ran a finger over the rich fabric at its centre, where a circular golden boss separated the four decorated quarters. It wasn't just similar to the symbol on the Empire, it was exactly the same.

'What do you think the four sections are?' said Toby.

'Hard to say,' said Lucy, 'but *these* three look as though they've been deliberately damaged. There used to be a symbol in each one of them, but all that's left now is the beetle.'

She ran her fingers briefly over the brilliantly embroidered insect, and then turned her attention to the other quadrants, where the coloured silk threads had been unpicked. Nothing now remained of the symbols that had been there, as if this was a flag for a country with a capital region and three others that people no longer travelled to – or which no longer existed.

'Well I hope we're in the place with the bright thread,' said Toby, 'because I don't like the look of those others.'

Lucy put a finger hold on Toby's nose and pinched hard.

'Ouch! Hells *bells*, Luce, what are you doing?'

'Lily always pinches herself when she can't believe her eyes. But I thought I'd pinch you instead – it's less painful.'

'Yeah, well thanks a lot,' said Toby.

'Never mind thanking me,' laughed Lucy, 'let's get to the conclusion of the experiment, shall we? Can you still *see* all of this stuff?'

'Of *course* I can.'

'That's a pity,' said Lucy, 'so can I.'

'So we're here for real?'

'It looks that way,' replied Lucy. She picked up one of the huge leather-bound books that Toby had moved to gain access to the flag. It was at least three feet square, but only half an inch thick, and had a beetle symbol embossed on the cover.

'Smegley Pratt's Skule Atlas,' she read aloud, 'being a complexe and compleet mappe of ye worlde and its formes in all their peculier and individual entirety. Hmm – it sounds like we've come to a place where spelling is optional.'

'Suits me,' said Toby, 'if maths is an option too I might even consider staying.' He was smiling as he said it, but suddenly realised that his joke might hide an unpleasant truth.

'Erm, we *can* get back, can't we?'

'I don't know,' said Lucy. 'I've been before, and I always went back whenever I fell asleep – but this time it feels different.'

'Oh, *great*,' said Toby. 'Being stuck in a strange world, well that's not *too* bad, is it? But being stuck in a strange world in a glorified cupboard? That's a bit hard to bear that is.'

'Like giving birth to a pineapple,' smiled Lucy.

'A *what?*' grinned Toby.

'Percy always says that when he's straining to come up with new ideas for his advertising campaigns. This is like trying to fart coconuts, he'll say.'

'Yeah, right,' laughed Toby, 'well remind me not to call at your house when he's trying to work. Now, are we going to have a look inside that atlas? It might help us to find out where we are.'

'*Oh,*' she said, opening the cover. 'It's not much of an atlas, is it? There's just one map, and it's completely circular.'

She opened the book out flat and placed it on top of a barrel. The light from the high window was improving with every passing minute now, and she was eager to examine the map in detail.

'It looks incredibly old,' said Toby.

'I don't think so,' said Lucy, 'it's an old style, but the cover looks quite new, and so does the inside page.'

'You're right,' said Toby, peering closely at the surface. 'It looks like someone made a forgery but forgot to soak it in cold tea.'

'So it's probably up to date then?' suggested Lucy.

'I expect so,' said Toby, 'shall we rip it out and take it with us?'

'It's bound into the cover,' said Lucy, 'and in any case, what would you *do* with it? We can only get as far as the door, and I don't think we need a map for that.'

V⸮⸮⸮⸮⸮

'Maybe,' said Toby, 'but we're going to be getting out soon, and when we *do, then* we're going to be needing it.'

'Well you can be the one to carry it then,' said Lucy, noticing for the first time that the design appeared to be hand drawn.

'It's like those maps of imaginary places we did at school,' said Toby.

'Yes, you're right,' said Lucy thoughtfully. She ran a finger over the skin-like surface, following a circular wall that enclosed a huge forest. There were settlements dotted here and there amongst the greenery, but the largest concentrations of buildings were at the four main compass points, with a much larger cluster of civilisation in the middle. Unlike the other parts of the map, the central area was inked in black, spidery lines, as if the artist's hand had been shaking. Lucy reached out and touched it, and felt a cold chill run down her spine.

'*Tower of Merciful Blades…*'

'And how did you know that then?' said Toby.

'How did I know *what?*'

'You just said the name,' said Toby.

'No I didn't.'

'But didn't you *hear* it?' said Toby.

'Hear what?' said Lucy vacantly.

'Do it again,' said Toby. 'Just touch the map, and *listen.*'

Lucy did as he suggested and this time they both heard it – a soft, musical voice, reciting the name of the place she was touching.

'*Tower of Merciful Blades…*' it whispered.

'Wow,' giggled Toby, 'a talking map – try it again.'

Lucy prodded a finger at random.

'*Courtyard of Extreme Vanity,*' whispered the map. The voice sounded like the sycophantic servant of some dark lord, although it was possible they were imaging that bit.

'Get it to speak up,' said Toby. 'Try pushing harder or something.'

Lucy pushed harder at another random place in the city.

'*Starr Gazey Dome and the Green-Witch Astrolabe,*' it whispered.

'Harder,' said Toby.

'It doesn't make any difference *how* hard you punch it – *look.*'

Lucy hammered her fist down, expecting to hear just a single name. Instead, the map-voice began to reel off a whole list of locations, each in the same infuriating whisper.

'*Run-a-long passage.*'

'*The Sign of the Gryphon and Pikestaff.*'

'*Euphemia Pongspittle – Her Privatt Howse.*'

'*The Gloppages and Pie Crust Lane.*'

'Whoops,' grinned Toby, 'I wonder how you stop it?'

'Apparently you don't,' said Lucy, prodding an area outside the walls. She'd guessed it was the key, because of the symbols, but the map-voice was unimpressed and continued its soft recitation of place-names.

'*The Institute of Predictory Science.*'

'*Dread Black Lane, leading to Stretch-My-Neck Gallows.*'

'*Department of Extreme Vengeance.*'

'*Cleaver and Marrowbone Orchestra rooms.*'

'*Counting House and Taxonomy Hall.*'

'*Sign of the Ratt Catcher.*'

'*Sign of the Barrel Organ.*'

'*Sign of the Lick Spittle.*'

'*Sign of the Stretched Weasel.*'

'*Sign of the…*'

'Shut *up*, will you?' shouted Toby. He reached in front of Lucy and mashed his palm down on a blank area outside the city walls. Mercifully, the random listing stopped, only to be replaced by an alternative announcement.

'*Farperoo,*' whispered the map-voice.

Toby pressed it again, just to be sure.

'*Farperoo,*' it said.

'That's done it,' he said, pressing once more for luck.

'*Farperoo and the Great Beeyond.*'

'Beyond?' grinned Toby. 'Did it say *beyond?*'

'Something like that,' said Lucy. 'Do it again.'

Toby pressed the spot.

'*Farperoo,*' it whispered.

'I reckon it must be broken,' he said.

'It's the size of your finger,' said Lucy. 'You're probably pressing more than one thing.'

'You're right,' said Toby, bashing the map to no great effect. 'None of this is helping, is it? Let's just concentrate on escaping, and then we can actually *see* the place, instead of just looking at some dusty old map.'

'That's the best idea you've had all day,' said Lucy. 'I tell you what, now that there's enough light, why don't we have a look out of the window? It might give us some ideas for getting out.'

'Alright,' said Toby, 'it's a bit high though, so we'll need to balance on some of this old furniture.'

'After that display we witnessed at the auction rooms?' said Lucy. 'I don't *think* so, do you? Did you *see* the state of that grey person-thing when it hit the floor? There was blood everywhere.'

'Do you *mind*?' said Toby. 'I go all faint when people talk about that stuff.'

'What, *blood* you mean?' grinned Lucy.

'I *said*, do you *mind*?' Toby swayed slightly, as if he was going to fall over.

'Alright,' she laughed, 'we won't pile up the furniture, in case we see something you don't like and faint on me.'

'What if I stand on your shoulders then?' said Toby.

'I'll stand on yours,' suggested Lucy, 'I'm lighter.'

'Alright, but I still don't think it'll work. Even with my height plus yours, you *still* won't be able to see anything.'

'I will,' said Lucy, 'if I use this.' She picked up a hand mirror from a nearby shelf, rubbing the thick dust off onto her tacky and still-smelly clothes.

'Let's do it then,' said Toby.

He braced himself against the wall and Lucy climbed onto his shoulders, using his cupped hands as stirrups. There was a great deal of moaning about how Lucy had managed to find all the softest parts of his body with all the hardest parts of hers, but eventually she managed to stand up straight with her back against the wall.

'Can you see anything?' grunted Toby, straining to stay upright.

'Just sky,' said Lucy, angling the mirror above her head.

'What about to the left?' asked Toby.

'Sky.'

'*Right* then?'

'Sky.'

'Look down,' he suggested. 'Can you see down?'

'Yes,' said Lucy.

'Well?' said Toby. 'Can you *see* anything?'

'Yes,' said Lucy.

'What?'

'Sky – and erm, just a few clouds.'

'Right,' said Toby. 'So not a lot of actual ground then?'

'Not a lot,' said Lucy, jumping down onto a pile of sacks.

'So now what do we do?' said Toby. 'Fall asleep and go home?'

'I *told* you it's different this time. For one thing it got light – when I came before, it stayed dark the whole time.'

'What else?' said Toby.

'I can't be sure,' said Lucy, 'but it feels as though this place is lived in. It's not like some old place that's been abandoned.'

'You're right,' said Toby, 'it's like my dad's garden shed – even when it's empty, you know it gets used.'

'It's like Percy's garden shed too,' said Lucy, 'even down to that big old armchair that looks as though it's been rescued from the dump.' She pointed at the unremarkable piece of furniture that had served as her bed, then stood gaping, as some tiny detail caught her eye.

'What is it, Luce?'

'Something we should have spotted earlier,' she said. 'Only we were so enthralled with unusual things that we looked straight past the ordinary items.'

'*What*? What have you ... Oh, I *see* it now.'

Toby imagined someone sitting in the chair, then gradually getting tired and slumping down into it with their arms draped over the side. And there, just where the phantom might have laid their right hand, was a metal cup.

'I think there's something in it,' said Toby. He picked it up and smelt the contents. 'Oh *God*, Luce, it's *disgusting* – like something Lily would serve.'

'It can't be *that* bad,' said Lucy, 'what does it taste like?'

VꟼⳤVⵣ๒⅂

'*Taste?*' said Toby. 'I'm sorry Luce, but that stuff isn't going anywhere *near* my mouth.'

Lucy took the cup and sniffed at it. He was right, it *did* stink rather badly, but she was going to taste it all the same. If she couldn't experience the sights or sounds of the world outside then at least she could find out what it tasted like. She raised the cup to her mouth, trying not to inhale the fumes or imagine what might happen when the stuff entered her mouth. Just as the smelly fluid was about to touch her lips though, she froze, staring at Toby over the rim of the cup. They had both hoped for it and both heard it, but now that the time had arrived, they weren't actually certain they wanted it.

Someone was *outside*, and they were turning a key in the lock.

The Shew Stone

Lucy's heart was beating in her mouth as they waited for the key to turn. And when *that* was done, there was the long, drawn-out process of knob turning that seemed to take forever. As it rotated, the polished metal surface caught the window-light and spun eerie reflections against the walls – and finally, the door began to swing, creaking like a leather corset.

'I wouldn't drink *that* if I was you. But I'm not you, so go ahead and have a taste – I'll be off getting some salt water and a sicky-puke-bucket.' The voice belonged to a small leather-faced man who might have been a walnut at one time but had then stayed out in the sun too long and got even wrinklier. That would account for the way he appeared to have shrunk too, withered up by the strong actinic rays until he was no taller than Lucy.

'Who are you?' she said, carefully replacing the cup under the chair.

'*I'm* supposed to be the one asking the questions,' said the walnut. 'This is my room after all, and I *seem* to remember leaving it locked. So who are *you*, and where did you come from?'

'Erm, from the *corridor*?' suggested Lucy hopefully.

'I *see*,' said the man, deciding to ignore the fact of the locked door for now, 'and from which direction might that be?'

'Erm, that way,' said Lucy, moving to the door and pointing left. She was desperate to see something – anything really, just as long as it gave her an idea of what to say next. She examined the man's face for clues, but he was giving nothing away – any expression that *might* have been there was hidden in the mass of wrinkles.

'Erm, we came from Farperoo,' said Lucy, moving into the corridor.

'Farperoo?' said the man lifting a hairy eyebrow. '*Interesting.*'

'Yes,' said Lucy, guessing that it was impossible to make matters any worse.

'We came in from Farperoo on the ornithopter and got lost on our way down the passage.'

'Ornithopter?' whispered Toby.

Lucy pointed at a sign on the wall.

"To the Ornithopters."

'Ah, well that explains it then,' said the walnut-faced man. 'It's easy to get lost around here. There are miles of corridors, even in *this* remote wing, and it would be *so* easy to go into a locked room by mistake, *if* you were wandering around – and *if* you were from Farperoo.'

'Mmm,' said Lucy. It was better than saying yes, because if she should have said no then she could claim that was what she meant by 'Mmm'. In any case, she knew the old wrinkly didn't believe a word of it. She liked him already though, despite the fact that he was uglier than all twelve Professor Haddocks put together.

'So *where* did you say we were going again?' asked Lucy. They were walking down a corridor that seemed to be losing height rapidly.

'I didn't,' said the wrinkled man. 'There are very strict rules here at the Braneskule and I don't want to get caught on the wrong side of them, not again – my name is Gusset by the way.'

'Gusset what?' said Toby rudely.

'Just Gusset,' he replied, 'it's enough of a name for me.'

'So, these rules, Mr. Gusset, have we broken any?' asked Lucy.

'Not yet,' he said. 'But I've a feeling you'll have stretched a few of them to breaking point by teatime.'

'Oh?' said Lucy, 'and why's that?'

'Just a vague feeling,' said Gusset. 'I get them all the time when strange-looking children from Farperoo appear in locked rooms.'

'*Ah, right,*' said Lucy, not wanting to push the point too far.

Gusset nodded and gave a little smile – at least it *looked* like a smile – he might just have been suffering from indigestion.

'Come on,' he said, 'let's get you to a classroom – we can discuss the whys and wherefores of keys later.'

'I told you it was a school, *didn't* I?' whispered Toby. 'I just *knew* I could smell custard.'

At the end of the corridor, they came across a spiral staircase where great beams of slightly redder-than-usual sunlight streamed in through tiny portholes. The windows were placed so high up in the walls though that it was impossible to see out of them.

'Do you really think this is a school?' whispered Lucy as they started down the stairs. 'It feels more like a prison.'

'Could be,' grinned Toby. 'Maybe *that* was the custardy smell?'

They descended the first couple of flights against the outer wall, but eventually Toby's curiosity got the better of him and he wandered towards the heavy banister that protected the drop on the inside of the spiral.

'Mind you don't fall,' said Gusset, grinning at them both.

Toby glanced over the edge, expecting to see the bottom a few floors down – instead he was almost sick at the sight that greeted him. There were *thousands* of steps, winding away into a cold, dark nothing that seemed to go on for ever – a bit like Lucy's mother in that respect.

'Quarter of a mile,' said Gusset.

'To the ground floor?' said Lucy. 'Wow – that's a *very* long way.'

'It certainly is,' said Gusset. 'But that's not what I meant – it's a quarter of a mile to the bottom of this particular staircase, but there's more after that. Not that you'll need to go down *that* far – I expect you'll be stopping somewhere close by.'

'Close by what?' said Toby. He moved gingerly away from the banister, trying not to make it seem too obvious.

'The place you'll be needed,' said Gusset. 'New arrivals always get brought up here – you just had the good fortune to be here already, what with coming from Farperoo and all. And while we're on the subject of arrivals, I'll tell you something else. There's no escaping – not here.'

'That's a pity,' said Toby, 'because it doesn't sound like the kind of place we'd want to be stopping in.'

'It's not up to you,' said Gusset, 'nor me either.'

'Can I ask something about your room, Mr. Gusset?' said Lucy.

'It's just Gusset, Missy – and what's your name anyway?'

'I'm Lucretia and this is Tobermory,' she lied smoothly. 'Only I was just wondering about the window. We tried to look out of it with a mirror but all we could see was sky and clouds.'

V?x̣ṿx̣ḅ⁊

'*Mirror? Sky? Clouds?* My, you *have* been busy, haven't you? And all because of a wrong turn? You must move like lightning you two, *mustn't* you? Anyway, no matter, as I said, it's not my lookout where you came from and why – I only know it's not from round here, because if you *were* then you'd know the answer to your own question.'

'Which is?' said Lucy, as politely as she could.

'You can only see sky because we're on the rim,' said Gusset.

'Oh,' said Lucy, looking at Toby for inspiration.

'Don't look at me,' he said, 'it was your question.'

'Well aren't you going to tell us any more?' said Lucy.

'Nope,' said Gusset. 'You'll find out soon enough, and the less of it you hear from me the better. I'm not exactly what you'd call popular right at this very minute – sort of persona-nun-grater, you might say.'

'Sounds like fun for the nuns,' giggled Toby.

They descended a couple of flights in silence, and then left the staircase to join a dim corridor, which was lit by smoking firebrands. At the end of the passageway, silhouetted against a barred window, a confident looking figure was approaching. It was slimmer and taller than Gusset and moved in a sinuous way that suggested intelligence and poise.

'They've got women then,' whispered Toby.

'That's a matter of opinion,' said Gusset, who obviously had ears with built-in amplifiers.

'Who have you there?' said a soft voice. 'Two strangers by the look of it – have they just come in?'

'I expect so,' said Gusset, obviously not so good at making up stories.

'Yes,' said Lucy, 'we came in from Farperoo on the ornithopter.'

'*Did* you now?' said the woman, narrowing her eyes. 'And are you alone?'

'Erm, yes,' said Lucy, 'my brother and I are orphans.'

'*Excellent,*' said the teacher.

'*Is* it?' said Lucy, examining the woman's face. She was quite pretty, apart from her bony beak-like nose.

'Erm, yeah,' said Toby, '*is* it?'

'Of course,' said the woman, 'the Braneskule prides itself on never turning anyone away. *Turnaway Ibus, Nulli Gobilus* as we say in the upper-level staff room.'

'Pardon?' said Lucy.

'It's Lattinn,' said the teacher, 'it means we take in anyone.'

Lucy turned to Toby, suddenly worried by what she was hearing.

'That wasn't Lattinn,' she whispered. 'I think she just made it up.'

'Never mind that,' said Toby, 'it's the being *taken in* part I don't like the sound of – have you seen the size of the bars on those windows?'

'Let's get you to a temporary class,' said the teacher, 'until we can sort out how you might fit into this august institution of ours.'

'Great,' said Toby, already looking for a way to escape.

'I'm Miss Niblock by the way,' said the teacher. 'I'm chief of cuisine and head of boats.'

'That means she's in charge of custard,' whispered Toby.

Miss Niblock overheard him and frowned, giving Toby the sort of look an eagle might spare a mouse, just prior to the commencement of dinner. She seemed to be sniffing too, and staring hard at the stains on Lucy's dress.

'Head of boats?' said Lucy, trying to distract her. 'What's that?'

'*Ah*,' said Miss Niblock. 'Well I was rather hoping you wouldn't ask, because the exact history of it isn't all that clear. And neither is the meaning of the word 'boat' come to think of it. There are some who think it should be spelt 'bote', and those who argue for 'bowt'. One particularly deranged individual even insists that it begins with a silent 'f' and is a form of transport that floats on water. Although heaven *only* knows where one might find so much water in one place.'

Toby started to say something, but Lucy guessed it was going to be some form of boat explanation and dug him in the ribs. It wasn't the right time to be giving secrets away, however insignificant – not when this new world had so many of its own to keep.

'Gusset?' said Miss Niblock.

'Yes missus?'

'I think our new friends will go to Mr. Creeps' for the moment, *if* you could arrange that? And without any mistakes?'

'I'll see what I can do, Missus,' said Gusset. When he thought she wasn't listening, he carried on mumbling to himself. 'Only nobody's perfect, are they? Who *knows* what might end up happening?'

'*What* was that last thing Gusset?'

'Nothing, Missus – I was just whistling through my teeth.'

'Hmm,' said Miss Niblock, spinning on a heel and preparing to leave them. 'I've heard you do a lot of that – you'd better be careful.'

'As long as you're careful with these young pigeons,' said Gusset.

Miss Niblock turned again and came back to face Gusset – and this time there was a much darker look in her eyes.

'Do you think they might come to some harm?'

'It's been known,' said Gusset. 'And if anyone knows how I feel about *that* Feazle, then it's you – I don't rightly agree with none of it.'

'You don't rightly agree with *any* of it,' corrected Miss Niblock.

'That as well,' said Gusset.

'Well fortunately,' said Miss Niblock, 'it's no concern of yours *what* happens to the pupils.'

'*Someone's* got to look out for them,' hissed Gusset.

'But that person isn't you, *is* it? If I were you Gusset, I would keep my mouth shut – it was that kind of talk that got you reduced from teacher to janitor, and if certain *authorities* find out you are repeating former blasphemies then there will be worse to follow. You *know* what I mean, don't you? Watch what you say, and who you say it to. Walls have ears – and eyes too I shouldn't wonder.' She looked up and down the corridor, as if they were being watched. 'But not bums,' she whispered behind her hand, 'walls have never had bums – at least not to *my* knowledge.'

Gusset forced a smile, but he was in no mood for laughter.

'I don't care who hears what I've got to say about it,' he said, 'as long as they take notice and put a stop to it – what's wrong is wrong.'

'Whether it's wrong or not, a single voice like yours will never influence matters,' said Niblock. 'These things take place at a much higher level than a simple janitor could ever understand.'

'I reckon they must,' said Gusset, 'because I'll never comprehend this thing as long as I live.'

'Which might not be as long as you think,' said Miss Niblock.

'Doesn't matter,' said Gusset. 'We all get chucked in the Morty Lakes sooner or later.'

'Well you'd better pray it's not sooner,' said Miss Niblock, finally turning to go. 'And when you've found a change of clothing for the girl, kindly bring me her dress for cleaning.'

As Miss Niblock left, Gusset sniffed the air, pretending he hadn't noticed the smell on Lucy's clothes.

'Yes, Missus,' he said, tipping a cap he wasn't even wearing. 'Come on – you heard the all-powerful Niblock; you're to come with me – *again*.'

'What was all *that* about?' said Lucy. 'What is it you don't agree with?'

Gusset stroked Lucy's hair, as if it might be the last time he would ever see her. 'Nothing for you to worry about,' he said.

They stood for a while in a draughty corridor as Gusset performed some kind of bizarre breathing exercise to calm his nerves. There was a classroom on the other side of the crystal door, and although he couldn't be seen, the faint voice of a teacher was audible – even through the thick milky glass. Lucy stared at the door, and was surprised to see that it became more transparent the harder she concentrated.

'It's made from thinking glass,' explained Gusset.

Lucy smiled and peered into the classroom where there were three rows of double desks, laid out two in each row. Seated at the desks were seven pupils, all of them craning their necks to get a look at the new arrivals.

'Where's the teacher?' whispered Toby.

'You'll be seeing him soon enough,' said Gusset, easing the door open so carefully that the tutor didn't even notice.

'...and what *else* do we know that's made of carbon?' said the teacher, oblivious to their presence.

'Erm, what about soot sir?' said a girl's voice.

'*Good*,' said the teacher. 'Now, is there anything else?'

'Very small pieces of meat?' suggested a boy.

'No, I don't *think* so, do *you* Bingo Sprocket?'

'Erm, what about those very small red flowers then?' said the same boy.

'No,' said the teacher, 'not those either.'

'Coal sir,' said the girl, 'and diamond as well.'

'*Excellent*,' said the teacher.

'Erm, *sir*?' said the one called Bingo. 'How can all these things be made of some other thing?'

'*Elements*,' said the teacher, with some satisfaction. 'That's the way the creator decided things should be, all those years ago. Now, if you'll excuse me, I think we have some visitors.'

'But sir...'

'Just write these things down in your jotters,' he snapped.

'But *sir*, does that mean you could make a diamond out of old bits of wood?' said Bingo.

'If those old pieces of wood were carbon, then *yes*,' said the teacher, 'but they aren't, *are* they?'

'But what if you burned them first?' said Bingo.

'Just write things down as you were told,' hissed the teacher, 'or you'll be getting a taste of the Lokey Pole.'

And with *that,* the classroom fell completely silent.

'And whom have we *here*?' said the teacher, staring intently at Lucy. The rather bizarre idea that you might be able to make a diamond from old bits of wood had left his mind completely.

'Erm, *sorry* Mr. Creeps,' said Gusset. He hovered in the doorway rather than stepping inside the classroom. 'Erm, what were your two names again?' he said.

'Lucretia and Tobermory,' said Lucy, realising that there was no point in having false names. 'But you can call us Lucy and Toby for short.' She stared back at Creeps, wondering who he reminded her of – and then she recalled the man who stood out on Grimston Promenade in all kinds of weather. He looked like Professor Ordinax, only his black silk robes were quite dry, and there was no sign of any seaweed hanging from them.

'Lucretia and Tobermory you say? *Well,* you'd better come in then,' said Creeps. 'Not *you* though, Gusset – you can go, thank you very much.'

'Don't mention it,' said Gusset, breathing in through his teeth.

'And by the way, *don't* do that.'

'Do what?'

'That thing with your teeth,' said Creeps. 'It sounds like the north wind whistling between tombstones. Don't you *ever* breathe through your nose like normal people?'

'Only when it's foggy,' said Gusset, slamming the door on his way out.

Lucy smiled at Creeps and headed for the empty desk in the front row. She could see that the three pupils sitting alone wanted her to come and sit next to them, but for now it was important that she and Toby stayed together, at least until they knew what they were dealing with.

'Lucretia? Tobermory? *What* is it that we never do?' demanded Creeps.

'Erm, I don't know,' volunteered Toby. 'It's a bit early to be asking us questions, isn't it? We've only just arrived.'

'Yes,' said Creeps, 'you *have* only just arrived, and presumably from a region of the city where good manners are considered old fashioned.'

'Sorry,' said Toby. 'What *is* it that we never do, Mr. Creeps?'

'That's *better*, Tobermory. We never mix, *that's* what we never do. I don't know how these things are handled where *you* come from, but here at the Braneskule, siblings are never seated together.'

'Siblings?' said Toby.

'Brothers and sisters,' sighed Creeps, making a note in his diary. 'And where *do* you come from, just as a matter of interest?'

'Farperoo,' said Lucy confidently. She moved back to the middle row, and sat next to a boy with no front teeth. He was smiling as though he'd only just discovered how to do it, and didn't dare to stop in case he forgot.

'*Farperoo?*' said Creeps.

There was an outburst of laughter from the other children, but it was quickly quelled by the master, who pointed a crooked finger at each of them in turn.

'Yes, that's *very* good,' said Creeps. 'I *like* a child with a sense of humour. Now, tell me, where are you *really* from?'

'We're from Farperoo,' insisted Toby.

There was another tiny laugh, but it quickly disappeared as Creeps spun around to see where it was coming from.

'*Silence,*' he hissed. 'And *you*, erm, *Lucretia*, take that bag thing of yours and hang it with the others.'

Lucy smiled and did as she was told, not wanting to draw attention to her rucksack – at least it was hanging somewhere she could see it.

'Now,' said Creeps, 'where did we get to last time? Phyllida Mugwort, can you tell us?'

'Erm, we didn't,' said the one called Phyllida. 'This is supposed to be the first lesson of creation studies.'

'*Is* it?' said Creeps. 'Then that's where we'll begin. It's a very good place to start, isn't it? Especially with creation.'

The rest of the pupils nodded, and Lucy and Toby joined in, both wearing satisfied grins. This was the *perfect* way to find out where they were, and without arousing suspicion.

'Now class,' said Creeps, 'who can tell me how *old* the world is?'

Lucy put her hand up as usual, and instantly realised her mistake. All *she* knew about was Grimston and her own world.

'Yes, Lucretia?'

'*Oh*,' she said, 'erm, yeah, *well*, is it about, erm, four billion years?'

'Hmm,' frowned Creeps. 'Do you recall earlier, when I said I liked a child with a sense of humour?'

'Ye-es,' said Lucy.

'Well it wasn't an invitation to have a joke at my expense,' said Creeps.

'Erm, sorry,' said Lucy, 'but I wasn't joking.'

'I see,' said Creeps with a frown. 'Well four billion is a very large number, isn't it? Especially for such a small girl – at least I *think* it's large.'

'Yeah, it's quite big,' said Toby helpfully.

'Indeed,' said Creeps. 'But it's not the correct answer. Can anyone help?'

The girl sitting in front of Lucy leapt to her feet and shot a hand into the air. She was younger than the others, probably only about nine, or ten.

'The world is thirteen years old sir.'

'Very good, Neeba Spatchcock. The world is thirteen years old. Now, shall we write that in our jotters?'

Toby looked back at Lucy with the most quizzical expression he could muster. '*Thirteen?*' he mouthed silently.

'Is there something wrong, Tobermory?'

'Erm, no sir.'

'Oh, I think there *is*, don't you?' said Creeps. 'We seem to have two new comedians in our midst. The Emperor *will* be pleased. Now why don't you share the joke with us?'

'Well,' said Toby, 'it's just that you said the world is thirteen years old.'

'Ye-es,' said Creeps.

'Well,' said Toby, 'my father has shirts older than that.'

'Your *father*? But I seem to recall you telling us you were an orphan?'

'*Oh*. Erm, *yes*, well he *had* shirts that were older than that,' said Toby, 'before he sadly passed away in the erm, the *mincing* machine accident.'

Lucy shook her head and glared at Toby, silently urging him not to be so clever. She'd begun to sense danger, like the smell of burned toast on the air.

'Get to the point boy,' said Creeps, 'otherwise you might find yourself in detention on your first day at the Braneskule.' He slapped his cane down on Toby's desk, glaring firstly at him and then at the pole that was propped in the corner of the room, as if it would scare the boy.

'Erm, right,' said Toby, trying to sound apologetic. 'I just thought the world would be a tiny bit older than that sir.'

'And why do you think that?' said Creeps.

'Erm, well it's just that Lucy and me, *we're* both thirteen. And as you're the teacher you're probably a *bit* older than that, and, well, it's erm…'

'I'm forty-two years old,' said the teacher. 'Is that a problem?'

'I *think* what Tobermory is trying to work out,' said Lucy, 'is how you could possibly be twenty nine years older than the world you live in.'

'Hmm,' said the teacher, returning to glance inside his lift-top desk, 'you're obviously more intelligent than you look, young man.'

'Oh, thanks a *lot*,' said Toby.

'Yes, *most* interesting,' said Creeps. 'It's most unusual for one so young to have even a basic grasp of the universal mysteries.'

'It's not a mystery at all,' said Lucy, watching the teacher closely. 'It's just simple arithmetic.'

'And *that* is where you are wrong,' said the teacher. 'Because if there's one thing we *all* know, it's that arithmetic is *never* simple.'

There was a furious round of nodding. For once, everyone in the class agreed, and to prove it they were all pulling books out of their desks, eager to show them to Lucy.

'Look,' said the boy sitting next to her. 'This is my arithmetic book – and it's empty.'

'Well I can't help it if you're slow,' said Lucy. She was ignoring the boy's empty jotter, because she had just noticed a tiny head – it was mounted in a glass cabinet on Creeps' desk. The container wasn't much bigger than a bar of soap and looked like a miniature version of Byron's Mumtaz mind reader.

'There's no need for that, Lucretia,' said Creeps, 'You should never mock those with less talent than yourself.'

'I didn't mean to,' apologised Lucy, 'it's just that where I come from…'

'Never mind where you come from,' said Creeps impatiently. 'You're here now, and *that's* what matters. The goings on at the north rim are of very little interest to us here.'

'The north rim?' said Lucy.

'Yes child, the north rim. Obviously, your great understanding in arithmetic has been gained at the expense of ability in other areas. You said you were from Farperoo, didn't you?'

'Erm, yes,' said Lucy.

'And this is obviously a lie,' said Creeps.

'Is it?'

'Of *course* it is. Everyone from the north claims to come from Farperoo. It makes them sound more mysterious, because Farperoo is a mythical place, which is completely outside the world, as you well know.'

'*Do* we?' said Toby.

'Yes, you do,' said Creeps. 'People claim to hail from Farperoo so they don't have to admit where they *really* come from. And as long as they don't have to admit the truth and we don't have to hear it then everyone is happy.'

'Are they?' said Lucy.

'Good *grief* girl. I can see why you've been sent to us. You need to learn a thing or two. Do you know *nothing* about the world you live in? Were you perhaps raised in a shoebox?'

'Erm, no,' smiled Lucy, thinking about her tiny bedroom. 'Sorry.'

'*Are* you?' said Creeps.

He opened his desk again and took out a huge sheet of paper that looked like someone's skin. Then he made a microscopic note, right at the top of the page, as if he might need to cram rather a lot in.

'I *think* we might have a short break,' he said, staring intently at Lucy. 'I suddenly find that I have something *important* to attend to.'

As soon as Creeps closed the door, Toby and Lucy became the centre of attention – but the girl who had known the age of the world was the only member of the class who dared to approach.

'That's done it,' said Neeba. 'He's gone to fetch the Old Haddock.'

'Who's the Old Haddock?' said Toby.

'The headmaster,' said Neeba, 'and nobody *ever* goes to see the head during class time – not unless it's urgent.'

'So what do we do now?' said Lucy. 'Is there a way out of here?'

'Well if there *is*,' said Neeba, 'then *I* don't know it. We can see what's going on though, if you like.'

'Where?' said Lucy.

'In the Beak's study of course.'

'And how do we do that?' said Toby.

Neeba directed the one called Fred Ogle to keep lookout on the door.

'They think we don't know about this,' said Neeba. '*Look.*' She groped about in the various under-layers of her grotty smock and eventually pulled out a small piece of glass. It could have passed for a gypsy's crystal ball, if you closed one eye and squinted hard with the other.

'What is it?' said Lucy.

'It's a shew stone,' said a thin girl who'd been sitting at the back of the class. 'It doesn't *belong* to Neeba though; she sneaked it out of her great uncle's library.'

'I did *not,* Pixy, you flipping-well liar.'

'You did – you told me you pinched it, when he was busy doing one of those sperry-mint things.'

'I didn't,' said Neeba, putting the stone away again.

'Did,' said Pixy.

'Didn't.'

'Did.'

'Didn't,' insisted Neeba.

'Did, did, did, did, did, and *did*,' said Pixy, turning to speak to Lucy. 'Her great uncle has a huge house Lucretia, over by the Morty Lakes. And that's where he does all his angel talking.'

'*Does* he?' said Lucy with a start. 'Erm, I think I might like to *meet* your great uncle. What did you say he was called?'

'I didn't,' said Neeba.

'Doctor Dee,' said a boy with eyebrows like hairy black caterpillars.

'You *shut* it, Ned Gullet. We don't even *know* these two and you're already giving our secrets away. If you're not careful I might give away some of yours. *You* know what I mean.'

The boy called Ned suddenly went very quiet, eager to keep his private things private – and Neeba gave a triumphant smile.

'Are you going to show us this stone thing then?' said Lucy. 'Or did you just get it out for fun?'

'I don't know if I *want* to now,' said Neeba sulkily.

'Go on,' said Pixy, 'we were only kidding.'

'Yeah, go on,' said Ned.

'Alright,' said Neeba, 'but we'd better be quick.'

She extracted the stone from her underclothes again and handed it to Lucy. It was still warm from the heat of her body, but it radiated another sort of warmth too, as if it possessed some kind of internal fire.

'Why is it called a shoe stone?' said Lucy. 'Did you find it in a shoe?'

'I thought you were supposed to be clever?' laughed Phyllida. 'It's called a shew stone because it shews you things stupid, s, h, e, w, 'shew', *now* do you understand?'

'Can't *anyone* around here spell?' grinned Toby.

'Never mind how they spell it,' said Lucy with an anxious glance towards the door. 'Let's see how it works.'

'There's no time,' said Neeba. 'Creeps will be back any minute.'

'There *is* time,' said Phyllida. 'Come on.'

'Hold it steady then,' said Neeba, 'and just look into it.'

'No, it's all over the place,' said Lucy. 'I'm going to be sick.'

'You're not holding it steady enough, that's why – keep it *still*.'

Lucy held the stone as still as she could, concentrating on the picture that floated in the midst of the glass.

'I can see it now,' she said. 'Oh, wait a minute, no, it's just this room.'

'Yes,' said Neeba. 'But you're not seeing *through* the glass, you're seeing *into* it. Just keep looking, and imagine yourself walking towards the door.'

'I am,' said Lucy, 'nothing's happening.'

'She can't do it,' said Phyllida cockily. 'Most people can't.'

'Yes I can,' said Lucy, 'let me have another try.'

'Why don't you let me have a go?' suggested Toby.

'Go on then,' said Lucy, admitting defeat. 'But don't throw up on me if the movement makes you ill.'

Toby took the stone and stared deep into the glass.

'There's a corridor,' he said, 'it's all cloudy and blue, and it's shaking like mad – but it looks like the one outside the classroom.'

'Go to the end, and turn left,' said Neeba. 'Then take the next right.'

'Are you there yet?' said Lucy.

Toby looked up briefly, to find every eye in the room riveted upon him.

'There's a painting,' he said, looking back into the glass. 'I can't see much, because it's even shakier now, but it looks like one of the Haddocks.'

'See? You're there already,' said Neeba. 'That painting is hanging outside the Beak's study.'

'So *now* what?' said Toby.

'Go in,' said Neeba.

'But the door's closed.'

'Just go through it,' said Neeba.

'Oh, *wow* Luce, we have just *got* to get one of these. I just walked through a solid wooden door.'

Lucy tried looking over Toby's shoulder but couldn't see anything.

'We've only got your word for that,' she said, pretending to sulk.

'Honest Luce, I can *see* them. They're a bit blurred, but there are two shadows. One of them is Creeps and the other one looks like the bloke in the Haddock paintings.'

'Can you see what they're doing?' said Neeba.

'They're just talking,' said Toby, 'and now they're walking in front of a big bright window, like silhouettes. Hey, wait, is that the city in the map that's outside the window?'

'What did you expect?' said Neeba, sounding surprised. 'Haven't you seen it before?'

Toby looked up from the stone, and when he looked back the image had gone, lost in a swirling blue cloud.

'Erm, yeah,' he said, 'of course we have, *haven't* we, Luce?'

'That's right,' said Lucy, 'we...'

Suddenly, everyone except Lucy and Toby rushed back to their desk and sat down – a floorboard had creaked in the corridor.

'…seems to be some kind of arithmetic prodigy,' said Creeps, opening the door.

'What are you doing out of your seat girl?' said the Old Haddock, pointing at Lucy. 'And *you* boy? Copying I suppose?'

'We thought you were coming to speak to us,' said Lucy.

'*Did* you now?' said the Haddock. 'And why would we wish to do that?' He looked just like all the other Haddocks, but with the addition of a pair of wiry and apparently glassless spectacles perched on the end of his nose.

'We thought you wanted to talk about arithmetic,' said Toby, slipping the shew stone into his pocket.

'Bless the holy sky, *no*,' said the Haddock. 'I simply wanted to observe Mr. Creeps' class today – and I, erm, er, have brought Miss Niblock along with me. She *often* accompanies me on such activities.'

Miss Niblock was waiting in the corridor and had obviously been listening to the conversation, because she came into the room just as her name was spoken – and this time she looked even less friendly.

Lucy smiled sweetly, but deep inside she was thinking what a dirty stinking rotten liar the Haddock was. If there was one thing she *knew* about it was stories and inventions. And the thing she knew the absolute *best* about them was when people were telling lies.

'Interesting, isn't it?' said the Haddock. 'Pupils seem to believe that the world revolves around *them*, just as the glory that is our sun revolves around the city – as if they believe the world was made for their own private use.'

'*Absolutely*,' said Creeps, with a sycophantic smile. 'I could not have put it better myself, headmaster.'

'Indeed you *couldn't* have,' said the Old Haddock. 'And *now*, Creeps, *what* did you say was the subject of the next lesson?'

Mappa
Mundi

Niblock, Creeps and the Old Haddock had crammed themselves behind Creeps' high wooden desk, and were now sitting shoulder to shoulder on three very spindly and uncomfortable looking stools. Just for a moment, Lucy considered giggling, but there was a menacing look on each of their faces, so she decided to sit up straight and keep quiet, like the others. All eyes were upon the teachers as they fiddled with their notes, adjusted their glasses, and filled up their pens – anything, it seemed, other than look directly at Lucy and Toby.

'Erm, shall we begin, Mr. Creeps?' said the Old Haddock.

'Ye-es, an *excellent* idea,' said Creeps. 'Children, I want you all to take out your *Tomes of Invention* and turn to The Fable of the Botes and the Isis.'

There was a great scraping of feet and opening of desks as the pupils searched for their reading books. Lucy followed their lead and opened her desk, where she found something that looked like a dried-up orange, and a pile of slim leather-bound volumes. She slid aside the top book, entitled *Merrie Japes in the Anciente Citie* – and below it found the one she needed, hand tooled with a familiar circular symbol – before she could pick it up though, there was a loud croak and a slimy green-skinned creature jumped into her lap.

'What is it *now,* Lucretia?'

'Erm, I think it's a frog,' said Lucy.

'A *what?*' said Creeps, looking puzzled.

'It's *not* sir,' said the boy next to her, 'it's a Loppit.'

'And *where*, might I ask, did you get one of *those?*' said Creeps. 'You've only *been* in the school for ten minutes.'

'I didn't,' protested Lucy, 'it was already in the desk.'

'*Well?* What are you waiting for?' said the teacher. 'Give it to *me* child.'

Lucy handed the creature to Creeps who returned to his own desk and placed it beside the tiny head cabinet. The Loppit was determined to make an escape though, and Lucy knew exactly how it felt.

'Here,' said Miss Niblock, her eyes narrowing into bird-like slits. '*I'll* take that.' She grabbed the runaway creature and crammed the poor thing into her mouth, chewing enthusiastically, as if her next meal was by no means guaranteed. As she crunched on a particularly gristly bit, her mouth dropped open slightly and the doomed Loppit managed a pathetic croak before finally disappearing for good.

'And let that be a lesson to you all,' she said. A stream of greenish-blue fluid leaked from between her lips and she wiped the slimy mess off her chin with the back of her hand. 'No food is to be brought into the classroom,' she said. 'How many times must you be told?'

Toby turned towards Lucy – he'd turned the same colour as the Loppit, and looked as though he might vomit at any moment.

'I can hardly wait for teatime,' said Lucy to the boy sitting next to her.

'Me too,' he whispered, 'it's Loppit Surprise tonight.'

'Wonderful,' whispered Lucy, 'and I bet I can guess what the surprise is.'

'Stop *gossiping* there,' shouted Niblock.

'And pay attention to the next lesson,' said the Haddock. 'Which erm, I *believe* is The Fable of the Botes and the Isis. Is that right, Mr. Creeps?'

'Indeed,' said Creeps. 'You will all take turns to read from the fable, and any hesitation or mispronunciation will be met with a punishment. And just in case anyone is in doubt, this *is* a fable. There is no such thing as a river, *or* a bote, because if there *was* then we would all have seen one by now, *wouldn't* we?'

Everyone nodded, including the teachers – everyone except for Toby and Lucy that was, who were looking slightly puzzled.

'You need to agree,' said Lucy's partner, 'I didn't agree last time and I had to go without dinner.'

'Well *that's* worth knowing,' whispered Lucy, nodding her agreement.

'Be *quiet*, Ned Gullet,' said Creeps. 'In fact why don't you start for us?'

Lucy opened her book at the front, and found to her relief that the contents page was written in Ingulesh.

'*Tome of Invention - being a compendium of fables as told to the author, the esteemed Eponymous Nurk.*'

She turned over, expecting a list of contents, but there was yet another introductory page.

'*Stories and inventions told by the sad folk at the Institute of Bended Myndes, being the babblings and descriptions of what might have been observed from the walls of our Citie.*'

'*Part the first – Lunatick Inventions as seen with the naked eye.*'

'*Part the second – General Madnesse, being observations with the Telescope.*'

Lucy skimmed the pages over, desperately searching for the story they were supposed to be reading. She stopped briefly to look at a picture of a dragon without wings.

'*The Dragon who Spread his Winges,*' said the title.

'That's not it,' hissed the boy next to her. 'You want part two.'

'Thanks,' said Lucy, flipping rapidly through the book – everyone was staring at her, including Toby.

'Come *on*,' he mouthed at her.

With great relief, she began to read the list of contents to herself.

'*Fable the First: Citie of Gasse Baggs with attendant ropes and floating things. A place of greate sadnesse and much thinking.*'

'*Fable the Second: The Tale of the Aquarium Citie, being the former realm of the Grand Dogus and home to the Council of Nine.*'

'*Fable the Third: Various comings and goings neere the Great Dome at a playce called the Fire Mines of Ignia, deepe in the darke interior.*'

'Lucretia?' said Creeps. 'Are you actually *with* us yet?'

She turned hurriedly to the next page and finally found what they were supposed to be reading – The Fable of the Botes and the Isis.

'I've found it, Mr. Creeps.'

'And about time,' said Miss Niblock. 'If you had only thought to mark the page Lucretia then we'd all be started now, wouldn't we?'

Lucy ignored the obvious retort and nodded, turning to the beginning of the story. It was accompanied by a helpful picture of what a bote might look like, just in case there was any doubt. Whoever had drawn it had obviously never seen one though. It was like the ancient pictures Byron had shown her – drawn by people who'd never actually *seen* a rhinoceros, an elephant, or a giraffe, but used their over-active imaginations to make up for it – a bit like the people at the Phibber.

'*The Fable of the Botes and the Isis,*' said Ned. '*It is said that once there was a river in the Citie, and that the river was full of water…*'

'Very good,' said Creeps, 'carry on please, Mashie Niblick.'

'*…coming from a place that nobody knew and flowing to a place that nobody knew either,*' continued Mashie.

Creeps pointed at the boy sitting in front of Lucy, just to her left.

'Bingo Sprocket,' said Creeps, '*you* next – come *on*, boy.'

'*And there was two skules,*' said Sprocket.

'*Were* two skules,' corrected Creeps, making a note of the boy's name.

'*And there were two skules,*' said Sprocket, '*both claiming to be the best, so they erm, er, decided to race their botes, on the river…*'

'Next,' said Creeps, pointing at Neeba.

'*There were eight men in each bote,*' said Neeba, '*sitting one on top of the other, and they were piled up so high that the top man had to use oars that were fifty feet long…*'

'Tobermory?' said Creeps.

Toby was about to read the next section when it all seemed to get a bit much for him.

'Erm, wait a minute, *that* can't be right, surely,' he said. 'A boat like that would topple over.'

'Then it's proof that the story is just a fable, *isn't* it?' said Creeps. 'Now, why don't you just carry on reading, or I'll make sure you're last in the queue for Grundly Liver.'

'I thought it was Loppit tonight?' said Ned, sounding disappointed.

'It *is* whatever we *say* it is,' said Creeps. 'Now, are you ready Tobermory?'

Toby noticed Niblock frowning again and wondered what was going on inside her head. Whatever it was, she wasn't thinking of stupid boats – she would know about those already, what with being 'head' of them. There was *something* going on though, because she kept whispering in the Beak's ear, and scribbling some very energetic notes.

'Tobermory?' she said, pointing her quill at him.

'*They rowed like fury,*' said Toby, '*with eight sets of oars pushing their boat frantically through the water…*'

'Pixy Scalybeak – carry on.'

'…*hurtling along, at five times the speed of a man walking.*' said Pixy.

'Fred Ogle,' said Creeps. 'Fred Ogle? Wake up boy…'

'…*but the botes were far too high, and kept crashing into the bridges, so…*'

'Lucretia? Your turn.'

Lucy looked up at the teachers, who were staring at her intently. And when she turned the page, she found out why – it was completely and utterly blank, and was obviously some kind of test.

'…*one year,*' said Lucy, deciding to make the best of the opportunity, '*the brightest scholars in the school created a new boat, a long thin one that could fit under bridges. And when they reached the Barnstorm Bridge, the boats did just that. Instead of being smashed to pieces they continued downstream, hurtling past the bandstand and the giant wardrobe store, and finally reaching a place called Puntknee without so much as the breadth of a hair between them.*'

Lucy looked up. The Niblock was writing so furiously that the feather on her quill cleaved the air like a wing, humming like a bird in flight. When she noticed the reading had stopped, Niblock paused for a moment, staring at Lucy and pointing her quill. It was an instruction to continue, but Lucy hesitated, inviting a stormy-black look from the Loppit gobbler. Just for the briefest of moments, she'd imagined the feather attached to Niblock's hand, not just held in her fingers, but actually growing out of her body.

'Yes, erm, well,' Lucy continued. '*The man in charge of the finishing gun was so surprised that he forgot to fire it and the boat crews took this as a signal. They thought they were being told to continue the race until one of the vessels pulled clearly ahead and could be judged the winner. Erm, yes, so, everyone on the bank started to run, following them past churches and warehouses and docks and under more and more and more bridges until finally they lost sight of the boats as they headed out towards the great wide sea…*'

The Beak began to cough violently, as if he'd inhaled a passing insect – and Lucy stopped reading, suddenly fascinated by the thought that the Loppit might still be croaking away inside Miss Niblock.

'*Sea?*' said the Haddock. 'Erm, yes, well I think we can probably stop there, don't you agree? Mr. Creeps? Miss Niblock?'

'Yes, I think we can,' said the Niblock, resting her quill.

'But why?' said Lucy, 'there's more.'

'I'm sure there is,' said Creeps, 'and frankly my dear, that's what worries us.'

'*Indeed,*' said the Haddock, 'but we're intrigued by your story, and wish to know more about this *sea* you mentioned.'

'What do you want to know?' said Lucy innocently.

'Well,' said the headmaster, 'do you, for instance, mean the *letter* C?'

'No,' said Lucy. 'That wouldn't make sense, would it? I meant the water.'

'River water?' said Creeps. 'But there's no such thing – it's a fable.'

'No it isn't,' said Lucy, 'but I didn't mean that anyway – I meant sea water.'

'Is that another name for drinking water?' said the Old Haddock.

'Of course not,' said Lucy. 'It tastes of salt, like the ocean.'

'I think we've heard *quite* enough of this,' whined Creeps. 'Don't you agree headmaster? This whole charade is nothing more than a diabolical attempt to disrupt my class. And I don't care if you are an arithmetical genius – I simply will not stand for it.'

'But I'm *not* an arithmetical genius,' said Lucy. 'And I'm not trying to upset your class either.'

'Then explain to us immediately what a *sea* is,' spat Creeps.

'And *what* in the name of all that's holy is an ocean?' said the Haddock.

Toby screwed his finger around at his temple, and fortunately for him, nobody had a clue what the sign meant.

'An ocean is just a big sea,' said Lucy, wearing an incredulous grin. 'Have you got a map? I'll show you – they're usually shown in shades of blue.'

'We *have* got maps, yes,' said Creeps, 'thank you very much for asking. And for *your* information it's the sky which is represented in blue.'

'The sky?' said Lucy. 'I don't think I've ever *seen* a map with sky on it. What about the land? What colour do you draw that?'

'Land?' said the headmaster, 'do you mean the city?'

'She means the country where the city *is*,' said Toby. 'And the other countries that surround you – what colour are they?'

'There *are* no other countries,' said Creeps. 'The only land that exists in the world is that which the city is built on. Whatever lies outside the city is part of the universal mysteries, and is therefore something that we can confidently leave in the hands of our betters.'

Miss Niblock smiled sagely at this point, as if she was one of those betters, or at least knew someone who was.

V𝑥v𝑥b⌐

Suddenly there was a lot of eager hand waving, which Creeps chose to ignore. Pixy Scalybeak was unable to wait though, and burst out chattering before he gave her permission to speak.

'And that's one of the great mysteries sir, isn't it? Just exactly how far down does the groundlings go?'

'*Do* the groundlings go,' corrected Creeps.

'Yes,' said Pixy. 'How far down do the groundlings go?'

'So,' said Lucy, ignoring this extra bit of confusion and shaking her head. 'Are you saying that the city is the whole world?'

'Absolutely,' said the Old Haddock.

'Well I'm sorry,' said Lucy, 'but that just *has* to be the biggest load of twaddle I've ever heard.'

There was an intake of breath around the class as the pupils considered this extremely unwise bit of cheek. Glassbone and Niblock began by scowling at Lucy, but their eyes soon moved to follow Creeps as he made his way to the corner of the room. He picked out an item that was too thin for a window pole and too thick for a cane, glancing back at his fellow teachers, as if seeking their approval. Niblock gave him a broad smile, and as she did so, Lucy noticed a fleck of Loppit blood on her lips.

Everyone knew what was coming and shrank visibly from Niblock's gaze, their eyes fixed on the battered desk lids. Lucy had gone too far, and was suddenly afraid. She lowered her gaze to the desk top, trembling at the thought of the unknown. And it was then that she noticed a trickling sound and the smelly pool of liquid at the feet of the boy sitting next to her.

'Lucretia, take note that you are to be punished,' said Creeps.

He took the tiny head cabinet from his desk and carefully screwed it into the top of the pole, making it into a kind of wand. Then he presented it to Miss Niblock, who marched slowly around the room, showing it to each of the innocent pupils. Nobody dared say anything – they simply sat in a frozen trance until she removed it from their faces, sighing with relief as she walked towards the next victim.

When it came to Lucy's turn, Miss Niblock stopped directly in front of her and rested the pole on the floor. The shrivelled face in the box was staring straight at her, like a dried up prune.

'*Stand,*' she said. 'And cup your hands at the side of your face. We don't want others to suffer for your misdeeds, do we?'

Lucy shook her head.

'*Do* we?' said Niblock, smashing the heavy base of the pole into the floor.

'Erm, no,' said Lucy nervously. She placed a hand on each temple, and looked at the floor. Her whole world consisted of just three things now – Niblock's feet, the bottom of the pole and an ever-expanding pool of wee.

'Look *up,*' the teacher commanded.

Lucy looked up as she'd been instructed, and Niblock moved the pole closer so that she could see every tiny detail of the face inside the cabinet. It was like a real person's head, but shrunk to the size of an egg – and it still had eyes. Before she had chance to examine it further though there was a flash of light and Lucy was no longer in the classroom. She tried to feel the rest of her body, but all she was aware of was her head. It was mounted inside a cabinet, staring out into an unfamiliar street through a dirty pane of glass. There were people passing by, and as they walked near the cabinet, a look of fear came over their faces and she found herself saying things to them. The worst part of it was that they were things she didn't believe, and she was unable to stop. Regardless of the efforts she made to stem the flow, the words just kept coming and coming, running out of her mouth like a polluted river.

Suddenly she was back in the classroom.

'A fraction of a second,' said Niblock with a vicious smile. 'Less time than it takes to gut a vangolin. *Now,* just imagine spending the rest of eternity like that, correcting your blasphemies by preaching truth to others. Would you *like* that?'

'No,' said Lucy, truthfully. 'I wouldn't – I feel sick.'

It was true. This was the worst she had felt since the day in the auction room when she saw the lining of Raziel's coat. That had been a particularly joyous experience, but when he closed the garment up, she felt just as she did now, as if someone was squeezing her soul, wringing every tear out of it, so they could drink her sorrow.

'Good,' said Niblock, sounding satisfied. 'Now pay attention to the rest of the lesson.' She glanced at the Haddock and then at Creeps – they were both wearing grins, as if they'd enjoyed the spectacle of torture immensely.

'*You,* boy,' said Creeps, 'Fred Ogle – get me the map.'

'Which one?' said Fred.

'Which *one,* boy? Do *you* want to see the truth as well?'

'Ner, ner, ner, *no* sir,' pleaded Fred.

'Then what have we been talking about? The map of the world of course – the *Mappa Mundi.*'

Fred ran to the cupboard as if his life depended on it and fetched back a roll of vellum that was at least three feet taller than he was. Then he stood beside Creeps, quietly awaiting his next command.

'*Desks,*' cried the teacher.

The children leaped to their feet and dragged the desks to the edges of the room, trying hard not to look at the damp floor in case it reminded them of the Lokey pole. When the space was cleared, Creeps rapped his truth wand against the floor and a circular section of it began to rise, stopping when it reached waist height.

'The *map,* boy,' commanded Creeps.

As soon as Fred Ogle had slapped the vellum onto the platform, Creeps began to unroll the map. As he did so, eight regularly spaced slots opened around the periphery and a set of bony fingers emerged from each, their long nails curling over the edge and digging into the pliable surface of the map. Lucy was taken aback by the sudden appearance of the skeletal hands, but even more surprised when a bright light appeared in the air near her shoulder. It fizzed slightly, smelling of sulphur, and shone a warm, reddish light over the map, hinting at where the shadows might fall if only there were buildings to cast them.

'This is the Mappa Mundi,' said Creeps. 'Otherwise known as the Map of the World. It was drawn up by our most eminent cartographer, Smegley Pratt. *Now* Lucretia, do you recognise anything?'

Lucy moved closer, keeping a careful eye on the nearest set of fingers. The map was blue around the edges, just as the master had promised, and displayed the legend '*Deepe Skye Abysses*' everywhere outside the city walls.

'This is Farperoo,' said Lucy, indicating the blue area.

'On a child's map, yes,' said Creeps. 'Children of a certain tender age are told that out beyond the walls of the city lies the land of Farperoo – it's just a tale though, for infants – and *you* two apparently.'

'We were just joking,' said Toby.

'Yes,' said Creeps, 'I *know* you were, because nobody can actually come from Farperoo, *can* they?'

'No, they can't,' said Lucy, eager to avoid a second taste of the wand.

'*And*,' said Creeps, 'as you will readily see from the map, there is no such thing as a river.'

'And beyond the city walls you will observe nothing but the holy sky,' added the Old Haddock. 'There is absolutely no sign of a sea *or* an ocean.'

'And why should there be,' said Niblock, 'when we have everything we need within these stout walls?'

'When you put it like that,' said Lucy, 'I don't suppose you *do* need anything else, do you?'

Toby scowled, disappointed that all the fight had suddenly been sucked out of his friend. Lucy returned his look and knew what he was thinking. It was alright for *him* though, wasn't it? *His* soul didn't have the truth wand's teeth marks in it. She leaned inwards, pointing at various locations on the map and listening as a familiar voice announced their names.

'*Frembley Craddock's Fried Pig-a-Torium.*'

'*The Howse of the Musitians in Threepenny Grunt Lane.*'

'*Honk Smallpiece – his Privatt Howse and Dunny Hole.*'

'*Snurdly Boggs' Loppit Lavatory.*'

'*The Sorcerer's Great Howse, down by the Morty Lakes.*'

'It's just like the other one,' said Lucy.

'The one that Gusset showed us,' said Toby, jumping in quickly. If the teachers knew they'd been in his room on their own there was no telling what trouble it might cause.

'Gusset has no business to show you anything,' said Haddock. 'His teaching days are long gone.'

'It was just a simple childrens' model,' said Lucy. 'I'm sure it couldn't show us *half* the things that the Mappa Mundi can.'

'You are correct,' said the headmaster proudly. 'This map is perfect down to the last detail. Who for instance, would imagine that we would be able to see the tiles on the roof of the Emperor's palace?'

'Or count the red velvet seats at the Theatre of Misery and Great Sadness?' said Creeps.

'Or be able to make out the dried-up remains of a river?' suggested Lucy. She drew her finger along an area of the map that hadn't been shown on Gusset's version. In fact, she wasn't entirely certain it had been on *this* one until a few moments ago. The broad brown line stretched all the way from one side of the map to the other, twisting and turning like a snake, erasing any suggestion of the houses and buildings in its path. Plenty more sprang up in the wake of her finger though, sprouting to the north and south of the serpentine form. They rose from the fabric of the map like iron filings attracted to a magnet, complete in every detail and casting shadows in the light from the artificial sun. It was almost as if they could swoop down and peer through each microscopic window, to spy on the tiny inhabitants.

'And where did *those* come from?' hissed Creeps.

'It's like a snake,' said the Old Haddock, 'a line of ants, all following…'

'*Sacrilege,*' hissed Niblock. 'That's what it is…'

As Lucy finished tracing her finger from west to east, she finally came to the edge – where her imaginary river would flow into the unknown. And that was where she dwelled for a moment, in the knowledge that the map had something more to tell them.

'*The Meanderings of the River Isis,*' said the familiar, soft voice, '*and the Boddy Pittes of the Morty Lakes.*'

A shocked silence took hold of the classroom as everyone held their breath – even the three traumatized teachers. But eventually, everyone had to let go, and with a loud gasp of air, the spell of the Isis was broken. The houses disappeared from the map, swiftly followed by the churches and the warehouses and the new-born river – and then the sun winked out too, and the map rolled up with a plop, as if the bony hands had suddenly decided it was too dangerous to touch.

Niblock stared at Lucy, her soft copper hair suddenly looking a lot wilder. Her eyes had narrowed to thin, carnivorous slits and were focussed completely on the young storyteller.

'Erm, I *think* it might be time for tea,' said the Old Haddock, somewhat nervously. He was quite pale and seemed to be having difficulty standing up.

'Erm, ye-es,' agreed Creeps, trembling slightly. 'Or perhaps we might even take something a little stronger?'

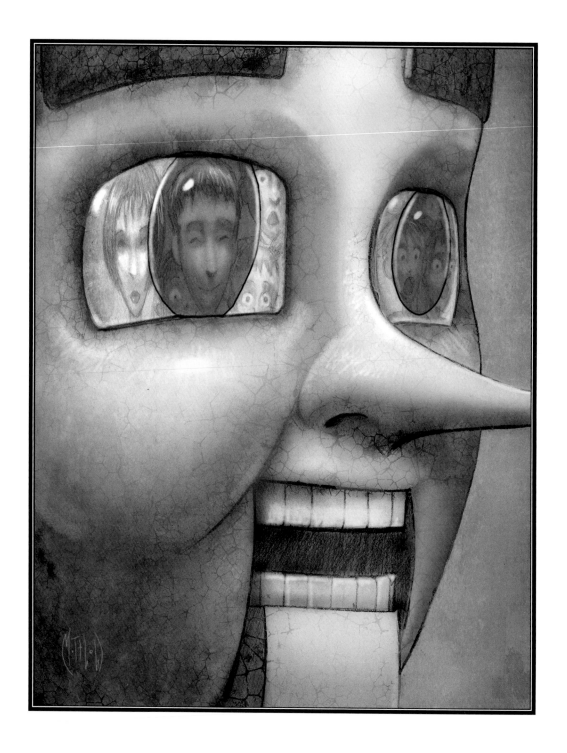

Venter

Lokey

'*How* many steps did you say there were?' said Toby. He paused for a moment to listen for the answer, and made the mistake of leaning on the tightly curved wall. It felt like ice, and set his teeth on edge.

'Four hundred,' shouted Pixy, from somewhere up ahead.

'And how many have we done?' shouted Toby. 'I'm getting dizzy.'

'I don't know,' said Pixy, 'I can only count up to seventeen.'

'Great,' said Toby, waiting for Lucy to catch up. 'In that case I suppose I'll have to ask our arithmetical genius. Luce? Are you alright back there?'

'Ask me when we get to the top,' breathed Lucy, peering around the upward curve of the spiral. Her new smock felt like it had once contained potatoes. In fact it was so uncomfortable there was a possibility that some of them might still be in it. On balance, she preferred the fit and the smell of her old dress, but suspected she'd seen the last of it.

'Nice sack you're wearing,' grinned Toby.

'Thanks,' said Lucy. 'I'll ask if they've got one in your size.'

'Right,' he smiled, 'but listen, I've been thinking.'

'Well don't,' grinned Lucy, 'you know how dangerous that can be.'

'No, *seriously* – we don't need to follow the rest of them – we're last in line, so we could just turn round and go back down.'

'And then what?' said Lucy, 'I'm pretty sure they locked the door at the bottom, and I don't know about you, but I haven't seen any windows for the past three hundred and fifty steps.'

'Me neither,' he admitted, 'and I don't expect there'll be any up ahead. So now what?'

'I think we should just play along,' said Lucy.

'Good idea,' said Toby. 'We can't come to any harm if we stick with the others, can we?'

'Don't bank on it,' said Lucy. 'Just keep thinking about that wand.'

'Oh, yeah, *that*,' said Toby, 'it looked painful.'

'It wasn't just pain,' said Lucy. 'It went a lot deeper than that, like having something thinking inside you. Anyway let's try to be positive.'

'A bit difficult,' said Toby, 'given the circumstances.'

'At least they let me keep the bag,' said Lucy. 'When Creeps had a look inside it in the dining hall, I could have sworn he was going to confiscate it.'

'Yeah,' said Toby, 'that *was* weird, wasn't it? He didn't bat an eyelid.'

'He probably sees bags with vent dummies and ancient manuscripts inside them every day,' grinned Lucy.

'But he *can't*,' said Toby, 'and that's why I reckon there's something fishy going on. I just haven't managed to work it out yet.'

'Well I've worked out at least one thing,' said Lucy.

'Oh,' said Toby. 'What's that?'

'My stepmother's a *brilliant* cook compared with this lot.'

'Too right,' agreed Toby. 'I hope you've still got that emergency food because I'm starving. One part of *my* dinner had an ear, and I'll swear it was listening to me – and there was another bit too, with suckers.'

'Lovely,' said Lucy.

'Yeah,' said Toby. 'I stuck it to the underside of the table.'

'I gave all *my* food to Pixy,' said Lucy. 'So maybe she'll repay us with a favour.'

'I wouldn't count on it,' said Toby, 'if someone did *me* a favour like that I'd throw up on them. The meals in this place are disgusting.'

'I know,' giggled Lucy. 'I stopped looking at mine when it began blinking. I can't *stand* food that wears eye makeup. But if you get the sucky special again you should hang onto it. We might be able to attach it to our hands and knees and use it to climb down the walls.'

'Yeah, *right*, that sounds like a great idea,' said Toby. He returned to the climb, and with each weary step, he tried to imagine hanging from the outer wall of the Braneskule with nothing but a piece of soggy dinner between them and a painful death.

'Come on,' shouted Neeba, 'we have to find you some beds.'

Toby emerged from the stairwell and stepped into the dormitory, closely followed by Lucy.

'That's the best idea I've heard for a long while,' he said. 'I feel as though I haven't slept for a week.'

'And you think you'll get sleep in *here*?' said Lucy.

'*Wow*,' said Toby looking up at the roof. 'It's *enormous*. When they said the dormitory was in the attic, I imagined something like we've got at home – full of cardboard boxes and those old toasters my dad tried to fix.'

'You'd need more than a few toasters to fill this place up,' said Lucy. 'But if you could get them working then at least we'd have some heat.'

'Yeah,' said Toby, breathing out purposefully, and watching his words condense in the cold air. 'There's just one slight flaw in that plan though.'

'And what's that?' said Lucy.

'Haven't you noticed yet? They don't have Lectric.'

Lucy's brow wrinkled as she tried to think of all the places they'd been in the Braneskule.

'Hmm, you might be right,' she said. 'There was nothing in Gusset's room, was there? And nothing in the classroom either.'

'And the food was cooked on flaming great stoves,' said Toby. 'I peeked into the kitchen when the doors were swinging, and I reckon the most advanced thing they had in there was a hammer for mashing potatoes.'

'What's Lectric?' said Neeba.

Lucy smiled, recalling what their physics teacher often said about cramming science into the heads of innocent babes. Now it seemed, she was faced with the same task.

'It's a sort of magic fluid,' she said, winking at Toby. 'It flows down pipes and you can burn it in lamps to make light.'

'Like goose oil?' said Pixy.

'Something like that,' replied Lucy.

'Yeah, well we don't get given oil to bring up here,' said Neeba.

'That's right,' said Pixy. 'When it gets dark that's it.'

The thought of being without light suddenly worried Lucy and she scanned the dormitory, trying to familiarise herself with the layout. Even without a firm plan, it was always a good idea to know where you fitted into the landscape. The apex of the roof was about fifty feet above the floor and the beams supporting it were at least four-feet thick, carrying slates the size of snooker tables. It was difficult to imagine how they might have been lifted up there even if they had been on the first storey, but if Gusset was to be believed then the roof was more than five thousand feet from the ground.

'This is the highest place in the world,' said Neeba, noticing the way they were both looking round. 'Apart from the Tower of Merciful Blades that is.'

'We've heard of that,' said Lucy, 'we saw it on a map.'

'Ah, but you ain't seen it for real though, have you?' said Neeba.

'And we're not likely to, up here,' said Toby. 'Unless you've got a window we don't know about.'

'Why don't we show them?' said Pixy. 'Before the light goes?'

'And how are you going to do that?' said Lucy. She had been trying to work out how to reach the high, vaulted windows – and unless Toby had been studying acrobatics in secret, they weren't going to be a great deal of help.

'You won't see out of *them*,' said Phyllida. 'But you won't *need* to, not if you're heavy enough.'

'Come on,' said Phyllida, pointing at a flagstone that seemed slightly lighter in colour than the others, 'we've all got to stand on this slab.'

'And then what?' said Toby.

'Then we pray,' said Pixy.

'Really? What exactly are we praying for?' said Lucy.

'How heavy are you?' said Phyllida.

'About seven stone,' said Lucy.

'Me too,' said Toby, 'give or take.'

'Then we have to pray that two times seven is enough,' said Phyllida.

'That's twelve,' said Toby, grinning at Lucy.

'*Is* it?' said Phyllida. 'Thanks, I'll try to remember.'

Lucy glared as they gathered on the slab, obviously not impressed with Toby's little joke. There was no time to reproach him though, because as soon as they were all in position the roof slates began to move, bobbing and floating out of the way, like plastic ducks on a fairground stall.

'Neat,' said Toby, sounding impressed. 'Now what?'

As if it had been lurking above them and waiting for the question, a spiral staircase appeared, turning and lowering itself through the gap like a huge corkscrew.

'Not *bad*,' said Toby.

'Wait till you get outside,' said Pixy, '*then* you'll see.'

The whole class mounted the stairs and climbed the fifty or so steps, eventually emerging onto a flimsy rooftop platform. There was a faint breeze, and the air was cool against their exposed skin.

'Is it safe?' said Toby, shivering already. He tested the strength of the structure with springy little jumps.

'Oh, yes,' said Neeba. 'It's perfectly safe – it's *you* that's in danger, especially if you keep doing *that*.'

'Very funny,' said Toby, 'I'm going to take your name down, just in case I need to complain about plummeting to a painful death.'

'Well whilst you're in the complaints department can you get them to do something about the cold?' said Lucy. 'Or maybe we could bring your dad's toasters out here?'

'What's a toaster?' said Neeba.

'Something I wish I hadn't mentioned,' laughed Lucy. 'Look, are you *sure* this thing is safe?'

'Well it's been up here since the beginning of the world,' said Pixy. 'And there's no real wind today, so I *think* we're *definitely* safe.'

'That's good to know,' said Toby, still not convinced. He studied Pixy's expression closely and eventually decided she was serious – they actually believed that the world was only thirteen years old.

Lucy walked to the edge of the platform where a rope had been stretched across to stop people dropping off. It would be a simple matter for her to step over it though, and after that, there was nothing at all, just a mile of plummeting, screaming, and waiting for the ground to come up and hit her in the face.

'It's so *quiet*,' she whispered, as she peered over the edge.

She had expected to hear the sounds of the city rising up to meet them but realised now that it was all too far away. Instead, there was a dense wall of silence, far quieter than anything she had ever known.

'This is *amazing*,' she said, gathering her arms around her to keep the cold at bay. 'It's *huge*, like something out of a dream.'

'Nightmare, more like,' said Toby.

'If you get a clear day,' said Neeba, 'you can see the whole world from up here. It's not so good now though. The northern rim is covered in mist, so the Great Winding Crayns are hidden – but you can make out the other quadrants easily enough.'

Lucy grinned at Toby, finally beginning to believe what they had been told all along. The maps they had seen really *did* show the whole of the world, or the city, or whatever it was they wanted to call it. Which meant that the void beyond the city walls really *was* Farperoo. Percy *would* be pleased, she thought, if only he could be here to see it.

'You haven't mentioned the Tower of Merciful Blades,' said Lucy.

'And I shan't,' said Pixy, staying well away from the edge. 'It's cursed, and anyone that talks about it gets cursed as well.'

'It's just a building,' said Toby. 'A pretty impressive one, I'll grant you that, but it's just a pile of bricks and mortar. So it can't be cursed.'

'That's all *you* know,' said Pixy.

'She's right,' said Neeba. 'The tower *is* cursed – and it isn't made out of bricks and mortar neither.'

'So what *is* it made of then?' said Toby.

'Don't know,' said Neeba. 'I've never been anywhere near it. No one has, except people from the olden days and they're all gone now.'

'So you can't just walk up to it then?' asked Lucy.

'You can't even get close,' said Fred. 'My uncle tried it once, a long time ago, and he got turned back by the guards when he was over a mile away. This is the best view of it you'll ever get.'

Lucy was still trying to get over the sheer height of the Braneskule, and wasn't really ready for the tower yet. It was ready for her though, and simply demanded to be looked at. Even from this great distance, it dominated the skyline, dwarfing every other building in the city, threatening them and pressing them into the ground with its massive bulk. Lucy estimated that it was twice as high as the Braneskule, which would make it around ten thousand feet to the point of its sharpened-looking spire.

'What is it for?' she said. 'And why is it so high?'

'And what does it look like during the day?' said Toby.

'The night is the best time to look,' said Pixy. 'The curse won't get you if you look at it in shadow. But if you're *really* interested in seeing it then you can come up here tomorrow morning. The sun's the other way round then and you can see all you like – I won't be coming though.'

'Me neither,' said Neeba. The others seemed to agree and were all shaking their heads.

'It's bad luck,' said Fred.

'It's worse than that,' said Pixy. 'I *told* you, the Migdal is cursed.'

'The Migdal?' said Lucy.

'Ignore her,' said Neeba, 'she's showing off – it's just another name for the tower.'

'Oh,' said Lucy She was thinking about things that had more than one name. For some reason Harry and his pigeons sprang to mind, and one of the birds in particular – she was thinking of Lilith.

'Lots of things have more than one name,' said Lucy.

'Yeah,' said Toby, guessing what she was up to. 'And I'll bet you anything that your name for the city is different to ours.'

'I don't think so,' said Pixy. 'Assiah – that's the only name we know.'

'Ah, so it *is* the same as our name,' said Lucy with a wink. 'See Toby? You owe Pixy anything she wants.'

'Right,' grinned Toby.

'So tell me,' said Lucy, 'was the city actually *designed* like this?'

'Yeah,' laughed Toby, 'or did you have an earthquake?'

'Oh, *no*,' said Pixy, quite seriously. 'I think this is how it was intended.'

The sky-borne mass of the Migdal was supported on four huge legs that looked as though they belonged to some monstrous creature accustomed to carrying heavy weights. They were *still* buckling under the strain though, and as a result, the tower leaned at a perilous angle. It wasn't on its own in this respect though, because the majority of the city's buildings were tilted in the same haphazard fashion. Fortunately, they were all interlinked by bridges and walkways, so if any of them felt like leaning a bit too far the others would hold them up. It was almost as if Assiah had been built straight but then been left in the melting sun or subjected to some strange twisting curse.

'So let me get this straight,' whispered Toby to Lucy. 'Their spelling is optional, their arithmetic is non-existent, and their geometry is completely open for discussion.'

'Well I like it,' whispered Lucy, 'straight lines aren't everything, are they? In fact, I think the threat of imminent collapse makes it all the more beautiful – it's like some delicate spider's web that might get blown away at any moment.'

'Yeah,' said Toby, 'it's a pity for the people who used to make the set-squares and rulers though, – they probably went out of business years ago – just look at all those swoops and curves and sharp sticky-out bits.'

'Perhaps they're sleeping dragons?' said Lucy.

'Oooh, like in the tome?' giggled Pixy.

'I don't know,' said Lucy. 'I didn't get a chance to read that particular story, but that's what they look like to me.'

'Erm, *Lu-cre-tia*?' said Pixy. 'Please will you tell us another story, like that one about the botes?'

'Yeah, go on,' said Phyllida and Fred together. They sat down on the platform, gathering their thin clothes around their shoulders as the cold of night descended.

'Yeah,' said Ned. 'We never get to hear any new stories. Just the ones in the tome, and they're boring. But that one you told us in the classroom Lucretia, well it was sort of amazing, like it was real.'

'It *was* real,' said Pixy enthusiastically. 'Go on, tell us about the dragons.'

'Do you mean the Weary Dragons of Farperoo?' smiled Lucy.

'If that's what they're called,' said Neeba with a shiver. The rest of the children nodded. If Lucretia's dragons had to have a name then it was as good as any other.

'Well,' said Lucy, 'if we're looking for a story about the scaly hordes then we need to go back to the beginning of the world.'

'What?' said Pixy, 'thirteen years back?'

'Goodness me, *no*,' said Lucy, 'it was *much* further back than that – in a time when the River Isis flowed as free as milk and the city was just a dream in the minds of a wandering tribe.'

'Was that before the world was created then?' said Neeba.

'It was,' said Lucy seriously, 'around the same time that the wars between the dragon lords and the hordes of heaven were coming to an end.'

'*Oh*,' said Pixy, sounding as though she was falling into a trance.

'It's hard to imagine in these *modern* days,' said Lucy, winking at Toby, 'but try to visualise the sky if you can, blackened by the presence of thousands of scaly winged creatures. Just picture them all, hanging there in the dusk, flapping in from the Great Beeyond at their slowest speed.'

'But *why* were they coming?' said Pixy.

'They were looking for a place to rest,' said Lucy. 'These were the battle dragons, injured and bleeding from the wars – every one of them limb-weary and wing-tired, from all those endless years spent in the air.'

'*Oh*,' said Pixy. 'Were there a lot of them then?'

'Of course,' nodded Lucy. 'They came in dribs and drabs at first, but soon they were gathering in huge numbers, all of them desperate to find a haven where they could safely lay their heads.'

'And they found this place?' suggested Pixy.

Lucy nodded again and smiled. It was a long time since she'd told a story to such an appreciative audience.

'They circled around at first,' she said, 'waiting for the fire-elders to decide if the place was suitable. But the old smoke breathers couldn't make up their minds, so the fighters had to keep circling, all the time getting weaker and weaker. Nearly a year went by, and the decision *still* wasn't made.'

'Did they fall out of the sky?' interrupted Pixy.

'No,' said Lucy, 'they didn't fall, but they knew that they couldn't fly for much longer.'

'So they landed?' said Pixy.

'There was no other choice,' said Lucy. 'They flared their great wings out to gather the pure-born air and glided down to the earth – *our* earth.'

'What happened next?' said Pixy, breathless with anticipation.

Lucy paused to examine her audience. Their mouths had dropped open in wonder, and every eye was fixed upon her, eager to hear what happened next – she was telling stories, and she was *so* happy.

'Some of the dragons wanted to celebrate the landings,' she smiled. 'But eventually they realised they were too tired for all that frolicking, so they just settled on the ground, tucked their great heads in and folded up their wings.'

'And then what?' said Fred.

'They fell asleep, stupid,' said Neeba.

'That's right,' said Lucy, 'they went into a deep slumber, dreaming of the day they would wake and continue their odyssey. But all those battles and the long flight back from the wars had left them feeling drained – so much so that they slept for two and half millennia.'

'Is that a long time?' said Neeba.

'If you're a dragon it's not so bad,' explained Lucy, 'but it's a long time in the lives of men.'

'I know,' said Neeba impatiently. 'I bet something happened when they were asleep.'

'That's right,' smiled Lucy. 'When they finally woke from their slumbers the dragons discovered that a great city had been built – it was all around them, and even on top of them.'

'*This* city?' said Pixy, her eyes alight with wonder at the new story.

'Yes,' said Lucy, '*this* city – just look at all those low buildings – can you see how they follow the contours of the sleeping dragons? And there's more evidence in the high spires and the towers – do you see the way they echo the points of their tails and claws?'

Everyone except Toby and Fred seemed to agree that they *could* see a similarity and they nodded eagerly, gazing down into the city in a search for telltale signs of the hidden beasts.

'So have *all* the buildings got dragons beneath them?' said Pixy.

'Of *course* not,' said Lucy, 'that would be far too much of a good thing. The secret of a good story is to leave little pockets of mystery, so the listener will always be left wondering.'

'That's us,' said Neeba, 'we're the ones doing the wondering.'

'And we don't know which buildings hide dragons,' said Pixy. 'Some of them are just built in the *style* of dragon sharps, but others have got *real* claws poking from their cornices and *real* dragons sleeping beneath them.'

'So now you know,' said Lucy. 'That's the story of the dragons.'

'But why don't they just fly away?' said Pixy, apparently not satisfied that they had come to the end.

'Yeah,' laughed Toby, 'why don't these famous dragons just fly off?'

'Because the buildings are far too heavy,' snapped Lucy. 'And there's another reason too,' she said, glaring at Toby. 'Do you see all those things that look like bats flying around the spires?'

'They don't just *look* like bats,' said Pixy. 'They *are* bats.'

'That's what *you* think,' said Lucy, 'but those are the scales from the dragons' wings, and as you'll probably know, the race of Draco can't fly without them.'

'Could they fly if they got their scales back?' said Pixy.

'We'll never know,' said Lucy, 'because nobody can remember the secret sound that's used to summon the scales.'

'And nobody cares,' said Fred, 'because it's all just a load of rubbish.'

'Well *I* care,' said Pixy.

'You *would*,' said Fred, 'you believe in all sorts.'

'It's better than not believing,' said Pixy. 'Will you tell us what happened to the dragons next, Lucretia?'

'No,' smiled Lucy. 'I think you have to imagine the rest yourself.'

The sun was beginning to set now, flooding the city with a blood-red tide, as if the spires and sharp-edged roofs had ripped open the belly of the fading sunlight. With no wind to speak of, columns of smoke rose vertically from every chimney, mingling as they climbed and forming a transparent blanket that hovered above the city. It was just as Lucy had described in her story – the buildings looked exactly like sleeping dragons, the smoke forming a veil that hung like a canopy over their massive bed.

'That was brilliant,' enthused Pixy, 'and there *are* dragons out there – real ones – I can see them.'

'No you can't,' said Neeba, 'it was just a story.'

'That's right,' said Lucy with a smile, 'and now it's your turn – you have to tell Toby and me a tale.'

'But I don't *know* any,' protested Pixy.

'Then tell us something that's true,' suggested Lucy, 'about the city.'

'Alright,' said Pixy, 'see over there? Well that's where I used to live when I was little.' She pointed to a huge building to the east of the tower, right at the end of the arterial road that led to the rim.

'My mother was Ocular Prefect at the Great Observatory. She was in charge of looking for other worlds.'

'*Other* worlds?' said Lucy, suddenly intrigued. 'And erm, what happened?'

She peered into the distance, trying to get a better look at the observatory. The place was in ruins, in common with quite a few others.

'It was closed down when the belief came,' said Pixy. 'Nobody was bothered though, because they never managed to find anything – just loads of clouds.'

'Closed down?' said Toby. 'It looks a bit more final than that. I'll bet Adam Knox gave them a hand to burn it down.'

'It *was* burned down,' said Pixy, 'but it was the Vooghul who did it. I don't think anyone called Knox was involved.'

'Ignore him,' said Lucy, 'He's just being stupid, *aren't* you Tobermory? Why don't you tell us what happened to your mother, Pixy?'

The young girl's eyes had reddened as she described the burning of the observatory, and they were filling with tears now as she remembered the loss of her mother. Her eyes were like fiery, water-filled marbles, and each time she blinked, a pair of warm tears spilled onto the ground.

'The *Vooghul* took her,' sobbed Pixy, 'they came to the ocular room one night, when we were polishing the lenses on the Mundus Magni-Ficat. They smashed everything up and set fire to it – they *even* burned the written records, which as you know are sacred.'

'Erm, *are* they?' said Lucy.

'Of course,' scoffed Neeba, 'everything that's written down is sacred – didn't you know that? It's how things are created.'

'Oh,' said Lucy. 'I didn't realise – erm, and who are these Vooghul?'

'Bad people,' said Neeba, '*very* bad people.'

'I see,' said Lucy, 'and is that all you know?'

'That's enough, isn't it?' said Phyllida.

'They took *my* parents too,' said Fred. 'They worked in the Ministry of Impossible Regions, until it got burned to the ground.'

'My parents have gone as well,' said Neeba. 'They were doing secret work for the Emperor, just like my great uncle. I lived with him for a while after they disappeared, but the Emperor had me sent away, so he could get on with his work – he's a famous sorcerer.'

'Yeah, *right*,' said Toby. 'I think you mentioned him once before.'

'You don't believe me, do you?' said Neeba. 'Well he lives over *there* on the western rim.' She pointed to the left of the great tower, following a gap in the buildings that suggested the route of the dried up river.

'That's right,' said Lucy, 'I remember it from the lesson with the Mappa Mundi, *The Sorcerer's great Howse, down by the Morty Lakes.*'

'*See?*' said Neeba. 'It *says* it on the Mappa Mundi.'

'And on Smegley Pratt's Skule Edition as well,' said Pixy, drying her eyes on the hem of her smock.

'It doesn't prove he's a sorcerer though,' said Toby. 'Do you remember the advert Percy did for Grimston Corporation Lucy? It said *Grimston-on-Sea, a great place to come for a holiday,* and *that* wasn't true either.'

'It doesn't matter *what* her great uncle does for a living does it?' said Lucy. 'He could be one of those people who go down sewers in thigh length waders for all I care. We're not likely to be visiting him, *are* we? I'm more interested in finding out what's going on round here – for instance, why were everyone's parents taken away by the Vooghul?'

'*What?*' said Toby. '*All* of them?'

'Of course,' said Pixy, 'everyone in the Braneskule is an orphan because their parents were taken away.'

'And the teachers study us all the time,' said Neeba. 'To see if we can tell stories.'

'And what if you can?' said Lucy.

'Don't rightly know,' said Fred. 'The ones who *can* tell them never come back.'

'Just like our parents,' said Neeba.

'So what happened to them?' said Toby.

'Nobody knows,' said Neeba. 'Why don't you tell us what happened to *your* parents Mister Nosey?'

'Mine passed away in a tragic mincing machine accident,' grinned Toby.

'Oh yes, I remember now,' said Neeba seriously. '*Sorry.*'

Lucy glanced at Toby and counted off a score of four on her fingers. He grinned, apparently pleased with the way his storytelling abilities were improving.

'What about yours, Lucretia?'

'You can call me Lucy,' she said with a laugh. She was trying to think of a way to explain what a ferry funnel was, but in the end, she decided that the truth was probably just a little bit too complicated.

'My father choked to death on a gherkin and pineapple doughnut,' she said. 'The person who was chewing it before him lost their false teeth and they got stuck in his throat.'

'Oh,' said Neeba, looking slightly confused.

'And my mother disappeared from a locked room,' said Lucy, thinking that this would be quite ordinary compared to her father's untimely exit.

'*No!*' shouted Pixy, obviously in some shock.

'Maybe she thinks *you'll* disappear as well?' suggested Toby.

'Disappear?' Pixy yelped. 'You can't do that, can you?'

'Hey, don't panic,' said Toby, 'I was only joking.'

'Were you, really?' said Pixy.

'Of course,' he said, 'we can't disappear, can we, Luce?'

'Not so's you'd notice,' said Lucy, 'at least not yet.'

'Well perhaps *you* can't disappear, but *they* can,' said Pixy.

'Oh, not *this* again,' said Fred.

'What? Who?' said Toby.

'I'm talking about the angels,' said Pixy. '*They* do it all the time.'

'No they don't,' said Ned, the boy with the famously empty arithmetic book. 'They don't do anything of the sort, because they don't exist.'

'They do *so* exist,' insisted Pixy.

'They don't,' said Ned, 'it's just made-up stories. My mum says it's a load of rubbish. Or at least that's what she *used* to say, before they came to the Faculty of Unusual Occurrences and took her away.'

'Yeah?' said Fred, 'Well my Uncle Philebas has actually seen one – and he actually *spoke* to it.'

'And I'll bet he was *actually* asking it to buy him a drink,' said Ned. 'That's the only way that *he* ever sees angels, when he's soaked up to the eyeballs in snot-ale – they always disappear when he sobers up.'

'Toby?' said Pixy. 'Do you have angels where you come from?'

They stopped for a moment to look towards the horizon where a huge blue-tinted moon had just begun to show itself. Lucy looked at Toby and smiled, as if to reconfirm that they were still really here. Just as they became accustomed to one part of the world, up popped another thing to keep them guessing.

'Erm, Luce, I think you'd better answer that one,' said Toby.

Lucy frowned, wondering what to say. It was what Percy would call a loaded question, because there were all sorts of traps it might spring. Where did she and Toby come from, for instance? And how did they get here? And if she confirmed the existence of Raziel, well, that was a completely different minefield…

'I don't know,' she said eventually. 'It's one of those things you can't be sure about, isn't it?'

'Yes,' said Pixy. There was a pause and Lucy knew instantly what they were all thinking. She had claimed to come from Farperoo and now they wanted to know the truth.

'It's a place called Grimston,' she said, without waiting to be asked.

'Is that near the Winding Crayns then?' said Pixy. 'None of us has ever been that far.'

'Yes,' said Lucy, breathing a sigh of relief and winking at Toby.

'I *knew* it,' squealed Pixy, 'they're from the same place.'

'The same place as who?' said Lucy.

'The *girl* of course.'

'What girl?' asked Lucy.

'The girl you're looking for.'

'Who?' said Toby. 'We don't know…'

Lucy elbowed him in the ribs.

'Who do you *think* we're looking for?' said Lucy.

'There was this girl,' said Neeba. 'We were all talking about it at dinner and I bet my next three plates of snork livers that you'd be looking for her. She's about your age, with freckles and long blonde hair – she went through about a week ago.'

'That sounds like our *friend*,' said Lucy with a wink.

'It does,' said Toby. 'When did you see her? Was she in your class?'

'Just for a while,' said Neeba.

'And where she is now?' said Lucy.

'She could be *anywhere*,' said Toby. 'You can go a long way in seven days.'

'Eh?' said Neeba. 'There's *nine* days in a week, *stupid*. Didn't they teach you any-fink at your last school?'

'Apparently not,' grinned Toby, 'I must have been away that day.'

'What was she called?' said Lucy. 'You must remember *that*, surely?'

'Dunno,' said Pixy. 'She hardly spoke – she was only here a few hours, then they came and took her away, just like Creeps threatened.'

'She spoke to me,' smiled Fred. 'It was the day I ate three servings of Loppit all in one go, do you remember? I threw up all over the place.'

'How could we forget?' said Pixy.

'Yeah, well, she said she could see inside me,' said Fred. 'She reckoned my guts were all twisted.'

'They *were*,' said Neeba. 'And we can still remember the stink you made when they *untwisted*.'

'That sounds like Fenny,' said Lucy. 'Do you know where she went?'

'*I* might do,' said Neeba, turning to go back downstairs. 'And I might even tell you, but only if you show us what's in the bag.'

'Hmm,' said Lucy, 'erm, alright then – but it's getting a bit cold up here. Shall we go back inside?'

They all trooped down the stairs, and when the last of them stepped away from the spiral, it disappeared through the hole in the roof, which promptly re-sealed itself.

'It's getting a bit dark,' said Lucy, 'shouldn't we wait until morning?'

'No,' insisted Pixy, 'we want to see it now, *don't* we?'

Everyone nodded, eager to see what mysterious artefacts the inhabitants of far-flung Grimston might carry around on their back.

'Come on,' said Fred, 'let's get on with it – then we can get some sleep.'

They dragged some beds together to form an impromptu theatre, and as they sat down, an expectant hush descended on the room. Lucy remained standing and made a great show of removing her rucksack and searching inside, as if she was having great difficulty finding something.

'Don't you *dare* bite me,' she said suddenly.

'I non't gite you,' said a voice from the bag.

'*Aaagh*, it's *alive*,' screamed Pixy. She leapt from the bed and jumped away from Lucy, pointing at the shape that was moving inside the rucksack.

'Od *course* I'n alide,' said the voice.

'Pixy's right,' shouted Fred, 'it's *alive*.'

Lucy pulled Genjamin out with a triumphant gesture, expecting to get some applause – so it came as a bit of a shock when she finally *did* get a reaction.

'Aaaahh, *no*,' screamed Neeba, 'put it away – *put it away*.'

'Can I hag a choc-lit giscuit kleese?' said Genjamin, winking one of his huge eyebrows.

'No,' shouted Fred, standing up on the bed. 'Take it away.'

'He only wants a biscuit,' said Toby, 'and if you haven't got a chocolate one then I'm sure a plain one will do.'

'No it gluddy non't,' said Genjamin. '*Choc-lit, choc-lit, choc-lit, choc-lit, choc…*'

'Stop it,' screamed Pixy. 'Stop it. Stop it. Stop it.'

'Alright, *alright*,' said Lucy, turning the puppet face down so that nobody had to look at his ugly mug. Even so, his mouth continued to move, whispering *choc-lit, choc-lit, choc-lit*, over and over.

'*There*,' said Lucy. 'I've stopped – alright?' She returned the puppet to the bag and pulled the drawstrings tight, making it obvious to them all what was going on.

'He won't get out of *there* in a hurry, *will* he Toby?'

'No, he's well and truly locked up,' grinned Toby.

'Don't *do* that,' screamed Neeba.

'What?' said Toby.

'*That*,' said Neeba, 'treating us like children.'

'Oh,' said Toby, 'but I thought…'

'We *know* it's just a puppet,' said Pixy. 'It's the Venter Lokey we don't like – you *know* what that is, don't you? Venter Lokey means to speak from the stomach – we did it in Lattinn studies.'

'Actually that's right,' said Lucy. 'The vicar told me the same thing. Venter means stomach and Loqui means to speak.'

'Yes, and it's completely *evil*,' said Neeba. '*That's* what it is, *evil*. All those stories coming straight out of your soul. Because that's where your soul is you know, in your stomach – that's why it burns when you're frightened or if you're excited.'

'But I thought you *liked* stories?' said Lucy, somewhat puzzled. 'You let me tell you about the dragons, didn't you?'

'That was different,' said Neeba. 'The dragons came out of your head, didn't they?'

'I don't know,' said Lucy, 'I *suppose* so.'

'Well you'd best pray they did,' said Neeba, 'because the Sisters teach us that stories that come from your soul are evil.'

'I see,' said Lucy. 'And these Sisters you mentioned, are they anything to do with that thing on Creeps' desk?'

'We *think* so,' said Pixy, 'but nobody has ever seen them.'

'And nobody wants to,' said Fred.

'But what about Creeps' pole?' asked Lucy.

'That's evil too,' said Neeba, 'he calls it his Spiritu Loqui.'

'Speaking from the spirit?' suggested Lucy.

'From the *soul*,' said Neeba. 'He says that that's what happens if you don't believe – there are *real* Spiritu Loqui boxes out in the city, with real people's heads in them.'

'Erm, you don't think that's true though, *do* you?' said Pixy, nervously.

'I'm certain it's not,' said Lucy, trying to spare the girl's feelings. There was an awful memory inside her that disagreed though, because she had *been* in just such a cabinet. And it was all too easy to imagine Pixy's mother in that same situation, her head stuffed in a glass box, beneath a badly painted sign that read *'Madame Ocular Prefect'*.

Seeing
Stars

Lucy was unable to sleep, and lay with her hands clasped behind her head, watching the stars through the high attic windows. The fact that they were almost at the top of the world should have made it easy to recognise the constellations, but there was nothing even faintly familiar. Even the Milky Way was missing, replaced by a faint red band of light that looked like dust and served to confirm the fact that she was a long way from home.

Until now, there had only been the sound of creaking beams and the low, soft moan of the wind. There was the sound of children breathing too, which was reassuring, but now there was a gentle movement of feet – unmistakable and secret, and very, *very* close. Lucy sat up with a start, suddenly aware of a shadow right next to her bed.

It was Gusset.

'You must come with me now,' he whispered, placing a wrinkled hand over her mouth.

'Hey, what's going on?' said Toby, stirring in the next bed.

'Apparently we've got to go,' whispered Lucy, freeing her mouth from the taste of Gusset's skin.

'And what if we don't want to?' hissed Toby, 'it's the middle of the rotten night.'

'Then I'll have to take you by force,' whispered Gusset.

'You're not big enough,' said Toby, getting out of bed and trying to make himself look taller. 'You wouldn't be able to fight us both at once.'

'Well I was *hoping* that wouldn't be necessary,' said Gusset.

'But can't it wait until morning?' said Toby. 'I was dreaming about triple beef sausages and soggy chips with brown sauce – and it wasn't that filthy fart-flavoured Snogg's stuff either.'

'Well that's most unfortunate for you,' said Gusset, 'but we *must* go now. If you hadn't made such a fuss we might have had a few days grace, but you went too far this afternoon. You riled the teachers when you should have been sitting and learning, and now you're going to reap the consequences.'

'No we're not,' said Toby, 'because we're not coming.'

'Then I'm going to have to use my backup plan,' said Gusset.

'Oh?' said Toby. 'And what's that?'

The wrinkled janitor disappeared, but he returned moments later with a large sack and a rather splendid looking truncheon.

'I can assure you,' he said, 'that this is going to be for your own good.'

When Toby recovered consciousness, he found himself and Lucy in that very same sack, wriggling furiously in an attempt to get out.

'Hey, watch what you're doing with that elbow Blake, you nearly had my eye out.'

'Watch it yourself,' screamed Lucy, 'and keep *still* when I'm trying to rescue us.'

'Well can you do it a bit more quietly?' said Toby. 'I'm right next to you, remember?'

'*So?*' screamed Lucy.

'So there's no need to shout,' said Toby. 'And another thing, it *stinks* in here – where do you think we are?'

'I don't know,' snapped Lucy, 'but if you've still got that pen-knife you got for your birthday then we can find out.'

'Here,' said Toby, 'help yourself – I'm just going to sit here and relax until he lets us out. Erm, he *is* going to let us out, isn't he?'

'I wouldn't count on it,' said Lucy, selecting the biggest and jaggiest blade she could find.

'Well I was sort of hoping,' said Toby. 'Hey, wait a minute – why are we swaying around? And why is the air so cold?'

Lucy was too busy hacking at the sackcloth to think of a sensible answer.

'Maybe we're outside?' she said idly.

'But it's freezing.'

'So?' said Lucy.

'So stop hacking,' said Toby. 'I need time to think.'

'There's nothing to think about,' said Lucy. She had made a hole about the size of a tennis ball, and was poking her hand through.

'Luce, *stop*. I think I know where we are, and you're not going to like it.'

'Erm, I think *I* do too,' said Lucy, pulling her hand back inside, 'and you're right, it *is* freezing out there.'

'So where do you think we are we then?' said Toby.

'You first,' said Lucy, examining the damage she'd done to the sack. Their combined weight was putting a strain on the weakened cloth and the edges of the hole were beginning to unravel.

'We're dangling over the edge of the Braneskule,' said Toby.

'That's what *I* thought,' said Lucy, 'only I was hoping you were going to say something else. This is all *your* fault, Lindstrom.'

'Erm, actually I don't *think* so,' shouted Toby. '*You're* the one with all the stories about boats and maps and dragons and things.'

'Well it was your knife that made the hole,' said Lucy.

'And it was you that did it,' said Toby, unable to believe the logic he was hearing. 'Rotten-stinking *girls*,' he screamed, 'I should have just ignored all that rubbish you told me in the saleroom and I should never have come with you to your uncle's laboratory – it's all *your* fault.'

'Well we couldn't possibly ignore what happened, could we?' said Lucy. 'We were meant to come here – it was all intended for *us*.'

'Yeah, great,' spat Toby, 'and just look where it's got us.'

'Arguing in a sack?' suggested Lucy.

'Yeah,' he muttered, a little more calmly. The mood didn't last though – it was interrupted by the faint ping-ping-pinging sound of stitches unpicking themselves.

'We've *had* it,' he shouted. 'The bloody rotten sack is unravelling.'

The hole beneath them had increased to the size of a football now, and despite their frantic efforts to hold the edges together the sack was fraying rapidly. Toby's knuckles were white with strain and the air was blue with the sound of his cursing. Lucy thought she could hear his heart beating, but then realised it was her own – like a pair of elephants jumping down stairs three at a time.

'It's going,' she screamed, the tears suddenly pouring out of her.

'We're going to fall,' shouted Toby, echoing her screams. 'I can't hold…'

V⸖V⸖Ꝺ

Rrrrrrriiiiiip…..

And off they went, falling through the air, rolling and tumbling end over end, the wind whistling in their ears and the bitter cold shrinking the skin from their faces.

Turtles

and Pulleys

'You *might* have waited,' said Gusset, as they dropped the last ten feet or so into a waiting hay cart. 'That was one of my best sacks.'

'Oh, *brilliant*,' said Lucy, realising she had just wasted an entire lifetime's worth of emotion. 'We just *had* to fall into a hay cart, *didn't* we?'

'Well *there's* gratitude,' said Gusset. 'I suppose you'd have preferred some hard packed mud, would you? Or a few stone slabs?'

'No,' said Lucy, 'but a *hay* cart? It's just like those old films, isn't it?'

'Films?' said Gusset.

'Yes, where they fall out of windows and, erm, oh don't worry,' said Lucy, realising her mistake. 'I'll tell you in four hundred years or so, if either of us is still around.'

'Good,' said Gusset, 'I'll look forward to it – now let's make a move before we're discovered.'

'Discovered by whom?' said Toby.

'The *Vooghul*,' said Gusset. 'I heard they were going to move you tonight, so I thought I'd save them the trouble.'

'But who *are* they?' said Lucy, 'and why do they want to move us?'

'Yeah,' said Toby, 'and *where*?'

'So many questions,' said Gusset, 'and like the ones we find in all the best examinations, they have such long and tedious answers.'

'Well *I* want to hear them, however long they are,' said Toby. 'I *still* don't trust you, and I'm not moving from here until we know.'

'Even if you don't know where *here* is?' said Gusset.

'I don't care,' said Toby, 'you knocked us out.'

'And tied us inside a sack,' added Lucy.

'Yes,' said Gusset, 'but I *told* you, it was for your own good.'

'We've only got your word for that,' said Lucy, 'unless you feel like telling us where we are and why we need to escape?'

'We're standing at the foot of the Braneskule,' sighed Gusset. 'The major quadrant building on the south rim.'

Toby gazed into the deepening blue sky, where the shadow of the Braneskule dominated everything in their field of vision. The monstrous structure masked one complete half of the heavens – its upper reaches dividing the sky into two distinct parts – stars and no stars, as if a black velvet blanket had been draped above their heads.

'And what's that hanging out of the hatch?' said Toby.

'Have you never seen a rope before?' said Gusset.

'*Rope?*' squealed Toby, 'it's more like a tree trunk.'

'It goes a long way up,' said Gusset, 'so it has to be strong.'

'And I suppose there are pulleys up there?' said Lucy, following the line of the cable up inside the hatchway.

'You *are* a clever girl, aren't you?' said Gusset. 'There *are* pulleys, lots of them in fact, and they go all the way up.'

'So it's like the story about the turtles then?' smiled Lucy.

'Oh no,' said Toby, 'not *that* one again.'

'Turtles?' said Gusset.

'Never mind,' said Lucy, 'we haven't got time – if we *are* in danger then we need to get moving.'

'There you go again with all that danger stuff,' said Toby. 'We're *still* not certain we're in trouble – we've only got *his* word for it.'

'If you could see what was going on up there, then you'd *know* alright,' said Gusset. 'And if you could get inside people's heads and see the black thoughts they harbour then you wouldn't hesitate.'

'Well, we *can't* look inside their heads, can we?' said Lucy.

'We might be able to use the shew stone,' suggested Toby.

'*Might* we?' said Lucy. 'I thought that belonged to Neeba?'

'It does,' admitted Toby, 'but I didn't give it back.'

'But that's stealing,' said Lucy

'I forgot,' said Toby. 'I'll give it back next time we see her.'

'*If* you see her,' said Gusset. 'And *if* we get out of this place in one piece.'

'Do you *really* think we're in that much danger?' said Lucy.

'Use the stone,' said Gusset impatiently, 'and see for yourself.'

'But it's too far,' said Lucy, 'the dormitory is *miles* away.'

'Five thousand feet,' said Gusset, beginning to sound annoyed.

'Then we've got no chance,' said Toby. 'I got sick last time I used it, and the Beak's study was close by. So unless we've got something to steady it…'

'Like a gimbal?' suggested Lucy.

'What's that then?' said Gusset. '*Science?*'

'I suppose so,' said Lucy. 'It's like a sort of mount with gears on, for keeping things like telescopes steady. And do you know what? I've just realised where I can get one.'

'What, right now?' said Toby. 'Well that's a bit of luck.'

'*No* stupid, not right now. We'll have to make the best of what we have.'

'I'll have a go,' said Toby. 'But why do you think we should be looking in the dormitory?'

'Just a feeling,' said Lucy, watching Gusset nod in agreement. She found a patch of soft earth and pressed the shew stone into it, half in, and half out of the ground.

'There,' she said, 'that should be enough support – why don't you try it?'

'Ingenious,' said Gusset. 'I would never have thought it possible.'

'But you're a teacher, aren't you?' said Lucy.

'Yes,' said Gusset, 'but not of science.'

'What then?' said Lucy.

'I was a master of creation studies,' said Gusset, 'until I started asking questions.'

'*Ah,*' said Lucy, 'I'm beginning to understand.'

'Hey, I can see corridors,' said Toby suddenly. 'No, erm, wait I'm in a classroom now. And now there's a store room – not yours though Gusset, it's another one, full of cabinets.'

'Get *out* of there,' said Gusset. 'And don't go looking at what doesn't concern you.'

'Alright,' said Toby, 'keep your hair on, I don't know my way around like you do.'

'No, of course you don't,' said Gusset. 'Sorry.'

Toby gave a few assorted *oohs* and *aahs* as he explored the rooms far above them, gently nudging the shew stone around in the soft earth when he wanted to change his point of view. There were rooms filled with mist and others that appeared to contain stars. Then there was a large room that seemed to overflow with brilliant light, and another, dark-walled and empty, except for a device that looked like a perch for a giant parrot. Finally, though, he went very quiet, refusing to speak, even when Lucy prodded him.

'What is it?' she said.

'I don't like to say,' said Toby.

'Tell us,' said Gusset, 'come *on*, what is it?'

'Trouble, by the looks of it,' said Toby, staring into the stone.

'Toby, *tell* us,' said Lucy, 'what do you see?'

'Things,' he said finally, 'floating in a black mist.'

'What about their faces?' said Gusset, 'can you make them out?'

'They're indistinct,' said Toby, 'like a sort of swirling fog.'

'The *Vooghul*,' hissed Gusset, 'the frigging, floating, filth-ridden servants of the Sisters.'

'I *see*,' smiled Lucy, 'and what are these Vooghul doing?'

'They've already done it,' said Toby. 'They're standing around my bed.'

'And?' she said.

'Well,' said Toby, 'it looks like there are pillows in our beds.'

'I put them there,' said Gusset. 'To make it look as though you were still sleeping.'

'Well I'm glad we're not,' said Toby. 'The one in *my* bed has got a huge spiky pole stuck right into the middle of it.'

Lucy sank to her knees, suddenly realising that the game was over. Whatever they had *thought* they were doing here, it had all changed now. They could laugh and joke on the outside, but at the *back* of the stage where this bright comedy was unfolding, something sinister was lurking behind the curtain.

'Give me your knife,' she said.

'You've still got it,' said Toby.

Lucy looked down at her hand as it slowly unfolded to reveal the weapon. The blade was still open, and at certain angles, even by mere naked starlight, she could see it glinting.

'Luce, don't do anything stupid.'

V♭xVxb╕

'This doesn't make complete sense,' said Lucy, 'not even to me, but it's certainly not stupid.'

She drew the blade sharply across the pad of her upturned thumb and winced as the skin parted. For a moment, there was just pink flesh visible, but then the gap filled with a crimson river that gushed and dripped away into the soil, seeking whatever lay beneath. Toby fainted when he caught sight of the red flood, but Gusset simply smiled and nodded, as if he understood.

When Toby regained consciousness, he was relieved to see that Lucy had wrapped the wound in a handkerchief.

'So what the *hell* was *that* all about?' he said.

Lucy smiled, first at Gusset and then at Toby.

'It was to prove that we can *die* here,' she said solemnly.

'I could have told you that,' said Gusset, 'folk die here every day, and I reckon the same rules apply to you two.'

'Alright, so we can die,' said Toby. 'So what?'

'I wanted to prove to myself that it's not a game we're playing,' said Lucy. 'I don't know about you, but *I'm* quite keen on staying alive.'

'Well she's right about that,' said Gusset. 'This is no game.'

'So what is it then?' said Toby.

'I don't profess to understand,' admitted Gusset. 'And I don't necessarily *want* to, but I *do* know we have to keep you away from the Sisters – and if I can help to do that and help to get your young friend back then I'll have done my part.'

'You *know* about her then?' said Lucy.

'Only that she's presently in a lot more danger than you are,' said Gusset.

'Oh,' said Lucy, trying to imagine the sort of peril that threatened their friend. She felt sorry for Fenny, but after a moment's thought she began to feel sorry for herself as well, stuck in this place, perhaps forever, and with far worse to come.

Gusset examined their long expressions, searching for the remnants of a smile where there was none to be had. He took hold of each of their faces in turn, and used his tough little fingers to squeeze their sad features into interesting shapes.

'Goldfish, anyone? Or how about the turned-up pig's nose? Or the fat-lipped chicken?'

None of the face-shapes seemed to work, because as soon as he let go their expressions returned to the same miserable state.

'Why don't you tell me about those tortoises?' he suggested.

Lucy smiled weakly, lacking the spirit to correct his mistake.

'Come on Luce,' begged Toby. 'Tell him about the rotten turtles and get it over with. I'll even promise not to groan on account of having heard it eighty-nine times already.'

Lucy smiled, more broadly this time, realising that they needed to support each other if they were to get through the coming ordeal.

'Alright,' she said. 'There are these two ladies, and they're talking about how the world is supported.'

'You mean what the world sits on?' said Gusset.

'Yes,' said Lucy.

'Ah, so it's more science then?' said Gusset.

'If you like,' said Lucy. 'Anyway, the first woman says that the world just floats around the sun, minding its own business.

'And the second woman?' said Gusset, ignoring the fact that the sun was supposed to go around the world. 'Is she also of a scientific mind?'

'No, she isn't,' said Lucy, 'that's the whole point.'

'So what does *she* think?' said Gusset.

Toby grinned, relishing the difficulty that Lucy was getting into.

'The second woman reckons that the world is a flat plate,' said Lucy, 'if you can imagine such a thing. She reckons that this flat plate sits on the back of a giant elephant, which in turn stands on the back of a huge turtle.'

'Right,' said Gusset. 'I saw some engravings of those turtles and elephants in the tomes of invention when I was a child – not that I can recall what shape they were, or even what colour come to that.'

'Erm, ye-es,' said Lucy, pushing on to the end. 'So the first woman asks what the turtle is standing on.'

'And it's another turtle,' said Toby helpfully.

'*So*,' said Lucy, frowning at her friend, 'the doubting woman asks what *that* turtle is standing on.'

'I see,' said Gusset, 'and what was the reply?'

'You can't fool me, she says — it's turtles all the way down.'

Gusset studied Lucy's face, trying to decide whether he should laugh.

'Sounds reasonable,' he said after some thought.

'Yeah, that was a *great* story,' grinned Toby, 'but I'll bet you won't be telling it around here again, will you?'

'Erm, probably not,' admitted Lucy. 'I think it lost a bit in translation.'

'No, it was an excellent tale,' said Gusset. 'I didn't understand the finer scientific points, but it'll come to me eventually — now are we ready to go?'

'I suppose so,' said Lucy.

'Good,' said Gusset, 'because we have to reach the Forest of Skeels before deepnight.'

The Forest of Skeels

'You can come out now,' said Gusset. 'We'll travel on foot beyond the forest gate.'

'Great,' said Toby, 'just when we were getting comfortable on these rock-hard boards.'

He and Lucy jumped down from the cart, feeling somewhat the worse for wear and picking bits of hay from their clothes and hair.

'Yes, thanks for the lovely ride,' smiled Lucy, gazing up at the trees.

They had seen them before of course – first as a flattish green area on the Mappa Mundi, and then later when they surveyed the city from the dormitory platform. Suddenly though, the forest had turned from a distant carpet of greenery into a dense, dark mass of timber leviathans that towered into the night.

'But the road carries on through the gate,' said Toby, following the route of the track into the forest.

'The *road* might,' said Gusset, 'but Equusnoctus doesn't.'

'And what's that?' asked Lucy.

'Not what, *who*,' said Gusset. 'It'd be a very special kind of horse that went into the Forest of Skeels at night.'

'Oh, I *see*,' said Lucy, 'and she *isn't* I suppose?'

'She's friendly, but not brave,' said Gusset. He handed Equusnoctus a carrot and when she finished the treat, he unhitched her from the wagon and sent her away with a slap on the rump.

'She'll find her way alright,' said Gusset.

'But what about us?' said Toby. 'I can't say I'm that keen – especially if the horse is scared to go in.'

'We have no choice,' said Lucy. 'We're probably being followed.'

'There was never any doubt of that,' said Gusset, 'but I was hoping we'd get further than this – *listen.*'

'What?' said Lucy. 'I can't hear anything.'

'*Exactly,*' said Gusset, 'no sound of hooves, no creaking of branches and no rustling of leaves – even the shriek owls are quiet, and those things fear nothing and no one.'

'So we *are* being watched?' said Lucy with a shiver.

'Did you ever get a feeling that people were looking at you,' said Gusset, 'even when there's nobody around? Well I'm getting it now, in my long bones. They're waiting for a chance to take all three of us.'

'Then we'd better not stand around,' said Toby, with a slight edge of fear in his voice.

Lucy led the way through a massive iron gate that marked the entrance to the forest, shuddering as they passed beneath the great parabolic archway. She tried not to look at the decorative gargoyles, because if *they* were any indication of what they might find on the old forest road then they were in for a hard time. She strode purposefully for a dozen or so yards, but soon realised that the old rutted track would provide them with very little cover.

'Are there any other paths?' she said.

'There's a multitude,' said Gusset. 'But you don't want to be taking any of them – there are tales.'

'I *like* tales,' said Lucy, forcing a smile.

'Not these you wouldn't,' said Gusset. 'If you manage to keep out of the dwellers' way and avoid getting eaten by prowlers, you'll probably end up being swallowed by one of the kiosks.'

'*Kiosks?*' laughed Toby. 'What are they selling?'

'*Selling?*' said Gusset. 'They don't sell anything as far as I know – but folk have disappeared inside them right enough, and never been seen again.'

'Are we talking about the same thing?' smiled Lucy. 'Where *we* come from, erm, in Farperoo that is, a kiosk is a little wooden hut where you can buy sweets.'

'That's *them* alright,' said Gusset, 'only without the sweets.'

'Well I vote we look anyway,' said Toby. 'I'm starving.'

'Me too,' said Lucy. 'But I'm still not hungry enough to eat Lily's sandwich.'

'Definitely not,' said Toby, pretending to retch. 'We'd have to be *really* desperate to touch that thing.'

'So where *are* these kiosks?' said Lucy.

'They're deep inside the forest,' replied Gusset. 'But we can't afford to stray that far from the paths – not at deepnight.'

'Maybe not,' said Lucy, 'but we need somewhere safe to sleep.'

'*Safe?*' said Gusset. 'Didn't I just *tell* you? Folk have disappeared.'

'I'd rather disappear than get caught by the Vooghul,' said Toby.

'Perhaps,' said Gusset. 'But first of all you need to *find* a kiosk – and then you have to work out how to get inside.'

'Ah,' said Lucy, 'and I suppose you're going to tell us that's not easy?'

They eventually left the old road and took a rough-hewn path through the western forest, following on silently behind Gusset. The place was like a mausoleum, full of twisted shapes – memorials to trees that had once been tall and upright. Something had happened though, and the tree-faces had been frozen in time, their grimaces preserved as a warning to anyone mad enough to venture into the forest at night.

'This one looks like you,' grinned Toby, pointing at a particularly gnarled specimen.

'Yes, and here you are,' said Lucy, 'with knobbly green bits all over you.'

'So who does that one look like then?' said Toby, indicating another gruesome example. 'Erm, not that I was saying…'

'It doesn't look like anyone,' said Lucy diplomatically. But they were thinking the same thing – if Gusset were to stand against the tree, he'd more than likely become invisible against the leathery, wind-worn bark.

'Are we there yet?' said Toby, trying to change the subject.

'Maybe,' said Gusset. 'It all depends on whether I can find a tree with a twisted four-part trunk and a face like Glassbone Haddock the third.'

Each time they came to a junction Gusset would stand and scratch his head, apparently considering the possibilities. Then he would suddenly make his mind up, seemingly at random, and forge off down the new path.

'I think we're horribly, horribly lost,' said Toby eventually. 'And I could do with that bed.'

'Me too,' said Lucy, 'and I think that deepnight thing has finally arrived too – it's as black as the inside of Lily's book depository in here.'

'Well *that's* lucky,' said Gusset, 'because we've arrived.'

'Where?' said Toby, looking about and finding nothing.

'Erm, well I could swear it was around here somewhere,' said Gusset.

'*Lost,*' said Toby with a nod in Gusset's direction.

'Hopelessly and completely,' agreed Lucy. 'I vote we have a sleep now.'

'Ah-*hah,*' said Gusset triumphantly. 'Then why don't we do it over there?' He pointed into the dark, where shadows shaped like smiles seemed to be laughing at their quest.

'There's nothing there,' said Toby. 'I vote we stay here.'

'It's just trees,' said Lucy, straining to see into the darkness.

'Then what do you call *this?*' said Gusset, somewhat distant.

'Where's he gone?' said Toby.

'This way,' called Gusset. 'I'm over near the kiosk.'

Toby and Lucy wandered towards the source of the voice – and sure enough, Gusset had found what they were looking for. It was more like a miniature pavilion though, made from wood and painted green to blend in with the forest. It reminded Lucy of a police telephone box with its little tiled roof and four gable ends.

'They're closed for the day,' said Toby, rattling the door.

'That's a pity,' said Gusset. 'I wouldn't mind seeing inside one of these.'

'Or even sleeping inside one,' suggested Lucy.

'Or finding a bacon sandwich inside one,' said Toby. 'Maybe we can break the door down?'

'Not a chance,' said Gusset. 'Have you *seen* the size of that door?'

'What about giving it a good kicking?' said Lucy. 'That's what I always do with our bathroom door at home.'

'A *room* with a bath?' said Gusset. 'What a wonderful idea.'

'Yes,' said Lucy, 'it's full of beauty preparations – you'd love it.'

'Go on, Luce,' said Toby with a grin. 'Give it a go.'

Lucy took hold of the knob and twisted it sharply as she gave the bottom of the door an almighty kick. It groaned slightly but stayed exactly where it was, leering at them in a way that had been mastered only by the most obstinate and inflexible of entrances.

VᚣVᚣbᚎ

'I know,' smiled Lucy, 'I forgot the password.'

'Uh-oh,' said Toby, 'stand back.'

'*Please?*' shouted Lucy, giving the door another massive kick.

It didn't budge – and from the way it just sat there not budging she could tell it was feeling pretty pleased with itself.

'Right then,' she said. 'I'll try the other password. You know, Toby, the really *secret* one.'

'Which one's that then, Luce?'

'*Pretty please?*' she screamed. The shout was accompanied by a kick that would have knocked a lesser door completely off its hinges.

'Hey, that's *it*,' said Toby as the door swung open.

'An interesting technique,' said Gusset. 'And just *think* of all those years I wasted using keys.'

'Me first,' grinned Toby, 'I want first pick of the beds.'

They crowded through into the darkened space beyond, but in the rush to get inside nobody had the sense to hold the door and it slammed behind them with an ominous thunk. From the sound it made, they knew at once that there was no going back.

'It's going to need more than a kick *this* time,' said Toby grimly.

'Yes, it did seem a bit too easy,' said Gusset.

'Well I didn't hear anyone complaining when we were on the other side,' said Lucy.

'Yeah, but that was before you brought us into *this* coalhole,' said Toby. 'I wish I'd brought a torch.'

There was a sound of metal scraping on stone, and moments later Gusset's wrinkly face was illuminated by a tiny glass lantern.

'I never go anywhere without my Pockalumo,' he said. 'You never know when you'll need one, do you?'

'I'll say,' said Toby, his mouth hanging open in surprise.

They were standing in a tiny square hallway, barely six feet on each side. There was a black-and-white tiled floor, just like in Lily's kitchen, but with only six tiles in each direction. At the edges of the tiled square were four familiar words, written in symbols that Lucy recognised – Lucal, Sobol, Babage, and Raas – north, west, south, and east. It brought to mind her bedroom at home, but with doors in place of windows – not so much a

Panopticon as a Panviatron. Instead of *seeing* anywhere, you could *go* anywhere – perhaps.

'Hey,' said Toby. 'This is like your bedroom Luce, only with different coloured doors instead of four different windows.'

'*Amazing,*' giggled Lucy, 'you could go on the stage with a mind-reading act like that.'

They fell silent for a moment, each examining a different aspect of the confined space. Gusset seemed to find something of interest on the floor, whilst Lucy examined an all too familiar design on the ceiling. In the meantime, Toby was interfering with things. To the right of each door was a varnished wooden pole standing in a brass-lined hole. And perched on top of each pole was a glass phial, like a small lantern. He tapped one, and all four of them suddenly burst into life, flooding the tiny room with light.

'Sorry,' he said.

Gusset closed the Pockalumo and examined the wand nearest to him.

'*Serpents,*' he said. 'There are two snakes floating inside this red light.'

'You're right,' said Lucy. 'And look, the bluish one has a crocodile – but it has wings.'

'Yeah, but they're just moving pictures,' said Toby. 'They're not real – erm, *are* they?'

'This is *truly* dark magick,' hissed Gusset. 'The natural world could never bear to contain pictures such as these. '

'Maybe not,' said Lucy. 'But I don't think there's any magick involved.' She wandered over to the other wands and peeked inside. The one that glowed yellow contained a representation of an eagle or some similar bird of prey. And the green one shone with the image of a beetle, this one glowing much more brightly than the others.

'Hey, look at the ceiling,' said Toby. 'It's just like the flag.'

'Flag?' said Gusset.

'Erm, yeah,' admitted Toby. 'The one we found in your room.'

'As far as I can remember it wasn't lost,' said Gusset. 'Although the last I saw of it, someone had kindly pulled it off the pole.'

'Oh, erm sorry,' said Toby, 'that was me.'

'We just wanted to have a good look at it,' said Lucy.

'And did you?' said Gusset.

'Beautiful embroidery,' said Lucy.

'Yeah,' said Toby, rattling the eagle wand.

'Well *one* part is beautiful,' said Gusset.

'We were going to ask you about that,' said Lucy. 'Why was only one of the panels sewn in bright thread?'

'Maybe the seamstress ran out?' said Gusset with a weak grin.

'That was careless of her, wasn't it?' said Lucy with a frown. 'To go to all that trouble and *then* run out of silk?'

'I don't know about that,' said Gusset. 'But what I *do* know is we should be thinking about moving out of this porch.'

'Great,' said Toby, 'I get to choose.'

'Erm, do you think that's wise?' said Gusset. 'We don't even know…'

Before he had chance to finish, Toby had yanked open the door guarded by the serpent wand.

'Erm, it's another porch,' he said, staring into the space beyond with a look of deep disappointment.

'And what did you *expect* to find?' said Gusset.

'I erm, well, I suppose I don't really know,' said Toby sticking his head through the door. 'It looks exactly the same as this one.'

'Breathing,' said Lucy.

'What?' asked Gusset.

'Eh?' said Toby.

'*Breathing*,' she hissed. 'I can *hear* it, on the other side of the door we just came through.'

They all held their breath and listened for the disturbance. It was like a wild boar with a head cold and a snout full of snot.

'I vote we move now,' said Toby. He stepped through the red door and into the next porch, but Lucy pulled him back.

'No,' she said, 'this way.' She rattled the crocodile door, but it wouldn't open, and neither would the one guarded by the eagle wand.

'It *has* to be this one then,' said Gusset, 'we've already got it open.'

'*No*,' snapped Lucy, 'try closing the serpent door first.'

Toby did as he was told and Lucy tried the crocodile again. This time it opened without a fuss, and they stepped into the next hallway without even thinking. Anything was better than facing the thing they'd heard snuffling through the green keyhole.

'Let's take another,' said Toby, 'every time we go through a new door, whatever's out there has got less chance of following us.'

'I know,' said Lucy. 'I was in that maths lesson too, remember? But I just need to find something first.'

'*Luce,*' hissed Toby, 'for pity's sake, hurry *up.*'

Lucy fumbled in her bag, looking for a pencil. And then, when Toby was fit to burst from anxiety, she fumbled even more, this time looking for a piece of paper. All she could find was a page that had been torn from one of Tarquin's books. It was printed with a list of numbers and names like *Isinglass* and *Night Hawk* and *Robert the Devil.*

'Right,' she said. 'If we're going to get lost we might as well do it properly. Can you remember what we've done so far?'

'Green, then red, then blue,' said Gusset.

'No,' said Toby, 'green then blue – we didn't go through the red one.'

'That's right,' said Lucy, writing the steps down. 'We didn't.'

'Come *on,*' said Toby, 'unless you want to find a pencil sharpener too?'

'Funny,' said Lucy, 'but not funny enough – right, let's *go.*'

Each time they burst through another door, Lucy scribbled the details of their move on the paper fragment, so they'd be able to retrace their steps. By the time they reached the twentieth porch-way though, she realised that something was seriously wrong.

'I think we've been in some of these rooms before,' she said.

'Circles,' said Gusset helpfully, 'they have no beginning and no end.'

'Yeah, well that's the sort of thing that's *really* going to cheer us up, isn't it?' said Toby. 'Do you *really* think we're lost, Luce?'

Lucy took the knife and scratched a number 'one' in the corner between the serpent door and the one with the eagle.

'That might help,' she said.

'Until we run out of numbers,' said Gusset in a grave tone.

'I don't think that will be a problem,' said Lucy. 'We've got some seriously big numbers where we come from.'

'And some really awful sandwiches,' said Toby. 'So let's get on with it, shall we? I want to find a hallway with a bacon butty dispenser.'

'*Butty*? What's a butt…oh,' said Gusset, as the next door swung open. '*What* the flipping Holy Son of Harold is *that*?'

Lucy had expected to find another porch-way, but was stunned into a sudden silence. In front of them lay a milky crystal passageway and a gently sloping staircase that rose towards a fuzzy, distant glow. The walls, ceiling, and stairs were fashioned from the same kind of glass they'd seen in the Braneskule, only *this* time nobody was expecting to see a classroom on the other side.

'Lucretia?' said Gusset. 'Erm, *what*…'

'*I* don't know, do I?' said Lucy. 'You're the one who lives here.'

'But this is all *your* doing,' said Gusset.

'I don't see why,' said Lucy, 'this is your forest, isn't it?' She stepped onto the staircase, and as her foot touched the first tread, the whole passageway turned from milky to clear.

'Holy *creator*,' shouted Gusset. 'What in the name of confounded muck-scraping tarnishment have we *found* here?'

'Amazing,' laughed Toby, 'this place just gets better and better.'

Lucy was standing on a transparent staircase and surrounded by invisible walls, which meant that she appeared to be floating in thin air. Far below her were clouds and storms and weather systems of every kind. And drifting amongst them were pockets of deep-blue space sprinkled with stars, the whole lot floating around a central fire, like an inferno fused into the bottom of a huge glass bowl.

'It's *beautiful*,' said Gusset. 'I've never seen anything like it.'

'It's like a planetarium,' said Toby.

As if their thoughts were linked, three pairs of eyes drifted skywards, tempted by the sight of cathedral-sized clouds and swirling sea-mists, all intertwined with galaxies and star-fields and glowing clouds of gas.

'I think this must be what heaven is like,' said Gusset.

'I reckon,' giggled Toby. 'It's *amazing*, isn't it Luce?'

'Mmm,' said Lucy absently. She was staring at the brilliant blue glow at the centre of it all, wondering how the ceiling could appear so close, yet the things it encompassed could appear so far away. Directly opposite them was another door, about four hundred yards away. And to their left and their right, about two hundred and eighty yards away, if her mental arithmetic was up to scratch, were two more doors. The four access points were evenly spaced around the sides of a globe, just slightly below the centre.

'Do you think those other doors have staircases?' said Toby.

'They would if I had designed it,' said Lucy.

'Designed?' said Toby. 'You mean this thing was built?'

'Well it's not *natural*, is it?' said Lucy.

'Perhaps we might discover more if we climbed to the centre?' suggested Gusset.

'Hey,' said Toby, 'I was going to say that.'

In the centre of the spherical space, but slightly above them, was a cage shaped like two bandstands joined back to back, so that it appeared to have two roofs. The structure was made of the same milky glass as the staircases, and had eight equal sides. Lucy guessed that there were four staircases leading up to it, one from each of the doors. All she had to do now was prove it, which meant stepping out into thin air, and praying that the stairs would carry her.

'I'll be waiting here,' said Gusset, realising what Lucy was planning.

She was already a good way up the invisible stairs when Toby plucked up courage to follow, gingerly feeling for walls he couldn't see and treading lightly on steps that were as insubstantial as the Zephyr's wings.

'Not far now,' said Lucy.

'Yeah,' said Toby, trying not to look down.

'Just concentrate on the cage,' said Lucy. 'Then you won't worry… Erm, *hey*, have you seen *that*?'

Toby stopped right behind Lucy who was now staring directly up into the heavens. It hadn't been visible before, but now they could make out a stream of glowing particles, falling from the brightest part of the sky and flowing down onto the octagonal roof. It didn't stop though; instead, it passed straight through the cage and flowed out from the centre of the lower roof. Here it continued its journey, dropping towards a light blue mist and finally being engulfed by the sea of fire and lava beyond.

As they reached the top of the stairs and stepped into the milky glass enclosure, the ceiling, walls, and floor disappeared, leaving just a suggestion of the edges where they joined. They were hanging in an invisible cage now, suspended at the centre of an imaginary sky in the midst of a most unlikely universe.

'Erm, I think I'm feeling a little sick,' said Toby.

Lucy looked down through the floor, following the path taken by the stream of particles. It was like being dangled over the mouth of a furnace, watching a waterfall as it disappeared into the flames.

'Sit down,' she said, 'and close your eyes.'

'And miss it?' said Toby. 'I'd rather see everything and be sick.'

'Charming,' said Lucy, 'but do it over the side, will you?'

She sat on the floor and gazed up through the crystal-clear ceiling, her heart pounding with the beauty of it all. The blue stream continued to fall from the heavens, and in a moment of madness, she lay on her back, directly underneath it. High above her, or perhaps it was right in front of her, sparks pretended they were lightning – or was it far-off lightning pretending to be sparks?

'Luce, what the *hell* are you doing?' hissed Toby.

'It's alright,' she said, 'look.' She held her hands up towards the stream, as if lying beneath a column of falling water. The particles were falling much slower than that though, filling, and then overflowing her cupped hands in slow motion, like a million dandelion seeds descending.

'It doesn't hurt,' she said.

'Maybe not,' said Toby, 'but I still don't think it's a good idea. It might be like X-rays – and you're not wearing your lead-lined underskirts.'

'And how would *you* know?' grinned Lucy.

'Luce, just *stop* it will you? You're worrying me.'

'Alright,' said Lucy. She stood up and waved to Gusset who waved back and then disappeared into the hallway.

'Erm, he's not *going*, is he?' said Toby.

'I'm the one with the directions,' said Lucy. 'And I don't think he'd be mad enough to leave without those.'

'*If* he's on our side,' said Toby. 'We still don't know for certain, do we? He might have been trying to lure us here all along – he might even have wanted you to lie down under that thing.'

'And turn me into a beetle?' said Lucy. 'Or a serpent?'

'It's possible,' said Toby.

'I don't think so,' said Lucy. 'Gusset wants to know what's behind those other doors just as much as we do.'

'But we're not even sure there are stairs going down to them,' said Toby.

Lucy felt her way around the invisible walls, gradually making her way to a side where she thought a staircase might be. When she found the gap, she knelt down and felt outside the cage.

'Well there's at least *one* step,' she grinned, locating a solid tread. And without waiting for Toby to complain she stepped out onto it, gently feeling for the next one with her toes.

'There's another one,' she said, stepping down, 'and another, and...'

Toby stood with his hands over his eyes, peeking between his fingers as Lucy cautiously made her way towards the red door. When she reached it, he let out a great sigh of relief.

'It's a curtain,' she yelled, 'and there's a pair of inter-twined serpents embroidered into the fabric.'

'What's behind it?' yelled Toby.

Lucy tried to pull the curtain aside, but it was attached on all four edges and refused to budge. She briefly considered trying to cut it open, but on closer inspection found that the cloth was woven from a fine metal thread.

'I don't know,' she shouted. 'I'm coming back.'

As Lucy ran back up the staircase, she was already thinking about exploring the other possibilities. But when she reached the cage, Toby tried to pour cold water on her enthusiasm.

'Luce, we've got to go back *now*,' he said. 'I'm getting this funny feeling in my hair – and I think it's the blue stuff that's causing it.'

'It's harmless,' said Lucy, beaming all over her face. '*Look*.'

She held out her hand and placed it under the stream, allowing the sparkling blue particles to gather in her palm before spilling over the sides and continuing their journey. 'Although, now you mention it, my hair *is* starting to tingle a bit.'

'Right, so we're going back then?' said Toby.

'Yes,' smiled Lucy, '*after* I've seen the blue door.'

'Luce, *no*,' he hissed.

She was enjoying herself *far* too much to listen. Instead, she located the gap, checked the first few steps were present, and then walked down them just as calmly as if she were at home.

'Luce, come back,' shouted Toby, 'my hair's doing funny things.'

'Mine too,' Lucy whispered to herself.

On reaching the door, she discovered that it was made from a dark, unpainted wood, as if this were the natural colour of the tree. The frame surrounding the portal was ornately panelled and decorated with carvings of sea-mammals and monsters, like something out of a gothic mansion. And the multi-faceted doorknob was equally elegant, fashioned from brilliant blue crystal with an animal design embedded inside. It was a crocodile – and once again, the river creature appeared to have sprouted wings.

'*Nice,*' whispered Lucy. She gave the knob a turn, even though she knew it wouldn't open. Then she turned towards Toby, and set off up the stairs again, wearing a disappointed expression. She stopped though, just for a moment, imagining for a second that she had heard the sound of crashing waves. Then the silence returned, and she was alone with her thoughts.

'That one was locked too,' she said, climbing into the cage just slightly out of breath. 'So there's just one more.'

'Erm, do you *really* think that's a good idea?' said Toby. 'Your hair is standing up now, and the last staircase might have some steps missing. And before you know it, it'll be thank you and goodnight Lucy Blake, it's been nice while it lasted, – you know the sort of thing.'

'That's why we're both going,' she grinned. 'And anyway, it's only the last staircase because we tried the others first.'

'Well there's no arguing with *that,*' grinned Toby. 'But the stream has got bigger Luce, and *stronger.*'

Lucy took hold of her friend's hand and drew him towards the side of the cage where she knew the fourth staircase would be. And without even checking for a step she began to run, pulling Toby behind her as she took to the air.

'*Whoo-hooo,*' she screamed. '*Whoo-hoo-hoo-hoo, I'm flying...*'

And she was *still* screaming and shouting when they ran full speed into the door at the bottom.

'*Whoo-hooo-hooo, thump…*'

'*Ow*,' said Toby. 'Erm, *that* was a bit solid, wasn't it?'

'Well look on the bright side,' smiled Lucy. 'We didn't fall down any non-existent invisible steps, did we?'

'True,' said Toby, examining the door. From a distance, it had looked yellow, but now they were closer it looked suspiciously like gold. Lucy ran her finger across the dull metallic surface, following the engraved outline of a vast wing-spread eagle. Suddenly they heard Gusset, calling out from the entrance door and waving his arms.

'What's he shouting about?' said Lucy.

'Something about noises,' said Toby, cupping his ears. 'He says we're supposed to be running away, not messing around.'

'Is that *all*?' said Lucy.

'No,' said Toby, 'there was something about breathing.'

'Uh-oh – so they're *back* then?' said Lucy. 'Are you *sure* we can't open it?'

Toby battered his shoulder against the door but it didn't move, not even a fraction of an inch.

'I think I've broken it,' he said, rubbing his arm. 'And I don't mean the door. Anyway, even if it *did* open, we couldn't just run off and leave Gusset.'

'Not unless it was absolutely necessary,' said Lucy.

'Oh, *charming*,' said Toby, examining her for a smile. 'You're not joking, are you?'

Before Lucy could answer, the air was filled with the sound of water falling from a great height onto solid stone. It was like a radio that had been tuned between stations – a deep, roaring hiss, like a million angry snakes. The heavenly blue trickle had turned to a torrent now, and was no longer confined to the area covered by the cage. It was falling over the eight sides of the roof now, tumbling in miniature cascades, and although the four staircases *still* couldn't be seen, their continuing presence was confirmed by the waterfalls that divided and then flowed around them.

'Erm, Luce, I hate to say 'I told you so', but the flow is getting wider. It's spreading towards the walls – and towards *us*.'

Lucy glanced over at Gusset who seemed to have grasped the danger quicker than they had. Their walnut-faced guide paused just long enough to wave, then stepped back into the porch-way and closed the door.

'Erm, I hope that wasn't a goodbye,' she said.

'Well if it was, you've only got yourself to blame,' said Toby.

'But I wasn't *really* going to leave him,' said Lucy uncertainly.

'I believe you – but we've got other things to worry about now. The particles are getting closer.'

'Get back against the door,' said Lucy, 'and hang onto something – it won't harm *us*, will it?'

'I wouldn't be so sure,' said Toby. 'You were alright before, when it was just a tiny trickle – but *now* look at it.'

The stream was rapidly increasing in diameter now; occupying almost the entire central area and raising a roar that made the surrounding air feel almost solid. The view of heaven was soon obscured, and as the edge of the stream reached the door-ledge, the vision of hell soon winked out as well. They were trapped now, pinned between the immovable 'eagle' door and a solid blue wall of particles that had completely swallowed the stairs. When Lucy looked more closely though she saw that the curtain of particles wasn't solid after all – in the depths of that teeming stream was a peacock-coloured mirage that reminded her of someone's coat.

'Any ideas?' shouted Toby. He was pressing his back up against the door – the thunder of the Lectric waterfall just inches from his face.

Lucy did have *one* idea, but the noise was going to make it difficult to explain, so she just went ahead and did it. She placed her hand against the roaring stream, fully expecting that she would feel nothing. For a moment, that was exactly what she *did* feel, but there was a sudden loud explosion and she was knocked backwards by a massive wave of pressure. It felt like a huge elephant was sitting on her chest. In fact, it felt like *several* elephants were sitting on her, all desperate to be the one that squeezed the very last bit of breath out of her body.

'And what did you want to do *that* for?' asked a voice in the dark.

'Erm, I thought it would be alright,' said Lucy. She opened her eyes and found Toby looking down at her with a concerned expression.

'Yeah, well don't do it again,' said Toby. 'Whatever it was that hit you, it hit me just as hard – but thankfully my skull is a lot thicker than yours.'

'No comment,' smiled Lucy. She dragged herself into a standing position, and as her head cleared, she realised the room wasn't dark after all – but it wasn't anything like she had expected either. It was similar in size to the hallways they had explored with Gusset, completely bare, except for the door they came through and the one behind them, which contained a small window.

'How did you get the golden door open?' she said.

'Oh, it was *easy* really,' said Toby. 'I thought I'd just stand back and let you stick your hand in that stream – what the bloody hell were you *thinking?*'

'It was harmless enough, wasn't it?' said Lucy, rubbing her bruised ribs. 'At least I *thought* it was. Anyway, we got the door open, didn't we? So where are we?'

'Have a look for yourself,' said Toby. He indicated a bright metal door behind them. It looked as though it had come from a high-security bank.

'We won't be getting *that* open in a hurry,' said Lucy. She looked through the tiny porthole and leaped back in surprise, almost knocking Toby back into the particle stream.

'Good, isn't it?' he said.

'Erm, ye-es, but what *is* it?' said Lucy.

'I thought it looked a bit like your uncle's laboratory,' said Toby.

Lucy went back for another peep, this time taking care not to dent her nose on the glass. The thick fishbowl window distorted the view, but she could still make out most of the details. It *did* look like a laboratory, but it was far more advanced than Byron's scrapheap. There were *things* in there, just floating in the air – strange, formless things that she didn't have a name for – and there were lights too, and knobs and levers, all begging to be pulled, prodded, and lit up.

'Very nice,' said Lucy, 'but how are we going to get out of here?'

'I don't know,' said Toby, 'but you haven't finished with the lab yet. Just keep your eyes on that window beyond the equipment racks.'

Lucy returned to the porthole and fastened her gaze on the huge window on the far side of the laboratory. There were clouds outside, which seemed quite normal, even if they *did* look a bit too pink. There was sky too – just a slightly paler shade of blue than she would have expected – and then she noticed what Toby had wanted her to see.

'*Ropes*,' she gasped, 'and an *airship* – or perhaps it's part of a big balloon? Or maybe…'

Lucy ducked down from the window.

'Hey,' she hissed, 'you didn't tell me there was someone in there.'

'I didn't know,' said Toby.

They flattened themselves against the sides of the cubicle as a shadowy figure approached the armoured window.

'What did they look like?' whispered Toby.

'I just saw a hand,' said Lucy, 'on one of those control knobs.'

'Erm, *Luce*, did you say control knob?'

Lucy turned towards the staircase, where the stream was still roaring past the door, and blocking their escape. Just below the level of the door ledge, a huge grid had appeared, like a safety net but made from criss-crossed steel wires. She guessed that it had been there the whole time, but something had happened to make it visible. And now, as the hand on the knob moved and the glow on the grid changed, the flow of the particle stream began to change in sympathy. She desperately wanted to see who the hand belonged to, but didn't dare lean forward in case they were discovered. All she could make out were four long grey fingers – they were grasping the dial quite firmly now, and turning the knob as far as it would go.

'It's cut off,' said Toby, 'erm, we can go, *can't* we?'

Lucy turned back and stared at the grid. The metal wires were fizzing so energetically now that the stream was no longer falling into the fire. It had doubled back towards the heavens, repelled by a swarm of dancing sparks.

'Run,' she shouted, 'run like mad, before they turn it back on.'

Toby didn't need to be told twice – he burst into a run, stopping to breathe only when he reached the safety of the cage. Lucy wasn't far behind, but tripped, suddenly realising that the walls were no longer there. If she happened to stray over the edge of the staircase now, she'd had it. All of a sudden, she was far more aware of the fizzing mesh of wires below her. The sparks were still dancing across the woven metal surface, but any second now, they might disappear and allow the blue stream to fall again.

'Luce, stop messing about and get up here. The yellow door has closed again. And Gusset's door is still shut. We're *trapped*.'

Lucy picked herself up and sprinted towards the cage, and then, without pausing for breath, she grabbed Toby by the hand and ran headlong down the stairs towards the green door. When they reached the bottom, she battered her fists against it, still too breathless to shout.

'Gusset,' she yelled eventually. 'Gusset, it's *us* – open up.'

There was no response – just a feeling that their hair was made of hot needles and wanted to get back inside their heads.

'It's starting again Luce – the stream's coming back.'

'Oh great,' hissed Lucy. '*Gusset*!' she screamed. 'Open the stinking-rotten *door* will you?'

Nothing happened, except for an increase in the roar that signalled the stream's activity. This time it meant business – there was a scream in the air, as if the particles wanted to tear every molecule out of the atmosphere.

'Gusset, *please*,' screamed Lucy. '*Let us in.*'

She fell against the door sobbing, and it was then that she came face to face with the symbol set in the glass hemisphere. It was a beetle, with a gold head and a brilliant-green iridescent shell, and even though they were about to be fried alive she felt drawn towards the glassy dome - the insect looked almost alive, as if it might fly out to meet them if the glass were ever broken.

'*Gusset*, for goodness sa…'

'Oh,' she gasped, as the door flew open and she fell into the porch-way. 'Well *you* took your time.'

'Never mind telling him off,' shouted Toby. 'Get out of the way.'

A shower of sparks flew past, threatening to sear him in two – so he launched himself into the air and landed on Lucy.

'Thanks,' he breathed, as Gusset slammed the door shut.

'*Oof*, yes,' said Lucy, 'and thanks for using me as a landing mat.'

'You'll get your breath back eventually,' snapped Gusset. 'Now why don't you start by telling me what all *that* was about?'

'But we don't *know*,' gasped Lucy, 'we've never seen anything like it.'

'And we don't ever want to see it again,' said Toby.

'Hmm,' said Gusset, 'and what about those other doors?'

'Locked,' said Lucy.

'Yes,' said Gusset, 'but you're good with locked doors, aren't you?'

Lucy gave Toby a look that meant '*say nothing*', but Gusset intercepted it and wrinkled his forehead in a deep frown.

'If we're going to get out of here we need to work together,' he said.

'We *are* working together,' said Lucy. 'You know as much about those doors as we do. And I'm not lying – all three of them *were* locked.'

'*That's* true,' said Toby with a smile.

'I wish I could believe that,' said Gusset. 'There are dangerous places in this city, and if you can't trust the folk standing behind you…'

'Trust us later,' said Lucy. 'But first we have to get out of the kiosk.'

'And find Fenny,' said Toby. 'And to do *that* we have to find Ra…'

'*Thank* you,' hissed Lucy. 'A little *too* much information I think?'

'*See?*' said Gusset. 'There you go *again* with your little secrets.'

'We just want to rescue Fenny and go home,' said Toby, trying to make amends.

'But first you must find her,' said Gusset. 'And for that you need to know a little bit about how she got here.'

'Yes,' said Toby, 'how *did* she get here? Was it through your cupboard?'

'Ah-*hah!*' said Gusset triumphantly. 'I *knew* you two came here by some strange means.'

'*Lindstrom*,' said Lucy, heaving a great sigh, 'you have *such* a big mouth.'

'Sorry,' said Toby, 'I wasn't thinking.'

'No, you *weren't*,' said Gusset. 'But to answer your question, *no*, I didn't find your friend in my map store.'

'Then how?' said Toby.

'I reckon she was brought here by one of *them*,' said Gusset.

'*Them?*' said Toby.

'The Sisters,' said Gusset. 'All *I* know is that she turned up completely out of the purple, just like you did. Only she wasn't spouting off a load of gibberish about how she'd arrived on an ornithopter from Farperoo.'

'Yeah, that'd be *your* department, Luce,' grinned Toby.

'Yes, *thank* you,' said Lucy sharply. 'We all have a few tales to tell, don't we? So why don't you tell us about the people who brought Fenny here? The children at the Braneskule mentioned the Sisters, but they never explained what they meant.'

'And neither will I,' said Gusset. 'It's not for me to be putting things like that inside your head. All I know is that she was *brought*, under most irregular circumstances.'

'It was the bed stabbers, wasn't it?' said Toby. 'Those things I saw in the shew stone.'

'Perhaps,' said Gusset. 'I told you, I never saw her being fetched, and that's the way I like it. But if I *was* to see such a thing then I'd prefer it was a Vooghul – they say that if you look the Sisters in the face you'll never live to tell the tale.'

'So nobody knows what they look like?' said Toby.

'There are certain *drawings* available,' said Gusset, 'but I don't know which of them are accurate – none probably.'

'You've seen Toby's bed stabbers though?' said Lucy.

'*Everyone* has seen the Vooghul,' hissed Gusset. 'They do the Sisters' dirty work.'

'That's right,' said Toby. 'I could tell they stank, even though I couldn't smell them. And now we're trapped in here, it's twice as bad.'

'I know what you mean,' said Gusset. 'The thought of being tracked by those aberrations is quite enough, but in here, it seems all the more serious.'

'They're going to kill us twice you mean?' smiled Lucy.

'Don't *ever* joke about such things,' said Gusset. 'Not until you know what you're talking about.'

'Yeah, Luce,' said Toby. 'You haven't even seen one.'

'And I don't particularly want to,' said Lucy, 'but I'd still like to know what they are and what they want.'

'What they *are* is simple,' said Gusset, 'but what they *want*, well that's a completely different thing.'

'So what *are* they?' said Toby.

'Are you sure you want to know?' said Gusset. 'It's not pleasant.'

'Yes,' said Lucy, 'we do.'

'They serve the Sisters,' said Gusset, breathing through his teeth. 'But before they became servants they were just ordinary folk, like you and me.'

'*Before?*' said Toby.

'Before whatever gets done to them – *if* you get my meaning.'

'Yes, *very* clear,' grinned Toby, 'and what is it that gets done?'

'I'm not even sure it *is*,' replied Gusset, 'because *that* would mean that someone is responsible – for all *we* know it might just happen.'

'Then what *happens*?' said Lucy. 'Do they die?'

'Some folk reckon they do,' said Gusset. 'But I think it's worse than that – you'll see one soon enough, and *then* you'll know. They wear hideous, rotting clothes and their faces are hidden by some kind of gaseous mask. Sometimes you might even think you recognise them, but their features get swirled away at the very last moment.'

'Oh,' said Lucy. 'They sound charming.'

'It gets worse,' said Gusset. 'They smell of decaying flesh.'

'And they don't have any feet,' added Toby.

'And that is *very* bad,' said Gusset, 'because if they were living then they'd be needing those feet, wouldn't they?'

'And you've *seen* one of these floating things?' said Lucy.

'Plenty,' said Gusset, 'but you never forget the first time. It was a warm enough day, but my bones were chilled through like glass rods – and the *stench* was unbearable – I nearly vomited up my mid-day sucky-mess.'

'I know the feeling,' smiled Toby.

'But it didn't harm you?' said Lucy.

'It wasn't paying attention to me,' said Gusset. 'I was out searching for berries with Fennel Shank – and *he* had this theory that if you ever came across one of them you could persuade it to speak about its former self.'

'How?' said Toby.

'By distracting it,' said Gusset.

'Did it work?' said Lucy.

'*Poor* Fennel,' sighed Gusset.

'What happened?' said Toby. 'Did it kill him?'

'I don't know,' admitted Gusset. 'I ran away and never saw him again. He sometimes visits my dreams though – howling like the wind, and calling me a coward for saving my own skin.'

Lucy turned her eyes towards the ceiling as Toby made a pathetic attempt to imitate the sound of howling wind.

'That's *rubbish*,' she said, 'even Tarquin could do better than that.'

'Erm, maybe he *could*,' said Toby nervously, 'but that wasn't me.'

The blood drained from their faces as they realised that the sound was coming from the behind the scarab door.

'*Uh-oh,*' said Lucy. As she spoke, the knob on the green door began to turn – she had to think fast.

'Open one of the other doors,' she shouted. 'You can only have one open at once, so if we…'

The green door opened, just a crack, but she was the only one there to see it – Toby and Gusset had already disappeared.

A dark, dank-smelling shape forced its way through the door, brushing the tattered rag-ends of its clothing on her face and leaving a cold, wet dew on her skin. Lucy was desperate to rub it off, but even more eager to get away, so she turned and fled.

The serpent door led to another hallway, where the wands and tiles were just as she expected. There was a difference though, because there was an elephant's-foot walking-stick stand and a pair of shoes. There was no time to stand and wonder about it though, because the Vooghul had followed her, breathing in a way that suggested it was about to speak. Lucy ducked beneath it and opened another door, then another and another, slamming each one shut as she ran headlong through the maze. Her mind was an absolute mess of detail. She was trying to put the creature's smell out of her thoughts whilst remembering the sequence of wands – all the while wondering where her companions had gone.

'*Luce,*' cried Toby suddenly, grabbing his friend as she flew past. '*Stop –* it's us - you're safe.'

'We're *not* safe,' she screamed, 'that bloody thing *touched* me – I can still feel it on my face.'

'Don't worry, it'll wash off,' said Gusset.

'No it *won't,*' screamed Lucy. 'It wasn't a smell it left behind, it was a feeling, and it'll *never* wash off. I could *feel* what it was thinking and it was overflowing with sadness – it *hates* what it's doing.'

'But it's going to keep doing it?' said Toby.

'It doesn't have the will to resist,' sobbed Lucy. 'There's nothing left but blind obedience. There *was* intelligence once, like a creative fire, but all that's left now is a few embers of thought and some very confusing ideas.'

'About itself *maybe*,' said Gusset, 'but it will have a very clear idea about what the Sisters want it to do.'

'Then we'd better keep moving,' said Toby.

'Good idea,' sniffed Lucy, 'only I *think* it knows what we intend.'

'I'd be surprised,' said Gusset. 'I don't think *we* know, do we?'

'Well let's do something different anyway,' said Toby. 'If *we* don't know what we're doing, then how will *they*?'

'It's a plan,' said Gusset, 'just not a very good one.'

Lucy opened a door without even looking to see where it led, and when the others followed, she closed it and opened another, squinting her eyes so that even the colours of the doors became a faded mystery. Each time they entered a new hallway she steadfastly refused to memorise what she was seeing, choosing a new door at random.

'Well,' said Toby, 'you've certainly got me fooled.'

'Me too,' said Gusset. 'I don't have the numbers to count the doors we just passed through, but it was certainly a lot.'

He sat down on the tiled floor with his back to the eagle door, and Lucy slumped down against the green door opposite. Toby remained standing, but only so he could twiddle with the serpent wand. It was the first opportunity he'd had to examine one closely, and when he did, he wished he hadn't bothered. The carved shaft of the wand was crude and badly painted, and the coloured glass of the lamp was pitted and cracked, as if the maker had been in a hurry. Then he realised why – if the maze went on for as far as he imagined then there must be thousands of them.

'*So*,' said Gusset eventually, 'what exactly did you see back there?'

'I told you,' said Lucy. 'It was one of the Vooghul.'

'I meant what did you see *inside* it?' snapped Gusset.

'You believe me then?' said Lucy.

'Not at first,' said Gusset. 'But I changed my mind when you mentioned the mental flame – the word *Vooghul* means '*Empty Lantern*' in the old language.'

'That makes sense if they're dead,' said Toby, 'their thoughts are like a light that has been put out.'

'That's not all,' said Lucy, 'there was something else.'

'Something *else?*' said Gusset. 'Well, I *am* impressed – obviously our simple mysteries aren't quite mysterious enough for a girl of your talents.'

'There were shadows,' said Lucy plainly, 'in the creature's thoughts.'

'I see,' mumbled Gusset, 'and what exactly does *that* mean?'

'It was trying to stop me seeing what it was thinking,' said Lucy. 'But I could sense everything, as if its mind was this big empty church, and there were just a few small candles lighting up certain memories. But there were other things too – things it had been instructed never to reveal.'

'And these things in the shadows,' said Toby, 'what were *they?*'

'*Wings,*' said Lucy. 'It was trying to stop me seeing them.'

'Wings belonging to what?' said Gusset.

'I couldn't *say* for certain,' whispered Lucy, 'but they might be angels.'

'I don't think so,' laughed Gusset. 'Those things are just myths. The children talk about them all the time, but there's no *truth* in it.'

'Well they aren't exactly overflowing into the streets where *we* come from,' said Lucy. 'But that's what I saw – huge, dusty wings, flapping in the darkness.'

'Children's stories,' said Gusset, 'that's all.'

'Perhaps,' smiled Lucy, 'but there can be a *lot* more to a story than what you see on the surface.'

'I'll vouch for that,' grinned Toby.

'So, do you *know* something about angels then?' said Gusset.

'Not nearly enough,' admitted Lucy, 'that's why we're here – because we're running away from one.'

'I see,' said Gusset. 'Well perhaps you ought to let me in on a few of your secrets? Once we get to somewhere safe?'

Hours later, they emerged into the darkness of the forest again, having seen no further sign of the particle-sphere or elephant's-foot walking-stick stands, and only once coming across a hallway where Lucy had scratched a number seventeen onto the tiles. There had even been something strange about that though, because the mark had moved to the opposite corner.

'I vote we stop for a rest,' said Toby. 'We were wandering around in those hallways for ages – and I think both my feet have dropped off.'

Without answering, the others sank to their knees, eager for a break themselves. They had come to a small clearing with a dry brush floor and plenty of fallen branches they could use as cover.

'This is ideal,' said Gusset. 'Gather up the wood, and we'll make a hide.'

Nobody felt like arguing, so they spread out to collect wood, keeping a close eye on the shadowy trees that surrounded them. For once though, luck was on their side and they were left undisturbed. When they had gathered enough branches, they piled them up in a haphazard way and crawled beneath the camouflage to get some sleep.

Lucy lay back with her hands behind her head, staring up through the branches and the canopy of trees towards the stars. She smiled as she recognised the familiar red smudge, and in her head, she began to sing a happy tune as she inhaled the fragrance of wild heather and thyme. But the peace didn't last.

'Luce? Is that a firefly?' said Toby. 'Or a star?'

'It's a firefly,' said Lucy, 'now get some sleep.'

'I can't,' said Toby. 'Do you think we'll ever get home?'

'Yes,' said Lucy, biting her lip. 'I'm sure we will.'

'Erm, can you smell chips?' said Toby.

'No, I *can't*,' hissed Lucy, 'now do you *mind*?'

'I wish I had a bacon sandwich,' said Toby.

'So do I,' said Lucy, 'at least it would stop you talking.'

'Not for long it wouldn't, I'm *starving*. Erm, I don't suppose you've got Lily's sand… erm, no, on second thoughts, maybe not.'

'We're not going to get any sleep at all, are we?' moaned Gusset. 'Not with *him* blathering all night.'

'I can't help it,' said Toby, 'my limbs feel like jelly.'

'Mine too,' said Lucy. 'I'm never going to drop off with all *this* spinning around in my head.'

'And there's that buzzing noise as well,' said Toby. 'It's like an elephant snoring – but with a pillow over his head.'

Gusset glanced towards the previously silent treetops, where there was now an obvious humming of wings above the canopy.

'What *is* that?' said Toby.

'As long as it doesn't get any closer you don't want to know,' said Gusset, snuffing his Pockalumo. 'Things that hum in the dark are best left alone.'

Toby looked at Lucy with a sly grin, knowing that she'd be thinking about the confuser.

'That's right,' he said, 'that's how we got into this mess.'

'*Mess*,' hissed Gusset, 'yes, that just about describes it.' He disappeared for a moment and came back laden down with a huge pile of branches. 'Here, I thought we might need extra.'

'Are you *still* worried about us being found?' said Lucy.

'Yeah,' said Toby, 'do we need extra cover because of the humming?'

'This is where you expect me to say no, isn't it?' said Gusset. 'And then you want me to tell you that everything will be alright in the morning.'

'Hopefully,' giggled Toby, 'yeah, that would be great.'

'Well it's going to get worse,' growled Gusset. 'I *know*, because my leg bones are twitching.'

'And why's that?' said Lucy.

'I wasn't going to say anything, not *yet*,' said Gusset, 'but since you ask, there's the small matter of what went on at the Braneskule – all that stuff about the age of the world and so on.'

'Ah, *that*,' said Lucy.

'Yes, *that*,' said Gusset, 'now call me suspicious if you like, but I don't reckon you should go blabbing that kind of thing to the first person you meet.'

'But *you* were the first one we met,' said Toby.

'In that case you didn't want to go blabbing it to the second person you met,' said Gusset, 'or the third – and *especially* not to teachers, and *double* especially if one of those teachers was Feazle Niblock – she's a sly one and no mistake.'

'But didn't *you* used to be a teacher?' said Lucy.

'I *was*, back when Glassbone Haddock was the Beak – but we had a *slight* disagreement about the new creation theories – and I had to hand in my robes.'

'We can still trust you though, can't we?' said Toby.

'You can trust me double,' said Gusset, 'but times are changing, and just trusting me isn't going to keep you safe.'

'So what's the humming?' said Lucy.

'Nothing for you to worry about,' said Gusset.

'It is,' said Lucy.

'It's just bats,' insisted Gusset.

As if they'd been waiting for the signal, thousands of bats suddenly rose from their roosts and flooded the sky — an inky green blanket that folded itself this way and that, looking for somewhere to settle. And when the curtain of wings was finally gone, so was the humming.

'There's an ancient roost somewhere in the forest,' said Gusset. 'But every time they take off in search of it, a few of them die and are never replaced. At one time they used to cover the Forest of Skeels completely, but their numbers have been dwindling for centuries.'

'Since before the world began?' suggested Toby.

'Yes,' said Gusset, frowning, '*long* before that.'

'Well that's not what Lucy told them, back at the Braneskule.'

'Oh?' said Gusset.

'No,' said Toby, 'she said the bats were scales — from dragons.'

'Dragons eh?' said Gusset. 'And where did she get *that* idea?'

'Luce?' said Toby. 'Where exactly *did* you get that idea?'

There was no reply — just the sound of a young girl snoring — and above her, in the canopy and in the sky, the sound of infinite movement and wonder.

Rootspank and Nine-Tails

'This is *it*,' said Gusset. 'I'm certain of it.'

'But you *said* that the last three times,' moaned Lucy. 'In fact you've said it every time we come to something that looks even *remotely* like a clearing.'

'It's the mist,' grumbled Gusset, 'it isn't exactly helping.'

'Neither are you,' whispered Toby.

'I *heard* that,' said their guide. 'Perhaps *you* might like to try?'

'Sorry,' said Toby, 'but we don't know where we're going or what we're looking for so I don't think I'd be much help.'

'Alright,' sighed Gusset, 'we're heading for the Bright Byrde — and for now that's all I'm going to say — and to get there we need to find a long rope bridge — it's one of the filaments that join the city plateau to the surrounding plains.'

'So why don't we just wait until the mist rises?' suggested Toby.

'An *excellent* idea,' said Gusset, snurking up a bit of loose phlegm. 'And when it clears and *we* can see the bridges, those stinking Vooghul will be able to see *us*.'

'*Ah*, good point,' said Lucy, feeling a sudden shiver on her spine.

'I thought there was just one of them?' said Toby.

'If there's one there'll be two,' said Gusset, 'and if there's two…'

'We get the idea,' said Toby.

'Yes, we understand perfectly,' said Lucy, recalling the wraith's damp, rotting-meat stink. 'So we need to find a bridge — *now*.'

'Yes, but not just any old bridge,' said Gusset. 'There are twenty-one.'

'*Oh*,' said Lucy.

'But we've been looking for *ages* and we're *tired*,' yawned Toby. 'We haven't slept properly for days — can't we just rest for a *little* while?'

'We're *all* tired,' said Gusset. 'Especially those of us who laid awake all night listening to stories about something called a bacon sandwich.'

'Erm, yeah, sorry about that,' said Toby. 'Actually now you come to mention it, I don't suppose there's any chance…'

Gusset growled like a chain saw, and Toby decided the sandwich could wait. But *only* if he could plaster huge piles of brown sauce on it, when it finally materialised.

'Erm, *wait* a minute,' said Toby. 'You did say *bridge*, didn't you?'

'*Rope* bridge,' said Gusset. 'It *has* to be a rope bridge.'

'Yeah, right,' said Toby, 'so will *that* one do?' He pointed to where there had been an impenetrable bank of fog just moments before. Suddenly though they were standing in a ring of vapour-free air, and for the first time since entering the mist they were granted an uninterrupted view of the sky — and the strangely patterned yet comforting stars.

'Erm, how, did *that* happen?' said Gusset.

'You *really* don't want to know,' said Lucy smiling at her friend. 'It wouldn't do to have the answer to everything, now would it?'

'I reckon not,' said Gusset, his eyes fixed firmly on the weather-lifter.

'So is this the one?' grinned Toby.

As they approached the edge of the clearing a series of thick, shadowy beams emerged from the thinning mist. Each was tethered by a dozen or so thick ropes, which in turn were lashed to a series of huge, squat boulders. It reminded Lucy of a picture-book giant, flat on his back and pinned to the ground by myriad tiny cables.

'It certainly *looks* like it,' said Gusset.

As they got even closer to the web-like network of beams and ropes, they were able to discern more of the structural details. Hundreds of smaller beams had joined forces to support a pair of massive wooden pillars, which were driven into the ground at an angle. And these in turn supported the ends of four huge ropes that simply disappeared off into the mist, carrying a shaky-looking wooden path upwards and out of sight.

'This is *it*,' said Gusset with a huge smile, 'we've *found* it.'

'*We?*' said Toby. 'Erm, it was *me* that found it, wasn't it? Only I'd like a *bit* of credit for rescuing us.'

'But how do we know it's the right one?' said Lucy.

'*Tintinnabulations*,' said Gusset with a broad grin. '*Listen.*'

'Tin *what?*' said Toby.

'*Shhh.* I can *hear* it,' said Lucy. 'It's like tiny bronze bells in the mist.'

'It's the *suspense-chimes*,' said Gusset enthusiastically. 'Listen carefully to their pattern – they sing a different song for each bridge.'

'Like lighthouses,' suggested Toby.

Ting-te-te-ting-ting – tong – ting-te-te-ting-ting…

They could all hear it clearly now – a subtle, metallic sound, suspended in the air all around them – a distant, yet enchanting piece of music that seemed to permeate the entire universe.

Ting-te-te-ting-ting – tong – ting-te-te-ting-ting…

'It's like Morse-code,' said Lucy, 'only much prettier.'

Ting-te-te-ting-ting – tong – ting-te-te-ting-ting…

Ting-te-te-ting-ting – tong – ting-te-te-ting-ting…

'It's my favourite crossing,' smiled Gusset. 'The Green Witch Suspense was the nineteenth bridge to be built, back in the second year of the world.'

'We believe you,' laughed Toby as he stepped onto the first slippery-looking slat. 'But just remember who it was that *found* it.'

'Erm, *actually*, it doesn't feel particularly safe,' said Lucy as they edged away from the great pillars.

'No,' admitted Gusset, 'and it gets worse – you'll need to keep a tight grip on the hand-rope.'

'*Great*,' chimed Toby and Lucy together.

Gusset was right – it *was* worse further on. As the main pillars gradually disappeared behind them, the moss covered support ropes began to sway violently, even though there was no trace of wind. There *was* a howling sound though, like a hunting pack in the chasm, however far down *that* was.

'Try not to walk in step,' said Lucy. 'It'll interrupt the swinging motion.'

Sure enough, when they broke the synchronisation of their footsteps the bridge stopped bucking about and their passage became a lot calmer. It still creaked and groaned every time they moved though – like the stays in an opera-singer's whalebone corset. Lucy gave a sudden grin – it was like listening to Aunt Violet under full-sail, her huge undergarments billowing in a hurricane-force storm, her bony ship's timbers protesting under the strain.

'You alright?' said Gusset. 'Only I could swear I saw you smile.'

'You did,' she laughed. 'I was thinking about that *thing* wiping its slimy trailers on my face – but then I had this picture of one of my stepmother's awful sisters, and for a moment the thought of it went away.'

'*See?*' said Gusset. 'Even *troublesome* relations can be of use sometimes.'

'Actually that's the first time,' said Lucy, a little more seriously. 'And from what I can remember of my Aunty Violet, it'll probably be the last.'

When the companions finally emerged from the mist, their journey's end was just visible as an indistinct smudge in the pre-dawn light. Even so, Lucy could tell there was something strange about it – it wasn't at all like the other end of the bridge – more like a single huge pylon growing up out of the mist.

'Don't worry,' said Gusset, 'you'll *like* it.'

'Percy said that about my last birthday present,' said Lucy. 'And I *hated* it.'

As they covered the last quarter-mile of ropeway a faint glow appeared in the east, and gradually, as the dark blue of night turned towards the pink of dawn, the dark shape became clearer.

'That's the Master's Crook,' said Gusset helpfully. 'It supports the whole northern end of the bridge.'

Toby and Lucy stared in awe as they realised what was holding the bridge up. Before anybody said anything though, they continued for a hundred yards or so, finally stepping off the long, heavy rope-sling that had carried them all the way from the forest clearing. They were on solid ground at last, with a powdery red rock beneath their feet.

'It's like a huge, bony finger made out of stone,' said Toby, peering out over the edge.

'*Precisely,*' said Gusset, 'and that's why this is my favourite bridge.'

'Well it's not mine,' said Lucy. 'I feel like an ant on the end of someone's finger – someone thin, and not very nice to know.'

'Yeah,' grinned Toby, thinking of Lucy's stepmother. 'And if she decides to pick her nose, we've *had* it.'

Lucy moved to the indistinct shoulder of rock at the edge and looked down. There was nothing to see but mist, and nowhere to go except back to the forest, or forwards toward the city. Everything else was a sheer drop into the unknown.

'Let's get a move on,' she said. 'This place feels dangerous – and I don't just mean dropping off into the mist.'

There was another short length of rope-work that joined the slender finger of rock to the edge of the chasm, and this was by far the shakiest section they'd encountered. The wooden slats were uneven and slippery and the ropes that bound them together didn't seem to be that well tied.

'Erm, you first,' said Toby, trying a cautious toe on the first step.

'Don't worry,' said Gusset, practically skipping across, 'it's perfectly safe.'

'Yes,' said Lucy, cautiously picking her way over, 'and where have we heard *that* before?'

They stood in silence as Toby edged his way across, and then, with just the slightest of sideways glances at the strangely carved pillars, they walked across the rock-strewn plain towards the city gates. As they did so though, they paused for a moment, their necks tingling with apprehension.

'I can *feel* something,' said Toby.

'Me too,' said Lucy.

'Then don't look,' said Gusset, with a slight shiver. 'It's probably just that imagination of your playing tricks.'

'Probably,' said Lucy, facing straight ahead.

'Yeah, that'll be it,' said Toby.

Gusset turned, but there was nobody there. The deserted walkway creaked and groaned in the slight breeze. Further back, beyond the rocky finger, the main span of the bridge was just as empty. Suddenly, the wind dropped and even the bridge was silenced – the only remaining sound was that of the chimes.

Ting-te-te-ting-ting – tong – ting-te-te-ting-ting...
Ting-te-te-ting-ting – tong – ting-te-te-ting-ting...

Ahead of them lay the faint outline of the city walls – vast piles of greenish-blue stone that stretched east and west, just as far as the morning-haze permitted them to see. The barricade and the spires of the buildings inside it were exactly like the structures they'd seen from the Braneskule – all armed to the teeth with swooping, bladed edges and sharp, jagged spikes. As they got closer though, their attention was diverted to the gate. The more Lucy looked, the more it seemed to her like an animal lying in wait – like a giant wolf in fact, with its head draped over the wall. The curved doors formed an arch that looked like a nose, and there was a round opening in each one that might have been a nostril. Further up, set into the wall itself, were a pair of elliptical windows that looked like eyes. There was a dim yellow light burning in each one, giving the impression that they were being watched by some dozing, glint-eyed monster. It was probably listening too, because the portal was flanked by a pair of towers that looked suspiciously like pricked-up ears.

'Erm, that's *quite* a gate,' said Toby nervously. He looked suddenly pale, having noticed a frowning, beak-like expression on the left-hand tower and a mocking, almost maniacal grin on the other. 'Erm, who exactly does it keep out?'

'*Us*, for the moment,' said Gusset.

'But I thought this was where we were heading?' said Lucy, watching Gusset closely – he kept looking back at the bridge, when he thought she wouldn't notice.

'We saved time coming through the kiosks,' he said, 'so we're early.'

'Shouldn't we knock or something?' said Toby. He was watching the tower-faces, just in case their expressions changed.

'You can *try*,' said Gusset. 'But you won't get an answer whilst there are tintinnabulations in the air.'

Toby strode up to the huge nail-studded doors and rapped his knuckles on the ironclad timbers. It hurt – and whilst he was still wishing he hadn't knocked *quite* so hard, one of the wolf-eye windows opened and a bucket of stinking slops was poured out.

Ting-te-te-ting-ting – tong – ting-te-te-ting-ting...

'Right,' he shouted, leaping aside just in time. 'Erm, we'll be down here when you need us – and thanks very much for your time.'

'Told you,' said Gusset with a smug grin. 'The bells chime between sundown and sun-up – and whilst they ring the doors stay shut. It's the rules – and there are no exceptions.'

Ting-te-te-ting-ting – tong – ting-te-te-ting-ting...

Toby wanted to see how the bells worked and returned to the gate, this time making sure he didn't walk under the eye. The chiming mechanism was mounted in a niche to the right of the archway and consisted of a wheel divided into six parts, each supporting a tiny metal disc that sounded a '*ting*' or a '*te*' or a '*tong*' as it passed a fixed striker. The whole affair was kept in motion by a continuous loop of string that appeared through a hole in the wall and disappeared through another.

'Hey Luce,' he called, 'this is like the message pole I used to send you those notes when you were locked in the Panopticon.'

Ting-te-te-ting-ting – tong – ting-te-te-ting-ting…

'*Luce?*'

Ting-te-te-ting-ting – tong – ting-te-te-ting-ting…

'Erm, ye-es, I sup-pose,' she said, somewhat distracted. 'But how long before they stop?'

Ting-te-te-ting-ting – tong – ting-te-te-ting-ting…

'Not long,' smiled Gusset. 'Are they getting on your wick?'

Ting-te-te-ting-ting – tong – ting-te-te-ting-ting…

'No, they're beautiful,' replied Lucy. 'But the Vooghul have caught us up.'

'Where?' said Toby.

'Look past the finger and down the slope of the main bridge,' said Lucy. 'Do you see where it drops into the mist? Now come forwards about two or three hundred feet.'

'*Uh-oh,*' said Toby. He began shaking his head, and a feeling of panic quickly overtook him. He was trembling. Lucy took hold of his hand, even though she felt the same fear. With Aunty Violet's help, she had managed to forget them just for a while, but the creatures were *much* more resilient than that – they simply refused to be pushed to the back of their victims' minds.

'It's *them* alright,' mumbled Gusset.

'How long?' said Lucy. She stared glassy eyed at the three wraith-like forms that were gliding towards them, like dark, stringless kites, guided by the bridge ropes.

'I think it's time we knocked again,' said Gusset.

'But what about the tintinnabulation things?' said Toby.

'*Sod* the ruddy tintinnabulations,' said Gusset. 'There's no cover outside these walls – we need to get inside, *now*.' He stepped up to the wolf-nose door and put his hand through a tiny flap near the ground.

'What's he up to?' whispered Toby.

'Maybe that's where they leave the key?' said Lucy with a nervous smile.

Gusset cursed and then sprawled himself in front of the gate, jamming his entire arm into the aperture. He was feeling around for something on the other side – and eventually he found it.

'*Wee-ow, wee-ow, wee-ow, wee-ow, weeeeee…*'

'What on earth was *that*?' said Lucy. 'It sounded like a wild cat.'

'Wild?' grinned Gusset, dusting himself off. 'It was absolutely *furious* – I gave it a *right* old tail-pulling.'

'So now what?' said Toby.

'We wait for Rootspank to get out of bed and see who's messing with her pussy,' said Gusset. 'She's the gatekeeper, and she *hates* it if anyone interferes with old Nine-Tails.'

'Well I hope she's a light sleeper,' said Lucy, glancing at the bridge.

They studied the progress of the wraiths for a moment, but then, as if someone had whispered the same idea to each of them, they lifted their eyes towards the horizon. Their gaze followed the route of the bridge to the point where it descended into the mist, and from there it travelled across the brilliant white quilt-of-morning, flying all the way to the southern rim. And there, rising from a cauldron of its own private clouds, was the Braneskule. It seemed to be waiting for something, like a lonely, twisted grandparent, lurking behind a lace curtain.

'We're never going back there, *are* we?' said Lucy.

'Not if *I* can help it,' replied Gusset. He gave the gate a swift kick and shouted Rootspank's name, but the doors remained resolutely closed. There wasn't even a bucket of sludge to acknowledge his efforts.

'So how far *did* we come?' said Toby, trying to take his mind off their approaching fate.

'About thirty miles,' said Gusset, holding a wet finger in the air.

'It seemed more like a hundred,' said Toby nervously. The Vooghul had reached the end of the main span now and were floating across the tip of the Master's finger.

'Nope,' said Gusset, 'because if we *had* come that far then we'd be floating in the Skye Abysse – the world is only sixty-four miles across, see?'

'Why am I not surprised?' said Toby. 'I suppose if it's only been here for thirteen years they haven't had time to build out any further.'

'There *is* no further,' said Gusset, picking up a rock and examining it as though it were a jewel. 'This is all the world we have.'

'We heard,' said Lucy. Her eyes were fixed firmly on the Vooghul. They were crossing the short bridge now, and would soon reach the rock-plain.

'Yeah,' said Toby, 'there were *lessons.*'

'There are lessons *everywhere,*' said Gusset solemnly, 'and enemies too, like the Vooghul, queuing up to teach them.'

'Look, I don't want to worry anyone,' said Lucy, 'but those things are getting *awfully* close – how are we doing with the gate?'

'I'll give the cat another yank,' said Gusset.

'Erm, wait a minute,' said Lucy, 'what's that smell?' She opened her lips slightly and allowed the tip of her tongue out to sample the atmosphere. It hesitated though, like a reluctant bird in a cuckoo clock. The morning air was suddenly thick with the stink of rotting meat.

'It's the Whiff-of-the-Smiff,' said a relieved Gusset. 'Look, the gates are opening.'

'Yeuk – I never thought I'd be glad to smell something like *that,*' said Toby, trying to squeeze through the gap. 'Quick, let's get inside.'

'*Halt* – whom have you there?' The challenge came from a stocky little woman clad in light leather armour. She walked with a slight limp and bore a striking resemblance to Gusset. *He* didn't have a dumpy little sword though, or a brass-hoop necklace strung with dozens of ornate keys.

'Rootspank, stop messing about will you? It's *me*, Gusset.'

'I *know*,' laughed the gatekeeper. 'No-one else would dare to mess with my little Nine-Tails. And I see you've brought trouble with you, as usual.'

'Erm, yes,' said Gusset, 'these are, erm…'

'I *know* who they are,' snapped Rootspank. 'Word travels fast.'

'And so do the Vooghul,' said Gusset.

'They're on the bridge,' added Lucy breathlessly.

'No they aren't,' said Toby glancing over his shoulder. 'They're *off* the rotten bridge. Can you stop them? *Please?*'

'Quite the little team, *aren't* you?' smiled Rootspank.

'Yes, we *are*,' said Lucy, 'so can you *stop* them?'

'What do *you* think?' grinned the gatekeeper. She waved her sword at the chain-master and moments later the gates slammed with a peal of thunder, dislodging mortar from the framework and flushing out a couple of birds who were nesting in the wall. They flapped and fluttered in front of Lucy for a moment, and then, satisfied that they were amongst friends, went back to their roost.

'Phew, now *that* was what I call close,' said Gusset. He was busy trying to disentangle a rather annoyed Nine-Tails. The cat was extracting his sweet revenge by perching on the janitor's head, using his rather attractive-looking claws as grappling irons.

'Nice hat you've got there,' smiled Toby.

'Yes, *very* attractive,' grinned Rootspank, 'but I'd dispose of it if I were you – there's a new tax on headgear.'

Just then, a small boy turned up with a storm-lamp. It cast a welcome light into the gloom, illuminating the high stone arch that formed the roof of the tunnel. At the far end of the archway were a pair of inner-doors, and beyond that was a gloomy looking courtyard.

'*Everyone*, stay where you are,' hissed a feeble voice. It belonged to a sad, doe-eyed creature who was slumped over a stationary treadmill set into a wall niche. He looked exhausted, but still had enough energy to speak.

'*Trundle*, shut your mouth and get back to your rotten bell-work.'

The man in the shadows was seated behind a large, wooden counting table. It looked as though it had recently been dragged out under the arch, because the tracks in the dirt were still fresh.

'But it's daytime,' moaned the treadmill creature. 'We don't *need* the bells.'

'Then go and *polish* them or something,' said the bean-counter. He looked like a ferret with the flu, only not as handsome, and with fewer teeth.

'And who are you?' said Gusset. There was a faint moaning coming from outside the walls, but they all pretended not to hear it. As long as the gates remained closed, they were safe – relatively speaking.

'I am Bogstride Pongsqueal,' said the bean-counter, twitching his narrow-pointed nose, 'and I only happen to be the Chief Imperial Taxonomist and the Emperor's personal Rassenprufer – so if *anyone* is going to tell people to stay where they are then it's me.' He nodded slowly, as if trying to convince himself of the truth of his own words. Then, with a certain amount of pride, he patted the cloth-covered items on the table, as if they were symbolic proof of his authority.

'Go on then,' said Gusset. 'Why don't you tell us?'

'Stay where you are,' said Pongsqueal, 'by order of his Imperial Majesty.'

'Yeah,' said Toby. 'I bet you feel *much* better after that, don't you?'

'Don't be insolent,' said the bean-counter, 'or I'll have you locked up.'

'Look, we'd love to stay and argue,' said Gusset. 'But we have to…'

There was another moan from outside the walls. This time it was louder and there were words attached. Nobody listened though, in case they heard what was being said. Instead, they paid attention to the treadmill creature, who was more concerned with events at the other end of the tunnel.

'You mustn't go,' he hissed. '*Listen to the sky – not safe to travel beyond.*' He dragged himself from the treadmill and cautiously approached the inner gates, pushing one of them open and cocking an ear into the sky.

'Hey, it's the humming noise,' said Toby, 'the one from the forest.'

'And it spells trouble, with a capital *truh*,' said Rootspank.

'A-*hem*,' said Pongsqueal, 'can we *please* get on with official matters? I need to know *who* you are, *what* you are and where you're going and why.'

'That's *our* business,' said Gusset, beckoning Toby and Lucy away from the inner gates. He was obviously treating Trundle's warning as genuine.

'You'd best listen,' whispered Rootspank. 'He's had *orders*.' She winked at Gusset, as if he might know what kind of orders she meant.

'Humph, *alright* then,' said Gusset. He took the lamp from the boy and held it towards Pongsqueal, eager to remember every detail of his face.

'That's *better*,' said the bean-counter smugly. 'Now, who's first? I know, we'll start with *you* – the one with a face like a three cart pile-up.'

'Gusset, I think he means you,' smiled Toby.

'Of course I do,' said Pongsqueal. 'Now, what *are* you? Above or below?'

'Below,' said Gusset, hanging his head, 'but I used to be a teacher.'

'*Used* to be?' sneered the tallyman. 'Well '*used to be*' doesn't count.' He lifted one of the cloths to reveal a rough wooden box with five holes in the top. Then he shifted the other rag, uncovering a tray of assorted marbles.

'What are those for?' said Gusset.

'I don't *answer* questions,' said Pongsqueal. 'I *ask* them.' He took a brown marble from the tray and posted it through the central hole – there was a mute ring, like a bell in a sweetshop.

'And *these* two?' he said with a sickly-weasel grin. 'What of *them*? Above or below?'

'Oh, very definitely above,' said Gusset.

'They couldn't be anything else, could they?' said Rootspank. 'Just look at their bright eyes – and their pale skin.'

'I can *see* that,' said Pongsqueal, staring at Lucy and casually fingering a green marble. 'But I'm suddenly intrigued by the girl's bag. What exactly do you have in there young lady?'

'Nugging,' said a muffled voice.

'*Nugging*?' said Pongsqueal. 'You said that without moving your lips.'

'Erm, it was me,' said Toby. 'I coughed, and that's how it came out.'

Lucy gave a smile and held three fingers up against her smock.

'Yes, *very* funny,' said the official. 'Well, since we're all in *such* a good mood I think we ought to call the guards and take a look, don't you?'

'If you insist,' said Lucy. She was trying hard not to look at Gusset, who had sneaked behind the bean-counter and climbed onto a gunny sack. She tried even harder as he reached into his pocket and removed his number three truncheon. And she tried her *absolute* hardest as the weapon whooshed through the air and Pongsqueal tumbled, face first, into his marbles.

'Suddenly, I feel a *lot* better,' said Gusset, without a flicker of a smile. 'I find it's always a pleasure to cut through unnecessary red tape.'

'Fetch a bag,' shouted Rootspank, pointing at the unconscious official. 'One about *that* size should do it. Oh, and thanks a *lot* Gusset. I'm assuming you'll be gone when he wakes up?'

'I'm afraid so,' said Gusset.

'Well be *careful*,' she said. 'Things have begun to happen, just as we thought.' She looked at Lucy with a mixture of anger and compassion, as if the mysterious 'things' that were happening were all her fault.

'Hey,' said Toby suddenly, 'look, he's coming around again.'

Gusset whipped out his truncheon again, and with a slight trace of a smile he gave the bean-counter another swift whack around the head.

'Three cart pile-up *indeed*,' he snorted.

'As I was saying,' said the gatekeeper, 'there's a lot of activity at the erm, the *wotchermacallit* – nowhere is really safe any more.'

'Ah,' said Gusset. 'And these, 'goings on', at the erm, the *wotchermacallit* – what form do they take exactly?'

'Certain forces are gathering,' spat Rootspank. She pulled her short sword out of its sheath and banged it flat against the tallyman's table, scattering his coloured marbles in the dirt. 'And we *all* know who's going to come off worst, don't we?' she added.

'Quite possibly,' said Gusset. 'But we *also* know what's at stake.' He watched as Rootspank and the lamp-boy shoved the bean-counter into the sack, then he stepped forward to tie it up – extra *tight*, of course.

'Erm, this *wotchermacallit* that nobody wants to talk about,' said Lucy nervously. 'Do you mean the Migdal?' Suddenly all she could think of was bony fingers digging into map-vellum.

'And who told you about *that* place?' snapped Rootspank.

'We saw it on a map,' said Toby.

'Best place for it,' said Gusset, ducking as Nine-Tails swung through on the end of a rope. He expected the cat to swing back as well, but it leapt off suddenly and scuttled towards the main gate.

'But we must be quite near to the tower now,' said Lucy.

'Yeah,' said Toby. 'We'll probably see it on the way to the Bright Byrde.'

'*Gusset?*' said Rootspank. 'What *have* you been telling these two?'

'As little as possible,' replied Gusset. 'But they're nosey little sods – you can *tell* by looking at them, can't you? Especially *that* one.' He grinned and pointed at Lucy, but was suddenly distracted by Nine-Tails. The cat was sniffing at the door-flap and making a horrific yowling noise, like a faulty air-raid siren.

'But we *will* see the Migdal, won't we?' said Lucy.

'Not unless you can fly over the rooftops,' said Rootspank. 'And even if you *do* happen to find a clear view, you *still* won't see it – not unless you believe.'

'Eh?' said Toby. 'You mean it's *there*, but we won't be able to see it unless we *believe* it's there?'

'Erm, that's right,' said Gusset, studying Nine-Tails closely.

'*What?*' said Toby. 'But we've already…'

Lucy gave him such a violent dig in the ribs that it knocked the wind out of him, probably cracking a few bones in the process.

'*Shhh,*' she hissed.

'*Wee-ow, wee-ow, wee-ow, wee-ow, weeeeee…*'

'The *cat*,' said Gusset urgently. 'I think he's trying to tell us something.'

'Erm, those doors, they *are* quite solid, aren't they?' said Lucy.

'The finest in the city,' said Rootspank proudly, 'except perhaps for the ones at the New Gate of course – on account of them being new.'

'Erm, ye-es,' said Lucy, 'but what about the cat-flap?'

'*Uh-oh,*' said Gusset.

'Where's Nine-Tails?' shouted Rootspank. 'Where has my *pussy* gone?'

There was a pitiful wail from the other side of the gate, followed by the sound of splintering bones and a horrendous scream that made Lucy's blood run cold. No one was in any doubt as to what had happened – brave little Nine-Tails had just breathed his last – and the merciless creature that had ended his life was trying to squeeze through the cat flap.

At the Sign
of the
Bright Byrde

When the humming finally stopped they said their various goodbyes, and with a sad-eyed blessing from the treadmill creature, they ventured out from beneath the arch. Gusset positioned himself at the centre of the tiny courtyard and took a long, deep breath – and as he drew the meaty stink down into his lungs, he grinned, like some demented hyena guarding its newly discovered dinner.

'Such an *exquisite* whiff,' he smirked. 'I'd recognise it anywhere. Even if you were to wrap me up inside ten gunny sacks, and then put those sacks inside a big metal box with locks on the outside, and then sink the box into the swamp on the end of a big hairy piece of rope. Even *then…*'

'Yeah, said Toby. 'You'd recognise the smell – I *think* we get the picture.'

'So this is the famous Smiff's Fields then?' said Lucy, turning to wave at the gatekeeper. Rootspank was standing on a lumpy-looking sack, smiling broadly, as she ground her heels into it.

'This is *it* alright,' said Gusset proudly, 'it's unmistakeable.'

'It's certainly *that*,' smiled Toby.

'Well I think it's a *lovely* place,' said Lucy. She winked at him and gave a little wrinkle of her nose, then stepped smartly to one side to avoid the bucket of red slops that had been thrown at their feet.

'Yeah,' said Toby, holding his nose, 'remind me to pick up a holiday brochure as we leave.'

'*If* you leave,' snapped Gusset. 'They won't be able to keep Pongsqueal in that bag forever you know, and when he finally *does* get out, there'll be trouble from the Imperial guard — not to mention any *other* kind of trouble we might find.' He glanced furtively into the clear, silent sky, as if from habit.

'Hey, what was that?' said Toby. He pointed at the middle of the cobbled yard, where an iron cover was dropping back into place. 'I'll *swear* someone was watching us from the sewers just then.'

They wandered over to the manhole and kicked at the octagonal plate. It was encrusted with filth, and looked as though it hadn't been opened for a hundred years.

'That's a good imagination you've got there,' said Gusset. 'This is just a key-tile — there's nothing underneath it.'

'Oh *isn't* there?' said Toby. 'And what about those sneaky eyes I saw? I'm telling you, there was *somebody* in that sewer, and they were watching us.'

'So *you* say,' grumbled Gusset. 'And what *is* a sewer? A new invention?'

'Erm, no,' smiled Lucy, 'not where we come from.'

'What then?' said Gusset.

'Over to you Luce,' grinned Toby. 'You're the expert when it comes to explanations.'

'Erm, yes, well, I *do* hope Rootspank doesn't get into trouble,' she said. 'It was bad enough that she lost Nine-Tails.'

'*Most* unfortunate,' agreed Gusset, apparently just as eager to drop the subject of the sewers, 'especially for the cat.'

'But at least he warned us in good time,' said Lucy.

'Yeah,' said Toby. 'All we have to do now is get out of here, before those stinking wraiths find a way to get past the gate.'

'Erm, they won't be able to get through the flap will they?' said Lucy. She ducked as a flock of pure white birds swooped down, eager for a look at the newcomers.

'Dunno,' said Gusset. He positioned his huge feet across the design on the manhole, as if to discourage them from looking at it.

'But we blocked it with Pongsqueal's table,' said Toby. 'They'll never be able to shift that from the other side.'

'They won't need to,' said Gusset sombrely. 'There are those on *this* side of the wall who'd be only too willing to help. We're probably being watched by some of them right now.'

'We *are*,' said Toby, 'from the sewers.'

'It doesn't matter *where* they are,' snapped Gusset. 'We must reach safety before mouths begin to flap.'

Lucy glanced up at the eaves as they entered an alleyway between two crumbling houses. The sun was up properly now, kissing the bizarrely shaped rooftops and threatening to fill the whole of the world with light.

'Watch your step in here,' said Gusset, 'and try not to stand out from the crowd. Oh, and watch out for carpets.'

'Erm, *right*,' said Toby, glancing back towards the manhole. 'So how far *is* it to the Bright Byrde?'

'Not far,' said Gusset. 'It's over by a place known as Bartolemius Fair – it's only called that on a Froggsday mind – the rest of the time it doesn't have a name.' Before they could ask the obvious question, he turned and led them away into a narrow maze of passages, most of which were less than a stride-and-a-half wide. 'I almost forgot,' he added. 'There's something very important you need to remember in here.'

'And what's that?' said Toby.

'Just a single word,' smiled Gusset. '*Balak.*'

'And what does *that* mean?' asked Lucy.

'You'll see,' said Gusset. 'If you *do* hear it, just get out of the way. Dive into a doorway if necessary, but *whatever* you do, don't just stand there.'

Suddenly there was a shout in the distance. It was dulled by line after line of tatty, timeworn washing, but even so, it sounded suspiciously like the new word that Gusset had just taught them.

'See?' he said with a grin.

Balak!

'Hey, you! *Balak*!'

Lucy turned in the direction of the scream and spotted a bundle of rolled-up tapestries hurtling towards her. The whole width of the passage was occupied by the load, the ends of the rolls brushing the flaking paint off the walls and raising a thick cloud of dust and debris. There was nowhere to go it seemed, and only seconds to get there.

'What is it?' shouted Lucy. 'What's a Balak?'

'*Shift* yourself, *quick*,' shouted Gusset. 'Find a *doorway*.'

At the Sign of the Bright Byrde

The air was filled with the sound of thunder now, a dull but not very distant rumbling that shook the foundations of the surrounding shops and threatened to vibrate the cobbles out of the ground.

'But what *is* it?' screamed Lucy. She ducked below the dust cloud and spotted Gusset leaping into a doorway. Whatever the identity of the creature at the midst of the storm it knew nothing about giving way. She could either go beneath the animal's feet or get crushed between the carpets and the wall.

'Never mind *what* it is,' screamed a distant voice. 'Just get out of its way.'

Lucy fell back into an entrance just as the mysterious tapestry carrier reached the opening. As the creature drew level with the door it turned and grinned at her with two ugly heads, each slug-like face drawing its lips back to reveal an impressive mouth filled with yellow teeth.

'Buying?' said a voice behind her.

'*Eh?*' said Lucy. 'Erm, no, I'm hiding – from *that* thing – or *those* things.'

She wanted to see more of the creature that was attached to the heads, but the owner of the shop was busy pulling her inside. He was a wizened old thing who reminded her of Gusset - only smaller and much uglier.

He *seemed* to be expecting her.

'Come,' he said, beckoning her towards the rear of the shop. The whole place was only about six feet wide, and half of *that* was taken up with monstrous wardrobes that looked as though they hadn't been opened for a hundred years.

'Erm, I don't actually want to *buy* anything,' she said, squeezing past the great wooden goliaths. 'I was just trying to avoid being run over by a load of carpets – and getting slimed by the thing that was carrying them.'

The shopkeeper ignored the explanation and ushered her into a tiny back room, where an old woman sat rocking a cradle – she *also* had a face like a slimy walnut.

'This is my family,' said the man with a nervous grin. 'And this is my child.' He took the infant from its bed and presented it to Lucy.

'Erm, yes, it's *beautiful*,' she lied, 'but I was just hiding…'

'*Maga, maga, mag, mag,*' cried the child. '*Magga, magga, magga, magga…*'

Lucy patted the infant on the head, trying not to look at it too closely. As babies went, it was probably the ugliest she'd ever seen – like a shrivelled up version of its mother.

'Magga, magga, magadala…' it gurgled, over and over.

'Yes, well, erm, thank you for showing me your child,' said Lucy, trying not to look at its staring eyes. 'But I really must be going now.'

'You must,' said the shopkeeper, 'and thank you for your blessing.'

'Erm, *yes*,' said Lucy with a puzzled stare, 'don't mention it.'

When she emerged into the narrow thoroughfare, Gusset was already waiting and Toby was just squeezing his way out of a shop on the other side of the passage. He was covered with some kind of gooey amber liquid, which smelt disgusting.

'Don't even ask,' he said. 'Just take a good look at the shop I came out of and remember it – and if you ever see it again, stay outside.'

'Don't worry,' said Gusset. 'The smell will fade in a few hours and the melly-flux will dry off, *eventually*.'

'Well next time I'll take my chances with the carpet carrier,' said Toby.

'Me too,' said Lucy, still puzzling over the ugly baby. 'So that thing with two heads and the bad teeth was a Balak, was it?'

'Of course not,' said Gusset. 'Balak simply means get out of the way. Now let's get a move on, shall we? We need to get to the other side of the market.'

Despite the early hour, the market traders were in full cry, screaming the benefits of their wares to anyone who would listen. Bartolemius Fair was packed with people and animals and rough wooden stalls, most of them decorated with bright canvas awnings and hung with bits of animal that Lucy preferred not to look too closely at. Many of the stalls were selling cooked or raw food, whilst others displayed shoes, hats, or quaint-looking clothes. One of them even featured a puppet show, which reminded Lucy of the Punch and Judy man on Grimston beach. It was all so distracting that she very nearly didn't duck in time.

'Look out,' shouted Toby.

Lucy crouched as a gruesome severed head swung out in front of her on the end of a rope. It was fastened to a bent iron hook, and missed her by inches.

'Hey, you want to watch it there,' said the stall-keeper. 'I don't want my stock getting damaged by your thick head, now *do* I?'

Lucy screwed her nose up and gave him a sickly smile. Then her gaze fell on the stall, where hundreds of different sized heads were arranged in rows and columns.

'What *are* they?' she said, feeling slightly sick. She was reminded of Mr. Eastman and his pig's head mirror. 'Or what *were* they, when they were alive?'

'Look at the sign,' said Gusset. He pointed to an old piece of wood that had been nailed up on the wall behind the stall.

Vangolins – lovely, lovely Vangolins, fresh from the Smiff's Fields.
We repair them. We move them. We buy them. We sell them.
And occasionally we steal them.

The bit that mentioned stealing them had been crossed out, and the word 'sorry' had been written over the top instead.

'But that still doesn't explain what they are,' said Lucy.

'You should be able to tell from the way they're laid out,' said Gusset. He accepted a piece of bone from the stallholder and then tapped various heads, getting a different note from each.

'Oh,' said Lucy, 'so it's a musical instrument then?'

'Correct,' said Gusset, 'but you can eat them too.'

'Wonderful,' said Lucy, 'you must let me have the recipe some time.'

'Hey, *Luce*,' shouted Toby, 'come and look at these entertainers.' He grabbed his friend's hand and dragged her towards the eel-pie bakery, where dozens of long, thin crusts were on display in the window. Four brightly dressed harlequins were standing in front of the shop, looking like suspects in a police line-up.

'Not a lot of activity then,' said Lucy.

'No, but look at their costumes,' hissed Toby.

Each of the performers was wearing a different coloured costume and his face was painted to match the clothing – and each of them had a symbol embroidered on his tunic.

'They're the same as the wands in the kiosks,' said Toby.

'Erm, yes,' said Lucy. 'But we might have to think about that later. We appear to have attracted some attention.'

A tall, lank-haired man dressed in rags had appeared from the shadows – and from the way he dangled his hat under their noses, he was obviously expecting some kind of donation.

'Sorry, we haven't got time for that,' said Gusset, pushing the hat away.

'Hey, watch it,' said lank-hair, 'and don't go scaring our customers off either – we need the money. Eel pies don't come cheap you know.'

'They're new around here,' said Gusset, flipping a silver coin in the direction of the hat. 'And they haven't *got* any money.'

'A *groat?*' said lank-hair, biting the currency. 'For *that* you can have the full show my friend.'

'I told you,' said Gusset, 'we haven't got time.'

'That's a pity,' said lank-hair, 'because Salmandis is a fine fire-breather, and the boy Undia is a dab hand at juggling water.'

'Really,' grunted Gusset. 'And what do the other two do?'

'You want to see them at work?' said lank-hair. 'That'll be a groat.'

'No, I *don't*,' said Gusset, 'and even if I did, I've already paid, remember? I just want to know what they do.'

'Yeah,' grinned Toby. 'Tell us, and we'll get off and leave you in peace.'

'Well,' said lank-hair. 'Sylph here can juggle all manner of things – insects mainly, but he can loft just about anything.'

'And what about this one?' said Lucy. She indicated the smallest of the four actors who appeared to be weighing a pile of pig dung in his hand.

'That's *Gnom*,' said lank-hair, 'he's an earth flinger.'

'Good for him,' said Gusset, waving them all away.

'Yeah, great,' said Toby, eyeing the dung. 'You won't be offended if we don't ask for a demonstration, *will* you?'

'No,' said lank-hair, pocketing the coin, 'I suppose not.'

They walked for another thirty minutes or so, pressing their way through the crowds to the sound of hand bells and barrel organs and the occasional vangolin serenade. They saw charm sellers and head-massagers too, and suspicious looking characters who were coiling brightly coloured snakes on sticks. The only time they stopped to rest was when their route was blocked by a densely packed crowd. The onlookers had gathered around a quack doctor whose gaily-painted sign promised the secrets of eternal life and a cure for warts on the privates – all apparently from the same bottle.

'Watch out for pickpockets,' said Gusset. 'And keep a special eye on that bag of yours – I reckon the thieving scum round here would love to know what you have in there.'

'I'll bet,' said Lucy. She watched Gusset closely, suddenly wondering if *he* might not be feeling a little curious too.

'It's just like a history lesson,' grinned Toby as he stopped to look at a stall selling wooden puzzles. 'Where do you think we are, Luce? And *when?*'

'I haven't a clue,' said Lucy. 'People keep telling me I'm no good at history and I've started to believe them.'

'Erm, it's the year thirteen,' said Gusset helpfully.

'Yes, that's *here,*' whispered Toby. 'But what about *real* years?'

'I'd say it was about 1583,' joked Lucy. 'September the third.'

'Hmm,' said Toby. 'I *suppose* that sounds about right.'

'And how would *you* know?' smiled Lucy. 'You came below me in history, didn't you?' She picked up one of the puzzles and began fiddling with it, trying to discover the secret of the four-coloured pieces. The stallholder leaned over to demonstrate the solution, but Gusset pulled her away.

'Just another fifty yards and we'll be at the Bright Byrde,' he said. 'I want to get you inside before too many people notice.'

'It's a bit late for that,' said Toby. 'Every eye in the place is following us – even the glass ones.'

The Bright Byrde had *very* ropey paintwork, *lots* of broken windows, and hundreds of missing roof tiles, which according to Gusset lent the place a charm all of its own. All they had to do now was *find* that elusive charisma – which was probably buried somewhere beneath the dense atmosphere of tobacco smoke and ale fumes.

'Can't we go to the Black Eyed Puke?' said Toby. 'It looks like fun.'

'I reckon not,' said Gusset, glancing at the tavern next door where the customers were happily vomiting out of the windows. 'The ale is fine, but the food is rotten.'

'Ah,' said Toby, 'well in that case…'

'Erm, are we actually allowed inside?' said Lucy, sniffing the rancid air.

Vᶻᵥᵡᵇ⅂

'Allowed?' said Gusset. 'Of *course* – it's a public tavern, isn't it?'

He pushed the rough door just a *little* too hard, smashing it against the inner wall and attracting precisely the sort of attention they didn't need. Everyone turned and stared, apart from the four drinkers at the corner table.

'Come on, Limbo,' screamed one of them, 'you can do it.'

'Yeah, go for it,' screamed another.

'Right then,' said Limbo. 'Here goes. *Ubar, mubar, farty-bonk and poo, loo-bar, coo-bar, slimy-fink and nooh. Seff... Te-punko... Clanko... Umbargo... Hey, wait a minute, who's that staring at us?*

Lucy had seen a cowboy film once, where a stranger walked into a saloon and the whole place went quiet. She was guessing the four drinkers had seen the same film, because they suddenly stopped shouting and spun around in their seats. After a tense moment though the silence was broken – one of them had recognised the Braneskule janitor.

'Nah,' said the man in the leather jerkin and skullcap, 'it's nothing to worry about – it's only old Gusset.'

'Oh, yeah,' said another. He wore a shabby-looking smock and had a dome-shaped leather hat, with flaps that hung down over his ears. 'How's it going Gussy-boy? We didn't recognise you without your teacher's robes.'

'It's going very well, Mongy Twelvetrees, and thank you for asking. Now if you *don't* mind we'd like to get our stomachs on the outside of some drinks.'

Gusset's urgent need for ale seemed to satisfy them and they went back to their conversations, ignoring the fact that Toby and Lucy looked suspiciously like the two children they had heard about. If Gusset and his companions wanted to get tanked up then that was alright by them – no questions asked.

'What was all *that* about when we came in?' said Lucy.

'It's a drinking game,' said Gusset. 'They have to recite an old nursery rhyme and then count backwards from four. But they have to do it in the old language. *Seff, Te-punko, Clanko, Umbargo.*'

'Is that difficult then?' said Lucy.

'Depends how much you've had to drink,' said Gusset. 'Most of them can only count when they're sober, and then only up to three, so doing it backwards is a bit of a challenge.'

'I just *love* this place,' grinned Toby. 'I love it so much I'm thinking of coming to live here.'

'*Are* you?' said Gusset. 'But I thought... Oh, never mind.'

'Yes, never *mind*,' hissed Lucy. When Gusset turned his back, she drew a finger smartly across her throat, signalling Toby to stop blabbing.

Lindstrom had been distracted though – a sly-looking man at the counter had just climbed down from his stool and was shuffling past them, staring intently at Lucy. He was dressed in an old sack and smoking a long clay pipe like Percy's – only the tobacco reeked far more than Belly Wind ever did. Just for a moment, it reminded Lucy of home.

'Don't worry,' said Gusset, 'he's just a spy – the place is full of them.'

'*Really?*' said Lucy, 'and erm, that's *good*, is it?'

'You think we haven't been spotted a dozen times already?' said Gusset. 'Now, what's more important, running from spies or having a drink?'

'Erm, running from spies?' suggested Toby.

Gusset shook his head slowly from side to side. To a casual observer it might have looked like he was messing around, but Lucy could see his eyes flickering about the place, weighing up the situation.

'Having a drink?' said Lucy.

'Correct,' said Gusset. 'So what's your poison?'

'I'll have a lemonade,' said Lucy, realising they were hungry *and* thirsty.

'Me too,' said Toby, watching the sly creature as he sneaked out.

'Lemmernade?' said Gusset. 'Never heard of it – you'll be having ale of some kind – all you have to do is decide which one.'

Toby located a list behind the bar and started to read it aloud, just in case he was missing something important.

"Stinking bird-weed."

"Stinking hog-snot."

"Stinking blue-pharts."

"Merry-go-Lightly-Around."

'Erm, are those real choices then?' he said.

'Of *course*,' said Gusset, 'these are some of the finest ales in the world.'

'I see,' said Toby, 'and what's the Merry-go-Lightly made with?'

'Erm, I think it's stinking Loppit spawn,' said Gusset.

'Lovely,' said Lucy, 'erm, I'll have the one that stinks the least.'

'Or perhaps we could have nothing?' suggested Toby.

'If you don't take ale then you can't stay in the tavern,' said Gusset. 'Don't worry about the stink though. There's no actual smell when you drink it – the name is more sort of related to how your head feels the next morning.'

'In that case we'll have two bird weeds,' said Toby. 'And go easy on the pong.'

Gusset ushered them towards a deep, dark alcove where they sat and watched the customers come and go, waiting for their guide to return with the ale. Nobody paid them much attention, and despite Gusset's comment about spies, they felt comparatively safe – until the sly man in the sackcloth returned. This time he seemed to be *looking* for something, scrutinising every movement in the room whilst pretending to be interested in the food.

'I'll have a platter of snork brains,' he said, pushing in front of Gusset. 'And I want gulloby sauce too, *lots* of gulloby sauce – and don't go sneaking any groop juice in either – *I've* heard the stories.'

The man behind the bar spat in a glass and then used a grimy-looking cloth to wipe it out.

'You can wait your squatting-well turn,' he shouted. 'Gusset was here first.'

The man picked his nose and glanced towards their alcove, looking away again as soon as he caught Toby's eye.

'Nice people,' said Toby. He turned to Lucy, but she'd slipped away into an even darker corner – and she was beckoning him over, eager to show him what she'd found.

'Gusset told us to sit tight,' hissed Toby as he joined her.

'We won't find Fenny by drinking ale, *will* we?' said Lucy. 'Anyway, come and have a look at this.' She dragged him further into the gloom and showed him the cabinet – it was a good two feet taller than either of them.

'It's a full-size version of that thing on the end of Creeps' wand,' said Toby.

'Yes,' said Lucy, 'but what *else* does it remind you of?'

Toby knew what she meant, but took time to study the thing before answering. It was a fortune teller, just like Byron's machine, but it was more realistic than that, like a mechanical gypsy whose head was frozen in ice. And that was what worried him. It looked too lifelike – an image of a real face, but projected onto a porcelain death mask.

'Princess Mumtaz,' he said finally, 'only the woman inside looks like she's alive – do you think we can get her out?'

'No,' said Lucy, 'because I don't think she's really there.'

'You reckon?' said Toby, 'she looks real enough to me.'

'Yes,' said Lucy, 'gruesome, isn't it? But I don't think she's actually inside the box.'

'So where is she?' said Toby.

'Do you remember when Niblock zapped me with that wand?' said Lucy.

'How could I forget?' said Toby. 'You were like a zombie for ages – it was like all your spirit had been sucked out.'

'And that's exactly what it felt like,' said Lucy. 'I don't know where my body was, but it felt like my head was inside something just like this.'

'Stuck in a box you mean?' grinned Toby.

'I know it sounds silly,' said Lucy, 'but it gives me the creeps.'

'Me too,' said Toby, 'let's get out of here – unless of course you want to hang around and find out what she's going to say?'

'Not really,' said Lucy.

'*Tower of Merciful Blades,*' whispered the head.

'Eh? What was that?' said Lucy.

'Something about the Tower of Merciful Blades,' said Toby.

'Are you sure?' said Lucy. She pressed her face up against the cabinet, her breath forming a subtle mist on the outside of the glass.

'It's breathing,' shouted Toby. 'Erm, no wait a minute, that's *you*, isn't it? But I still don't like it Luce, even if she isn't breathing. It's like you said in the confuser room – they've been put in a cabinet for saying things that other people didn't agree with.'

'Well if they have then it's not *my* fault,' said Lucy.

'I wouldn't be so sure about that,' said Toby. 'I think it happened because you said it.'

'Don't be so *stupid*,' hissed Lucy. 'That's ridiculous.'

'Yeah? Well it's no more ridiculous than us ending up in *this* place,' said Toby. 'Or is this sort of thing normal in your weird family?'

'We're not weird,' said Lucy. 'At least *I'm* not.'

'You *are*,' shouted Toby. 'Otherwise we wouldn't be in this place. I wish we could get out of here right now.'

'Be careful what you wish for,' said a woman's voice. 'And if *I* were you I'd stay away from those cabinets too.'

Toby and Lucy spun round in surprise, thinking they'd been alone.

The woman was sitting in a private alcove, watching them with great interest. As they approached, she dealt some large dog-eared picture cards onto the table in front of her. Lucy recognised them at once, suddenly relieved to see something familiar. It was similar to the Tarot deck that Lily used; only this one seemed to have been painted by hand.

'Who are you?' said Toby.

The woman scratched her bird's-nest hair with one of the cards, and then pointed to a painted sign that leaned against a nearby roof pillar.

"Miss Exotica Pubrane - official fortune teller (accept no bird-men)"

'So, can I help you?' said Miss Pubrane.

'Erm, no,' said Toby, staring at the cards. 'Unless you want to tell us what you're playing?'

'*Playing*?' said Miss Pubrane. 'This is not a *game* young man – the cards fall in a pattern that is capable of revealing the past, the present and the future.'

'I know,' said Lucy. 'But only if you know how to interpret the meanings and relative positions of the pictures.'

'Ah, so you *know* something of the ways of the Tarot,' said Exotica. 'Would you care for a reading?'

'Erm, no,' said Toby, 'we're just waiting for someone.'

'Then why not wait here?' said Miss Pubrane.

'We'd best not,' said Lucy, 'we were warned not to talk to strangers.'

'Why don't you just take a look?' said the fortune teller, turning a card. 'It can't hurt just to look, can it?'

The gaudy piece of pasteboard was painted with the rough outline of a robed woman sitting on a throne. She appeared to be casting a net whilst trying to balance a piece of exotic and highly decorative headwear. The crown was fashioned from a pair of horns – and a model of the sun was caught between the two.

'The Two of Trumps,' said Miss Pubrane. 'Known by some as The Priestess.'

'And what does that mean?' said Lucy.

'Nothing at all,' said Miss Pubrane, 'because the reading is not for you child. I was simply twiddling with the cards – you of *all* people should know that. For the reading to work properly the subject needs to concentrate.'

'And was I not?' said Lucy.

'I think you might have been distracted,' said Miss Pubrane, 'by something *nearby* perhaps?'

'You *could* say that,' said Toby. He'd spotted a movement on the chair next to fortune teller's table. 'Erm, what exactly *is* that?'

He pointed at a handbag that appeared to be made from the skin of a baby crocodile. The legs of the victim were folded into the corners and the head was draped over the front, like the tongue of a satchel – but the *eyes* were wide open, and watching every move they made.

'This is Henbeg,' said Miss Pubrane. 'Say *hello* Henbeg.'

'*Grrrrraarraarr…*'

Toby leapt back as the bag growled and spat, flashing four rows of razor sharp teeth and imparting a serious wobble to the chair it was sitting on – or lounging on. It was impossible to tell, because it was difficult to see where the outline of the animal finished and the design of the handbag began.

'Nice doggie,' said Toby, attempting to stroke the creature.

'*Grrrraarraarr – raaarr – raaarr,*' growled Henbeg. He shook his head so violently that his decorative tassels seemed ready to fly off.

'*Don't* do that,' said Miss Pubrane.

'What?' said Toby innocently.

'You were thinking about poking him.'

'Was I?' said Toby.

'The cards reveal all,' smiled Exotica. 'Now, why don't you tell me your names? I don't think I've seen you before, have I?' Her eyes were like Henbeg's, but sharper and quicker than the crocodile's and watching far more than just Lucy and her movements.

'He's Tobermory and I'm Lucretia,' said Lucy. 'We've just come from the Winding Crayns.'

'And you haven't been taken in by the Braneskule?' said Exotica.

'Erm, no,' said Lucy, immediately regretting her instinct to lie.

'Hmmph – I find that *most* unlikely,' said the fortune teller. She looked them up and down, as if trying to decide whether to call the watchman or take them into her confidence.

'It's true,' said Lucy, still wishing she'd said nothing.

'You're lying,' said Miss Pubrane plainly. 'But we all do it, *don't* we? The important thing is who we lie to, and why – wouldn't you agree?'

Lucy said nothing. If the lamp-stand had accused her like this, she'd be fighting back by now, but this was different. There was a certain matter-of-factness about the bony Miss Pubrane, and Lucy felt drawn to confide in her.

'Erm, yes, but we don't know who to trust,' she said plainly.

Miss Pubrane snorted and rubbed the side of her nose. A flurry of dried powder flaked away and fell like snow towards the dark pit of the floor.

'*Nobody* knows who to trust child – not since the belief started.'

'The belief? What's that?' said Toby.

'If I could give you an answer in less than a moon cycle then I might try,' said Exotica. 'Unfortunately, there is no explanation for the minds of the masses – especially when they *need* something to believe in.'

'What do you mean?' said Lucy. 'What's happened?'

'Too much,' said Miss Pubrane. 'And as usual there are those who will profit by it and fight to prevent the world going back to how it was before.'

Lucy began to ask another question, but Miss Pubrane brought a bone-skinned finger up to her lips, sealing the words inside.

'Not in here,' she said, 'you don't know who's listening.'

'And even if we did know,' said Toby, 'we don't know who they are.'

'Quite,' said Miss Pubrane.

'Yeah,' said Toby, suddenly feeling confident. 'We don't want the ears in the walls listening to us, do we? *Or* their bums.'

Miss Pubrane gave a little frown, screwing her face up as if someone had put a turd under her nose.

'*Must* you?' she said.

'Hey, I've been looking for you two,' shouted Gusset. 'I *thought* I told you to stay put? There are folk round here who'd slice you up into licky-strips if there was money to be made from it.' He glowered at Miss Pubrane, who turned a card over and gave him a little smile. He deliberately didn't look at it though, and turned to usher Toby and Lucy back to their seat.

'You two sit here for a while and sup your ale,' said Gusset, 'and *whatever* you do, don't *talk* to anybody, right?'

'Right,' said Lucy. She took a swig of foul-tasting ale and nearly choked. 'Erm, and where will you be?'

'Making enquiries about your friend,' said Gusset.

'Can *we* come?' said Toby, sipping carefully at his stinking bird weed.

'You'll be safer here,' said Gusset, 'relatively speaking – just don't go talking to anyone, and *especially* not the fortune tellers. I know you haven't got money, but they'll work out some scheme to have it off you anyway.'

As Gusset left, every eye in the tavern followed him – all except the ones belonging to the sackcloth spy. He was busy tucking into a steaming plate of brains, apparently minding his own business – but as soon as the janitor closed the door though his eyes swivelled round to stare at Lucy. She poked her tongue out at him, and then took the rucksack off, resting it on the table and looping her arm through the strap, just in case.

'Something valuable in there?' said a voice. It belonged to an old man who was shaped like a snake but looked like a very old passion fruit. He was carrying a large tray, but deliberately tilting it away, to hide his secret.

'*Valuable?*' said Lucy, pulling the bag close to her chest. 'Erm, no, we don't have anything of like that, *do* we, Tobermory?'

'No,' laughed Toby, 'we lost it all playing cards.'

'It's of no consequence,' said the man, 'I have something to give, not to take. Do you want to see?'

'No,' they said together.

'We're waiting for someone,' said Lucy. 'And he told us not to talk to anyone, especially fortune tellers.'

'Well if you don't mind me saying so,' said the man, 'I reckon that's a foul slur on an ancient and honourable profession.'

He fiddled underneath the tray for a moment, and then folded out a flimsy wooden leg to support the weight of it. Hanging from the front of the tray was a tatty box covered by a lid, whilst at the back were three birds, each imprisoned in a wicker cage. The front half of the tray was empty, but judging by the scratches and discolouration, this was where the birds did whatever they did.

V⸮V⸮ᚦꟼ

At the Sign of the Bright Byrde

'All you need to do is choose a bird,' he said. 'Or better still, let the bird choose you.' He pointed at each in turn, indicating the crude hand-painted signs above the cages. 'Which will it be?' he said. 'Ariel perhaps, or Cielo or Speranza?'

'We don't have any money,' said Lucy truthfully.

'Then you're in good company,' said the man, 'because neither do the birds – all you need to do is choose.'

Lucy dithered, watching the birds dancing and flitting about in their cages, each hoping to be the one that was picked. Finally, she chose Speranza, but at the very last moment, she changed her mind and opened the right-hand door. Ariel stayed inside though, venturing out only when the man tapped his fingernail on the tray.

The yellow-green finch emerged from the cage, looked at Lucy briefly, and then paused again, waiting for his master to lift the lid off the box. When it was removed, he examined the contents in a way that only a bird might, staring intently at the metal foils with a sideways tilt of the head. Most of the packets were made from lead, with just a dozen or so silver pieces and even fewer gold ones. They were folded up into tiny wraps and arranged tightly in the compartments along each side of the container.

'He will choose for you,' said the man.

'But what is he choosing?' said Lucy, suddenly worried that the man was trying to sell them something.

'Your *future*,' said the bird-man.

'What, *another* one?' said Lucy. 'Why is everyone round here so obsessed with telling us the future? They can't *all* be right, can they?'

'It depends how many futures you have,' said the man seriously.

The bird ignored their speculations, pecking with such precision that the packet he delivered to Lucy's hand really *did* seem predestined. After all, that was the idea, wasn't it? The message she received was bound up with her fate – ever since the note was written and placed in the metal foil, her life and its scribbled contents had been wrapped together.

'Ah,' said the fortune-teller, 'the young lady receives a lead-coloured foil.'

Lucy sighed – she'd hoped for a gold one, and knew the disappointment was showing in her face. Nevertheless, she closed her fingers around the prize and began searching for a pocket so she could put it away.

'No,' said the bird-man, 'you must open it now.'

'Why?' she said, noticing that his hands were shaking.

'Because you don't know how to interpret the signs,' he said. '*Look.*'

He took the packet from her and unfolded the envelope to reveal a number of seeds, each from a plant of a different type. Lucy didn't recognise them, so it was probably just as well she'd handed the prediction back.

'*Ah,*' said the fortune teller with a satisfied smile.

'*Ah?*' said Lucy.

'Yes, *ah,*' said the bird-man. 'It's the kind of thing we predictors say when we're trying to appear thoughtful. After that we usually switch into a sort of wise appearance.'

'And that would be what?' said Lucy. '*Oh?*'

'No,' said the bird-man, 'more a sort of *Aaah*. Then I might raise my eyebrows – and if I wanted to scare you, then I might shake my head very slowly from side to side, like *this.*'

He shook his head just as he'd described, which seemed to be a source of worry for some of the tavern's more curious clients. They had been having a good nosey at the goings-on, but when the bird-man's head began to shake they turned back to their ale – nobody in their right mind would want to get involved in *that* kind of prediction.

'So it's all just a sham then?' said Lucy.

'On the contrary, this is a *very* serious business,' said the teller. 'Think of the seeds you found inside the envelope, for instance. Sometimes *life* might be like that, enclosing one thing inside another, so that some unpleasant or frightening thing can be presented in a more acceptable way.'

'Like a metaphor?' said Lucy.

'Quite,' said the man, not quite understanding. '*Like* a metaphor – and there are very good reasons for this, because not everyone can stand the bare truth. On the other hand, they might simply prefer a bit of entertainment to wrap the machinery of prediction – like the mechanical peacock, which plucks such a wonderful tune. We *all* want to hear the enchanting music and see the graceful movements of the bird, but we don't necessarily want to watch the spring unwind, *do* we?'

'Yes, I see,' said Lucy, 'I *think* I understand now.'

Toby looked puzzled but thankfully made no comment.

'Good,' said the bird-man, turning his attention back to the seeds. He thought for a few seconds and then said 'Aaah.'

'Wisdom?' said Lucy.

'No,' he replied, breaking into a nervous smile. 'That would be *Aaah*. This is more like surprise. Do you see the way the poppy seeds have formed a crescent, just to the left of the Umbai kernel?'

'Is that the purple thing?' said Lucy.

'Yes, next to the Plumbinia,' he said, pointing at a yellowy-orange seed that looked like a tiny peach stone. 'And from this configuration I can gather certain interesting facts.'

'Such *as?*' said Lucy, with a sceptical look.

'The seeds suggest that you might be a person who is fond of telling lies.'

'Oh,' said Lucy. Suddenly, everyone in the world knew about her talent for telling porkies – *both* worlds in fact.

'And what's more,' said the teller, 'they seem to indicate that certain parts of your apparel are burning fiercely – a hat perhaps? No, wait, it's lower than a hat – pantaloons perhaps?'

'Knickers actually,' said Lucy.

The fortune teller looked confused. He seemed increasingly anxious too, and kept looking at the door.

'They're *like* pants,' explained Toby, 'but we sometimes give them a different name – a bit like life in that respect.'

'Ah, the companion *speaks*,' said the bird-man. 'But I have no need of a bird to tell *his* fortune – his fate is written in the skies.'

'Is it?' said Toby.

'I can see dark weather, deep inside you. I see it just as clearly as I see the young lady here with her pants on fire.'

'That's very good,' said Lucy. 'You might have something there – but on the other hand I want to make it perfectly clear that I only make inventions when it's absolutely necessary.'

'Of course,' said the bird-man. 'Now, just be quiet for a moment will you, and take another slip? Sometimes, even when the bird has looked deep into your soul, his tiny beak may falter and select the wrong foil.'

'What do you mean?' said Lucy. 'How can it be the wrong one?'

'Not *wrong* exactly,' said the man, 'but belonging to the wrong period of your life. I believe for instance that this picture of you dancing with your erm, *knickers* in flames, belongs to the present.'

'It was the very recent past,' said Lucy.

'Then select another bird,' said the fortune teller.

Lucy opened the left-hand cage and Cielo, a small red bird, made his way onto the stage. He pecked Ariel on the back of the neck and chased him back inside, and then waited for a tap of the bird-man's finger.

Once again, Lucy frowned and gave a little sigh. The bird had delivered a silver packet – and she had *so* much wanted a gold one.

'Go on then,' grinned Toby, 'let's *see* it.'

Lucy opened the foil to reveal the seeds, smoothing the edges down so they could see more clearly. And in doing so, she realised that by disturbing the paper she could re-arrange them – and at the same time presumably, reorganize her entire future.

'Erm, what exactly is the *point* of all this?' she said.

'*Ah...hem,*' said the bird-man. 'So you've started to *think*, have you?'

'Possibly,' said Lucy, 'the seeds can go anywhere, can't they?'

'But it was *you* who placed them there. And if you re-arrange them, even now, then it is *still* you who have placed them there. Do you understand?'

'Yes,' said Lucy.

'Erm, no,' said Toby.

'*This* is your past,' said the bird-man, ignoring Toby, and turning his attention back to the silver-foil envelope.

'And what can you see?' said Lucy, eager to hear what she must by definition already know.

'A few Gloobai seeds,' said the bird-man, 'dotted amongst the mustard grains – and...'

'Yes, but what does it *mean*?' insisted Lucy.

'Ah, so once again, you believe that it means something?'

Lucy nodded, still eager to hear about her past.

'Tell me,' said the bird-man, 'do you have any notion of how the universe is built?'

'Erm no,' said Lucy. 'Not especially.'

'Yeah,' grinned Toby, 'but we *do* know it's not thirteen years old.'

V𝑥V𝑥b𝑙

354

'*Well*,' said the teller, 'it's not for me to be giving lessons in cosmology, but it's said by some that there are four spheres of existence. There are others who claim a fifth, but that's just superstition.'

'And these four spheres of existence,' said Lucy. 'Are they *worlds*?'

'Something like that,' said the bird-man. '*Possibly*.'

'And can you tell us anything about them?'

'Only that we live in the one, whilst the other three exist as fables.'

'He's talking about the Braneskule stories,' said Toby, sounding suddenly enthusiastic.

'And the flag, said Lucy. 'It had four sections, but only one was brightly embroidered – the others were all faded, and the stitches were picked out.

'So it's all *true* then?' said Toby.

'It's not for me to say,' said the fortune teller.

'I don't like this at all,' said Lucy. 'It's starting to form a picture.'

'You're right,' said Toby, 'and when the jigsaw comes together I don't think we're going to like it.'

'No,' said Lucy. 'I don't think we will – this is all because Raz…'

'All *what*?' said the bird-man.

'Nothing,' said Lucy. 'I made a mistake.'

The bird-man gave a thin smile as if trying to guess Lucy's meaning.

'Look,' he said, 'I erm, wasn't going to tell you this, especially in view of the circumstances.' He rubbed his sweating palms together and looked nervously at the door again. 'It's something I saw in the seeds,' he said. 'And something the birds have just told me.'

Toby grinned, but for once, he decided to keep quiet and listen.

'You are connected to *all* of these four spheres,' said the bird-man. 'But you are bound by none of them, and *this* is the part I cannot understand. You belong to a *fifth* place – one that even the Umbai kernels cannot see.'

'And why's that?' said Lucy.

'Because it does not literally exist – it is a combination of the other four.'

'Great,' said Toby. 'I'm glad that's all cleared up. So what's next?'

'Another bird,' said the fortune teller.

'He's *good*, isn't he?' smiled Lucy.

'Am I?' said the teller.

'Yes, you *are*,' said Lucy eagerly. 'The next bird is the future, isn't it?'

'If you like,' said the bird-man plainly.

Lucy was extremely disappointed when Speranza, the bird in the middle cage, delivered another lead packet. It was filled with tiny white seeds that seemed to get brighter as they watched, as if they contained a thought that was getting stronger and stronger, feeding on the very air that surrounded them. Eventually they were burning like distant beacons, twinkling like the lights on the ships that sailed past Grimston in the night.

'*Oh!*' said the fortune teller.

'Wisdom?' suggested Lucy.

'Or surprise?' said Toby.

'*Death,*' he replied, turning a ghostly pale colour.

'Death?' said Lucy. 'But…'

The fortune teller held up a hand to stop Lucy speaking – and with great, warm tears flooding his eyes he opened the cages and encouraged the birds to take to the air.

'Erm, what exactly is going *on*?' said Toby.

'Freedom, for *some*,' said the bird-man.

As the birds circled around the tavern and found new perches in the rafters it soon became clear that something was seriously wrong.

'Hey, *wait* a minute,' said Lucy. 'I thought fortune tellers were bound by a strict code of ethics?'

'Indeed we *are*,' said the bird-man nervously. 'I assume you are referring to the rule about not discussing the client's mortality?'

'That's the one,' said Lucy. 'If you see death in a person's future you're not supposed to mention it, are you?'

'I can see why you might be concerned,' he said, shaking visibly. 'But you needn't worry – I wasn't speaking about *your* death – I was referring to my own.'

'*Khepri, akorpa, beelonga…*' screamed a voice near the door. It sounded like a woman, but the screech was so piercing it was hard to tell.

'*What* the hell was *that*?' shouted Toby.

Lucy ducked, flinching away from a great, dark shape she'd seen out of the corner of her eye. She had a vague impression of a small black tent, ripped from its mooring and flying across her field of vision in a gale.

'I don't know,' she said, diving on the floor, 'but it's coming back.'

'Uh-oh,' shouted Toby. 'I just *knew* this was a bad idea.'

A huge, dark beetle swooped back over their heads, clipping Lucy's hair with its extended claws and beating fifty crow's worth of sound out of the air. It had a hard, leathery body that resembled iridescent armour plating, and it was supported on the air by huge, transparent wings that were shot through with pulsing, crimson veins.

'Get down,' screamed Lucy. 'It's after us.'

'I can *see* that,' shouted Toby, diving beside Lucy. 'That thing must be at least three feet across the wingtips.'

'More like four,' yelled Lucy, as she scrambled under a nearby table. Toby squeezed in beside her, narrowly missing the sharpened claws that skimmed the air near his face.

'Alright then, *four*,' he shouted. 'Now, have you got any ideas on how we can avoid becoming that thing's dinner?'

'Well you can get your stupid *head* in, for a start,' cried Lucy.

The scarab came back for another run, clipping the tabletop as it passed, and filling the air with the foul stink of its breath. The tough wings beat with enormous ferocity, generating so much pressure that their eyes felt as though they were being forced from their sockets. Lucy tried to speak, but her mouth filled up with stinking air and she had to push her cheeks in with her fingers to force it back out.

She felt like being sick, but then something happened to take her mind off the stench of insect breath. The down-force from the creature's wings had upset the fortune teller's table and the air was thick with metallic packets and the seeds that had spilled out of them. It was like a magical display of light, swirling in the eddies of air that the beast had left in its wake.

'They're beautiful,' she whispered.

The seeds were still glowing, even as they flew, but the distance between them was increasing rapidly, stretching whatever links had bound them and destroying whatever story they might have told.

'Yeah, right,' said Toby, 'it's *lovely*, now get your head down.'

The insect turned for another run, this time coming in low and using the great whip-like protrusions on his head. The air pressure increased again as it skimmed past, but this time Lucy kept her mouth closed and covered her ears. She nodded at Toby who did the same, the pair of them bracing for an impact that never came. Instead, the scarab shot past at speed, flailing and cracking its whips.

'Erm, it *missed* us,' said Toby.

'It wasn't aiming for us,' said Lucy. 'Look.'

There was a scream from above. It was followed by a sickening crunch as the fortune teller hit the floor in front of them, his throat glistening with two deep red slashes. He was bleeding heavily, but still able to speak.

'Had to betray,' he gurgled, 'otherwise family get hurt.'

'*What?*' said Toby.

'No time for details,' said the man, obviously in pain.

'Don't talk,' said Lucy, 'we'll get help.'

'No,' he said, 'there *is* no help for this – I have seen it in the seeds.'

'Shush,' said Lucy, 'you're hurt.'

'Must tell,' whispered the bird-man. 'Beware the Vooghul, and beware the Sisters – and know *this* – there are great darknesses at work.'

'Darknesses?' said Toby, diving to avoid the beetle. He wiped some of its stinking spit from his face, suddenly realising how close it had come.

'Do you mean people?' said Lucy. 'But *who?*'

'I see no *names* in the seeds,' gurgled the bird-man, 'only shadows – but they are made from the deepest black, and know where you are.'

The air shuddered as the creature swooped past again, gouging at the bird-man's back with its razor-sharp claws. He screamed and tried to raise himself, but fell again, his wrinkled face thumping into the blood-soaked floor.

'In the seeds, I saw you in a nursery,' he gurgled, 'you played with four coloured blocks, then you took them and made a fifth, binding them up.'

'Shush,' said Lucy. 'Don't speak. Toby, try to drag him under the table.'

'There's no room,' yelled Toby.

'And no time,' hissed the bird-man. 'Listen to me…'

'Maybe we *should* listen,' said Toby, 'it might be important.'

'*All* is important,' he wheezed. 'You took the fifth block in your hand and reached towards a dark place, and then you were gone.'

'So that's it?' said Toby. He was watching the scarab – it was set in a hover and eyeing them, like a lizard watching flies.

'And *then* what happened?' said Lucy.

'I followed in spirit,' he gurgled. 'I flew behind you in the darkness – I saw the killing of birds, and the sorting of the weak from the strong.'

As he spoke, some of the seed packets fell back to earth, covering his bloodied back with gold and silver medallions.

'It's *Harry*,' said Lucy. 'Do you remember the old man I told you about? The one with the pigeons?'

'*Not* one man,' groaned the fortune teller, 'a hundred, or a thousand – I saw them all, with many heads and wings, just as the sorcerer Dee has described. They were like the Saraph and accompanied by great flame – and one of them, his name is R…'

'*Raziel?*' gasped Lucy. 'Is one of them called Raziel?'

There was no reply – the bloodied corpse of the fortune teller was finally stilled. All that remained now was the noise of leathery wings – and behind that sound, almost inaudible, the mournful song of three birds, as they twittered amongst the roof beams.

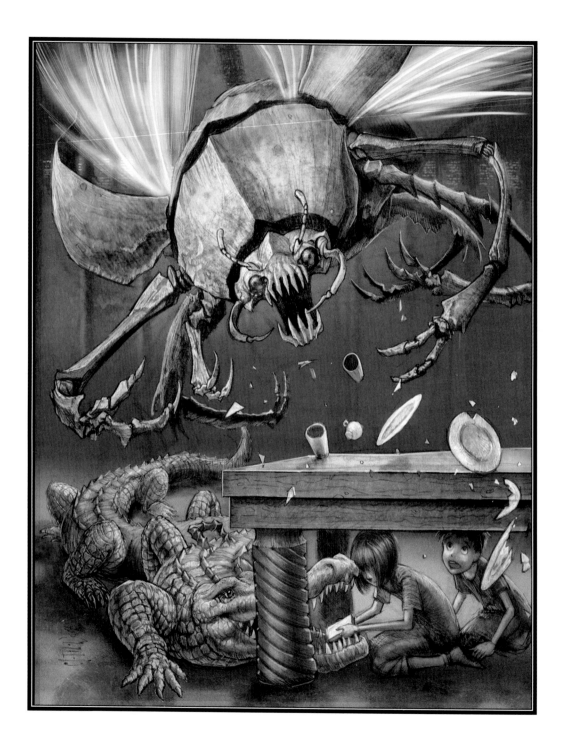

Khepri

'If you value your lives stay on the floor,' screamed a high-pitched voice.

Toby stuck his head up anyway, and spotted the Tarot woman on the other side of the room. She was hiding under a table, just as they were.

'It's Miss Pubrane,' he shouted.

'I told you to stay *down*,' screamed Exotica. 'Lucretia, can't you keep that boy under control?'

'*Toby!*' snapped Lucy. 'Get down here will you? I don't want you getting your head bitten off – just think of all the mess.'

'I can't say I'm keen on it myself,' said Toby. '*Hey*, wait a minute though, what *is* that mad card-woman doing?' He poked his head up again and nearly had it taken off as the insect swooped past.

'I'm *helping*,' shouted Miss Pubrane. 'Now get back underneath.'

With that, she darted out from under her own table and grabbed the handbag from the chair. Then she began to spin around on the spot, swinging the ugly thing around her head like a hammer-thrower. Finally, she let go and it came sailing towards them, hurtling across the room with a terrifying squeal.

'*Eeeee… aaaaahhh… aaaagggagrararaa… grunnnfff…*'

Henbeg screamed, grunted, and squeaked whilst he was in the air and finally gave a hefty grunt as he hit the stone floor in front of Toby.

'Actually I prefer flowers on a first date,' whispered Toby as he pulled the surprisingly heavy bag under the table.

'Listen to me,' shouted Miss Pubrane. 'This is no joke – we must act quickly – the Sisters are coming.'

'The *Sisters*?' yelled Toby, 'erm, but *Gusset* said…'

'Isn't that one of them at the door?' shouted Lucy.

'No, child it is *not*,' shouted Miss Pubrane. '*That* is a Khepri Mistress – she merely controls the insect beast.'

'A *what* mistress?' shouted Lucy.

'There is no time for explanations,' shouted Miss Pubrane. 'Just *listen* to me, and consider what you said earlier, about having nobody to trust.'

'We're listening,' said Lucy.

The scarab was still hovering, but had begun to edge forward now, tilting his snout down like a helicopter, and staring at them from unblinking multi-faceted eyes. The noise and the pressure from the insect's wings was almost unbearable, and Lucy had difficulty staying rooted as the insect pushed its dripping jaws closer and closer towards her face.

'Ah, *no*, go away, *shoo...*,' she screamed, grabbing hold of a table leg.

'*Shoo?*' yelled Toby. 'I think it might take something a bit stronger than that.'

'Well *you* tell it then,' screamed Lucy, 'because actually I'm quite busy at the moment.'

The Khepri Mistress had instructed the scarab to land in front of them, and it was squatting on five of its legs now, ripping at Lucy with its one free claw. The table provided good protection though and was low enough to prevent the scarab getting underneath – at least whilst it still had its wings unfolded. The insect could still prevent them from getting *out* though, so for now all they could do was curl up and protect themselves. The Khepri Mistress soon realised this, and screamed another command, causing the scarab to lower its gauzy wings and fold them inside the huge armour-plated elytra. The wing-covers reflected deep, vibrant blue and brilliant sea-green and every shade in between, and in other circumstances, Lucy might have been tempted to stop and consider how beautiful they were.

'*Uh-oh,*' she said. She held the rucksack out in front, shielding herself from the slobbering snout that was now pushing its way under the table. Toby did the same with the handbag, and from the amount of snarling and growling, it was clear that Henbeg wasn't too keen on the idea. The scarab was more interested in Lucy though, and had already torn a great slash in her rucksack – and now it was trying to put a matching gash in *her*.

'Luce, *watch* it,' shouted Toby. 'He's using that old boxing trick.'

'And which old boxing trick might that be?' shouted Lucy, fending off a vicious slice with her bag.

'You need to get further under the table,' said Toby. 'He's making you think his reach is shorter than it really is.'

Before Lucy could react, the scarab lashed out again, the half-split claws slicing the air like razors and catching her completely off guard. They were already streaked with the bird-man's blood and now they had claimed some of Lucy's, opening up a neat pair of grooves in her right cheek. They were shallower than the ones that killed the fortune teller, but no less crimson, and no less painful. She screamed in agony, and in a panic driven by sheer terror, she tried to wipe away the blood, smearing it on her face and hands and getting it into her eyes in the process.

'*Toby!*' she yelled, 'I can't *see* – are you still there?'

'Of *course* I am Luce, I wouldn't leave you…' He was gagging at the sight of the blood though, trying hard not to faint.

'You *must* leave her,' shouted Miss Pubrane, 'and you must listen to *me*.'

'No,' shouted Toby. 'She needs help – the bird-man *died* from wounds like that – don't you *see?*'

'I *do* see,' screamed Miss Pubrane, 'but if you don't listen then we will *all* die – you must leave her for a moment, and do exactly as I say.'

There was something in Exotica's voice that commanded obedience, like his and Lucy's favourite teachers at St. Frideg's. Not the arrogant ones that nobody listened to, but the gentle, intelligent creatures whose knowledge and empathy earned them respect.

'Alright then,' yelled Toby. 'What do you want me to do?'

'That's better,' shouted Miss Pubrane. '*Now*, I suspect that you have something they want, and whatever it is we must protect it at all costs.'

'*Ah*,' sighed Toby, suddenly suspicious again.

'*Well?*' shouted Miss Pubrane. 'What is it?'

'How do I know you don't just want to take the *light?*'

'*Light?*' shouted Miss Pubrane. 'I know nothing about any light – all I know is that the Sisters want whatever you have – are you still listening?'

'Yes,' said Toby.

'Then I have one word for you,' said Miss Pubrane. '*Trust.*'

'*Do* it,' hissed Lucy. 'Give her the *light* – I'd do it myself if I could see.'

'But *Luce*, we hardly know her.'

'And we've got lots of other options, have we?'

'Erm, no,' admitted Toby, 'not now you come to mention it, but…'

Lucy patted the surrounding ground, searching for Toby so she could strangle some sense into him. And *that* was when the scarab saw its chance, slashing at her outstretched hand with a razor sharp claw. In a single, savage movement, it sliced the little finger clean off her right hand.

'Oh, *no*,' yelled Toby, 'there's going to be even more bloo…'

Lucy screamed in agony as the pain ran like wildfire from her hand to her brain and back to her hand again. It felt like the bloodied mess had been plunged into burning coals – and even without the benefit of sight, she knew she had lost something very dear to her.

'That was my favourite *finger*,' she sobbed. 'I *wanted* that. I had plans for it. We were going to have a lovely life together, and now it's all ruined.'

'Eh?' said Toby. 'What on *earth* are you talking about?'

Lucy screamed, suddenly more aware of her pain and the stupid things it was making her say. Then she remembered Toby and his aversion to blood, and with the tears pouring out of her like running water, she pushed the bleeding stump into her mouth. As she sucked at it, she couldn't help thinking that the thick red fluid had the taste of defeat.

'Erm, *Luce*, I don't feel well,' said Toby.

'And how do you think *I* feel?' she gurgled, her mouth filled with a thick red tide.

'It's all this rotten *blood,* Luce – I think I want to throw up.'

'Close your eyes then,' said Lucy, 'and *neither* of us will see death coming.' She continued sucking at the stump in an attempt to staunch the flow, but was desperate to see what was happening too, and fought to clear the blood-filled eyes with her one free hand. As she did so, a clot of blood slid from the gathering pool in her mouth and slipped down her throat, making her want to vomit.

'Alright,' shouted Toby to the Tarot woman. 'We agree.'

'And about time,' yelled Miss Pubrane. 'Henbeg? *Henbeg?*'

At the sound of its name, the handbag seemed to perk up, as if it had been waiting for a word of command.

'*Eeeeekaah, Henbeg*,' shouted Exotica. '*Eeeeekaah-feekah-mallybash-derookah.*'

'Toby?' said Lucy. 'What's happening?'

'Erm, I'm not sure you'd believe me,' he replied, 'but if I was making it up you'd give me a six at least.'

'Don't bank on it,' said Lucy, still fighting to clear the blood.

'Believe me, Luce, you *would* – maybe even a seven.'

Khepri

It was almost as if the handbag had been wired up to Lectric terminals and was now discovering what it would be like to have ten thousand volts crackling up its trouser legs. Not that it was *wearing* any trousers, but if it *had* been then they would certainly be doing a fair bit of crackling. Henbeg shot ten feet into the air and exploded like a Chinee firecracker, unrolling himself into a blurred green shape on the way down.

'Tell me what's happening,' asked Lucy.

'Erm, it sort of *unfolded*, like some kind of complicated origami puzzle.'

'*What* did?' hissed Lucy.

'Oh, no,' said Toby, almost hypnotised by the enigma that was taking shape before him. 'Luce, I don't *believe* it – it's got eight legs.'

'*What* has?' hissed Lucy, '*talk* to me you idiot.'

'It's a crocodile,' laughed Toby. 'At least I *think* it is – but it has eight legs, and I'll swear it only had four when it was a handbag.'

'Oh I *see*,' sneered Lucy, 'well thank goodness for that – it's all beginning to make *sense* now.'

'I'm not making it up, honest Luce. The handbag has turned into a crocodile, and now I think he *wants* something from us.'

'Of course he does,' said Lucy, 'he wants to take you to the loony bin.'

Henbeg seemed to be smiling, but Toby was in no mood for smiling back. He was too busy taking in the full extent of that huge scaly body, wondering what it might be like on the inside. And he wasn't the only one who had noticed the transformation. The surrounding air was vibrating again as the scarab backed off and took to the air, suddenly aware of a new and much greater threat.

'*Khepri, akuba, heeka, eeka...*' the insect mistress shouted. '*Akuba, eehara, pora...*' Just for a moment, every eye in the place was upon the scarab as it lifted off vertically, wobbled for a moment, and then flew backwards until its position stabilised.

'*Now* what?' said Toby, ducking to avoid the scarab's first fly-by.

Henbeg gave a little grunt and opened his mouth wider than seemed possible for an animal of his size – or even a handbag of his size.

'Place the item inside,' shouted Miss Pubrane.

'What, in his *mouth* you mean?' said Toby. 'But that's disgusting.'

'Toby, what's happening?'

'Erm, I'm not sure Luce.'

'Do it now,' screamed Miss Pubrane.

Henbeg gave another encouraging grunt, and when Toby *still* didn't react, he started doing eight-legged press-ups. Then he nudged himself even further under the table and placed the tip of his snout just inches from Toby's face.

'Erm, *hello*,' said Toby nervously. 'Erm, *good* Henbeg…'

The handbag gave a quick snap of his jaws and then opened them again. And this time Toby couldn't help but notice how sharp the rows of yellow teeth were, and how black his tongue was, even though crocodiles weren't supposed to have them.

'*Now,* child,' screamed Exotica. 'Do it now.'

'*Alright,*' shouted Toby, 'just *wait* a minute will you? We're trying to fight off beetles as well you know.'

'*Toby?*' whispered Lucy.

'I'll tell you later,' said Toby. He took the *light* from Lucy's bag and was about to put it in Henbeg's saliva-filled mouth when he realised his mistake.

'Erm, wait a minute Luce – *you've* got to do this, haven't you? The *light* must be given freely, remember?'

He handed Lucy the manuscript and helped her to find Henbeg's eager and extremely smelly mouth. And when Henbeg was satisfied the Grobbley was in the proper position he flipped it into the air and swallowed it, following up with a deep, malodorous belch. Toby wrinkled his nose in disgust – obviously there was no such thing as toothpaste for handbags.

'*What* is that *stink*?' said Lucy.

'I keep *telling* you, Luce,' said Toby, 'but *will* you believe me?' He grabbed hold of Genjamin and stuffed the dummy into Henbeg's mouth too – and then, as an afterthought, he followed up with Lily's emergency rations.

'*Excellent,*' shouted Miss Pubrane. 'Now hold out your hands and let him smell you.'

'*Smell* us?' shouted Toby. 'Is that really necessary?'

'Do as you're told,' yelled Exotica.

They held out their hands so that Henbeg could get a nose-full of their scent, and when he was satisfied, he turned and ran. He didn't head for Exotica though, as they might have expected. Instead, he sprinted under tables and dived between legs, pausing for a moment at the door to vomit on the Khepri Mistress's feet – it was a disgusting mess of lumpy, green sick that looked suspiciously like Lily's emergency sandwich.

'See?' grinned Toby. 'Now *that's* what I call proof – he's sicked up the lamp-stand's special.'

'*Henbeg*,' screamed Exotica. 'Go boy – *go* – you mustn't stop to throw up whenever you feel like it – *feeky-derookah-eeky-pernookah*.'

'Too late,' grinned the Mistress, her expression turning to hatred as she examined her puke-covered feet. She slammed the door, trapping Henbeg by his head and forcing an ear-splitting squeal from the poor creature.

'*Khepri – akuba, heeka*,' she screamed.

The insect didn't *need* telling – it had followed the Henbeg's progress as he slithered amongst the tables, and now the prey was out in the open it was relishing the opportunity for a kill. It wheeled in a tight turn, clipping its wings against the ceiling and accelerating the full length of the tavern before swooping down and burying all six claws in Henbeg's back. The handbag gave a soul-rending shriek, crying out for his mother in the long-lost crocodilian tongue. And as he shed his pathetic tears, the scarab let out a victory wail, forcing its talons deeper and deeper into his flesh. In the blink of an eye, the fashion accessory had been reduced from a heroic gear guzzler to a pathetic, squealing lump.

'He would have *made* it through that gap if you hadn't given him too much to digest,' cried Miss Pubrane. 'What *was* that horrible thing? Or *who*?'

'Erm, it was a puppet,' admitted Toby. 'But it was the emergency rations that tipped him over the edge.'

'You *idiot*,' screamed Miss Pubrane. 'You mean we're endangering our lives to save a block of wood and some sandwiches?'

'Sorry,' shouted Toby, 'it just seemed like a good idea at the time.'

'Oh, just *look* at him,' cried Exotica. 'Look what you've done.'

Streams of yellow blood were pouring from Henbeg's back now as the scarab continued to drive its talons into his scaly green flesh.

'*Khepri, keepa-kenaba*,' screamed the Mistress. '*Keepa-kenaba*.'

The command sounded like a recall, but the scarab obviously hadn't been listening during obedience classes. He had the smell of blood in his nostrils now and wanted more, regardless of what the keeper said. He wanted to take his prize away and eat it, and began to flap his great wings, trying to take off with the handbag still in his grasp.

'We have to *do* something,' said Toby, realising that he'd finally managed to ignore the sight of the crocodile's blood. He made a move towards the creature, but the Mistress blocked his path, placing her back up against the partially open door and driving her foot down onto Henbeg's rump. Then, without taking her eyes away from Toby, she delivered a vicious back-heel kick, grinning as she managed to force a squeal from the hapless creature. He was severely weakened now, his resistance reduced to tiny body-twitches and weak flicks of his tail.

'Don't you *dare* do that,' screamed Toby. 'You're killing him – it's cruel – in fact it's more than that, it's *evil*.'

'Death is not cruel,' said the Mistress. '*Life* is cruel. *People* are cruel.' And she kicked out at Henbeg again, as if to prove the point.

'I *told* you,' shouted Toby. 'Leave him alone, or I'll…'

'Or *what?*' hissed the insect handler.

'Or I'll, erm, er…'

Lucy had finally managed to clear the blood from her eyes and the first thing she noticed was that the tavern appeared to be empty, apart from the three of them and the Khepri Mistress. Then she looked closer and spotted a row of heads peeping out from behind the bar.

'Aren't you lot going to *help?*' she shouted.

The nine assorted heads began to shake in unison, as if someone had nailed them together with a long plank of wood.

'They're scared of what might happen to their families,' shouted Miss Pubrane. 'I'm afraid we must deal with this on our own.'

'Indeed you *must*,' hissed the Mistress. 'But do not worry, you will not have long to wait.' She aimed another vicious kick at Henbeg, who gave a pathetic squeal. It was so quiet that it could only be a matter of seconds now before he expired.

Toby was filled with grief for an animal he'd known just a matter of minutes, and was desperate to find a way to help. If *only* he could get the scarab off Henbeg, the crocodile might just be able to squeeze through the door. If only he had a stick to beat the insect with, or something heavy that he could throw at it.

Khepri

He was about to fall on his knees and beg for Henbeg's life when he remembered the shew stone. It was certainly very heavy, and fitted nicely in his hand too – and it was still in his pocket.

'What are you *doing*?' screeched the handler. 'Take your hand *out* of there.'

'Erm, *what* hand?' said Toby innocently. 'Out of *where*? Out of my pocket you mean?'

'And what is *that*?' said the Mistress, as Toby withdrew the stone.

'Something heavy,' said Toby, weighing it in his hand.

'*No!* shouted Lucy. 'You *mustn't*, it's too valuable.'

'But we have to save the *light*,' shouted Toby.

'And Henbeg too,' yelled Miss Pubrane.

'And ne too,' shouted a muffled voice. It came from somewhere near Henbeg. In *fact*, it sounded as if it was coming from *inside* him.

Toby glanced across at Lucy, unable to believe that she could be joking at such a time.

'Well don't look at *me*,' she said with a shrug.

'And don't you *dare* throw that thing at my *cherished*,' screamed the Khepri Mistress, 'or the Vooghul will have your soul. They will be here soon, I know it. The Khepri can smell their spirit, and so can I.'

She inhaled deeply, as if she really *could* smell something coming. For a moment, the scarab sniffed the air too, waving its feelers as if collecting evidence of an approaching scent.

'Yeah,' said Toby. 'Well *we* can smell them too, and they *stink*.' And with the insect mistress's threat still ringing in his ears, he drew back his arm and took aim, calling upon every available bit of strength as he let the stone fly.

Sweeeeeooossshhhh...

The shew stone whistled through the air, and when it eventually found its mark thirteen pairs of eyes blinked in disbelief. It smashed straight into the leather-armoured head, knocking the creature senseless. Unfortunately, though, the unconscious scarab simply slumped down onto Henbeg's back.

'Oh, *great*,' said Toby, seeing that Henbeg still couldn't move.

Lucy was more concerned about the shew stone, gasping as it bounced away from the scarab and hit the floor with a loud clatter. For a moment, it seemed that everything was alright – but suddenly it exploded, showering the inn with millions of fine blue dust fragments.

'You *idiot*,' she screamed, 'we *needed* that.'

'Yes,' shouted Miss Pubrane, 'but not as much as you need Henbeg.'

'Erm, and now we've got them both,' said Toby. 'One of them in billions of tiny pieces and the other one pinned under a dirty great scarab thing.'

'Yes, we *have*,' sighed Lucy.

'*So*,' said Toby, 'erm, has anyone got any good ideas?'

As if responding to his plea, the scattered fragments of the stone took to the air, raised by a sudden draught that blew under the door. As they became airborne, the floating remains enveloped the entrance, hiding Henbeg and the Khepri Mistress in a kaleidoscopic cloud that displayed images from the shew stone's memory. There was a picture of the Beak's study, as recently seen by Toby, then another, packed with the dark creatures that had impaled his bed. And orbiting that, like a group of glowing asteroids, were dozens of views of the inside of Toby's pocket. The recent visions soon dispersed though, replaced by scenes from a distant past that nobody recognised. There were glimpses of great libraries and strong-rooms and palaces – and at one point, Lucy thought she saw a tiled floor, like the ones they had seen in the kiosks. This was a floor like no other though – it covered acres of ground, and there were hundreds of shadowy figures there, surrounded by majestic vaults that were frustratingly fuzzy. Then, as clear as anything, they saw an airship, and a flooded city made from iron, and a laboratory filled with ancient apparatus.

'Amazing,' said Toby.

'*Absolutely* amazing,' said Lucy, 'and now it's all bloody-well *gone*.'

'Yeah, *well*,' said Toby. 'I did it for Henb… erm, uh-oh, *Luce*, what the hell is *that*?'

An aerial image of Henbeg had appeared at the centre of the historic swirl – he was thrashing about like a mechanical paint mixer in a desperate effort to free himself from the claws that were locked deep into his flesh.

'It must be the final vision of the stone,' said Exotica. 'We can see what's happening inside the dust cloud.'

There was a cheer from the faces behind the bar when they saw what was going on and this gave the handbag the encouragement he needed. He paused to gather what little strength he had left, and then, with a single huge convulsion, he rippled every remaining ounce of power through his body and twisted out from beneath the dead weight of the insect. There was another rousing cheer of celebration, but as the dust cloud settled, the image of Henbeg began to fade, and when it finally disappeared, there was a huge sigh. He was gone from the doorway and gone from the shew-dust, and suddenly the place was empty and silent.

'You will suffer for this,' hissed the Khepri Mistress. '*All* of you.'

There was a huge cheer as Henbeg's snout appeared once again at the bottom of the doorway. It was only a flying visit though, just long enough to give a triumphant squeak and sink his teeth into the Khepri Mistress's ankle.

'He *made* it,' sobbed Miss Pubrane. 'My precious baby made it.'

'*Baby?*' said Lucy with a brief smile. 'If that's the baby, I wouldn't like to meet the mother.'

Exotica's tears of joy left deep, dark furrows in her makeup, and just for a moment Lucy found herself imagining her face as a strange map, full of forgotten waterholes and dried-up riverbeds.

'Well *he* might have made it,' said Toby, 'but I don't think *we* did – *look*.'

He pointed at a dark shape that was hovering in the open doorway.

'*Run*,' shouted one of the brave heads behind the bar.

'Where to?' screamed another, 'there's only one door.'

'Run anyway,' yelled someone else.

'No,' shouted a third voice, 'get behind the bar, and let *them* four worry about it. It hasn't come for us. We're just indolent bystanders, aren't we?'

'Yeah, but there's only three of them,' said the first voice.

'Five,' said another. 'And I should know, 'cause *I* can count.'

Lucy managed a brief smile, but inside she knew it was her fear that was laughing. Waves of deep, soul-destroying sadness were radiating from the dark figure that floated in the doorway – a creature that understood the nature of terror and knew how to spread it. It was at least two feet taller than her, its body swathed in drab grey veils that trailed on the ground, leaving a trace of dark, brown slime wherever they touched. The figure was holding a truth wand in one bony hand and pointing at Lucy with a single finger of the other. The sharp black nails reminded her of Lily, and the pale grey skin brought to mind the ridiculous wardrobe perchers. Now though, as she faced her newest nightmare, the sale of curiosities and the safe haven that was Grimston seemed so very far away.

Khepri

'It's a *Vooghul*,' hissed Lucy, 'and it's got a Spiritu Lokey.'

'I'm afraid I have let you down,' whispered Miss Pubrane. 'I *had* hoped to take you away before this, but we have been betrayed.'

'*Silence*,' hissed the figure. The words echoed about them, as if they were all standing in a church. '*You there, blood-face*, come with me now.'

It was pointing at Lucy, who stood motionless, transfixed by the sight of the glowing truth wand. She knew that if she succumbed this time it would be far worse than the punishment that Niblock had administered.

'Wh-wh-what do you want?' she said, unable to stop herself trembling.

'*You*,' hissed the wraith.

Lucy tore her eyes from the Lokey pole, so she could look the creature in the face. Gusset had been right though – there *was* no face, just a gaseous, smoking mask that concealed even the slightest feature or expression.

'*Come with me*,' it said, beckoning a crooked finger. 'Or resist us, and *die*.'

Lucy was paralysed with fear, like a rabbit hypnotised by car headlamps, the stench of rotting flesh filling her senses. All she could think about was spending the rest of her life inside a cabinet, feeling as though her soul had been sliced away and preaching a faith she had no belief in. The death promised by the stinking Vooghul seemed almost merciful in comparison.

'No,' she said finally. 'I don't think I *do* want to go, not just yet.'

She wanted to be sick, just to get rid of the smell, but guessed that the time she took to do it might be all the creature needed to trap her.

'Then you will *die*,' said the Vooghul, 'but first you will experience incredible pain. It will be like standing in the midst of a raging fire and having your heart gouged out by rusty blades. For *you* the pain will last an eternity, but in *this* place just a few seconds will have elapsed.'

Lucy trembled uncontrollably, and as the words of the threat faded, she felt the soul-cutting pain of the cabinet all over again, as if the mere description of the punishment had the power to inflict it. Then she realised it was not just her *own* pain. She had shared the Vooghul's thoughts in the maze, and now it was happening again. Somewhere inside this dark creature was the person it used to be, and she was bound up with their fears.

'You *hate* doing this, don't you?' said Lucy.

'Do *not* try to distract us from our allotted task,' hissed the Vooghul.

'Why not?' said Lucy. 'Are you *afraid* to remember your former self?'

Khepri

'We are not afraid,' hissed the Vooghul. 'Our personal wishes are no longer important – the will of the Sisters is *all*.'

The gaseous cloud shimmered slightly and just for a moment, Lucy saw the outline of a woman's face. It disappeared almost immediately though, leaving just a ghost in her memory.

'You were standing in a dome,' said Lucy. 'I *saw* you, just now when your thoughts slipped – you were surrounded by stars and lenses and mechanisms with wheels.'

'No longer,' hissed the Vooghul. 'The creature you speak of has gone for ever – all that matters now is the will of the Sisters.'

'Yes, I believe you mentioned that just now,' said Lucy. She had started to feel slightly more confident since glimpsing the face, but her poise soon evaporated as she noticed the smell of burning oil – so strong now that she could taste it. There was a crackle in the air too, and a familiar blue fizzing sound – a signal that they were on the edge of something magical.

'Don't just stand there *talking* to the bloody thing,' shouted Toby. 'Run.'

'No,' said Lucy. 'I want to understand – that's why we're here.'

'Oh, *great*,' said Toby. 'Un-be-bloody-well-lievable – she wants to sit down and get friendly with the stinking thing.'

'And what do you wish to know?' hissed the creature. She settled slightly, lowering herself to Lucy's height and trailing her smelly rags over the body of the scarab. The insect twitched, then sank back to the floor, its rotting flesh oozing out between the armoured plates. Lucy clamped her hand over her nose and mouth, trying to block the stench of the scarab's guts. And as the pain of the severed finger came back to her, she suddenly realised what a strange conversation she was having. She hadn't expected a reasoned discussion. She'd expected unrelenting violence, and lots of it.

'*Well?*' hissed the Vooghul.

'I want to understand what you are,' she said. 'And I want to know who the Sisters are.'

'There will be time *enough* for that, Lucy Blake,' said the wraith.

'*Oh*,' said Lucy. 'You know my name?'

She had heard a story once, about the bravest of men who had been reduced to cowardice, simply because the enemy had discovered his name. Somehow, this dark aberration knew who she was, and it terrified her.

'Of course I know your name,' said the Vooghul. 'Does the hunter seek her prey without knowing its identity?'

'I don't know,' said Lucy absently. 'Wait, will you? I'm thinking.'

'*Thinking?*' hissed the Vooghul.

'About the truth wand,' she replied, suddenly more confident.

'*Ye-es?*' said the wraith.

'And the way you hide your face behind a mask,' said Lucy.

'*Luce,*' shouted Toby, 'for *God's* sake, stop talking and *run,* will you?'

'What of it?' hissed the Vooghul.

'I'm imagining a pair of those old fashioned scales,' said Lucy, 'the kind where you place a known weight on one side and then balance it against something on the other.'

'I begin to see your point,' said the wraith. 'The power of the Sisters on one side of the scales against you and your own puny abilities.'

'Exactly,' said Lucy, sucking the bloodied stump of her finger.

'So this is a form of surrender?' said the Vooghul. 'A submission where you maintain your dignity by admitting inferiority?'

'*Something* like that,' said Lucy. 'Only I was thinking more along the lines of what Harry told me once.'

'*Harry?*' hissed the wraith.

'He's just an old man who loves pigeons,' said Lucy.

'I see,' said the creature, 'and what did this spirit lover tell you?'

'That I shouldn't try to fight something I don't understand.'

'A wise man,' said the creature, '*come* – I accept your surrender.'

'But I'm not surrendering,' said Lucy with a nervous smile, 'I'm *running* – but I promise to come back when I understand – and *then* I'll fight.'

The wraith seemed to comprehend what was about to happen and raised the Spiritu Lokey, tilting the face in the tiny cabinet towards Lucy.

'*Luce,* get down,' shouted Toby. 'It's going to…'

The tip of the wand puffed thousands of tiny seeds into the air, and before Lucy could register what was happening they had burst forth shoots which began to grow at an alarming rate.

'*Luce,* look out.'

The mass of plant growth was expanding so rapidly and gaining weight so quickly that it threatened to drag the pole from the Vooghul's grasp. It soon reached the floor though, which relieved the pressure, and then it began putting out tendrils that wrapped and smothered and choked everything in sight – and it was then that the main mass of greenery ceased to grow, and the plant began to flower.

'It's like the manuscript,' Lucy whispered. 'All those plant forms in the book – this is something to do with them, isn't it?'

There was no answer from the Vooghul – and as the cycle of growth prepared to begin once again with the death of the blossom, Lucy realised why. The Khepri Mistress and the wraith had been sent merely to delay her. Somewhere in the echoing dome of the creature's mind, she had sensed a tiny idea, like a single candle glowing behind a dark lace curtain. And she had swept the veil aside to reveal what the woman was thinking – one of the Sisters was coming to take her away.

As the pure white petals began to wither, they curled at the edges and turned brown, as if the show had all been for nothing. But then they began to fall, turning and floating in the same breeze that had held the shew-stone fragments aloft. As they twisted and turned in the draught they gradually transformed into feathers, first gathering into four distinct groups and then combining to make a single ball of fluff that evolved into a pure white dove.

The beat and motion of the bird's wings was graceful, hypnotic almost, as though it had come from heaven with a personal and very urgent message. Lucy had no time though – she needed all her concentration for something else.

'Hey! What's she *doing?*' said one of the heads behind the bar.

'*Eh?*' said Toby. He'd been paying so much attention to the tendrils and the flowers that he'd taken his eyes off Lucy. She was standing with her head turned towards the ceiling now, her eyes sealed tightly shut.

'*Zildar de tergonias,*' she whispered.

As the words emerged from her lips, a picture of her mother formed in Lucy's mind. She had successfully summoned a few more fragments of her childhood.

'*Nooooo,*' shouted Toby, guessing what was happening. His cry sounded like the howl of a dog, separated from his pack by the wiles of the forest.

Khepri

The expression on Lucy's bloodstained face was resolute though. Her eyes were tight-shut, but even so, a single tear managed to escape and trickle down her bloodstained cheek.

'*Zildar de tergonias, ad majorem dei gloria, …*' she whispered softly.

The image of her began to shimmer and fade, as if she were simply a figment of Toby's imagination. Her body had become suddenly transparent, wrapped in a fluttering curtain of lights that reminded him of the confuser. But whatever beauty he witnessed in the transformation was blotted out by the thought of what she was doing.

'Luce, *please*, don't leave us,' he pleaded, noticing the drop of blood that had oozed from the stump of her finger.

'Luce, don't *leave* m…'

Before the crimson droplet had hit the ground, Lucy Blake was gone, her shimmering image absorbed by a cloud of blue smoke.

All that remained was the sound of distant thunder, the magical smell of Lectric, and a heart-rending impression of absence.

Welcome Home, Lovely Daughter

It was dark – *extremely* dark in fact, and cramped too – very, *very* cramped. Lucy hadn't known what to expect when she'd uttered the words of flight, but it certainly hadn't been this. It was comfortable for one thing, and there were muffled voices too – like listening to a couple of secretive sheep holding a conversation through ten feet of army-grade wadding. It was the *smell* that kept her guessing though, at least to begin with – for some reason it reminded her of men digging up roads in summer. She took a deliberate breath and filled her lungs with the strangely familiar scent, allowing herself to be transported by the memories it kindled. And in a flash, she knew exactly where she was. The smell belonged to the coal-tar soap that Lily insisted on buying in bulk, and the slats forcing themselves into her back were the rough wooden shelves that Percy had built. All that remained now was the mystery of the voices – and she *already* had a sneaking suspicion about those. They became slightly clearer as she pushed a pile of scratchy 'guest' towels out of the way, and finally, as she elbowed a couple of feather pillows onto the floor every shred of doubt evaporated – it was dear, lovely Tarquin, and his friend Warren, the boy genius.

'I *heard* something,' said Warren. 'I *tell* you.'

'What? From in *there*?' said Tarquin.

'That's right,' he said, 'behind that door.'

'But it's locked,' said Tarquin. 'Mum *always* locks it to stop the guests stealing sheets.'

'I don't care,' insisted Warren. 'I *still* heard it.'

'Alright then,' said Tarquin, 'so what did it sound like?'

'Like a mouse eating a cough sweet.'

'A *what*?' grinned Tarquin.

'Well *I* don't know, do I?' said Warren. 'It was just a noise.'

'Hey, do you know what?' said Tarquin. 'I think you're right – there *is* something funny going on – there's a weird smell, like short-circuited Lectric.'

'Yeah, right,' enthused Warren, 'so let's break the door down.'

'Are you *thick* or what?' said Tarquin. 'My mum'll kill me if we damage the house – it's going to be hers soon, remember?'

'Oh yeah, sorry, I forgot.'

'Well *don't*,' said Tarquin. 'Now bunk me up so I can reach the key.'

Lucy pushed herself into the deepest recesses of the airing cupboard, wondering how she was going to explain her presence. As the key turned in the lock she decided on the only possible course of action – she'd pretend that nothing could be more natural.

'*You!*' squealed Tarquin, as the door swung open. 'I don't *believe* it.'

'Well you had *better* believe it, child nightmare,' said Lucy. 'I'm back.'

'Erm, yeah,' said Tarquin, staring at Lucy's sackcloth smock. 'Well just wait until you find out what's been happening while you were away.'

'Such as?' said Lucy.

'No clues,' smirked Tarquin. 'I wouldn't want to spoil the surprise.'

'Yeah, that's right,' grinned Warren. 'I can't *wait* to see your face.'

'It's not Doctor Veraciter again, is it?' said Lucy anxiously. She'd only been back a matter of seconds, and there were already new things to be worrying about.

'Nope, it's *much* better than that,' grinned Tarquin. He scratched furiously at the back of his head, trying to cure an itch that couldn't be reached. It was buried inside the plastic collar that was supposed to be keeping his neck straight.

'Yeah, you'll *never* guess,' grinned Warren.

'Oh?' said Lucy, struggling down from the shelf. 'And how would *you* know, brainy boy?'

Warren gave her a wicked smile, then cupped both hands around his mouth and turned to face down the stairs.

'MRS. WINNET-BLAKE,' he bellowed, 'come and look at what me and Tarquin have found in the airing cupboard.'

'Oh, well that's just *great*,' said Lucy, 'thanks a lot, Warren.'

Ω⅄⅋⅀⅄⅂⅄⅄C

Welcome Home, Lovely Daughter

'I wish she'd hurry up,' grinned Tarquin. 'I can't wait 'til she sees those horrendous clothes and all that blood – it *is* blood, isn't it?'

'Erm, *yes*,' said Lucy, realising it was pointless to deny a truth that was painted all over her face. 'I'd forgotten about that.'

'Oh *God*, this is *brilliant*,' grinned Tarquin. 'Mum's going to go absolutely ballistic – we'll have to get a big gang of hairy workmen to come and scrape her off the ceiling with one of those giant spatula things.'

Lucy had been back for less than a minute and already the memory of Assiah had begun to fade, as if it had all been a bad dream. But now that Tarquin had reminded her about the blood it was all flooding back again, as if an anaesthetic had just worn off. Her eyes filled with tears as she recalled the slashes in the fortune teller's neck and the gashes in her own cheek. And poor Henbeg too, who'd practically been torn to pieces – and her severed finger – how had she managed to forget *that*?

'Right,' she said, hiding her damaged hand, 'I'm going to wash this lot off before Lily sees me.'

'There's no time,' grinned Tarquin, 'she's coming.'

'No she isn't,' said Lucy, listening for footsteps on the stairs.

'She *will* be,' grinned Warren. 'If we keep shouting about blood she's going to be up those stairs like a hamster up a drainpipe.'

'MUM, MUM, MUM,' screamed Tarquin, wanting to get in first. 'Come and have a look upstairs – there's BLOOD *everywhere*.'

Lucy rushed to the bathroom and turned the taps on full pelt. She tried to lock the door too, but Warren stuck his foot in the way, so she set about getting rid of the evidence instead. The water gushed out in torrents, sluicing the blood away like magic, and turning the frothing water into a pink transparent lake.

'MUM! Hurry up – she's washing the BLOOD off.'

'Too late,' said Lucy, triumphantly grabbing a towel. 'Hey, wait a minute though, what's all *this*?'

'Erm, oh yeah, *those*,' admitted Tarquin. 'Mum had them extended a bit.'

'You don't *say*?' said Lucy.

During her absence the bathroom cabinet had gained five extra shelves, each one groaning under the weight of Lily's favourite beauty preparations. There were at least twenty tubes of Spot-e-Gone, six extra-large tubs of

Miracle-Wrinklo-Zap, and a dozen maxi-strength canisters of Lippy-Puff. In pride of place though was a huge stash of the ultimate in beauty preparations – an entire shelf crammed with giant-size jars of Completely-Nu-Face by the Slappiton Company of Lundern and Parris.

'And how can we suddenly afford all *this* expensive stuff?' said Lucy. 'Have we had a sudden rush of visitors?' She smiled briefly, thinking about the time a coach-load of Sleepwalkers Anonymous members broke down outside the door. They had all tramped inside wanting somewhere to kip, and every day for a week afterwards Lily had celebrated with a new hair-do.

'Well?' she said. 'Has the cat got your tongue?'

Tarquin stood with his mouth wide open, gazing down at her hand.

'*Mum!*' he screamed. 'Quick – Lucy's got a *FINGER* missing.'

'*Right*,' she said, quite calmly. 'That's enough of your messing around – I've got some serious business to attend to.'

'Yeah, right,' laughed Tarquin, 'serious business – in the airing cupboard.'

'Just listen very carefully,' said Lucy, 'and as you do, take a good look at my cheek.'

Tarquin took a long, hard look, and then gulped like he was trying to swallow a golf ball.

'Ah,' said Lucy, 'so I've finally got your attention, have I?'

Tarquin nodded, unable to take his eyes off the crimson stained gashes.

'Good,' said Lucy, 'now *listen* – I swear on Uncle Byron's life that if you mention my missing finger once more I'm going to introduce you to the beast that slashed my face and ate part of my hand – alright?'

Tarquin nodded again.

'Y, y, y, yes, alright, Luce,' he said. 'Anything you say – but how are you going to hide it?'

'I don't know,' said Lucy, 'but I'll think of something.'

Warren turned and ran down the stairs, suddenly aware that he had been promoted to the top of the Blake girl's hit list. And he didn't particularly want to be around if she was going to be introducing people to creatures like *that*.

'The same goes for you,' she shouted, as he reached the bottom of the stairs and barrelled into Lily. The lamp-stand was bowled for six, but quickly picked herself up though and reached the landing far more rapidly than Lucy had expected.

'Ah-hah,' said Lily, 'so you've decided to come *back* have you?'

'It would appear so,' said Lucy, hiding her injured hand up her back. 'And *yes*, I'm fine – thanks a lot for asking.' She leaned back slightly, peeking through Lily's bedroom door – there was a bizarre new bedspread in there that looked as though it might once have belonged to a giraffe.

'She was washing off BLOOD,' said Tarquin.

'Yes, *thank* you Tarquin,' said Lily, pulling the bedroom door shut.

'I fell,' said Lucy, scowling at her soon-to-be-dead stepbrother. 'Honest, it's nothing – I've been living in the shed, and I must have walked in my sleep and bumped into that two-pronged dibbler.'

'We haven't *got* a two-pronged dibbler,' said Tarquin. 'And anyway the shed's always locked.'

'Tarquin, *shush*,' said his mother. 'If Lucy says she was living in the garden shed then that's what happened.'

'*Is* it?' said Lucy, totally stunned.

'Of *course* it is, darling,' said Lily with a sickening smile. 'Come on now – let's get those little scratches cleaned up shall we?'

'*Little?*' squeaked Tarquin. 'They're not little, they're massive, and anyway she's got a finger…'

Lucy stamped on Tarquin's foot, hoping to hear some of the tiniest bones in his body breaking. Unfortunately, his squealing masked the sound. It was like listening to a couple of pigs stuck inside an industrial-size vacuum cleaner – and they were having an argument over who could stand at the nozzle end.

'Of *course* she's got a finger,' frowned Lily, 'now Tarquin, why don't you run along and play like a good boy?'

'That's right,' smiled Lucy, enjoying herself for the first time in days. 'Why don't you just run along?'

Tarquin stared at them both for a moment, wondering what was going on. Then one of his thirty-seven brain cells started to work and he sensed that he might be interfering with one of his mother's schemes.

'Erm, alright then,' he said meekly. 'If you need me, I'll be out taking my goldfish for a walk.'

'What an excellent idea,' said Lily. 'And *now*, Lucy, shall we go and find Percy and tell him the good news?'

'Erm, what good news is that then?' said Lucy with a frown.

'Why, *darling*,' said Lily, 'the very fact that you're *back* of course – what could be better than having our lovely daughter home?'

Lily skipped down the stairs like a happy schoolgirl, and Lucy followed, wearing a puzzled expression and mumbling to herself about strange goings-on and mysteriously changed personalities.

'What was that dear?' said Lily. They had stopped on the half-landing so the lamp-stand could admire herself in the ghastly new mirror. And it was then that Lucy noticed how scrunchy it felt underfoot.

'Erm, is this a new stair carpet?' she said.

'Of *course* it is,' said Lily dismissively. '*Now* where did Percy get to?'

When they reached the hallway Lily stood scratching her head, as if she had misplaced her husband like most people lose bunches of keys.

'The stuffed animal heads look a lot brighter,' said Lucy.

'They've been cleaned,' said Lily. 'And they've all been given new eyes.'

'Oh,' said Lucy, 'I didn't realise there was anything wrong with the old ones.'

'There wasn't,' said Lily, 'but new is always better, isn't it?'

Lucy didn't bother to answer. Things had changed since she went away, and it had all happened so quickly. There was a vast new collection of carved walking sticks and umbrellas in the lobby. And there was a strange porcelain head too, sitting in pride of place on the hall table.

'What on earth is *that*?' she said.

'It's a Phrenology Head, darling,' said Lily. 'It tells you what the bumps on your head mean.'

'No comment,' whispered Lucy, moving in for a closer look. The glazed surface of the head was covered with thousands of tiny cracks and marked out in various sections, each purporting to tell something about the owner of the bumps. On the right of the head, just a few areas were outlined, designating things like *Moral and Religious Sentiments* and *Domestic Propensities*. The other side though was a mass of smaller areas, with titles such as *Benevolence*, *Destructiveness* and *Secretiveness*. There was even a section entitled

Love of Family, which was a good clue as to why Lily might be interested in such a strange thing – she had such a great deal to learn from it.

'*Ah*, I've just remembered where I left him,' said Lily, shouting into the front garden. As she opened the door, Lucy caught sight of the old Four Havens sign – it had been repainted, and there was no mention of cruet.

'*Percy*?' screeched the lamp-stand, 'it's Lucy – she's *back*.'

'Who?' said Percy, sounding quite distant.

'Did he say *who*?' snapped Lucy. 'I haven't been away *that* long.'

'Actually darling, you *have*,' said Lily. 'I know *you* might not consider a month to be a long time but *we* do. And what's more the police tend to agree – and Doctor Veraciter too, I shouldn't wonder.'

'A *month*?' said Lucy, 'But I erm…'

'*Yes,* darling?' said Lily.

'Erm, I, er, erm…'

'*Yes,* darling?' repeated Lily.

'I'm lost for words,' said Lucy, desperately trying to think where the time had gone. 'And I'm going to hold my breath, until the dream goes away.'

'Yes, dear,' smiled Lily, 'you do that.'

As Lucy continued with her breath-holding, Percy appeared at the door, clutching an adjustable spanner and an oily rag. When she finally gasped it all out, things *still* weren't making any sense. How could she possibly have been away for a month?

'Are you working on a new oil campaign?' she said, looking at the rag.

'Never mind boring old campaigns,' said Percy. 'What about *you* old girl? It's marvellous to have you back. Lily? *Tell* her – it's good to have her back, isn't it?'

Lily nodded reluctantly, her face hardening into a fixed expression. It looked as though the smile she was wearing belonged to somebody else – she was just looking after it for them whilst they were away on holiday.

'But where the flipping-heck have you been?' said Percy. 'And *what* the screaming bejasus has happened to your face?'

Lily shook her head. She'd intended that only Percy would notice, but Lucy was watching her *far* too closely for that.

'Come on,' said Lily, 'let's go and have a nice cup of tea in the residents' lounge, and you can tell us all about it.'

'About what?' said Lucy.

'*You* know,' said Percy, '*it* – your adventure, or whatever.'

They went through into the newly decorated sitting room where a couple of elderly guests were studying a railway timetable and reading about the attractions further down the coast in Crapston Magna. Lily glared, and they quickly gathered up their belongings and left.

'I see our welcome policy hasn't changed,' said Lucy. She perched herself on the edge of a hideous leopard-skin settee, which had probably looked a *lot* better when it was holding a leopard together. It was brand-new, along with everything else in the room.

'We've been absolutely frantic looking for you,' said Lily, settling down next to her.

'That's right,' said Percy, searching for his pipe. 'The whole town has been turned upside down.'

'And I'm afraid the police are involved,' said Lily. 'So come on, Lucy – erm, *darling*. Why don't you tell us where you've been?'

'I've been in the airing cupboard,' she replied. At least *that* bit was true – just as long as they didn't ask how long she'd been there.

'No darling,' said Lily, her voice like a whole sickly tin of syrup. 'I don't think you have. I put some freshly crisped guest towels in there just this morning and I *think* I would have noticed.'

'Yeah, and so would I,' said Tarquin. He was standing in the doorway, grinning like an ape and scratching inside his collar with a twelve-inch ruler.

'*Tarquin?*' snapped Lily. 'I thought I told you to go out and play?' There was a brief look of thunder on Lily's face, but it soon passed, replaced by a smile made entirely of sugar. 'Now, Lucy,' she said, 'tell us where you've been – and we'll promise not to be angry.'

'I can't,' said Lucy, walking over to the window.

'Why not, old girl?' said Percy with a smile.

'Because you wouldn't believe me.'

'We *will* believe you, darling,' said Lily. 'Go on, *tell* us.'

'Are you *sure?*' said Lucy, raising an eyebrow. She had just noticed a new car parked outside. There was a silver mascot on the radiator, like the one on Doctor Veraciter's Alvis.

'Yes, darling,' said Lily, 'we promise, *don't* we, Percy?'

Welcome Home, Lovely Daughter

Lucy winced. She *hated* it when Lily was nice to her. It meant she wanted something – only with the amount of new stuff in the house it was difficult to imagine what she could possibly need. A new garden perhaps? The old one was still there for the moment, but Tarquin was doing his best to change that, hacking his way through the privet bushes with a kitchen knife. He was dragging the trampoline into position again, even though his neck hadn't healed from his last experience.

'Alright then,' said Lucy, 'I'll tell you, but first you have to tell me why all those things are up there in the airing cupboard.'

'And which things are those, darling?' said Lily.

'My *mother's* things,' said Lucy. She tightened her fist into a ball and wrapped her other hand around it to hide the stump – it had begun to bleed.

'Erm, *mother's* things?' said Lily innocently.

'I'd recognise them anywhere,' said Lucy, 'even in the dark.'

'Oh,' said Lily, '*those*.'

'Yes, *those*,' said Lucy. 'Byron told me that *he* had to look after them because you couldn't be trusted – and suddenly there they all are, piled up beneath the sheets – you even took the photograph album from my room.'

'Well *that's* rich,' spluttered Lily, 'especially coming from him. Did you hear that Percy? Saying that *we* can't be trusted? I think I'll be having a few words with that lovely Byron – *if* the police ever find him that is.'

'Erm, ye-es,' said Percy, smiling nervously at Lucy. 'Actually old girl, we have a bit of unfortunate news for you on that score.'

'About Uncle Byron?' said Lucy.

'Ye-es,' said Percy. 'The police believe that he kidnapped Fenny.'

'But that's nonsense,' hissed Lucy, 'he didn't do anything of the sort.'

'Well that's what they reckon,' said Percy, 'and they say he probably took Toby Lindstrom too.'

'Do they?' said Lucy, trying to sound as innocent as possible.

'The boy's been missing for ages,' said Percy. 'Erm, about a month actually, now you come to mention it.'

Lily was shaking her head slightly, as if she wanted Percy to change the subject. Eventually he noticed, but Lucy had seen it too.

'Right,' he said, tucking his pipe away. 'There'll be plenty of time for that later, won't there? Why don't we have a nice pot of tea and some fancies?'

Welcome Home, Lovely Daughter

'Erm, just tea thanks,' said Lucy. She was starving, but still not desperate enough to eat one of Lily's cakes.

'Then let's go and get some nice fresh tea,' smiled Lily.

'Lovely,' said Lucy with a weak smile. One day, she was thinking, when she had more time, she'd invent a brilliant new name for her stepmother's special brand of baking. But for the moment, there was more important business to attend to – like working out what the lamp-stand was up to, and then thinking of a scheme to stop her.

As they wandered towards the kitchen, Lily took up position at the head of the procession, closely followed by Lucy, with Percy trailing on behind. Every few feet the parade would stop though, and Lily would stop to hug her stepdaughter, pinching her cheek as if she was a five-year-old.

'It's good to have you back, darling,' she kept saying.

Lucy was about to throw up from the overdose of sugar, but as they stepped over the kitchen threshold an unfamiliar voice stopped her dead.

'HiLow Meeesis Weeenit-Blike anna how are *yew* tewday?'

'I'm very well thank you,' said Lily, 'and thank you for asking.'

'Erm, who's *this*?' said Lucy, her mouth hanging open like a pedal bin.

The young woman in question was quite attractive, with long blonde hair and eyes like a cat. She was preparing food of some kind, although it was difficult to say exactly what. Judging by the ingredients it was going to consist mainly of strawberries, garlic, whelks, pineapple and some suspicious pieces of blubbery grey meat that Lucy preferred not to look at too closely.

'I am the Hoolia,' she said, 'fromma de Vulgararia.'

'She's a Rooska, aren't you?' said Percy.

'*Nyet*, Percy, *not* Rooska – Vulgararia – is *different*.'

'I *see*,' said Lucy, 'and what exactly is she doing here?'

'She's our new housekeeper,' said Lily.

'So you don't do the housework any more?' said Lucy.

'Yes, of *course* I do,' said Lily, 'but most of what *I* do is invisible.'

'That's handy,' said Lucy.

Lily smiled again, and that was when Lucy *really* knew that things had turned strange in her absence. A month ago, or perhaps it was only a few days ago, Lily would have had a *lot* more to say if she'd answered back.

'Lucy?' said Lily. 'Why don't you help Hoolia to make the tea?'

'Oh?' said Percy. 'And where are you going, dear?'

'I have to make an important telephone call,' said Lily. She blew Lucy a kiss and disappeared towards the hall, leaving them alone with the new housekeeper. Lucy waited until the lamp-stand was dialling the number before pouncing on Percy with her question.

'*Housekeeper?*' she said, leaving her mouth hanging open again.

'Oh, yes,' answered Hoolia. 'De swipp-op, de klining, de weshing. All manner of de keeping of de house. I am de housekeeper - werry much.'

'Erm, she's just temporary,' whispered Percy, 'at least I *hope* so.'

'I see,' said Lucy, struggling to take it all in.

'Are you alright Luce?' said Percy. 'You seem a bit flushed.'

'Erm yes,' said Lucy, 'I'm just a bit surprised that's all.'

'Yes, well things have changed since you went away.'

'So I see,' said Lucy. 'And how did all this come about? Have you had a win on the football pools?'

'Don't worry about that now,' said Percy. 'Let's get you settled in first.'

Lucy glanced down at the slow river of blood that was seeping between her fingers. And as she watched the red stain emerge, she found herself thinking about Assiah and the scene of carnage that she had so bravely run away from – an injured crocodile, a dead fortune-teller, and a friend about to be captured and possibly killed by a shadowy wraith – she had been *so* brave.

'Where did you get to just *then,* Luce?' said Percy. He'd produced a pipe and begun sucking on it. 'You looked as though you were miles away.'

'Nowhere,' said Lucy, squeezing the aching stump. 'I'm tired, that's all.'

'*Kipper tie,*' squeaked Hoolia. 'This what you want iffa you feeling tired juringa thee die – I fetch thee vicar teapot, no?'

'Yes, Hoolia,' said Percy. 'Get the vicar's teapot out. I think we could all do with a cup, couldn't we?'

Lucy nodded, eager to get the taste of bird-weed ale out of her mouth.

'Anda thee fancy,' said Hoolia. 'Meeesis Weeenit-Blike, you know she show me how to mekka the fancies? All die long, after the cleenup, anna thee polish I mekka these very special Ingulesh recipe. You try them, yes?'

'No thanks,' said Lucy, thinking of Henbeg. 'I've heard they can be very bad for the digestion.'

'Yezzbut you see special one I have here, for thee digestion. Eez exclusive ingredient, send by my brutha fromma Vulgararia – this you will like.'

'I don't think so,' said Lucy.

'No,' insisted Hoolia. 'This you *will* like, hokay?'

Lucy frowned at the housekeeper, eager to show her who was boss – only it didn't appear to be working.

'Yes, Lucee – you *will* like – and you will *eat* – is fish eggs, anda brine anda thee sheep tonsil, all mash up widda green thing. You too, Percy – I *know* you like.'

'Erm, yes,' said Percy nervously, 'well now we know the ingredients, it doesn't sound too bad, does it?' He tasted a bit from the end of his finger and gave a sort of sickly smile. Lucy recalled the vicar using exactly the same expression the day that she and Genjamin were introduced.

'The brine sounds alright,' said Lucy. 'Salt water is good for making you sick.'

'But is notta salt water,' said Hoolia, 'brine, in Ingulesh issa what the *peeg* he theenk with – *brine*.'

'Erm, do you mean brain?' said Percy, turning slightly grey.

'Already I have said this,' said Hoolia, 'brine – for the *theenking*.'

'Right, that's *it*,' said Lucy, 'I'm definitely going to throw up now.'

'Hey, Lucy,' shouted Tarquin from outside the back door. 'I bet you haven't seen the new motor, have you?'

Lucy frowned, resisting the temptation to go outside and belt her dear stepbrother. Instead, she turned to Percy with a serious look – he was holding a hand over his mouth and looking decidedly ill.

'Percy? What *is* going on? How can you afford a new car?'

'Ah, erm, *yes*, the car,' said Percy, ushering Lucy over to the window. 'Do you like it? It's an Alvis Firefly – the same make as the doctor's, but a much sportier model.'

'Yes, I *do* like it,' said Lucy, 'but how did you pay for it? Has the holiday trade suddenly improved?'

'I'll tell you later,' said Percy, trying not to look at Hoolia's preparations.

'You'll tell her *what* later?' said Lily, stepping in from the hall.

'Just what's been going on while she's been away dear, that's all.'

'Well don't go boring her with *everything* Percy, *will* you?' Lily gave a kind of feline look at Hoolia, as if something was passing between them.

'Who were you calling just now?' asked Lucy.

'Just the vicar,' smiled Lily. 'He's been an absolute God-send since you, erm, since you went away – he's been round here every day.'

'That's right,' sighed Percy, 'every blinking day.'

'That's funny,' said Lucy, 'I thought you might have been speaking to Doctor Veraciter.'

'Who?' said Lily innocently. 'Oh, *him* – goodness me, no, we haven't spoken to him for ages darling – there's no need for his services any more, *is* there, Percy?'

'If you say so,' said Percy, sucking at his empty pipe.

'I *do* say so,' smiled Lily. 'In fact I think that we should make a promise to Lucy here and now – a promise that we will never ask Doctor Veraciter to visit us, ever again.'

'That sounds like a good idea,' said Lucy.

'*Provided* of course that certain conditions are observed,' added Lily.

'Ah,' said Lucy, 'well in *that* case I suppose it depends on the conditions.'

'*Excellent,*' said Lily, 'that's almost a yes, isn't it? All we have to do now is clear up a few points of mystery – such as where you've been all this time and where Toby and Fenny have got to.'

'And then we can all get back to normal,' said Percy.

'And we can havva thee tea,' said Hoolia, rattling the vicar's pot. 'But *first,* Lucy, you will tell Meeesis Weeenit-Blike where issa thee Fenny anna thee Toby gone? You tell her strite away where the uncle he has kidnapped them – anda you also tella how much ransom he wanting.'

'Hoolia, *no,*' said Percy, 'that's quite enough of that kind of talk.'

'But she *does* have a point,' said Lily. 'And it certainly wouldn't hurt if Lucy were to tell us why Byron might want to kidnap innocent children.'

'But he hasn't kidnapped anyone,' protested Lucy.

'That's not how the police see it,' smiled Lily. 'It's only natural that you defend your uncle, of *course* it is, but you *really* must tell us, if only for the sake of those poor, dear children.'

Welcome Home, Lovely Daughter

'Toby's *alright*,' said Lucy suddenly. She'd decided not to mention Fenny, but as soon as Toby's name crossed her lips, she was wishing she hadn't mentioned him either.

'Oh? And how do you know that?' snapped Lily.

'Because he was with me,' said Lucy.

'Really?' said Lily, the line of her thin mouth hardening slightly. 'And where exactly was that? The *truth* now.'

'Do you *really* want the truth?' said Lucy.

'Of course, darling,' smiled Lily. 'Friends and families must always share the truth, *mustn't* they, Percy?'

Lucy gazed around at their expectant faces. Lily wore an eager, hard-edged smile, whereas Hoolia was managing to look curious and threatening at the same time – and Percy just looked plain nervous.

In a sudden moment of inspiration she decided to tell them everything. It didn't really matter if they believed her or not – the important thing was to get away from them as soon as possible – and if she needed to distract people, then what could be better than confusing them with the truth?

'We were in a city,' said Lucy.

'City?' said Percy. 'Which one? Lundern? Eboracum?'

'Neither,' said Lucy. 'Actually, we went to this huge orphanage called the Braneskule first, and *then* we went to the city. We were being chased by the Vooghul – the servants of the Sisters. But we managed to escape through a maze of kiosks and we ended up in this tavern where we met a fortune teller. No, wait, there were *two* fortune-tellers. One of them was killed by a giant scarab though, and that's how I got the cuts on my face. And that's where Toby is – so we have to go and rescue him, don't we?'

'Erm, ye-es, I see,' said Percy. 'But if Toby and Fenny are still in this fabulous city then why did you come back?' He shot a glance at Lily – she was fuming already, unable to disguise her growing rage.

'Because it was getting too dangerous and I needed time to think. Harry told me not to fight unless I understood – so I ran away.'

'And who's this Harry?' said Percy.

'Never *mind* who bloody-well Harry is,' screamed Lily. 'Can you *believe* this ridiculous child? She's *still* at it, isn't she? Won't you *ever* learn, Lucy?'

'Eez flyming-well terribul,' cried Hoolia. 'You make a *werry* beeg upset of Meeesis Weeenit-Blike, with horrybool, spitefool lies. You are *werry* bad girl.'

'No,' said Percy, 'she's not bad, just…'

'Oh, but she *is*,' said Lily, 'and that's *it* for me I'm afraid – she's gone much too far this time.'

'But we *need* her, don't we?' said Percy. 'For the…'

'Shut *up*, Percy,' hissed Lily.

'Yezz, shut *up*,' snapped Hoolia. 'You not say nothing more Percy, otherwise you have *beeg* problems.'

'And you still haven't even seen the best bit,' said a voice at the window. 'Have a look at her right hand if you don't believe me.'

'What's that my precious?' said Lily.

'Look at her fingers,' grinned Tarquin, 'there's one missing.'

'Oh my *God*,' screamed Lily, 'you're *right*, Tarquin darling – she's lost one of her fingers. Have you *seen* this, Percy?'

'*Percy?*'

'Yes, I've *seen* it,' he replied, frowning at both Lily *and* Hoolia.

'Well don't just stand there gawping,' shouted Lily. 'Call the police at once – and tell them to bring some extra-strong handcuffs.'

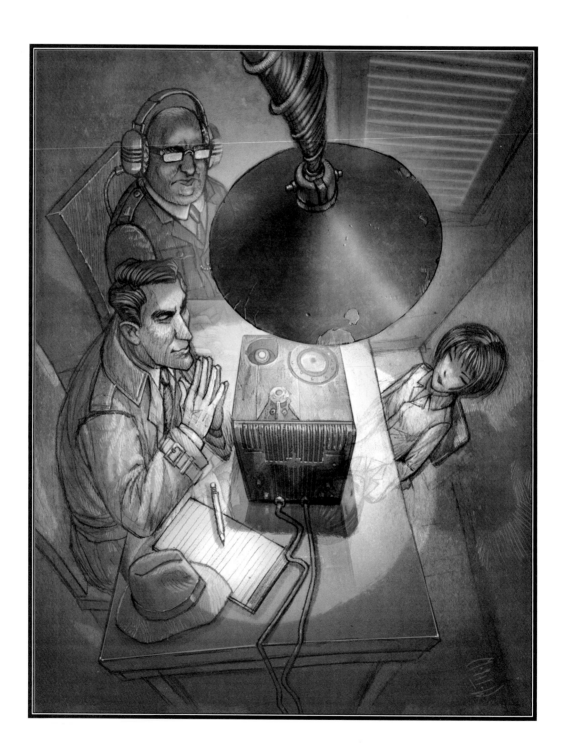

UnWarranted

Interference

'*Mum*?' shouted Tarquin, his face glued to the front-room window. 'The police are here – and they've brought the handcuffs – *big* ones.'

'About time too,' screeched Lily. 'I don't want that lying minx in my house a moment longer.'

'But this is *my* house,' protested Lucy.

'You're quite right,' said Lily, her narrow, powdered face floating before Lucy like an apparition. 'It's yours for *now* – but I think you'll find it's going to be changing hands rather sooner than you expected.'

'*Mum*?' grinned Tarquin, 'does that mean I can have Lucy's bedroom?'

'*No*, it bloody-well doesn't,' screamed Lucy, 'you just keep out of there, or I'll set a scarab on you.'

'You've got to find one first,' said Tarquin, leaning over to whisper in Lucy's ear. 'You know that lock on your trapdoor? Well I've got a key – and I'm going up there now to look through your stupid collection – what's *left* of it that is, because I've sold most of it.'

'Percy? Please, no, *tell* him,' screamed Lucy. 'Tell him to stay out of the Panopticon, and tell him not to touch my things.'

Tarquin poked his tongue out, and then pulled one of Maggie's playbills out of his pocket. It was already crumpled up, but the sight of it being torn in half sent Lucy flying into a rage.

'*Percy*, get that filthy liar off my boy,' screamed Lily, 'or I'll swing for her, I *swear* it.'

'Erm, sorry,' said Percy, pulling her away, 'but I can't have you doing that to your brother – anyway we need the space, so we can rent Tarquin's room out to holidaymakers.'

'He's *not* my brother,' screamed Lucy, 'and it's October, so there won't be any need to rent the room out.'

'Not normally,' said Percy, 'but every boarding house in Grimston is crammed full – it's because of the…'

'*Percy*?' screeched Lily. 'Flapping *mouths*, dear.'

'Flapping mouths?' said a man at the door. 'Well we don't want any of *those*, *do* we? At least not until we get to the police station, and then we positively encourage them, *don't* we Homburg?'

Lucy thought the stranger looked like Dick Barton, even though she'd never seen her hero from the radio. But if she *had* seen him then this was almost certainly what he'd look like, with a big brown trench coat and a fedora hat. His sidekick, who wore thick pebble glasses, looked nothing like a policeman though, and she began to suspect some kind of deception.

'I'm Inspector Trembley,' said the man in the trench-coat, 'and this is Homburg, my sergeant.' He flashed some identification papers that looked fairly convincing. There was a photograph of someone who certainly *looked* like the man standing before her, and there was an official-looking stamp too – it *might* just have said 'Grimston Police' – but it was smudged.

'How do I know you're a real policeman?' said Lucy.

'Eh?' said Trembley. 'But I just showed you my papers, didn't I?'

'They might be forgeries,' said Lucy. 'I could make a card like that with my junior printing kit.'

'No you couldn't,' grinned Tarquin. 'I sold it, along with your collection of theatre tickets and the bullet that killed Chung Ling Soo.'

Lucy let out a loud howl, then gritted her teeth and ran at Tarquin – but Homburg grabbed her by the shoulders and spun her round to face Inspector Trembley.

'If we run out of cards I'll give you a call,' said the inspector. 'But in the meantime you can assume the documents are real. I think you *knew* that already though, didn't you? I've heard all the stories you know.'

'I hope they were good,' said Lucy.

'Not exactly,' said the inspector. 'Now, are you going to come quietly?'

As they got out of the squad car, the rain began to fall quite heavily and Lucy shivered with the sudden cold. She sighed and gave a little shake, as if to flick the drops of rain from her back. It was the oddest sensation, and was followed by an even stranger one. Just for a moment, she had the impression that she was looking down onto the roof of the police station. But it was worse than that – she could see *herself* down there, just about to enter the front door, with Trembley on one side and Homburg on the other. She shook her head in disbelief and the vision vanished, and a fraction of a second later she walked head-first into a swing door – she staggered back, half-senseless, falling heavily onto the concrete path.

'Are you alright?' said Trembley, looking rather concerned. 'That was a nasty bump – you should pay more attention to where you're going.'

She nodded, but was too groggy to reply, so Trembley took her by the hand and sat her on wooden bench near the front desk. A kindly looking sergeant emerged from behind the counter and promised to make her a cup of tea.

'Five sugars alright for you, is it?' he said. 'I always find five sugars are best for shock – I'll put an extra one in though, just to be safe.

'Nnn,' said Lucy, still not quite with it.

'Yep,' he said, 'it's made from hardwood that door – although I expect you *noticed* that.'

'Yes, I *did*, thanks,' said Lucy finally. She leaned forwards and rested her head in her hands, praying to be rid of the headache and fretting about the vision. Life at the moment was bad enough, without suffering hallucinations as well.

'Why don't you try the long-wave button?' said an unfamiliar voice.

'*Pardon?*' said Lucy. She dragged her throbbing head up to look for the source of the sound, but there was nobody around. She was overhearing a conversation from somewhere behind the counter.

'I've *tried* it,' said the desk sergeant's voice. 'I've tried them *all* at least a dozen times – long-wave, short-wave, in-be-rotten-well-tween-wave, but none of them seem to work any more. All I get is that infernal racket and a load of idiots spouting rubbish.'

'Well you'd better let *me* hear it then,' said the other voice. It sounded as though he believed himself to be a bit of an expert.

The desk sergeant must have twiddled the tuning knob, because there was a familiar '*Weee-oo-free-oo*' whistling noise followed by a strange-sounding voice. It wasn't clear like radio transmissions normally were – it sounded as though it was coming from a very long way off.

'*...and Mister Tibbles, my cat – I do hope you're taking good care of him...*'

'See what I mean?' said the desk sergeant. 'It does that all the time.'

'Yeah?' said the expert. 'Well try the big cream-coloured knob then.'

Zzzzz, Weee-oo-free-oo, Zzzzz, Weop...

'*...yeah, it was a pity about me getting shot like that Vern, but never mind, eh? You can't have everything, can you? Now you know what to do, don't you? Tell Dingo and Masher and Grot-face that the loot's stashed at the back of the old barn, and make sure my missus, erm, no, my widow, gets my share...*'

'It sounds like the afternoon play,' said the unidentified expert.

'I don't care *what* it is,' said the sergeant. 'I just want my music back – it's absolutely ages since I've heard Tonk Marbley and his Crapston-Magna Roof Orchestra.'

'I reckon you must have done something to it,' said the expert. 'Radios don't just stop working for no reason, do they? Now what about *this* knob? The one with the red paint on?'

'Don't touch that,' said the sergeant. 'I did once and got a Lectric shock.'

'Yeah?' said the expert. 'Well you should be more careful then.'

Fzzzz, Weee-oo, Weee-oo, Snappp...

'*...Oooh, I don't really know Shirl, it's a lot darker than I expected, and there's an awful lot of rules. I was fined for walking on the grass the first day I was here. And the prices are simply shocking...*'

'See?' said the sergeant's voice, 'I *told* you not to twiddle with it, – it's started spouting rubbish again.'

'Well you must have done *something* to upset it,' said the expert. 'You haven't been cleaning it, have you? These old monsters can be very temperamental if you try to clean the gubbins.'

'I never touched it,' insisted the sergeant. 'All I know is it just *went* – it worked fine for years, and then suddenly it was on the blink.'

'And when *was* this?' said the expert. He was beginning to sound like a doctor with a very sick patient.

'It's been like it for about a month,' said the sergeant. 'I *know* that for certain, because about three or four weeks ago there was this programme about that new attraction at the Winter Gardens and I couldn't get a thing out of it then.'

'Have you tried adjusting it?' said the expert.

'What, *tuning* it in you mean?'

'No, adjusting it,' said the expert, 'like *this.*'

Wham. Smash. Crump.

Tinkle…

'Oh, bloody *marvellous,*' said the desk sergeant. 'Now that has *really* done the trick, hasn't it? There's nothing at all coming through now.'

There was a burst of swearing followed by the sound of a slamming door, and then the sergeant appeared again, looking somewhat annoyed.

'Sorry about the delay with your tea Miss, we were having a bit of trouble with the old Burpy-Phonic Mark Five.'

'So I heard,' said Lucy. 'Is it a valve job, or one of those new transferred-resistance things?'

'Valves I think,' said the sergeant. 'At least it *was*, when it was working. Now it's gone and went and died it's just a pile of junk.'

Lucy smiled, thinking back to Toby's description of Byron's laboratory.

'Erm, I don't suppose *you* know anything about them?' he asked.

Lucy shrugged. She *did* know a bit, but only what Byron had taught her, and she wasn't really in the mood for re-socketing valves or cleaning contacts or de-fluffing the air-spaced tuning capacitors.

'Nope,' she lied smoothly.

'No, I didn't think you would,' he said. 'It's not really a girl thing, is it, messing with radios? Anyway, here's your tea – drink it quick mind, because they'll be here soon.'

Lucy sat quietly and sipped from the giant porcelain mug. There were at least ten sugars in the bright-orange tea but she didn't mind in the least because there was a double-decker jammy dunker too – the first *real* food she'd seen for days.

'Right,' said the sergeant, checking off the day's cases in his desk diary, 'let's see what people are up to.'

'Missing parrot – *flew into station and told us his address.*'

'Stolen bicycle – *front light found, still looking for the rest.*'

'Missing Numerologist – *still no news we can count on.*'

'Stolen pigeons – *flown the coop.* No, best be serious. *Still missing.*'

'Ah, here it is – interview with Lucy Blake regarding kidnapping. Erm, is this *you* Miss?'

'Lucy Blake?' she said. 'Erm, ye-es, that's me. *Why?*'

'*Blimey,*' he said, leaning over the counter and wagging his pencil. '*Kidnapping* – you don't mess about, do you?'

'I was the *victim,*' said Lucy indignantly.

'Oh, were you?' said the sergeant. 'Sorry, I should have known by the state of your face. Anyway, how was your tea?'

'Fine,' said Lucy, pouring the dregs into a pot plant.

Suddenly there was a shadow standing over her.

'Would you mind not doing that?' said Inspector Trembley. 'The plants don't like it, especially when Stan makes the tea. Now, shall we go and have our little chat?'

'Do I have a choice?' said Lucy.

'Not really,' said Trembley, 'how's your head by the way?'

'I'll live,' said Lucy, rubbing the bump on her forehead.

She got up rather unsteadily and followed the inspector through a maze of corridors, each turn taking them to a darker part of the building. They called in at some shadowy offices on the way and picked up Sergeant Homburg and a woman Lucy had never seen before. There were no introductions, and to her frustration the woman fell in behind them, as if she didn't want Lucy looking at her too closely. Eventually they reached a dismal room that might once have been a broom cupboard. It was illuminated by a single dim bulb in a battered metal shade, and contained the absolute minimum of furniture. There was a simple wooden table, three chairs, and a moveable screen like the ones they had in hospitals. And sitting atop the table was one additional object – a rather interesting piece of equipment that Trembley seemed slightly in awe of.

'Just one thing before we sit down,' said the inspector. 'What on earth is that sack thing you're wearing? It looks like a museum exhibit.'

'It is,' said Lucy. 'The kidnappers took all our clothes, so we had to wear anything we could find.'

'You were being held captive in a museum?' said Trembley.

'You *could* say that,' said Lucy.

'Hmm,' said Trembley, 'then what's this I hear about you visiting another world?'

'Erm, it just *seemed* like another world,' smiled Lucy. 'I was confused.'

'So it would seem,' said the inspector.

'And I was in a state of shock,' added Lucy.

'Not to mention being in an airing cupboard,' said Trembley. 'The exact details of which I'm sure will eventually become clear. As will the mystery of the slashed face and the missing finger. First, though, we'd like to look at the clothing. So if you could just slip behind the screen with this lady and get yourself changed?'

The unidentified woman flicked her long red hair and gave Lucy the kind of smile that people used when they were obliged to be polite. She was quite pretty, with green eyes and large freckles, but there was something *else*. She was watching and waiting, and quite possibly dangerous. And if she wasn't, thought Lucy, then she definitely knew somebody who *was*.

When Lucy emerged from behind the screen, she was wearing a neat white boiler suit and looked as though she'd come to clean the toilets.

'Take a seat,' said Trembley, 'and allow me introduce you to Morana – she'll be your escort, as your parents refused to come to the interview.'

Morana gave another polite smile as she sharpened her pencil.

'I didn't want them here anyway,' said Lucy, her eyes fixed firmly on the pencil point.

'And why is that?' said the inspector. 'Actually no, don't answer that yet. We need to do this officially. Homburg? Set the machine going, will you?'

'What, *this* thing?' said Lucy with a smile. She pointed at the squat gunmetal cabinet, which dominated the tabletop. It was plugged into the wall, so it clearly ran on Lectric, but there was no clue as to its function. The sides of the cabinet were painted a uniform grey, and whatever works it had were covered by a solid metal lid.

'It's a wire recorder,' growled Homburg. 'Not that you need to know – all *you've* got to do is talk.'

'Now, now, Homburg,' said Trembley. 'Remember to be polite. Miss Blake is helping us, that's all – she's not a criminal, is she?'

'Not yet she isn't,' grunted Homburg under his breath. He removed the lid from the recorder, and revealed various dials and knobs, like a stage-magician expecting some applause. He left the room and returned moments later with a spindly-looking metal stand – there was a huge microphone dangling from it, which he positioned so that it hung between Lucy and the inspector.

'The Gecko Supa-Sensitive Ampliphonic Ribbon Microphone,' said Lucy, reading the label. 'Erm, I thought *micro* meant that things were small?'

'It's the best we've got,' grunted Homburg.

'*Is* it?' grinned Lucy. 'I'd hate to see the worst – does it work?'

'It works very well thank you,' said the inspector. 'Now, do you see those two green lights on the recorder? Well when they move that's your voice.'

'So how does it know the difference?' smiled Lucy.

'What do you mean?' said Trembley.

'How does it know I'm the one speaking?' she asked.

'It doesn't,' said Homburg.

'So the lights move when it's your voice as well?' said Lucy.

'Yes,' said the inspector, clasping his forehead with both hands. 'I suppose they do.'

'Just checking,' said Lucy. 'I like to know what's going on.'

'Funnily enough, so do *I*,' said Trembley, 'and that's precisely why you were brought here, so we can find out *exactly* what's going on. Is the machine running, Sergeant Homburg?'

Trembley's sidekick had perched a pair of Bakelite headphones on his ears and was now fiddling with the controls. It was the closest Lucy could come to describing what he was doing, because 'operating' was well wide of the mark – he seemed to be flicking switches and turning knobs almost at random.

'What if it doesn't work?' said Lucy.

'Then we'll have to look at my notes,' replied Trembley. 'Which *reminds* me.' He pushed a small pile of paper to one side and reached under the desk, pulling out a much larger pile. 'Morana, go and get me another bottle of ink, will you? I think we're going to be needing it with this one.'

Lucy smiled and reached up, pulling the microphone close to her face. It was heavier than she expected and bounced slightly in its cradle of protective rubber cords.

'Testing, *testing*,' she said, speaking into the Gecko.

'Oh my *God*,' said Homburg, 'I think I've gone deaf.'

'No you haven't,' said Trembley, pulling the microphone towards himself. 'NO YOU HAVEN'T,' he said, almost shouting into the thing.

'Ouch,' squealed Homburg, ripping the headphones off.

'There you are,' said Lucy, 'I *told* you it looked dodgy. If you want it to work properly, you need to switch the input gain attenuator to minus twenty decibels – that should just about do it.'

'*Oh*,' growled Homburg. 'So you're an *expert* now, are you? Ten minutes ago you didn't have a clue what the thing was, and *now* all of a sudden you're recommending input game thingy tenuators.'

'I'm a quick learner,' smiled Lucy.

'Yes, you most certainly are,' said the inspector, checking his notes. 'Most of the criminals we get in here don't know half as much as you do about breaking the law.'

'Am I in a bit of trouble then?' said Lucy.

'Oh, well let's *see*, shall we?' said Trembley. 'Homburg, what have we got on young Lucy's rap sheet?'

'Not much,' grinned Homburg. 'Just the stuff your average twelve-year-old gets up to. Stealing a book worth half a million pounds, breaking out of hospital custody, accusing her parents of plotting to steal an inheritance, you know the sort of thing.'

'Yes, *quite*,' said Trembley, scribbling a note.

'I didn't do any of that,' said Lucy, 'and I'm not twelve either.'

'Thirteen then,' grunted Homburg, '*sorry* – I'm sure that extra year makes all the difference, doesn't it?'

'It does when you're my age,' said Lucy. 'A lot can happen in a year.'

'Hmm,' said the inspector. 'Well if it was up to me I wouldn't leave you unattended for anywhere near that long. Heaven only knows what you might get up to.'

He waved a sheaf of papers under Lucy's nose, implying that she'd caused him an awful lot of work. She tried to look at the details as they swooped past but it was like trying to read on a bus – it made her feel sick.

'And we haven't even got to the most interesting bit yet,' said Trembley.

'What's that?' said Lucy, thinking they'd covered all the worst bits.

'The small matter of your appearance in a locked airing cupboard,' said Trembley, 'whilst being soaked in blood and having various parts of your body either damaged or missing – or will you be denying that as well?'

'*Ah*, no,' said Lucy, 'I'll own up to that one – there were witnesses.'

'Indeed there were,' said Trembley, 'and I'm sure we'll be hearing from them, just as soon as they get over the shock. Now, why don't we go through these items one at a time?' He began sorting through his notes, wearing the strangest expression and with his tongue planted firmly in the corner of his mouth. Lucy thought he looked like a dog that was having a hard time choosing its favourite bone of all time.

Finally, he pulled out a single sheet and smoothed it down onto the desk.

'*Right*,' said Trembley, 'let's talk about these people on the wardrobe.'

'What about them?' said Lucy.

'They were your accomplices, *weren't* they?'

'Were they?' said Lucy innocently. She watched the busy green lights on the recorder as they flickered briefly in response to her voice.

'Without a shadow of doubt,' said Trembley, 'but you did a superb job of training them, didn't you?'

'Did I?' said Lucy with a smile.

'Absolutely,' said Trembley, 'we couldn't get either of them to squeal, even after a couple of weeks in the cells.'

'But there was nothing to squeal about,' insisted Lucy, 'and they definitely weren't my accomplices.'

'Hmm, *strange*,' said Trembley, 'that's exactly what *they* said, once we managed to stop them shouting about the *light* and someone called Mister Raziel. A person who, incidentally, is not listed in the Grimston-on-Sea telephone directory.'

'So are they still arrested?' asked Lucy. She was trying not to smile at the idea that anyone who wasn't listed in the phone book was somehow immune from detection.

'They *would* be,' said Trembley, 'if I had my way – but those interfering idiots down at the Daily Phibber started a campaign to release them – they said we didn't have enough evidence.'

'That's right,' shouted Homburg, the earphones still clamped over his head. 'NO EVIDENCE.'

Trembley pulled out his wallet and handed Lucy a newspaper clipping. His hands were shaking, as if he'd taken the whole thing personally.

'That's me,' he said, pointing at a blurred picture of his hat. Underneath it, the caption read:

"Loser cop doesn't know when to stop."

'And this is *them*,' said Trembley. He produced another picture that showed the pair from the saleroom.

"Free the wardrobe men…" screamed the caption in two-inch-high letters.

'So you had to let them go?' said Lucy.

'Eventually,' said the inspector. 'We dragged our heels for as long as possible, but we couldn't find any real evidence, so the newspaper finally got its way.'

'So you don't actually *know* anything about them?' asked Lucy.

There was a pause whilst the inspector did some serious thinking. The silence was filled by a squealing, scraping kind of noise from the recorder. It had almost reached the end of the spool.

'Oh yes, *very* clever,' he said eventually.

'What?' said Lucy, innocently.

'Very clever indeed Miss Blake. I thought *I* was the one doing the interview, but it seems that I've given *you* far more information than you've given *me*.'

'Sorry,' said Lucy with a wicked grin.

'Can we rub that bit off?' said Trembley, turning to Homburg. His sidekick had put the headphones back on now – they didn't seem to be working though, because the sergeant didn't hear his boss and Trembley was obliged to pull the microphone over again.

'I SAID, can we rub that bit off?'

'Ouch,' said Homburg, fiddling with the full spool. 'Are you doing that on purpose?'

'I wouldn't worry,' said Lucy, 'those things never work, especially if you overload the inputs like that. You're probably picking up radio broadcasts from all over the place.'

Homburg pulled the headphone plug out of its socket and sure enough, they heard something that sounded a lot like the radio. It was one of the plays that Lucy had heard earlier, featuring the same distant-sounding voices.

Tzzz, Bzzz, Fzzz…

'*…I put the new will in a safe place, but dearie me, do you know I can't for the life of me think where that safe place was…*'

There was a pause, as if there was another part to the conversation that they couldn't hear, and then the radio play started up again:

Zizzz, Flimp, Bzzz…

'*…well there's no need to take that attitude. I left you your grandfather's cornflake collection, didn't I?…*'

'See? I *told* you,' said Lucy, 'you're picking up the afternoon play. You should get your desk sergeant in here. *His* radio has packed up so I'm sure he'd be interested in listening to yours.'

Trembley lunged over and pulled the plug out of the wire recorder, just in time to prevent them hearing someone's theory about how life was wasted on the living.

'Right, that's *it*,' he said, 'the gloves are *off*. I don't want any more of your messing around Miss Blake; I just want you to tell me straight.'

'About what?' said Lucy. She looked across at Morana, who was sitting quietly in the corner – *she* was taking notes too, but in a way that reminded her of someone else.

'I'm *talking* about the book, Miss Blake.'

'Oh, well that's *easy*,' said Lucy. 'It was a present.'

'Ah-*hah*,' said Trembley. 'So you admit you have it then?'

'Not exactly. The last thing I remember, someone was putting it in a handbag.'

'So it's safe then?' said Trembley.

'It's *very* safe,' said Lucy, 'just so long as we can find the handbag.'

'I see,' said Trembley, scratching another note. 'And the fact that you claim it was a gift?'

Lucy went through the whole story – describing in detail how she took the manuscript from the saleroom to prevent it falling into the wrong hands, and how she'd finally tracked Harry down and how he'd given her the book as a present.

'So,' said Trembley, 'let me get this right. You claim that a book worth half a million pounds was given to you by a man who keeps pigeons in a shack near the railway tracks?'

'Erm, ye-es,' said Lucy.

'I see,' said Trembley, 'and do you happen to know if this *Harry* person has a swimming pool at the aforementioned location? And perhaps a large garage, to house his collection of Moles Noyce motor cars?'

'Probably not,' said Lucy. 'I know it sounds unlikely, but it's true.'

'It sounds *most* unlikely,' said Trembley. 'But fortunately we don't even need to check your story – we already have a statement from the *real* owner of the Grobbley manuscript.'

'You do?' said Lucy, raising her eyebrows. 'But *who*? And *how*?'

'Oh, it was quite *simple* really,' said the inspector. 'The person spoke some words using his mouth and lips and we listened to the words as they came out and wrote them down on a piece of paper. With a *pen* –and some *ink*.'

'Yes,' said Lucy. 'I know what a statement is.'

'I'm sure you do,' said Trembley, 'and *I* know how the green voicy thing on a wire recorder works – *annoying*, isn't it?'

Lucy smiled. In other circumstances, she might have liked to befriend the inspector. As it stood though, it was 'one-all' on the 'being extremely picky' score-chart. She'd need to be careful though if he wasn't to go one ahead.

'So who's claiming to be the rightful owner then?' she asked.

'Claiming?' replied Trembley. 'He's not simply *claiming*, Miss Blake – he *is* the undisputed owner. We've checked very thoroughly and his paperwork is all in order.'

'So who *is* this person with all the orderly paperwork?' said Lucy.

'I shouldn't really tell you,' said Trembley, 'but I don't see that it can do any harm – it's Mr. Bumblebee, the auctioneer.'

'*No*,' screamed Lucy, 'that's *impossible* – it belongs to Harry, erm, no; I mean it belongs to *me*. And that rotten Mister Bumblebee, well he's just, erm, he's just a *dirty, filthy, stinking, rotten liar*.'

'Strangely enough that's just how he described you,' said Trembley, 'although his language wasn't *quite* so colourful. He was most helpful in describing the events leading up to the theft of the manuscript though. And he helped with our investigation into the wardrobe men too.'

'They're *not* my accomplices,' said Lucy.

'Perhaps not,' said Trembley, 'but they certainly provided you with the distraction you needed.'

'So I could steal the Grobbley?' said Lucy.

'Ah,' said Trembley, 'now we're getting somewhere.'

'No we aren't,' said Lucy. 'I'm just saying what you're thinking – I'm not admitting anything.'

'Right,' said the inspector, crossing out the last line of his notes. 'So you still deny it then?'

'I admit that I took it,' said Lucy, 'but then afterwards it was *given* to me – I've already told you all that.'

The inspector gave a huge sigh, as if he was trying to inhale every sheet of paper on the desk.

'This is very hard work,' he said, 'shall we change the subject?'

'If you like,' said Lucy. She looked over at Morana, who was still busy writing notes. Occasionally she looked up, like a large bird of prey surveying its dinner – she reminded Lucy of Miss Niblock.

'Where's your uncle?' said Trembley.

'I don't know,' said Lucy.

'Alright then, where's the boy? And the girl, Fenny?'

'Sorry, but I can't tell you that,' said Lucy.

'Or you *won't* tell us?' said Morana. She stood up and walked over to Lucy, standing over her with a clipboard, as if she were conducting some kind of scientific experiment.

'You do know that wasting police time is a very serious offence, don't you?' said Trembley.

'This is no good,' said Morana. 'I *told* you what she'd be like. The girl is an accomplished liar – there's absolutely no way she'll crack under *this* kind of feeble questioning.'

Trembley looked disappointed, as if he was imaging the headlines they'd print about him this time.

"Dumb cop fails to crack potty kidnap girl."

"Valuable book still missing."

'Erm, you're not *really* a policewoman, *are* you?' said Lucy.

'Did anyone say that I was?' said Morana.

'Then who are you?' asked Lucy.

'I think I'll let my driver answer that,' said Morana. She pulled the microphone towards her and used a name that was all too familiar to Lucy.

'Bruno?' she said. 'Bring the car to the front door, will you? I think we need to go for a little talk – a *proper* talk that is.'

'It'll be a pleasure, Miss Fay,' said a voice from somewhere deep inside the wire machine.

Saint Mallydick Mirabilis

'You *do* know where we're going, don't you?' said Morana as she slammed the car door.

Lucy screwed her nose up at the leathery smell of the seats, and realised that from this day forward Veraciter's car would remind her of the stink of scarab's wings.

'I think I can guess,' she said. She rubbed at the painful red marks Bruno had left on her arms as he threw her onto the back seat.

'Good,' said Morana, 'then there's no need for small talk is there? I can't *bear* that. Can you bear it Bruno?

'What's that, Miss Fay?' said the driver, climbing into his seat.

'Small talk,' said Morana. 'I can't abide it.'

'I never use any other kind,' whispered Bruno under his breath. He slotted the car into gear and accelerated hard, forcing the passengers back into their seats.

'May I call you Lucy?' said Morana, holding Lucy's gaze with steady eyes.

'No, you can call me Miss Blake.'

'Oh, so it's going to be like that, is it?' said Morana, flicking her long hair. 'Well in that case *you* can call me Miss Fay – and you needn't expect any special treatment either, even if you *are* famous.'

'Am I?' said Lucy, 'I didn't realise.'

'Oh, but *yes*,' said Morana. 'Thanks to those wonderful people at the Phibber everyone in Grimston knows about the disappearing schoolgirl who also happens to be a master criminal. I'm surprised Zenda Freggley hasn't already spirited you off to a secret hideaway, so she can get an exclusive story.'

'She didn't have the chance,' said Lucy. 'As soon as I got back my lovely step-parents called in the police.'

'Yes, you *do* seem to have a busy schedule, don't you? First, an airing cupboard, then the police station and now you're off to pay a visit to Saint Mallydick's. It's just one big social whirl for you, isn't it?'

'Is it?' said Lucy. She was unable to get over the impression that Morana was somehow jealous. 'We can swap places if you like.'

'I rather think not,' said Morana. 'You see *I* know what's going to happen to you next.'

'Oh,' said Lucy, 'and what's that?'

'You don't think I'm going to give *that* sort of information away do you? I'm not some gullible policeman you know – I have qualifications.'

'I see,' said Lucy. She sat in silence as they turned onto the promenade and followed the same route they'd taken the day she escaped from Doctor Veraciter. It had continued to rain whilst they were in the police station and it was *still* hammering down now, bouncing off the pavements in huge crystal marbles.

They drove quite quickly past the soaking whelk stalls and the fishing boats but slowed down as they approached the pier, first passing the Bleevit and then the orange box where she'd seen Kolley Kibber. With each familiar landmark that passed her heart grew a little heavier though. She was happy to be back in Grimston, but Toby and Fenny were still in danger, and all *she* had done was allow herself to be captured – it *wasn't* a very good start.

'Feeling sorry for yourself?' said Morana, misinterpreting Lucy's sad expression. 'Look, that's where you escaped last time,' she said, pointing out the box.

'It's nice of you to take an interest,' said Lucy.

'Oh, I'm *very* interested in *you*. A *lot* of people are, which is why you won't be escaping on *this* particular trip – *will* she, Bruno?'

Bruno twisted in his seat, keeping one eye on the road as he replied – as he turned, the skin on his neck folded like a hippo's hide.

'Nope,' he grinned. 'Absolutely no chance of escape this time – no Kolley Kibbers, no piers, and *especially* no chess machines to hide in.'

Lucy raised an eyebrow.

'Yeah,' grunted Bruno. 'We managed to work it out eventually.'

'So I'm not going to escape?' asked Lucy, with just a hint of challenge.

'Not while I'm around,' said Bruno. 'All *you've* got to look forward to is the welcoming embrace of Saint Mallydick's.' He started to laugh, but it turned into such an embarrassing session of snorting and guffawing that Morana told him to belt up.

Lucy smiled and contented herself with the picture of Grimston as it floated past the window. Every so often though she caught sight of Bruno's eyes in the rear-view mirror – he was watching her very carefully. Escape, it seemed, would have to come later.

'Just as a matter of interest,' said Morana, 'what *did* you do with those children?'

'Nothing yet,' said Lucy. 'We're waiting until the price for kidnap victims goes sky high and then we're going to flood the market with them.'

'Very funny,' said Morana.

'*I* thought so,' said Lucy, slightly hesitant. She'd just seen Zenda Freggley waiting to cross the road. More to the point, Zenda had spotted *her*, and there was no doubt that she remembered the face. The reporter had whipped off her high-heeled shoes and was sprinting behind the car as if her life depended on it. She wasn't fast enough to keep up with a speeding motor though, and as they picked up speed Lucy turned to look out of the back window. Zenda was leaning on a lamppost, struggling for breath.

'Well *somebody* took those kids,' said Morana, 'and the police seem to think it was you – or perhaps your mysterious uncle.'

'I can't help what people believe,' said Lucy, suddenly uncomfortable with her choice of words. 'I told Inspector Trembley the *truth*.'

'You *do* know the Lindstroms are willing to pay a good ransom, don't you?' said Morana. 'His parents are quite rich by all accounts.'

'Are they?' said Lucy. 'I didn't know.'

'They've offered to pay for the Savage girl too,' said Morana, 'as long as Toby is returned safely.' She looked at Lucy for a clue, as if the information she was laying out was some kind of bait in a trap. Lucy said nothing.

'Of course your family knows *all* about disappearing, don't they? First your mother, then your father and now you. Only you decided to come back, which is more than can be said for either of your parents.'

'Oh look, we're nearly there,' said Lucy, trying to change the subject. It *still* hurt whenever people goaded her about Maggie's disappearance.

'Come on,' said Morana, 'you can tell me – what's the big secret?'

'You'd *like* that, wouldn't you?' said Lucy, wishing she knew the answer herself. 'It'd be quite a feather in your cap if you managed to get all the information Doctor Veraciter wants. He might even give you a pay rise.'

'He almost certainly would,' said Morana, as they passed through the hospital gates. 'And what's more I could share it with you – you could move out of that boarding house and get somewhere of your own.'

'The boarding house *is* somewhere of my own,' said Lucy. She watched closely as Bruno manoeuvred the car into Veraciter's parking space. 'But actually I *am* interested in the money.'

'*Are* you?' whispered Morana, ensuring that Bruno didn't overhear.

'I need some getaway cash,' said Lucy, 'so give me fifty pounds and we've got a deal.'

Morana considered the proposal for a moment, then nodded and shook Lucy's hand. She soon drew away though, when she noticed the raw finger stump.

'But I don't want Bruno to hear us,' said Lucy quietly.

'Yes, of *course*,' whispered Morana, eager to hear the secret information.

'And there's just one more thing I want you to do, before I tell you,' whispered Lucy.

'Yes? What's that?' whispered Morana, leaning closer.

'I want you to GET LOST,' yelled Lucy, as loud as she could.

Morana recoiled as if she'd been bitten by a snake. Her head whipped back and hit the window, and when she recovered her poise, Lucy noticed that she was wearing a rather disquieting expression.

'We'll *see*, shall we?' said Morana calmly.

'Welcome to Saint Mallydick Mirabilis,' said Bruno with an evil leer. He leapt out of the car to open the door for Lucy. He wasn't being polite though, he just wanted to make sure she didn't escape.

'Thanks a lot, Mr. Pharty,' said Lucy. She was desperately looking for somewhere to run – but first she needed to escape Bruno's iron grasp – and it had just tightened considerably.

'Don't you go saying my name like that,' growled Bruno.

'But that's how it's pronounced, isn't it?' she said.

'It *is*,' said Bruno. 'But there are ways of making it sound…'

'Like a phart?' said Lucy. '*Ow*, get off you pig, you're hurting me.'

'Then behave yourself,' said Morana. 'Try to make new friends around the hospital – that way your stay with us will be much more pleasant.'

'Sorry,' said Lucy defiantly, 'but I won't be stopping that long.'

'They *all* say that,' said Bruno, 'but we have a pretty good record on escapes.'

'Oh?' said Lucy.

'An *excellent* record,' laughed Morana. 'None whatsoever, nix, nil – the total number of successful escapes is less than one.'

'I'll admit that does sound fairly final,' confessed Lucy. 'But I *do* like a challenge.'

She looked up at the huge black stone entrance and found herself believing every word of it. Even the skies were suddenly more threatening, sitting like a suffering crown over the black slate roof. Saint Mallydick's had been the manor house at one time and featured in most of the local tales of disappearances and strange goings on. None of them was true of course, but if you needed a house to feature in a blood-curdling tale then this was the one to have.

'Come on,' grunted Bruno, 'there's someone waiting for you inside.'

The foyer looked more like it belonged to a hotel rather than a hospital but the corridors leading off it gave the game away. They were highly polished and squeaky; the kind of passageway where you could hear people coming ages before they appeared. And they were lined with dozens of doors, all of which opened outwards so the inmates couldn't barricade themselves into their cells.

'What a charming place,' said Lucy nervously. She was trying to keep her spirits up, but there didn't seem to be much to laugh about.

'I'm glad you approve,' said Morana, 'because you'll be spending quite a while here if I have anything to do with it.' She stopped a man in a white coat who was just about to cross their path.

'Snatch? Which room is Miss Blake assigned to?'

The attendant dutifully checked his clipboard, running down the list of possibilities and moving his lips silently as he read the entries. It was like watching Genjamin in reverse. The lips were moving furiously but not a single sound emerged. Lucy though she saw the word 'nutcase' form there once or twice but couldn't be sure.

'She'll be in one of the rooms in E wing,' said Snatch finally, pointing up at the signs on the wall.

'Apple wing,' he said, just in case Morana couldn't read. 'Banana wing. Cherry wing. Damson wing.'

'Epricot wing?' suggested Lucy, still trying to be cheerful.

'*Experimental*,' hissed Morana.

'Oh,' said Lucy, her heart sinking again.

'Yes,' grinned Morana. 'I *thought* that might take the wind out of your sails. I suppose you think it was funny, did you – shouting at me like that?'

'I thought it was mildly amusing,' smiled Lucy.

'Good,' said Morana. 'Then here's something to wipe the smile off your face. I had a little talk with your stepmother earlier – and I found her to be a charming conversationalist.'

'*Charming?*' said Lucy. 'Are you sure you went to the right house?'

'Quite sure,' said Morana, 'we spoke for ages – it was *most* illuminating.'

'So?' said Lucy.

'So don't go thinking that you're the only one with eyes and ears and the intelligence to use them. For instance, Mrs. Winnet-Blake was telling me how you've grown rather attached to certain items once owned by your birth-mother.'

'*Oh,*' said Lucy. Her heart began to sink, until finally it hit a place where it could go no lower. It felt as though it was resting in cold, dirty water at the bottom of an abandoned well.

'Ah,' said Morana. 'We've finally begun to realise the seriousness of the situation, have we?'

It was true. Lucy had managed to convince herself that she was the only one with enough wit to see what was going on – but Lily had been noticing things as well. Just because she didn't like her stepmother, it didn't mean the lamp-stand was stupid, did it? It all went back to what Harry had told her, about not underestimating the enemy.

'They're of sentimental value,' lied Lucy. 'Those things are all I've got left of my real mother.'

'Aaaah,' said Morana, mockingly, 'is *that* so?'

'Yes,' said Lucy. A cold feeling in her stomach told her that the lie had completely failed.

'Well that's what you'd *like* us to believe, isn't it?' said Morana. 'But think again, Miss Blake.'

'What are you trying to tell me?' said Lucy. 'Just spit it out will you and stop playing cat and mouse?'

'Very well,' said Morana, 'I'm *saying* that you won't be performing your magical disappearing act any more, because your mother's things have been put away, in a safe place.'

'Where?' said Lucy, not really expecting an answer. She found it difficult to believe that Lily had worked it all out so quickly – she must have had help, mustn't she? From Raziel perhaps?

'They have gone to a very special place,' whispered Morana. 'In fact they're *so* safe that I'll even tell you where they are, because you haven't a hope in hell of ever reaching them.'

'Alright then,' said Lucy. '*Where?*'

Morana leaned over to whisper the secret location into Lucy's ear.

'SOMEWHERE YOU'LL NEVER FIND THEM,' she screamed.

Everyone within hearing range stopped what they were doing and spun round to see what all the shouting was about.

'She'll never find what?' said a familiar voice. It was the fish-faced Doctor Veraciter. He was dressed in a dung-brown suit and wearing shiny black shoes, squeaking his way down a side corridor towards the foyer.

'*Oh*, Doctor,' said Morana. 'I didn't see you there.'

'Apparently not,' he sneered. 'So what were you talking about?'

'Erm, my parents,' said Lucy, jumping in to stop Morana blabbing. 'Miss Fay was saying that I'm never likely to find my parents.'

'I'd say that was almost certain,' said Veraciter, 'since they're both dead.'

'Good point,' said Morana with a sly look at Lucy.

'*And*,' said Veraciter, 'if I find out that either of you has been lying to me there'll be trouble. *Now*, Miss Blake, shall we start again? It was very good of you to come.'

'Was it?' said Lucy. 'I didn't realise I had a choice – so if I'm free to go…'

'You *didn't* have a choice, *bless* you,' said Veraciter. 'But now that you're here it doesn't hurt to be polite, does it?'

Lucy smiled thinly, all the time trying to imagine how she was going to escape. They wouldn't be fooled so easily this time, and in any case, there was nowhere to run. Every window was barred, and all the doors were doubled up, just like the ones at the Braneskule.

'Shall we pay a visit to the experimental wing?' suggested Veraciter. He picked up a clipboard and set off down the squeaky corridor, jingling a huge bunch of keys as he went. Bruno pushed Lucy into place behind the doctor, and then stood back, allowing Morana to go next.

'I'll be right behind you Blake,' he grunted. 'Just in case you were thinking of making a run for it.'

'I wouldn't dream of it,' said Lucy. She was busy studying the back of Veraciter's podgy head, aware that some sort of change had come over him since their last meeting. He was still the same little piggy-eyed toad she remembered, but he was nervous now, twitchy almost, as if he had something far more important to worry about.

'So why have I been brought here?' said Lucy. As they walked, she examined every aspect of their route, just in case it might provide her with a way out.

'Don't you remember the conversation we had at the Four Havens?' said Veraciter. 'There are important things that need to be sorted out – issues of truth, for one.'

'Yes, but how does that affect me?' said Lucy. They were walking past a cell with a sign on the door that read *'thinks he's invisible'*.

'It affects *you* because you're at the centre of it all,' said Veraciter.

'Am I?' said Lucy. 'But my stepmother keeps telling me I'm not that important.'

'On the contrary,' said Veraciter, 'you *are* important – I didn't believe it myself at first, as you might recall – but then you managed to escape from us against all the odds – incredible, don't you think?'

'Unbelievable,' said Lucy. 'But why should you want to bring me here?'

'Because your escape convinced me that there might just be a grain of truth in those stories about your mother,' said Veraciter. 'And what's more, Professor Rasmussen agrees with me.'

'Lectrical Therapy

Bruno's bony fingers exerted such a powerful grip on Lucy's neck that she found it difficult to swallow, but she was determined not to make a sound, no matter *how* hard he squeezed. She was relieved when they reached the metal door though, and gave a loud gasp as he pushed her inside. She half-ran and half-fell into the dark space beyond, expecting to feel a cold stone floor and hear the slamming of a door. But to her surprise, Veraciter followed her in, and so did Morana, shutting the door behind them and switching on the subdued lighting.

Lucy's first impression was how quiet the room was, as if the walls had been designed to absorb the sound of their voices. The floor was springy and slightly soft underfoot, and a heavy velvet curtain covered one complete wall, currently concealing whatever lay behind. In front of the curtain was a desk that looked like something from a broadcast studio. It was full of switches, knobs, and readouts, and Lucy couldn't but think that this was what the confuser *should* have looked like, instead of being thrown together with old bits of junk. In front of the desk was a large, leather operator's seat, currently turned away from them. Lucy sensed it was occupied though – and by someone who was waiting for just the right moment to reveal themselves.

'Oh, *very* impressive,' said Veraciter, as if seeing the place for the first time. 'Will we be able to see it working soon?'

'*That* rather depends on our young visitor,' said a strained voice.

The seat rotated slowly to reveal a man in a peculiar black suit, his face almost completely covered in bandages.

'We meet at last,' he said, leaning forward and offering Lucy a claw-like hand. It was just possible that he was grinning, but it was difficult to tell through the layers of cotton dressings. 'Excuse me for not getting up, Miss

Blake, but I have certain *physical* problems. Certain temporary *afflictions* you understand, through no fault of my own.'

'It's *you*, isn't it?' hissed Lucy.

'And who else could I be, but myself?' said the man. 'I have been *so* looking forward to meeting you in the *flesh*. And speaking of flesh, I see that you also have been in the wars.'

He touched Lucy's cheek with the back of his scaly hand, and for a moment, she found herself imagining that he could heal her wounds. But if he could do that, then surely he would have healed himself?

'Perhaps I should explain?' said Veraciter. 'The professor was involved in an accidental fire at his home in Lundern. It was a bread-toasting appliance, wasn't it, Professor?'

'I believe they are known as Lectric muffin swelterers,' said the seated figure. 'My living quarters were turned into an inferno when the device burst into flames – I barely escaped with my life.' He paused, staring at Lucy through the slits in his bandages. 'I managed to survive however, through sheer force of will.'

'Yes, of *course* you did,' said Lucy with a frown.

'And now he's making a miraculous recovery,' said Veraciter. 'Which is *most* fortunate for Saint Mallydick's – because the professor is a world authority on the perception of truth.'

'Indeed I am,' said Rasmussen.

'Yes, well that's *very* convenient,' said Lucy. 'And how lucky for us that you ended up *here* in Grimston.'

'Where else?' said Rasmussen. 'The sea air is *such* a valuable aid to the recuperation and regeneration of the skin.'

'And we have some fine auction houses too,' said Lucy, 'so *handy* for picking up a bargain, if you like that sort of thing.'

'I really *don't* see where this conversation is leading,' said Veraciter, somewhat puzzled. 'We *have* come to see the new machine, haven't we?'

'Indeed,' said the bandaged man, 'so why don't we begin?'

Rasmussen pulled himself out of the chair with some effort, limping over to the curtains and indicating to Bruno that he should take the vacated seat.

'Oh, *excellent*,' said the doctor, rubbing his hands excitedly. 'I've really been looking forward to this. We expect great things from the professor's machine, *don't* we, Professor?'

'Yes, I *do*,' said Rasmussen, pulling the curtain cord. The drapes moved silently aside to reveal a room behind a large picture window. It was difficult to determine the size of the space because of the dim lighting, but its intended purpose was amply demonstrated by a pair of bright spotlights. One of them shone down on a familiar-looking cabinet, whilst the other illuminated a stout wooden chair. It was built like a primitive throne, but fitted with leather straps and vicious-looking harnesses.

Lucy's hand went up to her mouth to stifle a scream. The chair was quite threatening enough, but it was the other device that set her heart racing. It was just like the one they had seen in the Bright Byrde, except for the sliding cover that hid the glass front.

'Oh, God, *no*, it's a Spiri…' she said, cutting off the words as though they were made of hot lead.

'It's a *what*?' said Veraciter.

'Nothing,' said Lucy, realising her mistake. 'I haven't a clue what it is.'

'But of *course* you don't,' crowed Veraciter. 'There are just two people in the world who know the secret of this machine, and one of them is me.'

'Quite,' said Rasmussen.

'Indeed,' said Veraciter. 'The Extraction of Truth is a *very* serious affair, isn't it? We can't have just *anyone* knowing about it, now can we?'

'Extraction of truth?' said Lucy. 'Is *that* what you think it does?'

'All Spiritu Lokeys are capable of extracting Truth,' said Rasmussen with an evil grin, 'and the new *Lectro* Lokey is no exception. It employs different methods to the devices which were fashioned in ancient times, but its capabilities are similar to those you have already witnessed, Miss Blake.'

'And there are going to be more,' said Veraciter gleefully. 'Lots of them.'

'Indeed,' said Rasmussen. 'We must replace those ancient cabinets which have either been lost or destroyed by fools with no interest in the Truth.'

'Erm, *ye-es*,' said Veraciter uncertainly, 'that too.'

Lucy was stunned. Just moments before, she had believed the Spiritu Lokey to be one of her deepest buried secrets. Suddenly though, she felt as if she was wearing a silly hat with the words *'I've been to a secret world called Assiah...'* printed on the front.

'It was only a matter of time Miss Blake,' said Rasmussen matter of factly. 'It's the way the havens are constructed.'

Lucy was eager to know what he meant by this, but events beyond the window had overtaken her curiosity. The angel signalled to Bruno who pressed a button on the control desk, causing the wooden chair to rumble away from the pool of light on a squeaky track. It returned moments later though with a child strapped into it, the leather bonds cutting deep into the exposed arms and legs, and an iron band restraining the brow of the cloth-covered head.

'Are we ready?' said Rasmussen.

'Absolutely,' said Veraciter. 'Erm, but what was that you were saying just now about ancient cabinets?'

Rasmussen ignored the question and nodded to Bruno who flicked another switch on the panel. The cover on the cabinet slid down to reveal a glass window, behind which was the familiar blank-faced mannequin.

'We are ready to listen to the truth,' said Rasmussen.

'Yes, but *whose* truth are we going to be hearing?' said Lucy.

'Be quiet,' hissed Veraciter. 'You know nothing of these things.'

'Yeah,' grunted Bruno, 'you know *nuffink* – now *shut* it, or I'll come over there and squeeze your scrawny little neck.'

He turned back to the control panel and pressed a large red button. The child in the chair twitched violently, as if being electrocuted – and seconds later a face appeared in the cabinet, projected onto the porcelain mannequin.

'It's Adam Knox,' gasped Lucy. Although she'd known the boy was here in the hospital it was still a shock to see him staring out of the machine, the image of his frightened face jumping and flickering like some sixty-year-old film.

'An old friend of yours I believe?' said Rasmussen.

'*No*,' said Lucy positively. 'He's *not* my friend and never has been. Adam Knox is a sadistic, destructive creep, and if anyone deserves to be in this place then it's him.'

'*Excellent,*' said Rasmussen. 'I *do* like someone who knows their own mind. So, you won't be too worried about what happens to him, *will* you? Purely in the interests of science of course.'

'Erm, *Professor,*' said the doctor, 'I hardly like to mention this, but erm, what *exactly* are you planning to with the boy?'

'Just a little experiment, Doctor – to prove that the machine works.'

'You mean it hasn't been tested?' shrieked Morana. 'But that's downright irresponsible. I'm all for the advancement of science, but we shouldn't be trying out untested equipment on our patients, should we?'

'A good point,' said Rasmussen. 'And one that I hope you'll bear in mind later on. I, however, have absolute confidence in the machine.'

'And how do you know *that,*' demanded Lucy, 'if it's never been tested?'

'Because it was constructed by a craftsman with something valuable to protect,' said Rasmussen. He smiled at Lucy, as if she might know who he was talking about. 'And in return, I promised that his precious thing would never be harmed.'

'*Pardon?*' said Veraciter. He was obviously seeing a side of the professor that had so far remained hidden. 'Is that entirely legal, Rasmussen old boy? It doesn't sound ethical to me.'

'Indeed?' said Rasmussen. 'I always thought that a person's view of ethics depended on where they stood in order to examine them?'

'I'm sure you're right,' said Veraciter, 'but threats of violence? I don't think we can put up with that sort of thing here at Saint Mallydick's.'

'You can accept other forms of malpractice, *can't* you, Doctor? Or have you forgotten our little arrangement?'

'What arrangement is that?' said Morana, sensing an opportunity.

Veraciter was too embarrassed to look her in the face.

'It was nothing,' said Rasmussen. 'There were certain irregularities in the good doctor's accounts, so it was a simple matter to persuade him that he needed help here in the hospital.'

'Oh?' said Morana. 'What sort of help?'

'You'll find out,' said Rasmussen. 'Bruno? Give him the first level.'

Bruno turned the knob just a fraction, and Knox's head kicked back as he arched his spine and screamed out in pain. The face in the cabinet rocked from side to side like a mad puppet, the eyes staring straight ahead, seeing nothing. It was clear the boy was in agony, and although the glass blocked every bit of sound, Lucy had no difficulty imagining his grief-stricken screams.

'I thought we were supposed to ask him a question?' said Veraciter.

'*A question?*' hissed Rasmussen. 'And what could a child like *that* possibly know that we do not?'

'Rasmussen, *no,*' said Veraciter, 'I'm sorry, but I can't be part of this. The boy is obviously in tremendous physical pain. I can agree to the use of certain experimental drugs, but this is more like torture. Why don't you stop for a moment and tell us what you hope to achieve with this madness?'

'Don't you *know?*' said Lucy. 'I though you were in charge?'

'I *am,*' said Veraciter firmly.

Raziel gaze the doctor a long hard stare that suggested otherwise.

'In matters of day-to-day running,' said Raziel, 'the doctor is in charge, but in cases such as this, *my* judgement is final.'

'But, but, he, you, I, erm…' Veraciter's face turned purple as he struggled to find the words. And as Lucy recalled what he had put her through at the Havens, she actually found herself enjoying the spectacle.

'You don't actually *know* anything about him, *do* you?' she said. 'He might have just dropped in from heaven for all you know.'

Through the narrow gap in his bandages, Raziel appeared to be smiling. It seemed that even angels appreciated a little irony.

'On the contrary,' said Veraciter recovering his poise, 'the professor has an impeccable background, – his research is extremely well known.'

'And how long have you known that?' said Lucy. 'Did you look inside his coat and suddenly feel as though you'd known him all your life?'

'Coat?' said Veraciter. 'I erm, I don't seem to recall a coat, do I?'

'*Look* at me,' said Lucy. 'Do you actually *know* who this man is?'

'This is Professor Rasmussen,' replied Veraciter.

'No, he *isn't,*' hissed Lucy. 'This is the angel Raziel.'

Bruno and Morana stared at each other for a moment and then broke into fits of uncontrolled laughter. They were accustomed to hearing such lunatic outbursts from the patients, but it was always *such* a nice treat when one of them came out with something original.

'Do you *see* now?' said Raziel. 'Do you begin to understand why conventional methods are doomed to fail with this girl? She is a classic delusional. She sees faces everywhere, and each one of them is an angel.'

'Not *all* of them,' spat Lucy, 'just *you*.'

'A little more *pain* I think,' said Raziel. 'Don't you agree, Bruno?'

The driver grinned and turned the knob just a fraction – and Lucy watched in horror as Knox's gaping mouth framed another perfect scream.

'*No*! Don't hurt him,' she cried. 'Hurt *me* instead.'

'Hurt *you*, you little fool?' snarled Raziel. 'Do you think I would *ever* consider that?'

'Why not?' yelled Lucy. 'You threatened me once before.'

'A mere tactic,' said Raziel. 'I never carried out that threat, *did* I?'

'Erm, *no*,' admitted Lucy. She looked over at Veraciter and Morana, willing them to listen in detail to the conversation – because if they *did*, they would see she was right and realise that Rasmussen really was an angel.

'I didn't hurt you,' said Raziel, 'because our kind *cannot* hurt each other.'

'*Our* kind?' said Lucy. 'But I'm nothing *like* you.'

'That's right,' said Raziel, 'you *are* nothing like me – but to prove that *I* am a little like *you* I will stop if you ask me to.'

'You'll stop?' said Lucy. 'Just like that?'

'Say the word,' said Raziel, 'and I will cease.'

'And then what?' said Lucy.

'Then nothing,' said Raziel. 'If you instruct me to spare the life of this worthless individual then I will not harm him any further.'

'*Life*?' said Veraciter. 'Oh *dear me*, no, really, this has to stop.'

'Then I *command* you to leave him alone,' said Lucy, with all the authority she could muster.

'As you wish,' said Raziel. 'Bruno? You heard her – release the boy.'

Lucy heaved a sigh of relief as Bruno switched off the machine and went to remove Adam Knox's limp body from the straps. She gave the boy a half-hearted smile as the driver dragged him past the window, noticing his scowl and the deep look of shame in his eyes. She'd saved him from the pain alright, but at the cost of letting her see his tears.

'There,' smiled Raziel, 'are you happy now?'

'Yes,' said Lucy, 'but I still won't give you what you want.'

'Not immediately,' said Raziel, 'but I shall find a way to make it so eventually. *Now*, shall we continue with the rest of your lesson?'

'*Lesson?*' said Lucy. She thought of Gusset and what he'd said about enemies – the way they would queue to teach her lessons.

'Did you really think it would be that simple?' said Raziel.

'I don't know,' said Lucy, 'but I have a feeling you're about to explain.'

'The universe is full of wonders Lucy; you *know* that, don't you? And in time, you might even come to appreciate how it all works. Take the great physical laws for instance, like the rule of action and reaction.'

'I see,' said Lucy, turning suddenly pale. 'So who is it going to be?'

'Oh, you *are* a quick thinker, aren't you?' said Raziel. 'I shall have to watch my step with you, shan't I?'

'*Who* is going to take Knox's place?' demanded Lucy. She spun round, looking for Morana, but only herself, Raziel and Veraciter remained. Miss Fay was gone. She turned to face the window again and watched in horror as Bruno kicked the door open and dragged Morana in by the hair. He was wearing a sadistic grin and clearly enjoyed the look of shock on Lucy's face. As he went to grab the leather straps though, Morana broke away and ran to the window, beating on the thick glass in a desperate cry for release. With Raziel blocking the door though, Lucy was powerless to help – all she had to offer was her tears.

'Why don't you *do* something Doctor?' cried Lucy, her eyes flooding like warm pools. 'You *know* this isn't right, *don't* you?'

Veraciter shrugged. He seemed to have given up the fight, now that he'd seen what Rasmussen was really like.

'And you – why are you *doing* this?' she screamed, turning on Raziel.

'I'm *doing* it because I am unable to harm you directly,' said Raziel, 'but also because you and she are so much alike.'

'We are *not*,' protested Lucy. 'I'm absolutely *nothing* like her.'

Bruno had forced Morana into the chair now and was lashing the straps around her limbs, as if trying to amputate them. She was screaming, but the glass blocked every last desperate cry.

'Oh, but you *are*,' said Raziel. 'You have absolutely nothing in common with the Knox child, but there is a *great* deal of similarity between you and

Miss Fay. You are both very intelligent and you are both incredibly sly – perhaps one of you even more than the other.

'Rasmussen, *no,*' said Veraciter, finally finding some courage. 'This really *is* too much. Even if you have no intention of harming poor Morana, this is still mental torture as far as Miss Blake is concerned.'

Lucy began to sob uncontrollably – she had guessed the outcome of Raziel's dangerous little game before Veraciter had even managed to learn the rules.

'If I don't *intend* harm?' said Raziel. 'Oh, but I *do* intend it.'

He nodded to Bruno who returned and seated himself at the controls.

'*Bruno!*' screamed Veraciter. '*Listen* to me – you work for *me.*'

'I work for whoever pays me best,' grinned Bruno. 'And Professor Rasmussen here pays very well indeed.' He flicked an entire row of switches, and as each one clicked into position, a corresponding light came on above it. After a few moments delay, the entire console was lit and the air was filled with a familiar sound.

'*Thermionics,*' said Lucy.

'It's a *pleasant* sound, isn't it?' said Raziel. 'When you're not trapped inside the machine of course.'

'Ready Professor?' grinned Bruno.

'I have never been *more* ready,' said Raziel. 'And now we shall see what the machine can *really* do.'

Bruno grasped the largest of the control knobs and pushed a small button mounted on top of it. The dial lit up and began to rotate, and when he took his hand away, it continued to do so, as if some invisible force was in command.

Lucy cried out for mercy on Morana's behalf, but Raziel was already enjoying the show, grinning beneath his bandages as Morana's face appeared as a projection on the mannequin. The picture was flickering and rather indistinct, but the hazy features were still recognisable, twisting and writhing in agony as the cabinet worked on her mind, her gaping mouth screaming obscenities that thankfully nobody could hear.

'Would you like to hear what Miss Fay has to say?' said Raziel. 'She *might* even be able to convince you to co-operate – to hand over certain articles that do not rightly belong to you.'

Bruno leaned over and pressed a button marked 'mute' – and as it popped up the room was filled with the sound of Morana's screams.

'Nooooo…, *please no, I'll do anything…*' she shrieked, '*anything you want, pleeeeeeease…*'

'Let her *go*,' pleaded Lucy, 'she hasn't done anything to hurt you.'

'She hasn't done anything to assist me either,' said Raziel, 'but she's making up for that now, by demonstrating that I can reach you through others.'

'*You rotten, slime-ball, scum-sucking, crap-in-your-pocket weasels – help, meee…*,' screamed Morana. '*I'll see you in hell Rasmussen, you creepy, arse-faced, toe-rag.*'

'Yes,' said Raziel, 'well I think that's enough of th…'

'*Exner Heelo,*' screamed Morana. '*Ex-ner Hee-lo…*'

'What was that?' said Lucy. '*What* did she say just then?'

'*Nothing,*' screamed Raziel. '*Bruno?* Switch that thing off – *now.*'

Even at a distance, Lucy could see the pain reflected in Morana's eyes. And from her own fraction of a second inside a Spiritu Lokey, she knew exactly what that agony was like – she *had* to put a stop to this torture.

'I'm begging,' she screamed, 'stop it – *please.*'

'Begging?' said Raziel.

'Yes,' said Lucy, 'stop it, right now.'

'Then beg me again,' sneered Raziel.

'Alright, I'm *begging* you,' said Lucy, kneeling in front of the angel. 'On my bended knee – please don't hurt her any more.'

'Very well,' said the angel, nodding at Bruno, 'that will be sufficient.'

Bruno wrenched the dial back to its minimum setting, looking decidedly disappointed.

'Thank you,' she said, sighing with relief as Morana's expression returned to normal.

'For what?' said Raziel.

'Your compassion.'

'Ah, *yes,*' sighed Raziel, 'what a *pity* your sentiments are so often wasted on those who don't appreciate them.'

'What do you mean?' said Lucy.

'Your consideration of others is a weakness,' hissed Raziel. 'And it will eventually be your downfall Miss Blake. Remember, the only reason you were able to show *me* compassion was because you first tried to fry the wings off my back.' He leaned over to the panel and wrenched the big dial all the way to its upper region. Then he took his hand away and smiled at Bruno, as if giving him a present.

'*No*,' screamed Lucy, 'you *can't.*'

'I *can*,' said Raziel, his bandages stretching to accommodate a broadening sneer. 'And what's more, I *have.*'

Lucy's attention was torn away from Raziel's contemptuous grin as the machine began to work its evil on Morana. Bruno had strapped her down hard into the torture throne, but her body *still* managed to kick and reel in pain. Her skin was blackening and her eyes had begun to steam, and her beautiful red hair was standing on end, forming a soft, smoking crescent around her once-pretty face.

'*I'll do anything you ask*,' screamed Lucy.

'I *know* you will,' said Raziel with an evil smile.

'Then stop it now,' she pleaded.

Morana's body stopped twitching, just for a moment, and Lucy turned her attention to the face that was projected in the cabinet – and from the torment and suffering displayed in that flickering, smoky image, she knew that Miss Fay's mind was being torn apart.

'I'm afraid it's rather too late for that,' he sneered. 'Things have already gone *much* too far – all that remains now is for you to *watch*, and *learn.*'

'*No*,' screamed Lucy, 'you *must* be able to save her.'

'It's *such* a pity about Miss Fay,' said Raziel, ignoring her plea. 'She had qualifications you know.'

The image in the cabinet slowly winked out, like innocent stars snuffed out by gathering clouds. And as Morana's physical body kicked and twisted in a final heart-breaking spasm, Lucy let out a huge heart-rending sob. She slumped to the floor with her face resting against the angel's feet, the tears flooding out of her in unrestrained torrents. But then, in a sudden moment of calm she managed to gather her anger. She squeezed her fingernails into the palms of her hands and gritted her teeth so hard she feared they might splinter, filling her mouth up with hundreds of sharp little knives.

She picked herself up and stared Raziel directly in the eye, and as he took a single pace back from her she realised that her life had changed direction once again. She had glimpsed her destiny and seen Raziel there, surrounded by death and destruction. Finally, she knew what she must do.

When the opportunity presented itself, and she was certain that it would, she was going to kill an angel of God.

Trouble
with Nuts

Lucy had never tasted a chauffeur before and as she spat out a large piece of flesh and a clump of dark arm-hairs, she vowed silently never to try it again. Bruno looked down at his forearm and for some reason decided to wait a short while before screaming out in agony. Lucy thought that perhaps it was normal for someone like him, where the messages from the nerves to the brain were sometimes delayed by more important issues – such as strangling schoolgirls or torturing doctors' assistants. Whatever the reason, it gave her the opportunity to pull away from Bruno's iron grip and make for the door. To her great surprise, Veraciter simply stepped aside, as if he no longer approved of what was going on and actually *wanted* her to escape.

'*Stop* her,' barked Raziel, 'or you'll regret it.'

The doctor winced and shrank slightly in the face of the threat, but then folded his arms in defiance and set his piggy little eyes into a determined squint. From the nervous twitching of his mouth it was clear he wasn't sure where that action might lead, but it was obvious he'd had enough.

'Stop her yourself,' he said. 'I want nothing more to do with it.'

'Bruno?' shouted Raziel. '*Get* the girl – and this time I want no mistakes. The doctor here might be willing to tolerate failure, but *I* am not.'

Bruno was still gaping at the hole in his arm – an ugly patch of raw flesh, surrounded by a pair of bloodstained crescents that Lucy's dentist would have been proud of. He stuttered, unable to believe the amount of damage such a slightly built girl had managed to inflict – and then the words burst out of him like red-hot magma spewing from a volcano.

'I'm going to b-b-bleeding-well *have* you,' he bellowed. 'I *am* – I'm going to frigging-well *kill* you.'

'You'll have to catch her first,' smiled Veraciter.

'Yeah,' screamed Bruno, 'and when I *do* catch the little toe-rag and squeeze the frigging brains out of her then I'm going to come back and have *you* too.'

Raziel grinned encouragement at Bruno who started an ungainly lumber for the door. Lucy was already in the corridor though, wondering where to run. The only option for the moment seemed to be a blind dash in the direction she was already facing.

'You've got nowhere to go,' shouted Bruno. He was lagging behind already and sounded distinctly out of breath.

'I'll just keep running then,' said Lucy, 'and when you finally run out of steam and collapse with exhaustion I'll come and jump up and down on that big fat belly of yours.'

'Not in *that* direction you won't,' grinned Bruno. 'But you can go ahead and try – and when you eventually come back I'll give you a bloody-good hiding for that crack about my belly – and *then* I'll kill you.'

A voice in Lucy's head was telling her she needed more information – and, rather helpfully, it was suggesting that the breathless Bruno might be the ideal person to supply it. Like Harry had once said, to defeat an enemy, you must first understand them.

'Why don't you come and get me then?' she smiled, hoping to goad him into giving away something useful.

'All in good time,' snarled Bruno. 'Pleasure delayed is pleasure multiplied, isn't it? And I want to give you *plenty* of time to think about what a snapped neck feels like.'

'Take as much time as you like,' said Lucy. 'It'll give me more time to find a way out.'

'Well you won't be escaping from the offices, *will* you?' he grinned. 'There's heavy doors and barred windows on the lot of them – all except for the doctor's, and *that's* on the third floor – so you might as well give up.'

'I don't think so,' said Lucy, 'but thanks for the information – it was just what I needed.'

'Yeah, well you won't be thanking me when I catch up with you,' said Bruno, cracking his knuckles.

Lucy turned and ran, crashing her way through a pair of big swing doors before finally reaching the stairwell. There was a helpful sign placed high up on the wall, offering to point her towards the 'Institute of Truth'. But what she was *really* interested in was the picture of a gloved hand indicating the way to Veraciter's office.

She took the stairs two at a time, aware that every second she gained on Bruno was another second to think. How she was going to get out of a third-storey window was anyone's guess, but she wouldn't be able to tell until she got there, would she? Miss Mountshaft, her biology teacher, had written 'unbearably optimistic' on last year's report, and that was exactly what she needed to be now, because the alternative didn't bear thinking about. As she reached the third floor landing though she found herself thinking about it anyway. She was almost certainly going to get some broken bones from Bruno, and only *then* would she be allowed to suffer whatever Raziel had in mind.

She paused for a moment at the top of the stairs and listened. Bruno was clearly still in pursuit because she could hear his heavy breathing, even above the sound of his footfalls. Then, his great, fat fingers appeared on the handrail as he leaned out into the stairwell to look up at her.

'Give up now and save us both some trouble,' he wheezed.

'I'll take the trouble,' she shouted, 'I like my bones just the way they are.'

'Yeah, well they won't be that way for long Missy – not when I get hold of your slender little neck.'

Lucy pushed her way into the third-floor corridor, allowing the heavy doors to swing closed behind her and desperately looking for a way to block them. There was a bench seat about ten yards away and with all the strength she could muster, she dragged it over, squealing it across the highly polished lino. She jammed it up behind the doors, hoping that it might be enough to stop Bruno in his tracks. She couldn't be sure though, and was suddenly filled with doubt. An uneasy feeling was growing inside her – it was accusing her of not trying hard enough – and that was something *else* that Miss Mountshaft had kindly pointed out in her last report.

'Can I help you?' said a gawky-looking assistant. He'd appeared out of nowhere, complete with white coat and official-looking clipboard.

'Escaped patient,' hissed Lucy, coming out with the first thing she could think of.

'Who? *You?*' he said.

'Not *me*, you idiot, *him* – I'm just a visitor.' She jerked a thumb towards the door, indicating that the escapee was ready to break through at any moment.

'Visitor?' said the assistant. 'Hmm – well I'm not so sure about that, visitors aren't allowed up here you know.'

'I know that *now*,' sighed Lucy, 'but I didn't stop to consider it when your violent patient started chasing me, did I?'

'Erm, I'm still not sure,' he said, 'I'd best go for help.'

'Through *this* door?' said Lucy. 'Have you *heard* all the fuss that madman is making on the other side?'

'Open this bloody-bollocking-well door,' screamed Bruno, bellowing like a wounded elephant. 'I'm going to bloody-well kill you, you sodding little freak, just wait, and see if I don't. I'm going to wring your scrawny little neck until your pretty little eyes pop out of their sockets. And when they do I'm going to stamp up and down on them until they squelch, and I'm going to enjoy every single second of it.'

The assistant was suddenly convinced that Lucy was telling the truth and promptly sat on the seat, adding his weight to the barrier. Then he produced a key and locked the door, just to be sure. Lucy smiled, silently thanking Bruno for his outburst.

'Now what?' he breathed, suddenly concerned for his own safety.

'We need to get to Veraciter's office,' said Lucy. 'That's what he shouted when this lunatic started chasing me. *Get to my office*, he said, it's the only one without bars on the window.'

'Hmm, *yes*, that's right,' said the assistant. 'It *is* the only one without bars – I wonder what he had in mind?'

'Well we're not going to find out sitting here,' said Lucy. 'Why don't you let me in with your pass key – we can work out what to do next when we've got the door safely locked and barred.'

'Good thinking,' said the assistant. 'I'll just make a note of that.' He began scribbling on his clipboard, but Lucy grabbed the pen and hurled it down the corridor.

'*Now*,' she screamed, 'unless you want him to stamp on *your* eyes too?'

They sprinted off down the corridor, following a series of 'pointing hand' signs, each of which was slightly larger than the last. After passing a dozen or so though Lucy stopped. Away in the distance, they could hear Bruno beating the door down, but she still couldn't resist looking at the photographs on the walls. There were hundreds of them, stretching into the far distance – each one containing a mad face. Some of the expressions were so twisted their owners looked barely human, whilst others seemed quite happy in their strange nether-world, staring vaguely into space, like pupils in a calculus lesson.

'The cabinet of freaks,' explained the assistant. 'It's just a perfectly harmless collection of curiosities.'

'I suppose it is,' frowned Lucy, 'if you don't happen to be in the picture.'

She began to run again, afraid to look at the photographs and hoping that speed would blur them out of existence. But no matter how quickly she went they were still there, racing past in the corner of her eye. Mercifully, though, the gallery of twisted faces was eventually exhausted, indicating that they had finally reached their destination.

The heavy oak door bore the doctor's name in gold letters, followed by a long list of qualifications. Lucy examined them closely, but none of them identified the office as belonging to someone who might allow rogue angels or their servants to run amok in his hospital. But if there was time, and she could find a small pot of gold paint, well, anything was possible…

The assistant produced his key chain and was about to open the door when an expression of doubt crept across his face.

'I'm not sure about this,' he said, 'it's not really *allowed* you know.'

'Neither is chasing the professor's grand-daughter around the hospital,' said Lucy. 'But the escaped loony hasn't been told the rules.'

'You're Rasmussen's grand-daughter?' said the assistant, 'oh, well that's *different* then – why didn't you say?'

'I just did,' said Lucy, adopting the same air of superiority that she imagined Rasmussen's granddaughter might assume.

'Hey, wait, what was that noise?' he said.

'It's the nutter,' hissed Lucy, 'he's broken through the swing doors.'

The assistant fumbled nervously with the keys, trying each of them at least three times before finally locating the right one.

'For God's sake, hurry up,' screamed Lucy as the door squealed open.

'*Now* what?' breathed the assistant as they dived into the office. 'Why do you think the doctor wanted you to run here?' He slammed the door and re-locked it and they both leaned with their backs up against it, just in case.

'I don't know,' said Lucy, pretending to look for clues. 'I think we should start with *this* though. She picked up a glass paperweight from Veraciter's desk and showed it to the assistant.

'A present from Grimston-on-Sea,' he said, looking first at the picture of the pier and then reading the label inside the glass. 'Very nice, if you like that sort of thing.'

'Yes, well I don't,' said Lucy, recalling the one she'd thrown into the garden at home. 'I'm making it my job to rid the world of every one of them.' And with that, she threw the paperweight through the window.

'Oh,' said the assistant, cringing at the sound of breaking glass. 'Erm, I don't think you should have done that.'

'My grandfather won't mind,' said Lucy, 'not if my safety depends on it.'

'Your safety?' said a voice at the door.

'*You?*' said Lucy, 'erm, er, but *how?*'

'We have a large staff here in the hospital,' said Raziel, 'and they are well accustomed to dealing with such situations – surely you were *told?* Nobody has *ever* escaped from Saint Mallydick's'

'Ah, Professor,' said the assistant, trying to attract Rasmussen's attention. 'I just wanted to say that I took good care of your grand-daughter.'

'This isn't my granddaughter, you *idiot*,' said Raziel. 'This is the escapee – now *go* – I'll deal with you later.'

The man with the clipboard shot a disappointed look at Lucy, as if he had been deeply hurt by her lies and was going to get his revenge later – perhaps when she was in his sole care and he had a selection of large needles and some time to kill. Lucy felt guilty for deceiving him, but mainly she felt sorry for herself, now that Raziel had caught up with her.

'You almost made it,' said Raziel, 'how *very* resourceful.'

'There's still time,' said Lucy, ever hopeful.

'I doubt that *very* much,' said Raziel, grinning at Bruno.

'Can I have her now?' panted Bruno. He leaned on the doorframe, wheezing like a set of ruptured bagpipes.

'No, you cannot,' said Raziel. 'You can sit quietly and think about how you were outwitted and outrun by a mere ten-year-old – not once, but twice.'

'I'm *thirteen*,' insisted Lucy, suddenly realising that nobody really cared – all *they* were concerned about was that she didn't get any older.

Bruno grabbed a chair and turned it round so he could lay his arms on the backrest – then he simply sat there, growling and glaring, as if Lucy's appointment with fear had merely been delayed. The bite-wound she had managed to inflict dripped blood onto Veraciter's carpet in large, ruby-coloured drops.

'So Lucy, what do you think you achieved?' asked Raziel. 'And how did you convince that poor soul I was your aged relation?'

'I lied,' said Lucy.

'I think it was a little more than that,' said Raziel. 'The fool believed you completely, *didn't* he?'

'Then I must have lied well,' said Lucy.

'Do *not* underestimate me a second time,' hissed Raziel. 'We *both* know that there is more to your storytelling than a simple talent for lies.'

'I *knew* it,' said Veraciter, appearing in the doorway. 'I was *right* all along.'

'Be *quiet*,' hissed Raziel, 'unless you want to sample some of Miss Fay's special treatment?' He sat down in Veraciter's chair, obviously still in pain from the burns he'd received in the confuser. It seemed to Lucy that he was creaking inside the bandages, if that was possible, as if they were too tight and the flesh they bound was unnaturally compressed. Eventually though, he managed to settle, pausing for a moment to enjoy the look on Veraciter's face. Rasmussen had taken control of the hospital, and his occupation of the big leather chair was merely the final insult.

'If you're so interested in my lies,' said Lucy, 'then why don't we exchange stories?'

'Exchange?' grinned Raziel. 'Do you think this is the kind of situation where you can barter? I think in this instance *I* have all the cards. However, as a mark of respect for the so-called *Architect Elect* I will allow it.'

'Not with *him* here,' said Lucy, pointing at Bruno. 'He wants to hurt me.'

'Perhaps it's something we both want?' said Raziel.

'Yes,' said Lucy, 'but first you want to talk – I *know* you do. And I'm not going to talk with *him* here.'

'Very well,' said Raziel, 'but before he leaves, you must give me a solemn promise that you will not attempt to escape again.'

Lucy considered the angel's suggestion for a moment, the image of poor, smouldering Morana still fresh in her mind. Finally, she reached a decision based on what she had seen in the Lokey room.

'Alright then,' she said. 'I *promise* – solemnly.'

'Bruno?' said Raziel. 'Go and wait outside the door.'

The driver scowled and turned his gaze on Lucy. It was a look filled with gurgling breath and snapping bones and the sound of her screams. If there had been any doubt before there was none left now – if Bruno ever caught her, she was going to end up dead. And *that* would be a great pity for a number of reasons – for one thing, she'd never find out what Raziel had meant when he referred to her as the *Architect Elect*.

'So,' said Raziel, as the door clicked shut, 'you want to exchange stories.'

'Tell me why the *light* is so important,' said Lucy, 'and in exchange, I'll tell you where it is.'

'Ah,' said Raziel, with a satisfied sigh, 'progress at last.'

'Then tell me,' demanded Lucy.

'Very well,' said Raziel, 'the *light* is *not* important.'

Lucy studied the angel's bandages. They were seeping a sticky yellow fluid where they overlapped, as if Raziel was sweating golden blood.

'Now *you're* the one who's lying,' said Lucy. She looked across at Veraciter who was listening with extreme interest. The poor man didn't have a clue what was going on, but Lucy could see that his brain was working overtime. The gigantic filing cabinet in his head was swallowing up various little pieces of information, and later he was going to pull them all out again and try to assemble them into a coherent story.

'Very well,' said Raziel. 'I admit it – the manuscript *is* important – but it can always be written again.'

'*Can* it?' said Lucy with a suspicious squint.

'Of course,' replied Raziel.

'And how long would *that* take?'

'A year perhaps?' said Raziel, his eyes looking slightly unsteady.

'No it *wouldn't*,' said Lucy. 'Even *I* know it would take a lot longer than that. It's not just a collection of writings and pictures. There are feelings in there – *deep* feelings – and *memories* – and other things that I can't even begin to put a name to.'

'Ah,' said the angel, 'so you *know* about these things?'

'I've been developing a special emotion for them,' said Lucy.

'So it would seem,' said Raziel. 'In that case I will tell you the truth. It would take a billion years to recreate the *light* – perhaps even ten billion. The true answer is that nobody knows – it is unique and irreplaceable.'

'Now *that* sounds more like it,' said Lucy, 'but it still doesn't tell me what I need to know.'

'You need to know nothing,' said Raziel, 'once you have willingly handed the book to me then *that* will be an end to the matter.'

'But I need to know where it came from,' said Lucy.

'Heaven,' said Raziel suddenly. 'The constancy we call the *light* is the only book ever to have been prepared in heaven.'

'Oh,' said Lucy, recalling the last known whereabouts of this object of infinite beauty and immeasurable value. It had just been digested by a cross between a crocodile and a leather goods accessory.

'Is that all you have to say?' said Raziel. '*Oh?*'

'No,' said Lucy. 'I want to know who created it.'

'It has *always* been extant,' said Raziel after some consideration.

'But somebody must have created it,' said Lucy. 'It hasn't *always* existed, has it?'

Lucy studied Veraciter for a moment. His eyes were staring out of his cake-mix face like a pair of wrinkly, protruding things – and his mouth was hanging open to display a tongue that couldn't keep still. It kept popping out, like a greasy gooseberry coming out to sniff the air.

'It was *created* in heaven,' insisted Raziel, 'and therefore it has always been extant. And now it is *your* turn, Lucy Blake. You were going to tell *me* something in exchange.'

'Was I?' she smiled.

'Don't be coy,' hissed Raziel. 'You promised to tell me where the manuscript was.'

'That's right,' said Lucy, 'but you killed poor Morana, didn't you?'

'And what if I did?' said Raziel. 'A promise is a promise – surely you must know that?'

'Alright then,' said Lucy, deciding it wouldn't make any difference whether Raziel knew or not. 'But you'll never find it though – it's tucked safely inside a lady's handbag, and even I don't know where *that* is – the thing has a mind of its own.'

'Excellent,' said Raziel, with a sudden look of satisfaction. 'So you have entrusted the *light* to Henbeg, have you? And whose idea was that? Miss Pubrane's I suppose?'

Lucy swallowed hard. What Raziel had told her in the confuser room appeared to be true – there *were* no places he didn't know about.

'You have underestimated me once again, *haven't* you, Miss Blake? Just as I underestimated you, when I allowed myself to become entangled in that contraption of your uncle's.'

'And how do you know it belonged to my uncle?' said Lucy nervously.

'I know *many* things. I know for instance that you were entrusted with the constancy we call the *light*, and that just a few moments later, relatively speaking, you managed to lose it again.'

'I *didn't* lose it,' said Lucy. 'I gave it away, but I intend to get it back.'

'We agree on *that* point at least,' said Raziel. 'You *will* get it back – I intend to make quite sure of that.'

'*Professor*, what on *earth* are we talking about here?' said Veraciter. 'What's all this about the *light*?'

'Nothing that concerns you Doctor,' said Raziel. 'This is all to do with young Lucy here.'

'And why is she so important?' asked Veraciter. 'She's just an ordinary girl with an aptitude for lying. A *great* aptitude I admit, but an ordinary girl when all's said and done.'

'*No*,' hissed Raziel, 'she is *not* ordinary – she might be many things, but ordinary is not one of them.'

'Then why don't you tell us *both* what's going on?' said Veraciter. 'Because it's clear that Miss Blake is as much in the dark as I am.'

'You think so?' said Raziel. 'If you could look inside this girl's head you might be surprised by what she has seen and heard these past few weeks. And that is the only reason I have preserved her for so long. If it were not for the help she might provide then I would have rid the world of her long ago.'

'You intend to kill her then, just as you disposed of Miss Fay?'

'I could,' said Raziel, 'not personally of course, because I cannot harm her directly – and in any case I would be destroying my best hope of finding the *light*. Disposing of Miss Blake is a minor aim, and can be done at any time. My foremost task is to return the *light* to its rightful place.'

'Which is?' asked Lucy.

'Why don't you ask your friends?' said Raziel.

'I don't have any friends who might know,' said Lucy.

'No?' said Raziel. 'What about your assistants from the auction room?'

'Not *you* as well,' protested Lucy. 'I'm tired of telling people this – I don't *know* them, alright? I've never seen them before.'

'You haven't?' said Raziel. 'Then *look* at me, child, and tell me again.'

For some reason Lucy did as she was told, repeating her denial in the knowledge that she wasn't going to come to any harm as a result.

'You have told the truth,' said Raziel, examining her closely. 'They have failed to make contact, which is truly *excellent* news.'

'But who are they?' said Lucy.

'It no longer matters,' grinned Raziel, 'soon they will be nobodies – *most* unfortunate for them of course, but they knew the risks they were taking when they came here.'

'Came from where?' said Lucy. 'Are you all from the same place?'

The sound of Raziel's laughter echoed inside Lucy's head, as if a much bigger creature was laughing in a much larger space.

'Do you really think I would tell you such a thing?' he said. 'What could it profit me to reveal secrets that I need not? All you need to know is that we are going to search for the *light* together – you and I.'

'I don't think so,' said Lucy.

'We *are*,' said Raziel, 'if you want to see your friend again.'

Lucy's confidence was suddenly washed out of her, like blood wrung from a damp cloth. She had dreaded this moment – always praying that Fenny's disappearance and Raziel's presence was just a horrible coincidence.

'So it *was* you,' she said, trying to hide her surprise. 'I might have known.'

'Yes, you *might*,' said Raziel, '*if* you had stopped to consider it a little longer. Your thinking is a bit cloudy now, *isn't* it, Lucy?'

'No it isn't,' she said, suddenly realising what had been staring her in the face all along. 'You wanted *me*, didn't you? But you got Fenny by mistake.'

'Oh, *well done*,' said Raziel. 'Yes, I took her by accident, but things worked out eventually didn't they – because here you are, stuck in my honey-trap, and with no means of escape.'

'I wouldn't say that,' said Lucy, 'there's always hope.'

'You really *are* unbearably optimistic, aren't you?' said Raziel. 'But the time has finally come for you to co-operate. If not then I will search for the *light* on my own – and you know what *that* means.'

'Yes, I do,' said Lucy, 'so why don't you go and look on your own?'

Raziel's face turned from a satisfied smile to a storm in the blink of an eye. For a moment, Lucy thought her time had come, but then she remembered what he'd said about not being able to harm her directly. It wouldn't take him long to call Bruno though, and then she really *would* be in trouble.

'Alright,' she said, suddenly appearing to give in. 'I'll help you, but on one condition.'

'Only one?' said Raziel. 'And what might that be? Mercy for your friends? A stay of execution for your family?'

'*No*, you rotten *pig*,' she snarled, suddenly erupting with anger. 'I want to know what happened to the rest of the Empire.'

She had been looking around the room for some time now, desperate to find something that might help her escape. And she had just noticed a small wooden frame on the wall – it blended in so well with Veraciter's certificates that she had almost missed it.

'Ah, the toy theatre,' said Raziel, 'well, as you can see, the good doctor here couldn't fit the whole thing into the frame, so he was obliged to chop it up. He kept the best part though, don't you think?'

'And how did you end up with it in the first place?' snapped Lucy, realising that her outer calm had just disappeared in a puff of smoke. 'That's my very own personal property.'

'Some of your possessions were confiscated by the police,' said Veraciter. 'But I managed to get them to hand it over as a personal trophy. I didn't tell *them* that of course. I said it might provide vital clues that would lead to the location of the missing children. They were quite eager to help after that, bless their little cotton socks.'

Lucy went to the wall and took the frame down – then she ran to where Veraciter was standing and kicked him hard in the shin. He creased up in pain, and as he reached down to rub the wounded leg she brought the frame crashing down on his head.

'Well if you like it so much,' she screamed, 'then why don't you take a closer look?'

'Miss Blake, *please*,' said Raziel, 'this is getting us nowhere.'

'No?' shouted Lucy. 'Well you won't mind if I try anyway, will you?'

She knocked the frame on the corner of Veraciter's desk, breaking the wooden edges away to release the one remaining part of the Empire. It was the flat piece of plywood that had formed the stage floor, complete with the peanut iris and the decorated emblem.

'I'm going now,' she said, running to the window and preparing to jump.

'I wouldn't do that if I were you,' smiled Raziel. 'Not unless you learned to fly whilst you were away on your little holiday?'

'No,' said Lucy, 'that was one thing I *didn't* learn.'

'Then come away from there and *give* me that,' said Raziel. He attempted to stand, but was hindered by his bandages and fell back into the chair.

'*Mag*,' said Lucy.

'*What?*' said Raziel, looking slightly puzzled.

'*Mag*,' repeated Lucy.

'*What?*' he said. 'Is this some kind of trick?'

'*Mag, mag, mag…*' hissed Lucy.

'What *are* you talking about you stupid child?'

'*Mag, mag, mag*,' said Lucy, angling the stage so that the iris faced out of the broken window. '*Phenuuuuuuu…*'

After the usual worrying delay, there came the familiar sound of thunder and a crackling of energy that signified great things at work – and *finally*, the delivery began. Lucy struggled to keep the fragment of the Empire steady as it bucked and tossed in her hands, but even so she couldn't help grinning as the stream of nuts exploded from the iris in a huge, noisy hailstorm.

'Oh my *God*,' squealed Veraciter. 'The Crested Eagle is parked directly under that window.'

'Then I hope you like nuts in your upholstery,' smiled Lucy.

She knocked the remaining glass out of the window frame and leaned out, searching for some sign of the Alvis. It had already disappeared though, beneath the biggest pile of peanuts Grimston had ever seen – and by the time Veraciter had begun to move she was already perched on the windowsill, ready to jump.

'No, not my lovely car,' cried Veraciter. '*Please* no.'

'Sorry,' grinned Lucy, 'but I have to go now.'

She smiled at Raziel and stepped out from the stone ledge as if it were a perfectly normal thing to be doing. Half a second later though, when she hit the pile of nuts, she realised it was anything but. The impact was a *lot* harder than she would expected and she sank waist-deep into the pile before pitching forwards and disappearing again, this time head first. Eventually though she managed to fight her way out, sliding rather unceremoniously towards ground level.

'You won't get away,' yelled Raziel, shouting down from the window.

'I think I just *did*,' shouted Lucy. She dusted herself down and tried to look casual as she extracted a peanut shell from her ear. Then she patted her arms and legs, just in case. It didn't *feel* like there were any broken bones, but the feeling of elation in the pit of her stomach just *might* have been masking the pain.

'But you gave a solemn promise not to escape,' screamed the angel.

'You're right,' she yelled back, 'but a promise requires honour on *both* sides, and you don't have any – and if you have any doubts on that score then perhaps you ought to ask poor Morana?'

Raziel hissed some incomprehensible curse as he tried to raise a leg onto the windowsill. For a moment, it looked as though he was going to jump down after her, but his injuries put paid to *that* particular idea.

'*Bruno?*' he screamed. 'Get back in here this instant.'

There was an enthusiastic smashing sound as the driver separated the office door from its hinges. By the time he made it to the window though, Lucy had already sprinted across the perfectly manicured lawns and reached the evergreen woods that surrounded the hospital.

'Get out there and *find* her,' hissed Raziel. 'I don't care if it takes you ten years, just *do* it.'

ΩχεχϽχϲ   448

'Oh, I'll *find* her alright,' snarled Bruno, 'and when I *do* I'm going to rip her pretty little head off and shove it right up her...'

'Just bring her to me *alive*,' hissed Raziel, 'and when *I'm* finished with her, *then* you can have your little bit of pleasure.'

Tales by the Sea

The next morning, Lucy woke to the sound of fairground rides and seagulls and the distant swish of the sea as it lapped the shore at low tide. Even so, it took her a moment to realise where she was, and how she had got here. It had been a good plan. It *must* have been good, because she had made her escape, then slept for a few hours and she was still breathing the air of freedom – even if it *did* smell of fried fish. Somewhere above her, the famous pier café was blowing warm air through a pipe – and that had kept the cold of night at bay. She knew exactly what Toby would say if he were here. It would be something about her smelling like a bag of chips – because if there was one thing he was impressed by, it was soggy newspaper stuffed with fried potato. But he *wasn't* here, was he? She had abandoned him at the Bright Byrde and now she had to get back there and make amends.

'*Hello*,' said a weedy voice. 'I know where you can get flat stones.'

'Do you?' said Lucy, wiping the sleep from her eyes. 'Well good for you.'

'Shall we go and get some then?' insisted the voice. It belonged to a small boy with red hair and freckles. He wore heavy black glasses and carried a brand-new satchel and was wearing a cap that still hadn't had the house badge ripped off – all that was missing was the row of assorted pens and pencils in his blazer pocket.

'*Well?*' he said. 'Do you want to come and get some?'

'Actually no,' said Lucy, 'I'm a bit busy at the moment.' She suddenly recalled the events of the previous day and struggled to hold the tears back.

'Busy running away?' said the boy, missing an excellent opportunity. He *could* have asked Lucy what she was busy *at*, bearing in mind that she was just sitting under the pier and staring out to sea.

'And what makes you think I'm running?' said Lucy.

'I *saw* you, yesterday,' said the boy. 'You came hurtling out of Saint Mallydick's with a piece of wood.'

'Oh,' said Lucy, 'you *saw* that, did you?'

'Yeah, and I followed you through the woods and across the squelchy marshes – and I was hiding in the reeds when you talked to those birds.'

Lucy blushed, embarrassed that the child had eavesdropped on such a personal moment. She had stopped to watch a skein of geese as they honked their way across the wetlands – and she'd found herself talking to them as if they understood. They hadn't bothered to stop and answer her though, and before she knew it their orderly vee formation had disappeared from view, leaving her with her *own* thoughts of freedom.

'So why *are* you running away?' enquired the boy.

'I'm *not*,' said Lucy, 'I'm enjoying a quiet time on the beach – or at least I was, until you turned up.'

'Yeah, but you *were* running,' insisted the freckled child.

'Well I'm not *now*, am I?' said Lucy, wiping another tear. 'So why don't you just push off and leave me alone?'

'Are you *sure* you don't want to go for some flat stones?' said the boy.

'*Look*, shouldn't you be in school or something?' sniffed Lucy. 'And isn't it a bit late in the year to be wearing shorts?'

'My mother makes me,' he replied. 'That's why I'm bunking off school, because my friends take the mickey out of me.'

'Nice friends you've got,' said Lucy.

'Yeah,' said the boy. 'And they nicked my special set of assorted pens and pencils too – my mum'll kill me when she finds out.'

'I *see*,' said Lucy, suppressing a reluctant smile.

'Was there something funny about my pencils?'

'Erm, *no*,' she grinned.

'Yeah, well *anyway*,' said the boy, '*you* can talk.'

'About pencils?' said Lucy.

'About wearing funny clothes – and *you* should be in school too.'

'Good point,' she admitted. 'I've lost track of things since I got back, and you're right – I *should* be in school.'

'But not dressed like that,' said the boy.

'I'm not wearing these by choice you know,' said Lucy, frowning down at the police-issue dungarees.

'I can't imagine anyone who would,' grinned the boy. 'Where have you been anyway? You said you came back from somewhere.'

'You wouldn't believe me if I told you,' said Lucy. 'But actually you've just given me a good idea.'

'You've changed your mind about the stones, haven't you?'

'No,' said Lucy, 'but I might come and look for some later. Firstly though, I'm going to show you a magic trick. What's your name?'

'Sniffy Morton,' said the boy.

'Right Sniffy, my name's Lucy, and I want you to close your eyes.'

'Alright,' said Sniffy obediently, 'but don't give me a Chinee burn, will you? I don't like those.'

'Neither do I,' said Lucy. 'Now, you're not looking are you?'

'No,' said Sniffy.

'Good – now whatever you hear and whatever happens you're to keep your eyes closed, otherwise the trick won't work.'

'Alright,' he agreed.

There was a whisper of *Empaaah*, which Sniffy almost didn't hear.

'Erm, hey, what was that?' he said nervously.

There was no reply. Lucy had gone, leaving Sniffy in charge of the final remaining fragment of the Empire. It was a bit of a chance, trusting him with so much, but it was a gamble she felt obliged to take.

'Erm, hello, are you there?' said Sniffy nervously. '*Hello?*'

His eyes were still tightly shut, but he was thinking of opening them any minute now. There was a limit to how long even *he* was willing to sit under a draughty pier with his eyes closed.

'Erm, Lucy? Are you there? I'm going to open them,' said Sniffy.

'Go on then,' she said.

Sniffy opened his eyes and gasped, unable to believe the transformation. Lucy was wearing a clean red dress and a long, dark coat that made her look slightly sinister.

'Wow,' he said, 'just wait till I tell my friends about *this*.'

'Erm, *no*,' said Lucy, trying not to sound too worried. 'I don't want you to do that, not just yet anyway. You can tell them anything you like once I'm safe, but for now we need to keep this a secret, alright?'

'Secrets cost money,' said Sniffy.

'Do they?' sighed Lucy. 'There's a price on everything these days, isn't there? Alright then, I'll pay, but it'll have to be with a story.'

'Nah, don't like 'em,' said Sniffy, 'they're boring.'

'And how do you know that if you haven't heard it?' asked Lucy. 'They can't *all* be boring, can they?'

'Tell me how you did the trick,' said Sniffy, 'was the coat buried in the sand?'

'So where was it before I buried it?' said Lucy. 'You followed me from the hospital remember, and I didn't have it then, did I?'

'Oh yeah,' said Sniffy, 'so how *did* you do it?'

'Easy,' said Lucy, 'my stepmother told me I couldn't keep the coat, so I made arrangements to keep it somewhere safe.'

'Where?' he asked. 'Under the pier?'

'I left it in a special secret world that nobody else knows about,' smiled Lucy. 'It's just like this one, only there are no people in it.'

'Wow,' he gasped, 'so you got the coat from a shop in this other world?'

'You're not listening, *are* you?' said Lucy, 'I took it there myself – but now you come to mention it, that's not a bad idea – getting things from the shops I mean. If there are no shopkeepers then it's not really stealing, is it?'

'Is that the story then?' said Sniffy. 'Because if that's the best you can do I'm off to find my mates and tell them all about you.'

'I thought you didn't like them?' said Lucy. 'Didn't they steal your pens?'

'That was before I knew about your secret world,' said Sniffy. 'They'll be my absolute best friends when I tell them about that. I'll probably even get my pencils back.'

'I see,' sighed Lucy, 'well in that case I suppose we'd better go for a walk.'

'And get some flat stones?'

'If you insist,' said Lucy.

'*See?*' grinned Sniffy. 'I *knew* you wanted to get some skimming stones – only they're called *flatties*, right?'

Lucy nodded and smiled, happy to be free again and equally content to join him in a spot of stone throwing. In fact, she realised, it was the perfect cover – her pursuers would never dream of finding her dawdling at the water's edge and skipping stones.

'It's good this, isn't it?' said Sniffy. He'd managed to bounce a stone twice before it sank.

'Yes, it is,' agreed Lucy, skimming a 'triple' out across the oily-smooth surface. As the stone sank, a shadow passed over them, and they raised their eyes – a pair of Fulmars was wheeling above them in the clear blue sky.

'That reminds me,' said Lucy, suddenly enjoying the feel of sand between her toes, 'I promised to tell you a tale, didn't I?'

'Yes, you did,' said Sniffy. 'What's it about?'

'It's called The Legend of the Ornithopter,' said Lucy, selecting a stone.

'And what's one of *those*?' Sniffy asked impatiently. 'Is it what gave you the scratched face? Or the thing that bit your finger off? Or is it…'

'Well, if you'll *shut up* for a moment I'll *tell* you,' said Lucy.

She waited for a gap in the waves and pitched the stone with all her might, judging the angle perfectly. It skimmed over the surface of the water, skipping once, twice, and finally three times before finally succumbing to the pressing call of gravity. And as Lucy began to tell her tale, it sank without trace, in the flat, cool waters of the Cherman Sea.

Bentley Priory – Private Dick

'Would you mind awfully if I had another look through your window?' asked Lucy.

'Be my guest,' said the shabby man seated behind the desk. 'Are you hoping to see anyone in particular?'

Lucy moved the filthy lace curtain as gently as possible and peered into the street below – there was nobody there *again*. All the way here she'd been plagued by the sound of footsteps, but every time she turned around they had faded away to nothing. It was like being followed by an invisible camel with a passion for carpet slippers.

'I'll know them when I see them,' said Lucy, wondering if she'd done the right thing in coming to this place. She'd found the address on a printed card that had been nestling deep in the pockets of the borrowed coat. And she'd distinctly remembered the name 'Bentley Priory' from the newspaper.

'If you do see who you're looking for, be sure and let me know,' said the man. 'I'll come and have a look myself.'

Lucy had another squint, just to be certain, and this time there *was* someone there. It was Sniffy with a group of his so-called friends – and they were just about to walk past a huge advertisement hoarding. She was pleased to see her new acquaintance had his pencils back, but unfortunately that could mean only one thing. The boy with the freckles had told his friends about her, and quite possibly re-ignited a trail that she hoped had gone cold.

Suddenly, the advertisement burst into song:-

Yakky, yakky,
yakky, yakky Morto,
If you haven't even used it yet
then we really think you aughto...

'Oh no,' she sighed, 'not *another* singing advert – the one they had near the railway station was bad enough, screaming about Snogg's sauce at all hours.'

'*Tell* me about it,' he said, dropping his unshaven face into his hands and sticking a little finger in each ear. 'Let me know when it stops, will you?'

As the group of boys disappeared, Lucy breathed a sigh of relief. They *hadn't* been following her after all. There was more to come from the automatic advertisement though, which had now noticed someone else walking past. As the woman with the pram drew level with the movement detector, the Lectric speaker burst into life – this time blaring out a different but equally annoying, message :-

Yakky, yakky,
yakky, yakky, yakky
Come on now,
and give it a go,
it really isn't tacky...
(despite what you might have heard to the contrary)...

'What on *earth* is a Yakky Morto?' said Lucy, reading the poster again, to make sure there was no mistake.

"Visit Grimston's newest attraction…"
"Now showing at the Winter Gardens..."
"This is the one to get all the family talking..."
"And we mean that literally…"

'Believe me; you *really* don't want to know. It's just some silly scheme designed to part idiots from the contents of their wallets. I can tell you about it if you like, but I think you might have more important things on your mind.'

'Oh?' said Lucy. 'And how do you know that?' She remembered now where she'd seen him before. His car had been parked across the street from Byron's laboratory – and it was *his* coat she was wearing.

'I'm a detective,' he said, 'so I can usually work these things out – and when a young girl comes into my office and starts acting suspiciously, I tend to put two and two together and get five. It's what we in the detecting trade call a 'nose for the job'.'

Lucy examined him closely for the first time since she'd entered the office and found him hiding a coffee cup behind a cushion. He hadn't shaved for days and his eyes were sunk so deeply into their sockets she doubted whether he'd bothered to sleep either. With the addition of an old-fashioned hat like Inspector Trembley's, he would have made the perfect film detective.

'Two and two makes *five?*' laughed Lucy. 'They'd *love* you where I've just been – they'd probably make you a professor of advanced mathematics.'

'At the hospital?' asked the detective.

'Of course not,' said Lucy, wondering how he'd guessed. 'I erm, visited a place called the Braneskule.'

'Not in Grimston then?'

'No,' she said, 'not really.'

The detective studied Lucy's face for a moment, and then focused his attention on the coat. He'd recognised it immediately of course, but chose to ignore the discovery, along with the scarred cheek and the not-quite-complete hand.

'I'm Bentley Priory,' he said. 'You might have noticed my name written on the door as you came in.'

'I did,' said Lucy, 'but it said *entley Pri ry ivate dick.*'

'Some of the letters got rubbed off,' said Bentley.

'So I noticed,' she added, 'but even if they hadn't, it's still quite a strange name, isn't it?'

'How kind of you to say.'

'No, I didn't mean it like that,' said Lucy, squirming slightly.

'Nobody ever does,' said Bentley. 'Have you got an appointment?'

'Erm, no I haven't,' said Lucy, 'but why does your door say private dick?'

'It's better than the alternative,' said Bentley. 'Now, shall we see about that appointment?'

He leaned towards the box on the desk, which, judging by the number of frayed wires sticking out of it was some kind of Lectric device. It appeared to have been involved in an argument with something very much bigger and sharper than itself, so it wasn't really in peak condition. He seemed oblivious to the dangers of Lectrocution though and selected a coloured button, apparently at random. He pressed it quite hard, and the machine emitted a harsh, metallic squeal, like some poor soul having their gold-rimmed spectacles filed down with a cheese grater.

Amazingly though, a blue light came on.

Zzzz.

'Philandra? *Hello*? This is Bentley on erm, yes, blue. Are you there?'

'Erm, there was nobody there when I came in Mr. Priory.'

'Please, call me Bentley,' he said. 'Everyone else does – at least the polite ones do. *Hello? Philandra?*' he shouted, trying another button. 'Are you there? I'm on red now.'

Zzzz. Zzzz.

'Philandra? For *God's* sake woman, where are you?'

'Why don't you try the yellow switch?' suggested Lucy.

'*Yellow?*' laughed Bentley, getting gradually more enthusiastic with his button pressing. 'Don't be *ridiculous* – nobody is *ever* on yellow.'

Zzzz. Zzzz. Zzzz.

Lucy studied the path taken by the dozens of wires that sprouted from the back of the Lectric intercom machine. They snaked across the top of the desk and coiled down the leg, then looped their way around a waste-paper basket before finally ending up in the corner of the room. And that was where the trail ended – the bare wires were connected to absolutely nothing.

'She's not *out* there,' insisted Lucy.

'Oh,' said Bentley, 'do you know Philandra then?'

'*Know* her?' said Lucy, raising an eyebrow.

'Well you must at least know what she looks like,' said Bentley, 'otherwise how would you know she's not out there?'

'*Nobody* is out there,' she laughed. 'It's like a cowboy picture I went to see once – the whole town was completely deserted and there were these great big weeds tumbling down the street.'

'Ah, it's got as bad as that has it? Oh well, she did mention that she might be nipping out to the heel bar – something about having a key cut...'

'There's been nobody out there for *months*,' insisted Lucy. 'They'd have left a trail in the dust otherwise – the windows are filthy and the floor is all covered in soot – it looks like you've had a bird in the chimney.'

'Soot?' grinned Bentley. 'Oh, don't go worrying about that – I'm waiting until I've got enough to make a diamond.'

'Well don't go making one on Philandra's account,' said Lucy. 'I *told* you, she's gone.'

'*Ah,*' said Bentley, his face suddenly filled with sorrow. 'So the beautiful Philandra has finally left — she was always threatening to do that, especially when I didn't pay her regularly. Women can be so picky, can't they?'

'Erm, yes, well I'm sure she'll be back soon,' said Lucy, realising how badly it was affecting the detective.

'Do you really think so?' he said, looking slightly more cheerful.

'She's probably just popped out,' said Lucy.

'There you are, you see? I *told* you she was just out for a moment.'

Bentley went to press the yellow button, despite having assured her that nobody was ever on yellow. Lucy put her hand over the switch though — she'd seen enough of the amazing intercom to last a lifetime.

'Erm, ye-es,' said Bentley, realising what she was trying to say. 'Perhaps I'll give her a call after lunch. Now, what can I do for you? Have you come to deliver my cheese sandwich?'

'No,' said Lucy, 'but I'll bring you one next time if you like.'

'Then what do you want?' said Bentley. 'Can't you see I'm busy?'

Lucy scanned the room, eager to spot something that wasn't covered in half an inch of dust. There was a rather bored-looking tortoise on the desk that was being used as a paperweight, and *that* looked fairly shiny.

'Erm, I can see you're rushed off your feet,' said Lucy, having second thoughts. After all, the poor fool hadn't even recognised his own coat, had he, so what possible use was he going to be?

'No, wait, don't go,' said Bentley, thumbing through a diary. 'I can fit you in — I've got a window — I know that, because someone dressed in a blue overall keeps charging me ten bob to clean it.' He threw the diary over his shoulder and it disappeared into some dark corner, never to be seen again.

'Here, hold this,' he said, handing Lucy the tortoise. Then he started shuffling through the papers it had been holding in place.

'His name is Arcadia by the way.'

'Whose name?' said Lucy.

'The tortoise of course, who else? *Right*, now I just need to find a blank case form and then I can take some details.'

He leafed through a pile of brown, dog-eared folders, moving them with tantalising slowness so that Lucy was able to read the titles. As each was placed gently to one side, she realised that she *had* come to the right place after all. If anyone could sort out what was happening in Grimston it was the famous Bentley Priory.

"Case of the Nose in the Mince."
"Case of the Partially Constructed Pier."
"Case of the Missing Wife."
"Case of the Pax Beetle."
"Case of the Missing Bicycle Parts."

'Case of erm, the erm, hmm, I can't make out the title on this one,' he said, pitching the offending folder into the waste-paper basket.

'Case of the Lizard Skin Folio?' suggested Lucy.

She walked over to the window again and squinted into the street, as if narrowing her eyes might protect her from being spotted. Someone was lurking in the shadows, but she couldn't see enough to identify them.

'Lizard skin?' said Bentley. 'I don't remember that – was it one of mine?'

'No, it's alright,' said Lucy, 'it was just my little joke.'

'*Very*,' said Bentley, 'can you warn me next time so I know when to laugh?'

'Sorry,' said Lucy.

'Right – here's a blank form – let's take some details shall we? Name?'

'Lucy Blake.'

'Not yours,' said the detective. 'The name of the missing party.'

'How do you know there's a missing party?' asked Lucy.

'There always is,' said Bentley. '*Name?*'

'Fenny Savage,' she replied.

'*Ah*,' said Bentley, flopping the file closed.

'Erm, what are you doing?'

'There's no point taking any further details,' said Bentley. 'The police are out looking for that girl – it was in the paper.'

'You read the Daily Phibber then?'

'Of *course*,' he grinned. 'I scan it every day, with religious fervour. Where *else* could you find so many bizarre stories packed into such a small space? Some of my very best cases started off as three-line articles in that paper.'

'Well *that's* good,' said Lucy, 'because they mentioned Fenny too.'

'They did,' said Bentley, 'but I make a point of never taking on a case where the police are involved – I steer *well* clear of those.'

'But the police aren't going to find her,' said Lucy.

'Oh?' said Bentley. 'And why not?'

'Because it's not the usual kind of disappearance,' said Lucy. 'That's why I came to you – the article in the Phibber said you had extraordinary talents.'

'And an extraordinary bank overdraft,' said Bentley. 'I haven't had a decent case in months – but even so, I can't get involved in...'

'Police cases?' Lucy finished. 'Yes, but they won't find her – I *know* they won't.'

'*Ah*,' said Bentley, 'now that sounds like inside information.'

'Maybe,' said Lucy, 'so will you do it, just for me?'

'Give me one good reason,' said Bentley.

'It's fate,' she replied, 'you know, the *coat* and everything?'

'Ah, yes,' said Bentley, 'I was wondering when you'd mention that. I hope you've been taking good care of it.'

'Of course,' said Lucy. 'I stored it in a *very* special place.'

'Alright,' said Bentley reluctantly. 'I'll take some details – but I'm not promising anything.'

'Brilliant.'

'Name?' said Bentley. 'Ah, no, wait, we've done that.'

'Right, *suspect*?' he said.

'Pardon?' said Lucy.

'The person you suspect of having done the deed. There always *is* one, even if it's just a vague notion.'

'Veraciter,' said Lucy, after a moment's thought.

'Ah,' said Bentley, 'the mental doctor.'

'You know him then?' said Lucy.

'Who doesn't?' said Bentley. 'You can't miss him – he drives around in a whacking great turquoise Crested Eagle.'

'Actually it's peacock-blue,' said Lucy.

'*Is* it now? So you know him as well, do you?'

'Of course not,' grinned Lucy, 'I just made his name up at random.'

'Very funny,' said Bentley, 'and why do you suspect *him* of all people?'

Lucy wanted to say it was because the seats in his car smelt of giant scarabs and he had walnuts for eyes, but instead, she told the truth. It was *good* to tell the truth occasionally, just so her poor brain could remember what it felt like.

'He's sinister,' said Lucy, 'and so are the people around him.'

'There's someone else then?' said Bentley.

'Someone called Raziel,' said Lucy. She wanted to tell Bentley that Raziel was the real villain, but didn't dare, fearing that he might need something slightly more solid to start with – and catching Raziel would be like trying to sieve the lumps out of moonlight.

'Hmm,' said Bentley. '*Raziel*, you say? Never heard of him. I thought I knew everyone in Grimston but that's a new name for sure. Spell it for me just to be certain – and pass me that jotter, will you? The one labelled Universal Mysteries.'

'*Is* it?' said Lucy, unable to hide her surprise. She passed the book over to the detective, pausing just long enough to confirm the title – and there it was, written in smudged green ink. 'Funnily enough, that's exactly what Creeps said about arithmetic – he reckoned it was one of the universal mysteries.'

'Creeps?' said Bentley. 'He sounds like a teacher.'

'He is,' laughed Lucy. Whatever teachers were called it seemed that they were instantly recognisable by their names.

'Right,' said Bentley, licking his pencil, 'what was that name again?'

As Lucy spelled the angel's name, she got the strangest feeling that Raziel was aware of what she was doing. Or at least that he knew she was saying his name. There was something else too – a deep feeling of guilt, because she had given Bentley the name without warning him what Raziel was like. But if she told him *that* then she'd have to tell him everything. Sometimes, Byron had said, innocence was the best form of defence – and then he'd gone and spoiled it all by adding that it was also a good way to end up being slaughtered.

'When was the girl last seen?' enquired Bentley. 'No, wait, don't tell me. She was with a group of her friends on the pier. I know – I read it in the paper.'

'It won't help,' said Lucy. 'You remember that inside information you thought I had?'

'Erm, ye-es,' said Bentley.

'Well I know where Fenny is – *that's* how I know the police won't find her. What *I* want to know is how she got there, and more to the point I want to know why the place is there to begin with.'

'Ah, now that *is* different,' said Bentley grinning from ear to ear. 'I'm beginning to see why you came to me with this case. And I suppose any further tiny little niblets of information would be out of the question?'

'Of course,' said Lucy. 'I read somewhere that you like a challenge.'

'I do,' said Bentley, 'but let's not stretch the point *too* far – now, is there anything else you wanted to know?'

'Erm, yes,' said Lucy. She described the Assiah gateway in detail, conveniently leaving out the bit about how she'd found it in her mother's photograph album and then used it to travel to another world.

'I see,' said Bentley, 'so what exactly do you want to know about it?'

'Where it's being kept,' said Lucy, 'and then I need to get it back.'

'So it's yours then?'

'It belonged to my mother.'

'I see. And do you have even the remotest idea of where it might be?'

'Somewhere safe,' said Lucy, repeating Morana's taunt.

'Now *that's* what I like to hear,' grinned Bentley, 'good solid clues – I find there's nothing like them to get a case like this one solved nice and early. Now, are you *sure* there's nothing else you can tell me?'

'All I know is that it was put somewhere safe,' said Lucy.

'Right,' said Bentley, 'and who told you that?'

'Morana Fay.'

'Ah,' said Bentley, with a faraway look, 'the dear lovely Morana.'

'Do you know her as well then?'

'Not as well as I'd *like* to,' said Bentley, waggling one eyebrow.

The corners of Lucy's mouth turned down slightly – an involuntary reflection of her innermost sadness. Moments later, her chin quivered almost imperceptibly, and a single tear dripped onto her scarred cheek. Bentley noticed it immediately, which was surprising, because even the most obvious things seemed to pass him by – as if he was tuned to a slightly different frequency than everyone else.

'Have I said something wrong?' he asked.

'No,' sobbed Lucy, recalling Morana's final agonising moments.

'It's alright,' said Bentley, offering her a hankie. 'You can tell me.'

'I don't think I can,' said Lucy, 'not just yet anyway.'

'Alright,' he said, 'whenever you're ready. Now, was there anything else?'

'Erm, yes,' said Lucy, recalling the words Morana had called with her dying breath. 'I need to find out what *Exner Heelo* means.'

'*Ex-ner-hee-low,*' said Bentley, writing the phrase in his mysterious school jotter. 'Alright, I'll see what I can do.'

'Is that all the information you need?' asked Lucy.

'What else could there possibly be?' he smiled broadly. 'I don't *really* think your shoe size is all that relevant, but if you think it would help.'

'You're the expert,' said Lucy.

'That's right, I *am*,' laughed Bentley, 'and expert advice costs money.'

'*Ah,*' said Lucy.

'Although I don't expect you'll *have* much of that,' he said, 'what with being a nine-year-old?'

'I'm thirteen,' said Lucy crossly. 'I'm just a bit small for my age.'

'Nine, thirteen, whatever,' he said. 'It makes no odds, does it? And don't worry about the money – next time you come to visit, just make sure you bring me a cheese sandwich, and if it's a good one I might just have some information for you.'

'A cheese sandwich?' said Lucy.

'The very thing,' said Bentley. 'Now, are there any *more* questions?'

'Erm, ye-es, why is your tortoise called Arcadia?'

'Oh *that,*' said Bentley, 'well it's a sort of play on words – oh, and one other thing,' he said, suddenly looking very serious.

'What?' said Lucy, expecting a vital piece of information.

'That sandwich you're going to bring.'

'Ye-es?' said Lucy.

'I like white bread, but not the kind with round corners,' he said, 'and I don't want it smothering with great loads of onion either.'

The Eighth Hour
of the Night

Lucy had cried quite often since returning to Grimston – usually when taken by surprise in a quiet moment, the tears flooding out of her in an uncontrollable torrent. She *could* be strong, and frequently was, but every so often she glimpsed the wall of circumstance that was building up around her and began to feel trapped.

And now, in a place where she'd least expected it, the tears were falling once again – only this time it wasn't herself she was feeling sorry for. She'd made her way to the loft in the hope of seeing a friendly face and to hear the anxious beat of hundreds of pairs of wings. Instead, she found the whole place in confusion – the fabric of the building had been smashed beyond repair and every bird except one slaughtered in the vilest and most brutal way she could imagine.

Without looking, she knew who the survivor would be. She could hear him, scratching around in his roost box – she even imagined that she could sense him thinking. There were just two things occupying his tiny spirit mind – the freedom of the skies and the fate of Lilith, his mate.

'Can I help you, dearie?' said a frail-sounding voice.

Lucy jumped as the damaged door scraped open. Her gaze darted back and forth like a shuttle, taking in the woman's kindly, grey features, then returning to the blood, the feathers, and the message of hate they were sending.

And suddenly, there was another level of panic.

'It wasn't me,' she said desperately, 'it *wasn't,* – I wouldn't do it.'

'Shush dear,' said the woman with a compassionate smile. 'I know you wouldn't – I *know.*' She pulled Lucy's face into her breast and stroked her hair, and in the midst of this sadness, all Lucy could think of was the fact that her tears were dampening the stranger's blouse.

'I came here the other day,' she said. 'I was looking at the birds – and I spoke to Harry.'

'The other day?' said the woman, regarding Lucy with slightly more suspicion. 'No chick, I don't think so. The ruin you see here was created a good while ago – weeks ago, it was.'

Lucy took another look at the carnage and burst into tears again. They were all so beautiful. They *had* all been so beautiful, and now they were gone, flying in some other sky, far beyond life.

'Anyway,' said the woman, 'it doesn't matter *when* you came, does it? Why don't you come to the house? I'm sure Harold would be pleased to see you.'

'Won't he be coming up here then?' asked Lucy.

'I don't think so, luvvie. I can't imagine anything that might bring him back into the loft now – not even if it was filled to the brim with birds.'

'I see,' said Lucy, picking up a single flight feather, 'then we should go and see *him*, shouldn't we?'

'Yes chick, we should – but *prepare* yourself. All this upset has taken a toll on his health – I'm Avis, by the way.'

Lucy introduced herself in turn and followed Avis down a winding path towards the house, noticing on the way how bare all the trees were. So Lily had told the truth – she *had* been away for a long time – and time obviously flowed quicker in Grimston than it did in Assiah.

'Sorry it's such a tip,' said Avis.

Lucy smiled. She had often seen the houses as they passed on the train, and had always believed them to be derelict.

'Harold?'

Avis called through the back door, but the kitchen beyond it was empty.

'*Harold?* There's a girl to see you. She's been to the loft and seen the birds.'

Lucy was amazed that people could actually live in such a mess. The house contained enough bric-a-brac to fill a dozen junk shops – with the leftovers being sufficient to keep Bumblebee's auction rooms going at full tilt for a whole month. Ah *yes*, thought Lucy, *Bumblebee*, that rotten stinking liar – someone *else* she wanted to have a word with.

'This is Harold's collection,' said Avis, 'and as you can see he's a bit mad on birds. Sometimes I think he only married me because of my name – it means 'bird' you know.'

'Yes, I know,' said Lucy, 'it's Lattinn, isn't it?'

Everywhere she looked there were paintings of birds, photographs of birds, photographs of Harry with birds, bird trophies, and bird rosettes. There were even stuffed birds imprisoned under glass domes, although she couldn't imagine him having anything to do with such an abhorrent idea.

'Harold? Are you awake love? It's the girl.'

Lucy followed Avis into the front parlour where they were greeted by even more bird paraphernalia – or perhaps it was parrot-phernalia? She smiled briefly at the thought, but her jaw dropped when she saw Harry in what was obviously his favourite chair. He was slumped right down, his arms hanging over the sides like they belonged to a rag doll – and all the light had gone from his eyes.

'I told you, didn't I?' whispered Avis. 'It's affected him badly.'

'No it hasn't,' insisted Harry quietly. 'I can always get more birds.'

He sounded as though he meant it, but his eyes gave away the lie – Lucy always knew when people were lying.

'I knew you'd come back,' he said unsteadily.

'I always intended to,' said Lucy.

'Have you returned because you understand?'

'No,' admitted Lucy, wondering how much she should reveal. 'But I *am* beginning to see the world in a new light.'

'*Are* you indeed?' chuckled Harry. 'Then we have something to celebrate – would you like some tea?'

Lucy nodded, and without waiting to be asked Avis went through to the kitchen to prepare the feast.

'She knows,' said Harry, as Avis left the room.

'Knows what?' said Lucy.

'When to go and make tea,' he said, sitting up slightly. 'When you've been together for as long as we have it gets like telepathy. You know what the other one's thinking.'

'And Avis knew that you wanted to be alone?' said Lucy.

'Just for a moment,' he said.

The Eighth Hour of the Night

There was an awkward silence whilst Lucy considered what to say. Harry smiled and gently took the feather she was holding, rubbing it against his cheek – then he began to cry.

'I've seen the loft,' said Lucy.

'I know,' whispered Harry. He slumped into the seat again, and Lucy began to wonder if she'd done the right thing. He had tried to put the darkness of slaughter behind him, and she had brought it all back, like a cat bringing a dead mouse to the kitchen door.

'Sorry,' she said.

'Don't be,' said Harry, 'it's not your fault.'

'But I still feel responsible,' said Lucy.

Harry smiled and looked her up and down, as if considering purchasing her in an auction.

'From the marks on your face I'd say you've had an interesting time.'

'You could say that,' agreed Lucy. 'Has anything happened here, apart from erm…'

'I had a new chick,' said Harry. 'You would have liked her.'

'*Would* have?' asked Lucy.

'She came out of her nesting box too early,' said Harry, 'so the others pecked her to death, – they were jealous of her, see?'

'Why?' said Lucy. 'How could an animal become so jealous that they'd want to kill another?'

'She was too beautiful,' said Harry. His eyes glazed over at the thought of that one death amongst hundreds, but then he recalled why he was telling the young girl the story. 'Remember when I showed you that new-born chick and you said it was beautiful?'

'Yes,' said Lucy, 'I remember.'

'I told you they was always ugly, *didn't* I?' said Harry. 'But I was wrong, because this new chick was luminous right from the start. She dazzled 'em all with her brilliance and they hated her for it. She had bright feathers too, right from birth, and they knew that when she moulted them off and got her adult plumage, she'd be the most radiant bird in the loft. Perhaps even the most beautiful in the world.'

'So they murdered her?' said Lucy. She was desperate to hear the answer, but Harry had slumped. He was sound asleep with his mouth wide open – and he was slobbering all over his tatty pullover.

'He's exhausted,' said Avis, returning with a tray of tea things. 'I think we'd better let him rest.'

As she poured the tea, Lucy turned her attention to the huge painting that hung above the mantelpiece.

'That's his favourite,' said Avis, 'it's called The Annunciation.'

'It's amazing,' said Lucy. She was mesmerised by the image of the angel, but at the same time she wondered why it had just a single pair of wings. Then she realised – it was because the artist had probably never seen one.

'Does Harry like angels then?' she said.

'I couldn't say,' said Avis, 'but he certainly loves birds.'

Lucy looked again, trying to see the picture through Harry's eyes. There was a thin ray of light shining like a message from heaven – and it was passing right through the middle of a pure white bird.

'It's beautiful,' she said.

'It *is*, duck, but that's not what's on your mind, is it?'

Lucy considered the dozens of questions that were floating around inside her head – so many in fact that they were fighting with each other for the opportunity to dance across her lips. In the end, the least important of them sneaked out of her mouth whilst the others were still squabbling.

'Can I sleep here tonight please?' she asked.

'Of *course* you can,' said Avis, 'you look as though you need it.'

Lucy had been unable to sleep, and although the sun had not risen, she found herself in the garden, walking barefoot on the dew-laden grass. She knew the birds had all but gone from the loft, but was still drawn towards it, as if Lucifer was calling her name.

The scene inside had changed overnight though. The rotting bodies had been removed and the clean feathers gathered into a respectful pile. The bloodstained ones were collected up too, but they were heaped unceremoniously next to a shovel – and obviously intended for burial.

Lucy went to Lucifer's box and listened. There was nothing but silence.

'Are you there?' she said aloud.

There was no reply, just a creak from the broken framework of the loft as it shifted in the breeze. But there *was* no breeze – it was early morning and the wind still hadn't stirred – only pale moonbeams disturbed the air.

'*Lucifer?*' she hissed. 'Is that you?'

There was another creak, this time slightly louder, and Lucy knew exactly where it was coming from. She bent down and swept the filth-strewn floor with her hands, searching for the recessed ring in the trapdoor. There was yet another creak as she located it, and then silence as she lifted the trap.

'*Ah,*' she said, staring into the hole, 'well I didn't expect to be seeing *you* two again.'

There was no reply, just the sad, blinking eyes of the creatures she had last seen perching on wardrobes at Bumblebee's auction rooms – or rather throwing themselves off.

'*Well?* What are you doing here?' she asked.

The moonlight was so weak and the pit was so dark that she could only make out their heads and shoulders – the rest was hidden by the shadows. But what she *could* see of them told a harrowing tale – they were drawn and thin, ghostly almost, one of them much more so than the other.

'What are we *doing?*' said the strongest-looking one. 'We are squatting in stinking spirit-filth and waiting to die – *that* is what we are doing.'

'I *see,*' said Lucy, 'and, erm, who exactly *are* you? Only everyone I meet these days seems to think I know you already.'

'I am Thomax,' said the stronger creature, 'and this is my companion Hanoziz – and together we have the honour of serving under Narcoriel.'

'And should I know him?' said Lucy. 'This, erm, Narcoriel?'

'He is an angel of the eighth hour of the night,' said Thomax, 'and we both have the honour to serve under him.'

'Yes, you mentioned that,' said Lucy, 'and what else was it? Something about waiting to die?'

'We await the dark, dreamless night where nothing stirs,' said Thomax.

'I *see,*' said Lucy, 'and why did you choose *this* place?'

'You think to *question* me?' hissed Thomax. 'Are you so enamoured of your power already?'

'Erm, no, *sorry,*' said Lucy, looking a shade embarrassed. 'It's just that this all seems a little bizarre – but then again so does everything else these days.'

'Our likenesses were stolen by a fiend who carries the power of lightning in a box,' hissed Thomax. 'And from that instant our joint fates were sealed.'

'You mean photographs, don't you?' said Lucy. 'Are you talking about the smudger from the Phibber?'

'The *same*,' said Thomax. 'I speak of Tenby Yates – the *executioner*.'

'Are you *serious*?' laughed Lucy. 'You think you might be dying just because he took your photograph?'

'Just so,' said Thomax, his eyes blinking white in the shadows.

'But that's just a load of silly superstition,' said Lucy.

'Is it?' said Thomax. 'Then we must be imagining our approaching fate.'

He tried to climb out of the hole but slipped back and put out his hand for Lucy's help. She pulled him up and then stepped back, screaming silently into her hand as he in turn helped Hanoziz. She thought she'd imagined it when her hand seemed to slip through him, but now it was all too clear why he'd seemed so insubstantial.

'I can see through you,' she mumbled, her hand still covering her mouth.

'As I said Lucy Blake – we are dying.'

'And the camera did all that?'

'I'm afraid so,' said Thomax. As he spoke, Lucy could see the words forming in his throat – not on the surface of his neck, but deep inside, as if he were an automaton made from glass. Everything about him was visible – the pumping of his heart, the squeezing and relaxing of his arteries, the expansion and contraction of his lungs – every aspect of his physical being was laid out for her inspection.

'Hanoziz was photographed first,' he explained, 'and most frequently, so he is the weaker of us, and the least visible.'

'So I see,' said Lucy. She was going to add 'so I *don't* see', but it seemed unnecessarily cruel. And of course there was still the small matter of the information she needed from them. 'So tell me,' she said. 'Who are you, and where are you from?'

'You already know who we are,' said Thomax. 'I have *told* you our names, and even told you our allegiance.'

'Then *what* are you?' said Lucy, suddenly frustrated with his pickiness.

'We are the same as you,' said Thomax. 'Simple flesh and blood.'

'Really?' said Lucy. 'I don't think so, do you? You might be flesh and blood, but you're not simple.'

'Just as *you* are not ordinary,' said Thomax.

'Raziel keeps saying the same thing,' said Lucy, 'but I *still* don't know what's going on.'

'And nor *should* you,' said Thomax.

'You don't seem very surprised that I know about Raziel,' said Lucy.

'Why should I?' said Thomax. 'You were both at the auction – it was only a matter of time before you met once again. And Raziel, as you have probably discovered, is very resourceful – he is also *very* dangerous.'

'I've noticed,' said Lucy.

'Good,' said Thomax. 'Now tell me, have you *been* anywhere recently?' He tried to make the question sound like an innocent enquiry, but Lucy knew there was only one place he could mean.

'I *might* have,' she said.

'Then you have exposed the means of transfer – that is good. And from your reluctance to answer directly I see you have also discovered the use of caution – that is also good. You will need your wits about you, Lucy Blake, if you are to be successful against them.'

'Them? Who are *them?*'

'You will know soon enough,' said Thomax. 'In the meantime it's best that you discover things for yourself. You will find that the universe has a habit of unwinding at its own pace.'

'So everybody keeps telling me,' said Lucy. 'I just wish there was some way of speeding it up a bit.'

'And what would that achieve?' said Thomax. 'In the grand scheme of things it does not matter if you discover yourself in two weeks time or two years time. From a point ten billion years in the future the two instances will be inseparable.'

'I can hardly wait,' said Lucy.

Thomax smiled, but it was an expression he obviously wasn't accustomed to. It looked as though he'd just sat down on a sharp metal spike – but was far too polite to say anything.

'They *did* say the Architect Elect had a sense of humour,' he said, 'and now I have seen it for myself.'

'Oh, so they *said* that, did they?' said Lucy.

'Which is just as well,' said Thomax. 'You will need it, if you are to succeed where we have failed.'

'You were sent here to retrieve the *light*, weren't you?' said Lucy.

'Were we?' said Thomax.

'You were sent, just as Raziel was,' said Lucy. 'So there must be opposing sides, mustn't there? Otherwise they'd only need to send one person.'

'Not necessarily,' said Hanoziz. The weaker angel sounded like a thin, reedy reflection of Thomax, as if his image and his voice had been bounced around an infinite number of mirrors.

'Oh, he *speaks,* does he?' said Lucy.

'Don't be insolent,' groaned the weaker angel. 'You must show respect for your elders — has nobody ever taught you that? Surely good breeding has a place in this world, just as it has in...'

'*Hanoziz*?' said Thomax. 'Be *silent* and remember our instructions.'

'Ah,' grumbled Hanoziz, 'yes, the famous *instructions* — how could we ever forget *those*? How could we possibly overlook the orders which have brought us to the very brink of death, when we should rightly have lived for aeons?'

'We chose to come of our own free will and accord,' said Thomax, 'or have you forgotten? We came for the good of heaven, not to improve our own lot — try to remember that.'

'So, reading between the lines,' said Lucy, 'there are two groups trying to get hold of the *light*. Am I right? Otherwise you'd be working *with* Raziel and not against him, wouldn't you?'

'Two groups?' laughed Hanoziz, 'if only things were that simple.' He clutched at his side, or at least he *would* have, if his hand hadn't passed through his body. There was a strange stirring of his internal organs as the flesh from his arm negotiated its way through his inner being. It moved the palpitating masses this way and that, never actually splitting them, but stretching them to the point where it looked as though they might.

'I think I'm beginning to understand,' said Lucy, suddenly feeling ill at the sight of their pulsating bodies.

'Then at least we have achieved something by our efforts,' said Thomax. His transparent eyes flickered slightly, and when she followed their direction,

Lucy saw the loft door opening. The sun had just risen, and their visitor was ushered inside by a pale pink light and the growing sound of birdsong.

'I see you've found each other again,' said Avis. She stood there smiling, as if the discovery of foul-smelling angels in her husband's pigeon loft was an everyday occurrence.

'You knew they were here then?' asked Lucy in surprise.

'Of course I did chick, there's not a lot gets past me.'

'No,' said Lucy, 'I don't suppose there is – and do you know why they're here?'

'I do,' said Avis, 'but if *they* won't tell you then it's not my place to say.'

'I suppose not,' said Lucy, 'only if I *did* know it might help.'

'Things have a habit of unfolding on their own,' said Avis, almost as if she knew what was troubling Lucy. One thing was certain though; she was definitely working to the same script as the angels. All that stuff about things happening at their own pace – it was *so* frustrating.

'I'm sure things will become clear eventually,' said Lucy, 'but that doesn't make me feel any better now.'

'Perhaps not,' said Avis, 'but *this* might.' She handed Lucy a postcard with a picture of Mimsy Muggeridge and her Mumbling Marionettes on the front.

'It was stuck in the window at the post office,' said Avis, 'and it made me think of you.'

Lucy took the card and turned it over, and as she recognised the spidery writing, her heart gave a little leap.

"For Sale or Auction. Are you feeling Lucyk?
Cheese and Onion Sandwich.
One careful owner, only nibbled at weekends.
Apply on The Promenade, Grimston-on-Sea.
Saturday, 9a.m. You'll know where."

'Do you remember that detective you told me about?' said Avis. 'I think it might be a message from him. Look, he's even mis-spelt the word 'lucky' so that it looks like your name.'

'You're right,' said Lucy, 'but how did you get hold of the card?'

'The post-mistress is an old friend of mine,' said Avis. 'I thought it might be a good idea if certain people didn't see it, so I asked her to take it out of the window as soon as I spotted it.'

'*Saturday*,' said Lucy with a vague look on her face. Just for a moment, she had a mental image of a highly trained snake licking a postage stamp. 'Erm, that's three days from now isn't it – so what am I going to do in the meantime?'

'You slept for a good while longer than you thought,' said Avis. 'It's Saturday today my chick, so you'll have to fly if you're going to catch him.'

'Oh,' said Lucy, somewhat taken aback, 'and erm, those people who you didn't want see the card – did you mean anyone in particular?'

'There are two of them hiding in the bushes over the road,' said Avis. 'They'll do to be going on with.'

'I see,' said Lucy, 'and has one of them got a camera by any chance?'

'I *think* so,' replied Avis.

'The *executioner* has returned,' hissed Hanoziz.

'I think it's time I was going,' said Lucy. 'Avis, could you possibly take them some tea whilst I slip out the back?'

'You do that dear, and take this, to remind you of us.'

She handed Lucy a picture of herself and Harry who was cradling his favourite bird. Lucifer was staring out of the snapshot as if he could actually see Lucy, even from the confines of his photographic prison.

'Thanks,' said Lucy, 'I'll treasure it.'

'Yes duck, and mind you keep yourself safe – and erm, before you go, why don't you put some shoes on?'

'Good idea,' said Lucy.

She turned back to bid farewell to Thomax and Hanoziz, but they had already taken their leave of her. The trapdoor had been fitted silently back into place, and now, for all anyone knew, the angels loyal to Narcoriel might never have existed.

The Yakky Morto Machine

Lucy did her best to mingle with the sea-front crowds, pretending to play on the fruit machines and watching the Punch and Judy show, but no matter how hard she tried to blend in she was unable to shake off the feeling of being watched. At three minutes past nine, when the tiny car screeched to a halt in front of her, all hope of remaining inconspicuous was finally lost. Bentley sounded the horn and rolled down the window to shout her over, and dozens of pairs of eyes followed her movements as she leaned inside the vehicle.

'I think you've just blown our cover,' she said.

'Don't worry,' grinned Bentley, 'it's part of the master plan.'

'Well it must be an *amazing* plan then,' said Lucy, 'and erm, how did you know you'd be able to reach me with that silly postcard?'

'*Silly*?' said Bentley indignantly, 'how do you work that out? You're *here*, aren't you?'

'But the chances of me seeing it were…'

'Were exactly one chance in one,' interrupted Bentley. 'I used the same idea to locate someone who'd been lost in the Ammazons for five years. I just nailed a postcard to a tree and a couple of hours later we were sipping tea in my canoe.'

'That's the problem with people who get lost in the jungle,' said Lucy, 'they get out of the habit of using cups.'

'I'll pretend I didn't hear that one,' said Bentley. 'Now, are you going to get in or not?'

'It's not exactly an Alvis Crested Eagle, is it?' said Lucy, grinning as she climbed into the cramped passenger seat. 'But I *suppose* it'll do.'

'It's all I can afford,' said Bentley, 'but I'll tell you what I *could* do – what about getting a stuffed chicken, and mounting *that* on the bonnet?'

'Sorry – I didn't mean to offend you,' said Lucy. 'I *like* your little car – and I particularly *don't* like crested eagles, because Doctor Veraciter has one – it's the Mayfair model – or at least it *was*.'

'Ah, so it *was* you,' said Bentley.

He pulled an old newspaper out of the tiny glove box and pressed it into Lucy's hands. She gasped as she unfolded it and read out the headline:-

"Grimston lunatic in suicide leap from third-floor window."

"Idiotic girl saved by the sudden and miraculous appearance of seven tons of peanuts."

'Brilliant,' she laughed. 'I've *always* wanted to be in a newspaper headline. Although I was rather hoping they weren't going to include the word 'idiot' in the same sentence.'

'Never mind,' said Bentley, 'you got your wish – splashed all over the front page, and a picture too – which reminds me, you'd better put these on.'

He handed Lucy a pair of black-silk opera gloves and some strange-looking glasses – the kind that opticians use to test their patients' sight. They were equipped with tiny supplementary lenses that could be swung into position on adjustable arms.

'It's a disguise,' explained Bentley. 'The more conspicuous you are, the less people will look at you.'

'I suppose it might fool people who don't know me,' said Lucy, 'but if we run into Lily or Percy then we've had it.'

'*Right*,' said Bentley, 'in *that* case we'll just have to drive very quickly.'

They hurtled off down the road, zooming in and out of the crowds of holidaymakers and attracting *lots* of unwelcome attention. Lucy wasn't entirely sure about the detective's conspicuosity theory, so she decided to reinforce her disguise by hiding behind the newspaper.

'It's quite nippy for a single carburettor model, isn't it?' said Bentley, as they hurtled across a zebra crossing and clipped a pedestrian with the wing mirror.

'Erm, ye-es,' said Lucy, suddenly feeling quite ill.

'Oh, and that reminds me,' he said. 'If you really must vomit, can you try to catch it all in the newspaper?'

'Normally I'd agree straight away,' said Lucy.

'And why not now?' said Bentley, adjusting the driver's exterior mirror and changing gear at the same time.

'Well, the Phibber certainly *deserves* to be covered in sick,' said Lucy, 'but just this once I'm actually quite interested in what they have to say.'

'I know, it's *great,* isn't it?' chuckled Bentley. 'I've never been featured in the headline story.'

'Erm, you *still* haven't,' said Lucy. 'I don't think they mention you.'

'Don't they?' said Bentley, sounding rather disappointed. He leaned over to check the paper – and in the process, he managed to drive round the wrong side of a traffic island and bounce the car into the kerb.

'Concentrate on the road,' screeched Lucy.

'I *am,*' grinned Bentley, 'you should see me when I'm distracted.'

'I'd rather not thanks.'

'Are you absolutely *sure* I'm not in?' he said, leaning over for another look at the headlines. 'Why don't you read me a bit?'

'Good idea,' said Lucy. 'That would be *much* safer.'

She checked the inside pages, desperate to find even a single mention of the detective. He'd obviously fallen out of favour though, because there was nothing even remotely connected with him – just a *lot* more rubbish about her escape from the hospital – so she read that out instead.

"In our next exciting edition, we'll reveal more about the nuts.

Were they, as one source has suggested, ready salted?

And if they were, then where did all that salt come from?

Also, the new problem caused by huge flocks of foul-smelling birds near Saint Mallydick's. Is their sudden appearance linked to the mystery snacks?"

'They didn't waste much time getting *that* story, did they?' said Lucy.

'Erm, well actually *I* told them,' admitted Bentley as he drove through a red light. 'I heard a couple of rumours and a few other bits of news after you left my office, and I put two and three and five together and ended up with fifty-nine.'

'I see,' smiled Lucy, '*more* advanced arithmetic?'

'It seemed like a good idea at the time,' said Bentley. 'I needed the money to buy petrol.'

'Why?' said Lucy. 'Where are you going?'

'Where are *we* going, do you mean? After our last conversation, I thought we might need to fire up the old banger – in case something turns up.'

'Another opportunity to grass me up to the newspapers you mean?'

'*Ahem,*' said a rather embarrassed Bentley, 'you needn't worry about that. We have enough petrol to last a while – and in any case, I didn't tell them how I got the story or where they could find you.'

'*Great,*' said Lucy, 'well *that's* certainly a bonus.'

As they turned off the promenade towards the Winter Gardens, Lucy caught sight of a newspaper seller shouting about today's big headline story.

'*Kidkers-bakken-dissup-eersegen.*'

Bentley stopped next to paper-seller and Lucy wound the window down, trying to make out what he was saying.

'*Kidkers-bakken-dissup-eersegen,*' he shouted, much louder this time.

'That's about you, *isn't* it?' said Bentley.

'I don't know,' said Lucy, 'I can never understand what they say.'

'*KIDKERS-BAKKEN-DISSUP-EERSEGEN.*'

'Yes, *thank* you,' said Lucy to the paper-seller, who had just shouted directly into her ear.

'It's easy,' said the detective, 'if you know the secret.'

'And what's that?' said Lucy.

'You either need to be drunk, or else not really trying to hear the words,' said Bentley. 'It's like a sort of heavenly music – you just pick up the feeling from the tune.'

'So what *is* he saying then?' said Lucy, winding the window up again.

'*Kidkers-bakken-dissup-eersegen.*'

'I think what he's trying to say is that a child came back from somewhere but unfortunately they seem to have disappeared again.'

'Oh,' said Lucy, 'so it *is* about me.'

'So it would seem,' said Bentley. He drove a few yards and then stopped again. 'And so, I believe, is *this.*'

He parked the car opposite the great glass-roofed bulk of the Winter Gardens, a place where the holidaymakers gathered to be entertained when the weather in Grimston was being unkind. This of course meant that the gardens were always busy, because the weather was always horrid – except for today.

'Erm, is it just me,' said Lucy, 'or has there been another accident with the weather?'

'The sun, you mean?' said Bentley. It's been fine for about a month now, on and off. That's why the town is packed out with all these Emmets and their screaming kids.'

'But people are still flocking to the Winter Gardens,' said Lucy, 'to see this Yakky Morto thing presumably?'

'That's right,' said Bentley. 'I've been meaning to tell you about it since we set off, but what with one thing and another it completely slipped my mind – anyway, we're here now.'

'No thanks to your driving,' laughed Lucy. 'Have you ever considered walking?'

'Tried it once,' said Bentley, 'couldn't get along with it.'

They got out of the car and stood on the pavement opposite the Winter Gardens, shielding their eyes from the sun and trying to read the huge posters that were pasted up on the billboard. There were so many people walking past that the Lectric speakers were going the whole time.

Yakky, Yakky,
Yakky, Yakky,
Yakky, Yakky Morto,
If you haven't even used it yet
Then we really think you aughto...

'It's a catchy campaign,' said Lucy, 'I'm hooked already.'

'*Are* you?' said Bentley. He stuck a finger in each ear and hummed loudly.

'No,' smiled Lucy, 'not really, but I think I recognise the style – and I'm beginning to realise why you've dragged me down here.'

Yakky, Yakky,
Yakky, Yakky,
Yakky, Yakky, Yakky,
Come on now, and have a try,
It's much, much better than baccy,
(or beer or bingo)...

'Do you know what annoys me most about these jingles?' said Bentley. 'They don't even rhyme properly.'

'So they'd be alright if they rhymed, would they?' smiled Lucy.

'Erm, no,' said the detective. 'I see what you mean.'

'Anyway,' said Lucy, 'rhyming was never really Percy's strong point.'

'*Ah*! You've guessed then?' said Bentley. 'About him being involved?'

'Judging from the quality of the advertising I'd say he's in it up to his neck,' said Lucy. 'He's not clever enough to be running the show though, so someone else must be doing all the brain work – and I *think* I can guess who that might be.'

They crossed the road and stood on the pavement near the grand entrance, bathing in reflected sunlight and the glow from the hundreds of incandescent bulbs that surrounded the main doors. As they gazed in awe, Lucy realised that she and Bentley were the only ones standing still. Everyone else was pushing and jostling, trying to squeeze themselves into the already crowded foyer.

'Look, it's the inventor of the Yakky Morto,' shouted a smelly man as he pushed past Lucy.

'Is it?' she said to nobody in particular. 'I wonder who that could be?'

'Not your Uncle Byron, *I'll* bet,' said Bentley.

'I should think that's very unlikely,' said Lucy, pushing forwards with the rest of the rude and inconsiderate crowd.

'I got a signed photograph,' screamed a woman who was heaving herself in the opposite direction. 'The inventor of the Yakky Morto *touched* me.'

'Wow,' said Lucy, 'I wonder what he does for an encore?' She spotted a piece of paper on the floor and bent down as best she could, surrounded by crushing bodies on all sides. Unfortunately, when she got down far enough to pick it up she was unable to stand again – the space she had previously occupied was filled by bellies of every size, shape, and fitting.

'I'll just sit here then, shall I?' she muttered.

'Lucy?' shouted Bentley. 'Where are you?'

'Don't worry,' she replied. 'I'm in the skirt and trouser department, but I'm heading for the front entrance.' She crawled on her hands and knees to the thinnest part of the crowd, eventually managing to stand up again and get a look at the piece of paper. It was a cheaply printed flyer, advertising the Winter Gardens' newest attraction.

The Fabulous…

The Wonderful…

The Marvellous Yakky Morto…

The Eighth Wonder of the World…
Amaze your friends by talking to their dead relations!
You'll be gob-smacked by all the secrets they're willing to divulge.
After all, they're dead, so what do they care what the living think?"
'Oh, *marvellous,*' sighed Lucy, 'this is *exactly* what we need.'

'I managed to get as far as the booking office,' said Bentley, pushing his way back through the crowd. 'Then I thought I'd best get back to you. It's lucky you didn't come with me, because it's just as you suspected. Your stepmother and Percy are running the whole show. Only they don't seem to be taking any money at the moment. Your step-dad is just sitting there behind the till, signing photographs of himself.'

'Bentley?' said Lucy. 'I've got a really horrible feeling about this. I think I know what's going on, but I need to be *sure.*'

'I know,' he said, 'and I just *happen* to know the way onto the roof.'

As they climbed hand over hand up the rusty ladder, Lucy found herself looking everywhere except up. As they gained height, she caught a glimpse of the sea between the buildings to her left, and then, as they finally reached the roof, she spotted the boarding house. Unfortunately, it seemed to have been painted purple in her absence.

'Something wrong?' said Bentley, noticing her screwed-up features.

'Nothing that a few tins of paint couldn't put right,' scowled Lucy.

'Yes, drab isn't it?' said Bentley, thinking she was talking about the roof gardens. 'They've seen better days, that's for sure. When this place was new, people would come up here just to stare at the domed windows. Although I *think* they probably came up the main stairs, not the fire escape.'

Lucy admired the four rusting domes for a moment, then leaned on the nearest one so she could look down into the main hall.

'Don't press too hard on the glass,' said Bentley. 'And don't let the sun get behind you – they'll see your shadow on the floor.'

'I won't,' said Lucy, peering down through the huge curved panel.

'You know, it's funny,' said Bentley, 'but I expected you to be jittery coming up that iron ladder – I know *I* was.'

'I've never been afraid of heights,' she said. 'I've got a good sense of balance too, like those native Mericans who build skyscrapers. They walk along tiny little planks in the sky, just as if they were on the ground.'

'And you think you could do the same?' said Bentley.

'I've stood on top of the Braneskule,' smiled Lucy, 'and that was at least a mile high.'

'Hmm,' said Bentley, rubbing his stubbly chin, 'nothing wrong with your imagination, is there? So what do you reckon is going on below?'

'Hard to tell,' said Lucy, squinting through another panel. 'I *think* they're attempting a component transplant – there's gubbins everywhere.'

'Gubbins?' said Bentley.

'It's technical talk,' said Lucy, 'you need a minimum of a clipboard and a really bad haircut if you're going to understand it.'

'Really?' said Bentley. 'So what about you then?'

'That's different. It's cool for girls to understand technical stuff – it makes the boys go weak at the knees.'

'And you understand *that* thing?' asked Bentley.

'I might,' said Lucy. She took another look, even though she didn't really need to. She knew every single piece of the machine they'd installed in the grand hall. Somehow, Lily and Percy had managed to move Byron's confuser out of his laboratory – and somehow, God alone knew how, they had managed to get it working again.

'And they say miracles never happen,' said Lucy.

'Do they?' said Bentley.

'Well they must have had *some* kind of divine help,' said Lucy. 'There are thousands of delicate components in the confuser, and they could go '*puff*' at any moment.'

'It looks like quite a few of them already have,' said Bentley, 'or is it supposed to be all black and charred like that?'

'Nope,' grinned Lucy, 'scorch marks were never part of the design – so it looks like they're in serious trouble.'

'You're not going to help them fix it then?' Bentley asked.

'Are you *kidding*?' spat Lucy. 'That's *exactly* why I'm running away, only I hadn't realised it 'til just now. That's why the lamp-stand and Percy were so sweet to me when I came back from, erm, *away*. They've been making loads of money with the machine, and now they've managed to break it.'

'And they reckon you can fix it?' said Bentley.

'Probably,' she replied, 'that's what Percy was going to say when Lily shut him up. And that rotten housekeeper as well, 'Hooley' or whatever she calls herself. It didn't take *her* long to get her feet under the table, did it?'

'So what exactly are they *doing* with it?' said Bentley. 'I thought the publicity was just the usual showman's blarney – you know the sort of thing, like those travelling fairs that advertise a man-eating chicken in a cage.'

'And it's a man sitting in a cage, eating some chicken,' laughed Lucy.

'That's right,' grinned Bentley, 'those showmen will say *anything* to get paying customers through the doors – or the tent flaps.'

'Only *this* time I don't think they're exaggerating,' said Lucy seriously.

'*Really?*' said Bentley. 'You mean all those things they're saying about dead people are actually true? You really can *talk* to them?'

'It's beginning to look that way,' admitted Lucy. 'It seems the Yakky Morto is a machine for talking to the dead, just like the lamp-stand said.'

'Are you *sure?*' said the detective. He leaned on the window, and then had to scrape the pigeon and seagull poo from his hands.

'I suppose I knew all along,' said Lucy, 'but I didn't want to admit it, because of what else it means.'

'Which is what?'

'There's a switch on the control panel,' said Lucy. 'You can't even see it from way up here, but it's there alright.'

'And what does it do?' said Bentley.

'It depends,' she said, not really wanting to go into the details of how you could fry angels with it. 'One of the positions is marked with letters instead of words.'

'An acronym?' suggested Bentley.

'Yes,' said Lucy. 'And I'm willing to bet it was Percy who worked out what it means – he's good when it comes to crosswords.'

'And you've just worked it out yourself, have you?' said Bentley.

'I *think* so,' said Lucy. 'It reads CWPWHPO and OKAD in brackets.'

'And what does it mean?'

'Well I *think* it means Converse With People Who Have Passed Over

(Otherwise Known As Dead).'

'Which fits nicely with the Yakky Morto idea,' said Bentley.

'And everything I know about Byron,' smiled Lucy. 'I can just imagine the grin on his face as he made it up – but it's sad too, because it means that none of them are coming back.'

'None of who?' said Bentley.

'My Uncle Byron for one,' she said in a very quiet whisper. 'I think he's dead, and I think I know who killed him.'

'Then we should get down off this roof and tell the police.'

'Erm, no thanks,' said Lucy. 'I've had quite enough of the police – they'd probably just take me back to Saint Mallydick's.'

'So who do you think killed your uncle then?'

'Someone who made him a promise,' said Lucy. 'I think Byron was trying to protect me, and that's why he co-operated with them. They made him build a machine and then killed him anyway.'

'And do you *know* someone like that?' said Bentley, suddenly very serious.

'Yes,' said Lucy, climbing onto the ladder, 'unfortunately I *do.*'

'I see,' said the detective, following her down the fire escape. 'Well that *is* bad news, especially for your uncle.'

Lucy stopped for a moment and looked down into the alley. She thought she'd heard a noise in the gloom, but apart from the rats, it was quiet.

'Hey,' said Bentley, as they continued their descent. 'I've just thought of something that might take your mind off your uncle – I managed to locate that piece of paper you were interested in.'

'Oh, *have* you now?' said a coarse female voice. 'Well you'll just have to tell her about it later, *won't* you?'

'Eh?' said Bentley, peering down from his perch. 'And who the hell are you?'

'*Uh-oh,*' said Lucy.

'I'm Zenda Freggley,' said the woman. She was standing with her arms folded and flashing a superior smirk at them as they climbed down into the darkened alley. 'The Phibber's finest,' she added, 'at your service.'

'I doubt *that* very much,' said the detective crossly.

'I don't care whether you doubt it or not,' said Zenda, '*now,* I have some business with Miss Blake, so *if* you don't mind?'

'If I don't mind what?' yelled Bentley.

'Just run along like a good boy, will you? Otherwise Zenda will ask her friends to pay you a visit.'

'Erm, are they big then, these friends of yours?' said Bentley.

'Actually they *are*,' said Zenda, 'so if you don't mind just shoving off?'

'Erm, don't *I* get a say in this?' asked Lucy.

'Actually, *no* dear, you don't,' replied Zenda.

'Oh,' said Lucy, 'well in *that* case I think we're going to say no to your very kind offer – come on Bentley, let's leg it.'

'I'm right behind you,' he said, sprinting after her. 'Erm, so I hope you know where we're going.'

'Why don't you just stop and *think* for a moment?' shouted Zenda. 'I'm offering you money if you co-operate and a prison cell if you don't. I wouldn't have thought it needed much intelligence to work *that* one out.'

She started to take her high heels off to run after them, but by the time she had stripped down to her stockings, the pair had disappeared.

'*Right*,' spat Zenda, 'so it's a *game*, is it? Well we'll soon see who knows the most hiding places in Grimston, *won't* we? Will it be the has-been detective and his snotty schoolgirl sidekick? Or will it be *La Gloriosa Freggley*, the stunningly attractive and daring female reporter who's chased more stories than she's had hot-pie-and-gravy dinners?'

'She's going to find us in here, I just *know* it,' whispered Bentley. 'We *really* should have run further before going to ground.'

'But we'd have stood more chance of being recognised,' Lucy whispered back. 'At least this way we get to watch something whilst we wait for the trail to go cold.' She settled down into her seat, wishing they'd stopped in the foyer to buy chocolate instead of rushing through as if the cinema was on fire.

'Do you like nuts?' said Lucy.

'In moderation,' said Bentley nervously, 'why, have you got some?'

'Not right at this minute,' giggled Lucy, 'but I could *get* some.'

'Depends how many you were thinking of,' grinned Bentley.

The man in front turned round and gave them both a huge *shush*.

'Will you two *please* shut up?' he added.

'Erm, sorry,' whispered Lucy, slipping even lower in her seat. As she did so, she happened to notice the symbol that was set into the proscenium arch above the flickering cinema screen.

'Bentley, do you see that thing up there – the symbol with the four sections? It's exactly the same as the one on my toy theatre.'

'And how is that significant?' he asked.

'I don't know,' said Lucy, 'but it's a bit creepy, don't you think?'

'Not if your toy theatre was modelled on this one,' said Bentley.

'*Ah*,' said Lucy, 'I didn't think of that.'

'Will you two please *shush*?' hissed the man in front.

'Simple explanations are always the best,' whispered Bentley.

'I suppose,' said Lucy, 'but they aren't always the most interesting.'

'*Right*, that's *it*,' yelled the angry man, 'I'm calling the manager.'

'*No*,' whispered Lucy, '*please* don't – we're hiding.'

'Yes,' said Mister Angry, 'I can see how that might be – and from whom are you hiding – the *noise* police?'

'No,' said Lucy, 'it's, erm, *hey*, wait a minute, what's *that*?'

She stood up and pointed at the cinema screen where a man was dangling from the minute hand of a giant clock. Far below him, in glorious black and white, people were wandering along the pavement, completely unaware of the drama that was unfolding above.

'*That* has just given me a really *brilliant* idea,' said Lucy.

'Well I hope it really *is* brilliant,' said Bentley, 'because the lovely Zenda has found us.'

Lucy slammed down into her seat and turned around, peering towards the back of the cinema – and there it was – the unmistakeable outline of their pursuer, silhouetted in the green glow of an 'exit' sign.

'Zenda rotten Freggley,' she hissed, 'the journalistic equivalent of having a Jack Russel terrier fastened to your trouser leg.'

'Keep down,' said Bentley, 'she might not see us.'

'*Miss*?' shouted the man in front. 'Hello? You know those people you're looking for? Well they're over here.' He stood up on his chair and began waving his arms, pointing at Bentley's hat.

'Oh, well thanks a flipping *lot*,' moaned Lucy.

'Don't mention it,' said the man in front. 'And *now* perhaps we can all get on with watching the film?'

'Hey, *you*, will you shut up?' The woman in front of their betrayer was standing on *her* seat now, shouting at *him* for shouting at Lucy.

'Hey, you two, get down off those seats,' yelled someone behind. 'I can't see what's going on.'

'Hey, leave it out, will you?' said another voice.

'Yeah,' shouted a gruff man right at the back. 'Shut your bleeding faces, *all* of you, or I'll come down there and shut them for you.'

'Erm, I don't like the sound of this,' said Lucy. 'We seem to be attracting rather a lot of attention – *again.*'

'I think that might be a bit of an understatement,' said Bentley, peering back into the stalls.

Suddenly everyone was at it, shouting about not being able to see, throwing popcorn, standing on seats or just generally getting in the way of the screen. And suddenly, right in the middle of the riot, the projector stopped. The picture on the screen froze, still showing the man dangling from the clock – moments later the film bubbled and melted and caught fire, and everyone cheered.

'I don't suppose we can we use that brilliant idea of yours, can we?' said Bentley. He sounded slightly desperate.

'Erm, ye-es, *probably,*' said Lucy, 'but first we need to do a bit of running.'

When Zenda emerged into the foyer, the girl who sold her the ticket was still sitting in the glass booth, trying to make the world's tallest-ever pile of half-crowns.

'No refunds,' she said, with a bored expression. 'I don't care *how* bad the film was – if the manager catches me giving you a refund, he'll set me on fire and then pee on the ashes. I know, because that's what he did with the last girl, and she was *not* happy.'

'I'm not interested in your stupid refund,' snapped Zenda. 'I just want to know where the young girl and the detective went.'

'Is that in a film then?' said the ticket seller.

'No, it's *not* in a bloody film,' spat Zenda, 'it's in real life – you *do* know what that is, don't you? Or do you live in that stupid cabinet permanently?'

'It's not my job,' said the ticket girl.

'*What* isn't your job?'

'Keeping a lookout for escaped customers,' replied the girl.

'Listen,' said Zenda, 'do you *know* who I am?'

'Dunno,' said the girl. 'Are you famous?'

'I'm Zenda rotten-well Freggley, *that's* who I am.'

'Yeah?' replied the girl. 'Well *I've* never heard of you.'

'But I'm the finest... no, *wait*, we're wasting time here – just answer the stinking-rotten question, will you? *Did you see a detective come this way?* He had a girl with him. She was wearing a long black coat, and she had a scar on her face, and I think she might be missing a finger too – she had a floppy glove.'

'*Scar? Finger? Floppy glove?*' said the ticket seller. 'Are you quite *certain* this wasn't in a film?'

'*Holy-Bloody-Pig-Snot*,' screamed Zenda, 'just answer the bloody-stinking question will you?'

'I *told* you,' said the girl, 'I'm not in charge of disappearances.'

And with that, she pulled the little canvas curtain down. It said 'closed', quite clearly, but Zenda read it aloud anyway – three times. And as she did so, a tiny light came on, somewhere deep inside her head.

'Of course!' she smiled. 'The story's already in the bag, isn't it? I can just see the headline now – it'll be a *huge* banner, splashed right across the front page.'

"Ace private detective has-been and slash-faced teenage art thief vanish from Grimston cinema. Police admit to being completely baffled."

'I can still hear you,' said the girl in the booth. 'This curtain is only thin – and I'm *still* not telling you.'

'Shut your spotty rotten face,' said Zenda. 'I've just realised I don't need you any more, you *twerp*.'

In the rush to get out of the cinema she barged an old gypsy flower-seller into the gutter, stepping on the woman's feathered hat as the victim fell between two parked cars.

'Well don't just *lay* there,' grumbled Zenda, 'get out of my way, can't you? I'm on important newspaper business.'

'Won't you buy a flower dear?' said the gypsy, still sitting in the gutter.

'Get lost you old bag, didn't you *hear* me? I'm in a hurry.'

'What about some pegs then? People always need pegs.'

Zenda stepped over the woman, grumbling about how inconsiderate people could be, and ignoring the tirade of curses that were shouted after her. Nothing mattered now except the story – and the sooner she got to the offices of the Phibber, the better it would be for everybody – but *especially* for her.

'And that'll be the best part,' she whispered under her breath, 'the bit about the police being baffled.'

She had no intention of telling the police of course. But if she *had* been thinking of telling them, then she felt certain they *would* have been baffled. So once again, the honour and the integrity of the newspaper profession had been upheld.

The Mysterious Bandstand

'I feel as though I should ask you what's going on,' said Bentley, his eyes out on stalks, 'swiftly followed by various questions about where we are, and how you got us here.'

'So why don't you?' said Lucy.

'Because I'd probably need a few notebooks to write the answer in, and I didn't bring any extra ones with me.'

'You want to write it all down?' said Lucy.

'Of course – things like this *have* to be written down,' said Bentley, 'they're a matter of history.' He was wearing a vaguely distant look, as if imagining the contents of his pile of buff folders.

'So you're not going to ask then?' said Lucy.

'No,' he replied, 'I don't think so – well, perhaps just *one* small thing.'

'Go on then,' smiled Lucy.

The detective squinted, as if trying to remember some significant detail.

'What was that machine thingy we saw in the white room? It looked like it had been hit by a bomb or something.'

Lucy grinned, thinking back to the feelings of triumph and freedom she'd experienced as she leapt out of Veraciter's window.

'I think I was a bit over-enthusiastic when I asked for that last pile of nuts,' she said, 'I suppose seven tons *is* quite a lot, isn't it?'

'It *is*,' laughed Bentley. He was gazing around the telescope room like a very small child in a very large toyshop. 'So is that where all the nuts that fell on Veraciter's car came from?'

'Yes, but I don't think we'll be using *that* particular feature again.'

'Is that a problem?' said Bentley.

'I don't know,' she replied, 'we'll think about it later - we've got less than twenty minutes.'

'Or else what?' said Bentley.

'All *this* lot disappears,' said Lucy, with a vague gesture in the direction of the window.

Bentley hesitated; still trying to work out was going on.

'Are you coming or what?' shouted Lucy. 'We have to pay a visit to the town hall – but first we have to climb down out of this room.'

'Who exactly are we going to see?' said Bentley as they walked through the deserted streets. 'You can't just wander into that place and *talk* to someone you know. I tried it once, when my dustbin wasn't emptied. I spent the whole day going from one wind-swept office to another, and finally ended up in a disused toilet in the attic.'

'I think we might get through a bit quicker today,' smiled Lucy.

'Yes, I *noticed* that,' said Bentley. 'It *is* rather quiet, isn't it?'

'I'll say,' laughed Lucy.

'In fact it's a bit too *quiet*,' said Bentley. 'What's going on around here? Where *is* everybody?'

'I'll explain later,' said Lucy, 'but just for now can we get to the town hall please – *urgently?*'

According to Byron, the huge green dome of the town hall had once been a sort of bronzy-gold colour – but the metal had oxidised over the years, gradually turned the colour of frog-sick by the weather. The four-faced clock still had a nice gleam to it though, perched at the very top of the dome with its huge porcelain dial indicating the time at each point of the compass.

'What's wrong?' said Bentley.

'Nothing,' said Lucy with a shrug. This was no time for outbursts of emotion – they had a job to do, even if she *had* just been reminded that she'd never see her uncle again. 'Come on,' she said, forcing a smile. She pushed her way through the heavy outer doors and into the grand entrance hall. 'Erm, I don't suppose you know where the stairs leading to the dome are?'

'Actually I do,' said Bentley, leading the way across the parquet floor. As they got to the door in the corner of the foyer though, he stopped to rub his chin and frown, staring down at the polished wooden tiles.

'Hmm,' he said, 'now I *seem* to recall a big fuss about this, years back. The wooden floor was ripped out and replaced with marble, but here it is again, all nice and wooden. I suppose you're going to explain *that* later as well, are you?'

'I *might* do,' grinned Lucy, 'but we need to get our skates on – and you need to bring *that* thing.' She pointed at the gold mayoral mace, which lived in a big display cabinet. 'You'll need to break the glass first though.'

'What?' said Bentley, 'but that's…'

Lucy heaved the cabinet over onto the floor, jumping back smartly as it disintegrated with a lot more ferocity than she'd expected. The mace stayed in one piece though – not that it would matter.

'There you are,' she said, 'and if anyone asks who did it you can tell them it was me. Now can we please *hurry up*? I reckon we've got about four minutes left at the most.'

'Is this something to do with the streets being deserted?' said Bentley.

'Three minutes thirty seconds,' said Lucy.

Bentley realised that further argument would be futile, so he shouldered the mace and followed Lucy – she had already kicked the door open and was climbing the narrow staircase that spiralled its way up to the clock room.

After a long, breathless haul, they emerged into the roof-space and located the tiny wooden platform tucked high up inside the dome. It looked like a cubical room, but had no walls, just a wooden framework suspended at the centre of the sphere on delicate wooden joists. It reminded Bentley of a wooden puzzle he'd enjoyed as a boy, where a glass ball was trapped by a nest of ropes and beams. The centre of *this* puzzle was occupied by the clock mechanism though, and directly above that were the four clock faces, sitting in the crown of the dome and connected to the works by a series of heavy chains.

'The four-faced liar,' said Bentley, peering into the furthest reaches of the dome.

'Who is?' said Lucy.

'The clock,' he replied, 'that's what everyone calls it, because none of the faces ever tells the right time.'

'Good,' said Lucy, 'so we'll be doing the town a service, won't we? Now, do you want to give me the mace? Or do you want to do it?'

'I'll let you have the honour,' said Bentley, 'especially as I haven't a clue what you intend.'

'I was thinking of something like *this*,' grinned Lucy.

She took the mace from Bentley, wilting slightly beneath the unexpected weight then heaving it onto her shoulder, where, just for a moment, the incredibly delicate filigree work caught her eye.

'It's beautiful, isn't it?' she said.

'If you like that sort of thing,' he replied.

Lucy smiled, and then, summoning all her available strength, she jammed the smallest end of the pole into the delicate clock mechanism. There was a horrendous grinding of gears and breaking of springs, like an explosion in the spare parts department at the Slepe-O-Matic bed factory – and a few moments later the four-faced liar was dead.

'There,' said Lucy, 'I think that's just about done it, don't you?'

'Erm, yes, I think it probably *has*,' said Bentley, 'and have you considered how we're going to pay for all this damage?'

As they threaded their way through the deserted streets towards the sea-front, Lucy explained as gently as possible why they were alone.

'So nobody lives here then?' said Bentley.

'I've never found anyone,' said Lucy. '*Yet.*'

'Well this is *definitely* one for my curiosities notebook,' said Bentley. 'But what was all that business with the mace?'

'I got the idea from the film,' said Lucy. 'It just didn't make sense for me to be here for just twenty minutes and then have to stand back and watch it all disappear – and then I saw the man hanging from the clock.'

'So what's the idea then?' said Bentley. 'It looks like someone has gone to an awful lot of trouble, but I can't see why they would bother.'

'It's like a puzzle that we have to work out,' said Lucy. 'Erm, actually no, I suppose it's a puzzle that *I* have to work out – no offence.'

'None taken,' said Bentley. 'Anyway, you're right – I don't know why, but the place feels as if it belongs to you. Does anyone else know about it?'

'Just my friend Toby Lindstrom,' said Lucy.

'The boy who was kidnapped?'

'Yes, only he wasn't,' she said, looking slightly sad.

'But that's *good* news, isn't it?'

'Not really,' said Lucy, 'when I left him he was in a great deal of danger – in fact he'd probably be better off if he *had* been kidnapped.'

'So where is he?' asked Bentley.

'If I had a moon cycle or more…'

'Moon cycle?' said the detective.

'Erm, yes, that was one of Miss Pubrane's phrases,' said Lucy.

'Have I met her?' said Bentley. 'I don't *think* I have – it's not the kind of name you forget in a hurry, is it – *Poo Brain*?'

'You might have seen her handbag,' smiled Lucy, 'it all depends on the kind of nightmares you have.'

When they reached the sea front, Lucy skipped down the wooden steps that linked the promenade to the beach. She broke into a run as soon as she hit the sand, and made straight towards the sea.

'Where are we going?' shouted Bentley, running after her.

Lucy waited for him to catch up, smiling, but still saying nothing, as if mere words might spoil the moment. Then she threw her shoes and socks off and waded in, thankful for the cold touch of the waters against her skin.

'Have you ever seen a bandstand in Grimston?' she said eventually.

'Erm, no,' he said, peeling his odd socks off, 'there isn't one, is there?'

'No,' said Lucy, 'and as far as I can work out it's the only thing you can find here that we don't have back in the real Grimston.'

'So is that where we're going then?' said Bentley.

'Once we've skimmed a few stones,' said Lucy, picking up a large, flat pebble.

'*Four*,' said Bentley, watching her pitch the stone and then counting the skips. 'Impressive.'

'I had a good teacher,' she said, 'come on, we need to head south.'

'Is all this really necessary?' said Bentley. 'Only I reckon we've been walking for about an hour now, and we appear to be running out of beach.'

'Did you have other plans then?' chuckled Lucy.

'Well,' said Bentley, 'now you mention it, we *could* be looking at my office.'

'Sorry,' said Lucy, 'but that's not as important as the bandstand.'

'And what if it turns out to be a mirage?' asked Bentley.

'We'll know that soon enough.'

'Good,' said Bentley, 'well let's hope it doesn't disappear in a puff of smoke just as we get there.'

'If you were *me*,' sighed Lucy, 'and I was my friend Toby, he'd probably be telling you to shut your moaning pie hole right about now.'

'Is he interested in pies then?' grinned Bentley.

'Only when he can't get chips,' said Lucy with a smile.

They were still a hundred yards or so short of their target, but even at this distance, they could see that the bandstand was a marvellous affair. And the pigeons and gulls that had followed them from the pier seemed to agree – they were circling above it now, in an unsettling echo of the day that Fenny disappeared.

'Erm, it looks freshly painted,' said Lucy with a frown. She had *wanted* to say something significant – about the curvature of the roof perhaps, or the splendid decorative pillars or the elegance of the finely gilded finials – but the *paint?*

'It *does* look rather fresh,' said Bentley, 'unlike the rest of the town, which is just as shabby and rundown as the real Grimston. I wonder why *that* is?'

'We'll soon know,' said Lucy, striding out towards the structure.

'One thing *I* want to know,' said Bentley, 'is how you knew it was here?'

'*Magni-Ficat*,' cried Lucy.

'Yes, I know it is,' said Bentley, 'but how did you know it was here?'

'No, *Magni-Ficat*,' said Lucy, 'that's the telescope we passed on the way in. Toby and me saw the bandstand through it ages ago, only we could never get anywhere near it.'

'Until now,' said Bentley, sharing in Lucy's triumph. 'And it was worth the trip too – just look at all that lovely fretted ironwork where it holds the roof up. You don't get workmanship like that nowadays, do you? This thing was built by a craftsman.'

Lucy nodded, staring in awe at what had obviously been a labour of love. There was stunning decorative detail everywhere, and the further she studied it, the more there was to find, as if the features went all the way to infinity – so small that they couldn't be seen with the most powerful microscope, yet still there, provided for the pleasure of those few with the ability to see.

'Octagonal base,' observed Bentley, 'just like the one down in Crapston. And a split post at each corner too, just like Crapston, and a domed roof covered in copper. Hmm, now they don't have *that* in Crapston Magna, do they? And the copper hasn't turned green either. Why do you think that is?'

'You're right,' said Lucy, 'copper doesn't stay that colour for long. It goes that sickly shade of green, like the dome at the town hall. But *this* roof seems to be as bright as the day it was made.'

'Perhaps today *is* the day it was made?' suggested Bentley.

'Maybe,' said Lucy, 'but that's not the question – what worries me is why it's here in the first place.'

'Perhaps it's a conversation piece?' said Bentley.

'A *what*?' said Lucy. 'Are you joking?'

'My great-aunt used to have an Erotocordion on her parlour table,' said Bentley, 'and it never failed to captivate her visitors – as soon as they laid eyes on it they were completely hooked. Can you imagine that? If *you* saw something as enigmatic as that you'd be absolutely *dying* to know what it was, wouldn't you?'

'I suppose so,' said Lucy, 'but what has that to do with your aunt?'

'*Ah*,' he said, 'well sometimes, when she was descended upon by visitors she didn't particularly like, she'd show them the Erotocordion and then very politely decline to tell them what it was used for – it drove them mad.'

'But this is a bit different though, isn't it?' said Lucy.

'I suppose,' said Bentley, 'in this case the whole town's a conversation piece – not that you get many visitors.'

Lucy's curiosity had peaked, and to Bentley's dismay she now seemed more interested in examining the bandstand than finding out what an Erotocordion was. She mounted the steps but stopped suddenly, as if a hungry lion had blocked her path.

The sky darkened, and just for a moment the birds ceased their chattering – as if they disapproved of Lucy's discovery.

'Erm, *Bentley*? I think you had better come up and have a look at this.'

The detective climbed the steps and stood next to her, suddenly more aware of the deep black skies and the pure unbroken silence that hung about them like a cloak.

'Hmm,' he said, staring at the floor. 'Well I don't know how you managed to get those nuts to come out of your little scrap of theatre, but can I just suggest one thing before we start?'

'What's that?' said Lucy.

'Don't try it here,' he grinned, 'that iris in the middle looks awfully big.'

'Ah, so you recognise the design then?' she asked, a note of superiority in her voice. 'Only when I pointed out the similarity between my toy theatre and the design in the cinema you said that simple explanations were best.'

'That was before you brought me here,' said Bentley. 'I'm willing to believe just about anything now.'

'Good,' laughed Lucy, 'because you might just need to.'

'Hmm,' he said, stroking his chin, 'you're *still* not telling me everything, are you?'

'Not yet,' grinned Lucy.

'So what's the story with the bandstand? Am I cleared to know that?'

'I don't know if there *is* one yet,' replied Lucy. 'We've only just got here, so you know as much as I do.'

'We could ask the birds,' suggested Bentley. 'They do seem to be trying awfully hard to tell us something.'

From their position underneath the canopy, they couldn't actually see the funnel of wings, but the beak-music had started up again and the mad cacophony was steadily increasing now, as more and more of their number joined the flock.

'The design's the same as the Empire stage,' said Lucy, 'apart from the symbols around the outside edge.'

'Yes,' said Bentley, 'but your theatre has the design painted on – this is all laid into the floor in metal and coloured glass.'

'Like a mosaic,' said Lucy. 'If you could release one of those pieces of glass it'd make a great conversation piece for your great-aunt's parlour table. Not that I'm thinking of trying anything like that.'

'Then what *are* you thinking of doing?'

'I'm open to suggestions,' said Lucy, glancing at the five-pointed star on the ceiling. 'But I reckon *this* is the original, and the ones on the Empire and in the cinema are the copies.'

'You're probably right,' agreed Bentley. He got down on one knee to inspect the glass inlays, whilst Lucy walked around the platform. She started at the edge where the steps joined the floor, and worked her way clockwise.

'There's a symbol for each of the eight sides,' she said, 'one for each compass point and four smaller symbols interleaved between them.'

'They're incredible,' said Bentley enthusiastically, 'look, this one's a beetle of some kind, and there's an eagle too, and a pair of coiled snakes – I've never seen anything like it, have you?'

'Erm, no,' lied Lucy, her eyes flickering over the symbols. They were arranged exactly like the wands in the Forest of Skeels, forming yet another part of a complex pattern that refused to emerge into the light. Once again it seemed, she had been driven to hide the truth, and once again she felt a sudden guilt, for not telling the detective everything he needed to know.

'I'll make a drawing,' he said, pulling out his trusty school jotter. 'Just in case we need to refer to them later.'

'Consider yourself the official artist then,' said Lucy.

Bentley began copying the symbols, noting every curl, swirl, and link, just in case they were significant. In the main, the symbols were made up of smaller symbols, some of them joined by lines and others standing alone, as if they represented letters and the symbol as a whole represented a word.

'I think I've got them all,' said Bentley, tucking his notebook away, 'so when we get back we can…'

'What on *earth* is *that?*' screamed Lucy suddenly.

'Erm, it *looks* a bit like a seat,' said Bentley, slightly hesitant.

'I can *see* that,' snapped Lucy, 'but where did it *come* from?'

'Underneath?' he suggested. 'I think it appeared when you walked over that beetle symbol.'

Lucy walked away from the scarab and sure enough the seat eventually slipped away again in complete silence. It didn't leave a hole though, just a certain mysterious 'lack', as it dissolved into the floor.

'Neat,' said Bentley, 'I don't suppose you feel like trying it again?'

Lucy approached the scarab again, and sure enough, the seat returned.

'I think it's intended for you,' said Bentley.

Lucy nodded and sat down. She'd been thinking exactly the same thing.

'It's warm,' she observed.

'Not only that, it seems to have taken a liking to you,' said Bentley. He pointed at the illuminations beneath the floor, and then indicated the way the seat seemed to be wrapping itself around Lucy's hips.

She stood up and the lights went out, and when she sat down they returned. Lucy estimated that perhaps one in eight of the lights was illuminated – then, suddenly curious, she counted them. *Exactly* one eighth of the lights were glowing, as if she was one-eighth part of an equation.

'Well *that* seems fairly conclusive,' she said, 'now what do we do?'

'What do *you* do, you mean? I'm just here by accident, remember?'

'Alright,' said Lucy, 'put your fingers in your ears.'

Without questioning, Bentley did as he was told.

'*Sobol*,' she whispered.

Nothing happened.

'*Raas*,' she whispered.

Nothing happened again.

'*Lucal*.'

Again nothing – *this* was getting a bit tiresome.

'*Babage*.'

Nothing.

'So much for that idea,' she said.

'Can I take my fingers out now?' pleaded Bentley.

Lucy shook her head, eager to try one last idea. It was a thought that had been ignited by a far-distant memory – a memory that featured her mother's photograph album.

'*Pasbs de Madriax*,' she whispered.

The words were spoken so gently that even *she* had difficulty hearing them, but some*one* or some*thing* had heard – there was a distant grumble from beneath the bandstand, as if some huge mechanism was preparing for action. The floor-lights dimmed slightly and *then* came a long, deafening silence – even the birds had stopped calling.

Above them, the ceiling turned suddenly and completely transparent, so that the geometry of the five-pointed star appeared to be floating

ᴇϽᴙᴇᴉ⅄Γ

unsupported in the air beneath the dome. Then, before they could even register their surprise, a faint squeal of oiled metal signalled the opening of the copper canopy. At first there was just the tiniest point of light at the apex, but soon the eight segments of the roof began to inch apart, peeling back like a sleepy flower that was seeking the sun after a long, cold night.

With the petals fully opened, a perfect circle of heaven was revealed. It was a violent, swirling sky though, stocked with black-bellied clouds and a gathering wind – and superimposed on that dark vision was the mysterious pentagram, glowing slightly, like a luminous clock-face.

Behind *that* were the birds, wheeling, diving, and watching *everything*.

'I hope you know what you've done here,' shouted Bentley. He still had his fingers firmly inserted in his ears, so he was speaking *much* louder than he needed to, threatening to destroy the magick they were witnessing.

'I haven't a clue,' whispered Lucy, 'but it's a bit too late to be changing my mind.'

Bentley seemed to understand and nodded, raising an eyebrow as the next part of the sequence began. There was a noise like thunder, followed closely by the familiar sound of trumpets and the smell of Lectric.

It was the vibration that worried them though. The great central iris in the floor was trembling, each of its eight leaves vibrating with a metallic jingle against its neighbours, as if anticipating some momentous event. Lucy took a deep breath, aware that she too was shaking – something momentous *was* going to happen – and she desired it and feared it in equal measure.

Without warning, the iris screeched open for just a fraction of a second. Then it closed again – like a giant camera taking a photograph of the sky.

Lucy gasped as she let her breath out, then ran towards Bentley, laughing with relief as the pent up emotions spilled out of her.

'Right, that's it,' he giggled, 'I'm taking my fingers out now whether you like it or not...'

'*Fantastic*,' grinned Lucy, 'did you see inside?'

'There was a door in some kind of underground chamber,' said Bentley, 'but I was too busy worrying about all the rumbling and vibrating to look for anything else. I was concerned about dying with my fingers stuck in my ears, when what I *really* wanted was to die as a tragic hero.'

'Or not die at all?' suggested Lucy with a smile.

'Even better,' agreed Bentley. 'Did *you* see anything?'

'The same as you,' said Lucy, 'only it must have been a different door, because we were on opposite sides of the opening.'

'Anything else?' said Bentley.

'Unfortunately no,' said Lucy, 'it was all over too quickly – and I *think* we used up our only try.'

'You don't think it's worth a second go then?' said Bentley.

'No,' said Lucy, still uncertain why she felt so positive about it, 'one try is all we get – like a demonstration.'

'So that's it?' said Bentley, sounding slightly disappointed.

'It's lucky we didn't blink, isn't it?' said Lucy.

'I saw *quite* enough thank you.'

'Me too,' laughed Lucy.

'And I *felt* enough too,' he said. 'Did you get a strange sort of feeling in the pit of your stomach whilst it was all happening?'

Lucy nodded, touching her belly, as if to confirm the burning excitement that was still roaring inside her. What they had seen was a mere taste of what was possible, and the thought of events yet to come had set her imagination alight.

'It was like those film trailers you see at the cinema,' she babbled. 'You get to see a tantalising glimpse of next week's feature and then you have to spend the next seven days agonising over it. Which reminds me, we came here from the cinema, so that's where we'll appear when we go back.'

'You think our friend Miss Freggley might be hanging around?'

'Almost certainly,' said Lucy, 'didn't you notice? She was wearing one of those fiery *I'm not giving up* looks.'

'Can't we just take a peep, to see if she's there?' said Bentley.

'It's a nice thought,' said Lucy, 'but it doesn't work like that.'

'So what's next?' said Bentley. 'You're the expert when it comes to popping into the world next door to borrow a cup of sugar.'

'I think we should stay here for a while,' she said, glancing up at the dark-laden sky. 'We'll find somewhere to sleep, and by tomorrow things at home will have cooled down. Do you fancy the beach?'

'I prefer a little more luxury,' said Bentley. 'There are some camp beds at my office – we could use those.'

'*Oh*,' she said with a smile, 'erm, ye-es, that's *right*, isn't it?'

With all the fuss over clocks and bandstands, Lucy had completely forgotten that they could now visit any place they liked. She could go and look in her own bedroom for instance, or explore the other rooms at the Four Havens and see if they were all exactly like she remembered. Only now that it was possible it didn't seem that important. She was still curious, and the idea *still* made her feel like a quivering jelly, but compared with the other possibilities it all seemed a bit frivolous.

'Alright,' she said finally, 'let's sleep at your office – and those fold-up beds of yours had better be comfortable.'

'There's absolutely zero chance of that,' grinned Bentley. 'Haven't you ever read those small advertisements in the Phibber? No matter what else they have for sale, there are *always* a couple of camp beds. I reckon they're the same ones, and they just get passed around.'

'Fine,' said Lucy, 'well in that case I'll sleep on the floor.'

The Grand Architect of the Universe

'*Wow*,' said Bentley, 'this is amazing – my key fitted perfectly, and the office is exactly the same, even down to the coffee-cup rings on the desk – only there aren't enough of them.'

'Yes, but that's because…'

'Erm, no, wait a minute,' said Bentley, 'something isn't right – it's *not* exactly the same after all.'

'That's what I'm *trying* to tell you,' said Lucy. 'This isn't the same Grimston we just left Zenda in – it's Grimston as it was thirteen years ago.'

'Wow, you're right,' said Bentley, 'look – this is Philandra's handbag.'

'So when was the last time you saw her?' asked Lucy.

'A couple of months ago.'

'Be *honest*,' said Lucy with a reassuring smile.

'Oh, *alright*,' admitted Bentley, 'it was about thirteen years ago – and ever since then I've been pretending she'll be coming back.'

'Well, you never know, she just *might*,' said Lucy, 'one day.'

'It's nice of you to say,' said Bentley, 'but I don't think so – not that I'd even know what to say to her. Which reminds me, I have something to tell *you*. I almost forgot, with all this excitement.'

'What is it?' said Lucy, settling into Bentley's chair.

'Do you remember those questions you asked the first time we met?'

'Of course I do,' said Lucy eagerly, 'have you found something?'

'As it *happens*,' said Bentley, fishing a few screwed-up notes from his battered wallet. 'I went to Lundern on the train, to do some research – that's seven pounds nineteen and six you owe me for the ticket by the way.'

'Put it on my account,' smiled Lucy. 'There's bound to be *something* left of my inheritance – even *after* Percy and Lily have finished siphoning it off.'

'I wouldn't bet on it,' said Bentley, 'you didn't see their faces when they were sitting in the Winter Gardens ticket office. Those two were just *made* to perch behind a cash register – erm, *now*, where was I?'

'In Lundern,' said Lucy.

'So I was,' said Bentley, 'and whilst I was there I called in at the Museum of Antiquities to meet an old friend of mine – he's a professor of something or other, at some university somewhere or other.'

'Does he have trouble finding his way into work?' laughed Lucy.

'Erm, *no*,' said Bentley, 'I'm the one with the poor memory, not him. *Now*, I wrote all the details down somewhere…'

He delved into his jacket-pocket and pulled out his school jotter – on the cover of which a much younger Bentley had scrawled *B. Priory. Form 1a*. When he opened the book there was more evidence of the detective in his early years. He'd written '*Maffs stinx*', on the inside cover, and underneath it, someone else had scrawled '*…and so does bent end priory*'.

'Erm, they wouldn't let me borrow any of the books,' he explained, 'so I had to copy everything out.'

He extracted a crumpled piece of paper and handed it over to Lucy.

She recognised the subject immediately, despite Bentley's crude drawing efforts. Her heart missed a beat as she touched the paper. Even though it was just a copy, the image seemed to have a power of its own.

'Where did you see *this*?' she gasped, her face suddenly turned white. It was a chilling representation of the thing she feared the most – a Spiritu Lokey cabinet.

'It was an engraving in a book called *Mythes and Legendes of Loste Worldes*,' said Bentley. 'There are only two known copies apparently, one in private hands and the one I saw at the museum.'

'And was there anything else?' breathed Lucy. 'This is *really* important.'

'Why's that?' said Bentley, obviously intrigued.

Lucy bit her tongue. She *still* wasn't ready to tell the detective about the world of the Braneskule and the Sisters. She trusted him; there was no doubt about that, but for the moment, the less people who knew about it the better. For instance, what if she told him everything and then Raziel caught up with him? Even now Morana's screams were echoing inside her head – and she didn't want to add Bentley's agony to the chorus.

'I copied all the stuff I could understand,' said Bentley. 'Most of it was in Lattinn, but some of it had been translated into Old Ingulesh. You know, the kind that looks as though it was written by a drunken spider?'

'And which bits did you understand?' said Lucy impatiently.

'The Angelic Cabinets,' said Bentley. 'It's all made up of course, unless you happen to believe in angels. Erm, you *don't* believe in them, do you?'

'Of course not,' said Lucy. Now *that* was a lie, plain and simple, with absolutely no invention required.

'I didn't think you would,' said Bentley, 'it's all a bit airy-fairy that angel stuff, isn't it? It made interesting reading though – do you want to hear about it?'

'Go on then,' said Lucy, trying not to sound too eager.

'Right,' said Bentley, 'well apparently there was some kind of big hoo-ha back in the middle ages – there were *lots* of arguments about whether angels existed or not. Some of the philosophers couldn't be bothered to argue though, because they were certain that angels *did* exist, so *they* kept themselves busy with various other things – like wondering how big the angels were.'

'I heard about that,' said Lucy, 'there were debates about how many angels could stand on the head of a pin.'

'Exactly,' said Bentley, 'and calculating how many angels dropped out of heaven at the time of the great fall.'

'I wouldn't have thought it was something you could work out,' smiled Lucy. She got up from the chair and walked over to the window where a pigeon was pecking on the glass. Beyond that, the sky was thick with birds, and especially so in the general direction of the bandstand.

'The Bishop of Tusculum did,' said Bentley. 'He came up with an exact number, which was supposed to be a third of all the angels in heaven.'

'And how many was that?' grinned Lucy.

'A hundred and thirty-three million, three hundred and six thousand, six hundred and sixty-eight.'

'Now *that* is a very precise number of angels,' smiled Lucy. 'I don't suppose he counted them again to double check?'

'Hardly,' laughed the detective.

'I thought not,' said Lucy, 'and what about the cabinets?'

'Ah, *well*,' said Bentley, '*those* were designed by the philosophers who argued that there *were* angels. As far as *they* were concerned, it was a complete waste of time sitting around and arguing about whether they existed or not. What *they* were interested in was getting their filthy hands on one – and that was the whole idea behind them. They were designed to lure unsuspecting angels, and capture their eternal souls.'

'Oh,' said Lucy, holding a hand up to her mouth. Bentley noticed the missing finger for what must have been the hundredth time, but once again he decided not to mention it. She'd tell him the rest of her story when she was ready – *hopefully*. 'But that's not all,' he continued, 'shortly after the first cabinet was constructed the philosophers discovered another use for them. They could hold angels alright, but they could also imprison something else. Something the book called *earth bounds*.'

'Ordinary people, you mean?' said Lucy.

'I suppose,' said Bentley, 'the book didn't go into detail, not in Ingulesh anyway. All I could gather was that the cabinet trapped the person's soul and thoughts, leaving their actual body to wither away and eventually die.'

'I *see*,' said Lucy, her voice ringing with sadness.

'Nice people, weren't they?' said Bentley.

'Not really,' said Lucy, thinking of Miss Niblock. 'So why haven't we heard of these things before?'

'Maybe the church wasn't proud of what it had done?' said Bentley. 'If *I'd* done something like that, I don't think I'd want anyone to know.'

'I suppose not,' said Lucy, realising that she'd never mentioned cabinets to Bentley in the first place. 'So, erm, how did you happen to come across all this information?'

'It was all thanks to my friend the professor,' said Bentley. 'I told him about your questions and he showed me where to look for the answers.'

'You found something else though didn't you?' said Lucy. 'I can tell from the way you're grinning at me. Was it connected with the cabinets?'

'It's more sort of connected with angels,' smiled Bentley. 'You remember that phrase you asked me about? *Exner-Heelo*? Well it's actually spelt Ex Nihilo – and it's Lattinn.'

'And what does it mean?' said Lucy. Her heart was pounding away inside her ribcage, and she felt sick with apprehension.

'It means *'from nothing'*,' said Bentley.

'Oh,' she sighed, 'I was hoping for a bit more than that.'

'So was I,' said Bentley, 'and luckily there *was* more. My professor friend introduced me to someone who lectures in comparative religion.'

'Really?' said Lucy. 'And what does *that* mean in words that ordinary people can understand?'

'It's to do with what people believe,' said Bentley, 'about God mainly.'

'Oh,' said Lucy. 'I never really got on with religious studies.'

'But you know about other things though, don't you?' said Bentley. 'Like Lectric and science?'

'I suppose,' said Lucy modestly.

'Good,' said Bentley, 'because what he told me was more to do with how the universe came into being.'

'Ah, *creation studies*,' smiled Lucy, suddenly reminded of a world that was just thirteen years old.

'Just so,' said Bentley, 'and as you might expect there are a few different ideas about how it all happened. For instance, there are some who believe that the universe was never created, because it has always been here.'

'Like the Grobbley Manuscript,' said Lucy, '*that* has always existed, because it was made in heaven.'

'I won't even ask,' smiled Bentley, 'it sounds incredibly complicated.'

'It is,' said Lucy. 'So what about the other idea? The opposite to the universe having always been there?'

'The only possible alternative is that it was created,' said Bentley.

'By God presumably?' said Lucy. She walked over to the window again, as if she might be able to shake off her feeling of unease by moving around. The pigeon was still there, looking at her as if she was an old friend.

'*Well*,' sighed Bentley, 'there are certainly quite a few people who'd agree with *that* idea.'

'And some who wouldn't?'

'Well according to the professor — that's the second professor you understand, not the first one — there are *some* who believe that the universe was created by an angel.'

'*Oh*,' said Lucy, 'well I certainly wasn't expecting *that*.'

'It came as a bit of a shock to me too,' said Bentley. 'I'd never heard of the idea before, but apparently it's quite well known in theological circles.'

'And do you know the name of this angel?' said Lucy nervously.

'I do,' said Bentley. 'He's called *Demiurge.*'

Lucy heaved a huge sigh of relief. For one horrible moment she'd had the strangest idea – that the creator of the universe might be called Raziel.

'And did your friend tell you anything else?' she asked. She could feel her heart beating again, much faster than usual now, as if she had run for miles and suddenly stopped to listen to the gushing of her own blood. '*Bentley?* Did he tell you anything else?'

'Erm, well *yes,* he told me another name for Demiurge.'

'*Well,* what is it?' hissed Lucy, desperate to hear the name. She'd started to perspire – the sweat was running off her forehead into her eyes.

'He's also known as the Architect of the Universe,' said Bentley.

'*No, that's impossible,*' she snapped, 'have you been talking to Raziel?'

'The chap you mentioned at the office? The *real* office I mean?'

'Yes,' said Lucy, '*him.*'

'Erm, no,' said Bentley, 'honestly, I've never met him.'

'Then how do you both come to use the same phrase? *He* mentioned something about architects as well.'

'It's probably just a coincidence,' said Bentley.

'But they're the same thing, surely? Architect Elect, and Architect of the Universe – it can't just be a coincidence, can it? It *might* have been, if Raziel was just an ordinary man, but he's not – because they're both…'

'Both what?' said Bentley.

'*No,*' said Lucy, 'sorry, I can't tell you – I have to do this on my own.'

'No-one has to do *anything* on their own,' said Bentley, 'that's why we have friends – and I'm *your* friend Lucy. I know we haven't known each other for long, but just look at what we've been through already.'

'You're right,' said Lucy, 'I wouldn't be here now if it wasn't for you.'

'And I *certainly* wouldn't be here if it wasn't for your wonderful piece of plywood – so why don't you tell me?'

'They're both *angels,*' said Lucy. She blurted the words out as if they were made from a fizzy gas that boiled inside her and could no longer be kept down. 'Raziel is an angel, and he mentioned someone called the Architect

Elect – and Demiurge is the Architect of the Universe – now *that's* not a coincidence, is it?'

'Not if it's true,' said Bentley, 'and before you say anything else, let me tell you this – I *believe* you.'

Lucy had been gritting her teeth, preparing to explode when Bentley questioned her story – but suddenly, all that effort was for nothing.

'You *believe* me?' she sighed. 'But I told you that I thought there was no such thing as an angel.'

'Of course I believe you,' smiled Bentley, 'because it all fits in with what the second professor told me about your phrase.'

'Well go *on* then,' said Lucy impatiently.

'In religious circles,' whispered Bentley, 'the phrase *Ex Nihilo* is usually preceded by the word *Creatio*.'

'*Creatio ex Nihilo?*' said Lucy. She rolled the words around on her tongue, feeling the correctness of them – and she *knew* that it was right.

'Literally speaking,' said Bentley, 'it means to create something from nothing.'

'Well *that* would explain a *lot*,' said Lucy. She was grinning so hard that she feared her face might split.

'It certainly would,' said Bentley, 'but unfortunately, it answers one question and asks about twenty more.'

'We could start with Kolley Kibber,' suggested Lucy.

'*Kibber?*' said Bentley, looking somewhat surprised. 'Hmm, now *that's* a name I haven't heard in a long time.'

'Oh yes,' said Lucy. 'I forgot to tell you about him, didn't I?'

'I remember him from way back,' said Bentley, 'but I'm surprised *you* do – it was *well* before you were born.'

'That's the whole point,' said Lucy. 'I heard a story about a man called Kolley Kibber, and then I made an invention with him in it, and the next thing I know I'm bumping into him on the sea front. That's how I escaped from Veraciter the first time round.'

Bentley was beginning to look puzzled, so Lucy explained the escape in detail, stopping only when she got to the bit about the auction rooms.

'I see,' said Bentley. 'And are we to conclude that you *made* all this happen?'

'I *think* so,' said Lucy. 'I haven't actually told anyone in as many words, but yes, I *think* I made him appear. But where was he before? And where did he go afterwards?'

'If I have it right,' said Bentley, 'then he was nowhere. That's what *Creatio ex Nihilo* really means – you don't just move a thing from one place to another, you actually create it from *nothing*.'

'Nothing at *all*?' said Lucy.

'All you need is the will to do it,' said Bentley. '*Think* about it Lucy – there are people who would *kill* for that sort of power.'

'I know,' said Lucy seriously, 'I've met them.'

'*Met* them?' said Bentley.

'Raziel,' she said.

'Hmm, yes,' mumbled Bentley. 'Now you come to mention him again I'm sure I saw that name somewhere – now where *was* it?'

Lucy's eyes widened at the prospect of further information, but judging from Bentley's expression his memory of the event had slipped into a deep chasm somewhere inside his brain and would never be heard of again.

'Ah! *Got* it,' he said suddenly, 'it was the *book* – the one that contains the fifteen-hundred keys to the universe.'

'*B-book*?' said Lucy, feeling a sudden shiver on her spine. 'Are you *sure*?'

'Erm, yes, it's full of indecipherable language,' said Bentley, 'which is probably just as well, if it really *does* contain all those secrets.'

'But how did Raziel's name remind you of that?' said Lucy nervously.

'Well if I remember it correctly,' said Bentley, 'then *he* was the character who stood on the opposite side of the curtain from God – and apparently he copied down everything he heard.'

'Spying on the Almighty?' said Lucy.

'Yep,' said Bentley, 'and when the book was finished he gave it away.'

'*Ah*,' said Lucy, 'well that doesn't sound like *my* Raziel – the angel I've met would never give anything away.'

'Maybe he lost it then?' said Bentley.

'*If* he ever had it in the first place,' said Lucy. She leaned back in the rickety chair and put her feet up on the desk, noticing with a smile that the wires from the intercom *still* didn't go anywhere. Then she noticed something else – there was a faint, pink glow on the wallpaper in that corner of the room. She sighed and turned towards the window and saw that same rose-coloured stain on the lace curtains – they had been talking all night, and the sun had come to remind them that tomorrow had arrived.

'It's the first time I've seen the sun rise here,' said Lucy. She was smiling, looking almost as radiant as the fireball that was growing in the east.

'And it seems to have made you *very* happy,' said Bentley. 'Which is good, because when we're happy we make bold decisions.'

'*Uh-oh*,' said Lucy, 'what kind of bold decision did you have in mind?'

'You remember those documents you asked me about?' said Bentley.

'My mother's things?' said Lucy eagerly.

'I found out where they're being kept,' said Bentley. 'They were taken to a solicitor's office for safe keeping.'

'*Oh*,' said Lucy.

'There's no need to look so glum,' he said. 'I've yet to come across a door that can't be opened with a bit of ingenuity and a comprehensive selection of lock-picks.'

'You mean we're going to break in?' grinned Lucy.

'I'm afraid I couldn't possibly comment,' laughed Bentley. 'Once you were in possession of a secret like that you'd become a major security risk and I'd be obliged to kill you.'

'I *see*,' said Lucy, 'well that's nice, but I'm afraid you might have to get in the queue.'

Dewey, Cheetham
and Howe

'*Heck-sclew-sive.*'

'*Hace-tecti-a-teen-idge-artfeef-disupeer-frcinma.*'

'*What* did that newspaper seller say?' asked Lucy.

'I'm not sure you want to know,' said Bentley, threading the little car through the traffic.

'*Heck-sclew-sive.*'

'*Hace-tecti-a-teen-idge-artfeef-disupeer-frcinma.*'

'It *sounded* like 'half a tectonic plate and an artist feeding peas to the enemy.'

'Erm, no,' smiled Bentley, 'it was about you and me doing a disappearing act from that cinema.'

'Ah,' said Lucy, 'Zenda didn't waste any time getting *that* story into print, did she?'

'But there's good news too,' grinned the detective. 'We *both* made it to the front page this time.'

'Then shouldn't you be wearing a disguise?' said Lucy.

'I'll bear it in mind,' said Bentley, 'but I don't really suit glasses.'

'You'll be needing *something*,' said Lucy, 'especially if we run into that cinema manager again. Do you *really* think he believed that story about us falling asleep and getting locked in?'

'He didn't have much choice,' said Bentley. 'There *we* were, locked inside, and there *he* was, with the only key – what other explanation *could* there be?'

'I'm glad they didn't find the Empire gate,' said Lucy, 'it was a bit of a risk just leaving it there on the cinema stage.'

'But appropriate,' said Bentley, 'bearing in mind your toy theatre was based on that same cinema.'

'*Might* have been,' said Lucy, 'we don't know that for certain.'

Dewey, Cheetham and Howe

As Bentley parked the car outside the solicitor's office, Lucy fished out the glasses and put them on, moving both of the accessory arms into position so that she looked like some kind of mad scientist.

'That ought to do the job,' said Bentley, 'even my own mother wouldn't recognise you.'

'But she doesn't know me,' said Lucy.

'Which just goes to prove what a good disguise it is,' said Bentley.

'Hmm,' smiled Lucy, 'I *think* I'll put the opera gloves back on too.'

They got out of the car and stood on the pavement for a moment, rehearsing the story they were going to tell. In the end though, they decided it would be better if Lucy invented something – that way there were no lines to get wrong.

The offices of Dewey, Cheetham and Howe were situated on one of the upper floors at 47 Kronk Street, which was a single shabby door, sandwiched between a smoke-filled laundrette and a newsagent. Behind the door was a tight corridor and narrow, threadbare carpets leading up the rickety stairs.

'Blimey,' said Bentley, 'I thought *my* office was bad, but it's a palace compared to this.'

'You should see Byron's place,' said Lucy, 'that's worse – at least it is now.'

'I think I might not bother then,' said Bentley, 'come on...'

After two flights of stairs, they found a sign saying '47C this way'. It pointed towards a glass-panelled door which Lucy opened just a crack so she could peer into the shabby office beyond. It was difficult to see if there was anyone home, because the place was crammed with furniture and box-files and stacks of old papers. Eventually though, stuck in a corner between a filing cabinet and a thousand-year-old ledger they spotted a thin, grey-faced man who was inspecting a leather bound book. He had warty skin and a big nose and his hair looked as though it had just been tested in a wind tunnel. Lucy smiled – she imagined the poor soul dying some time ago – at which point some kindly relative had propped him up in the corner until he was stiff enough.

'Erm, can we speak to Mister Dewey please?' she said.

'Who wants him?' said the corpse. He continued flicking idly through the pages of his book, throwing up thick clouds of dust.

'It's private,' said Lucy, wrinkling her nose.

'I'm *afraid* he's unavailable,' said the man, '*dead* in fact.'

'Ah,' said Lucy, slightly taken aback.

'Well *actually* we wanted Mister Howe,' she said, undeterred. 'I asked for the, erm, the *other* one by accident.'

'*Did* you now?' said the old man, '*hmmm – interesting.*'

'Yes,' said Lucy, 'it was a mistake – it's Mister Howe we *really* wanted.'

'*Dead.*'

'What?' said Lucy. 'Him as well?'

'Has been for years,' said the grey-skin. 'What was it you wanted to talk to him about? If it was *important* you could try the Winter Gardens. I believe they have a machine down there which allows one to speak to one's deceased relatives.'

'We know,' said Lucy, 'we've seen it.' She looked at Bentley for support, but the famous detective just gave a shrug.

'Erm, *right*, well can we speak to Mister Cheetham then?' said Lucy, sensing that she was on her own. '*He* must be here, *surely* – otherwise who's running the office?'

The grey-skin gave a violent cough, and was about to speak when Lucy interrupted.

'No, wait a minute,' she said, 'don't tell me – *he's* dead as well, isn't he?'

'You know him then?' grinned the old man. He adjusted his gold-rimmed spectacles so that he could stare at Lucy over the top of them.

'You mean he *is* dead?'

'As a doornail,' said gold-rims, 'about thirty years ago.'

'Erm, *right*, so this *sign* you've got outside,' said Bentley. 'Would we be right in thinking that it advertises a firm of solicitors who are all dead?'

'Well *they* can't help it, can they?' said the old man. 'The firm was taken over by the Swindlem brothers when old Mister Cheetham finally fell off his perch.'

'Ah,' said Lucy, 'well now we're *getting* somewhere. Can we speak to one of the Swindlem's please?'

'Which one? Snellgrove or the Major?'

'Snellgrove I think,' said Lucy, 'yes, *him.*'

'Why?' said the man. 'Do you know him?'

'Erm, no,' said Lucy.

The grey-skin began shuffling a pile of papers from a basket marked 'in' to a basket marked 'out'. He didn't bother to examine them though, and it seemed to Lucy like some kind of sign. If they didn't *know* Snellgrove, he seemed to be saying, then they weren't going to get to *see* him.

'Wait,' said Lucy, 'yes, on second thoughts I think we *do* know him.'

Bentley shook his head violently when the old man wasn't looking, but it was too late – Lucy had already committed herself.

'Oh, you *do*, do you? And are you sure about that?'

'Erm, ye-es,' said Lucy, not feeling very sure at all.

The man gave an awful grin, exposing a set of yellowy-green teeth which were all too obviously his own. Then he folded his face up into something that resembled a prune, but with extra wrinkles.

'*Ah*,' said Lucy, realising her mistake, 'erm, *you're* Snellgrove, *aren't* you?'

'Indeed I am,' he grinned, 'so what did you want to talk to me about?'

'Oh,' said Lucy, 'but I thought you wouldn't want to…'

'On the contrary, we never turn business away, *do* we Major?'

Lucy turned back towards the doorway, where a shadowy figure had just appeared. He was exactly how Lucy had imagined a major might be; only he wasn't wearing a military uniform. Everything else about him screamed 'army', from the fine pewter monocle and the brass-pointed swagger stick right down to the highly polished caps of his huge toe-crushing boots.

'I see you've noticed my boots,' he bellowed proudly.

'Yes, they're erm, very attractive, erm, *boots*,' said Lucy.

'I was up until two o'clock this morning *bulling* them,' said the Major. 'The trick is to start with a hot spoon, don't you know? You use it to smooth the old polish down to form a completely flat base – *then's* the time to come in with your other layers of polish, first of all you….'

'Yes, *thank* you,' said Snellgrove, turning to Lucy with an apologetic smile. 'He'd go through the entire spit and polish process if you'd let him.'

'That's alright,' said Bentley, 'we're interested, *aren't* we Lucy?'

'Erm, *are* we?' said Lucy.

'Yes,' said Bentley with a wink. 'I'd be very interested to hear about the Major's army days – which regiment were you in?'

'*Regiment?*' said the Major. 'I erm, *harrumph*, I was erm, *harrumph* in er...'

'I don't think he *was* in a regiment, were you Major?' said Lucy, winking back at Bentley. 'I think he was probably one of those soldiers of fortune.'

'That's right,' he blustered, '*ahem*, yes, I was a soldier of, erm, whatever it was *she* said.'

Snellgrove looked disapprovingly over the top of his glasses and the man with the shiniest boots in town responded by snapping to attention and saluting. Then he marched smartly out of the office, as if he was on a parade ground.

'Shall we get on with it?' said Snellgrove. 'What exactly can we do for you?'

'*Well*,' said Lucy, 'erm, this is my Uncle Gusset.'

'A most unusual name,' said Snellgrove.

'He's an unusual man, *aren't* you, uncle?'

'What?' said Bentley, absent-mindedly. 'Oh, yes, I expect so.'

'*Very* unusual, I'd say,' said Snellgrove, 'to be letting an eleven-year-old girl do all his talking for him.'

'I'm thirteen,' snapped Lucy, 'and there's a very good reason why he doesn't talk a lot, isn't there uncle?'

Bentley nodded as if there *was* an extremely good reason but he just didn't want to say. Actually, he was busy having a good nosey around the office, trying to work out where they stashed the valuables.

'I see,' said Snellgrove, 'and what might this reason *be?*'

'He's often busy thinking about important things,' said Lucy, 'so when he stops for an ordinary conversation he forgets his thoughts and it takes ages to get them back.'

'I see,' said Snellgrove, 'and what can *we* do to assist your extremely busy and forgetful avuncular relation?'

'*Eh?*' said Lucy.

'How can we help your uncle?' said Snellgrove.

'Ah, that's easy,' said Lucy. 'Uncle Gusset has some journals that contain all his best thoughts, and he needs a *very* safe place to keep them.'

'And?' said Snellgrove, pushing his spectacles back up his nose.

'And erm, *well*, we were sort of wondering if it was the kind of service you could provide?' said Lucy.

As if on cue, Bentley pulled a notebook and pencil from his pocket and scribbled a few notes. A satisfied look spread across his face, as if he'd just come up with a solution for squaring the circle or had an idea for a perpetual motion machine.

'Well, Miss Blake, as it happens we *do* provide such a service, and we'd be *more* than happy to look after your uncle's research notes. If you'd like to fill in a few forms we can take them into safe keeping straight away. I assume he has the notes with him?'

Bentley pulled out the jotter again and flicked through the pages, noting with surprise that it contained considerably more notes than he'd expected.

'Here it is,' he said tamely. He handed the book to Lucy who inspected the notes and seemed genuinely impressed with his scribbling.

'*My*, uncle, you *have* been busy, haven't you?'

'You know me,' said Bentley. 'I'm like the constipated mathematician – I'm always ready to work it out with a pencil.'

'Quite,' said Snellgrove, 'and now the forms, *if* you don't mind?'

'And then can we have a look at your storage facility?' said Lucy.

'I'm sorry?' said Snellgrove.

'The place where you keep all the valuables,' said Lucy.

'Ah, what we in the trade call the *safe*,' said Snellgrove. 'Yes of course you can – if you'd like to come this way?'

'Erm, ye-es,' said Lucy, somewhat hesitantly. 'Actually would you just like to *wait* a minute?'

'Is something the matter?' said Snellgrove.

'There *is* actually,' said Lucy. 'I was just thinking about earlier, when we were asking you about safe keeping.'

'Erm, ye-es?' said Snellgrove.

'Yes,' said Lucy firmly, 'you referred to me as Miss Blake.'

'Well?' said Snellgrove. 'That *is* your name, isn't it?'

'It certainly *is*,' said Lucy, 'but *I* didn't tell you that, *did* I?'

'That's right,' said Snellgrove raising a flat hand in acceptance of his defeat, 'you *didn't* tell me, did you? In which case I must have recognised you from the photograph your stepmother gave us.' He produced a tiny brown picture from his desk drawer – a square of expired light from some distant promenade that wasn't Grimston.

'You recognised me from *this* thing?' said Lucy, squinting at the snap.

'Actually *no*,' admitted Snellgrove. He grinned again and scratched some disgusting yellow gunk from his teeth with a paperclip. 'We were simply warned to expect someone coming to us with an extremely unlikely story. And lo-and-behold, here you are just as predicted, with your strange story and your smelly coat, wearing glasses that obviously don't suit you. Not to mention the fact that your face looks as though it has just lost a fight with a lawn mower. *Really* Miss Blake, you must think I was born yesterday.'

Lucy took a good look at the reams of wrinkles and the grey hair that sprouted from every orifice on Snellgrove's head.

'Hardly,' she muttered.

'Erm, I assume you've called the police?' said Bentley.

'You're the detective,' sneered Snellgrove, 'what do *you* think?'

'Yes, I rather thought you might have,' said Lucy, 'come on Uncle Gusset, I mean erm, Uncle Bentley, we'd best be going.'

'They'll catch up with you eventually you know,' said Snellgrove.

'They might,' said Lucy, 'but we'll be better informed by then, won't we?'

'Better informed about what?' said Snellgrove.

'Don't be so nosey,' said Lucy, 'and when you see my lovely stepmother, give her my love and tell her that whatever she's up to it won't work.'

'There's no point,' said Snellgrove, 'it already *is* working. Have you any *idea* how much money they're making with that Yakky Morto machine?'

'No,' said Lucy, 'but I've seen some of the things they've bought with the proceeds and if *that's* the best you can do with money then you can have the lot. Come on uncle dearest, we need to be off.'

In a surprising display of agility, Snellgrove leapt up from his seat and ran to block the doorway. Fortunately though, Bentley was bigger and stronger than the old man and simply lifted him to one side.

'Nice meeting you,' said the detective, 'some other time perhaps?'

'Remember what I told you,' shouted Snellgrove, 'you won't get far.'

'Yes, we heard,' said Lucy, shouting back up the stairs.

'*Now* what?' she hissed, as they ran out into the street.

'Erm, *run*, I suppose,' said the detective.

'Yes, but *where?*' said Lucy. 'We're running out of bolt-holes.'

'Wait, let's stop and think about this logically,' said Bentley. 'The boys in blue will be expecting us to leg it, won't they?'

'Erm, *ye-es?*' said Lucy uncertainly.

'Right,' he said, 'so why don't we do exactly the opposite?'

'Such as?'

Bentley glanced up and down the street to make sure they were not being watched, and then he looked up at the window of 47c – and *then* he smiled and pointed at a sign on the opposite side of the road.

"*Ye Long-Handled Spune – Home of the Choccy Glopp.*"

'Why don't we just go and sit in that café?'

'*Brilliant,*' said Lucy, 'I wish *I'd* thought of that.'

'Me too,' said Bentley, 'but actually it was my stomach that came up with the idea.'

Major Excitement
on Route 53

'It's *him* again,' whispered Lucy, 'the nosey one, with the striped apron.'

'Just nod and smile politely,' said Bentley. He was fishing around in a tiny purse for the last of his money.

'Another pot of tea was it?' said the waiter.

'Erm, yes, thank you,' said Bentley.

'You *like* tea, don't you?' said the striped apron.

'And whatever gave you that idea?' said Bentley.

'Well, that's the seventh pot you've had since you came in.'

'*Is* it?' said Lucy.

'Four pots of Assam, one of Darjeeling and two of that stuff that tastes like boiled socks,' said the waiter. 'I've been told I'm very observant, so I couldn't help but notice. You tend to *see* these things when you work with the general public.'

'As you say,' said Bentley, 'we *like* drinking tea.'

'Very much,' added Lucy, licking her lips.

'Yes, but nobody likes it *that* much, do they?' said the waiter. 'If I didn't know better I'd say there was something funny going on.'

'Oh dear,' whispered Lucy, 'he's *onto* us.'

She made certain her whisper was loud enough for the waiter to hear.

'Eh?' said Bentley, '*onto* us?'

'It's no use Boris,' she said, 'we have to let him in on the deal.'

'Erm, what deal's that then?' said the waiter, suddenly looking quite eager. It was clear that nothing exciting had happened in the café world recently and he was willing to listen to anything that sounded remotely interesting. Fortunately, Lucy was only too willing to oblige – she picked up the greasy menu and whispered to the waiter behind it.

'If we were both adults, they'd be onto us in a flash,' she said, 'so Boris brought *me* along, as part of his cover.' She swung one of the accessory lenses on her glasses out of the way, to show that it was just a clever disguise.

'I *see*,' said the waiter. He stared at Lucy's scar for a little longer than was polite, then scanned the café to see if anyone else was listening. 'But what are you *doing*?' he whispered.

'We're watching the people over the road,' whispered Lucy. 'The Major and the other one.'

'Snellgrove?' suggested the man in the apron.

'That's him,' said Lucy, gently drawing the waiter towards her by his lapels and whispering again. 'We think Snellgrove's the mastermind, but it's difficult to say at this stage. What we need is someone like you, to work on the inside.'

'Oh, *yes*,' shouted the waiter. He punched his fist into the air, obviously pleased with the idea. Then he came over all embarrassed as he realised that undercover agents probably didn't do that sort of thing.

'I bet they come in here all the time, don't they?' said Lucy.

'Never seen 'em before,' said the waiter.

'Oh, erm, *well*,' said Lucy, turning to Bentley. 'See?' she smiled, 'I *told* you they wouldn't use this place, didn't I? It's *much* too obvious – they'll probably make the drop somewhere else.'

'Erm, yes, I would think *so*,' said Bentley, raising a surprised eyebrow.

'What's all this about a drop then?' said the waiter. He sat down and dragged his seat up to the table. 'What exactly is going on?'

'It'd be quicker to tell you what *isn't* going on.' said Lucy. 'They're up to all sorts over there. He wouldn't believe it, *would* he, Boris?'

Bentley nodded, obviously enjoying himself.

'Erm, that's right,' he grinned, 'we've got case files thicker than your Double Choccy-Glopp pancakes back at HQ.'

'*With* the caramel sauce or without?' said the waiter.

'With,' said Lucy.

'Wow,' said the waiter, 'that *is* serious.'

'*I'll* say,' said Lucy. 'Obviously we can't tell you about the smuggling yet, not until you're officially made part of the team, but I can tell you about the murders now if you like.

'*Murders?*' gasped the waiter. 'Here in Grimston?'

'That's right,' whispered Lucy, 'we think they might have killed Mister Dewey and Mister Cheetham and Mister Howe, and then moved in on the solicitors' business. There's a distinct possibility that they've got the bodies walled up inside the office somewhere.'

'*No,*' gasped the waiter, 'what, all *three* of them?'

'Have you ever seen any of them in here?' said Lucy, realising she was taking a bit of a chance.

'I can't say I have,' replied the waiter.

'Well there you are then,' said Lucy, breathing a sigh of relief. 'That just about proves it, wouldn't you say Boris? If they don't come in here then they *must* be walled up in that office.'

'Incredible,' said the waiter.

'It certainly *is*,' said Bentley, pulling the skin down below his right eye. 'I can scarcely believe it myself.'

'And you can tell all *that* just by sitting here drinking tea?' said the waiter.

'Yes, well it's a combination of intensive tea drinking and modern detection techniques,' said Lucy triumphantly. 'Today's police force couldn't do without either of them. Now *remember*, when you go to sign the papers to get you onto the squad, be sure to ask for Inspector Trembley. I'll leave a message for him, describing how you'll be helping with our enquiries.'

'Great,' said the waiter, 'and is there anything I can do now?'

'We need some peace and quiet,' said Bentley. 'We're waiting for the brothers to go out, and then we're going to get the surveillance team in for a closer look at the offices.'

'I'll see you're not disturbed,' said the waiter, 'anything else?'

'Erm, *ye-es,*' said Bentley, finally getting into the swing of things. 'Why don't you bring us a couple of plates of those *Kreem-e-Krisp* biscuits? You can charge them to Inspector Trembley's account.'

'Has he got an account with us then?' said the waiter.

'He has now,' grinned Bentley.

'Right you are,' said the waiter, 'and would you like another pot of tea to go with that?'

Bentley was standing at the door of number 47, ready to go in as soon as Lucy gave the signal. She waved across at the waiter who gave an eager thumbs-up sign. Then she waved at someone down the street as if she was communicating with the other members of her crack police squad. To her surprise, the person she waved at smiled and waved back.

'It's going to be a good day,' she said to Bentley.

'It's certainly been an excellent day for drinking tea,' he said.

Lucy turned and gave another thumbs-up signal to the waiter. He grinned and gave her a double thumbs-up and then pretended to be clearing the tables, just as they'd arranged. It was lucky he wasn't a vital part of the plan, because suddenly he looked nothing like a waiter, even though he'd been doing it for years. Instead, he looked like a very bad actor who was *pretending* to be a waiter.

'That was really cruel,' said Bentley as they climbed the stairs to the offices.

'What?' said Lucy innocently.

'*You* know what I'm talking about – the way you conned that waiter into keeping lookout for us.'

'It was *you* that conned him out of all those biscuits,' said Lucy.

'Yes, but it wasn't me that had him watching the offices while we went for a sleep in the kitchens.'

'He was *enjoying* himself,' smiled Lucy. 'Did you see the grin on his face when he came and told us the brothers had gone out?'

'Yes, he *was* enjoying it,' laughed Bentley, 'and so were you.'

They stood on the landing for a moment, listening for signs of activity behind the glass-panelled door. The office of Dewey, Cheetham and Howe was as quiet as the grave though, which was just the way they wanted it.

'Right,' said Bentley. 'I want you to look away for a moment, because innocent young girls aren't supposed to know about things like this.'

'Things like what?' said Lucy.

'Breaking and entering,' said Bentley.

The mechanism gave a tiny click and the door sprang open slightly.

'There, now that wasn't too difficult, was it?'

'And where did you learn that?' said Lucy, pushing the door open and tiptoeing inside.

'Ask no questions, hear no lies,' he replied. 'Although perhaps I shouldn't be saying things like that in the presence of the greatest lie master the world has ever known.'

'They're not lies, they're *inventions*,' said Lucy. 'I keep *telling* people that, but do they ever listen? *No*, they flipping-well do *not*.'

'Right,' said Bentley, pulling up the last of the loose floorboards. 'I reckon it must be this one – we've looked everywhere else.'

'I think you might be right,' said Lucy peering into the inky void.

'Oh, *frig*,' hissed Bentley, 'it's a Grubb Type Seven.' He tapped the safe as if it might spring open spontaneously. It had obviously never heard of optimism though, and remained steadfastly shut.

'Is that good then?' said Lucy. 'A Grubb Type Seven?'

'Well,' said Bentley, 'it's *sort* of good – especially if you want to keep your private things out of other people's busy little hands.'

'And what if the busy little hands are ours?' said Lucy.

'Then it's *not* so good,' admitted Bentley, 'practically impossible in fact.'

'Oh,' said Lucy, 'well trust *us* to come up against a modern safe.'

'Ah, no,' said Bentley, 'that's the whole point you see – it's not modern at all. Now if it was one of the new *Theef-Stopp* Gold Label models or a *No-Nick* Safe-T-Soo-Preme then there'd be absolutely no problem.'

'So you can't open it because it's *old*? Is *that* it?'

'Precisely, said Bentley, 'I'm a whizz when it comes to handling tremblers and tumblers and nibblers and I can do absolutely *anything* with a rotary combination lock or a parallel snip-shaft, but I'm afraid these old ones with keys are the worst. And the Type Seven needs two keys – *Lectric* ones.'

Lucy's eyes suddenly brightened, filled with mischief at the sound of her favourite word. She looked round the office for a few moments, but it was clear to Bentley that her search had failed.

'Erm, I won't be long,' she grinned, 'I just have to pop out.'

Bentley watched in amazement as Lucy ran out of the office and back down the stairs – and a minute or so later he was *still* looking puzzled as the front door slammed and she appeared again, just slightly out of breath.

'Any minute now,' she grinned.

'What?' said Bentley.

'Don't be so impatient.'

The seconds ticked by, and for Bentley each one seemed like an entire week. Eventually though, there came the tiniest of delicate clicks from inside the safe.

'Erm, it's open,' said Bentley, with a look of astonishment, 'but *how*?'

'Easy,' grinned Lucy, 'I telephoned the Lectric board.'

'Uh-oh,' said Bentley. 'I don't think I like the sound of this.'

'Don't worry,' she said. 'I just told them about that crane driver who was getting too close to the overhead lines.'

'Crane driver?' said Bentley. 'I didn't see any, oh, yes, I see – but isn't that dangerous?'

'I don't think switching Lectric *off* is particularly dangerous,' said Lucy, 'but switching it *on* can be.' She thought for a moment about how she and Toby had fried Raziel in the confuser – but managed to balance her guilt by recalling what *he* had done to poor Morana.

'Anyway, this is important,' she said, 'it's a matter of life and death.'

'Alright,' said Bentley, 'I trust you – but won't your call to the Lectric people get you into even more trouble?'

'I don't think so,' said Lucy, 'I used my adult voice trick – and I told them it was Inspector Trembley calling.'

'Is *this* what we're looking for?' said Bentley. The top shelf of the elaborate safe was stacked with bundles of papers, one of them tied up with red ribbon and bearing the Blake family name.

'It's my mother's will,' said Lucy, unwrapping the packet and leafing through the contents.

'It certainly *looks* like a will,' said Bentley, sorting through another pile. 'And is *this* is the piece of paper you're looking for?'

'If only you knew,' said Lucy. She took the Assiah gateway from him and clasped it to her breast, feeling a wave of sadness creeping up on her.

'This is *so* much more than a piece of paper Bentley. It's, it's, erm, it's…'

The feeling of melancholy suddenly became too much for her and she burst into tears, unable to stop thinking about what she was holding. It wasn't just Toby and Fenny on the other side of those symbols – it was thousands of *other* lives too – clasped in hands that trembled at the thought of all that responsibility.

'Steady on, old girl,' said Bentley. 'It can't be *that* important, can it? It's just an old bit of paper.'

'You're wrong,' sobbed Lucy. 'I have to look after this above all else – I have to protect it with my life – and if *I* can't look after it then you must.'

'Alright,' he said, 'I'll see what I can do.'

'No,' said Lucy, drying her tears, 'that's no good – you must *promise.*'

'Erm, alright,' whispered Bentley urgently, 'but I think that might have to wait – there's someone coming – what is it going to be, window or cupboard?'

Lucy had a quick look out of the window. The street was only two floors below, but this time the peanut dispenser would be no help – it was almost certainly wrecked beyond repair.

'Cupboard,' she hissed, yanking the door open and suddenly realising how much room there *wasn't.*

'No time to change your mind,' said Bentley, 'in you go.'

They pushed, groaned, and grunted their way into the cupboard, juggling all sorts of packets and bundles and piles of paper until there was just enough room to fit. They closed the door just in time too, holding their breath as they heard the floorboards creaking on the other side.

'I *love* being in cupboards,' whispered Lucy, 'or wardrobes – actually I've been in quite a few recently, and I think I can safely say that this is the worst one yet – it smells of cat wee.'

'Well it's not me,' said Bentley, 'now shush, or they'll hear you.'

'You haven't made your promise yet,' whispered Lucy.

'Alright,' he whispered. 'I promise to look after your rotten piece of paper – now will you be *quiet?*'

'I can hear you talking in there,' said a voice outside.

'Oh,' said Lucy, no longer trying to whisper.

'Yes, *oh*,' said the Major, pulling the door open.

'Erm, *hello*,' said an embarrassed Lucy, 'erm, nice to see you again.'

'Never mind the pleasantries,' grumbled the Major, 'out you come young lady – and take those ridiculous glasses off. They don't suit you.'

'So I'm told,' said Lucy, 'but how did you know we were here?'

'Military intelligence,' said the Major. 'Some say that's a contradiction in terms, but a modern army can't do without it – and a successful commander never reveals his sources.'

'Why not?' said Lucy. She looked at Bentley who shrugged back. The safe was hanging open and there were loose floorboards strewn all over the place – even Warren Idiot could have worked *that* one out.

'Why *not?*' said the Major. 'I'll *tell* you why not – because blabbing secrets to the first person who asked wouldn't be particularly clever *would* it? Now hand over whatever it is you've got there.'

'I don't think so,' said Lucy.

'You'd *better,*' said the Major, 'company property and all that.'

'But it's *mine,*' said Lucy.

'Can't possibly be,' barked the Major. 'Why on earth would you bother to break in if it were your rightful property?'

'I needed it in a hurry,' said Lucy. She was glad Toby wasn't here, because that particular lie was worth one out of ten at the most.

'*Poppycock,*' blustered the Major, 'absolute flaming *balderdash* - now give it here this minute, or it's the firing squad for you both.'

'Nope, I don't think so,' said Lucy. 'We're going now and there's nothing you can do to stop us.'

'I don't need to,' said the Major. 'The guards will do that – there's a whole platoon covering the stairs, and a team of snipers on the surrounding rooftops. This place is tied down so tight you could hear a fruit fly fart.'

'No it *isn't,*' smiled Lucy, 'there's nobody out there, *is* there?'

'Erm, no,' admitted the Major, 'but *I* can stop you – I'm combat-trained.'

'No you *aren't,*' said Bentley, joining in the fun.

'Erm, no,' said the Major, 'actually you're right, I'm not – but I *would* have been, if it hadn't been for that damn-blasted medical. How was *I* to know my underwear had been too tight for all those years?'

'Right, well I think we'll be going now,' said Lucy, making for the door.

'I wouldn't do that if I were you,' said the Major. He began to make a tut-tut-tutting noise and shook his head very slowly, as if he knew something they didn't. Then he removed a metal box from his pocket and pressed a button on the front panel. A tiny red light came on, and shortly after that an old iron bed flopped down out of the ceiling and covered the window.

'*Bomb*,' he said proudly, pushing a second button. 'Only *now* it's an *armed* bomb.'

'No it *isn't*,' sighed Lucy. 'The box isn't even connected, *is* it? Except perhaps to some imaginary pile of explosives that came from the same army camp as your imaginary company of soldiers?'

'Platoon,' said the Major, 'let's keep things straight.'

'Alright,' said Lucy, 'platoon then – but it doesn't matter what you call them does it? A non-existent *platoon* of men is exactly the same size as non-existent *company* of men – it's exactly zero men.'

'True,' admitted the Major, 'but their non-existent commanding officer would need to be a different rank, wouldn't he? So there *is* a difference.'

'I give up,' said Lucy, 'come on Bentley, it's time we were going.'

'Take one more blasted-well step and the whole office goes up,' said the Major. 'I *mean* it – I have four tons of quarry-grade dynamite in the cellar and another three and a half in the attic. It was a *flip* of a job getting it up there, I can tell you, especially with my gammy leg – but it's up there now right enough, and it's just sitting and waiting for the little detonator to go *pop*.'

'And when it does,' said Lucy, 'you'll be going with it.'

The Major's thumb twitched – hovering over the largest of the buttons.

'*Lucy?*' said Bentley, sounding distinctly nervous. 'I think perhaps we ought to listen – he *might* be telling the truth.'

'Sensible man,' said the Major. 'I had a batman like you once, you know, officer's servant and all that? Marvellous feller he was – blew himself up whilst driving a gelignite truck through the Atlas Mountains – *terrible* business – terrible for him anyway. I got a replacement skivvy almost straight away of course. Now *he* was useless, I don't mind telling you – didn't have a clue how to put a decent trouser crease in…'

'*Prove* it,' interrupted Lucy. 'If you've got all that dynamite spread around the place then *surely* you must have some proof?'

'I've been told I've got an honest face,' said the Major. 'Will that do?'

'They say the same about me,' said Lucy, 'but I'm getting rather good at lying – erm, *and* making inventions.'

'Alright,' said the Major, 'if it's proof you want, what about *this*?' He kept his thumb positioned over the detonator button whilst he fiddled around in his trouser pocket with the other hand. Eventually he pulled out something that looked like a large stick of seaside-rock.

'But it's blue,' said Lucy, 'shouldn't dynamite be red?'

'Only if you've been watching too many cartoons,' said the Major. 'This is the real stuff – now, pass me that box of matches, will you?'

'No, *don't*,' said Bentley, moving the matches out of the way.

'I have no intention of passing him anything,' said Lucy, 'but that still doesn't mean I believe it's real dynamite.'

She tiptoed over to the window as if treading on hundreds of tiny, invisible explosives that might go off at any moment. It was covered by the metal grid now, but opened just enough for her to call down into the street.

'*Hey!*' she yelled, 'you down there, with the bobble hat.'

'What the *flip* are you playing at?' yelled the Major, 'and who the devil are you talking to?'

'Yes, *you*,' shouted Lucy. '*What?* Well there's nobody *else* wearing a bobble hat down there is there? So I *must* mean you then, mustn't I?'

'Come away from that window at once,' shouted the Major.

Lucy ignored him completely.

'I want you to take a message to Zenda Freggley,' she shouted.

There was a pause, as if someone in the street was answering.

'Yes, that's her,' said Lucy, 'she works at the Daily Phibber. I want you to get round there as quick as you can and tell her that Major Swindlem was never in the army.'

'*Nooooo*,' bellowed the Major, 'that's a complete flipping-well lie.'

'That's right,' shouted Lucy, 'and tell her that he parades up and down in front of the bedroom mirror in his underpants, pretending to be a military band.'

'How did you know… erm, no, *alright*,' said the Major, 'here, come away from the window – and here's the detonating box. Now just *go* will you?'

'With pleasure,' said Bentley, already sprinting for the door.

'We won't *really* need this will we?' said Lucy as she took the box from the Major.

'Take it just in case,' said Bentley.

'Right,' said Lucy, 'let's go.'

She pushed past the Major and charged downstairs behind Bentley, rushing out into the street and laughing fit to burst. The waiter was watching them from the café and waved as they approached the car.

'Are we going to let him in on the secret?' giggled Bentley.

'No,' laughed Lucy, 'he's got to go and see Inspector Trembley yet, remember?' She pocketed the toy detonator and was just about to climb into Bentley's car when they heard a familiar and most unwelcome voice.

'So, we meet again, Miss Blake.'

'Zenda rotten Freggley,' spat Lucy. 'What the hell do *you* want?'

'I want *you,* Miss Lucy Blake – and I want to know about your special talents. But let's start with the easy ones, shall we? Why were you shouting my name from an upstairs window?'

'Erm, what talents are those?' said Bentley, ignoring the question about Lucy's shouting.

'Don't come the innocent with *me* Priory,' snapped Zenda. 'I've been watching *you* just as closely as you've been watching me – and I've seen some *very* interesting things.'

'Yeah?' said Lucy. 'Such as what?'

'Empty cinemas for one thing,' replied Zenda.

'Well they *do* show some rubbish these days,' giggled Lucy. 'I'm surprised they aren't empty more often.'

'*Don't* insult my intelligence,' snapped the reporter. 'You know *exactly* what I mean, and exactly what I *want*. This is the biggest story ever to hit Grimston, and Zenda Freggley wants exclusive access to the girl at the centre of it all.'

'That'll be you Lucy,' grinned Bentley.

'*My,* you *are* quick, aren't you?' snarled Zenda. 'Now *look* Blake, I won't beat about the bush, I've had a word with my editor and he's prepared to go as high as a hundred pounds for the rights to your story.'

'Well,' smiled Lucy, 'that certainly is a *lot* of money for a story about a silly schoolgirl.'

'It *is* a lot,' said Zenda, 'and by my reckoning that means you'll be about forty pounds richer than you are now.'

'Excuse me?' said Lucy. 'Forty? But you just said a hundred didn't you? Not that I *want* the money, even if it *is* a hundred.'

'Let me explain,' said Zenda. 'You get forty pounds, right? And your agent gets the other sixty.'

'Agent?' said Lucy. 'But I haven't *got* an agent.'

'Of course you have,' said Zenda, '*all* famous people have an agent.'

'Well *I* haven't,' insisted Lucy.

'You have now,' said Zenda.

'Well I don't want one,' said Lucy, 'especially at *that* rate of commission – who *is* this bloodsucker anyway?'

'It's a Mister Percy Winnet,' said Zenda with a perceptive grin. 'I think you probably know him, don't you?'

'I'm beginning to wish I didn't,' said Lucy.

'Well then,' said Zenda, 'I think you should give the offer some serious consideration. A girl like you could do a lot with forty pounds – you could travel the world for instance.'

'I'll bear it in mind,' smiled Lucy, 'but the answer is still no.'

'Now that *is* a pity,' said Zenda, her expression hardening. 'I was rather hoping you'd accept the money and save us all the trouble.'

'All the trouble?' said Lucy. 'Erm, all *what* trouble?'

Zenda didn't bother to answer. Instead, she jammed her thumb and index finger into her mouth and let rip with one of the loudest whistles Lucy had ever heard. In response to the summons, two large men appeared from around the corner. Each of them was approximately the size of a small parcel delivery van, and had a face to match – suddenly, it seemed, there was a *lot* less sunlight.

'This is Lenny,' smiled Zenda, 'and *this* is Oliver.'

'Erm, hello,' said Bentley, staring up at them both. Lenny grunted, but Oliver wasn't quite so communicative.

'Lenny here used to be a bare-knuckle prize-fighter,' said Zenda, 'until he got thrown off the circuit for persistent brutality.'

'And what about Oliver?' said Lucy, 'or am I going to regret asking?'

'Ah, dear *lovely* Oliver,' grinned Zenda, '*he* was the one that did the throwing.'

'Erm, do these doors lock?' said Lucy, diving into the car beside Bentley.

'I hope so,' said Bentley, turning the engine over.

Oliver and Lenny stood either side of the car, battering on the windows with their huge ham-sized fists – after a word from Zenda though, they began to rock the car from side to side, obviously aiming to turn it over.

'Bentley? Start the car,' said Lucy, quite calmly.

'*Arr, arr, arr, arr…*'

The engine turned and turned, and then it wheezed and wheezed, like an asthmatic donkey pulling a tram up a hill.

'Start the *car*,' said Lucy again, not quite so calmly.

'*Arr, arr, arr…*'

'*Start the bloody car,*' screamed Lucy.

'*Arr, arr…*'

Eventually, the old rust-bucket decided to co-operate. The engine gave a final wheezing cough and then fired up, and with a well-practised crashing of the gearbox from Bentley, they were finally on the move. Lucy spun round in her seat so she could watch Zenda's reaction – but she and the gangsters had already piled into their own car.

'They're coming after us,' screamed Lucy, 'they've got a car.'

'I was hoping you'd say that,' said Bentley, checking the rear view mirror.

'*Were* you?' said Lucy.

'No, of course not,' he shouted. 'You *do* know their car's a lot faster than ours, don't you? They'll be on top of us before we get half a mile.'

Bentley stepped on the gas anyway, heading south on the wide road that led out of Grimston – he was praying that Lucy had some good ideas.

'We need to *do* something,' he said, 'once we get out of town there's nothing but mile after mile of straight road and nowhere to turn off or hide.'

'Alright,' said Lucy, spotting a small concrete structure up ahead, 'if we can't be faster then we've got to be cleverer – unless you can wind the rubber band in this thing a bit tighter?'

'Believe me, if I *had* one I'd *use* it,' said Bentley. 'How are we doing?'

Lucy turned in her seat and squinted out of the tiny rear window.

'Erm, very badly I suspect – either their car is slowly getting bigger or they're catching up – which do you prefer?'

'I prefer a brilliant and totally foolproof escape plan,' said Bentley, 'right about *now* would be a good.'

'Then stop here,' screamed Lucy.

'Where?'

'Right *here*,' she yelled, 'I've had an idea.'

Bentley screeched to a halt next to a bus stop where two elderly ladies were waiting. At this time of day Lucy guessed, they were probably waiting for the number forty-seven – or possibly a forty-four.

'Ooh, *Gladys*,' said one of the ladies as she pointed at the car, '*look*, it's the man who's always getting his name in the paper.'

'Oh *yes* Ethel, so it is,' said the other, 'it's Bendingo Priory.'

'This had better be good,' said Bentley, getting out of the driver's seat.

'Well I can't think of anything else,' said Lucy, turning to the ladies.

'It's Ethel and Gladys, *isn't* it?' she said.

'Oh, now that *is* good,' said Gladys, 'how did you know our names?'

'Just good customer relations,' smiled Lucy. 'Erm, we've been asked by the bus company to make sure that people waiting in their shelters are being taken care of properly.'

'Oh, *well* we are now, *aren't* we, Gladys?'

'We certainly are, Ethel. But we don't want to fill in any forms, do we? And we're not answering any questionnaires either.'

'It's nothing like that,' said Lucy, 'we've come to keep you entertained whilst you wait for the forty-four.'

'Oh *no*, love,' said Gladys. 'It's the fifty-three we're after; we just like to get here nice and early – it goes up by the cemetery you know.'

'Yes, I know,' said Lucy, checking the horizon for signs of Zenda's car. It was stuck behind a lorry at the zebra crossing, where, as luck would have it, Zenda was arguing with a pedestrian. It was obviously something she was very good at because she appeared to be winning.

'So what is it then?' said Gladys. 'What's the entertainment?'

'Erm, it's a free magic show,' said Lucy, 'but it's only for people who travel on the fifty-three.'

'*Oh, yes*,' yelled Ethel, punching the air with her fist, 'that's *us* – did you hear that Gladys? We've qualified for a free magic show. So when do we collect the tickets dear?'

'You don't need tickets,' said Lucy.

'No tickets?' said Ethel, 'but how will we get in?'

'You're in already,' said Lucy, 'and the show's about to start.'

'Where?' said Gladys.

'Right here,' grinned Lucy, 'in this very bus stop.'

'Well I've never heard of *that* before,' said Gladys. 'Is it legal?'

'Don't worry about that,' said Bentley, 'we won't be sawing anyone in half or anything like that, *will* we Lucy?'

'Not without anaesthetic,' said Lucy, 'and now ladies, I want you to watch the Great Boris here very closely – because he's going to make me disappear.'

'*What?*' hissed Bentley. 'Have you gone barking mad? This is exactly the sort of thing Zenda wants.'

'No, it's *not*,' whispered Lucy, 'just trust me.'

She turned to the ladies, who were obviously eager to get on with the show now that the offer had been made. 'I'll be with you in just a minute Gladys – we just need to sort out our props.'

'*Look*,' she whispered to Bentley. 'You told me that the more obvious you are, the less people notice you, so I'm making my disappearance really obvious.'

'Right,' said Bentley, 'only when I *said* that, I wasn't really thinking about conducting impromptu magic shows in bus shelters.'

'Well we're *doing* it,' insisted Lucy, 'unless you've got any better ideas.'

'No,' he admitted with a shrug.

'Right,' said Lucy, 'are you ready ladies?'

'Oooh, yes *please*,' said Ethel, clapping. 'We're ready for anything, aren't we, Gladys?'

'We certainly are,' said Gladys, 'and it had better be good.'

'I'll do my best,' said Lucy, handing the valuable parchment to Bentley.

'Just hold it still,' she whispered, 'and when I'm gone, guard it with your life. I haven't a clue what might happen if it was damaged, and I don't particularly want to find out.'

'Take care,' said Bentley, holding the page so that Lucy could touch it with the flat of her hand. He *still* didn't know what was going to happen, but after the visit to the bandstand, he was prepared for anything – well *almost* anything.

'Zildar de Babage,' whispered Lucy. '*Zildar de Babage…*'

Zap – the ladies' skirts flew up, and their hats blew off.

Poof – two hubcaps and a wing-mirror dropped off Bentley's car.

Bang – all the windows dropped out of the bus shelter.

'Oooh, *Gladys*, what's that smell? It's like when we had our house rewired, do you remember, when it caught fire the next day? I *told* Alfred that Lectrician was far too cheap, but he wouldn't listen, would he?'

'Erm, yes, *well* ladies, erm, that concludes today's show,' said Bentley.

'Absolutely *marvellous*,' said Gladys, suddenly reminded of what they were supposed to be seeing. 'The girl has disappeared, hasn't she? Oh, and is that for me? What is it – a souvenir program?'

Before Bentley realised what was happening Gladys had snatched the paper from his grasp and now she was wrestling with the buckle on her handbag, eager to get the booty safely stowed away.

'*No*,' he screamed, 'no, that's not for you at all – it's erm, oh *no*, it's just that it's very important and I'd be very grateful if...'

Just then, a car screamed towards them and mounted the pavement, screeching to a halt just inches from Gladys. The passenger side window rolled down to reveal Zenda Freggley, who was looking extremely pleased with herself.

'*I'll* take that, *if* you don't mind,' she grinned. And she snatched the Assiah gateway from Gladys, just as the old dear was about to stuff it into her handbag.

'No, *wait*, Zenda, you can't,' shouted Bentley. He raced to get back into his own car, but it was already too late – by the time he got the engine started, Zenda's more powerful vehicle had done its own disappearing act.

'Lucy is *not* going to be happy with this,' he mumbled. He sank down into the seat, his shoulders drooping, and his head resting on the bakelite steering wheel.

'Well I don't know about *that*,' said Gladys, leaning in through the window. 'We both thought the show went very well, didn't we, Ethel?'

'*Eh*?' said Bentley. 'Oh, yes – the magic trick – did you like it?'

'We certainly did,' said Gladys. 'It was a wonderful idea and we'd like you to thank the bus company for thinking of it.'

'I will,' said Bentley, wondering how he was going to make it up to Lucy.

'Good,' said Ethel, 'and now young man, since you've already got your engine running, do you think you might be able to give us a lift?'

'A lift?' said Bentley. 'I thought you were waiting for a bus?'

'We *were* dear,' said Gladys, 'but you've just given us an idea, *haven't* you?'

'Have I?' sighed Bentley.

'Yes, you *have*,' said Ethel, with a mischievous twinkle in her eye. 'You've gone and got us *thinking*.'